C. J. SANSOM

Heartstone

§

PENGUIN BOOKS

PENGUIN BOOKS

Published by the Penguin Group
Penguin Group (USA) Inc., 375 Hudson Street, New York, New York 10014, U.S.A.
Penguin Group (Canada), 90 Eglinton Avenue East, Suite 700, Toronto,
Ontario, Canada M4P 2Y3 (a division of Pearson Penguin Canada Inc.)
Penguin Books Ltd, 80 Strand, London WC2R 0RL, England
Penguin Ireland, 25 St Stephen's Green, Dublin 2, Ireland (a division of Penguin Books Ltd)
Penguin Group (Australia), 250 Camberwell Road, Camberwell,
Victoria 3124, Australia (a division of Pearson Australia Group Pty Ltd)
Penguin Books India Pvt Ltd, 11 Community Centre, Panchsheel Park, New Delhi – 110 017, India
Penguin Group (NZ), 67 Apollo Drive, Rosedale, Auckland 0632,
New Zealand (a division of Pearson New Zealand Ltd)
Penguin Books (South Africa) (Pty) Ltd, 24 Sturdee Avenue,
Rosebank, Johannesburg 2196, South Africa

Penguin Books Ltd, Registered Offices:
80 Strand, London WC2R 0RL, England

First published in Great Britain by Mantle, an imprint of Pan Macmillan,
a division of Macmillan Publishers Limited 2010
First published in the United States of America by Viking Penguin,
a member of Penguin Group (USA) Inc. 2011
Published in Penguin Books 2012

1   3   5   7   9   10   8   6   4   2

LIBRARY OF CONGRESS CATALOGING IN PUBLICATION DATA
Sansom, C. J.
Heartstone / C.J. Sansom.
p.   cm.
"First published in Great Britain by Mantle . . . 2010"—T.p. verso.
ISBN 978-0-14-312065-0
1. Shardlake, Matthew (Fictitious character)—Fiction.   2. Lawyers—England—London—
History—16th century—Fiction.   3. Great Britain—History—Henry VIII, 1509–1547—Fiction.
4. Portsmouth (England)—Fiction.   I. Title.
PR6119.A57H43 2012
823'.92—dc22
2011043101

Printed in the United States of America

Heartstone

Part One

LONDON

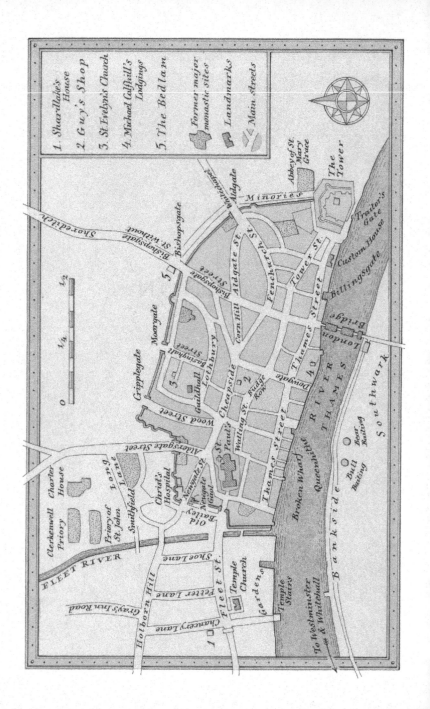

1. Shardlake's House
2. Guy's Shop
3. St. Evelyn's Church
4. Michael Calfhill's Lodgings
5. The Bedlam

Former major monastic sites
Landmarks
Main streets

Chapter One

THE CHURCHYARD was peaceful in the summer afternoon. Twigs and branches lay strewn across the gravel path, torn from the trees by the gales which had swept the country in that stormy June of 1545. In London we had escaped lightly, only a few chimneypots gone, but the winds had wreaked havoc in the north. People spoke of hailstones there as large as fists, with the shapes of faces on them. But tales become more dramatic as they spread, as any lawyer knows.

I had been in my chambers in Lincoln's Inn all morning, working through some new briefs for cases in the Court of Requests. They would not be heard until the autumn now; the Trinity law term had ended early by order of the King, in view of the threat of invasion.

In recent months I had found myself becoming restless with my paperwork. With a few exceptions the same cases came up again and again in Requests: landlords wanting to turn tenant farmers off their lands to pasture sheep for the profitable wool trade, or for the same reason trying to appropriate the village commons on which the poor depended. Worthy cases, but always the same. And as I worked, my eyes kept drifting to the letter delivered by a messenger from Hampton Court. It lay on the corner of my desk, a white rectangle with a lump of red sealing wax glinting in the centre. The letter worried me, all the more for its lack of detail. Eventually, unable to keep my thoughts from wandering, I decided to go for a walk.

When I left chambers I saw a flower seller, a young woman, had got past the Lincoln's Inn gatekeeper. She stood in a corner of

Gatehouse Court, in a grey dress with a dirty apron, her face framed by a white coif, holding out posies to the passing barristers. As I went by she called out that she was a widow, her husband dead in the war. I saw she had wallflowers in her basket; they reminded me I had not visited my poor housekeeper's grave for nearly a month, for wallflowers had been Joan's favourite. I asked for a bunch, and she held them out to me with a work-roughened hand. I passed her a halfpenny; she curtsied and thanked me graciously, though her eyes were cold. I walked on, under the Great Gate and up newly paved Chancery Lane to the little church at the top.

As I walked I chided myself for my discontent, reminding myself that many of my colleagues envied my position as counsel at the Court of Requests, and that I also had the occasional lucrative case put my way by the Queen's solicitor. But, as the many thoughtful and worried faces I passed in the street reminded me, the times were enough to make any man's mind unquiet. They said the French had gathered thirty thousand men in their Channel ports, ready to invade England in a great fleet of warships, some even with stables on board for horses. No one knew where they might land, and throughout the country men were being mustered and sent to defend the coasts. Every vessel in the King's fleet had put to sea, and large merchant ships were being impounded and made ready for war. The King had levied unprecedented taxes to pay for his invasion of France the previous year. It had been a complete failure and since last winter an English army had been besieged in Boulogne. And now the war might be coming to us.

I passed into the churchyard. However much one lacks piety, the atmosphere in a graveyard encourages quiet reflection. I knelt and laid the flowers on Joan's grave. She had run my little household near twenty years; when she first came to me she had been a widow of forty and I a callow, recently qualified barrister. A widow with no family, she had devoted her life to looking after my needs; quiet, efficient, kindly. She had caught influenza in the spring and been dead in a week. I missed her deeply, all the more because I realized how all these years I had taken her devoted care for granted. The contrast with the wretch I now had for a steward was bitter.

I stood up with a sigh, my knees cracking. Visiting the grave had quieted me, but stirred those melancholy humours to which I was naturally prey. I walked on among the headstones, for there were others I had known who lay buried here. I paused before a fine marble stone:

ROGER ELLIARD
BARRISTER OF LINCOLN'S INN
BELOVED HUSBAND AND FATHER
1502–1543

I remembered a conversation Roger and I had had, shortly before his death two years before, and smiled sadly. We had talked of how the King had wasted the riches he had gained from the monasteries, spending them on palaces and display, doing nothing to replace the limited help the monks had given the poor. I laid a hand on the stone and said quietly, 'Ah, Roger, if you could see what he has brought us to now.' An old woman arranging flowers on a grave nearby looked round at me, an anxious frown on her wrinkled face at the sight of a hunchbacked lawyer talking to the dead. I moved away.

A little way off stood another headstone, one which, like Joan's, I had had set in that place, with but a short inscription;

GILES WRENNE
BARRISTER OF YORK
1467–1541

That headstone I did not touch, nor did I address the old man who lay beneath, but I remembered how Giles had died and realized that indeed I was inviting a black mood to descend on me.

Then a sudden blaring noise startled me almost out of my wits. The old woman stood and stared around her, wide-eyed. I guessed what must be happening. I walked over to the wall separating the churchyard from Lincoln's Inn Fields and opened the wooden gate. I stepped through, and looked at the scene beyond.

☘

Lincoln's Inn Fields was an empty, open space of heathland, where law students hunted rabbits on the grassy hill of Coney Garth. Normally on a Tuesday afternoon there would have been only a few people passing to and fro. Today, though, a crowd was gathered, watching as fifty young men, many in shirts and jerkins but some in the blue robes of apprentices, stood in five untidy rows. Some looked sulky, some apprehensive, some eager. Most carried the warbows that men of military age were required to own by law for the practice of archery, though many disobeyed the rule, preferring the bowling greens or the dice and cards that were illegal now for those without gentleman status. The warbows were two yards long, taller than their owners for the most part. Some men, though, carried smaller bows, a few of inferior elm rather than yew. Nearly all wore leather bracers on one arm, finger guards on the hand of the other. Their bows were strung ready for use.

The men were being shepherded into rows of ten by a middle-aged soldier with a square face, a short black beard and a sternly disapproving expression. He was resplendent in the uniform of the London Trained Bands, a white doublet with sleeves and upper hose slashed to reveal the red lining beneath, and a round, polished helmet.

Over two hundred yards away stood the butts, turfed earthen mounds six feet high. Here men eligible for service were supposed to practise every Sunday. Squinting, I made out a straw dummy, dressed in tatters of clothing, fixed there, a battered helmet on its head and a crude French fleur-de-lys painted on the front. I realized this was another View of Arms, that more city men were having their skills tested to select those who would be sent to the armies converging on the coast or to the King's ships. I was glad that, as a hunchback of forty-three, I was exempt from military service.

A plump little man on a fine grey mare watched the men shuffling into place. The horse, draped in City of London livery, wore a metal face plate with holes for its eyes that made its head resemble a skull. The rider wore half-armour, his arms and upper body encased in polished steel, a peacock feather in his wide black cap stirring in the breeze. I recognized Edmund Carver, one of the city's senior aldermen; I had won a case for him in court two years before. He looked uneasy in his armour, shifting awkwardly on his horse. He was a decent enough fellow, from the Mercers' Guild, whose main interest I remembered as fine dining. Beside him stood two more soldiers in Trained Bands uniform, one holding a long brass trumpet and the other a halberd. Nearby a clerk in a black doublet stood, a portable desk with a sheaf of papers set on it slung round his neck.

The soldier with the halberd laid down his weapon and picked up half a dozen leather arrowbags. He ran along the front row of recruits, spilling out a line of arrows on the ground. The soldier in charge was still casting sharp, appraising eyes over the men. I guessed he was a professional officer, such as I had encountered on the King's Great Progress to York four years before. He was probably working with the Trained Bands now, a corps of volunteer soldiers set up in London a few years ago who practised soldiers' craft at week's end.

He spoke to the men, in a loud, carrying voice. 'England needs men to serve in her hour of greatest peril! The French stand ready to invade, to rain down fire and destruction on our women and children. But we remember Agincourt!' He paused dramatically: Carver shouted, 'Ay!', followed by the recruits.

The officer continued. 'We know from Agincourt that one Englishman is worth three Frenchmen, and we shall send our legendary archers to meet them! Those chosen today will get a coat, and thruppence a day!' His tone hardened. 'Now we shall see which of you lads have been practising weekly as the law requires, and which have not. Those who have not – ' he paused for dramatic effect – 'may find themselves levied instead to be pikemen, to face the French at close quarters! So don't think a weak performance will save you from going to war.' He ran his eye over the men, who shuffled and looked uneasy. There was something heavy and angry in the officer's dark-bearded face.

'Now,' he called, 'when the trumpet sounds again, each man will shoot six arrows at the target, as fast as you can, starting with the left of the front row. We've prepared a dummy specially for you, so you can pretend it's a Frenchy come to ravish your mothers, if you have mothers!'

I glanced at the watching crowd. There were excited urchins and some older folk of the poorer sort, but also several anxious-looking young women, maybe wives or sweethearts of the men called here.

The soldier with the trumpet raised it to his lips and blew again. The first man, a thickset, handsome young fellow in a leather jerkin, stepped forward confidently with his warbow. He picked up an arrow and nocked it to the bow. Then in a quick, fluid movement he leaned back, straightened, and sent the arrow flying in a great arc across the wide space. It thudded into the fleur-de-lys on the scarecrow with a force that made it judder like a living thing. In no more than a minute he had strung and loosed five more arrows, all of which hit the dummy. There was a ragged cheer from the children. He smiled and flexed his broad shoulders.

'Not bad!' the officer called grudgingly. 'Go and get your name registered!' The new recruit walked over to the clerk, waving his warbow at the crowd.

A tall, loose-limbed young fellow in a white shirt, who looked barely twenty, was next. He had only an elm bow, and an anxious look. I noticed he wore neither bracer nor finger guard. The officer looked at him grimly as he pushed a hank of untidy blond hair from his eyes, then bent, took an arrow, and fitted it to the string. He pulled the bow back with obvious effort and loosed. The arrow fell well short, thudding into the grass. Pulling the bow had set him off-balance and he nearly fell, hopping on one leg for a moment and making the children laugh.

The second arrow went wide, embedding itself in the side of the butts, and the young man cried out, doubling over with pain and holding one hand with the other. Blood trickled between his fingers. The officer gave him a grim look. 'Haven't been practising, have you? Can't even loose an arrow properly. You're going to the pikemen, you are! A tall fellow like you will be useful in close combat.' The lad looked frightened. 'Come on,' the officer shouted, 'you've four more arrows still to loose. Never mind your hand. This crowd look like they could do with a laugh.'

I turned away. I had myself once been humiliated in front of a crowd and it was not something I relished seeing others endure.

✝

BACK IN Gatehouse Court the flower seller was gone. I went into chambers, where my young clerk Skelly was copying out some orders in the outer office. He was bent closely over his desk, peering carefully at the document through his glasses.

'There is a View of Arms over at Lincoln's Inn Fields,' I told him.

He looked up. 'I've heard the Trained Bands have to find a thousand men for the south coast,' he said in his quiet voice. 'Do you think the French are really going to invade, sir?'

'I don't know, Skelly.' I smiled reassuringly. 'But you won't be called. You've a wife and three children, and you need your glasses to see.'

'So I hope and pray, sir.'

'I am sure.' But these days one never knew.

'Is Barak not back from Westminster?' I asked, glancing over at my assistant's vacant desk. I had sent him to the Requests Office to lodge some depositions.

'No, sir.'

I frowned. 'I hope Tamasin is all right.'

Skelly smiled. 'I'm sure it is only a delay getting a wherry on the river, sir. You know how busy it is with supply boats.'

'Perhaps. Tell Barak to come and see me when he returns. I must go back to my papers.' I went through to my office, little doubting Skelly thought me over-anxious. But Barak and his wife Tamasin

9

were dear friends. Tamasin was expecting a baby in two months, and her first child had been born dead. I dropped into my chair with a sigh and picked up the particulars of a claim I had been reading earlier. My eyes wandered again to the letter on the corner of the desk. I made myself look away, but soon my thoughts returned to the View of Arms: I thought of invasion, of those young men ripped apart and slaughtered in battle.

I looked out of the window, then smiled and shook my head as I saw the tall, skinny figure of my old enemy, Stephen Bealknap, walking across the sunlit court. He had acquired a stoop now, and in his black barrister's robe and white coif he looked like a huge magpie, seeking worms on the ground.

Bealknap suddenly straightened and stared ahead, and I saw Barak walking across the court towards him, his leather bag slung over one shoulder. I noticed my assistant's stomach bulged now against his green doublet. His face was acquiring a little plumpness too that softened his features and made him look younger. Bealknap turned and walked rapidly away towards the chapel. That strange, miserly man had, two years ago, got himself indebted to me for a small amount. Normally bold as brass, Bealknap, for whom it was a point of pride never to part with money, would turn and hasten away if ever he saw me. It was a standing joke at Lincoln's Inn. Evidently he was avoiding Barak now too. My assistant paused and grinned broadly at Bealknap's back as he scuttled away. I felt relieved; obviously nothing had happened to Tamasin.

A few minutes later he joined me in my office. 'All well with the depositions?' I asked.

'Yes, but it was hard to get a boat from Westminster stairs. The river's packed with cogs taking supplies to the armies, the wherries had to pull in to the bank to make way. One of the big warships was down by the Tower, too. I think they sailed it up from Deptford so the people could see it. But I didn't hear any cheering from the banks.'

'People are used to them now. It was different when the *Mary Rose* and the *Great Harry* sailed out; hundreds lined the banks to cheer.' I waved at the stool in front of my desk. 'Come, sit down. How is Tamasin today?'

He sat and smiled wryly. 'Grumpy. Feeling the heat, and her feet are swollen.'

'Still sure the child's a girl?'

'Ay. She consulted some wise woman touting for business in Cheapside yesterday, who told her what she wanted to hear, of course.'

'And you are still as sure the child's a boy?'

'I am.' He shook his head. 'Tammy insists on carrying on as usual. I tell her ladies of good class take to their chambers eight weeks before the birth. I thought that might give her pause but it didn't.'

'Is it eight weeks now?'

'So Guy says. He's coming to visit her tomorrow. Still, she has Goodwife Marris to look after her. Tammy was glad to see me go to work. She says I fuss.'

I smiled. I knew Barak and Tamasin were happy now. After the death of their first child there had been a bad time, and Tamasin had left him. But he had won her back with a steady, loving persistence I would once not have thought him capable of. I had helped them find a little house nearby, and a capable servant in Joan's friend Goodwife Marris, who had worked as a wet nurse and was used to children.

I nodded at the window. 'I saw Bealknap turn to avoid you.'

He laughed. 'He's started doing that lately. He fears I'm going to ask him for that three pounds he owes you. Stupid arsehole.' His eyes glinted wickedly. 'You should ask him for four, seeing how the value of money's fallen.'

'You know, I sometimes wonder if friend Bealknap is quite sane. Two years now he has made a fool and mock of himself by avoiding me, and now you too.'

'And all the while he gets richer. They say he sold some of that gold he has to the Mint for the recoinage, and that he is lending more out to people looking for money to pay the taxes, now that lending at interest has been made legal.'

'There are some at Lincoln's Inn who have needed to do that to pay the Benevolence. Thank God I had enough gold. Yet the way Bealknap behaves does not show a balanced mind.'

Barak gave me a penetrating look. 'You've become too ready to see madness in people. It's because you give so much time to Ellen Fettiplace. Have you answered her latest message?'

I made an impatient gesture. 'Let's not go over that again. I have, and I will go to the Bedlam tomorrow.'

'Bedlamite she may be, but she plays you like a fisherman pulling on a line.' Barak looked at me seriously. 'You know why.'

I changed the subject. 'I went for a walk earlier. There was a View of Arms in Lincoln's Inn Fields. The officer was threatening to make pikemen of those who hadn't been practising their archery.'

Barak answered contemptuously, 'They know as well as anyone that only those who like archery practise it regularly, for all the laws the King makes. It's hard work and you've got to keep at it to be any good.' He gave me a serious look. 'It's no good making laws too unpopular to be enforced. Lord Cromwell knew that, he knew where to draw the line.'

'They're enforcing this. I've never seen anything like it before. And yesterday I saw the constables sweeping the streets for the beggars and vagabonds the King's ordered to be sent to row on the galleasses. Have you heard the latest word – that French troops have landed in Scotland and the Scots are ready to fall on us too?'

'The latest word,' Barak repeated scoffingly. 'Who sets these stories running about the French and Scots about to invade? The King's officials, that's who. Maybe to stop the people rebelling like they did in '36. Against the taxes and the debasement of the currency. Here, look at this.' His hand went to his purse. He took out a little silver coin and smacked it down on the desk. I picked it up. The King's fat jowly face stared up at me.

'One of the new shilling coins,' Barak said. 'A testoon.'

'I haven't seen one before.'

'Tamasin went shopping with Goodwife Marris yesterday in Cheapside. There's plenty there. Look at its dull colour. The silver's so adulterated with copper they'll only give eightpence worth of goods for it. Prices for bread and meat are going through the roof. Not that there is much bread, with so much being requisitioned for the army.' Barak's brown eyes flashed angrily. 'And where's the extra silver gone? To repay those German bankers who lent the King money for the war.'

'You really think there may be no French invasion fleet at all?'

'Maybe. I don't know.' He hesitated, then said suddenly, 'I think they're trying to get me for the army.'

'What?' I sat bolt upright.

'The constable was going round all the houses in the ward last Friday with some soldier, registering all men of military age. I told them I'd a wife and a child on the way. The soldier said I looked a fit man. I flipped my fingers at him and told him to piss off. Trouble is Tamasin told me he came back yesterday. She saw him through the window and didn't answer the door.'

I sighed. 'Your over-confidence will be the end of you one day.'

'That's what Tamasin says. But they're not taking married man with children. Or at least, not many.'

'The powers that be are serious. I think there is going to be an invasion attempt, or why recruit all these thousands of soldiers? You should take care.'

Barak looked mutinous. 'None of this would be happening if the King hadn't invaded France last year. Forty thousand men sent over the Channel, and what happened? We were sent running back with our tails between our legs, except for the poor sods besieged in Boulogne. Everyone says we should cut our losses, abandon Boulogne and make peace, but the King won't. Not our Harry.'

'I know. I agree.'

'Remember last autumn, the soldiers back from France lying in rags, plague-ridden, on all the roads to the city?' His face set hard. 'Well, that won't happen to me.'

I looked at my assistant. There had been a time when Barak might have seen war as an adventure. But not now. 'What did this soldier look like?'

'Big fellow your age with a black beard, done up in a London Trained Bands uniform. Looked as if he'd seen service.'

'He was in charge of the View of Arms. I'd guess a professional officer. No man to cross, I'd say.'

'Well, if he's viewing all the mustered men, hopefully he'll be too busy to bother any more with me.'

'I hope so. If he does return, you must come to me.'

'Thank you,' he said quietly.

I reached for the letter on the corner of my desk. 'In return, I'd like your view on this.' I handed it to him.

'Not *another* message from Ellen?'

'Look at the seal. It's one you've seen before.'

He looked up. 'The Queen's. Is it from Master Warner? Another case?'

'Read it.' I hesitated. 'It worries me.'

Barak unfolded the letter, and read aloud.

'I would welcome your personal counsel on a case, a private matter. I invite you to attend me here at Hampton Court, at three o'clock tomorrow afternoon.'

'It's signed—'

'I know. Catherine the Queen, not lawyer Warner.'

Barak read it again. 'It's short enough. But she says it's a case. No sign it's anything political.'

'But it must be something that affects her closely for her to write herself. I can't help remembering last year when the Queen sent Warner to represent that relative of her servant who was accused of heresy.'

'She promised she would keep you out of things like that. And she's one who keeps her promises.'

I nodded. More than two years before, when Queen Catherine

Parr was still Lady Latimer, I had saved her life. She had promised both to be my patron and never to involve me in matters of politics.

'How long is it since you saw her?' Barak asked.

'Not since the spring. She granted me an audience at Whitehall to thank me for sorting out that tangled case about her Midland properties. Then she sent me her book of prayers last month. You remember, I showed you. *Prayers and Meditations*.'

He pulled a face. 'Gloomy stuff.'

I smiled sadly. 'Yes, it was. I had not realized how much sadness there was in her. She put in a personal note saying she hoped it would turn my mind to God.'

'She'd never put you in harm's way. It'll be another land case, you'll see.'

I smiled gratefully. Barak had known the underside of the political world from his earliest days, and I valued his reassurance.

'The Queen and Ellen Fettiplace in one day!' he said jokingly. 'You will have a busy day.'

'Yes.' I took the letter back. Remembering the last time I had visited Hampton Court, the thought of presenting myself there again set a knot of fear twisting in my stomach.

Chapter Two

IT WAS LATE AFTERNOON when I finished my last brief and sanded my notes. Barak and Skelly had already left and I set off up Chancery Lane for my house nearby.

It was a perfect summer evening. Two days ago had been Midsummer's Day, but the normal celebrations and bonfires had been curtailed by royal proclamation. The city was under a curfew now, with extra watches set through the night, for fear lest French agents set it alight.

As I reached my house, I reflected that these days I no longer felt the uplift on coming home I had when Joan was alive; rather, a worm of irritation stirred. I let myself in. Josephine Coldiron, my steward's daughter, was standing on the rush matting in the hall, hands clasped in front of her and a vacant, slightly worried expression on her round face.

'Good afternoon, Josephine,' I said. She curtsied and bobbed her head. A tendril of unwashed blonde hair escaped from under her white coif, dangling over her brow. She brushed it away. 'Sorry, sir,' she said nervously.

I spoke gently, for I knew she was afraid of me. 'How is dinner progressing?'

She looked guilty. 'I haven't started yet, sir. I need the boys' help to prepare the vegetables.'

'Where are Simon and Timothy?'

Josephine looked alarmed. 'Er, with Father, sir. I'll fetch them and get started.'

She scurried into the kitchen with her quick, tiny steps, like an agitated mouse. I crossed to the parlour.

Guy, my old friend and current house guest, sat on a chair looking out of the window. He turned as I came in, venturing a weak smile. Guy was a physician, a man of some status, but that had not stopped a gang of apprentices on the lookout for French spies from wrecking his house down near the Old Barge one night two months ago, tearing to shreds the medical notes he had made over the years and smashing his equipment. Guy had been out, or he might have been killed. No matter that Guy's ancestry was Spanish; he was a well-known foreigner with a dark face and a strange accent. Since I had taken him in he had sunk into a deep melancholy that worried me.

I laid my satchel on the floor. 'How now, Guy?'

He raised a hand in greeting. 'I have been sitting here all day. It is strange; I thought if ever I was without work time would pass slowly, but it seems to race away without my noticing.'

'Barak says Tamasin is feeling the heat.'

I was pleased to see interest come into his face. 'I am seeing her tomorrow. I am sure she is well, but it will reassure them. Him, rather. I think Tamasin takes it all in her stride.' He hesitated. 'I said I would see her here, I hope that was not presumptuous.'

'Of course not. And you are welcome here as long as you wish, you know that.'

'Thank you. I fear if I go back home the same thing will happen again. The atmosphere against foreigners grows more poisonous every day. Look out there.' He pointed through the diamond-paned window to my garden.

I moved over and looked out. My steward William Coldiron stood on the path, hands on his skinny hips and a fierce expression on his cadaverous, grey-stubbled face. My two servant boys, tall fourteen-year-old Simon and little twelve-year-old Timothy, paraded stiffly up and down in front of him across the garden, each with a broomstick over his shoulder. Coldiron watched them keenly from his single eye – the other was covered with a large black patch. 'Right turn,' he shouted, and the boys obeyed awkwardly. I heard Josephine call from the kitchen door. Coldiron looked up sharply at the study window. I opened it and called 'William!' sharply.

Coldiron turned to the boys. 'Get indoors and get master's dinner ready,' he shouted at them. 'Making me waste time giving you drilling lessons!' The boys looked at him, outrage on their faces.

I turned to Guy. 'God's death, that man!' Guy shook his head wearily. A moment later Coldiron appeared in the doorway. He bowed, then stood stiffly to attention. As ever, I found his face difficult to look at. A long, deep scar ran from his receding hairline to his eyepatch and continued down to the corner of his mouth. He had told me when I interviewed him that it was the result of a sword thrust received at the Battle of Flodden against the Scots over thirty years before. I had sympathized, as I always did with those who were disfigured, and that had influenced me in taking him on, though there was also the fact that, with two large instalments of tax due to the King, I had to be careful with money and he did not demand high wages. In truth I had not much liked him even then.

'What were you doing out there with the boys?' I asked. 'Josephine says nothing has been done to prepare dinner.'

'I'm sorry, sir,' he answered smoothly. 'Only Simon and Timothy were asking me about my time as a soldier. God bless them, they want to do what they can to defend their country from invasion. They pestered me to show them how soldiers drill.' He spread his hands. 'Wouldn't let me alone. It stirs their blood to know I fought the Scots last time they invaded us, that I was the man who cut down King James IV.'

'Are they going to defend us with broomsticks?'

'The time may be coming when even such callow boys may need to take up bills and halberds. They say the Scots are up to their old pranks again, ready to march on us while the French threaten us from the south. I believe it, I know those redshanks. And if foreign spies set fire to London—' He gave Guy a sidelong look, so quick it was barely noticeable, but Guy saw it and turned away.

'I don't want you drilling Timothy and Simon,' I said curtly, 'however great your knowledge of the arts of war. Those of housekeeping are your work now.'

Coldiron did not turn a hair. 'Of course, sir. I won't let the boys press me like that again.' He bowed deeply once more and left the room. I stared at the closed door.

'He made the boys go out and drill,' Guy said. 'I saw it. Timothy at least did not want to.'

'That man is a liar and a rogue.'

Guy smiled sadly, raising an eyebrow. 'You do not think he killed the Scottish King?'

I snorted. 'Every English soldier who was at Flodden claims he did it. I am thinking of dismissing him.'

'Perhaps you should,' Guy said, uncharacteristically for he was the gentlest of men.

I sighed. 'It's his daughter I feel sorry for. Coldiron bullies her as well as the boys.' I passed a hand over my chin. 'I am due to visit the Bedlam tomorrow, by the way, to see Ellen.'

He gave me a direct look, his face as sad as any man's I have seen. 'By going there every time she says she is ill – well, it may not be to the benefit of either of you in the long run. Whatever she is suffering, she lacks the right to summon you at will.'

✟

I LEFT EARLY next morning to visit the Bedlam. The night before I had finally come to a decision about Ellen. I did not like what I planned to do, but could see no alternative. I donned my robe and riding boots, collected my riding crop and walked round to the stables. I had decided to ride across the city, and my way lay down the broader, paved streets. Genesis was in his stall, nose in the feed bucket. Timothy, whose duties included the stable, was stroking him. As I entered, the horse looked up and gave a whicker of welcome. I patted his cheek, running my hand down his stiff, bristly whiskers. I had had him five years; he had been a young gelding then, now he was a mature, peaceful animal. I looked down at Timothy. 'You have been mixing those herbs with his fodder as I asked?'

'Yes, sir. He likes them.'

Seeing Timothy's smiling, gap-toothed face, I felt a clutch at my heart. He was an orphan, with no one in the world outside my household, and I knew he felt Joan's loss deeply. I nodded, then said gently, 'Timothy, if Master Coldiron sets you and Simon to play at soldiers again, you are to tell him I said no, do you understand?'

The boy looked worried, shifted from foot to foot. 'He says it's important for us to learn, sir.'

'Well, I say you are too young. Now, fetch the mounting block, there's a good lad.' I said to myself, that man will go.

✝

I RODE DOWN Holborn Hill and through the gate in the city wall at Newgate, the grim, smoke-blackened stone of the jail hard by. Outside the entrance to the old Christ's Hospital two halberdiers stood to attention. I had heard it was being used, like other former monastic properties, to store the King's weapons and banners. I thought again of my friend Roger's plans for the Inns of Court to found a new hospital for the poor. I had tried to carry on his work after his death, but the weight of taxation for the wars was such that everyone was pinching and sparing.

As I passed the Shambles a blizzard of small goose feathers swept out from under a yard door, causing Genesis to stir anxiously. Blood, too, was seeping into the street. The war meant a huge demand for arrows for the King's armouries, and I guessed they were killing geese for the primary feathers the fletchers would use. I thought of the View of Arms I had witnessed the previous day. Fifteen hundred men had already been recruited from London and sent south, a large contingent from the sixty thousand souls in the city. And the same thing was going on all over the country; I hoped that hard-faced officer would forget about Barak.

I rode on into the broad thoroughfare of Cheapside, lined with shops and public buildings and prosperous merchants' houses. A preacher, his grey beard worn long in the fashion now favoured by Protestants, stood on the steps of Cheapside Cross, declaiming in a loud voice. 'God must favour our arms, for the French and Scots are naught but the Pope's shavelings, instruments of the devil in his war against true Bible faith!' He was probably an unlicensed radical preacher, of the sort who two years ago would have been arrested and thrown in prison, but encouraged now for their hot favouring of the war. City constables in red uniforms, staffs over their shoulders, patrolled up and down. Only the older constables were left now, the younger ones gone to war. They looked constantly over the crowd, as though their rheumy eyes could spot a French or Scottish spy about to – what, poison the food on the stalls? There was little enough of that, for as Barak said much had been requisitioned for the army, and last year's harvest had been poor. One stall, however, was filled with what to my astonished eyes looked like a heap of sheep droppings until, riding closer, I saw they were prunes. Since the King had legalized piracy against the French and Scots all sorts of strange goods from impounded ships had turned up on the stalls. I remembered the celebrations in the spring when the pirate Robert Renegar had brought a Spanish treasure ship up the Thames, full of gold from the Indies. Despite Spanish fury he had been feted at court as a hero.

There was an angry tone, different from the usual haggling, in the many arguments going on up and down the market. At a vegetable stall a fat, red-faced woman stood waving one of the testoons in the stallholder's face, the white wings of her coif shaking with anger.

'It's a shilling!' she yelled. 'It's got the King's majesty's head on it!'

The weary-looking stallholder slapped his hands down and leaned forward. 'It's nearly half copper! It's worth eightpence in the old money, if that! It's not my fault! I didn't make this evil coinage!'

'My husband got paid in these! And you want a penny a bag for these scabby things!' She picked up a small cabbage and waved it at him.

'The crops have been damaged by the storms! Don't you know

that? It's no good coming to me making moan!' The stallholder was shouting now, to the delight of some ragged urchins who had gathered round with a skinny dog, which stood barking at them all. The woman threw the cabbage down. 'I'll find better somewhere else!'

'Not for one of those dandyprats, you won't!'

'It's always those at the bottom that suffer,' she said. 'Poor people's work is all that's cheap!' She turned away and I saw tears in her eyes. The dog followed her, jumping and barking round her ragged skirts. Straight in front of me she turned and aimed a kick at it. Genesis stepped back, alarmed.

'Have a care, goodwife!' I called out.

'Pen-pushing lawyer,' she yelled back. 'Robed hunchback leech! I warrant you don't have a family half starving! You should be brought down, the King and all of you!' She realized what she had said and looked round, afraid, but there were no constables nearby. She walked away, an empty bag slapping at her skirt.

'Quiet, good horse,' I said to Genesis. I sighed. Insults about my condition still felt like a stab in the guts after all these years, but I felt humbled too. For all that I, like other gentlemen, might rail against the taxes, we still had money to put food on the table. Why, I thought, do we all put up with the King squeezing us dry? The answer, of course, was that invasion was a worse fear.

I passed down the Poultry. At the corner of Three Needle Street half a dozen apprentices in their light blue robes stood with hands on their belts, looking round threateningly. A passing constable ignored them. Once the plague of the authorities, the apprentices were now seen as useful extra eyes against spies. It was such a gang of youths that had sacked Guy's shop. As I passed beyond the city wall again at Bishopsgate I wondered bitterly whether I was going to a madhouse, or coming from one.

✝

I HAD FIRST MET Ellen Fettiplace two years before. I had been visiting a client, a boy incarcerated in the Bedlam for religious mania.

At first Ellen had seemed saner than anyone else there. She had been given duties caring for some of her easier fellow patients, towards whom she showed gentleness and concern, and her care had played a part in my client's eventual recovery. I had been astonished when I learned the nature of her malady – she was utterly terrified of going outside the walls of the building. I had myself witnessed the wild, screaming panic that came over her if she were made even to step over the threshold. I pitied Ellen, all the more when I learned she had been incarcerated in the Bedlam after she was attacked and raped near her home in Sussex. She had been sixteen then; she was thirty-five now.

When my client was discharged Ellen asked if I would visit her and bring news of the outside world, for she had almost none. I knew no one else visited her, and agreed on condition she would let me try to help her venture outside. Since then I had tried any number of strategies, asking her to take just one step beyond the open doorway, suggesting I and Barak hold her on either side, asking if she could do it with closed eyes – but Ellen had procrastinated and delayed with a guile and persistence more than equal to mine.

And gradually she had worked that guile, her only weapon in a hostile world, in other ways. At first I had promised only to visit her 'from time to time', but as skilfully as any lawyer she had manipulated the phrase to her benefit. She asked me to come once a month, then every three weeks as she was so famished for news, then every two. If I missed a visit I would receive a message that she was taken ill, and would hasten round to find her sitting happily by the fire soothing some troubled patient, having made a sudden recovery. And these last few months it had dawned on me that there was another element in the problem, one I should have seen earlier. Ellen was in love with me.

✞

PEOPLE THOUGHT of the Bedlam as a grim fortress where lunatics groaned and clanked their chains behind bars. There were indeed some who were chained and many who groaned, but the grey-stone exterior of the long, low building was quite pleasant looking. One approached across a wide yard, which today was vacant except for a tall, thin man dressed in a stained grey doublet. He was walking round and round, staring at the ground, his lips moving quickly. He must be a new patient, probably a man of means who had lost his wits and whose family could afford the fees to keep him here, out of the way.

I knocked at the door. It was opened by Hob Gebons, one of the warders, a big bunch of keys jangling at his belt. A stubby, thickset man in his fifties, Gebons was no more than a jailer; he had no interest in the patients, to whom he could be casually cruel, but he had some respect for me, for I stood up to the Bedlam's keeper, Edwin Shawms, whose cruelty was not casual. And Gebons could be bribed. When he saw me he gave me a sardonic smile, showing grey teeth.

'How is she?' I asked.

'Merry as a spring lamb, sir, since you sent word you were coming. Up till then she thought she had the plague. Shawms was furious watching her sweat – and she did sweat – thinking we'd be quarantined. Then your message came and within an hour she was better. I'd call it a miracle if the Church allowed miracles now.'

I stepped inside. Even on this hot summer's day the Bedlam felt clammy. On the left was the half-open door of the parlour, where some patients sat playing dice round a scratched old table. On a stool in a corner a middle-aged woman was weeping quietly, a wooden doll clutched firmly in her hand. The other patients ignored her; here one quickly got used to such things. To the right was the long stone corridor housing the patients' rooms. Someone was knocking on one of the doors from the inside. 'Let me out!' a man's voice called.

'Is Keeper Shawms in?' I asked Hob quietly.

'No. He's gone to see Warden Metwys.'

'I'd like a word after I've seen Ellen. I can't stay more than half an hour. I have another appointment I must keep.' I reached down to my belt and jingled my purse, nodding at him meaningfully. I slipped him small amounts when I came, to ensure Ellen at least had decent food and bedding.

'All right, I'll be in the office. She's in her room.'

I did not need to ask if her door were unlocked. One thing about Ellen, she was never, ever, going to run away.

I walked down the corridor and knocked at her door. Strictly, it was improper for me to visit a single woman alone, but in the Bedlam the usual rules of conduct were relaxed. She called me in. She was sitting on her straw bed, wearing a clean, blue dress, low-cut, her graceful hands folded in her lap. Her narrow, aquiline face was calm, but her dark-blue eyes were wide, full of emotion. She had washed her long brown hair, but the ends were starting to frizz and split. It is not the sort of detail you notice if you are attracted to a woman. Therein lay the problem.

She smiled, showing her large, white teeth. 'Matthew! You got my message. I have been so ill.'

'You are better now?' I asked. 'Gebons said you had a bad fever.'

'Yes. I feared the plague.' She smiled nervously. 'I was afraid.'

I sat on a stool on the other side of the room. 'I long for news of the world,' she said. 'It has been more than two weeks since I saw you.'

'Not quite two, Ellen,' I answered gently.

'What of the war? They won't tell us anything, for fear it may unsettle us. But old Ben Tudball is allowed out and he saw a great troop of soldiers marching past . . .'

'They say the French are sending a fleet to invade us. And that the Duke of Somerset has taken an army to the Scottish border. But it is all rumour. Nobody knows. Barak thinks the rumours come from the King's officials.'

'That does not mean they are untrue.'

'No.' I thought, she has such a sharp, quick mind, and her

interest in the world is real. Yet she is stuck in here. I looked at the barred window onto the yard. I said, 'I heard someone down the corridor banging to be let out.'

'It's someone new. Some poor soul that still believes they are sane.'

The atmosphere in the room was musty. I looked at the rushes on the floor. 'These need changing,' I said. 'Hob should attend to it.'

She looked down, quickly scratched at her wrist. 'Yes, I suppose they do.' Fleas, I thought. I'll get them too.

'Why do we not go and stand in the doorway?' I suggested quietly. 'Look out at the front yard. The sun is shining.'

She shook her head, wrapping her arms round her body as though to ward off danger. 'I cannot.'

'You could when I first knew you, Ellen. Do you remember the day the King married the Queen? We stood in the doorway, listening to the church bells.'

She smiled sadly. 'If I do that you will press me to go outside, Matthew. Do you think I do not know that? Do you not know how afraid I am?' Her voice took on a bitter note and she looked down again. 'You do not come to visit me, then when you do you press and cajole me. This is not what we agreed.'

'I do visit you, Ellen. Even when, as now, I am busy and have worries of my own.'

Her face softened. 'Have you, Matthew? What ails you?'

'Nothing, not really. Ellen, do you really want to stay here for the rest of your life?' I hesitated, then asked, 'What would happen if whoever pays your fees were to stop?'

She tensed. 'I cannot speak of it. You know that. It upsets me beyond bearing.'

'Do you think Shawms would then let you stay out of charity?'

She flinched a little, then said with spirit, looking me in the face, 'You know I help him with the patients. I am good with them. He would keep me on. It is all I want from life, that and – ' She turned away, and I saw tears in the corner of her eyes.

'All right,' I said. 'All right.' I stood up and forced a smile.

Ellen smiled too, brightly. 'What news of Barak's wife?' she asked. 'When is her baby due?'

✝

I LEFT HER half an hour later, promising to be back within two weeks — *within* two weeks, not *in* two weeks, she had nudged our bargain in her favour again.

Hob Gebons was waiting for me in Shawms's untidy little office, sitting on a stool behind the desk, hands folded over his greasy jerkin. 'Had a good visit, sir?' he asked.

I closed the door. 'Ellen was as usual.' I looked at him. 'How long is it she's been here now? Nineteen years? The rules say a patient can only stay in the Bedlam a year, and they're supposed to be cured within that time.'

'If they pay, they stay. Unless they make a lot of trouble. And Ellen Fettiplace don't.'

I hesitated a moment. But I had made up my mind: I had to find out who her family were. I opened my purse, held up a gold half angel, one of the old coins. It was a large bribe. 'Who pays Ellen's fees, Hob? Who is it?'

He shook his head firmly. 'You know I can't tell you that.'

'All the time I've been visiting her, all I've learned is that she was attacked and raped when she was in her teens, down in Sussex. I've learned where she lived too — a place called Rolfswood.'

Gebons stared at me through narrowed eyes. 'How did you find that out?' he asked quietly.

'One day I was telling her about my father's farm near Lichfield, and mentioned the great winter floods of 1524. She said, "I was a girl then. I remember at Rolfswood . . ." Then she clammed up and would say no more. But I asked around and discovered Rolfswood is a small town in the Sussex iron country, near the Hampshire border. Ellen won't say anything else though, about her family or what happened to her.' I stared at Gebons. 'Was it someone from her family that attacked her? Is that why they never visit?'

Hob looked at the coin I still held up, then at me. 'I can't help you, sir,' he said slowly and firmly. 'Master Shawms is very particular about us not asking anything about Ellen's background.'

'He must have records.' I nodded at the desk. 'Maybe in there.'

'It's locked, and I'm not going to be the one to break it open.'

I had to get out of this tangle somehow. 'How much is it worth, Hob?' I asked. 'Name your price.'

'Can you pay me what it would cost to keep me the rest of my life?' he said with sudden anger, his face growing red. 'Because if I found out and told you, they'd trace it back to me. Shawms keeps that story close and that means he's under instructions from above. From Warden Metwys. I'd be out. I'm not going to lose the roof over my head and a job that feeds me and gives me a bit of authority in a world which is not kind to poor men.' Hob slapped the bunch of keys at his belt for emphasis, making them jingle. 'All because you haven't the heart to tell Ellen she's foolish to think you'll ever bed her in that room. Don't you think everyone here knows of her mad fancy for you?' he asked impatiently. 'Don't you realize it's a joke up and down the Bedlam?'

I felt myself flush. 'That's not what she wants. How could she, after what happened to her?'

He shrugged again. 'That only makes some women keener, from what I'm told. What else do you think she's after?'

'I don't know. Some fantasy of courtly love perhaps.'

He laughed. 'That's an educated way of putting it. Tell her you're not interested. Make life easier for yourself and everyone else.'

'I can't do that, it would be cruel. I need to find some way out of this, Hob. I need to know who her family are.'

'I'm sure lawyers have ways of finding things out.' He narrowed his eyes. 'She *is* mad, you know. It's not just the refusing to go out. All these fake illnesses, and you can hear her crying and muttering to herself in that room at night. If you want my advice you should just walk away and not come back. Send that man of yours with a message that you're married, or dead, or gone to fight the French.'

I realized that in his own way Gebons was trying to advise me for the best. My best, though, not Ellen's. Ellen mattered nothing to him.

'What would happen to her if I did that?'

He shrugged. 'She'd get worse. But if you don't tell her, she will anyway. Your way is just more drawn out.' He looked at me shrewdly. 'Perhaps you're afraid of telling her.'

'Mind your place, Gebons,' I said sharply.

He shrugged. 'Well, I can tell you that once they get ideas fixed in their heads, it's hard to get them out. Believe me, sir, I've been here ten years, I know what they're like.'

I turned away. 'I will be back the week after next.'

He shrugged again. 'All right. Hopefully that will content her. For now.'

I left the office and went out through the main door, closing it firmly behind me. I was glad to be away from the fetid air of that place. I thought, I will find out the truth about Ellen, I will find some way.

Chapter Three

I RODE BACK to my house, quickly changed into my best clothes, and walked down to Temple Stairs to find a boat to take me the ten miles upriver to Hampton Court. The tide was with us, but even so it was a hard pull for the boatman that sultry morning. Beyond Westminster we passed numerous barges going downriver laden with supplies – bales of clothing, grain from the King's stores, on one occasion hundreds of longbows. My sweating boatman was not inclined to talk, and I stared out at the fields. Normally by now the ears of corn would be turning golden, but after the bad weather of the last few weeks they were still green.

My visit to Ellen still lay heavy on my mind, especially Hob's words about lawyers having their ways of finding things. I hated the thought of going behind her back, but the present situation could not continue.

✝

AT LENGTH the soaring brick towers of Hampton Court came into view, the chimneys topped with gold-painted statues of lions and mythical beasts glinting in the sun. I disembarked at the wharf, where soldiers armed with halberds stood on duty. My heart beat hard with apprehension as I looked across the wide lawns to Wolsey's palace. I showed my letter to one of the guards. He bowed deeply, called another guard across and told him to take me inside.

I remembered my only previous visit to Hampton Court, to see Archbishop Cranmer after having been falsely imprisoned in the Tower. It was that memory which lay at the root of my fear. I had heard Cranmer was down in Dover; they said he had reviewed the soldiers there on a white horse, dressed in armour. It sounded extraordinary, though surely no stranger than anything else happening now. The King, I learned from the guard, was at Whitehall, so at least there was no risk of seeing him. Once I had displeased him, and King Henry never forgot a grudge. As we reached a wide oaken doorway, I prayed to the God I hardly believed in any more that the Queen would keep her promise and that, whatever she wanted, it be not a matter of politics.

I was led up a spiral staircase into the outer rooms of the Queen's chambers. I pulled off my cap as we entered a room where servants and officials, most wearing the Queen's badge of St Catherine in their caps, bustled to and fro. We passed through another room and then another, each quieter as we approached the Queen's presence chamber. There were signs of new decoration, fresh paint on the walls and the elaborately corniced ceilings, wide tapestries so bright with colour they almost hurt the eye. Herbs and branches were laid on the rush matting covering the floor, and there was a heavenly medley of scents; almonds, lavender, roses. In the second room parrots fluttered and sang in roomy cages. There was a monkey in a cage too; it had been clambering up the bars but stopped and stared at me, huge eyes in a wrinkled, old man's face. We paused before another guarded door, the Queen's motto picked out in gold on a scroll above: *To be useful in what I do.* The guard opened it and I finally stepped into the presence chamber.

This was the outer sanctum; the Queen's private rooms lay beyond, behind another door with a halberdier outside. After two years of marriage Queen Catherine was still in high favour with the King; when he had been away last year, leading his armies in France, she had been appointed Queen Regent. Yet remembering the fates of his other wives, I could not but think how, at a word from him, all her guards could in a moment become jailers.

The walls of the presence chamber were decorated with some of the new wallpaper, intricate designs of leaves on a green background, and the room was furnished with elegant tables, vases of flowers and high-backed chairs. There were only two people present. The first was a woman in a plain cornflower-blue dress, her hair grey beneath her white coif. She half-rose from her chair, giving me an apprehensive look. The man with her, tall and thin and wearing a lawyer's robe, put his hand gently on her shoulder to indicate she should stay seated. Master Robert Warner, the Queen's solicitor, his thin face framed by a long beard that was greying fast though he was of an age with me, came across and took my hand.

'Brother Shardlake, thank you for coming.' As though I could have refused. But I was pleased to see him, Warner had always been friendly.

'How are you?' he asked.

'Well enough. And you?'

'Very busy just now.'

'And how is the Queen?' I noticed the grey-haired woman was staring at me intently, and that she was trembling slightly.

'Very well. I will take you in now. The Lady Elizabeth is with her.'

✝

IN THE SUMPTUOUSLY decorated privy chamber, four richly dressed maids-in-waiting with the Queen's badge on their hoods sat sewing by the window. Outside were the palace gardens, patterned flower beds and fishponds and statues of heraldic beasts. All the women rose and nodded briefly as I bowed to them.

Queen Catherine Parr sat in the centre of the room, on a red velvet chair under a crimson cloth of state. Beside her a girl of about eleven knelt stroking a spaniel. She had a pale face and long auburn hair, and wore a green silken dress and a rope of pearls. I realized this was the Lady Elizabeth, the King's younger daughter, by Anne Boleyn. I knew the King had restored Elizabeth and her half-sister Mary, Catherine of Aragon's daughter, to the succession the year before, it was said at the Queen's urging. But their status as bastards remained; they were still ladies, not princesses. And though Mary, now in her twenties, was a major figure at court and second in line to the throne after young Prince Edward, Elizabeth, despised and rejected by her father, was hardly ever seen in public.

Warner and I bowed deeply. There was a pause, then the Queen said, 'Welcome, good gentlemen,' in her clear rich voice.

Before her marriage Catherine Parr had always been elegantly dressed, but now she was magnificent in a dress of silver and russet sewn with strands of gold. A gold brooch hung with pearls was pinned to her breast. Her face, attractive rather than pretty, was lightly powdered, her red-gold hair bound under a circular French hood. Her expression was kindly but watchful, her mouth severe but somehow conveying that in a moment it could break into a smile or laugh in the midst of all this magnificence. She looked at Warner.

'She is outside?' she asked.

'Yes, your majesty.'

'Go sit with her, I will call her in shortly. She is still nervous?'

'Very.'

'Then give her what comfort you can.' Warner bowed and left the room. I was aware of the girl studying me closely as she stroked the spaniel. The Queen looked across at her and smiled.

'Well, Elizabeth, this is Master Shardlake. Ask your question, then you must go to your archery lesson. Master Timothy will be waiting.' She turned back to me with an indulgent smile on her face. 'The Lady Elizabeth has a question about lawyers.'

I turned hesitantly to the girl. She was not pretty, her nose and chin too long. Her eyes were blue and piercing, as I remembered her father's. But, unlike Henry's, Elizabeth's eyes held no cruelty, only an intense, searching curiosity. A bold look for a child, but she was no ordinary child.

'Sir,' she said in a clear, grave voice, 'I know you for a lawyer, and that my dear mother believes you a good man.'

'Thank you.' So she called the Queen mother.

'Yet I have heard it said that lawyers are bad folk, with no morals, who will argue a wicked man's case as readily as a good one's. People say lawyers' houses are built on the heads of fools, and they use the tangles of the law as webs to ensnare the people. What say you, sir?'

The girl's serious expression showed she was not mocking me, she truly wished to hear my answer. I took a deep breath. 'My lady, I was taught it is a good thing for lawyers to be ready to argue the case of any client, indifferently. A lawyer's duty is to be impartial, so that every man, good or bad, may have his rights faithfully argued before the King's courts.'

'But lawyers must have consciences, sir, and know in their hearts whether the cause they argue be just or no.' Elizabeth spoke emphatically. 'If a man came to you and you saw he acted from malice and spite against the other party, wished merely to entangle him in the thorny embrace of the law, would you not act for him just the same, for a fee?'

'Master Shardlake acts mostly for the poor, Elizabeth,' the Queen said gently. 'In the Court of Requests.'

'But, Mother, surely a poor man may have a bad case as easily as a rich one?'

'It is true the law is tangled,' I said, 'perhaps indeed too complex for men's good. True also that some lawyers are greedy and care only for money. Yet a lawyer has a duty to seek out whatever is just and reasonable in a client's case, so he may argue it well. Thus he may indeed engage his conscience. And it is the judges who decide where justice lies. And justice is a great thing.'

Elizabeth gave me a sudden winning smile. 'I thank you for your answer, sir, and will think well on it. I asked only because I wish to learn.' She paused. 'Yet still I think justice is no easy thing to find.'

'There, my lady, I agree.'

The Queen touched her arm. 'And now you must go, or Master Timothy will be searching. And Serjeant Shardlake and I have business. Jane, will you accompany her?'

Elizabeth nodded and smiled at the Queen, looking for a moment like an ordinary little girl. I bowed deeply again. One of the maids came over and accompanied the child to the door. Elizabeth walked with slow, composed steps. The little dog made to follow her, but the Queen called to it to stay. The maid-in-waiting knocked on the door, it was opened, and they slipped through.

The Queen turned to me, then held out a slim ringed hand for me to kiss. 'You answered well,' she said, 'but perhaps you allowed your fellow lawyers too much latitude.'

'Yes. I am more cynical than that. But she is only a child, though a truly remarkable one. She converses better than many adults.'

The Queen laughed, a sudden display of white even teeth. 'She swears like a soldier when she is angry; I think Master Timothy encourages her. But yes, she is truly remarkable. Master Grindal, Prince Edward's tutor, is teaching her too and says she is the cleverest child he has ever taught. And she is as skilled at sporting pursuits as things of the mind. Already she follows the hunt and she is reading Master Ascham's new treatise on archery. Yet she is so sad sometimes, and so watchful. Sometimes frightened.' The Queen looked at the closed door with a pensive expression, and for a moment I saw the Catherine Parr I remembered: intense, afraid, desperate to do the right thing.

I said, 'The world is a dangerous and uncertain place, your majesty. One cannot be too watchful.'

'Yes.' A knowing smile. 'And you fear I would place you again amidst its worst dangers. I see it. But I would never break my promise, good Matthew. The case I have for you is nothing to do with politics.'

I bowed my head. 'You see through me. I do not know what to say.'

'Then say nothing. Tell me only how you fare.'

'Well enough.'

'Do you find any time to paint nowadays?'

I shook my head. 'I did a little last year, but just now –' I hesitated – 'I have many demands on me.'

'I read worry in your face.' The gaze from the Queen's hazel eyes was as keen as Elizabeth's.

' "Tis only the lines that come with age. Though not on yours, your majesty.'

'If you ever have troubles, you know I would help you all I can.'

'A small private matter only.'

'An affair of the heart, perhaps?'

I glanced over at the ladies at the window, realizing that all the while the Queen had kept her voice raised sufficiently for them to hear. No one would ever be able to report that Catherine Parr had had a privy conversation with a man the King disliked.

'No, your majesty,' I answered. 'Not that.'

She nodded, frowned thoughtfully for a moment, then asked, 'Matthew, have you any experience with the Court of Wards?'

I looked at her in surprise. 'No, your majesty.' The Court of Wards had been founded by the King a few years ago, to deal with the wealthy orphan children throughout the land who came under his control. There was no court more corrupt, nor one where justice was less likely to be found. It was also where any documents certifying Ellen's lunacy would be kept, for the King had legal charge of lunatics too.

'No matter. The case I would like you to take requires an honest man above all, and you know the sort of lawyers who make wards their speciality.' She leaned forward. 'Would you pursue a case there? For me? I wish you to take it, rather than Master Warner, because you have more experience in representing ordinary people.'

'I would need to refresh my mind about the procedures. But otherwise, yes.'

She nodded. 'Thank you. One more thing you should know before I bring in your new client. Master Warner tells me Wards' cases often involve lawyers travelling to where the young wards live to gather statements.'

'Depositions. That is true of all the courts, your majesty.'

'The boy concerned in this case lives in Hampshire, near Portsmouth.'

I thought, the way there from London lies through West Sussex. Where Ellen comes from.

The Queen hesitated, choosing her next words carefully. 'The Portsmouth area may not be the safest region to travel to these next few weeks.'

'The French? But they say they may land anywhere.'

'We have spies in France, and the word is they are headed for Portsmouth. It is not certain, but likely. I would not have you take on this matter without knowing that, for Master Warner tells me depositions may well be needed.'

I looked at her. I sensed how much she wanted me to deal with this case. And if I could go via Rolfswood . . .

'I will do it,' I said.

'Thank you.' She smiled gratefully and turned to the ladies. 'Jane, please fetch Mistress Calfhill.'

'Now,' she said to me quietly, 'Bess Calfhill, whom you are about to meet, was an old servant of mine when I was Lady Latimer. A housekeeper at one of our properties in the north and later in London. She is a good, true woman, but she has recently suffered a great loss. Deal with her gently. If anyone deserves justice, it is Bess.'

The maid-in-waiting returned, bringing with her the woman I had seen in the presence chamber. She was small, frail looking. She approached with nervous steps, her hands held tightly together.

'Come, good Bess,' the Queen said in a welcoming voice. 'This is Master Shardlake, a serjeant at law. Jane, bring over a chair. One for Serjeant Shardlake too.'

Mistress Calfhill lowered herself onto a cushioned chair and I sat opposite her. She studied me with her intent gaze, grey-blue eyes clear against the lined, unhappy face. She frowned for a second, perhaps noticing I was a hunchback. Then she looked at the Queen, her expression softening at the sight of the dog.

'This is Rig, Bess,' the Queen said. 'Is he not a fine fellow? Come, stroke him.'

Hesitantly, Bess leaned across and touched the animal. Its feathery tail wagged. 'Bess always loved dogs,' the Queen told me, and I realized she had kept Rig back to help relax her old servant. 'Now, Bess,' the Queen said, 'tell Serjeant Shardlake everything. Do not be afraid. He will be your true friend in this. Tell him as you told me.'

Bess leaned back, looked at me anxiously. 'I am a widow, sir.' She spoke softly. 'I had a son, Michael, a goodly, gentle boy.' Her eyes filled with tears, but she blinked them away resolutely. 'He was clever, and thanks to Lady Latimer's – I beg pardon, the Queen's – kindness, he went to Cambridge.' Pride came into her voice. 'He graduated and came back to London. He had obtained a post as tutor to a family of merchants named Curteys. In a good house near the Moorgate.'

'You must have been proud,' I said.

'So I was, sir.'

'When was this?'

'Seven years ago. Michael was happy in his position. Master Curteys and his wife were good people. Cloth merchants. As well as their house in London they had bought some woodland belonging to a little nunnery down in Hampshire, in the country north of Portsmouth. All the monasteries were going down then.'

'I remember very well.'

'Michael said the nuns had lived in luxury from the profits of selling the wood.' She frowned, shaking her head. 'Those monks and nuns were bad people, as the Queen knows.' Bess Calfhill, clearly, was another reformer.

'Tell Master Shardlake about the children,' the Queen prompted.

'The Curteyses had two children, Hugh and Emma. I think Emma was twelve then, Hugh a year younger. Michael brought them to see me once and I would see them when I visited him.' She smiled fondly. 'Such a pretty boy and girl. Both tall, with light brown hair, sweet-natured quiet children. Their father was a good reformer, a man of new thinking. He had Emma as well as Hugh taught Latin and

Greek, as well as sportly pastimes. My son enjoyed archery and taught the children.'

'Your son was fond of them?'

'As if they were his own. You know how in rich households spoiled children can make tutors' lives a misery, but Hugh and Emma enjoyed their learning. If anything, Michael thought they were too serious, but their parents encouraged that: they wanted them to grow up godly folk. Michael thought Master Curteys and his wife kept the children too close to them. But they loved them dearly. Then, then – ' Bess stopped suddenly and looked down at her lap.

'What happened?' I asked gently.

When she looked up again her eyes were blank with grief. 'There was plague in London the second summer Michael was with them. The family decided to go down to Hampshire to visit their lands. They were going with friends, another family who had bought the old nunnery buildings and the rest of the lands. The Hobbeys.' She almost spat out the name.

'Who were they?' I asked.

'Nicholas Hobbey was another cloth merchant. He was having the nunnery converted to a house and Master Curteys' family was to stay with them. Michael was going down to Hampshire too. They were packing to leave when Master Curteys felt the boils under his arm. He had barely been put to bed when his wife collapsed. They were both dead in a day. Along with their steward, a good man.' She sighed heavily. 'You know how it comes.'

'Yes.' Not just plague, but all the diseases born of the foul humours of London. I thought of Joan.

'Michael and the children escaped. Hugh and Emma were devastated, clinging to each other for comfort, crying. Michael did not know what would become of them. There were no close relatives.' She set her jaw. 'And then Nicholas Hobbey came. But for that family my son would still be alive.' She stared at me, her eyes suddenly full of rage.

'Did you ever meet Master Hobbey?'

'No. I know only what Michael told me. He said originally Master Curteys had been thinking of buying the nunnery and all the land that went with it, as an investment, but decided he could not afford it. He knew Master Hobbey through the Mercer's Hall. Master Hobbey came to dinner several times to discuss splitting the woodland between the two of them, which was what happened in the end, with Master Hobbey buying the smaller share of the woodland and the nunnery buildings, which he was going to convert to a country residence. Master Curteys took the larger part of the woodland. Master Hobbey became friendly with Master and Mistress Curteys over the sale. He struck Michael as one who adopts reformist positions when he is with godly people, but if he were negotiating the purchase of lands with a papist he would take some beads to click. As for his wife, Mistress Abigail, Michael said he thought she was mad.'

Madness again. 'In what way?'

She shook her head. 'I don't know. Michael did not like to talk to me of such things.' She paused, then went on. 'Master and Mistress Curteys died too quick to make wills. That was why everything was uncertain. But shortly afterwards Master Hobbey appeared with a lawyer, and told him the children's future was being arranged.'

'Do you know the lawyer's name?'

'Dyrick. Vincent Dyrick.'

'Do you know him?' the Queen asked.

'Slightly. He is an Inner Temple barrister. He has represented landlords against me in the Court of Requests occasionally over the years. He is good in argument but – over-aggressive perhaps. I did not know he worked in the Court of Wards too.'

'Michael feared him. Michael and the Curteyses' vicar were trying to trace relatives, but then Master Hobbey said he had bought the children's wardship. The Curteyses' house was to be sold and Hugh and Emma were to move to the Hobbeys' house in Shoe Lane.'

'That went through very quickly,' I said.

'Money must have passed,' the Queen said quietly.

'How much land is there?'

'I think about twenty square miles in all. The children's share was about two-thirds.'

That was a great deal of land. 'Do you know how much Hobbey paid for the wardship?'

'I think it was eighty pounds.'

That sounded cheap. I thought, if Master Hobbey bought Hugh and Emma's wardship he has control of their share of that woodland. In Hampshire, near to Portsmouth, where there would be much demand for wood for ships, and not too far from the Sussex Weald, where the expanding ironworks had brought constant demand for fuel.

Bess continued. 'Master Hobbey seemed minded to get his own tutor, but Hugh and Emma had grown attached to Michael. The children asked Master Hobbey to keep Michael on, and he agreed.' Bess lifted her hands, made a sort of helpless motion. 'Apart from me, the Curteys family were all Michael had. He was a lad full of generous emotion: he should have sought a wife but for some reason never did.' She composed herself again, continued in a flat voice. 'And so the children were moved, and the house they had lived in all their lives sold and gone. I think the proceeds were put in care of the Court of Wards.'

'Yes. It would be the trustee. So, Mistress Calfhill, your son moved with the children to Shoe Lane.'

'Yes. He did not like the Hobbeys' house. It was a small, dark place. And Michael had a new pupil. The Hobbeys' son David.' She took a deep breath. 'Michael said he was a spoiled and pampered only child, the same age as Emma. Stupid and cruel, always taunt-ing Hugh and Emma, saying they were in his house on sufferance, that his parents did not love them as they did him. True enough, I suppose. I believe Master Hobbey only took the children on to profit from their lands.'

'Is it not illegal to make profit from a ward's lands?' the Queen asked.

'Yes. Whoever purchases a wardship has custody of the ward's lands, but he is supposed to take care of them and not make profit for himself. Though that is not always what happens. And he would have control of the girl's marriage,' I added thoughtfully.

Bess said, 'Michael feared they wanted to marry Emma to David, so her share of the children's lands would pass to the Hobbey family. Those poor children. Hugh and Emma cleaved together, they only had each other, though they had a friend in my son. Michael told me Hugh had a fight once with David, over something improper he said to Emma. She would have been only thirteen. David was a big strong boy, but Hugh beat him.' She looked at me sharply again. 'I told Michael he was getting too concerned over Hugh and Emma, he couldn't be mother and father to them. But then – ' her face went blank once more – 'then smallpox came to the Hobbeys' house.'

The Queen leaned forward and laid a hand on Bess's arm.

'All three children caught it,' Bess continued stonily. 'Michael was forbidden their chambers for fear of infection. The servants were set to look after Hugh and Emma, but David's mother cared for him herself, weeping and crying to God for her boy to be saved. I give her credit for that; I would have done the same for Michael.' She paused, then said in a savage voice, 'David survived unmarked. Hugh lived, but with a pitted face that destroyed his handsomeness. And little Emma died.'

'I am sorry.'

'Then a few days later Master Hobbey told my son his wife would not live in London any more. They were going to their house in Hampshire for good and he would not be needed. Michael never saw Hugh again – he and David were still being kept isolated. They allowed Michael to go to poor Emma's funeral, that was all. He saw her little white coffin laid in the earth. He left that day. He said the servants were burning Emma's clothes in the garden in case they harboured the ill humours of the disease.'

'A terrible story,' I said gently. 'Death and greed, and children the victims. But Mistress Calfhill, your son could have done no more.'

'I know,' she said. 'Master Hobbey gave Michael a letter of recommendation, and he got other positions in London. He wrote to Hugh, but had only a stiff reply from Master Hobbey saying he should not write, they were trying to build a new life for the boy in Hampshire.' Her voice rose. 'The cruelty of it, after all Michael had done for those children.'

'That was hard indeed,' I said. Yet I could see Hobbey's point of view. In London the boy Hugh had lost his entire family.

Bess continued, the tonelessness returning to her voice. 'The years passed. Then at the end of last year Michael took a place down in Dorset, teaching the sons of a large landowner. But the fate of Hugh and Emma seemed to haunt him. He often said he wondered what had become of Hugh.' She frowned and looked down.

The Queen spoke again. 'Come, Bess, you must tell the last part, though I know it is the hardest.'

Bess looked at me, steeled herself. 'Michael returned from Dorset to visit me at Easter. When he arrived he looked terrible, pale and distracted, almost out of his wits. He would not tell me why, but after a few days he suddenly asked if I knew any lawyers. For what, I asked. To my amazement he said he wished to apply to the Court of Wards for Hugh to be taken from the Hobbeys' custody.' She took a deep breath. 'I told him I knew no lawyers, and asked why he should do this now, after six years. He said it was something not fit for my ears or any woman's, or man's either except a judge. I tell you, sir, I began to fear for Michael's reason. I can see him now, sitting opposite me in the little house I have, thanks to the Queen's goodness. In the light from the fire his face looked lined – old. Yes, old, though he was not yet thirty. I suggested if he wanted a lawyer perhaps he should visit Master Dyrick. But he laughed bitterly and said he was the last person he should go to.'

'That is right. If Dyrick was acting for Hobbey in the wardship, he could not act against him in the same matter.'

'It was more than that, sir. There was anger in Michael's voice.'

I sensed a new stillness in the room, and glanced over to the windows. The maids-in-waiting had stopped sewing, and were listening as intently as the Queen and I.

'It occurred to me that on the way back home from Dorset Michael might have visited Hugh. I asked him outright, and he admitted it was true. He had not made an appointment because he feared Master Hobbey might not receive him. He said when he arrived he found that something frightful had been done. He had to find a lawyer whom he could trust, and if he could not he would file the case in court himself.'

'I wish you had come to me, Bess,' the Queen said. 'You could have.'

'Your majesty, I feared my son was losing his reason. I could not see anything that could have happened to Hugh that would drive Michael to such a state. Shortly afterwards Michael said he had found a lodging of his own. He said he was not going back to Dorset. He – 'At last she broke down, burying her head in her hands and weeping. The Queen leaned over and held Bess close against her breast.

At length she regained her composure. The Queen had given her a handkerchief, which she twisted and squeezed in her hands. She spoke, but with her head bowed so low I was looking at the top of her white coif.

'Michael moved into lodgings down by the river. He visited me most days. He told me he had filed papers in the Court of Wards by himself and paid the fee. I fancied he looked a little easier then, but in the days that followed that old, drawn look returned. Then several days passed when he did not visit. The following morning the local constable came.' She looked up, eyes bereft. 'He told me my son had been found dead in his room, he had hanged himself from a roof beam. He left me a note – I have it. Master Warner said I should bring it with me for you to see.'

'May I?'

Bess produced a folded scrap of dirty paper from her dress. She passed it to me with a trembling hand. I opened it. *Forgive me, Mother,* was scrawled on it. I looked up at her. 'This is Michael's writing?' I asked.

'You think I do not know my own son's hand?' she asked angrily. 'He wrote this, as I told the coroner at the inquest, before the jury and all the curious public.'

'Come, Bess,' the Queen said gently. 'Master Shardlake needs to ask these questions.'

'I know, your majesty, but it is hard.' She looked at me. 'I apologize, sir.'

'I understand. Was the hearing before the London coroner?'

'Yes, Master Grice. A hard, stupid man.'

I smiled sadly. 'That he is.'

'The coroner asked me if my son had seemed unwell and I said yes, his behaviour had been strange lately. They brought in a verdict of suicide. I did not say anything about Hampshire.'

'Why not?'

She raised her head and looked at me again, defiantly. 'Because I had decided to bring that matter to the Queen. And now I have come for justice, by the Queen's good grace.' She sat back. I realized there was a thread of steel under Bess's pain.

I asked quietly, 'What do you think your son found in Hampshire that could have driven him to kill himself?'

'God rest and quiet his soul, I do not know, but I believe it was something terrible.'

I did not answer. I wondered if Bess needed to believe that now, had turned pain outwards into anger.

'Show Master Shardlake the summons from the court,' the Queen said.

Bess reached into her dress and pulled out a large paper, folded many times, and handed it to me. It was a summons from the Court of Wards, ordering all parties with business in the matter of the wardship of Hugh William Curteys to attend the court on the twenty-ninth of June, in five days' time. It was addressed to Michael Calfhill as petitioner – they would not know he was dead – and I noted a copy had also been delivered to Vincent Dyrick at the Inner Temple. It was dated near three weeks before.

'It reached me only last week,' Bess said. 'It arrived at my son's lodgings, was taken to the coroner, then he sent it to me as Michael's next of kin.'

'Have you seen a copy of Michael's actual application? It is called a Bill of Information. I need to know what he said.'

'No, sir. I know only what I have told you.'

I looked at Bess and the Queen. I decided to be direct. 'Whatever the application says, it is Michael's, based on facts within his knowledge. But Michael is dead, and the court might not hear the case without Michael there to give evidence.'

'I know nothing of the law,' Bess said, 'only what happened to my son.'

The Queen said, 'I did not think the courts were sitting, I heard they were dissolved early because of the war.'

'Wards and Augmentations are still sitting.' The courts that brought revenue to the King, they would sit all summer. The judges there were hard men. I turned to the Queen. 'Sir William Paulet is Master of the Court of Wards. I wonder if he is sitting himself, or has other duties connected with the war. He is a senior councillor.'

'I asked Master Warner. Sir William goes to Portsmouth soon as governor, but he will be sitting in court next week.'

'Will they make Master Hobbey come?' Bess asked.

'I imagine Dyrick will attend on his behalf at the first hearing. What the court will make of Michael's application will depend on what it says and whether any witnesses can be found to help us. You mentioned that when Master Hobbey applied for the wardship Michael sought the help of the Curteyses' vicar.'

'Yes. Master Broughton. Michael said he was a good man.'

'Do you know whether Michael saw him recently?'

She shook her head. 'I asked him that. He said not.'

'Did anyone else know about this application?' I asked. 'A friend of Michael's perhaps.'

'He was a stranger in London. He had no friends here. Apart from me,' she added sadly.

'Can you find out?' the Queen asked. 'Can you take the case? On Bess's behalf?'

I hesitated. All I could see here was a bundle of intense emotional connections. Between the Queen and Bess, Bess and Michael, Michael and those children. No facts, no evidence, maybe no case at all. I looked at the Queen. She wanted me to help her old servant. I thought of the boy Hugh who was at the centre of it all, only a name to me, but alone and unprotected.

'Yes,' I answered. 'I will do the best I can.'

Chapter Four

I LEFT THE QUEEN an hour later, with the suicide note and the summons in my pocket. I had arranged with Mistress Calfhill for her to call on me later in the week so that I could take a full statement.

Warner was waiting in the presence chamber. He led me up a flight of winding steps to his office, a cramped room with shelves of papers and parchments tied in pink ribbon.

'So you will take the case,' he said.

I smiled. 'I cannot refuse the Queen.'

'Nor I. She has asked me to write to John Sewster, the Court of Wards attorney. I will say next Monday's hearing should go forward, even though Calfhill is dead. I will say the Queen wishes it, in the interests of justice. He will tell Sir William so, and that should stop him from throwing the case out. Paulet is a man for whom political advantage is all — he would not wish to upset her.' Warner looked at me seriously, fingering his long beard. 'But that is as far as we can go, Brother Shardlake. I do not want to press the connection to the Queen too far. We do not know what lies at the bottom of this case. Maybe nothing, but if Michael Calfhill did find something serious, it may be a matter the Queen should not be publicly involved in.'

'I understand.' I respected Warner. He had worked as an attorney in the Queen's household for over twenty years, since Catherine of Aragon's time, and I knew he had come to have a particular affection for Catherine Parr, as most did who worked for her.

'You have been given a hard task,' he said sympathetically. 'Only five more days to the hearing, and no witnesses apart from Mistress Calfhill that we know of.'

'With the end of the law term I have time.'

He nodded slowly. 'The Court of Wards still sits. There are wards and money to be gathered in.' Like any lawyer with integrity, he spoke of Wards with contempt.

'I will do what I can to find witnesses,' I told him. 'There is that vicar who worked with Michael six years ago. My clerk will help me, he is skilled in such matters. If there is anyone, we will find them. But first I must go to Wards, see what Michael's Bill of Information said.'

'And you will need to talk to Dyrick.'

'After I've seen the papers, and found what witnesses there are.'

Warner said, 'I have met Dyrick.' The legal world of London was small, everyone knew everyone else by reputation at least. 'A strong opponent. No doubt he will say the case is a meaningless accusation from a madman.'

'That is why I wish to see more of how the land lies before visiting him. Tell me, what do you make of Mistress Calfhill?'

'Full of grief. Confused. Maybe looking for a scapegoat for her son's death. But I am sure you will do everything possible to root out the truth of it.' He smiled sadly. 'You were afraid it was politics. I saw that on your face when you came in.'

'Yes, Brother Warner, I fear I was.'

'The Queen always honours her promises, Brother Shardlake,' he answered reprovingly. 'And will always help an old servant in trouble.'

'I know. I should have trusted.'

'Queen Catherine holds old friends in more kindness than any since the first Queen Catherine.'

'Catherine of Aragon.'

'Yes. She, too, was kind, though she had her faults.'

I smiled. 'Her Catholicism.'

He looked at me seriously. 'More than that. But come, I say more than I should. Talk of politics is dangerous, even though the great men of the realm have no time for intrigue just now. Hertford,

Norfolk, Gardiner – all away on military assignments. But if we get through this war, I have little doubt it will all begin again. The Catholic party does not like Queen Catherine. You have seen her book?'

'*Prayers and Meditations*? Yes, she sent me a copy last month.'

He looked at me keenly. 'What did you make of it?'

'I did not know she had such sadness in her heart. All those prayers urging us to put up with the shafts of ill fortune that come to us in this world, in the hope of salvation in the next.'

'Her friends had to advise her to leave out certain passages – with a flavour of Luther. Fortunately she listened to us. She is always careful. For example, she will not stir from her chamber today because Sir Thomas Seymour is at Hampton Court.'

'That rogue,' I said feelingly. I had met Seymour at the time the King was pressing Catherine Parr to marry him; she had wanted to marry the dashing Seymour instead.

'The King has had him chasing round the south of England inspecting the armies. He's come to report to the Privy Council.'

'I am glad the Queen has loyal friends such as you,' I said sincerely.

'Ay, we'll watch out for her. Someone has to do the politics,' he added.

☩

I STEPPED OUT into the sunlit courtyard. The astronomical clock over the arch in front of me showed four o'clock. The red-brick buildings cast barely a shadow on the courtyard; the paving stones shimmered in the heat. Sweat pricked at my brow. A messenger in the King's livery rode fast through the courtyard, under the opposite arch, perhaps with some message for the military commanders.

Then I saw two men standing in a doorway, looking at me. I recognized both, and my heart sank. Warner had said Sir Thomas Seymour was at Hampton Court and here he was, in a bright yellow doublet, black hose on his long shapely legs, the handsome face above his dark red beard as hard and mocking as I remembered. He stood with hands on hips in a pose of courtly arrogance; the stance in which Holbein had painted the King. Beside him, short and neat in his lawyer's robe, stood Sir Richard Rich, his fellow member of the Privy Council, the King's willing tool in the dirtiest pieces of State business these last ten years. I knew Rich had been involved in the financial administration of the invasion of France the year before; rumour said he had been in trouble with the King for lining his pockets a little too heavily.

The two did not speak or move, just stood looking at me, Seymour with a contemptuous stare and Rich with his cold, still gaze. They knew a man of my rank could not simply ignore them. I took off my cap and approached, trying to keep my legs steady. I bowed low.

Seymour spoke first. 'Master Shardlake, it is a long time since we met. I thought you had gone back to the courts.' He smiled mischievously and waved a hand in an exaggerated, sweeping gesture. 'Gathering gold from the quarrels of poor silly folks, while strong true Englishmen fight to save their country from its enemies.' He pointedly looked me up and down, even glancing round a little at my back.

'God has given me my limitations.'

He laughed. 'Ay, that he has.'

I did not reply. I knew Seymour would soon tire of mocking me and allow me on my way. But then Rich spoke, quietly, in his sharp voice. 'What business have you here? I would not have thought you would dare come near the King's court again. After last time.'

He was referring to when he had had me put in the Tower on false charges to win a court case. Rich had then been in charge of the Court of Augmentations, which controlled the monastic lands seized by the King. I had brought a case on behalf of the City of London and, had I won, it would have reduced the value of some of the lands. Rich had used lying witnesses to have me imprisoned on false charges of treason. He would happily have seen me executed, but the charges had been proved false. Nonetheless the City Council had been so frightened they had withdrawn the case.

I begged my legs to be still. 'I am here on legal business, Sir Richard. For Brother Warner.'

'The Queen's lawyer. I hope she has not set you to defending heretics, as Warner did last year.'

'No, Sir Richard. Merely a civil case. For one of the Queen's old servants.'

'Which court?'

'Wards.'

Rich and Seymour both laughed, Seymour's bellow contrasting with Rich's rasp. 'Then I wish you a merry time,' Rich said.

'I hope you have a full purse for the officials,' Seymour said. 'You will need it.'

I expected that to earn a rebuke from Rich; he was a law officer and they took offence at mention of corruption in the courts. But Rich only smiled thinly. 'But who will fill that purse, Sir Thomas?' he asked. 'The Queen's servant, I hope. Were the Queen to pay herself that would be maintenance of someone else's case, which is not lawful.'

'You may be sure the Queen will see the proprieties observed,' I replied. 'She is a woman of probity.' It was a bold answer, but it was time to remind him who my patron was.

Rich inclined his head. 'I know this is not the first time her majesty has instructed you in legal matters. I find it a little strange, given the opinion the King showed of you at York.' He turned to Sir Thomas, smiling. 'Master Shardlake annoyed him there, and he suffered a public humbling for his pains.' He cast his neat little head on one side, and I saw that beneath his cap his hair was greying.

'I know that tale,' Seymour said. 'He called Shardlake a bent bottled spider before half of York.' He laughed again.

Rich bowed slightly, dismissing me. 'Take care, Master Shard-lake.'

I walked away, shaken, feeling their eyes on me. To meet those two together was a piece of ill luck. I had thought I was long since done with Rich. It frightened me to think his malicious eyes had been watching me all this time; but no doubt he watched all the little people, waiting to see whom he could entangle in his webs. Thank God I had the Queen's patronage. I waited till I had passed under the arch, beyond their gaze, before I wiped my brow.

✣

I WENT STRAIGHT HOME; I knew Tamasin was calling to see Guy and Barak would be with her. To my surprise when I entered the house the hallway was full of people. Tamasin sat at the bottom of the staircase, her swollen stomach prominent under her dress, her pretty pale face perspiring, blonde hair hanging limp around it. Coldiron's daughter Josephine had removed Tamasin's coif and was using it to fan her face with broad sweeps of her arm. Barak stood by, biting his lip anxiously. Coldiron stood looking on disapprovingly, while the two boys peered out from the kitchen doorway.

'Tamasin,' I said anxiously. 'My dear? What has happened? Where is Guy?'

'It's all right, Master Shardlake.' To my relief there was amusement in her voice. 'He's gone to wash his hands. I just felt strange when I came in out of the sun, I had to sit down.'

'She walked all the way here by herself,' Barak said indignantly. 'I said I'd meet her here but I thought Jane Marris would be with her. Walking alone, in this heat, and at too fast a pace if I know her. What if you'd fallen down in the middle of Chancery Lane, Tammy? Why didn't Jane come with you?'

'I sent her to the shops. She hadn't returned when I was due to leave. It's chaos in the markets with all the uproar over the new coins.'

'You should have told her to get back in time to fetch you here. Where are your wits, woman?'

'I didn't faint, Jack,' Tamasin replied irritably. 'I just had to sit down – ow!' She broke off as Josephine, fanning a little too wildly, accidentally hit her on the cheek.

Coldiron stepped forward, grabbing the coif. 'Watch what you're doing, you clumsy mare. Get back to the kitchen! And try not to break any more pots!' Josephine blushed and hastened away with her little scuttling steps, head bowed. Coldiron turned to me. 'She broke the big butter pot this morning. I've told her it'll come out of her wages.'

'It doesn't matter,' I said. 'Tell her I'll pay for a new one.'

Coldiron took a deep breath. 'If I might suggest, sir, that's not good for discipline. Women are like soldiers, they need to obey their superiors.'

'Get out,' I said irritably. 'I've enough to attend to here.'

Coldiron's single eye widened for a moment with anger, but he obeyed and followed his daughter back to the kitchen. The boys, who had been grinning, fled before him. I turned back to Tamasin. 'Are you all right?'

'Of course. There was no need for him to speak to her like that. Poor girl.'

Guy appeared, walking slowly down the stairs, drying his hands on a towel. 'Are you feeling better, Tamasin?' he asked.

'All well now.' Tamasin struggled to her feet, Barak hastening to help.

'Tell her, Dr Malton,' Barak appealed. 'Tell her she was stupid to walk here unaccompanied.'

Guy leaned down and felt her brow. 'You are very overheated, Tamasin. That is no good thing when you are with child.'

'All right, I won't walk out alone again.' She looked at Barak. 'I promise.'

'May I examine Tamasin in your study, Matthew?' Guy asked.

'Of course. Jack, I would like a word with you,' I added quickly as he made to follow Guy and his wife. Tamasin shot me a grateful smile over her shoulder. Reluctantly, he followed me into the parlour.

I shut the door, bade him sit, and took a stool facing him.

'We've some urgent work,' I said.

'The Queen?'

'Yes.'

His eyes lit up with interest as I told him of my meeting with the Queen and Bess. 'The Lady Elizabeth was there when I arrived,' I added.

'What is she like?'

'Astonishingly clever. The Queen and she are like mother and daughter.' I smiled, then frowned. 'Afterwards I met two old acquaintances. Rich and Thomas Seymour. I think they knew I was there,' I concluded. 'I think they were waiting for me to come out, to taunt me.'

'It was just ill chance. They were probably talking about war business when you appeared. If you go to a cesspit, you're bound to see some maggots.'

'You're right. But Rich has obviously been following my career.'

'It's no secret you've acted in cases for the Queen. He probably heard you were coming and decided to have a bit of sport with you.'

'Yes. I'm not important enough for him to take any real interest.'

'I'd heard Rich was a little out of favour.'

'I heard that too. But he is still on the Privy Council. His talents are valued by the King,' I added bitterly.

'Politics is like dice: the better the player, the worse the man.'

'Jack, we need to move fast. This hearing is on Monday.'

'We've never dealt with the Court of Wards before.'

'Many of its functions are not those of a court at all. You know the principle of wardship?'

He quoted slowly, a passage remembered from a law book. 'If a man holds land under knight service, and dies leaving minor heirs, the property passes in trust to the King till the ward comes of age or marries.'

'That's right.'

'And the King has the right to manage the lands, and arrange the marriage of the ward. But in fact he sells the wardships to the highest bidder. Through the Court of Wards.'

'Well remembered. Knight service is an ancient form of tenure which was dying out before the present King's reign. But then the Dissolution of the Monasteries came. And all the seized monastic lands that have been sold have been on terms of knight service. It generated so much wardship business they abolished the old Office of Wards and set up the court. Its main job is money. They check the value of lands subject to wardship through the feodaries, the local officials. Then they negotiate with applicants for the wardship of minor heirs.'

'Some wardships are granted to the children's families, are they not?'

'Yes. But often they go to the highest bidder, especially where there is no immediate family. Like this man Nicholas Hobbey in the case of the Curteys children.'

'I can see why he'd do it.' Barak was interested. 'If he could marry the girl to his son, he'd get her share of her father's woodland. But the girl died.'

'It is still worth his while to have Hugh. Emma's share would have passed to her brother. Hobbey will have control of Hugh's lands till he is twenty-one. There is a constant cry for wood in the south, for ships and for charcoal for the ironworks. Especially now with the war.'

'How much woodland is there?'

'I believe approaching twenty square miles in all. Hobbey owned about a third himself, but the rest will now belong to Hugh Curteys. And by law the value of his land should be preserved. But I believe those who have bought wardships often make illicit profits by cutting down woodland, usually hand in glove with the local feodary, who takes a share. The whole system is rotten from top to bottom.'

Barak frowned. 'Is there nothing to protect children under wardship?' A child of the streets himself, the plight of children in distress always moved him.

'Very little. The wardmaster has an incentive to keep the ward alive because if he dies the wardship ends. And he is supposed to ensure the child is educated. But he can marry the ward off to more or less whom he pleases.'

'The children are trapped, then? Helpless in the briars?'

'The court has a supervisory power. It is possible to apply for protection against bad treatment for wards, which is what Michael Calfhill did. But the court doesn't like interference, wardships are profitable. I will go to Wards tomorrow. I'll probably have to grease some palm to see all the papers. And while I'm at it — ' I took a deep breath — 'I'll try and get a copy of the document certifying Ellen's insanity. From nineteen years ago.'

Barak looked at me seriously. 'That Ellen is closing a vice on you. Weakness can give some folk a strange sort of power, you know. And she's crafty, as mad folk often are.'

'Finding out about her family may be a way forward. Maybe I can find someone who will care for her. Ease my burden.'

'You said Ellen was raped. Maybe it was a member of her family who did it.'

'Or maybe not. If the Curteys application goes forward, I may have to go down to Portsmouth to take depositions. Perhaps I could make a detour to Sussex on the way.'

Barak raised his eyebrows. 'Portsmouth? I've heard a lot of soldiers are going there. It could be a likely place for the French to land.'

'I know. The Queen warned me the King's spies say that is what is planned. But the Hobbey establishment is some miles north.'

'I'd come with you, but I can't leave Tamasin. Not now.'

I smiled. 'I won't hear of it. But help me with Michael Calfhill's hearing.'

'Strange he should kill himself just after making this application. When he might have been able to do something for the Curteys lad.'

'You mean he might have been killed? I thought of that. But his mother said no one else knew of the application, and she recognized his writing on the suicide note.' I passed the scrap of paper over to Barak. He studied it.

'Still strange. It would do no harm to go to where Michael lodged, ask a few questions.'

'Could you do that tomorrow?'

Barak smiled and nodded. This was the sort of work he liked, and was good at. Ferreting things out on the street.

'And visit the Curteyses' old church, see if their vicar is still there?'

'First thing.'

'Here, I'll write down the addresses.'

When I turned to give the paper to him he was smiling at me sardonically.

'What?'

'This one has got your juices flowing, hasn't it? I could see you were getting bored.'

Barak sat up at the sound of his wife's voice. We went to the door. Tamasin stood outside smiling. Guy looked happier than for some time.

'Everything is as it should be with my daughter,' Tamasin said. 'My little Johanna.'

'My little John,' Barak countered.

'But you are right heavy with the child, Tamasin,' Guy said warningly. 'You must take things easily.'

'Yes, Dr Malton,' she answered humbly.

Barak took her hand. 'You'll listen to Dr Malton, but not to your husband and master, eh?'

Tamasin smiled. 'Perhaps my good master will see me home. If you can spare him, sir.'

As they left the house, bickering amiably, Guy smiled. 'Tamasin says Jack is over-anxious.'

'Well, I have some new work that will keep him occupied.' I put my hand on his shoulder. 'That is what you need too, Guy, to get back to work.'

'Not yet, Matthew. I am too – weary. And now I should wash my hands again. Unlike some of my colleagues I believe it is important, to get rid of any bad humours.'

He went back upstairs. I felt a sudden weight of sadness, for Guy, for Ellen, for the unknown lad Hugh Curteys, for poor Michael Calfhill. I decided to walk round my garden to order my thoughts a little.

As I came round the side of the house I saw Coldiron chopping a pile of wood with an axe. His red face was slick with sweat; it dripped down past his eyepatch, onto his nose. Josephine was beside him, twisting her hands anxiously. She seemed on the point of tears. 'Hunchbacks,' her father was saying. 'Swart-coloured men, pregnant hussies falling and displaying their great bellies on the stairs.' He jumped and looked round at the sound of my approach. Josephine's eyes widened and her mouth dropped open.

I stared at him. 'Think yourself lucky Barak was not with me,' I said coldly. 'If he heard you talking of his wife like that you might find yourself on the wrong end of that axe.' I walked round him and away. I would have dismissed him on the spot, but the look of utter fear in Josephine's eyes had stopped me.

Chapter Five

AN HOUR LATER Guy and I sat down to supper. Coldiron was at least a good cook, and we dined on fresh river eels with butter sauce. His manner was obsequiously respectful and he kept his eye downcast as he served us.

When he had left the room, I told Guy about my meeting with the Queen and the Curteys case. I also said that if I were to go to Hampshire, it would be a way of investigating Ellen's past.

He fixed me with his keen brown eyes, hesitated a moment, then said, 'You ought to tell her you know how she feels about you and that there is no hope.'

I shook my head vigorously. 'I fear the effect on her. And if I stopped going to see her, she would be alone.'

Guy did not reply, only went on looking at me. I threw down my knife and sat back.

'If only love could always be mutual,' I said quietly. 'I loved Dorothy Elliard, but she could not return my love. While for Ellen I feel only – liking, yes. Pity.'

'Guilt? Because of what you cannot feel for her?'

I hesitated. 'Yes.'

He said quietly, 'It would take courage for you to tell her. To face her reaction.'

I frowned angrily. 'I am not thinking of myself!'

'Not at all? Are you sure?'

'The best way to help her is to find out the truth about her past!' I snapped. 'Then—'

'Then the problem may be handed over to someone else?'

'It does not belong with me. And finding out the truth can only help her, surely.'

He did not reply.

✝

AFTERWARDS I went upstairs to look at my commonplace books, notes on cases and aspects of the law going back to my student days. I needed to refresh my mind on the rules and procedures of the Court of Wards. First, though, I thought about Coldiron. I half-wished I had dismissed him in the garden, but it occurred to me that if I did and then had to go to Hampshire, there would be nobody left in charge of the house and the two boys except Guy, and it would be unfair to leave that responsibility with him. Better to set enquiries about possible stewards in motion round Lincoln's Inn tomorrow, and make sure I had someone to take his place before dismissing him. Yet Josephine worried me; I did not want to cast her out into the world with nobody but Coldiron. I cursed the day I had taken him on.

I spent the rest of the evening making notes, calling down to Coldiron to bring a candle as the light faded. I heard Josephine's footsteps pattering up the stairs: she brought in a candle, set it on my desk, and left with a quick curtsey. Her steps descended again, pitter, pitter, pitter.

At length I stopped writing and sat back to think. Master Hobbey had begun by purchasing a portion of this tract of woodland plus the monastic buildings, which he had converted into a house, then he had bought the children's wardship. The capital outlay for all these transactions would have been large, even for a prosperous merchant. It would be interesting to find out the sums involved. Emma, Bess Calfhill said, had not liked young David Hobbey; but my reading had made clear that only in the most exceptional circumstances would the court consider an appeal by a ward against a proposed marriage. The marriage partner would have to be far below her in social class, or a criminal, or diseased or deformed – I noted wryly that a hunchback counted – for the Court of Wards to disallow the marriage on the basis of 'disparagement'.

But Emma had died, and if that was Hobbey's plan it had come to naught. Her inheritance would have passed to Hugh and though by one of the law's oddities a girl, if unmarried, could apply to have her wardship ended at fourteen, a boy could not 'sue out his livery' until the age of twenty-one. According to Bess, seven years ago Hugh had been eleven; he would be eighteen now – three years till he could come into his lands.

I got up and paced the floor. Until Hugh was twenty-one Hobbey would be entitled only to the normal income his lands brought in, and if it was woodland there would be no income from rents. Yet, as I had told Barak, the owners of wardships were notorious for 'wasting' the lands of their wards, selling and profiting from assets like woodland and mining rights.

A book on my shelf caught my eye: Roderick Mors's *Lamentation of a Christian Against the City of London*, a diatribe against the city's social evils that had belonged to my friend Roger. I opened it, remembering there was a passage about wardship: 'God confound that wicked custom; for it is too abominable, and stinks from the earth to heaven, it is so vile.'

I closed the book and looked out over my garden. It was nearly dark; the window was open and the scent of lavender came up to me. I heard the bark of a fox, a flutter of wings somewhere. I thought, I could almost be in the countryside, back on the farm where I grew up. At that moment it was hard to believe the country was embroiled in crisis; armed men marching, armies forming, ships gathering in the Channel.

✞

NEXT MORNING I walked down Chancery Lane to catch a boat to Westminster Stairs. Crossing Fleet Street, I saw someone had placed handwritten posters all over the Temple Bar, calling on the mayor to beware 'priests and strangers' that would set fire to London. The weather was even stickier this morning; the sky had taken on a yellow, sulphurous look. I turned into Middle Temple Lane and followed the narrow passageway downhill between the narrow buildings. Along a side lane the old Templar church was visible. Vincent Dyrick practised in the Temple. I thought, only four days now until the hearing. I walked on past Temple Gardens, where the recent storms had laid great wreaths of petals under the rose bushes, and down to Temple Stairs.

The river was still crowded with supply boats heading east. I saw one barge laden with arquebuses, five-foot iron barrels glinting in the sun. The boatman told me all the King's ships had sailed out from Deptford now, bound for Portsmouth. 'We'll sink those French bastards,' he said.

At Westminster Stairs two barges were tied up, each with a dozen men leaning on the oars. I climbed up into New Palace Yard, under the huge shadow of Westminster Hall. A company of a hundred soldiers was drawn up beside the great fountain, resplendent in the red and white of the London Trained Bands. They made a magnificent display, as they were meant to. Their weapons were a stark contrast to their bright uniforms: dark, heavy wooden maces with heads full of spikes and studs in elaborate, brutal designs.

Facing them was a stocky officer on a black horse, with a surcoat in the royal colours, green and white, a plumed helmet on his head. A crowd of onlookers lined the square, the hawkers, pedlars and prostitutes of Westminster and some clerks from the courts. One of the whores pulled down her bodice to display her breasts to the recruits, and people nearby laughed and cheered. The officer smiled faintly.

The soldiers had a tense, expectant air, watching as the officer produced an impressive-looking parchment, held it up with a flourish, and began declaiming: 'By the faith I bear to God and King, I will truly obey the martial laws or statutes.' He paused and the men repeated his words in a loud chant. I realized this was a swearing in, men taking the oath binding them to full-time service, and I pushed my way through the crowd, a careful hand on my purse. Then, suddenly, I was in the narrow, dark lane between Westminster Hall and the abbey, deserted save for a white-headed old clerk walking slowly towards me, bent under the weight of a pile of papers.

I arrived at the group of old Norman buildings behind Westminster Hall, white stone shabby with soot. Instead of heading for the Court of Requests as usual, I opened a stout wooden door in the adjacent building and climbed a flight of narrow stone steps to a wide archway. Above it was a carved representation of the seal of the Court of Wards; the royal arms and underneath the figures of two young children bearing a scroll with the Latin motto of the court: *Pupillis Orphanis et Viduis Adiutor*. A helper to wards, orphans and widows.

✝

THE BROAD VESTIBULE of the court was dim, with the familiar law court smell of dust, old paper and sweat. A number of doors led off to one side, while on the other several people sat on a long wooden bench, their faces strained and tight. All were richly dressed. There was a couple in their thirties, the man in a fine doublet and the woman in a silk dress and a hood lined with pearls. A little way along sat a boy of about ten in a satin jerkin. A young woman in a dark, high-collared dress held his hand as she argued with a barrister I did not know.

'But how could they do that?' she asked. 'It makes no sense.'

'I have told you, my lady,' he answered patiently, 'here, it is expecting sense that makes no sense.'

'Excuse me, Brother,' I asked. 'Can you direct me to the clerk's office?'

He looked at me curiously. 'The door behind you, Brother. You new to Wards?'

'Yes.'

He tapped his waist where his purse hung. I nodded. The child looked at us with an expression of desperate puzzlement. I knocked at the clerk's door.

✝

INSIDE, a large room was divided in two by a wooden counter. On the far side, under a window through which the sky was still darkening, a thin, grey-haired clerk in a dusty robe sat working at a desk. A younger, thin-faced clerk was arranging papers on the shelves that lined the walls from floor to ceiling. The older clerk looked up, the steady scratch of his quill ceasing, and came across to me. His lined face was expressionless, but his eyes were sharp and calculating. He bowed briefly, then laid a pair of ink-stained hands on the counter and stared at me enquiringly, quite unintimidated by my serjeant's coif. The clerks held great power in all the courts, but usually they showed deference to barristers and serjeants. The Court of Wards, it seemed, was different.

'Yes, sir?' he asked neutrally.

I opened my satchel and laid Michael Calfhill's summons on the counter. 'Good day, master clerk. My name is Serjeant Shardlake. I wish to go on record in this case. I believe Master Warner, the Queen's attorney, has written to Attorney Sewster.'

He looked at the paper, then back at me, his expression a shade more respectful. 'Yes, sir. I was told to allow a late entry on the record. But Master Sewster also told me to say, sir, that evidence to support the plaintiff's case needs to be filed quickly.'

'I understand. Were you told the man that laid the Bill of Information has died?'

'Yes.' He shook his head sadly. 'The plaintiff dead, a lawyer instructed four days before the hearing, no depositions, no papers. Sir William will be placed in difficulties at the hearing. The proper procedures have to be followed. The interests of young children are at stake, you see.'

'I would be willing to show good appreciation for any help you can give me now. I hope to have fresh depositions shortly.' I slipped my hand under my robe, to my purse, 'Master –'

'Mylling, sir, under-clerk.' He turned his palm slowly upwards. I glanced at his young colleague, still putting away papers. 'Oh, don't heed him,' Mylling said. 'Five shillings in the new money to see all the papers about the wardship, three in proper silver.'

I blinked. The whole legal and government system was lubricated by bribes. Money or expensive gifts were passed to officials from parties to legal cases, merchants looking to supply the army, people wishing to buy monastic land. But usually these presents were made semi-covertly, described as gifts in token of personal esteem. And those who asked for too much too often, as rumour said Rich had done last year, got into trouble. For a clerk to ask a serjeant blatantly for money like this was remarkable. But this, I reflected, was the Court of Wards. I handed over the money. The young clerk went on with his filing, quite uninterested in what was clearly routine business.

Mylling's manner became friendly. 'I'll get you on the record, sir, and fetch the papers. But, sir, I tell you in your own interest, you need witnesses that can give some credibility to Master Calfhill's accusations. I am being honest with you, as I was with Master Calfhill when he came.'

'Michael Calfhill saw you when he made the application?' I asked.

'Yes.' Mylling looked at me curiously. 'Did you know him?'

'No. I only took instructions from his mother yesterday. What was he like?'

Mylling thought a moment. 'Strange. You could see he'd never been in court before. Just said terrible things had been done to this young ward, he wanted it brought before Sir William at once.' Mylling leaned his elbows on the desk. 'He seemed wild, distracted. I wondered if he was a bit brainsick at first, but then I thought, no, he is – ' he thought a moment – 'outraged.'

'Yes,' I said. 'That fits.'

Mylling turned to his assistant. 'The papers, Alabaster,' he said. The young man had been listening after all, for he immediately began rooting in the dog-eared piles, quickly fetching over a thick bundle tied in red ribbon. Mylling untied it and passed me the top paper.

A Bill of Information, filled out in a neat hand, the signature in the bottom corner the same as that on the suicide note. I read:

I, Michael John Calfhill, do humbly petition this Honourable Court to investigate the wardship of Hugh Curteys, granted to Nicholas Hobbey, of Hoyland Priory, Hampshire, anno 1539, monstrous wrongs having been done to the said Hugh Curteys; and to grant an injunction to avoid Nicholas Hobbey's possession of the ward's body.

I looked at Mylling. 'Did you help draft the application?' I asked. Clerks were not supposed to do that, but Michael Calfhill would not have known the legal formulae and Mylling would probably have helped for cash.

'Ay. I told him the bill should strictly be signed by a barrister, but he insisted on doing it himself, at once. I said he should tone his language down, but he wouldn't. I did try to help him. I felt sorry for him.' I saw, rather to my surprise, that Mylling spoke truly. 'I told him he'd need witnesses and he said he'd talk to some vicar.'

'May I?' I reached for the file. The paper beneath the application, as I expected, was the defendant's reply to the bill. Signed by Vincent Dyrick, it was a standard defence, bluntly denying that any of the allegations were true. The other papers were much older.

'Is there anywhere private I could look at these?'

'I'm afraid not, sir. Court papers may only be taken out of the office for hearings. You may lean at the desk here.' My hand went to my purse again, for leaning over that counter for any length of time would, I knew, hurt my back, but Mylling shook his head firmly. 'I'm afraid that is the rule.'

So I leaned over the counter and looked through the papers. Nearly all dealt with the grant of Hugh and Emma's wardship six years before; records of the application by Nicholas Hobbey, Gentleman, and valuations of the land from the local officers, the escheator and feodary. Hobbey had paid £80 for the wardship, and £30 in fees. That was a large amount.

There was also a copy of the earlier conveyance to Hobbey of the priory buildings and his minority share of the woodland he had bought from the Court of Augmentations. He had paid out £500 for those. There was a plan of the lands formerly under the nunnery's ownership; I looked to see whether there were any valuable rented properties, but all the land, both Hugh's and Hobbey's, seemed to be just an expanse of woodland – apart from the village of Hoyland, which Hobbey had bought with the priory buildings. He was lord of the manor, giving him an increase in social status. Hoyland was quite a small village, I saw, thirty households so perhaps two hundred people. There was a schedule of tenancies and I saw that although some households owned their land freehold, most held it on short leases of seven to ten years. I thought, the amount of rent will be minimal, not much profit for anyone there. Hoyland Priory was described as being eight miles north of Portsmouth, 'on the hither side of Portsdown Hill'. From the plan it lay very near the main London to Portsmouth road, ideal for transporting wood.

I stood up, easing my back. Hobbey had made a big investment, first in his portion of the land and then in the wardship. He had moved down there, so presumably he had sold his merchant's business in London. A successful merchant deciding to set himself up as a country gentleman – it was a common enough picture.

I looked up. Mylling was glancing at me covertly from his desk. His eyes skittered away. 'This wardship went through very fast,' I said. 'Barely two months from the original petition to the grant. Hobbey paid high fees. He must have wanted the wardship badly.'

Mylling got up and came over. He said in a low voice, 'If he wanted it put through quickly he would have been expected to show his appreciation to Attorney Sewster and the feodary.'

'Master Hobbey has lands in Hampshire next to the wards' property. And a young son.'

Mylling nodded sagely. 'That'll be it. If he married the girl to his son that would unite their lands. Draw up a pre-contract of marriage while they're still children. You know the gentry. Marry in haste, love at leisure.'

'The girl died.'

Mylling inclined his head wisely. 'Wardship has its risks like any other business. There's still the boy's marriage, though. He could make some profit from that.' Mylling turned away as the outer door opened and a fat, elderly clerk brought in a file of papers, depositing it on the counter. 'Young Master Edward's wardship to his uncle is confirmed,' he said. 'His mother was overruled.'

Through the door I heard the sound of a woman and a little boy weeping. The clerk stroked the dangling sleeves of his robe. 'His mother said the uncle is so ugly the boy runs away at the sight of him. Sir William told her off for insolence.'

Mylling called for Alabaster and he came over. 'Draw the orders, there's a good fellow.'

'Yes, sir.' Alabaster smiled cynically at the court clerk. 'No gratitude in Wards, is there, Thinpenny?'

The clerk scratched his head. 'That there isn't.'

Alabaster smiled again, a nasty smile I thought, then saw me looking and turned back to his desk. Thinpenny left and Mylling returned to his desk. I turned back to the Curteys documents. There was little more on the file: an exhibition setting out the amounts Hobbey undertook to pay for the children's education – another outgoing, I thought – and then a short certificate recording the death of Emma Curteys in August 1539. Finally there were half a dozen orders from the last few years, ordering that Master Hobbey be permitted to cut down a limited amount of woodland belonging to Hugh, 'the trees being mature and the demand for wood great'. Hugh's profits, like his inheritance, were to be held by the Court of Wards. The amount to be cut down was to be agreed 'between Master Hobbey and the feodary of Hampshire'. On each occasion sums between £25 and £50 had been remitted to court with a certificate endorsed by the feodary, one Sir Quintin Priddis. At last, I thought, the stink of possible corruption; there was nothing to prove that larger sums had not been split between Hobbey and this Priddis. But nothing to prove they had, either. I slowly closed the file and straightened up, wincing at a spasm from my back.

Mylling came over. 'All done, sir?'

I nodded. 'I wonder whether Master Hobbey will come to the hearing.'

'His barrister going to the initial hearing would suffice. Though I would go if I was the subject of an accusation like that.'

'Indeed yes.' I gave him a friendly smile. I needed Mylling for one thing more. 'There is a separate matter I seek information on. Not connected to this case. The record of a *lunatico inquirendo*, a finding of lunacy on a young woman. It would have been nineteen years ago. I wondered if you could help me find it.'

He looked dubious. 'Do you represent the guardian?'

'No. I want to find who the guardian is.' I tapped my purse.

Mylling cheered up. 'It's not strictly my department. But I know where the records are.' He took a deep breath, then turned to the young clerk. 'Alabaster, we're going to have to go to the Stinkroom. Go to the kitchens, fetch lanterns and meet us there.'

✝

THE PEOPLE waiting on the bench had all gone. Mylling led me through a warren of tiny rooms with a quick, bustling step. In one a clerk sat with two piles of gold coins on his desk, transferring angels and sovereigns from one pile to another and marking up a fat ledger.

We descended a flight of stone stairs. There was a landing and then another flight, leading down into darkness. We were below street level. Alabaster was waiting on the landing, holding two horn lanterns with beeswax candles inside, which gave off a rich yellow light. I wondered how he had got there before us.

'Thank you, Alabaster,' Mylling said. 'We won't be long.' He turned to me. 'This is not a place you'd want to spend too much time in.'

The young clerk bowed, then walked away with quick, loping

strides. Mylling took the lantern and handed one to me. 'If you please, sir.'

I followed him down ancient steps, carefully, for they were so old they were worn in the centre. At the bottom was an ancient Norman door set with studs of iron. 'This was once where part of the royal treasure was kept,' Mylling told me. 'These parts date back to Norman times.' He put his lantern on the floor, turned his key in the lock and heaved at the door. It creaked open loudly. It was enormously thick and heavy, and he needed both hands. Next to the door was half a flagstone. He nudged it into the doorway with his foot. 'Just to be safe, sir. Careful of the steps inside.'

As I descended after him into the pitch-black room, the smell of rot and damp made me gasp and almost retch. Mylling's lantern showed a small, dimly lit chamber with a stone-flagged floor. Water dripped somewhere. The walls were furred with mould. Piles of ancient papers, some with red seals dangling from strips of coloured linen, were stacked on damp-looking shelves and on the old wooden chests that stood piled on top of each other.

'The old records room,' Mylling said. 'The work at Wards grows so fast, the storage space is all taken up so we have put papers about wards who have died, or grown up and sued out their livery, down here. And all the lunatic cases.' He turned and looked at me, his face more lined and seamed than ever in the lamplight. 'There's no money in lunatics, you see.'

I coughed at the foul air. 'I see why you call it the Stinkroom.'

'No one can stay here for long — they start coughing and can't breathe. I don't like coming down here; I start to wheeze even in my own house in a damp winter. In a few years all these papers will be stuck together with mould. I tell them, but they don't listen. Let's get on, if we may. What date would this lunacy enquiry be, sir?'

'Fifteen twenty-six, I believe. The name is Ellen Fettiplace. From Sussex.'

He looked at me keenly. 'Is this another matter the Queen has an interest in?'

'No.'

'Fifteen twenty-six. The King was still married to Catherine the Spaniard then. That caused some stir, his divorcing her to marry Anne Boleyn.' He chuckled wheezily. 'A few more divorces and executions since then, eh?' He weaved his way through the chests to a far corner. 'This is where the lunatics are kept,' he said, stopping at a row of shelves piled with more damp-looking paper. He raised his lantern, and pulled out a stack. 'Fifteen twenty-six.' He laid them on the stone floor, bent down and riffled through them. After a while he looked up. 'Nothing here for Fettiplace, sir.'

'Are you sure? No similar names?'

'No, sir. Are you sure you have the year right?'

'Try the years before and after.'

Mylling rose slowly, wet marks from the floor on his hose, and returned to the stacks. As he ferreted through more papers, my nose and throat began to tingle. It was as though the furry, damp coating on the walls was starting to grow inside me. At least the clerk was thorough. He pulled out two more stacks and laid them on the floor, flicking through them with experienced fingers. I noticed a huge glistening mushroom growing between the stone flags next to him. At length he got up and shook his head. 'There's nothing there, sir. No one named Fettiplace. I've been a year back and a year forward. If it was here I'd find it.'

This was unexpected. How could Ellen be held in the Bedlam if there was no order of lunacy? Mylling rose, his knees creaking. Then we both jumped at the sound of a clap of thunder through the half-open door. Underground as we were, it was still loud.

'Listen to that,' Mylling said. 'What a noise. As though God himself were sending his fury crashing down on us.'

'He'd have cause, given what goes on in this place,' I said with sudden bitterness.

Mylling raised his lantern and looked at me. 'It's the King's wish, sir, everything that happens here. He is our Sovereign Lord and Head of the Church, too. What he orders must be enough to satisfy our consciences.' I thought, perhaps he believes what he is saying, perhaps that is how he is able to do this.

'I'm sorry I couldn't find your lunatic,' Mylling said.

'Well, sometimes knowing what is not on record can be useful.'

Mylling looked at me, eyes bright with curiosity and maybe some deeper emotion. 'I hope you find your witnesses for the Curteys case, sir,' he said quietly. 'What happened to Michael Calfhill? I can see nothing good, though Master Sewster wouldn't say.'

I looked at him. 'He killed himself.'

Mylling looked at me with his sharp dark eyes. 'I wouldn't have thought he'd have done that. He seemed so relieved to have made the application.' He shook his grey head, then led the way back into the corridors. I heard the chink of gold again.

Chapter Six

STEPPING OUTSIDE, I blinked in unexpectedly clear light. The flagstones of the passageway were covered with hailstones, shining under a sky that was bright blue again. The air was fresher, suddenly cool. I walked away carefully, crunchy slipperiness under my feet. In Palace Yard people who had taken shelter from the storm in doorways were emerging again.

I decided to walk to Barak's house, which lay on my way home, and see if he was back. By the time I reached the great Charing Cross the hailstones had melted away, the ground only a little damp underfoot. As I passed the fine new houses of the rich lining the Strand, my thoughts were on Ellen. How could she have been placed in the Bedlam without a certificate of lunacy? Someone had been paid well to take her in and was still being paid. I realized she was at liberty to walk out of the place tomorrow; but there was the paradox, for that was the last thing she could do.

I turned into Butcher Lane, a short street of two-storey houses. Barak and Tamasin rented the ground floor of a neat little house, painted in pleasing colours of yellow and green. I knocked at the door, and it was answered by Goodwife Marris; a stout woman in her forties, Jane Marris normally had an air of cheerful competence. Today, however, she looked worried.

'Is Mistress Tamasin all right?' I asked anxiously.

'*She*'s all right,' Jane replied with a touch of asperity. 'It's the master that isn't.'

She showed me into the tidy little parlour with its view on a small garden bright with flowers. Tamasin sat on a heap of cushions, hands cradling her belly. Her face was streaked with tears, her expression angry. Barak sat on a hard chair against the wall, shamefaced. I looked from one to the other. 'What's amiss?'

Tamasin cast a glare at her husband. 'We've had that officer back. Jack's only got himself conscripted into the army, the fool.'

'What? But they're looking for single men.'

'It's because he flipped his fingers at the man. And he answered him back today. Jack thinks he can do as he likes. Thinks he's still Thomas Cromwell's favoured servant, not just a law clerk.'

Barak winced. 'Tammy—'

'Don't Tammy me. Sir, can you help us? He's been told to go to Cheapside Cross in three days' time to be sworn in.'

'Sworn straight in? Not even sent to a View of Arms?'

Barak looked at me. 'He said he could see I was fit – lusty in body and able to keep the weather, he said. And he wouldn't listen to argument, just started shouting. Said I'd been chosen and that was that.' He sighed. 'Tammy's right, it's because I was insolent.'

'Recruiters are supposed to pick the best men, not indulge their disfavours.' I sighed. 'What was his name?'

'Goodryke.'

'All right, I will go to Alderman Carver tomorrow.' I looked at Barak seriously. 'The officer will probably want paying off, you realize that.'

'We've some money set aside,' he said quietly.

'Yes,' Tamasin shot back. 'For the baby.' Her eyes filled with tears.

Barak shrugged. 'Might as well spend it now. Its value's going down every day. Oh, God's death, Tammy, don't start throwing snot around again.'

I expected Tamasin to shout back at him, but she only sighed and spoke quietly. 'Jack, I wish you'd accept your status in life, live quietly. Why must you always fight with people? Why can't you be at peace?'

'I'm sorry,' he answered humbly. 'I should have thought. We'll be all right, Master Shardlake will help us.'

She closed her eyes. 'I'm tired,' she said. 'Leave me for a while.'

'Jack,' I said quickly, 'let's go out and discuss this case. I've some interesting news. I know where we can get a pie – ' Barak hesitated, but I could see Tamasin was best left alone for a while.

Outside the door, he shook his head. 'That was some storm,' he said.

'Ay. The hailstones were thick on the ground at Westminster.'

He nodded back at the house. 'I meant in there.'

I laughed. 'She's right. You are incorrigible.'

✝

WE WENT TO a tavern near Newgate jail frequented by law students and jobbing solicitors. It was busy already. A group of students sat drinking with half a dozen apprentices round a large table. The barriers of class, I had noticed, were becoming blurred among young men of military age. They were well on in their cups, singing the song that had become popular after our defeat of the Scots at Solway Moss three years before.

> 'King Jamey, Jemmy, Jocky my Jo;
> Ye summoned our King, why did ye so – '

And now apparently the Scots are waiting to fall on us, I thought, reinforced by thousands of French troops. Hardly surprising since the King had been chivalrously waging war on their infant Queen Mary for three years. Looking at the group, I saw an older man among them, and recognized the scarred face and eyepatch of my steward. Coldiron, his face flushed, was singing along lustily. I remembered it was his night off.

'Go to the hatch and get me a beer and a pie,' I told Barak. 'I'm going to sit there.' I nodded to a table screened from the body of the tavern by a partition.

Barak returned with two mugs of beer and two mutton pies. He sat down heavily, and looked at me apologetically. 'I'm sorry,' he said.

'Tamasin is in a great chafe.'

'She's right, I know. I shouldn't have given that arsehole a flea in his ear. Soldiers are touchy. Did you hear — a band of German mercenaries made a riot up at Islington this morning? Wanted more pay to go to Scotland.'

'The English troops are going quietly enough.'

'Can you get me out of it?' he asked seriously.

'I hope so. You know I'll do what I can.' I shook my head. 'I saw a hundred men from the Trained Bands setting out from West minster Stairs earlier. And at Lincoln's Inn I heard there are twelve thousand men in the navy. Sixty thousand militia on the Channel coast, thirty thousand in Essex. Twenty thousand on the Scottish border. Dear God.'

Beyond the partition, one of the carousing youngsters shouted, 'We'll find every last damned French spy in London! Slimy gamecock swine, they're no match for plain Englishmen!'

'He'd feel different if he had a wife and child.' Barak took a bite of his pie and a long swig of beer.

'If you were their age again and single, would you not be singing along with them?'

'No. I've never run with the crowd, particularly if it's heading over a cliff.' Barak wiped his mouth, took another swig.

I looked at his near-empty tankard. 'Slow down.'

'I don't drink much now. You know that. It was that which parted me from Tamasin. Not that it's always easy. It's all right for you to lecture that never drinks enough to drown a mouse.'

I smiled sadly. It was true I drank little. Even now I remembered my father, after my mother died, spending his evenings in the tavern. I would be in bed and would hear him being helped upstairs by the servants, stumbling on the steps, mumbling nonsense. I had sworn never to end like that. I shook my head. 'What did you find out today?'

'I think there's something odd about Michael Calfhill's death,' he said in a low voice. 'I talked to Michael's neighbours, saw the local constable. He's an old gabblemouth, so I took him for a drink. He said Michael had a spot of trouble with some local apprentices. Corner boys, standing around looking tough, with eyes peeled for French spies.'

'What sort of trouble?'

'The constable heard them shouting after Michael as he passed. Apparently the lads didn't like the way Michael looked at them.'

'What way?'

'As though he'd have liked to get into their codpieces.'

My eyes widened. 'There mustn't be a word of that at the hearing. What did the neighbours say?'

'There's a young couple in the room below Michael's. They didn't see him much, just heard him on the stairs, sometimes pacing in his room. The night he died they were woken by a crash. The husband went upstairs but couldn't get an answer, so he called the constable. He barged the door open and found Michael swinging from the roof-beam. Michael had cut a strip from the bedsheet and made a noose, then stood on a chair and kicked it away. That was what made the bang.' Barak leaned forward, animated now. 'I asked the young couple if they heard any footsteps going up or down the stairs. They didn't, but the room's only one storey up. And the constable said the window was open.'

'It's summer, that's no surprise.'

'I'm just saying someone could have got in while Michael was asleep, strangled him, then strung him up.' Barak smiled, his old conspiratorial smile. 'We can get into the room tomorrow if you like, take a look. It hasn't been let. The constable left the key with the young couple. I told them I might be back with someone.'

'I'll think about it. What about that vicar?'

'He's still at the same church, St Evelyn's in Fall Lane. Master Broughton. He wasn't there, the verger said to come back tomorrow at eleven.'

I smiled. 'Well done. We might have a witness after all. And we need one.' I told him about my visit to the Court of Wards. 'You got off lightly if you only had to pay out some some beer money. It cost me three shillings in good silver to get Mylling's help. We'll go and see the vicar tomorrow. And, yes, I'll have a look at Michael's lodging. Though his mother said the note was definitely in his hand.' I frowned. 'I wonder if whatever he found in Hampshire might have sent him out of his wits.'

The voices of the gang beyond the partition had grown louder, and now I heard Coldiron's voice, a grating shout. 'Men nowadays are too womanly! Sleeping out's all right! Get some branches and put blankets over them and you're as snug as a pig!'

'I'd rather huggle with my pretty pussy!'

Coldiron shouted above the laughter. 'Plenty of pussy in the army! Camp followers! Dirty girls, but they know what they're doing! Come lads, who's going to get me another drink?'

'You made a bad choice there,' Barak said.

'I know. I'm going to get rid of him as soon as I can find some-one else.'

Barak drained his mug. 'D'you want another beer? Don't worry, this'll be my last.'

'All right. But don't catch Coldiron's eye.'

While Barak fetched the drinks I sat thinking. When he returned I said, 'I found out something about Ellen at the Court of Wards. She has never been registered as a lunatic.'

'Then how did she get to the Bedlam?'

'That's what I intend to find out. Someone has been paying. Warden Metwys is in it, he has to be. And all the Bedlam wardens back nineteen years. The wardenship is an office of profit, sold to courtiers.'

Barak said, 'You'll end up more involved with her than ever.'

I shook my head. 'I won't. I can't.'

'Look, at the moment Ellen's got somewhere to live, a job of sorts. If you delve into family secrets, whoever's been paying the Bedlam might stop. Then the warden might kick her out. Where does she go then – your house?'

I sighed, for he spoke sense. 'I'll move quietly, carefully. But if I go to Portsmouth I can't miss the chance to find out what happened at Rolfswood.'

'Do you think you will?'

'If the case is allowed to go ahead next Monday, probably. Listen, tomorrow I will go and see Alderman Carver about this mess you've got yourself into. He owes me a favour. Then we can visit this vicar, see what he knows about the Curteys family. Bess will have to attend the hearing on Monday, by the way. I'm seeing her on Saturday. I don't want her to know about Michael giving those corner boys looks. If he did.'

'Maybe they decided to kill him.'

'For giving them looks? Don't be silly.'

'What if we don't come up with anything against Hobbey from the vicar?'

'Then it's more difficult. I'll have to rely on the severity of Michael's allegations and throw in the fact the wardship was put through very hurriedly. If need be I will say the Hobbey family need to answer interrogatories. If the court agrees, I'll probably have to go down to Hampshire and take them myself. I'll see Dyrick after we've found out whether there is any useful witness evidence.'

'You'll need someone with you if you go. This could be a dirty business. Ellen's matter too.'

'You're not going, not with Tamasin about to give birth. A gentleman might take a steward on such a journey, but I'd rather join the army myself than take Coldiron. I'll arrange something with Warner.' I shook my head. 'Wardship. Do you know what the motto of the Court of Wards is? Emblazoned above the door. "Pupillis Orphanis et Viduis Adiutor."'

'You know I'm no hand at Latin.'

'It means, a helper to wards, orphans and widows. There's a verbal reference to Maccabees, about the aftermath of a war: "when they had given part of the spoils to the maimed, and the widows, and orphans."'

'Now you're showing off.'

'It just struck me that whoever invented that had a dark sense of humour.'

Barak was quiet a moment, then said, 'I can think of a candidate.'

'Who?'

'I remember Lord Cromwell telling me he had been given an idea that could bring great revenue to the King. By granting out the lands of the monasteries on terms of knight service, bringing all the buyers within the scope of wardship.' He looked at me steadily. 'The man who gave him the idea was the head of the Court of Augmentations, which dealt with the monastic properties.'

'Richard Rich.'

'He was in charge of liveries in the old Office of Wards too. He put the two ideas together.'

'I'd forgotten Rich used to deal with wardships.'

'That rat has had a finger in every dirty pie. He betrayed my master that gave him office. Turned on him and condemned him when he lost the King's favour.' Barak clenched his fist, hard.

'You still remember Cromwell with affection.'

'Yes.' There was defiance in his tone. 'He was like a father to me. He took me off the streets when I was a lad. How could I not remember him well?'

'He was the hardest of men. Promoted many of the hard men we have over us now. Like Sir William Paulet.'

Barak shifted in his seat. 'I didn't like a lot of the things he got me to do,' he said quietly. 'Organizing spies and informers, occasionally frightening someone he thought needed it. But the people against him at court were no better, they hated him for his lowly origins as much as his radical religion. I sometimes still think of those days, my old work. Sometimes it used to make me feel alive.'

'Doesn't Tamasin make you feel alive? And the prospect of the child?'

He looked at me as seriously as he ever had. 'Yes. More than anything. But it's a different sort of alive. I know I can't have both.'

He was silent a moment, then stood. 'Come, I'd best get back or I'll be in more trouble.'

Beyond the partition the shouting and singing continued. As I walked past, I turned my head to avoid Coldiron's eye. One of the students was sprawled across the table now, dead drunk. Coldiron's voice sounded out again, slurred now.

'Twenty years I was a soldier. I've served in Carlisle, Boulogne, even in the Tower. All in the King's service.' His voice rose. 'I killed the Scottish King. At Flodden, that great and mighty battle. The Scottish pikemen ran down the hill at us, their cannons firing behind, but we did not flinch.'

'Englishmen never flinch!' one of the students shouted, and the group slapped their hands loudly on the table.

'Did you never want to settle down, Master Coldiron?' one of the apprentices asked.

'With this face? Never. Besides, who wants a woman bossing them around? Ever heard the saying, "There is but one shrew in the world and every man has her for a wife!"'

Laughter from the table followed us as we went out. And I thought, if you never married, then who is Josephine?

Chapter Seven

NEXT MORNING I set out for the Guildhall towards ten. I had sent Timothy round to Alderman Carver's house the previous night with a message, and he had returned saying Carver could not see me earlier. It was a nuisance, for I had much to do. I had then sent a note to Barak's house saying I would meet him outside St Evelyn's church at eleven.

After breakfast I again put on my best robe, coif and cap to impress Alderman Carver. I went into the parlour, where Guy, having breakfasted early as usual, was sitting at the table, reading his treasured copy of Vesalius's *De Humani Corporis Fabrica*. His first copy had been stolen two years before by his former apprentice, and it had taken him much cost and trouble to find another. He was running a finger down one of the beautiful but gruesome illustrations, a flayed arm.

'Studying again, I see, Guy.'

'The intelligence of this book never ceases to astonish me.' He smiled sadly. 'Coldiron saw me reading it the other day and was very interested. Favoured me with stories of how much he saw of men's insides at Flodden.'

'He would. Guy, what do you think of Josephine?'

He leaned back, considering. 'She is shy. Not happy, I think. But that is hardly surprising with Coldiron for a father. She too saw me reading Vesalius the other day. She turned away and looked quite sick.'

'I don't blame her. She doesn't have a young man, does she?'

'No. A pity, for she is good-natured and could be pretty enough if she cared anything for her appearance.'

'Coldiron is always criticizing her. That does little for her confidence.'

'I was in the hall a few days ago and heard him shouting at her in the kitchen. Calling her a silly, empty-headed wench for dropping something. She burst into tears. I was surprised to hear Coldiron speak to her in comforting tones then. He said, "You're safe with me." Calling her his JoJo like he does.'

'Safe from what?' I shook my head. 'I plan to dismiss him, but I wonder if there is any way of keeping her.'

'I fear she relies on him entirely.'

I sighed. 'Well, I must be gone. To try and save Barak from the soldier's life Coldiron brags about so.'

✣

AFTER THE STORM it was a cool, clear day with blue skies. As I walked along I thought about what I had discovered regarding Ellen. Like a good lawyer, I considered questions of organization, power. Some arrangement had been made with whoever was Bedlam warden in 1526, and kept going since. But by whom? Somehow, I did not know how, I had to *rescue* her.

I walked down Cheapside again. It was another busy morning, more angry arguments going on about the new coins. I heard a couple of traders say the hailstorm had flattened many of the crops round London so there would be a dearth of grain again this year.

I turned up to the Guildhall, and mounted the steps into the wide, echoing entrance hall. Master Carver was waiting for me, resplendent in his red alderman's robes. Beside him, to my surprise, stood the bearded officer from Lincoln's Inn Fields in his white and red uniform and with a sword at his belt. He looked at me grimly.

'Good morning, Serjeant Shardlake,' Carver said heartily. 'I am sorry to hear of your clerk's problem.' He turned to the soldier. 'Master Goodryke wished to be here, as the matter concerns him.' The officer's heavy brows drew together in a frown.

'Your man was impertinent, sir,' he said. 'His behaviour was a defiance of the King's authority. He does not possess a bow and did not even pretend to have been practising.'

'That seems to be true of many,' I answered mildly.

'It is no excuse. I'm told by the constable this Barak is of Jewish stock; perhaps that's why he shows no loyalty to England when we're about to be invaded.'

I thought, so that story's got round. I forced a smile. 'Barak can be – a little disrespectful. But he is a loyal Englishman; he worked for years for Lord Cromwell.'

'Who was executed for treason,' Goodryke countered sharply. 'I don't see any reason this man should be exempted because he used to work for a traitor.' He tilted his chin at me aggressively.

I tried again. 'He has things on his mind. His wife has a baby due in a few weeks, and they lost the last one.'

Alderman Carver nodded, looked sad. 'Ah, that is hard. Is it not, Master Goodryke?'

Goodryke was unmoved. 'He flicked his fingers at me and told me to piss off, as though I were any common churl and he could shirk his duty where he liked. Many of the soldiers I've seen are unfit for service, but he seems a good strong fellow. He could make a pikeman.'

'Well,' I said quietly, 'can we not come to some arrangement?'

'Yes,' Carver agreed eagerly. 'Master Shardlake has acted for the Guildhall many times, I can vouch for him. And I have seen this Barak, he must be in his thirties now. Old for service. If you could show latitude I am sure Serjeant Shardlake would be willing to show his appreciation. Some contribution to your company, perhaps – '

Goodryke reddened even further. 'This is not about money,' he said in a stern voice, causing passing merchants to turn and stare. 'That man is eligible to be called into service and needs to be taught discipline and loyalty.'

Carver bit his lip and looked at me. 'Serjeant Shardlake,' he said, 'perhaps we could have a little word, if Master Goodryke will allow us.' Goodryke shrugged, and Carver took my arm and led me to a corner.

'I miscalculated there,' he said. 'I thought he might be bought off. But Goodryke is a fierce fellow, he's got the bit between his teeth. He has been a whiffler for many years—'

'A what?'

'A junior officer in charge of training and discipline in military companies. He retired from the army, but joined the Trained Bands. He was only a watchman before and he is jealous of the authority the war has returned to him. He believes Barak has dishonoured our forces.'

'Alderman, the welfare of Barak and his wife are important to me. If you can resolve this I would be happy to contribute a goodly sum to Goodryke's company, though heaven knows I have little enough free cash with the next instalment of the Benevolence due.'

'Leave it with me.'

'Thank you.'

'I have not forgotten how you won those lands my cousin claimed from me, against the odds.' Carver raised his eyebrows. 'And I know how Barak must feel, the army wants gentlemen to be captains of companies and they asked me to lead a company of London men. I managed to persuade them I would be of no use. I'll talk to Goodryke's superiors. I know you get cases from the Queen: can I mention that?'

I hesitated, for I did not like to use the Queen's name too readily. But I nodded.

'As for Barak, make sure he doesn't get into any more trouble. I'll send a message as soon as I have news.'

'Thank you.'

Carver lowered his voice. 'I saw you looking on at the muster on Tuesday. To be honest I felt a fool sitting on that horse. This war – all because the King wants to hold Boulogne, which has no value.'

I nodded in agreement. 'Indeed. Do what you can, sir. Please.'
I turned away, nodding to Goodryke. He barely acknowledged me.

✝

I WALKED the short distance to Fall Lane. It was off Basinghall
Street. London Wall and the high towers of the Moorgate were visible
at a little distance. The houses were prosperous looking, with fine
windows of mullioned glass and beautifully carved doorposts, backing
onto the wide gardens of Drapers' Hall. A merchant's wife walked
past, accompanied by two armed servants, a cloth vizard covering her
face.

A small old church stood at the top of the lane. I saw the pointed
steeple with its gleaming weathercock was new; this was a wealthy
parish. Barak sat on the wall by the lych gate, looking pensive. He
stood as I approached. 'The verger says Vicar Broughton will be
along shortly,' he told me, then added, 'what news?'

I told him of my encounter with Goodryke. His face fell when he
realized the matter was not resolved. 'Tammy will have my guts.'

'Alderman Carver will do what he can. He's on our side. The
Common Council is weary of the King's endless calls for them to
raise more men. But they haven't forgotten what happened to Alderman Read.'

Barak laughed bitterly. 'I should think they haven't.'

Read's defiance had been the talk of London in January. The
King had requested a Benevolence from the tax-paying classes, a
'voluntary' tax to add to all the others he had levied for the war.
Read alone had refused, and for his pains had found himself conscripted into the army and serving with Lord Hertford's forces on the
Scottish border. He had been captured shortly after, and was now a
prisoner of the Scots.

'Has the Common Council no power left?' Barak asked, kicking
at a stone. 'Londoners used to walk in fear of the aldermen.'

I sat beside him on the wall, squinting in the sun. 'And they walk in fear of the King. And this Goodryke is acting in his name. But Carver will go higher up the chain of command.'

Barak was silent for a moment, then burst out, 'Jesus, how did we get to this? There was peace with France for twenty years till this started.'

'Perhaps the King sees keeping Boulogne as his last chance for glory. And he had his alliance with Emperor Charles last year.'

'Right worthless that proved. The Emperor made his own peace and now we face France alone.'

I looked at him. 'If they succeed in invading us they won't be kind. Nor will their Scots allies. And from what the Queen said, invasion is coming.'

'I won't leave Tamasin now.' He clenched his fists hard. 'They'll have to drag me away.'

I rose hastily as a man in a white cassock approached. Elderly, stooping, with a long grey beard. I nudged Barak. 'Quick, get up.' We bowed to the clergyman. His expression was serious, but his brown eyes looked kind. 'Master Shardlake?'

'Yes, sir. Master Broughton? This is my assistant, Barak.'

'It is about the Curteys family?'

'Indeed.'

'So,' he said, 'at last someone has come.'

✝

HE LED US into the church. The interior was bare, empty niches where statues of saints had once stood, stools set out for the congregation with copies of the King's compulsory new primer laid out on them. Broughton bade us sit, lowering himself onto a stool facing us. 'You are a lawyer, sir, I see. Do you represent Hugh Curteys? He was the only one of that poor family left.'

'No. Hugh still lives with Master Hobbey, down in Hampshire. I have not met him. But a complaint against Master Hobbey's conduct of his wardship has been laid by his old tutor, Michael Calfhill.'

Broughton smiled. 'I remember Michael well. An honest young gentleman.'

'Did he visit you recently?' I asked.

Broughton shook his head. 'I have not seen Michael in six years.' That was a blow; I had hoped Michael had come here more recently. 'How fares he?' the vicar asked.

I took a deep breath. 'Michael Calfhill died three weeks ago. I am sorry.'

The vicar closed his eyes for a moment. 'May his soul be received in Heaven, by Jesus's grace.'

'Shortly before he died, Michael laid a Bill of Information before the Court of Wards, alleging that some monstrous injustice had been committed against Hugh Curteys. According to his mother he had recently been in Hampshire and had visited him.'

'God help us,' Broughton said. 'What did he find?'

'His Information does not say. But there is a hearing on Monday. I am going to represent his mother. I need witnesses who know about this wardship, sir. Urgently.'

Broughton collected his thoughts, then looked at me directly. 'I knew that wardship was tainted. John and Ruth Curteys were my parishioners for years. When reform of the Church came they supported me in breaking with the old ways. They were stalwarts. I saw their children born, christened them, saw the family prosper. And then I buried John and Ruth.' His face twitched with emotion.

'Did they have any other family?'

Broughton clasped his hands on his lap. 'They came to London from Lancaster. Like many young folk John came here to seek his fortune. In time their parents died. When the plague took John and Ruth there was only an old aunt of Ruth's left in the north that she spoke of sometimes and wrote to. Michael came to me, concerned by Master Hobbey's interest in the children's wardship – I suggested he look for letters from her, and I would write to her. Sir,' he burst out suddenly, 'how did Michael die?'

I answered gently, 'The verdict was suicide. What he found in Hampshire may have disturbed the balance of his mind.'

'Oh, dear God.' Broughton put his head in his hands.

'I am sorry, sir. But please, tell me what you can about the wardship. What of the aunt?'

'Michael brought her address. By that time, he said, Nicholas Hobbey was already taking away papers and books of account. Michael argued with him, but Hobbey brushed him aside – Michael had no status.'

'It sounds as though you knew Michael well.'

Broughton sighed and shook his head. 'Michael came to church with the family every Sunday. But no, I never felt I knew him. Nor that he fully trusted me. I wondered if he was a secret papist, but I do not think so. Something troubled him though. But he loved those two children and did all he could to help them. We became – ' he smiled – 'conspirators, for the children's welfare.'

'Michael's mother said Hugh and Emma Curteys were close.'

'Yes. Serious, godly children.' He shook his head, his long beard trembling. 'I wrote to the aunt, paid for a fast messenger. It was already three weeks then after John and Ruth's death. Michael and I suspected Hobbey was after control of the children's lands, but not that it could be done so fast.'

'Usually it can't.'

'I waited every day for a reply from the north, but you know how long it takes to get messages from those wild places. Two weeks passed, then three. Michael visited me again, saying Hobbey was always at the Curteys house. And his lawyer too.'

'Vincent Dyrick.'

'Yes, that was the name. Michael said the children were afraid. He implored me to go and see Hobbey. So I did, I went to his house up at Shoe Lane.' Broughton frowned. 'He received me in his parlour, looked at me with the haughty arrogance of a man who worships Mammon, not God. I told him I had written to the aunt. Well, Master Hobbey only asked coldly how an old woman was going to drag herself two hundred miles and care for two growing children. He said he was the family's best friend and their neighbour in Hampshire, he would see justice done for Hugh and Emma. And then his wife came in. Abigail Hobbey.' There was anger in Broughton's face now.

'Goodwife Calfhill mentioned her. She said Michael thought her a little mad.'

'A screaming, raving shrew. She burst into the parlour while I was talking to her husband, screeching that I was a troublemaking ranter, making accusations against her husband when he wished only to help two orphaned children.'

'But you had made no accusations.'

'No, but when that woman started screaming at me, that was when I really began to fear for those children.'

'How did Nicholas Hobbey react to his wife's outburst?' I asked curiously.

'He was annoyed. He raised a hand, said, "Quiet, my dear," or some such words. She stopped yelling, but still stood with her eyes flashing fire at me. Then Hobbey told me to leave, saying I had upset his wife. Unwomanly creature. He added sarcastically that I should let him know if the aunt replied, but he had already made his application to the Court of Wards.'

'Did the aunt reply?'

'Two weeks later I had a letter from her vicar in Lancaster, to say she had died a year before.'

'I suspect Master Hobbey had already discovered that.'

'There seemed nothing else I could do,' Broughton said, spreading his arms wide. 'I talked to Michael. To be fair to Hobbey, Michael said the children were well taken care of, their needs looked after. But he said Hugh and Emma had no affection from Hobbey or his wife.'

'That happens often enough in wardship cases.'

'There was more to it than that. Michael feared Nicholas Hobbey planned to marry Emma to their son, and so unite their Hampshire lands.'

'That would be David Hobbey.'

'Yes. I saw him as I left the house that day. He was in the hallway outside, I am sure he had been listening at the door. He gave me an impertinent stare, a strange look for a child, something – triumphant about it.'

'He would have been – what – twelve then?'

'Yes. As ill favoured a boy as I have ever seen. Squat, fat-faced. Dark like his father, a wispy moustache already growing on his lip.' Broughton stopped, raising his hands. 'I am sorry, I should not have said that. He was only a child.'

'Almost a man now,' Barak observed.

I said, 'Unfortunately, to arrange such a marriage would be within Master Hobbey's rights once he had the wardship.'

Broughton shook his head in disgust. 'It is ungodly. The sacrament of marriage turned to a bargain. And Michael said – he told me David had put his hands on Emma. In a way he should not. Hugh had fought him over it.'

'So Michael's mother told me too. But then Emma died.'

'God rest the poor child. By then the wardships had been granted and Michael had moved with the children to the Hobbeys' house, out of the parish. I only saw him once more after that, when he came to tell me Emma had died and he had been dismissed.' Broughton shook his head. 'He said Abigail Hobbey showed no sadness at her funeral, looked on coldly as Emma was buried. I thought I saw despair in Michael's face then. And from what you say it seems I was right.' Broughton looked at me earnestly. 'Does this help you, sir?'

I thought. 'Only a little, I fear. Is there anyone else in your congregation who knew the family?'

He shook his head. 'Not well. It was only I that took an interest in the wardship. People do not like to interfere in such matters. But there was one thing I discovered. There were rumours that Master Hobbey was in debt.'

'Then how could he afford to buy the wardship? And he had just bought a monastic house and was having it converted.'

Barak grunted. 'Hoped to get Emma's share of the Curteys land by marrying her to his son. If so, he got a bad bargain.'

Broughton looked alarmed. 'He still has the right to make a marriage for Hugh. What if he plans to marry him to someone unsuitable? That could be what Michael discovered.'

I nodded thoughtfully. 'Possibly. Sir, I would be grateful if you could come to the hearing on Monday. At least you could testify you were unhappy with how matters were handled.' I needed every scrap of evidence I could bring. But there was still nothing a good lawyer for the other side could not easily dismiss. I got up, wincing at my stiff back. Broughton rose too.

'Sir,' he said. 'You will see justice done? Right whatever wrong is being done to Hugh?'

'I will try. But it will not be easy. I will send Barak back tomorrow to prepare a deposition for you. It must be lodged with the Court of Wards before the hearing.'

'God will not suffer injustice to children,' Broughton said with sudden passion. 'Our Saviour said, "Any wrong done unto these little ones is done also to me."' He quoted the Bible in a fierce voice; but then I saw he was crying, tears running down his creased face. 'I am sorry, sir,' he said. 'I was thinking of Michael. A suicide. In Hell. It is so – harsh. But God has decided that is where suicides must go and how can we question God?' Faith and desperation showed equally in his face.

'Justice may be tempered with mercy,' I ventured. 'That is an important principle, in earthly law at least.'

Broughton nodded, but did not speak again as he led us outside. 'What time should I come on Monday?' he asked as we parted at the church door.

'The hearing is set for ten, the Court of Wards at Westminster. If you could come early.'

Broughton bowed and returned to the dim interior of the church. As we walked through the lych gate Barak turned to me. 'Justice? He won't see that in the Court of Wards.' He gave a bitter laugh. 'Only harsh judgement, like he says God gives.'

'If Michael Calfhill deserves to be in Hell, perhaps even the Court of Wards' judgement is better than God's. Come, let's change the subject. We are talking heresy in the street.'

✝

MICHAEL CALFHILL'S lodgings lay at the other end of the city, in the warren of streets down by the river. The afternoon was well on as we turned into a narrow alley, where high old dwellings with overhanging eaves had been converted into lodging houses, old paint flaking onto the muddy ground. Chickens rooted in the dust. At a tavern on the corner a group of seven or eight apprentices in their late teens, many with swords at the belts of their blue robes, gave us hostile looks. The tallest, a fair-haired, heavy-set lad, fixed me with a hard stare. Perhaps he thought my lawyer's robe the uniform of a French spy. Barak put a hand to his own sword and the boy turned away.

Barak knocked on an unpainted wooden door. It was answered by a pretty young woman, an apron over her cheap wool dress. She smiled at him in recognition before giving me a deep curtsey. This must be Michael's downstairs neighbour; I guessed Barak had charmed her.

'I've brought Master Shardlake, Sally,' he said lightly. 'The lawyer that has an interest in poor Michael's affairs. Did Constable Harman give you the key?'

'Yes, sir. Come in.'

We followed her into a damp hallway, through an inner door into her lodging, a small room with dirty rushes on the floor, a table and a bed. An old iron key lay on the table. There was no glass in the windows, and the slats in the shutters were open. I saw the apprentices watching the house. Sally followed my gaze. 'They've been hanging around there for days,' she said. 'I wish they'd go away.'

'What guild are they from?' I asked. 'Their masters should keep them under better control.'

'I don't know. A lot of apprentices have lost their places with goods so dear. My husband worked as a messenger for the German traders at the Steelyard, but there's no trade now with ships being impounded everywhere. He's out looking for work.' Her face was weary.

Barak picked up the key. 'Can we have a look?'

'Yes. Poor Michael,' she added sadly.

I followed Barak up a flight of narrow stairs. He turned the key in the lock of a battered door at the back of the house. It creaked open. The shutters on the little window were closed, only dim shapes visible. Barak pulled them open. I saw the room was small, patches of damp on the walls. There was a narrow straw bed, a pillow with a torn sheet splayed across it. An old chest beside the bed was open, revealing an untidy heap of clothes. The only other furniture was a scarred table and a chair that lay overturned on the floor. A quill and a dusty, dried-up inkpot stood on the table. Looking up, I saw a strip of white sheet knotted to the roof beam, the end cut.

'Christ's wounds,' I said. 'It's been left as it was when he was cut down.'

'Maybe the coroner ordered it kept as it was for the jury's inspection.'

'Then forgot to tell the landlord he could clear it. That sounds like Coroner Grice.' I stared around the miserable room where Michael had spent his last days. Barak went to the chest and started searching the contents. 'There's only clothes here,' he said. 'Clothes and a few books. A plate and spoon wrapped up in a cloth.'

'Let me see.' I looked at the books – Latin and Greek classics, a tutor's books. There was also a copy of Roger Ascham's *Toxophilus*, his treatise on archery that the Queen told me the Lady Elizabeth was reading. I said, 'They should have taken all these things as exhibits.'

'The coroner was only here five minutes.' Sally was standing in the doorway. She looked around the room sadly. 'Isn't that why you're here, sir, to question the careless way the coroner handled matters?'

'Yes, that's right,' Barak said before I could reply. Sally looked round the room. 'It's just as I saw it that night. Constable Harman forced the door open, then he cried out. Samuel ran up to see what was happening and I followed.' She stared bleakly at the strip of linen hanging from the beam. 'Poor Master Calfhill. I've seen a hanging, sir, and I saw from his face he'd strangled slowly, not broken his neck.' She crossed herself.

'What was he wearing?'

She looked at me in surprise. 'Just a jerkin and hose.'

'Was he carrying anything at his belt? They would have exhibited it at the inquest.'

'Only a purse, sir, with a few coins, and a little gold cross his mother recognized as his at the inquest. Poor old woman.'

'No dagger?'

'No, sir. Samuel and I noticed he never wore one.' She smiled sadly. 'We thought him foolish. Master Calfhill didn't understand how rough it can be down here.'

I looked at Barak. 'So what did he use to cut up the sheet to hang himself?' Turning back to Sally, I asked, 'Did they say anything about that at the inquest?'

She smiled sadly. 'No, sir. The coroner just seemed to want to get through everything quickly.'

'I see.' I looked at the roof-beam again. 'What was Michael like, Sally?'

'Samuel and I used to jest that he lived in a world of his own. Walking about in fine clothes, which isn't really safe round here. I would have thought he could have afforded better lodgings. But he didn't seem to care about the dirt or the rats. He seemed lost in thought most of the time.' She paused, then added, 'Not happy thoughts. We used to wonder if he was one of those whose minds are perplexed about religion. Samuel and I just worship the way the King commands,' she added quickly.

'The constable told me he had some trouble with the corner boys,' Barak said. 'Was it the ones outside?'

She shook her head. 'I didn't hear that. It can't have been them. Those boys have only been there these last few days.'

'One question more,' I said. It was something no one had mentioned so far. 'What did Michael Calfhill look like?'

She thought. 'He was small, thin, with a comely face and brown hair. It was starting to recede though I doubt he was thirty.'

'Thank you. Here, for your trouble in helping us – '

She hesitated, but took the coin. She curtsied and left, closing the door behind her. Barak had gone over to the window. 'Come and look at this,' he said.

I went over. Directly underneath was the sloping roof of an outhouse, covered with mossy tiles, above a small yard. 'Someone could have climbed up there easily,' Barak said. 'I could get up, even now with all my easy living.' He patted his stomach.

I looked out. From here I could see the river, busy as ever with barges carrying equipment down to the sea. 'There are no tiles off the roof,' I said. 'They look old, someone climbing up would surely have dislodged a few.' I turned back to the room, looked up at the beam. 'If someone climbed up into the room and grabbed him in bed, there would have been a struggle.'

'Not if they knocked him out as he slept, then strung him up.'

'That would have left a mark on his head. The jury would have seen it at the viewing of the body.'

'Not if it was above the hairline, and they didn't look hard.'

I considered carefully. 'Remember what this case is about. The management of some lands down in Hampshire, maybe a fee for marrying off Hugh Curteys. In three years the boy will reach his majority and the lands will be his. Would Nicholas Hobbey order Michael killed just to protect that? When he could hang for it? A man with status and a family?'

'Maybe Michael discovered something Hobbey would hang for anyway.'

'Like what?'

'What about the missing knife?'

'It could have been lost or stolen in that shambles Grice calls the coroner's office.' I smiled. 'Come, have we not become too ready to see murder everywhere after all we have seen these last few years? And remember, the suicide note was in Michael's hand.'

'I still think there's a smell of bad fish here.'

'There's certainly a smell of rats. Look at those droppings in the corner.'

'Why would Michael leave his mother's house and come to a dog hole like this?'

I considered this. 'I don't know. But I see nothing here pointing to murder, except the absence of the knife, and that could easily have been lost. What we must do now is concentrate on Monday's hearing.' I took a last look round the miserable room, and the thought crossed my mind that Michael might have been punishing himself in some way by leaving his mother. But for what? My eye went to the strip of cloth again, and I shuddered. 'Come,' I said to Barak, 'let's get out of here.'

'Do you mind if I talk to the constable again?' he asked as we descended the stairs. 'I know where he'll be, in the tavern I took him to before. It's a few streets away. Maybe he will remember about the knife.'

'Won't Tamasin be waiting for you?'

'I shan't be long.'

☦

WE RETURNED the key to Sally and left the house. It was dusk now; looking down between the houses I saw the river shining red in the setting sun. The corner boys had gone.

'Can you prepare a draft deposition and take it to Broughton this evening?' I asked Barak. 'Then come to chambers tomorrow at nine. Mistress Calfhill is coming in.'

'All right.' He took a deep breath. 'Will you let me know when you get word from Carver?'

'At once.'

Barak went down towards the river, while I turned for home. As I walked along, I thought again about Michael's death. Barak had a nose for foul play.

I passed a dark alley, then jerked upright at a sudden rush of footsteps behind me. I turned quickly but got only a glimpse of young faces and blue robes, before a bag stinking of old vegetables was put over my head. Several pairs of hands seized me, hauling me into the alley. Robbers; like Michael I had carelessly advertised my wealth.

My back was slammed up against a stone wall. Then to my horror I felt hands around my neck, lifting me off the ground. My arms were held firm; my legs kicked helplessly against the stone. I was strangling, hanging. Then a hard youthful voice spoke into my ear.

'Listen to me carefully, master hunchback.'

I gasped, gagged. Little red flashes began to appear in the pitch darkness inside the bag.

'We could have you dead in a minute,' the voice continued. 'Remember that and listen hard. You drop this case, you forget about it. There's people who don't want this matter taken further. Now, tell me you understand.' The pressure at my neck eased, though other hands still gripped my arms hard.

I coughed, managed to gasp a yes.

The hands released me, and I dropped to the muddy ground in a heap, the bag still over my head. By the time I clawed it off they had gone. I lay in the dark alley, taking great sucking breaths to get some air back into my lungs. Then I leaned over and was violently sick.

Chapter Eight

I MADE MY WAY home painfully, pausing occasionally for I felt dizzy. By the time I stumbled through my front door my neck was so swollen it was painful to swallow. I went up to Guy's room. When he answered the door I could scarcely speak, my voice a croak. He made me lie down and applied a poultice, which brought some small relief. I told him I had been robbed, and he gave me a sharp look when he saw my purse was still at my belt; I felt guilty, but I had decided to keep what had happened to myself for now.

Guy told me to lie down and rest, but a short time later there was a knock at my door. Coldiron looked at me curiously as he told me I had a late visitor, Alderman Carver. I told him to show Carver into the parlour. Wearily, I went downstairs.

The set of Carver's plump face told me he had brought no good news. He, too, stared at my neck. 'Forgive my voice, sir,' I croaked. 'I was attacked earlier. Robbers.'

Carver shook his head. 'There are more and more robberies with so many constables away at the war. The times are mad. And I fear I have been unable to get a release for your man Barak.'

'But his wife—'

'I have spoken to Mayor Laxton and he has talked to Goodryke. But he is adamant he wants Barak. He has the bit truly between his teeth; Barak must have sorely annoyed him. Says the King has ordered sharp dealing with impertinence. Laxton said we could appeal to the Privy Council, but they are under orders from the King to veto any softness.'

'And I can't plead for the Queen to intervene with the King. My name has no favour with him.'

'His worship suggested one possible way forward.' Carver raised his eyebrows. 'Deal with the matter by stealth. Perhaps Barak could disappear somewhere for a while. He'll get orders very soon for swearing in.'

'He has already.'

'If he doesn't turn up, it's the council that would be asked to send constables to find him. Well –' he gave a politician's calculating smile – 'they need not try too hard. And if he is gone, well . . .'

'But where? Neither Barak nor his wife have any relatives alive. I have some in the Midlands, but Tamasin is seven months gone with child, she could not travel. And what if they come after him later for desertion? It's a capital offence.'

'Goodryke himself will be gone to the wars soon, surely.' Carver spread his plump, beringed hands. 'I can do no more, sir.'

'I understand. I will have to talk to Barak. Thank you for what you have done, sir, I am grateful.' I hesitated, then added, 'I wonder if I could impose on you further for some information. In connection with a case. You have sat on the Common Council many years.'

'Indeed. Near twenty.' Carver's plump figure swelled with pride.

'I hear the council has been negotiating with the King to take over the Bedlam.'

'For some time. We are trying to get the King to fund hospitals under the city's control; taking over the Bedlam would be part of the scheme.'

'The wardenship has been in the King's gift many years. I know Sir George Metwys holds it now. I know George Boleyn held the wardenship before, till his execution. Might you remember who held it before him? I need to go back to 1526.'

Carver thought. 'I believe it was Sir John Howard. I remember now, he died in office.'

So that connection to Ellen was gone. But any secret arrangements would have been passed on to subsequent wardens. 'One more thing,

Alderman. Do you remember a man who was in the Mercers' Guild some years ago? Nicholas Hobbey.'

He nodded slowly. 'Yes, I remember Master Hobbey. He worked his way up as an apprentice and set himself up in a small way of business. He did not involve himself much in Guild matters, though, his great interest was making money. He involved himself in importing dyestuffs, I remember, and his business suffered when the King broke from Rome and exports from the continent were embargoed. He closed his business and retired to the country.'

'I heard a rumour he was in debt about the time he moved.'

'I seem to remember people saying that.' Carver looked at me sharply. 'Sir, I should not really give you information on Guild members—'

'I am sorry, perhaps I should not have asked. But I am acting for the orphan son of another Guild member, who died some years ago and is now Master Hobbey's ward. John Curteys.'

Carver nodded sadly. 'I remember Master Curteys. A pleasant fellow, though a little stiff in religion. I did not know him well.'

'Well, sir, I thank you for your help.' I smiled. 'I will not forget my promise about a donation to the Guild.' I coughed and rose. 'Forgive me, but I should get back to bed.'

Carver stood and bowed. 'Take care of yourself, sir.' He shook his head. 'These times – '

✟

NEXT MORNING I walked to work slowly and painfully, for my neck and throat still hurt. As I crossed Gatehouse Court I nodded to a couple of acquaintances, who fortunately were at a sufficient distance not to see the raw bruised flesh above my collar.

I entered chambers and sat behind my desk. By the chapel clock it was just after nine. Barak was due shortly, and Mistress Calfhill in half an hour. I undid my shirt collar, to ease the chafing of my bruises.

From my window I saw Barak striding across Gatehouse Court.

I thought again how he was putting on weight. He knocked at my door and entered, then stared at my neck. 'God's nails! What happened to you?'

I told him in my still creaky voice. 'It's worse than it looks,' I concluded.

'Jesus. Who were they? Those lads hanging around outside Michael's house?'

'I didn't see. They made sure of that, jumping me from behind.'

'Is this Hobbey's work?'

'I don't know. Someone must have paid them well. Though there was little enough risk, there's no law left on the streets.'

Barak said, 'I wonder if Hobbey is in London.'

'If he isn't he has had no time to organize this. I only went on the court record two days ago.'

'What about Dyrick? He'll have been notified you're acting.'

'I doubt a barrister would risk his career by getting involved in something like this. Though it's not impossible.'

'When would he have got the papers saying you were on the record?'

I considered. 'Yesterday morning, I would guess. Whoever it was, they organized it fast.'

Barak looked at me keenly. 'Do you think the little arseholes meant to kill you?'

'They weren't so little. But no, I doubt it. Just to scare me off.'

'I still think someone could have killed Michael Calfhill.' Barak fixed me with his brown eyes. 'You shouldn't go to Portsmouth,' he said intently. 'Certainly not alone.'

'I agree. I have decided to talk to the Queen. I sent a message to Warner yesterday evening. She will find someone to travel with me if she thinks I should go.'

'So you'll still go if she wants you to.'

'I don't like a bunch of bluecoats trying to intimidate me.'

'Mistress Calfhill is due soon. Will you tell her what happened to you?'

'No. It would only frighten her without good cause. I'll see her, then I'll go down to the Temple and see Brother Dyrick. I sent a message last night.'

Barak slapped his knapsack. 'I've Broughton's deposition here.'

'Good.' I looked at him. 'But there is something else I must tell you now. Alderman Carver came to see me last night. I'm afraid it is not good news.' I repeated what Carver had told me.

'Shit,' he said fiercely. 'Tammy's right, I should have treated Goodryke with more care.'

'Why don't I come to your house later, and the three of us can talk about it?'

'I won't have Tammy leaving London, travelling over muddy roads,' he said firmly. 'I was scared shitless when she collapsed the other day.'

'I know. But we'll find some way through. I promise. Now, let me see Reverend Broughton's deposition.'

Barak opened his satchel and passed me the paper, written in his scratchy copyhand and signed by Broughton. He sat frowning, preoccupied, as I read. Broughton reiterated what he had told us about the Curteys family, the parents' death and Nicholas Hobbey's rapid intervention, his own and Michael's efforts on behalf of Hugh and Emma, and Hobbey's hostility to him. I looked at Barak. 'Nothing new, then?'

'No. He says that's all he remembers. I asked him if any of the Curteyses' neighbours could tell me anything, but he was sure not. The family do seem to have kept to themselves, as the godly folk will.'

I looked up as a shadow passed the window: Bess Calfhill, her face pale as parchment in the sunshine, paler even than her white coif. She wore a black dress again, though the mourning period was long past. 'Go and receive her,' I said to Barak, 'tell her my neck's been hurt in an attempted robbery. Gently. Someone with a bruised neck's the last thing she'll want to see.'

He went out, and I pulled the strings on my shirt tight again before taking the draft deposition I had prepared for Bess from my desk. Barak led her in, and she sat on the other side of my desk. She looked at my neck, shuddered slightly and dropped her gaze, twisting her hands in her lap. Then she looked up, her face determinedly composed.

'Thank you for coming, Bess.' I made my voice as strong as I could.

'It is for Michael, sir.'

'I have prepared a deposition based on what you told me at Hampton Court. If I may, I will read it over. We can make any necessary corrections, see if there is anything to add.'

'I am ready,' she said quietly.

We went through her story again. Bess nodded vigorously when I read out how close Michael and the two children had been, and said 'Yes' with quiet fierceness as I related Michael's attempt to resist Hobbey's taking over their affairs. At the end she nodded firmly. 'That is it, sir, that is the story. Thank you. I could never have formed the words so well.'

I smiled. 'I have training, Bess. But please remember that Michael's story, told to you, is hearsay. Hearsay is allowed in the case of a deceased person, but it does not have the status of first-hand testimony. And Master Hobbey's barrister may question you on it.'

'I understand,' she said firmly. 'Will Nicholas Hobbey be there?'

'I do not know.'

'I am ready to face them both.'

'We have spoken to Vicar Broughton, who has been helpful. He is coming on Monday. But he can confirm only that he and Michael tried to stop the wardship. Is there anything else you can think of that I have not included? About the children, perhaps.'

She shook her head sadly. 'Only little bits and pieces.'

'They would have been brought up by the women of the household till they were old enough for a tutor, I imagine.'

'Yes. Though John and Ruth Curteys delayed past the normal age to get a tutor. Michael thought they loved their children so much they did not wish to share them.'

'Did you meet Hugh and Emma?'

'Yes. Once Michael brought them to visit me and I went to him at the Curteyses' house and saw them many times. Master and Mistress Curteys were most civil to me, as though I were a gentlewoman. I remember Hugh and Emma coming up to Michael's room to meet me. They were laughing because Hugh had got nits from somewhere and had his hair cut close. His sister laughed at his shaven poll, saying he looked like a little old man. I told Emma tush, she should not mock her brother, but Hugh laughed and said if he were a man then he was strong enough to smack his insolent sister. Then he chased her round the room, both of them shrieking and laughing.' She shook her head. 'I can see them now, that poor dead girl's hair flying out behind her, Michael and I joining in their laughter.'

'Mistress,' I asked quietly, 'why do you think Michael left home towards the end?'

'I think it was because – ' her lips worked suddenly – 'because I fuss so.' She bowed her head, then said, 'Michael was all I had. His father died when he was three, and I brought him up alone. At Lord and Lady Latimer's house in Charterhouse Square. Lady Latimer, as she was then, took great interest in my son, who was fond of learning like her, and encouraged him. She too knows what a kind-hearted boy he was. Too kind-hearted, perhaps.'

'Well,' I said, 'let us see if we can get his kindness rewarded in court on Monday.' I exchanged glances with Barak. We both knew that if the case were allowed to go forward, it would be because of the Queen's involvement, not the merits of the evidence.

✞

A LITTLE LATER I walked again down Middle Temple Lane, my knapsack over my shoulder. I turned left, to the Temple church. Dyrick's chambers lay opposite, in an ancient building of heavy stone. A clerk told me he was on the third floor, and I trudged wearily up a wide staircase of heavy oak boards. I had to pause halfway up, for my neck was throbbing. I grasped the banister and continued. On the third-floor landing a board outside a door had Dyrick's name picked out in elegant letters. I knocked and went in.

All barristers' chambers are much alike. Desks, shelves, papers, clerks. Dyrick's had many bundles piled around on tables, the sign of a busy practice. There were two clerks' desks but only one was occupied, by a small young fellow in a clerk's short robe. He had a thin face and a long neck in which a large Adam's apple bobbled, and narrow blue eyes beneath straggling hair. He looked at me with insolent disapproval.

'I am here to see Brother Dyrick,' I said curtly. 'Serjeant Shardlake.'

An inner door was thrown open, and Vincent Dyrick stepped out, advancing quickly with outstretched hand. He was a tall, lean man around my age. Athletically built, he seemed to exude energy. He had a pale complexion and coppery hair worn long; he was not handsome, but certainly striking. He smiled, showing a full set of teeth, but his greenish-brown eyes were hard and watchful.

'Good morning, Serjeant Shardlake. We have met before in court. I beat you twice, I think?' His voice was as I remembered, deep and rasping, educated but still with a touch of London in it; a good voice for court.

'We lost one case each, as I recall.'

'Are you sure?'

'Yes.'

'Come to my room. You do not mind if Master Feaveryear, my clerk, sits with us?' He waved an arm at the young man.

'Not at all.' My strategy was to say as little as possible, and get Dyrick to reveal as much as possible.

'In you go, Sam.' Dyrick threw open the door to his office and waved Feaveryear in ahead of him. I followed. 'Please, sit.' Dyrick indicated a stool set before a large oak desk and took a chair behind it, motioning Feaveryear to another stool beside him. The clerk took up a quill that had been laid there, ready sharpened, and dipped it in an inkpot. Copies of Michael Calfhill's application and Dyrick's reply lay on the desk. Dyrick squared them carefully with his hands, then looked at me. His smile was gone.

'Brother Shardlake, it grieves me to see a lawyer of your seniority involved in such a case as this. I would call it frivolous and vexatious were not the man who lodged this garbled bill clearly insane. A suicide, God pardon him. This application will be thrown out, and there will be substantial costs.' He leaned forward. 'Who is to pay them? Has his mother means? I heard she was but some old servant.'

So he had been doing his research. Maybe paying for information from the Court of Wards, perhaps even from Mylling.

'Any costs will be paid according to the law,' I said. It was the same point I had made to Richard Rich. I made a mental note to write to Warner suggesting he find some substantial back pay due to Mistress Calfhill. 'If we lose, that is.'

'You will.' Dyrick laughed, glancing at Feaveryear, who looked up and smiled. I opened my knapsack.

'You should see these depositions, Brother. From Mistress Calfhill and the Curteys family's vicar.' I passed copies across. Dyrick read, occasionally screwing up his nose. Then he passed the papers to Feaveryear with a shrug.

'Is this all you have, sir?' Dyrick spread his arms. 'Insignificant hearsay. This man Calfhill, before hanging himself, made accusations of serious misconduct against my client. Though neither he, nor these depositions –' he leaned across the desk to emphasize the point – 'state what this misconduct actually is.'

He was quite right, and there lay our greatest weakness.

'Michael Calfhill made a serious claim – '

'Undefined, unspecified—'

' – sufficient I believe for the court to require further investigation. Remember the Court of Wards' motto. A helper to wards, orphans and widows.'

Dyrick raised his eyebrows. 'And what, sir, would that investigation consist of? Depositions?'

'Perhaps.'

'And who is to be sent to take them? All the way to Hampshire. And how much will that cost? Enough to bankrupt any servant woman.' His voice rose angrily. He frowned, bringing himself under control – or seeming to. It had struck me that everything Dyrick and his assistant did was a performance, though a skilful one.

'It would take a few days,' I said. 'Your client will only have to pay if he loses. And you say he will not. And my client has her own house.'

'Some hovel near the Butcheries, perhaps?'

'You should not cast aspersions on my client, Brother,' I said with asperity. Dyrick inclined his head. 'You should not, Brother,' I repeated. It hurt me to speak now, I had placed too much strain on my throat. 'I see no deposition from your client. Is Master Hobbey in London?'

'No, Brother Shardlake. Master Hobbey is a gentleman with much business in Hampshire. And there is nothing here for him to depose *to*, no allegation precise enough to warrant an answer.'

'Where a child is concerned, any allegation should be investigated.' I thought, so Hobbey is not in London. No time for him to give an order to have me attacked.

'A child?' Dyrick expostulated. 'Hugh Curteys is eighteen. A strong, fit lad; I have seen him when I have visited my client on business. And well cared for, I might add.'

'Still a minor. And under the control and custody of—' I had to break off at a spasm of pain from my throat. I gasped, put my hands to my neck.

'See, Sam,' Dyrick said to Feaveryear, 'Brother Shardlake's words stick in his throat.'

I glared at Dyrick, cursing myself for my weakness. Then I saw the anger in his eyes, fierce as mine. It was no act.

'I see you have scant answer, Serjeant Shardlake,' Dyrick continued. 'I thank you for these depositions, though they are out of time and I shall argue so on Monday—'

'I see Master Curteys' estate consists of a considerable acreage of woodland.'

'All dealt with properly. You have seen the papers.'

'But no accounts.'

'Those are kept by the feodary in Hampshire. You may not be familiar with the Court of Wards, Brother, but that is the procedure.'

'Tell me, Brother Dyrick, is any marriage contemplated for Hugh Curteys?'

'None.' He inclined his head and smiled. 'There is really nothing to investigate, Brother Shardlake.'

'These accusations must be looked into, and I think the court will agree.' My voice came scratchy, high-pitched.

Dyrick stood up. 'I hope your throat is recovered by Monday.'

'It will be, Brother.'

I got up and turned to leave. Dyrick's face was cold, stony. I glanced at Feaveryear. For the first time I saw him smile, not at me but at his master. A smile of pure admiration.

Chapter Nine

THE FOLLOWING MORNING I crossed the central yard of Hampton Court again. It was Sunday, a bright, cool day, the day before the hearing. The courtyard was quiet, only a few clerks around; no skulking courtiers today.

A letter from Warner had been waiting when I returned home from my encounter with Dyrick. Coldiron had been standing in the hallway, turning the thick white paper over in his hands, staring at the beautifully written superscription on one side, the Queen's seal on the other. He handed it to me with new respect in his eye, as well as aching curiosity. I dismissed him curtly and opened it; it asked me to attend the Queen again on the morrow.

I had been instructed to come to Warner's office, and once more I climbed the spiral steps. I wore my coif to hide my bruises. Warner's room had been freshly laid with new rushes, their sweetness overcoming the smell of dust and paper. 'Ah, Brother Shardlake,' he said. 'It is cold again. What a summer.'

'I saw, on my way here, that hailstorm has flattened much of the wheat.'

'It's worse in the north. And great winds in the Channel. By Christ's mercy the *Great Harry* and the *Mary Rose* have arrived safely in Portsmouth Haven.' He looked at me keenly. 'I showed your message to the Queen. She was disturbed, as I was, by the attack on you. You are recovering?'

'I am, thank you.'

'The Queen wishes to see you now.' Warner opened a side door and called in a young clerk. 'Serjeant Shardlake is here. Go, inform the Queen. She will just be leaving the chapel.'

The clerk bowed and ran from the room. His footsteps clattered on the steps, then from the window I saw him run across the courtyard. I envied his speed and grace. Warner invited me to sit. He stroked his beard. 'These are lawless times. Tell me what happened.'

I told him the story, concluding with my visit to Dyrick. 'He will fight hard for his client,' I said. 'And, to be frank, his arguments are strong.'

Warner nodded slowly. 'Do you think he is involved in what happened to you?'

'There is no evidence at all. When I first saw him I thought he was acting the part of the outraged lawyer. But then I sensed an anger behind the legal dancing, some personal feeling.' I hesitated. 'Talking of that, Mistress Calfhill told me the Queen was very fond of Michael.'

'That is my impression too.'

Warner frowned. I could see he wished himself, and the Queen, rid of this.

'One thing, Master Warner. There is a rumour that Master Hobbey was in debt at the time of his move to Hampshire. I spoke to Alderman Carver of the Mercers' Guild, but he was reluctant to talk about another member. Is there any way you could make discreet enquiry?'

'I will see what I can do.' He stood up, nodding at me to do likewise, as light footsteps sounded on the stairs. We both bowed deeply as the door opened. A maid-in-waiting stepped in and held it open for the Queen.

✝

QUEEN CATHERINE was dressed soberly for Sunday, in a plain dress of grey silk and a hood without jewellery. I thought they suited her less well than the bright colours she favoured, though they showed her auburn hair to advantage. She indicated that Warner and

I should sit. The maid-in-waiting took a stool by the window, folding her hands in her lap.

'Matthew,' she began, 'Robert tells me you have been attacked. Are you safe?'

'Quite safe, your majesty.'

'I thank God for it. And what of the case? I understand there is little new evidence.' Her eyes were full of sorrow. Bess was right. She had cared deeply for Michael.

I told her that apart from Broughton's confirming his and Michael's opposition to the wardship, I had discovered little. She sat, considering, then said quietly, 'One thing I know about Michael, have known since he was a child. He was a *good* man, full of the kindness and charity that our Lord wished us all to have, though few enough do. He would never have made up a story to harm Hobbey. Never, even if his mind was disturbed.'

'That is my impression.'

'If something bad has been done to that boy,' Warner said, 'this case could make a stir. To say nothing of inflaming opinion further against the Court of Wards. The King might not wish that.'

'No, Master Warner!' The Queen spoke with sudden fierceness. 'His majesty would not wish wrongdoing to go unpunished. Michael wished to protect the boy Hugh, the only survivor of that poor family, and so do I. For his sake, and his good mother's, and the sake of justice!'

I glanced at Warner. I thought his estimate of the King's likely response more accurate than the Queen's. She continued, 'Matthew, if the gathering of depositions is ordered tomorrow, do not feel you must take on this burden. Another barrister can be appointed to act from then on and travel south.'

'He would need to know everything about the case to deal with the matter properly.'

She nodded. 'That would only be fair to him.'

'Someone else might take it on for a good purse,' Warner said, 'but would he have Serjeant Shardlake's commitment?' I realized Warner wanted me to stay with the case. He trusted me, and the fewer who knew the Queen had got herself involved with such a jar of worms the better. He looked at me. I could almost feel him willing me not to withdraw.

'I will follow this through, your majesty.'

The Queen smiled again, a warm open smile. 'I knew you would.' Her mobile face grew serious again. 'But I remember all that happened the last time you plunged into dark waters when your friend Master Elliard was murdered. Before I was Queen.'

'That I do not regret.'

'But Hugh Curteys is not a friend; you have never met him.'

'I would like to help him if I can. I would ask, though, for someone to accompany me. My clerk cannot come and my steward is – unsuitable.'

She nodded. 'A good clerk, and some strong fellow to be at your side. Warner, you can arrange that?'

'I will do all I can.'

She smiled at him. 'I know you are uneasy, my good servant. But I wish this matter properly investigated. Because it affects me in my heart, and because it is right that it should be.' She turned back to me. 'Thank you, Matthew. And now, I must go. I am due for lunch with the King. Matthew – ' she held out her hand for me to kiss – 'keep me informed of what happens at the hearing.'

My lips brushed a soft hand, there was a whiff of musky scent, and then Queen Catherine was gone, the maid-in-waiting following and closing the door behind them. Warner sat down again, and looked at me quizzically.

'The die is cast then, Matthew.'

'Yes.'

'Let me know what happens immediately the hearing is over, and if you have to go, I can select good men to accompany you.'

'Thank you.'

Warner hesitated, then said, 'I believe you have acted for wronged children before.'

I smiled. 'Did not our Lord say we should suffer the little children?'

Warner inclined his head. I could see he was wondering why I was doing this. I was unsure myself, except that children in peril, and judicial wrong, were two things that touched me closely. As did the wishes of the Queen, for whom I realized I felt more than friendship. Though there was no point in dwelling on that. As I took my leave, I felt a new surge of determination, what Barak sometimes called my obstinacy.

✝

A FEW HOURS later I crossed the Bedlam yard once again. It had turned misty, deadening the clamour of the city, and warmer.

I had decided to visit Ellen that morning. The thought that she did not even have the formal protection of an order of lunacy had tightened my sense of responsibility even further. Two people had to know the truth: Warden Metwys and the keeper, Edwin Shawms. Metwys I had encountered during the case of my incarcerated client two years before; he was a typical courtier, who made no secret of the fact that the wardenship was for him nothing more than an office of profit. The sums that a man of his status would require to give up secrets were beyond my means. And Keeper Shawms was a tool of Metwys's. So I had decided, perhaps rashly, to see Ellen again, and try once more to find out what I could.

I knocked at the door. It was answered by one of the junior keepers, a heavy-set, slack-jawed young man called Palin. He nodded at me dully. 'I have come to see Ellen Fettiplace,' I said.

'Ah.' He nodded. Then he was pushed aside and Hob stood in the doorway. 'Master Shardlake,' he said in a mock-cheerful tone. 'I had not expected to see you again so soon.'

'I may be going away, I wished to tell Ellen.'

He stood aside to let me enter. The door of the office was open and I saw Shawms sitting behind the desk, writing. A fat, middle-aged man, he always seemed to wear the same slightly stained black jerkin. He looked up as I appeared, his expression stony. We were old adversaries.

'Come to see Ellen, Master Shardlake?' he asked in his growl of a voice.

'I have, sir.'

'Looks like someone's been at your neck,' he said. 'Some poor defendant had enough of being dragged through the courts?'

'No, just some common thieves, after money like all rogues. Thank you for your welcome, Master Shawms. It is always warm greetings at the Bedlam.'

'It's hard work for those who have to labour here. Eh, Hob?' He glanced sharply at Gebons.

'That it is, sir.'

'She is in the parlour. And you can tell her either to get old Emanuel to sign a receipt for his clothes, or sign it on his behalf. Tell her to bring it to me, and my inkpot.'

✟

IN THE PARLOUR Ellen was doing what she did best, talking reassuringly to a patient, her voice calm and encouraging. It was the tall, thin man I had seen in the courtyard on my previous visit. They sat at the large, scarred old table, a quill and inkpot between them. Ellen was studying a paper, while the new patient clutched a bundle close to his chest and looked across at her apprehensively. As I entered, they both looked up. Ellen's face was transfigured by a delighted smile. The patient, though, dropped his bundle onto the table, stood and waved a frantic hand at me. 'A lawyer!' he shouted. 'They've sent a lawyer, they're going to put me in the Marshalsea prison!'

'No, Emanuel,' Ellen said, grasping his shoulder. 'This man is my friend, Master Shardlake. He has come to see me.' She spoke with pride.

'I've paid all I can, sir,' Emanuel told me, wringing his hands. He backed away, becoming more agitated. 'My business is gone, all I have are the clothes I stand in and those in this bundle. The court allowed me those, they sent them—'

I raised a hand soothingly. 'I have come to see Ellen, sir. I know nothing of you—'

'You deceive me. Even the King deceives me, his silver is not real. I have seen it. All my true silver is taken.'

'Palin,' Ellen called, as Emanuel dodged her grasp and made for the door. The young man entered and caught him firmly. 'Come on, matey,' he said. 'Come and lie down. No one's after you.' He strong-armed a weeping Emanuel away. I turned to Ellen. She was staring at my neck with a horrified look.

'Matthew, what happened?'

'An attempt at robbery. I am quite safe,' I added, making light of it.

'Thank you for coming again. It has scarce been four days.' She smiled once more.

'There was something I wished to speak to you about. But Shawms said something about signing a paper for him.'

'Yes, it is this, a receipt for Master Emanuel's poor belongings. He will not sign it, so I must.' She did so, signing her name with an elegant round hand, proof she had had some education.

She returned the paper and inkpot to Shawms's office, and then I followed her down the long corridor to her chamber. She wore the same light-blue dress as on Wednesday, and I noticed it was threadbare in several places. We passed the chamber of the fat old gentleman who had a delusion that he was the King. His door was half-open, and one of the keepers was replacing the rushes on the stone floor, a rag over his face against the smell, for the old ones, heaped in a corner, stank mightily. The old man sat on a commode, a tattered curtain for a robe and his paper crown on his head. He stared stonily ahead, ignoring the common mortals who passed.

We entered Ellen's room. As usual, she sat on her bed and I stood. 'Poor Master Emanuel,' she said sadly. 'He was a prosperous gentleman until last year, a corn merchant. He accepted payment for a large load in new coins just after the last debasement and made a great loss. He tried to hide it by borrowing and now his business has gone. His wits, too.'

I looked at her. 'You care about the patients, don't you, Ellen?'

'Someone has to care for those nobody else cares for.' She smiled sadly.

'At the moment I am trying to help a young man in that position.' I hesitated. 'And to do so I may have to go away for a short while.'

She sat up at that, an anxious look on her face. 'Where? For how long?'

'To Hampshire, to take some depositions. A week, perhaps a little more.'

'So far? I will be alone.' Her voice became agitated.

'I have a case in the Court of Wards. Representatives often have to travel to where the ward lives.'

'I have heard Wards is an evil place.'

I hesitated, then said quietly, 'It is where orders of lunacy are kept as well.' I drew a deep breath. 'I had to go there on Thursday. About this case. I also — I also asked the clerk if your records were filed there.'

For the first time since I met her Ellen looked at me with anger. Her face seemed to change, somehow flatten and harden. 'How could you?' she asked. 'You had no right to look at papers about me. No right to see those things.' She shrank back, curling her hands into fists in her lap.

'Ellen, I only wished to ensure there was a proper record for you.' A lie.

Her voice rose, cracking and breaking with rage. 'Did you laugh? Did you laugh at what you read?'

'Ellen!' I raised my own voice. 'There was nothing to read! There is no record of you there.'

'What?' she asked, her voice suddenly dropping.

'You are not registered as a lunatic.'

'But I must be.'

I shook my head. 'You are not. You should never have been sent here at all.'

'Will you tell Shawms?' Now her voice was small, frightened. In an instant all her long trust in me seemed to have gone. I raised a hand soothingly.

'Of course not. But, Ellen, they must know already. I would like to protect you, Ellen, help you. But to do that I have to find out how you came here, what happened. Please tell me.'

She did not reply, just looked at me with terrible fear and distrust. Then I said something which showed how little, even then, I understood her. 'Ellen, the way to Portsmouth passes near the Sussex border, near the town of Rolfswood, where I know you come from. Is there anyone I could visit there who might help you?'

At the mention of Rolfswood Ellen's bosom heaved as though she were fighting for breath. Then she began not to shout but to scream hoarsely. 'No! No!' Her face reddened. 'They were so strong!' she shouted. 'I could not move! The sky above – it was so wide – so wide it could swallow me!' The last words were a shriek of pure terror.

'Ellen.' I took a step towards her, but she shrank away, pressing herself into the wall.

'He burned! The poor man, he was all on fire—'

'What?'

Her eyes were glassy now, I realized she was not seeing me, nor the room, but something terrible in the past.

'I saw his skin melt, turn black and crack!' she howled. 'He tried to get up but he fell!'

There was a crash and the door flew open. Shawms entered, furious looking. Behind him were Palin and Hob Gebons. Palin held a coil of rope in one hand.

'God's nails!' Shawms shouted. 'What the hell's going on here?' Ellen stared at them and instantly became quiet, quaking against the wall like a poor mouse trapped in a corner by a cat. Shawms grasped my arm in a meaty hand and pulled me away.

'It's all right,' I said. 'She's only frightened – ' And then, when it was far too late, I stretched out a hand to her, but she did not even see me as she shrank away from Hob and Palin. Hob looked at me over his shoulder, fiercely, and shook his head. Shawms jerked my arm again, pulling me to the door. I resisted, and he bent close, speaking quietly and savagely. 'Listen to me, master hunchback. I'm in charge here. You come out of this room, or I'll have Hob and young Palin put you out, none too gently. Want Fettiplace to see that, do you?'

There was nothing I could do. I let him lead me outside, leaving Hob and Palin to stand guard over Ellen as though she were a dangerous animal rather than a desperate, helpless woman. Then Shawms slammed the door on them, pulled the little square viewing window shut, and turned to face me. He was breathing hard.

'What happened in there, lawyer? We heard her screaming from the other end of the building. Her that's normally more quiet and biddable than any of them. What did you say to her, or maybe do to her?' His glare turned into a vicious leer.

'Nothing. I only told her I may be going away for a while.' I had to say as little as possible, for her sake.

'Well, that's the best news I've heard since they put Cromwell's head on a pike.' Shawms's eyes narrowed. 'That's all? I heard her screaming about burning men, the sky swallowing her.'

'She started shouting when I told her I was going, I didn't understand any of it.'

'They'll say any sort of crazy rubbish when they're riled.' Shawms leered again. 'Doesn't like the idea of you going away, does she?'

I heard muttering on the other side of the door, male voices, something being moved. 'What are they doing to her?' I asked.

'Tying her up. It's what happens to those who make scenes. Be grateful it's not the chains.'

'But she's ill—'

'And those who are ill must be restrained. Then perhaps they'll learn to restrain themselves.' He leaned forward. 'This was your fault, Master Shardlake, for coming here so much. I don't think you should come again for a while. If you're going away, maybe now she'll realize you're not going to order your life around her, and that may do her good. We'll keep an eye on her, make sure she does nothing stupid.'

'Maybe it would be easier for you all if she died,' I said quietly.

He shook his head and looked at me seriously. 'That it would not, Master Shardlake. We've kept her safe here nineteen years, and will go on keeping her safe.'

'Safe from what?'

'From herself.' He leaned forward and said, slowly and emphatically, 'The only danger to Ellen Fettiplace is from people stirring her up. It's best for everyone if she stays here, grazing like a contented cow. Go and do your business. Then when you come back, we'll see where we are.'

'Let me look in that room before I go. See that she's all right.'

Shawms hesitated, then knocked on Ellen's door. Gebons opened it. Palin stood by the bed. Ellen's feet were tied, and her hands too. She stared at me and her eyes were no longer blank, they were full of anger again.

'Ellen,' I said. 'I am sorry – '

She did not reply, just stared back, clenching her bound hands. Shawms closed the door. 'There,' he said. 'See the damage you have done.'

Chapter Ten

AGAIN I CLIMBED the stairs to the Court of Wards. Barak was at my side, the Curteys case papers tied in red ribbon under his arm. We passed under the carving of the seal: *Pupillis Orphanis et Viduis Adiutor.*

It was a beautiful, warm morning. I had walked down to Westminster, where I had arranged to meet Barak outside the court half an hour before the hearing. I found my assistant leaning against the wall, looking as worried as I had ever seen him.

'Goodryke called again last night,' he said without preliminary.

'By Mary, that man is obsessed.'

'Tammy answered the door, told him I was out. He ordered me to be sure to attend for swearing in in two days' time. If I don't they'll be after me as a deserter.'

'It's time to get you out of London,' I said firmly. 'It doesn't matter where.'

'Even if I go, Goodryke won't let it lie. You can hang for desertion now.'

Before I could reply I felt a touch on my arm. It was Bess Calfhill, dressed in black again. She looked nervous.

'Am I late?' she asked. 'I feared I was lost among all these buildings and alleyways—'

'No, Mistress Calfhill. Come, we should go in. We'll talk afterwards, Jack.'

We climbed the stairs, walked under the coat of arms. I was relieved to see Reverend Broughton sitting on the bench in his cassock. He looked solid, determined. A little further up the bench Vincent

Dyrick looked at me and shook his head slightly, as though amazed by the unreasonableness of the whole situation. Next to him young Feaveryear was ordering papers into a large bundle.

'Good morning,' I said to them, as cheerfully as I could for I had been worrying about Barak and Ellen for most of the night.

Bess looked anxiously at Dyrick. 'Where will the case be heard, sir?' she asked quietly. Dyrick nodded at the door to the court. 'In there, madam. But do not worry,' he added scoffingly, 'we will not be there long.'

'Now, Brother Dyrick,' I said reprovingly. 'You are for the defence, you are not allowed to talk to the applicant.'

Dyrick snorted. 'The *late* applicant's personal representative, you mean.'

Barak approached Feaveryear. 'That's some pile of paperwork you've got.'

'Bigger than yours,' Feaveryear replied in a tone of righteous resentment, staring at the much smaller bundle Barak carried.

'Oh, mine's always big enough for the job in hand. So my wife says, anyway,' Barak retorted. Feaveryear looked scandalized, then pointed a thin finger at the documents Barak carried. 'Those are tied in red ribbon,' he said. 'Papers for Wards require to be tied in black.' He nodded at the black ribbon round his own files.

Dyrick looked up. 'The applicant's bundles are in the wrong colour ribbon?' He stared at me. 'I have heard of cases being thrown out of Wards for lesser errors.'

'Then you must tell the Master,' I replied, cursing myself inwardly for my mistake. I had missed the rule in my haste.

'I will.' Dyrick smiled wolfishly.

The court door opened, and the black-robed usher I had seen in Mylling's office appeared. 'Those concerned in the wardship of Hugh Curteys,' he intoned. I heard a gasp of indrawn breath from Bess. Dyrick rose, his robe rustling as he strode to the door.

✞

THE COURTROOM was the smallest I had ever entered. It was dimly lit by narrow arched windows set high in an alcove, the walls undecorated. Sir William Paulet, Master of the Court of Wards, sat at the head of a large table covered with green cloth, a wooden partition behind him blank save for the royal coat of arms. Beside him Mylling sat, his head lowered. The usher showed Dyrick and me to places at the table facing the Master. Barak and Feaveryear sat beside us. Bess Calfhill and Reverend Broughton were waved to seats separated from the body of the court by a low wooden bar.

Paulet wore the red robes of a judge, a gold chain of office round his neck. He was in his sixties, with a lined, hoary face and narrow lips above a short white beard. His large, dark blue eyes conveyed intelligence and authority but no feeling. I knew he had been master of the court since its founding five years before. Before that he had been a judge at the trial of Sir Thomas More, as well as a commander of the royal forces against the northern rebels nine years earlier.

He began by giving me a thin smile. 'Serjeant Shardlake. Master Dyrick I know, but I think you are new to my court.'

'Yes, Master.'

He stared at me for a long moment, frowning. I guessed he was annoyed by the Queen's interference in his court. He nodded brusquely at the papers in front of him. 'These are strange allegations. Please explain the matter.'

Dyrick half rose. 'If I may mention a point of procedure, Master, the papers of the claimant's personal representative are not in the correct form. The ribbon should be black—'

'Do not be silly, Brother Dyrick,' Paulet said quietly. 'Sit down.'

Dyrick flushed but remained on his feet. 'And the papers, such as they are, were filed very late—'

'Sit *down*.'

Dyrick did so, frowning. He had hoped to earn me at least a reproving word from the judge. Paulet turned back to me. 'Yes, Serjeant Shardlake?'

I made the best of my weak case. Quills scratched as Barak, Feaveryear and Mylling took notes. I explained Michael's long association with the Curteys children, his good character and record as a tutor, and his serious concern about Hugh after his recent visit to Hampshire. I said his mother believed his complaint warranted urgent investigation.

When I had finished, Paulet turned and stared at Bess for perhaps half a minute. She flushed and shifted in her seat, but returned his gaze steadily. Broughton put his hand over hers, earning him a glance of disapproval from the Master. Then Paulet turned back to me.

'Everything depends on the mother's evidence,' he said.

'It does, Sir William.'

'The applicant's death is a strange matter. A suicide, he must have been sick in his mind.' There was a suppressed sob from Bess, which Paulet ignored.

I said, 'Master, something which may have tipped this man of good character over the edge of reason must be serious indeed.'

'*May* be serious, Master Shardlake. *May* be.' Paulet turned to Dyrick. 'I will hear from Master Hobbey's representative. Master Hobbey himself is absent, I see.'

Dyrick rose. 'My client is busy with contracts to supply the fleet and army at Portsmouth with wood, work of national importance.' He looked at me. 'From his own woodlands, I should add.'

Paulet considered a moment. 'I understand no marriage is in prospect for the ward.'

'No, indeed. Master Hobbey would not wish his ward to marry till he finds a lady of his own choice.' Dyrick's voice rose. 'As we know, the man who lodged this extraordindary bill is dead. His mother's evidence is mere hearsay. And Reverend Broughton's deposition deals only with allegations relating to the grant of the wardship many years ago.' His voice took on a reproving note. 'That wardship went through the due and proper processes of the Office of Wards, predecessor to this honourable court.'

Paulet nodded. 'Very true.' He stared at Broughton. 'I think you a naughty fellow, sir, to stir up trouble now over how the wardship was granted.'

Broughton rose. 'I have told only the truth, as God is my witness.'

'Do not bandy words with me, or I will have you in the Fleet for contempt.' Paulet did not raise his quiet voice but it cut like a knife. Broughton hesitated, then sat down again. Paulet turned back to Dyrick and sighed.

'Michael Calfhill's allegations, however vague, do, I think, merit some investigation. Do you wish to question the witnesses?'

Dyrick stared at Bess. She looked back at him, lifting her chin. Dyrick hesitated, then said, 'No, Master.' I smiled inwardly. Dyrick had realized that questioning Bess on her statement would only reveal her total sincerity. I understood then that I had won this stage of the battle at least, and from the angry set of his face Dyrick did too. But I took no credit. I had seen enough of Paulet to realize that if pressure had not been brought on him by the Queen he would indeed have thrown us out the door of his strange fiefdom in minutes.

'I think,' Paulet said, 'the court should order depositions from all persons currently concerned with Hugh Curteys' welfare.' He looked at me. 'Whom did you have in mind, Serjeant Shardlake?'

'Hugh Curteys himself, of course. Master Hobbey, his wife, perhaps their son, the steward of the household. Any current tutor—'

'There is no tutor,' Dyrick said. He stood again, his face red with suppressed anger. 'And David Hobbey is a minor.'

'Anyone else, Master Shardlake?'

'I would submit that a statement should be taken from the local feodary, and that he should make his accounts regarding Hugh Curteys' estate available.'

Paulet considered. 'Sir Quintin Priddis is feodary of Hampshire.'

I ventured some flattery. 'Your wide knowledge does you credit, Master.'

Paulet smiled thinly again. 'Not really. I am from Hampshire too. I am going down to Portsmouth in a few days, as governor, to bring some order to all the soldiers and sailors.' He reflected. 'A deposition from Sir Quintin: yes, I agree to that. But as for viewing the accounts – I think not. That could be considered a slur on Sir Quintin's honesty.' He stared at me with those large empty eyes, quite straight-faced, and I realized I had not won as much as I thought. If profits were being creamed off Hugh's estate, and the fact that Hobbey was cutting down woodland strengthened the notion, the local feodary was probably involved. Without accounts he could say anything and there was no way to test the truth of it.

'Now,' the Master continued urbanely, 'there is the question of who should take these depositions.' He looked at Dyrick, whose face was now almost as red as his hair. 'What about Serjeant Shardlake?'

'With due respect,' Dyrick answered, 'an impartial person is needed—'

Paulet leaned back in his high chair. 'I have a better idea. You and Serjeant Shardlake can both go.'

I saw what Paulet was doing. He was going to let the investigation go ahead, but handicap my enquiries by setting Dyrick to breathe down my neck as well as refusing to order disclosure of the accounts. Dyrick must have realized that, but he looked no happier. 'Master,' he said, 'that would give me difficulties. Family commitments—'

'It is your commitment to the court that matters, Brother. Master Shardlake, have you any objections to my suggestion?'

And then I had an idea. I stared at Barak, who looked back enquiringly. 'Sir William,' I said, 'if Brother Dyrick and I are both to go, then might I ask that we take our clerks to assist us?'

Paulet inclined his head. 'That seems reasonable.'

'Perhaps they could be named in the order to attend us. Merely to ensure fairness, equality of legal resources, in the investigation.'

Paulet turned to Dyrick. 'Any objection to that?'

Dyrick hesitated. Paulet drummed his fingers on the desk. Dyrick said, 'I have no objection, if Serjeant Shardlake wishes it.' I looked down at Barak and ventured a wink. If he was ordered by a court to travel to Hampshire the army could not touch him.

'What are the names?'

'Barak and Feaveryear, Master.'

'Note the names, Mylling.'

I saw to my surprise that Feaveryear was smiling.

Paulet leaned back. 'Now, I shall set a further hearing, let us say four weeks from today, to get this matter over and dealt with. I may be back myself, we should be able to see off the French by then, eh?' Mylling laughed at the joke, his head shaking with amusement over his quill. Paulet gave a wintry smile. 'If not, my deputy will take the hearing.'

Dyrick rose again. 'Master, if Serjeant Shardlake and I are both to go, the cost will be high. I must ask that Master Hobbey's costs be met in full, if, or rather when, these allegations are shown to be groundless.'

'If they prove groundless they will be, Master Dyrick, I shall see to that.' He turned to Bess. 'Do you have the means, Madam, to meet what may be very considerable costs?'

Bess rose. 'I can meet the costs, sir.'

Paulet gave her a long, hard look. He would guess the money would come from the Queen. I hoped Warner would be able to cobble together a plausible payment from the Queen's treasury. The Master turned and held my eyes for a long moment. 'This had best not be a mare's nest, Serjeant Shardlake,' he said very quietly, 'or you will be in bad odour with this court.' He turned to Mylling again. 'Draw the order.'

The clerk nodded, took a blank piece of paper and began to write. He had not so much as glanced at any of us. I wondered whether he could have given information to Dyrick about my involvement, whether it could have been Dyrick that set the corner boys on me. My opponent was putting his papers in order with rapid, angry movements. Paulet said, 'Master Dyrick, I would like a brief word.' He stood, and everyone in the court rose hastily. Paulet bowed, dismissing us. Dyrick gave me a nasty look, then went out after the judge.

✟

WE RETURNED to the vestibule. As soon as the door was closed Broughton seized my hand. 'The light of the Lord's grace shone in that court,' he said. 'With that hard judge I thought we must lose, but we won.'

'We have won only the right to investigate,' I cautioned.

'But you will find the truth, I know. These people who gather wardships. Men without conscience who flatter themselves with heaping riches upon riches, honours upon honours, forgetting God—'

'Indeed.' I looked at the court door, wondering why Paulet had called Dyrick back. Bess came up to me. She was pale. 'May I sit down?' she asked.

'Of course. Come.'

I sat her down on the bench. 'So Michael has obtained his wish,' she said quietly. 'An enquiry.'

'Be sure I shall question everyone in Hampshire closely.' I glanced at Barak, who was leaning against the wall, looking thoughtful. Next to him Feaveryear swept his lock of lank hair from his forehead. He still looked pleased at the prospect of the journey.

Bess sighed heavily. 'Thank you for all you have done, sir.' She looked at me. Then she reached round to the back of her neck and unclipped something. She opened her hand and showed me a small, beautifully worked gold crucifix. She laid it on the bench between us. I looked at the delicately crafted figure. There was even a tiny crown of thorns.

Bess spoke quietly. 'This was found with Michael when he died. It was Emma's, given her by her grandmother. The child wore it in the old woman's memory. After Emma died and Michael was dismissed he asked Mistress Hobbey if he could have some remembrance of Emma. She gave him that, with an impatient gesture, Michael said. He kept it with him always. Would you take it, and give it to the boy Hugh? I am sure Michael would wish him to have it now.'

'I will, of course,' I said. I picked it up.

'I pray you get the poor boy out of the hands of that wicked family.' Bess sighed. 'You know, in the weeks before he died my son had taken up his archery again. I think if he had lived he would have gone to the militia.'

'Did he fear being called up?'

She frowned. 'No, sir, he wanted to play his part in repelling the French. He was a good and honourable man.'

Reverend Broughton touched her arm. 'Come, good madam, I would be out of this place. May I accompany you home?' Bess allowed Broughton to lead her away. In the doorway she turned briefly, smiled at Barak and me and was gone.

☦

THE COURT DOOR opened, and Dyrick strode towards me. He looked in a cold fume.

'Well, Master Shardlake, it seems we must go to Hampshire.'

'It does.'

'Are you up to such a journey?' he asked with a hint of a sneer.

'Once I rode to York on a case.'

'I was hoping to spend these next weeks with my wife and children. I have two girls and a boy; during the law term I do not see nearly enough of them. Now I must tell them I have to disappear to Hampshire.'

'We will not be long away. Three or four days there and three or four back if we make haste, a few days in between.'

'You have no family, I think, sir? It is easier for you.' Dyrick leaned close to me and spoke quietly, fierce eyes on mine. 'I know why Sir William has done this. Normally he would throw such a tissue of unsubstantiated allegations out at once.'

'Perhaps he wished to do justice.'

'Just now he told me that Mistress Calfhill was for many years the servant of Lady Latimer, as she then was.'

'Even the servant of a Queen may seek justice, I think.'

'This is not justice. It is pestering, persecution.'

'Everyone in Hampshire will get a fair hearing.'

'Sir William told me that while the Queen may press for an investigation she cannot determine the outcome. The help she can give you stops here.' His voice rasped like a file.

I met his angry stare. 'We should consider the practicalities of our journey,' I said.

'I want to leave as soon as we can. The sooner we start, the sooner we return. And it will take more than three or four days to get there. The roads will be muddy after the storms, and there will be soldiers and supply carts on the roads south.'

I caught Barak's eye. 'I agree. What about the day after tomorrow?'

Dyrick looked surprised by my ready agreement. I continued, 'I suggest we take a boat as far as Kingston, that would be the quickest way, then hire strong riding horses so we can make the journey as fast as possible.'

'Very well. I will send Feaveryear down today to hire the horses.' He turned to the clerk. 'Can you do that?'

'Yes, sir.'

'That sounds sensible,' I said. 'But horses will be difficult to hire just now. There will be much demand for them.'

'Then we must pay above the normal rate.'

I hesitated. If we found nothing all those costs would be paid by Bess. Or, rather, by the Queen. But my horse Genesis was only used to short rides and this would be a long one. I had ridden him to York four years before, but that was by slow stages and he was younger then. I nodded agreement.

'Will you bring a bodyservant as well as your clerk?' Dyrick asked.

'Probably.' I was thinking about the man Warner had promised me.

'I will not. Feaveryear can do my fetching and carrying. We should travel as light as we can to make speed. I must send a letter by a fast rider to Master Hobbey, so at least he has some advance warning of this nonsense. I suggest we meet in Kingston on Wednesday. As early as possible – I will send you a note.'

'We agree on the practicalities, then,' I said, trying to lighten the discussion. After all, I would be stuck with Dyrick for well over a week.

He leaned in close again. 'Be assured, you will find nothing. And when we come before the court next month I will make you regret this nonsense. That is, unless the French land and we find ourselves cut off in a battle zone.' He sighed deeply, then looked at me. 'You could still pull out. Go after your client and advise her she will be bankrupted, which she will. Unless I find evidence the case is being maintained by the Queen, in which case Mistress Calfhill could find herself in prison.'

I met his gaze. I knew he was bluffing, he would never dare bring the Queen into this. He gave me a final vicious look and turned away. 'Come on, you,' he said to Feaveryear.

Barak and I were left alone in the vestibule.' Now,' I said, 'come. There are things we must discuss.'

Chapter Eleven

I TOOK BARAK to a tavern. 'That was a clever idea,' he said, 'getting my name on the order. But will it override Goodryke's orders?' The hand that held his mug was trembling slightly.

'Yes. It is an order of the court, instructing you personally to accompany me. Sir William Paulet has more power than any whiffler. Go back to Wards this afternoon and fetch the signed order, then take it round to Carver at the Guildhall. He can show it to Goodryke. And the day after tomorrow we will be gone.'

'Goodryke will know what you've done.'

'He won't be able to do anything about it. Paulet himself will be gone to Portsmouth and the clerks at Wards won't be interested.' I smiled bitterly. 'There's no money in it.'

'Did the idea just come to you in court?'

'Yes. Thank God Dyrick did not object.' I looked serious. 'I know I didn't want you to come, but it seems the only way to keep you safe. I'll tell Warner I don't need a clerk now, though a stout bodyservant would still be useful.'

Barak looked at me. 'Tamasin knows nothing about the attack on you, that warning from those apprentices.'

'Then don't tell her. I'm less worried for my own safety than I was. Dyrick knows I have the Queen's patronage, and I have no doubt he will tell Hobbey when he writes. If the danger came from them, they're not going to risk trouble from that quarter. Though I am less and less sure they set those boys on me. Dyrick is a nasty piece of work, but I don't think he'd do something that could cause him trouble at the Bar.'

'Didn't like the look of him at all. What's his history?'

'I've asked around Lincoln's Inn. He's a London fellow, his father was some sort of clerk. He did well at his examinations and chose to specialize in land litigation and the Court of Wards. He's a strange one; it's as though he knows no other way of being than aggression. Yet from what he said he'll miss his wife and children.'

'If not him, then who was it set those boys on you? And I still think there is something suspicious about Michael's suicide.'

I considered. 'There is no evidence for that. All we have is an empty room.'

'I suppose if those boys really wanted you out of the way they would have killed you, or hurt you badly.'

'Yes.' I looked at him. 'When we go south you are not to go chasing trouble. This man Warner has promised me can come with me to where Ellen lived when I go there.'

'You're still going to look into that?'

'Oh, yes.'

He raised his eyebrows. Then he said quietly, 'Tamasin must have the final word on this. Will you come home with me?'

☩

HALF AN HOUR later we were back at Barak's house, in the little parlour. Tamasin sat opposite us. Through the window bees hovered over her pretty flower garden.

'You must decide, Tammy,' Barak said.

She sighed deeply. 'Oh, Jack, if only you had dealt with that man civilly in the first place—'

'Tammy, I am more sorry than I can say.'

'With luck,' I said, 'we may be back in under two weeks. Well in time for the birth.'

She looked at Barak. 'At least I wouldn't have to put up with your fussing around.' Her tone was light but I could see she was blinking back tears. And I knew how frightened they both were that this baby might be born dead like their first, and how much they needed each other now. But I could see no better plan. Barak reached across and took Tamasin's hand.

'It is a hard journey to make in these times,' she said.

'We have travelled harder and longer,' Barak said. 'To York, where I met you.'

'You'd better not meet anyone else in Hampshire,' she said in mock-threatening tones, and I realized she had decided my plan was for the best.

'I won't.'

She looked at me. 'What if the French invade near where you are?'

'Hoyland, the place where we are going, is some miles from the coast. And I have just had another thought. There must be many royal post riders taking messages up and down between London and the troops on the coast. Trained men, with relays of horses waiting for them, and priority on the road. I am sure I could arrange with Master Warner for letters to go back and forth that way. At least you can send each other news. And I want to keep in touch with Warner.' I smiled. 'It will do no harm for me to receive one or two letters with the seal of the Queen's household.'

'What about your house?' Tamasin asked. 'That pig of a steward?'

'I will have to ask Guy to take charge of the household. I didn't want to trouble him, but I see no alternative. And I want him to keep an eye on someone for me.'

'Ellen?' Barak asked.

'Yes.'

'That woman,' Tamasin said. 'She only brings you trouble.' I did not reply, and she looked at Barak again. 'This is the only way to stop you being conscripted, isn't it?'

Barak nodded. 'I think so. I am so sorry.'

Tamasin looked at me again. 'Hurry back as soon as you can.' She clutched her husband's hand tighter. 'Keep him safe.'

'And you keep my son safe,' Barak said. 'My John.'

Tamasin smiled sadly. 'My Johanna.'

☦

THE FOLLOWING morning I returned to the Bedlam. I knew Keeper Shawms usually took a long lunch at a nearby tavern and was unlikely to be there. Hob Gebons answered the door. He did not look pleased to see me.

'God's nails! He told you to stay away! If he finds you—'

'He won't be back from the tavern for an hour.'

'You can't see her. He's ordered her kept tied up till this evening. No visitors.'

'It's you I wanted to see, Hob. Come, let me in. Everyone that passes through the yard can see us talking. It's all right, I'm not after information.'

'I wish I'd never set eyes on your bent back,' Hob growled, but he allowed me to follow him inside and into the little office. I heard a murmur of voices from the parlour.

'How is she?'

'Taking her meals. But she hasn't said a word since Sunday.' He gave his hard little laugh. I bit my lip; I hated the thought of Ellen being tied up, and because of things I had said to her.

'I am going away tomorrow. For ten days or so.'

'Good.'

'I want you to ensure Ellen is well looked after. That she's allowed to go about her business again. If she – if she becomes wild again, stop her being ill-treated.'

'You speak as though I run this place. I don't.'

'You are Shawms's deputy. You have day-to-day care of the patients and can make their treatment better, or worse.' I reached into my purse and held up a gold sovereign. Gebons's eyes fixed on it.

'There's another if I come back and find she's been well treated.'

'God's teeth, you're willing to spend enough money on her.'

'And I'm going to arrange for my doctor friend to visit while I am away and write to me about her progress.'

'That brown-faced fellow you brought when Adam Kite was here? He used to scare the patients.'

'Make sure he is allowed to see her.' I waved the coin.

Hob nodded. 'Where are you going?' he asked.

'To Hampshire, to take depositions in a case.'

'Make sure the Frenchies don't get you. Though my life would be easier if they did.'

I handed over the coin. 'Can I see Ellen? Not to talk to her, just see how she is?'

Hob hesitated, then nodded reluctantly. 'Just as well for you the ones that aren't locked up are having their lunch in the parlour under Palin's eye.' He stood. 'Quick, now.' He gestured me out, and led me down the corridor to Ellen's closed door. He pulled back the viewing hatch. Ellen was lying on the bed, in the same position as on Sunday, her bound hands in her lap. She seemed not to have moved at all. She stared at me, that same fierce accusing look. It unnerved me. It was as though a different person from the Ellen I knew lay there.

☦

THAT AFTERNOON I visited Hampton Court again, climbing the stairs to Warner's office. He was silent when I told him the investigation was to proceed, and looked relieved when I said that Paulet would countenance no further pressure from the Queen.

'You are sorry this matter is going ahead.'

'To be honest, yes. Though I am concerned for you as well. There is some news I should tell you. The King and Queen are going to Portsmouth next week, to review the King's ships that are gathering there. Half the Privy Council are going too. There is a great flurry at Whitehall to get everything organized, as you may imagine.'

'If the King and Queen are going there, it sounds as though the spies' reports were true and the French are heading for Portsmouth.'

'So it would seem. There is a great fleet gathering at the French Channel ports. It is as well you are going tomorrow, you will probably be on your way home again before the royal party gets to Hampshire. Your old friend Sir Richard Rich is to go too. I hear he has been given a position organizing supplies for the soldiers and sailors.'

'After the accusations of corruption against him last year?'

'The king always valued expertise.'

I took a deep breath. 'Well, I have to go. The die is cast now. Will you be accompanying the Queen south?'

He nodded.

'I was going to ask if you could arrange for letters to me and Barak to be brought to Horndean, near Hoyland, using the royal messengers.'

'I can do that. And if you wish to write to me, messengers will be calling on the royal party as it journeys south.'

'Thank you. By the way, I no longer need a clerk but would very much welcome a trusty strong fellow to accompany us on our journey.'

'I have a good man I can let you have. I will send him to your house tomorrow.'

'Thank you.'

'Safe journey,' he said.

I bowed. 'And to you.'

✠

THAT EVENING I spoke to Guy. I had already told him the outlines of the Curteys case and he knew I might have to go to Hampshire. I had been dubious about asking him to look after both Ellen and Tamasin, but to my relief he seemed pleased to have some responsibilities again. He said he was happy, also, to take charge of the household while I was away. I began to think, he is coming out of his melancholy. I had to tell him of Ellen's outburst, and I warned him not to press her about her past, which he agreed would only do harm just now.

I spent the next day in chambers, placing my papers in order and leaving instructions for Skelly. The last two days had been beautiful; the stormy weather seemed a distant memory. I hoped fervently that the good weather would continue.

I left chambers late in the afternoon. As I walked across Gatehouse Court, I thought again of Dyrick. I did not relish the time I must now spend with him and his strange little clerk. At least Barak would be with me. And I had sworn to myself that I would not involve him in my investigation of Ellen's past.

I was not pleased, on entering the house, to see Coldiron bent at the closed parlour door, obviously listening to a conversation within. He jumped up. 'I thought I saw mouse droppings on the floor,' he said quickly.

'I see nothing,' I answered coldly.

He put his hand to his eyepatch. 'My vision is not what it was, with only one eye.' He smiled obsequiously. Since the letter from Hampton Court his manner towards me had become full of awed respectfulness.

'I am going away tomorrow,' I told him, 'for ten days or so. To the south coast.'

He nodded eagerly, bringing his skinny hands together and performing a half bow. 'Is it royal business, sir? To do with the war, perhaps? Setting those Frenchies to rights?'

'Legal business.'

'Ah, I wish I was still young enough to fight those French gamecocks myself. As I did at Flodden. When I cut the Scotch King down the Earl of Surrey himself praised me—'

'Arrangements will need to be made for while I am away—'

'You can rely on me, sir. I'll keep everyone in order. The tradesmen, the boys, JoJo—'

'I am leaving Dr Malton in charge of the household.'

I enjoyed the sight of his face falling. He said in a whining tone, 'In my last place the steward was in charge when the master went away.'

'When there is a gentleman staying in the house, like Dr Malton, he should be in charge.' Coldiron gave me one of his quick, vicious looks. 'Now, I am hungry,' I said lightly. 'Go and see how supper is progressing.'

I entered the parlour, curious to see what he had been listening to. Guy was sitting at the table with Josephine. She had bared her right arm, showing a blistered red mark running from her hand up her wrist, which Guy was bathing with lavender oil. Its smell filled the room.

'Josephine burned her hand,' Guy said.

She stared at me anxiously. 'I am sorry, sir, only good Dr Malton offered to help—'

'I am glad he did. That burn looks nasty.'

'It is,' Guy said. 'I do not think she should use the hand for a little while. She should put oil on it four times a day.'

'Very good.' I smiled. 'Do light work only till Dr Malton orders otherwise.'

She looked frightened. 'But Father—'

'I will speak to your father. Do not worry.'

Josephine looked between me and Guy. Tears came to her eyes. 'You are so kind, sirs, both of you.' She rose, knocking a stoppered bottle of ointment off the table. Guy caught it deftly and handed it to her. 'Keep this safe,' he said.

'Oh, thank you, sir. I am so clumsy. I am so sorry.' She curtsied, then left the room with her hurried little steps. Guy looked at me seriously.

'That burn is three or four days old. She says her father told her to go on working. She must have been in agony handling things.'

'He is a brute. Guy, are you sure you are willing to have charge of him while I'm away?'

'Yes.' He smiled. 'I think so.'

'Handle him as you think fit. I will arrange for a new steward as soon as I return, then he can go.' I hesitated. 'Though I am concerned for Josephine.'

'She relies on him so utterly.' He looked at me. 'I am not sure she is quite as stupid as she seems. Only used to being afraid.'

I said musingly, 'I wonder if there might be some way of detaching her from Coldiron.'

'You have enough responsibility with Ellen.' He looked at me keenly, then asked quietly, 'What should I say, Matthew, if she tells me she is in love with you?'

I blushed deeply. 'Can you say you do not know the answer?'

'But I do.'

'Then tell her she must talk to me about it.'

He looked at me with his penetrating brown eyes. 'She may decide to do so. What will you do then?'

'Let me see what I can find out in Sussex.'

'I suspect it may be nothing good.'

I was relieved to be interrupted by a loud knocking at the front door. 'Excuse me,' I said.

A young messenger wearing the Queen's badge prominently on his doublet stood in the doorway. Coldiron had let him in and was staring with wide eyes at the badge.

'A message from Master Warner, sir,' the young man said.

I turned to Coldiron. 'The supper,' I said. Reluctantly he returned to the kitchen. The messenger handed me the letter. I read it. 'Damnation,' I breathed.

It was from Warner. He told me he could not after all send the man he had promised; like many of the stout bodyservants at Hampton Court, he had that day been conscripted.

'Is there a reply, sir?' the messenger asked.

'No reply,' I said. I closed the door. It was not like Warner to let me down, but there were even stronger pressures on those working at court than on those outside. I thought, we leave tomorrow morning, it is too late to find anyone else now. I was more thankful than ever that I had not told Barak about what Ellen had blurted out to me about men burning. Now I would have to try to deal with that matter on my own.

Part Two

THE JOURNEY

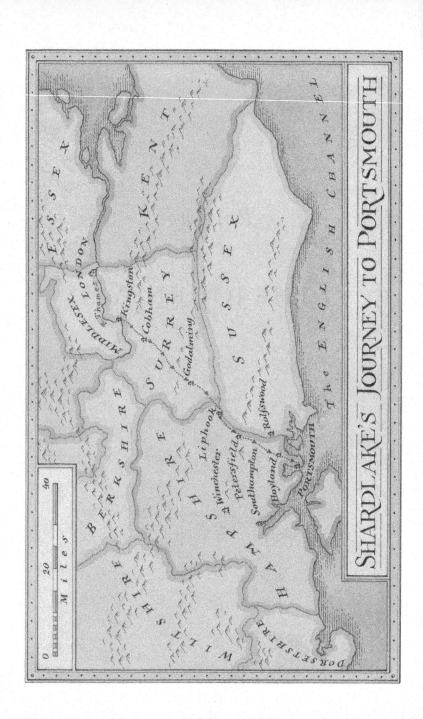

SHARDLAKE'S JOURNEY TO PORTSMOUTH

Chapter Twelve

I ROSE SHORTLY after dawn on Wednesday, the first of July. I donned a shirt and light doublet, pulled on my leather riding boots and walked downstairs in the half-light. I remembered how, whenever I had set out on a journey before, Joan would be up no matter how early the hour, bustling around to ensure I had everything I needed.

At the foot of the stairs Coldiron and Josephine stood waiting, my panniers on the floor beside them. There was too much for me to carry alone and I had ordered Coldiron to walk with me to the river stairs, where I was to meet Barak.

Josephine curtsied. 'Good morning, sir,' Coldiron said. 'It looks like a fine day for travelling.' His eyes were hungry with curiosity; he thought I was going on royal business.

'Good morning. And to you, Josephine. Why are you up so early?'

'She can carry one of the panniers,' Coldiron answered. Josephine gave me a nervous smile and held up a small linen bag. 'There's some bread and cheese here, sir, some slices of ham. And a sweet pastry I got at market.'

'Thank you, Josephine.' She blushed and curtsied again.

Outside, it was already warm, the sky cloudless. I walked down a deserted Chancery Lane, Coldiron and Josephine behind me. Fleet Street was silent, all the buildings shuttered, a few beggars asleep in shop doorways. Then my heart quickened at the sight of four blue-robed apprentices leaning against the Temple Bar. They detached themselves and approached with a slow, lounging walk. All wore swords.

'Special watch,' one said as he came up. He was a thin, spotty youth, no more than eighteen. 'You're abroad early, sir. It's another hour till curfew ends.'

'I am a lawyer going to catch a boat at Temple Stairs,' I answered shortly. 'These are my servants.'

'My master is on important business,' Coldiron snapped. 'You lot should be in the army, not making trouble here.'

The apprentice grinned at him. 'What happened to your eye, old man?'

'Lost at the Battle of Flodden, puppy.'

'Come on,' I said. We crossed the street. Behind us one of the boys called out, 'Cripples!'

We passed into Middle Temple Lane. A thin, chill river mist surrounded us as we walked through Temple Gardens. Barak was waiting at the stairs, his own pannier at his feet. He had found an early boatman, whose craft was tied up; the lantern was lit, a yellow halo in the mist.

'All ready?' Barak asked. 'This fellow will take us to Kingston.'

'Good. How is Tamasin?'

'Tearful last night. I left home quietly without waking her.' He looked away. I turned to Coldiron. 'Put those in the boat. Barak's too.'

As Coldiron descended the steps I spoke quietly to Josephine. 'Dr Malton is in charge while I am away,' I said. 'He will be your friend.' I wondered if she understood I meant she could appeal to Guy against her father, but she only nodded, her expression blank as usual.

Coldiron reappeared, panting in an exaggerated way. Barak stepped down to the boat. 'Goodbye, Coldiron,' I said. 'Take care to do everything Dr Malton asks.' His eye glittered at me again in that nasty way. As I descended the slimy steps I knew he would have liked to pitch me in the water, on royal service or not.

✠

ON THE RIVER the mist was thick. Everything was silent, the only sound the swish of the oars. A flock of swans glided past, quickly vanishing again. The boatman was old, with a lined, tired face. A large barge passed us, with a dozen men at the oars. Fifty or so young men sat in it, all in white coats with the red cross of England on the front. They were unnaturally quiet, their faces pale discs in the mist. But for the plashing of the oars it might have been a ship of ghosts.

The mist thinned as the sun rose, bringing a welcome warmth, and as we approached Kingston river traffic appeared. We pulled up at the old stone wharf. I looked across the river at the wooded expanse of Hampton Court Park. The Queen would already be preparing her household for the journey.

We walked down a short street to the marketplace. Dyrick had sent me a message to meet him and Feaveryear at an inn called the Druid's Head. Barak, who had shouldered two of the panniers, remained silent and thoughtful. I gave him an enquiring look. 'Thank you for getting me out of that mess,' he said quietly. 'That boat full of soldiers we saw, I could have been in one like that through my foolishness.'

'Well, thank goodness you are safe now.'

We entered the inn courtyard. There was a large stable, the doors wide open, several horses in the stalls. Next to it was a forge, where a sweating blacksmith hammered horseshoes at an anvil beside a glowing furnace. We turned into the inn. The parlour was almost deserted save for two men breakfasting at a table, their caps and two sets of spurs on the bench beside them. Dyrick and Feaveryear. We approached and bowed. Feaveryear half-rose, but Dyrick only nodded.

'Good, you're here,' he grunted. 'We should get started.'

'We left London at first light,' I answered pointedly.

'I travelled down last night, to meet Feaveryear and look at the horses. A man of countenance expects a reasonable horse.'

'We have four good horses, and a fifth for the panniers,' Feaveryear said smugly. Greasy hair hung over his forehead as usual. He looked tired, though Dyrick was his customary energetic self. He wiped his mouth with a handkerchief and stood up briskly.

'We should go. We need to reach Cobham tonight, nine miles away and I hear the Portsmouth road is full of soldiers and supply carts. Bring the panniers, Sam.' Dyrick reached for his cap and led the way to the stables. Barak smiled and shook his head, earning a look of rebuke from Feaveryear.

We entered the stable building. Dyrick nodded at the ostler. 'The others have arrived at last,' he said. 'Are the horses saddled and ready?'

'Yes, sir. We'll bring them into the yard.'

We went outside. The ostler and a boy led out five horses. They were all big, strong-looking beasts, with coats of brown and dappled grey. 'You have done well,' I said to Feaveryear.

'My master said not to spare the purse. It is five pounds for the return journey.'

'God's warts,' Barak breathed beside me.

'There's a premium on horses now,' the ostler explained.

'I suggest you pay the man, Brother Shardlake,' Dyrick said. 'You can reclaim it from your client when she loses. Or her pay-mistress.'

'I will pay half. That is what the court would expect. We can meet our own expenses till the outcome is known.'

Dyrick sighed, but fetched out his purse.

'Might we get to near Portsmouth in four days?' I asked the ostler.

He shook his head. 'You'll be lucky, sir. I'd plan on six or seven, the roads are so full.'

'There, Master Shardlake,' Dyrick said. 'I knew how it would be.'

We mounted, Dyrick and I in front and Barak and Feaveryear behind, the horse with the panniers secured to Feaveryear's horse with a line. As we rode into the street a rider sped into the inn yard, his horse's flanks sweating. I saw he wore the badge of the King's household. A harbinger, responsible for checking the King's route in advance of a royal journey.

⚜

WE RODE OUT of Kingston into the Surrey countryside. There were market gardens and cornfields on each side of the road, serving the insatiable demand of London, with the fenced-in woodland of Hampton Court behind them. Normally at this time of year people would have been garnering the hay and the cornfields would be turning yellow, but after the storms the half-flattened corn was still green. The people working in the fields must be praying for better weather. As the sun rose higher it became hot, and I was glad of my broad riding cap. The going was better than Dyrick had feared; the wide road was soft and full of deep ruts from loaded carts but the worst stretches had been repaired; the earth beaten flat, potholes filled with stones and layers of wattle fencing laid over muddy stretches. All our horses seemed strong and placid.

'We should make Cobham today,' I said to Dyrick.

'I hope so.'

'What is our route? I have never been to Hampshire.'

'Cobham tonight, Godalming tomorrow if we are lucky. Then across the Hampshire border the next day and on past Petersfield and Horndean.'

'Hoyland is seven or eight miles north of Portsmouth, I remember reading.'

'Yes. On the fringes of the old Forest of Bere.'

I looked at him. 'I gather you have visited Master Hobbey there before.'

'Yes. Though he usually consults me when he comes to London on business.'

'Is he still involved in the cloth trade?'

Dyrick looked at me sharply. 'No.'

'You spoke in court of his selling wood from Master Curteys' lands recently?'

Dyrick turned in the saddle. 'Impugning my client's integrity already, Brother Shardlake?' His voice took on its characteristic rasp.

'How Hugh Curteys' lands are managed is my concern.'

'As I said in court, some wood is being cut. It would be foolish not to take advantage of the market just now. But all is properly accounted for with the feodary.'

'Whose accounts I am not allowed to see.'

'Because that would impugn Sir Quintin Priddis's integrity as well as my unfortunate client's.' Again that undertone of anger. 'You will get the chance to talk to Sir Quintin, that should be enough for any reasonable man.'

We rode on in silence for a while. Then I said mildly, 'Brother Dyrick, we will be together for the next week or more. Might I suggest life would be easier if we could maintain some civility. That is normal practice among lawyers.'

He inclined his head, thought a moment. 'Well, Brother, 'tis true I am vexed by this journey. I was hoping to teach my son to improve his archery this summer. Nonetheless, the visit could be useful. Along with the lands he bought from the abbey, Master Hobbey obtained the manorial rights over Hoyland, the local village.'

'I know,' I said.

'We have been in correspondence about plans he has to acquire their commons, a tract of forest. The villagers will be compensated,' he added.

'Without their common lands most villages cannot survive.'

'So you have argued against me in court. But now I would ask you to give your word of honour not to involve yourself with the Hoyland villagers.' He smiled. 'What say you? For the sake of fellow-ship?'

I stared him down. 'You have no right to ask that.'

He shrugged. 'Well, sir, if you go hunting for clients among those villagers you cannot expect good relations with Master Hobbey.'

'I intend to hunt for nothing. But I will not be bounden to you in return for your civility. Either you will give that as a brother lawyer or you will not.'

Dyrick turned away, a sarcastic smile on his face. I looked back at Barak. I had heard him attempting conversation with Feaveryear, and overheard Feaveryear say, 'The Popish Antichrist,' in a sharp tone. Barak rolled his eyes at me and shook his head.

We continued to make good progress, halting once by a stream to water the horses. Already my thighs were becoming stiff. Dyrick and Feaveryear stepped a few paces away, talking quietly.

'This is going to be no pleasant journey,' I said to Barak.

'No. I heard your conversation with Master Dyrick.'

'I begin to think he is one who would start an argument with the birds in the trees were there no people around. What was that I heard Feaveryear say about the Antichrist?'

Barak laughed. 'Remember a while back we passed some men digging up a wayside cross?'

'Ay. There's few enough left now.'

'I said it looked like hard work for a hot day, to make conversation. Feaveryear said the crosses were papist idols, then started on about the Pope being the Antichrist.'

I groaned. 'A hotling Protestant. That's all we need.'

✝

A FEW MILES outside Esher our rapid progress ended. We found ourselves at the end of a long line of carts, held up while repairs were carried out to the road ahead. Men and women in grey smocks, probably from the local village, were beating flat a low-lying stretch of road scored with deep muddy ruts. We had to wait over an hour before we were allowed to continue, more carts lining up behind us, Dyrick fuming in the saddle at the delay. The traffic was thicker now, and for the rest of the morning we had to weave our way slowly past carts and riders.

At last we made it into the little town of Esher, where we stopped at an inn for lunch. Dyrick was still in a bad temper, snapping at Feaveryear when he spilled some pottage on the table. The clerk blushed and apologized. It astonished me how much he put up with from his master.

✝

THE AFTERNOON'S journey continued long and slow. There were more and more carts heading south, some full of barrels of food and beer, others loaded with carpentry supplies, cloth, and weapons – one with thousands of arrows in cloth arrowbags. Once we had to pull into the side of the road to allow a big, heavy-wheeled cart to pass us, full of barrels lashed tightly with ropes, a white cross painted prominently on the side of each. Gunpowder, I guessed. Later we had to allow a troop of foreign soldiers past, big men in brightly coloured uniforms, the yellow sleeves and leggings slashed to show the red material beneath. They swung confidently by, talking in German.

In the middle of the afternoon the sky darkened and there was a heavy shower, soaking us and turning the road miry. The ground was rising, too, as we left the Thames valley and climbed into the Surrey Downs. By the time we reached Cobham, a village with a long straggling main street by a river, I was exhausted; my legs and rear saddle-sore, the horse's sides slick with sweat. Barak and Dyrick both looked tired too, and Feaveryear's thin form was slumped over his horse's pommel.

The place was busy, carts parked everywhere along the road, many with local boys standing guard. Across the road, in a big meadow, men were hurrying about erecting white conical tents in a square. All were young, strong-looking, taller than the average and broad-shouldered, their hair cut short. They wore sleeveless jerkins, mostly woollen ones in the browns and light dyes of the poorer classes, though some were leather. Six big wagons were drawn up on the far side of the field, and a dozen great horses were being led down to the river, while other men were setting cooking fires and digging latrines. An elderly, grey-bearded man, in a fine doublet and with a sword at his waist, rode slowly round the fringes of the group on a sleek hunting horse.

'That looks like a company of soldiers,' I said. There were perhaps a hundred men in all.

'Where are their white coats?' Dyrick asked. Soldiers levied for war were usually given white coats with a red cross such as we had seen in the barge.

Looking over the field, I saw a stocky red-faced man of about forty, wearing a sword to mark him out as an officer, running over to where two of the young men were unloading folded tents from a cart. One, a tall rangy fellow, had dropped his end, landing it in a cowpat.

'You fucking idiot, Pygeon!' the officer yelled in a voice that carried clear across the field. 'Clumsy prick!'

'Soldiers, all right,' Barak said behind me.

'Heading south, like all the others.'

Dyrick turned on me with sudden anger. 'God's blood, you picked a fine time to land this journey on me. What if we end with the French army between me and my children?'

'Not very patriotic,' Barak muttered behind me.

Dyrick turned in the saddle. 'Mind your mouth, clerk.'

Barak stared back at him evenly. 'Come,' I said. 'We have to try and find a place for the night.'

To my relief the ostler at the largest inn said three small rooms were available. We dismounted and walked stiffly inside, Barak and Feaveryear carrying the panniers. Feaveryear looked as though he would drop under the weight of the three he carried, and Barak offered to take one. 'Thank you,' Feaveryear said. 'I am sore wearied.' It was the first civil word we had had from either him or Dyrick.

✟

I CLIMBED the stairs to a poky room under the rafters. I pulled off my boots with relief, washing the thick dust from my face in a bowl of cold water. Then I went downstairs, for I was ravenously hungry. The large parlour was crowded with carters drinking beer and wolfing down pottage at long tables. Most would have been on the road all day and they gave off a mighty stink. The room was dim, for dusk was drawing on, and candles had been set on the tables. I saw Barak sitting alone at a small table in a corner, nursing a mug of beer, and went to join him.

'How's your room?' he asked.

'Small. A straw mattress.'

'At least you won't have to share it with Feaveryear. We'd no sooner closed our door than he took off his boots, showing a pair of shins a chicken would think shameful, then knelt down by his bed and stuck his bum in the air. It gave me a nasty turn for a moment, until he began praying, asking God to watch over us on the journey.' He sighed heavily. 'If I hadn't been insolent to that arsehole Goodryke I'd be with Tamasin tonight, not him.'

'It'll be more comfortable when we get to Hoyland Priory.'

He took a long swig of beer. 'Watch that,' I said quietly. I realized the sight of the soldiers had reminded him again of the fate he had so narrowly escaped.

'Here's looking forward to passing time with good company,' he said with heavy sarcasm.

Dyrick and Feaveryear came in. 'May we join you, Brother Shardlake?' Dyrick asked. 'The other company seems rather rough.'

We called for food and were served some pottage, all the inn had. It was flavourless, nasty-looking pieces of gristle floating on the greasy surface. We ate in silence. A group of girls entered, wearing low-cut dresses. The carters hallooed and banged on the tables, and soon the girls were sitting on their laps. Barak looked on with interest, Dyrick with cynical amusement and Feaveryear with disapproval.

'Not enjoying the spectacle, Sam?' Dyrick asked him with a smile.

'No, sir. I think I will go upstairs to bed. I am tired.'

Feaveryear walked slowly away. I saw him look at the girls from the corner of his eyes. Dyrick laughed.

'He can't help hoping to see a pair of bubbies, for all his godliness,' he said, then added sharply, 'though Sam is keen and sharp enough to help ensure your case against the Hobbeys is shown for the nonsense it is.'

I looked over the room, refusing to rise to his taunts. One of the carters had his face buried in a girl's bosom now. Then my attention was drawn by an officer in a soldier's white coat, sword at his waist. He sat hunched over a pile of papers at the corner of a table, seemingly oblivious to the clamour around him. I stared harder, for I seemed to recognize that shock of curly blond hair, the regular features beneath. I nudged Barak.

'That officer over there. Do you recognize him?'

Barak peered through the dim room. 'Is it Sergeant Leacon? I'm not sure. But he was discharged from the army.'

'Yes, he was. Come, let us see. Excuse us, Brother Dyrick, I think I recognize an old client.'

'Some fellow you got lands for from his landlord?'

'Exactly.'

Barak and I weaved our way among the tables. The soldier looked up as we approached, and I saw it was indeed George Leacon, the young Kentish sergeant we had met four years before in York. I had done Leacon an injustice then, but put it right by wresting his parents' farm from a grasping landlord. Leacon had been in his twenties, but now he had lines around his eyes and mouth that made him look a decade older. His blue eyes seemed more prominent too, with a strange wide stare.

'George?' I asked quietly.

His face relaxed into the broad smile I remembered. 'Master Shardlake. And Jack Barak, too.' He rose and bowed. 'What are you doing here? By Mary, it must be three years since I saw you.'

'We are travelling to Hampshire on a case. You are back in the army?'

'Ay. They recruited me last year to go to France. They needed men with military experience. Even more so now, with invasion threatened. I am taking a hundred Middlesex archers down to Portsmouth. You probably saw them in the meadow.'

'Yes. They were putting up their tents. Who was the finely dressed old fellow on the horse?'

Leacon grimaced. 'Sir Franklin Giffard, captain of the company. One of the leading men in north Middlesex. He was a soldier in France in the King's first war thirty years ago. Unfortunately he is, between ourselves – ' he hesitated, then said, 'a little old for command.'

'He is certainly not young.'

'They need a gentleman of substance to keep the soldiers in awe, but I was recruited to go up there, select a hundred good longbowmen, and be his deputy. I am a petty-captain now, promoted last year on the battlefield outside Boulogne.'

'Congratulations.'

He nodded, but something blank came into his face for a moment. He said, 'How do you fare?'

'The law keeps me busy.'

'It is good to see you again.'

'Remember Tamasin Reedbourne?' Barak asked.

'Indeed I do.'

'We are married,' he said proudly. 'And a baby due next month.'

Leacon shook his hand warmly. 'Then it is you that deserves congratulation.'

'How are your parents?' I asked.

'Both well, sir. Still on the farm that is theirs thanks to you. But getting older, they find the work hard now. I should take over, but – ' he grimaced again – 'it is easier to get into the King's army than out of it just now.'

'Truly spoken,' Barak agreed with feeling.

Leacon gestured at the papers in front of him. 'My suppliers' accounts, for the men's food. They are supposed to be settled in every town, and I have money to pay for them. But with this evil new coinage the local merchants charge more.' He pushed the papers aside with an impatient gesture.

'How many men are going to Portsmouth?' Barak asked. 'The roads are full.'

'Six thousand are there or on the way, with many more local militia all along the south coast ready to be called out if the French invade.'

'Jesu.'

'And most of the King's ships of war are there, fifty or sixty of them, so there are several thousand sailors too. I have to get my men to Portsmouth in four days. March on the Sabbath if need be.'

'And the King himself is coming to inspect them all.'

Leacon looked at us seriously. 'Word is the French fleet is thrice the size of ours, loaded with thirty thousand soldiers. There could be a hot time coming. My company may be going to the ships, to do battle if the fleets grapple together.' He shook his head. 'I sailed on a warship last year, but many of my men have never seen a body of water larger than the village pond. But we must do all we can to beat off the invasion, we have no choice.' Something weary and almost despairing had entered Leacon's voice. He looked as though he were about to say something more, then changed the subject. 'Is it just the two of you travelling down?'

'Wish it were,' Barak answered.

'No, we travel with another lawyer and his clerk. Not easy companions.' I turned to look at Dyrick, but he had gone. 'My fellow lawyer was keen to make the journey in four or five days but it does not seem we will do that. Today we have been forever held up behind carts.'

Leacon looked at me. 'Perhaps I can help there.'

'How so?'

'I have orders to get my men to Portsmouth by the fifth. It is hard marching. I have the right to order carts aside, command the roads. If you and your companions wish to ride in front of our baggage train, that would speed your journey.'

'We should be very grateful,' I said.

'We start at five tomorrow, I warn you.'

I exchanged a glance with Barak. He nodded eagerly. The sooner we got to Hoyland, the sooner we would return home. 'We will be there,' I answered. 'Thank you.'

'I am pleased to do something to return the favour you did my family.' Leacon looked reluctantly at his documents. 'But now, if you will forgive me, I need to make some sense of these figures, then get over to camp.'

'You're not staying at the inn?'

'No. I sleep with the men.'

'Then we will leave you.'

We headed for the door. One of the carters had a girl on the floor now, the others cheering him on.

'I will call at Dyrick's room and tell him the news,' I said.

'Maybe the arsehole will show a bit of gratitude.'

'I doubt that.' I turned to him. 'Jack, what has happened to George Leacon?'

He shook his head. 'I don't know. Trouble, I can tell you that.'

I glanced back. The soldier's blond head was bent over the papers again as he ran his finger down a column of figures. His other hand, which rested on the table, trembled slightly.

Chapter Thirteen

M Y BACK AND LEGS were an agony of stiffness when I reached
my room. I had called on Dyrick on the way; he had been
sitting on his bed, papers from the case strewn over it and on his lap.
He glared at me, but when I told him of Leacon's offer he was quick
to accept. 'Well, your former client has come in useful,' he said,
which I took to be his nearest approach to thanks.

It was long before I slept, the continued carousing downstairs and
my aching limbs keeping me awake. Even after all was quiet I tossed
and turned. When at length I drifted off I had a fearful dream: I was
drowning, deep under water, hands at my throat keeping me under. I
grasped at them but they were like steel. I looked at who was holding
me and saw the hard face and cold eyes of Sir William Paulet, framed
by a steel helmet.

I woke with a start, my heart still thumping with terror. I often
had such dreams; two years before I had nearly drowned in a filthy
sewer with a murderer for company, and once before that I had myself
drowned a man who was trying to kill me. I crossed to the window
and threw open the shutters. Sunshine streamed in; from the long
shadows I guessed it was near five.

Outside the tents were being loaded onto carts with other
equipment under the supervision of the red-faced officer, whose
barking at the men I could hear from my room. The big horses were
already between the shafts, munching piles of hay. A little way off a
couple of dozen men were practising their skills with the warbow,
shooting at a doublet nailed to an oak tree at the far end of the field.
Arrows arced through the air, the men shouting when someone hit

the target — as most did, for they were all good shots. Leacon stood beside them, watching. I dressed hastily and hurried down to the parlour, deserted now save for Barak, breakfasting alone. I hurried across. 'Thank goodness you are still here.'

'The soldiers are still loading up. I've written a letter to Tammy, the innkeeper will give it to the next post rider going north.'

I breakfasted quickly, then we went outside. I saw a few of the soldiers did have white coats, including the red-faced man supervising the loading of the carts and a soldier who was strapping a drum round his middle. A trumpet hung from a baldric on his shoulder. We went over to Dyrick and Feaveryear, who were standing talking to the white-bearded man I had seen the night before.

'Ah, Brother Shardlake,' Dyrick said reprovingly, 'you have risen. I hope we will be off soon. Those carters will be sleeping it off with the whores. Captain Giffard here wants to be gone before them. Fourteen miles to Godalming today.' His tone was admonitory.

The white-bearded man turned to me. He wore a peacock-feather cap and a high-collared doublet with buttons patterned in gold leaf. His face was round, spots of colour in his cheeks, his blue eyes watery. I bowed. He gave me a haughty nod.

'You are the other lawyer my petty-captain has invited to travel with us? I am Sir Franklin Giffard, captain of this company.'

'Matthew Shardlake. I hope you do not mind us accompanying you, sir.'

'No, no. Leacon knows what he is doing.' He looked across to the archers.

'Those men shoot well,' I observed.

'They do, though hand-to-hand combat is the gentlemanly way to fight a war. But the archers won us Agincourt. Not much of an inn, was it?' he added. 'All that noise, those carriers. We must be gone. Please go and tell Leacon.'

I hesitated, for he had addressed me as though I were a soldier under his command. But I answered, 'If you wish,' and went to the field, passing the carts. In the nearest I saw a pile of round helmets and large, thick jackets that gave off a damp smell.

As I approached Leacon, I saw now how much thinner he was, his broad frame all gone to stringiness. I stood by him, watching the archers. A handsome dark-haired lad who looked to be still in his teens stepped forward with his bow. He was short, but stocky and muscular, with the heavy shoulders most of the men had. Like them he carried a warbow two yards long, with decorated horn nocks at each end.

'Come, Llewellyn!' one of the men called. 'Show us those of Welsh blood can do more than screw sheep!'

The boy smiled broadly. 'Fuck you, Carswell!' A number of arrows had been thrust into the grass and he pulled one out.

Leacon leaned forward. 'Llewellyn,' he said quietly, 'step away a little. Try to hit the mark from a sixty-degree angle, like we practised two days ago.'

'Yes, sir.' The boy stepped away a few yards and faced the tree at an angle. Then, in seconds, he had drawn his bow back nearly three feet, shot, and landed the arrow in the centre of the doublet. The soldiers clapped.

'More,' Leacon said. 'Make it six.' At a speed such as I had never seen, the boy loosed five more arrows, all of which hit the doublet. He turned and bowed to the appreciative crowd, a flash of white teeth in his sunburned face.

'That's how we'll feather them in the goddam Frenchies' bowels!' someone shouted, and there were more cheers.

Leacon turned to me. 'What do you think of my Goddams?' He smiled at my puzzled look. 'It's what English archers call themselves.'

'I have never seen such skill. George, Captain Giffard wants us to move off. I am sorry, I should have said at once, but I was so taken with that display.'

Leacon turned back to the men. 'No more, lads! We march!'

There was a grumbling murmur as the men set to unstringing their bows and I accompanied Leacon back to the road.

'Are your men all from the same district?' I asked.

'No. They come from all over north-west Middlesex. They're a varied bunch, sons of yeomen together with those of artisans and poor labourers. The commissioners are often accused of levying the dregs of the villages, but I was told to pick a company of strong, practised archers – principal archers we call them, and I have. Though there has been little time to train them to work together yet, most of the day is taken up with marching.'

'That fellow who shot last was remarkable, but he seemed young for service.'

'Tom Llewellyn is not nineteen, but he was the best archer I saw at the Views of Arms. A blacksmith's apprentice, son of a Welshman.'

'Are they willing recruits?'

'Some. Others less so. We had a few desertions in London, so we are four men short. And our company preacher was taken ill. We had no time to get a replacement.'

I laughed. 'You were unable to find a preacher in London? Now that does astonish me!'

'Not one willing to serve in the army, anyway.'

I nodded at the officer supervising the loading of the carts, which was now almost complete. He was still walking around, shouting and snapping.

'He is a choleric fellow.'

'Yes, Master Snodin, our whiffler. He is a seasoned veteran, he keeps the men well in order.'

'Ah.' I thought of Goodryke.

'He drinks, though, and gets in a fierce temper. I hope he does not have a seizure before we reach Portsmouth. He is the only other officer, apart from the vientinaries.'

'The what?'

'Companies are grouped into five sections of twenty, each with a corporal in charge whom I have nominated.'

'I was surprised not to see more men in uniform.'

He grunted. 'The store of white coats in the King's armouries has run out, and there has been no time to make more. Even the armour we have is a jumbled-up mixture. I'll swear some of it goes back to the wars between York and Lancaster, if not Agincourt.'

'I saw some ill-smelling padded jackets in one of the carts.'

Leacon nodded. 'Jacks. They give protection from arrows. But many have been shut up in church vestries for years and mice have nibbled at some. I am getting the men to mend them when they have time.'

I watched the men complete their loading. 'George,' I said, 'I understand our way goes near the Sussex border.'

'Yes, between Liphook and Petersfield. With luck we will reach there the day after tomorrow.'

'There is a small town on the Sussex side, Rolfswood. I have some business there.'

'I only know our stops along the road.' Leacon smiled. 'I'm a Kentishman, the less we know of Sussex clods the happier we are. You had best ask when we reach those parts.'

We had come up to the others. 'We must be off, Leacon,' Sir Franklin said.

'Nearly ready, sir.'

'Good. We should find our horses. And I want to talk to you about the men's buttons.'

'I thought we had settled that, sir.' A note of irritation had crept into Leacon's voice.

The captain frowned. 'We discussed it, sir, but did not settle it. Do you think I am of no good memory?'

'No, sir. But—'

'Come with me.' Sir Franklin turned and walked back to the inn, Leacon following, his straight-backed stride contrasting with Sir Franklin's slow, stiff-legged gait.

Dyrick shook his head. 'Buttons? What's that about? Silly old fool.'

We turned at the sound of shouting. The carts were loaded, and the recruits were fixing the large pouches containing their possessions to their belts, beside the long knives they all carried. Two soldiers by the carts had started fighting. The rangy fellow who had dropped the tent in a cowpat the previous evening and a big man with untidy fair hair were pummelling at each other with their fists. Other recruits gathered around eagerly.

'Come on, Pygeon. Don't let him get away with that!'

'What did you say to him now, Sulyard?'

The two men pulled apart, breathing hard, and circled each other. 'Come, Pygeon, you scabby freak!' the fair-haired fellow called out. 'Get your balance! Don't catch the wind with those great ears of yours or you'll fly up like a bird!'

There was more laughter. Pygeon was one of those unfortunates with large ears that stuck out from the side of his head. He had a narrow face and receding chin. He looked no more than twenty, while his opponent was some years older, with ugly, bony features, sharp malicious eyes and the taunting expression of the born bully. I was pleased when Pygeon caught him off guard, kicking out at his knee so that he howled and staggered.

The circle of onlookers parted as the red-faced whiffler Snodin pushed through, his face furious. He crossed to Pygeon and slapped him hard across the face. 'What the fuck's going on?' Snodin shouted. 'Pygeon, it's always you whenever there's trouble. You useless shit!'

'Sulyard won't let me be,' Pygeon shouted back. 'All the time insults, insults. I had to take it in our village but not now.'

Some in the crowd murmured agreement, others laughed. This infuriated the whiffler even more. His face grew almost purple. 'Shut up!' he bawled. 'You're King's men now, forget your damned village quarrels!' He looked malevolently over the crowd. 'This morning you can march in jacks and helmets. And Pygeon's section can wear the brigandynes. You can blame him.' There were groans from the men. 'Quiet!' Snodin shouted. 'You need to get used to them, you'll be wearing them when we meet the French! Front ten men, unload them!'

Ten men peeled quickly away from the crowd, ran up and unloaded the tight-fitting steel helmets from a cart, together with the jacks, and other jackets inlaid with metal plates that tinkled like coins: brigandynes, which I had heard could stop an arrow. Sulyard had got to his feet and, though limping slightly, gave Pygeon a victorious grin.

'The men must march in those?' I said to Barak.

'Looks like it. Rather them than me.'

Dyrick said, 'As the whiffler pointed out, they may have to fight in them. Look, here come Leacon and the captain. Come on, let's get moving.'

Leacon and Sir Franklin, mounted now, rode over to the whiffler. The three conversed in low tones. Leacon seemed to be disagreeing with the whiffler but Sir Franklin said, 'Nonsense! It'll teach them a lesson,' and concluded the discussion by riding back to the road.

The men donned the jacks, except for a group of twenty at the rear which included Sulyard and Pygeon as well as the young archer Llewellyn; they pulled on the brigandynes. Many of them were threadbare, like the jacks, some with the metal plates showing through. The section grumbled as they put them on; though Sulyard, who wore a new-looking brigandyne dyed bright red, the brazen studs holding the plates glinting, looked proud of what I guessed was a personal possession. The other men grumbled; the corporal, a heavy-set, keen-eyed young fellow with pleasant, mobile features, encouraged them. 'Come on, lads, it can't be helped. It's only till lunchtime.'

At a command from Snodin the soldiers drew up in rows of five. Sir Franklin, Leacon and the drummer took places at the front. The drummer began a steady beat and the men marched out of the field. I noticed again how young most were, almost all under thirty and several under twenty. All wore leather shoes, some old and battered. Snodin placed himself at the rear, in a position to watch the entire company. We four civilians mounted and took our places behind him; from the horse's back I had a view of his balding crown, with a glimpse of his blue-veined bottle nose when he turned his head. Behind us the carts creaked into position. As we made our way slowly down the empty main street of Cobham an old man leaned from the upper window of a house and called out, 'God be with you, soldiers. God save King Harry!'

✟

I WAS BEGINNING to grow fond of my horse, named Oddleg for his one white foot. He was placid, walked at a steady, unvarying pace and had seemed glad to see me that morning. The company marched into the countryside to the rhythm of the drum, the tramp of marching feet accompanied by the rumble of cartwheels behind us, the hoofbeats of our horses and, immediately ahead, an odd coin-like jingling from the brigandynes. One of the soldiers began singing, and the others took up the ragged chorus of an obscene variation of 'Greensleeves', each verse more inventive than the last.

After a while Leacon signalled the drummer to stop. We were climbing into the Surrey Downs now, the road mostly well-drained chalk. The marching men threw up much dust, and soon we at the back were grey with it. The countryside changed, more land farmed on the old system, with huge fields divided into long strips of different crops. The wheat and vetches seemed further on here, less battered looking; the storms must not have reached this far south. Peasants stopped work to look at us, but without much interest. We would not be the first soldiers passing this way.

The singing petered out after a couple of miles. The pace flagged and the drummer sounded the marching beat again. I decided to essay another conversation with Dyrick. Despite his wide-brimmed hat, his sharp, lean face was starting to burn as those of ruddy-headed people will. 'Poor caitiffs,' I said, nodding at the men in brigandynes, 'see how they sweat.'

'They may have to do more than sweat when we get to Portsmouth,' he replied grimly.

'Ay. Better the King had never started this war.'

'Maybe 'tis time for a final reckoning with the French. I just wish you hadn't got me caught up in the middle of it all.'

I laughed suddenly. 'Come, Brother Dyrick, there must be some topic we can agree on.'

He gave me a hostile stare. 'I cannot think of one.'

I gave up. Although it was discourteous, I fell behind so I could converse with Barak. Feaveryear gave me a disapproving look.

✝

WE MADE good progress; at a blast from the drummer's trumpet several carts, and once a gang of road menders, moved to the side of the road to let us pass. After two hours we stopped by a bridge to water the horses at the stream running under it. As we led the animals down to the water, the soldiers fell out and sat breakfasting in the road or on the verge, taking bread and cheese from the large pouches at their waists. The men in the jacks and brigandynes looked utterly weary.

'I don't think I could have stood up to this march like them,' Barak said. 'Five years ago, maybe. That arsehole Goodryke, he didn't care whether I'd make a good soldier or not. He just wanted to make an example of me.'

'Yes, he did.'

'That Snodin's another one. You can see he has it in for the jug-eared fellow.'

'He does.' I looked behind us, up the road. 'What's that?'

A plume of dust had appeared in the distance, men riding fast. Snodin ordered the recruits slumped in the roadway to move. Half a dozen riders passed us, all in the King's livery, heading south. At their head was a little man in a grey robe, his horse draped in a cloth of green and white, the royal colours. The party slowed to cross the bridge and I recognized the neat pale face of Sir Richard Rich.

Chapter Fourteen

As the morning wore on I found the journey increasingly wearying. For the marching men it was much harder, and I noticed those with old shoes were beginning to limp. In front of us dark sweat stains were visible on all the brigandynes now, outlining the metal squares sewn into the fabric. The soldiers slowed and the drum sounded to make them pick up the pace. Some were grousing by the time the trumpet sounded a halt just outside a village, beside a large pond fringed with willows. A couple of white-aproned old goodwives approached us and Leacon spoke to them, leaning down from his horse. Then he conferred briefly with the captain before calling back to the men.

'We stop here for lunch! The villagers have ham and bacon to sell. Purser, get some money! And the jacks and brigandynes can come off now!'

'Can we buy some women as well as food, sir?' It was the young corporal from the rear section. The soldiers laughed, and Leacon smiled.

'Ah, Stephen Carswell, never at a loss for a jest!'

'Hillingdon men are more used to donkeys than women!' the bully Sulyard shouted. He laughed loudly, showing a mouth half-empty of teeth.

The men fell out and sat at the roadside again, apart from a few who went to the carts and began unloading biscuit, cheese and a barrel of beer. I had to admire the smoothness of the company's organization. Leacon and the captain led their horses to the water, and we lawyers followed.

While the animals drank, Dyrick went to sit under the shade of a willow, Feaveryear following. Barak and I went over to where Leacon stood alone, watching his men. Some were straggling towards the village.

'Hard work, being in charge of a hundred men,' I observed.

'Ay. We have our grumblers, one or two rebellious spirits. Carswell there is our jester. A good man – I think he is one of those who will still joke as they march into battle.'

'That straw-haired fellow seems a nasty piece of work. He started the trouble with the other man this morning, you know.'

He sighed. 'Yes, Sulyard is a troublemaker. But Snodin dislikes poor Pygeon for his clumsy ways. Junior officers will sometimes take against a man for little reason.'

'You are right there,' Barak agreed feelingly.

'I think it was unjust,' I said.

Leacon gave me an impatient look. 'This is the army, Master Shardlake, not a law court. Snodin's job is to keep discipline and he may have to do that in battle, so I avoid gainsaying his decisions. Hard as he is, I need him. Sir Franklin is – well, you have met him.'

'What was that business about buttons earlier?'

'You may have noticed some soldiers have buttons on their shirts, while others tie them with aiglets. Sir Franklin believes only gentlemen should be allowed to wear buttons. It is, shall we say, something of an obsession.'

'Buttons?' Barak repeated disbelievingly.

'Yes. Not that he is altogether wrong, the men like keeping as many as they can of the social distinctions they had before. That is part of the trouble between Sulyard and Pygeon. They come from the same village – Pygeon is a labourer's son, Sulyard the son of a yeoman. Though only a second son.'

'Whose inheritance was ever what the cat left on the malt heap.'

'He was keen to join the company, and he is a good longbow-man.'

'Would there had never been need to recruit this army,' I said.

Leacon looked across to the village, then round to where a long field of strips crested the downland. People were hard at work weeding their rows. He spoke with sudden passion. 'We have to protect these people, Master Shardlake. That is why this army was levied. And now I must find where the captain has wandered off to.' He strode away.

'I think I offended him,' I said to Barak.

'He must know what people think of the war.'

'Yet in the end he is right about the need to defend ourselves. And he and his men are the ones who must do it.'

'Come on,' Barak said. 'Let's go to the village. I wouldn't mind a piece of bacon.'

✝

THE VILLAGE had no real centre; longhouses of various sizes were jumbled together at odd angles, paths weaving between them. In front of the bakehouse, a low square building, a table was loaded with bacon and thick slices of ham. Several soldiers were arguing with the women who had come out to us and now stood behind it. Sulyard was at the centre of the argument, shouting. More villagers were coming out of their houses.

One of the old women was waving a coin at Sulyard with just the air of outraged fury I had seen in Cheapside ten days before. 'This is no proper coin!' she shouted. 'It's not silver! Shame on you, the King's soldiers trying to cheat us!'

Sulyard bawled back. 'It's one of the new coins, you doltish country mare! It's a testoon, a shilling!'

A tall old man stepped up to him, grim-faced. 'Don't you insult my wife, ape!' He gave Sulyard a little push. Another soldier stepped forward and shoved him back.

'Don't you push Sulyard! Ape he is, but he's our ape!'

Carswell, the corporal, raised his hands. 'Come, lads. Don't make trouble, or we'll end marching in the jacks all day.'

'These clods don't understand the coinage!' Sulyard said with a mocking laugh. The growing crowd of villagers murmured ominously. Barefoot children looked on excitedly.

'Please,' Carswell called out, 'be calm! Our ape speaks true, these are the new coins of the realm!' Sulyard gave him a nasty look.

'Then pay in the old ones!' a young man called out.

The young archer Llewellyn stepped forward. 'They're all spent. Please, Goodwife, we've had scarce anything but bread and cheese for three days.'

The old woman folded her arms. 'That's your problem, my pretty.'

'We should send that old woman against the damned French,' Sulyard shouted. 'They'd flee at the sight of her.'

A couple of villagers, older men, stepped forward. Carswell looked round desperately, then saw me. He pointed. 'See, we have a gentleman with us, a lawyer. He'll confirm what we say.'

The villagers gave me hostile looks. I hesitated, then said, 'There is indeed a new coinage.'

'So soldiers take hunchback lawyers with them now to cheat folks!' Nothing could mollify the old woman. The villagers growled agreement.

I stepped forward. 'See, the coins have the King's head on them.'

'It's not silver!' the old woman shrieked in my face. 'I know how silver looks and feels!'

'It's mixed with copper. They are worth eightpence of the old money in London.'

'Ninepence!' one of the soldiers called out hopefully.

'Eightpence,' I repeated firmly.

The old woman shook her head. 'Don't care. Don't want that rubbish!'

'Come, Margaret,' one of the old men said. 'We killed Martin's pig to get this meat, we need to sell it.'

I took my purse. 'I'll pay, in the old money. Then the soldiers can repay me, eightpence for a new testoon.'

There was a murmur of agreement among the villagers. The old woman still looked suspicious, but said, 'You can have the lot for four shillings in proper silver. It should be five given the insults I've had, but we'll say four.'

It was a hard bargain, but I nodded agreement. The tension, which had been singing in the hot midday air, relaxed as I handed over a dozen silver groats, which the old woman examined ostentatiously before nodding and waving a hand at the meat. The soldiers took portions. The villagers returned to their houses, giving us hostile looks over their shoulders.

Carswell collected money from the recruits, then approached me. 'Thank you, sir, on behalf of the men. Here is their money. If we'd got into a fight we'd have been in the shit with the officers.' He hesitated, then added, 'It would be a favour if you did not mention this to Captain Leacon.'

'Ay,' Tom Llewellyn added. 'We know you are his friend.'

I smiled. 'Word has travelled fast.'

Sulyard swaggered by, giving us a dirty look. I noticed he wore pearl buttons on his jerkin, and remembered what Leacon said about the differences in the soldiers' clothes. He said, 'You stopped a promising fight brewing there, Carswell, you dog-hearted scut.'

'With old people and children?' Carswell asked. Sulyard was now attracting hostile looks from some of the other soldiers. He turned and swaggered away.

'Sorry about him, sir,' Carswell said. 'Come on, Welshy, let's get back.'

I looked at Llewellyn curiously. 'You are not Welsh, by your voice?'

'No, sir. But my father is. He trained me to the warbow,' he added proudly. A shadow crossed his face. 'Though I like my work at the forge too.'

Carswell nudged him. 'And your girly, eh? He's to be married at Christmas.'

'I congratulate you.'

'But where shall we be at Christmas?' Llewellyn asked sadly.

'We'll beat those Frenchies,' Carswell said confidently. 'You'll be happily in bed with your Tessy come Twelfth Night. If they have beds in Yiewsley village: I've heard you all still sleep with the cows.'

'No, that's Harefield men, like Sulyard.' Llewellyn looked at me. 'There are four of us here from our village.' He shook his head sadly. 'When we left, the girls garlanded us with flowers, everyone stood cheering as a lute player led us down the road. A far cry from our reception here.'

'Come on,' Carswell said. 'Let's get this bacon back to camp, before I start drooling.'

They walked away. 'That's got us well in with the troops,' Barak said.

'Jesu knows we need some friends on this journey.'

He looked at me. 'That was Richard Rich back there on the road, wasn't it?'

'Yes. Probably on his way to Portsmouth. The sooner we get to Hoyland Priory and back again, the better.'

✝

AFTER LUNCH the company rested for an hour, sitting out the hottest part of the day. Then the soldiers were called back into line.

We marched on steadily. By the time we reached Guildford, late in the afternoon, some of the recruits were drooping with exhaustion. We marched through the town without stopping, a few small boys running alongside and cheering, but most of the townsfolk barely looking at us; many companies of soldiers would have passed through these last weeks.

Not long after we mounted a crest of sandstone hills, then descended into a river valley. It was about six o'clock, the sun starting to sink. We saw Godalming at last, cradled by the hills and dominated by the tall spire of a large church. A man stood at the gate of a meadow, looking at us expectantly. At a signal from Leacon, the men fell out and sank exhausted to the roadside. Leacon rode back to us.

'I am leaving Snodin in charge of the men,' he said. 'That is the field allotted them to camp in tonight. I am riding into town with the purser to buy rations and see if I can find some new shoes. Some of the men are limping badly.'

'That they are.'

'I'll probably have to pay a high price. How merchants are profiting from this war. I'll return to stay with the men, but you and your friends may as well ride in with me and find an inn. We can pick you up on the main road as we march through tomorrow. At six, we have to keep up the pace.'

'We'll be ready,' Dyrick answered, though he was as tired and dusty as I.

☨

WE RODE INTO Godalming. Leacon and his purser left us to find the mayor, and we went to look for an inn. Most were full, but we found places at last. Barak and Feaveryear would have to share a room again. I went up to my chamber, took off my boots and lay down on the mattress, a feather one this time. I was almost asleep when there was a knock at the door and Barak entered.

'Come with me into town,' he begged. 'Let's find somewhere else to eat. I can't bear a whole evening with Feaveryear.'

I heaved myself to my feet, wincing at my sore back and thighs. 'Nor I with Dyrick.'

We found another inn, with better food than the night before. It was a companionable meal without Dyrick and Feaveryear. But as we stepped out into the street again I felt an urge to be alone for a while; I had been constantly in company for two days.

'I think I will look at the church,' I said.

'A spot of prayer?'

'Churches are good for contemplation.'

He sighed. 'Back to nestle with Feaveryear, then.'

I walked up the main street and into the church. The hushed space reminded me of childhood days, for this was as traditional a church as the law allowed. The evening sun shone straight in through the brightly stained west window, making the interior a dim red. A chantry priest recited Masses for the dead in a side chapel.

I walked slowly down the nave. Then I saw, in another side chapel, bent before the altar rail, a figure in a dusty white coat. George Leacon. He must have heard my footsteps stop for he turned round. He looked utterly weary.

'Forgive me,' I said quietly. 'I came to look at the church.'

He smiled sadly. 'I was trying to communicate with my Maker.'

'I remember at York you were working hard at reading the Bible.'

'I still have that bible.' He looked at me, his face anguished now. 'These days it strikes me how full of war the Bible is. The Old Testament, at least, and the Book of Revelation.'

I sat on the altar-rail steps. After that long day in the saddle I doubted I could kneel. 'Yes,' I agreed.

'I need to get *away* from images of war.' Leacon's tone was suddenly fierce. 'I read the New Testament, I pray for images of battle to stop crowding into my head, but – they will not.'

I wondered again at how the open boyish face I remembered had become so thin, so stark. 'You said you were in France last year,' I prompted gently.

'Ay.' He turned so he was sitting beside me. 'Those recruits, they have no notion what war is. When you knew me four years ago, Master Shardlake, I had had an easy form of soldiering. Garrison duty on the northern border or in Calais, or guarding the King's palaces. No war, only border ruffles with the Scots. Yes, I saw reivers there brought back dead for their heads to be displayed on Berwick Castle. But I had never killed a man. And then, you remember, I was dismissed.'

'Unjustly.'

'And so I returned to my parents' farm, which you saved for us in that court action.'

'I owed you a debt.'

'That was a good life, if a hard one. But my parents grew older, they could do less work and we had to hire labourers. Then, in the spring of last year, my old captain came. He said the King was going to invade France and they needed all the soldiering men they could get. The pay was good and I agreed.' He looked at me intently. 'I had no idea what it would be like. Does that not sound stupid, childish, coming from one who was a professional soldier?'

'What happened?'

Leacon now spoke with a sort of quiet, desperate fervour. 'I sailed first to Scotland with Lord Hertford's fleet. Did you know, the King ordered him to wage a war that would spare neither women nor children? Lord Hertford did not want to, but the King insisted. We landed at a place called Leith and sacked it, burned every house to the ground and set the women and children running into the countryside. My company stayed there so I saw no more action then, but the rest of the army went to Edinburgh and did the same, razed everything to the ground. The men came back laden with booty, anything of value they could take from the houses. The boats were so laden it was feared some might sink. But spoil is part of war — without hope of gain soldiers are reluctant to march into enemy country.'

'And now the Scots threaten to invade us, with the soldiers the French have sent them.'

'Yes. King Francis wants England humbled for good.' Leacon ran a hand through his curls. 'We sailed straight from Scotland to France. In July, just a year ago. I was in charge of a half-company of archers. They are all dead now.'

'All?'

'Every one. We landed in Calais and marched straight to Boulogne. The countryside between had already been ravaged by foraging soldiers. As in Scotland the fields had been trampled, villages burned. I remember local people standing by the road, old people and women and children in rags, everything they owned taken or destroyed. Starving in the rain, there was nothing but rain and cold winds in France last year. I remember how pale their faces were.' His voice fell almost to a whisper. 'There was a woman, a baby in one skinny arm, holding out the other for alms. As I marched past I saw her baby was dead, its eyes open and glassy. Its mother hadn't realized yet.' Leacon stared at me fixedly. 'We were not allowed to stop. I could see it affected the men but I had to encourage them, keep them marching. You have to, you have to.' He stopped, with a great sigh. 'And the French will do the same if they land, for revenge. Their captains will cry, "Havoc," and it will be the turn of their men to take booty from us.'

'All because the King wanted glory,' I said bitterly.

A spasm of disgust crossed Leacon's face. 'We marched right past Henry when we reached the outskirts of Boulogne. He was in his camp, all the splendid tents up on a hill. I saw him, a huge figure encased from head to foot in armour, sitting on the biggest horse I ever saw, watching the battle. Well out of range of the French cannons pounding our men from the city, of course.' Leacon swallowed hard, then continued. 'Our company marched uphill, under fire from the French – Boulogne is on a hill, you see. All our forces could do was hunker down under mud embankments, firing back into the town with our cannon, moving forward by inches. I saw Boulogne turned to rubble.' He looked at me, then said, 'You will not know what it is like to kill a man.'

I hesitated. 'I did kill a man once. I had to or he would have killed me. I drowned him, held him under the water of a muddy pond. I still remember the sounds he made. Later I was nearly drowned myself, in a sewer tunnel flooded with water. Ever since I have been terrified of drowning, yet felt it would be a kind of justice.'

'There is no justice,' Leacon said quietly. 'No meaning. That is what I fear. I beg God to take my memories from me but he will not.' He looked at the richly gilded statue of the Virgin Mary on the altar, her expression quiet, contemplative, immeasurably distant. He resumed his terrible story.

'When the part of Boulogne nearest us was blown almost to dust we were ordered to advance. The King had gone home by then; it was September, wetter and muddier than ever. Hundreds of us struggled uphill through the mud, French cannon firing down on us all the time. Then, when we got closer, their archers and arque-busiers fired from among the tumbled stones. The nearer we got to the town the more men fell. My company of archers shot many French cannoneers and archers. But we were a target ourselves, and many of my men were blown to fragments by the cannons.' He laughed suddenly, wildly, a terrible sound echoing round the dark church. 'Fragments,' Leacon repeated. 'A little word for such a meaning. All that great muddy slope covered with hands and bits of legs, great joints of meat in scraps of uniform, pools of bloody slime among the mud and tumbled stone. A friend's head in a puddle, still with the helmet on.' He cast his head down, gave a mighty sigh, then looked up.

'Enough survived to climb the rubble into the town. Then it was hand-to-hand fighting, swords and bills, hacking and crunching and blood everywhere. The French — and they are brave men, as good as ours — retreated to the upper part of Boulogne and held out another week. I was wounded slightly in my side, I passed out and woke shivering in pain in a leaky tent, trying to keep rats away from my wound.' He gave a harsh laugh. 'They said I had been a brave soldier and promoted me to petty-captain.'

'Brave indeed, in a situation so terrible I can barely imagine.'

'It isn't the fighting in the town I remember most,' Leacon said. 'Though I killed several Frenchmen then and was myself in mortal danger. It's that hill below, like the inside of a slaughterhouse. So many dead. Many nights I dream I am there again. I struggle through that landscape, looking for pieces of my men, trying to identify them so I can put them together again.' He took a deep breath. 'If we fight the French ships, if we board, that will be hand-to-hand fighting. I got Snodin to address the men on the second day, tell them what it might be like. I know he was at Boulogne too. I could not bring myself to do it.'

I could think of nothing to say. I put my hand on his arm.

'I'm a fine fellow to lead soldiers, eh?' He laughed bitterly. 'When I am like this within?'

'You lead them well. I can see they respect you.'

'They would not if they could see how I really am. I can control myself for most of the time. But then I think of what I may be leading those men and boys to. Some like Sulyard are keen to fight, but even they have no conception what it will be like.'

'George, if you were not leading them it might be someone with less care for his men, who would not trouble to get good shoes for them.'

'I hate the drums.' There was desperation in Leacon's voice now. 'When we marched uphill at Boulogne the companies were always led by drummers, beating as loud as they could to compete with the cannon. I hate the sound, I always hear it in my dreams.' He looked at me. 'If only I could go home, to the farm. But I can't, we are all sworn in. You should thank God, Master Shardlake, that you are a civilian.'

Chapter Fifteen

THAT NIGHT I slept deeply. When the innkeeper woke me at five I had a vague memory of a dream involving Ellen, which left me with a heavy, troubled feeling.

The four of us were waiting on our horses outside the inn when the company marched through. Dyrick was in one of his sulky moods again, perhaps because I had abandoned him the night before. Sir Franklin rode at the head of his men with a haughty expression, Leacon with his face set and closed.

We took our places at the rear as the soldiers tramped south once more. Many of the recruits looked dull-eyed with the long boredom of the march; but several who had been limping now wore new shoes. The whiffler Snodin was again marching just in front of me; he reeked like a beer keg.

Soon after leaving Godalming, we crossed the border into Hampshire. We were in the western fringes of the Weald, mostly flat, forested country, massive old oaks among elm and beech. Areas of hunting ground were fenced in with high, strong wooden palings. We marched through tunnel-like lanes where the trees sometimes met overhead, a green dimness with spatters of bright sunlight on the road. A rich loamy smell came from the woodland. Once I saw a dozen bright butterflies dancing in a patch of sunlight. On the march there had been a constant sound of birds flapping away at our approach, but the butterflies ignored us as we passed, many of the men turning to watch them.

Again we halted near midday, in a broad, wooded lane near a stream. The horses were led to the water and the men crowded round the carts to receive the rations bought at Godalming. I heard complaints that there was only fruit and bread and cheese again, though a fat man who was the company purser pleaded the limited buying power of the new coins. One man called out, 'We've got our bows, let's hunt our own supplies. Come on, Goddams, let's get some rabbits or partridges, maybe a deer!'

There were shouts of agreement. Sir Franklin, like Leacon still mounted, turned and stared with an outraged expression. Leacon dismounted hastily and went up to the men.

'No!' he called out. 'This land is fenced, it's the hunting ground of some gentleman or even the King! I won't have you breaking the law!'

'Come, Captain!' someone called out. 'We're country lads, we can soon catch something.'

'Ay! Master Purser's keeping us short. We can't fight on empty bellies!'

'And what if you meet a forester?' Leacon asked.

To my surprise Pygeon spoke up, his words tumbling over each other in his nervousness. 'God made the forests and game to serve man, sir, not to be fenced in for the sport of those who have full bellies!' There were more shouts of agreement, and for the first time I sensed a challenge to Leacon's authority. The whiffler Snodin marched across, purple-faced. 'Rebellious bastard!' he shouted right in Pygeon's face, adorning it with spittle.

'Drunken old cunt,' I heard Sulyard murmur. Several men laughed. Leacon stared them down. Many lowered their eyes but not all. Some crossed their arms and looked defiant.

'Maybe you're right!' Leacon said loudly. 'I'm a poor farmer's son myself, I've no time for enclosers of land! But if you take game and meet a forester then you'll hang, soldiers or no. And that'll be a fine thing to be said of a company of the warbow! I promise when we get to Liphook I'll make sure you get a good meal, if I have to hold Master Purser upside down and shake the last groat from his doublet!'

'Can I help you shake him, Captain?' Carswell called. As in the village the day before, his humour broke the tension and the men laughed.

After eating, many of the men went to a spot on the wattle fence enclosing the hunting park, ostentatiously pissing against it. After my own repast of bread and bacon, I walked over to where Leacon sat. He had handled the angry soldiers skilfully, and it was hard to realize this was the same man as the agonized figure I had spoken with the night before. 'How are you and your friends bearing up with the ride?' he asked. I sensed a new reserve in his voice.

'Stiff and sore, but that is only to be expected.'

'Your colleague's young clerk finds it hard, I think.'

'Feaveryear is managing. Just.' I looked at Leacon keenly, wondering if he regretted his confidences. 'A couple of men were arguing just now over whether a bowl was theirs or the King's,' I said to make conversation.

'Yes, some brought their own but many had to have bowls and spoons issued from the stores. A wooden bowl may be a prized possession in a poor family. It is the same with the bows: only those with good ones, like Llewellyn, were allowed to bring their own. Most are standard issue from the armouries. It is the poorer men who hadn't equipment to bring, and yet their pay will be docked. Strange, is it not?' He smiled mirthlessly.

Dyrick came up to us, nodding to Leacon before addressing me. 'Master Shardlake, I would speak with you confidentially, if I may.'

We sat together at the side of the road. The rest of us were tanned now, but Dyrick's face was still red, sunburned skin peeling off one cheek above the coppery stubble on his lean face. He said, 'Master Hobbey has turned part of the priory lands into a hunting park. Only a small one, but well stocked with game.' He gave me one of his hard looks. 'He is to hold his first hunting party in ten days' time. Many local gentlefolk will be present. It will be an important event for my client.'

'I hope we shall be gone by then.'

'But lest we are not, I trust you will not tell any of the local society the purpose of our visit.'

'As I said about the villagers, Brother Dyrick, I look to make no trouble for Master Hobbey. But I will make no commitments about what I may say or do.'

'I shall be watching you carefully, Brother Shardlake.' Dyrick's expression was intent, his green-brown eyes locked on mine. 'My client has come far, from wool merchant to country gentleman. Perhaps one day he may be Sir Nicholas. I will not see his prospects harmed.'

'All I want is to ensure Hugh Curteys' lands and welfare are properly looked after. Why can you not realize that?'

'You will soon see that they are.'

'Then all will be well, Brother.'

There was silence for a moment, then Dyrick asked, 'Have you ever hunted?'

'When I was young, once. Though it was not to my taste, the beasts harried along to their deaths. They have no chance.'

Dyrick laughed scoffingly. 'There speaks the Court of Requests lawyer. Even deer get your sympathy. Well, it will be my first hunt if we are still there, though like you I hope we will not be.' He grunted. 'I did not come from the class that hunts. I am the son of a poor clerk — I have had to struggle up the ladder of life. From Church school to a scholarship at the Temple, to a lowly job as a lawyer at the King's court—'

'You worked at court? Perhaps you met people I know. Robert Warner, for example?'

'The Queen's solicitor? No, I had a grubbing clerkly job. I left to test my wits in litigation.' He looked at me hard again. 'Master Hobbey comes from lowly origins too. But I hear your father was a rich farmer, Brother Shardlake.' There was a sneer in his voice.

'Not so rich, a yeoman only. And I was told my grandfather's grandfather was a serf. That is where most of us have come from in the end.'

'I admire those who come from nothing and aim high.'

I smiled. 'You are one of our "new-made men", Brother Dyrick.'

'And proud of it. In England we are not slaves like the French.'

We looked at the soldiers. A little group with Sulyard at its centre were talking in low voices and laughing unpleasantly, mocking someone no doubt, and Barak had struck up a conversation with Carswell and the Welsh boy. Dyrick stood, brushing grass from his rear. 'Another thing,' he added, 'your man Barak, like Feaveryear, will be expected to stay out of the house. Master Hobbey does not approve of over-familiar servants.'

He walked away. I watched him, reflecting with a sardonic smile that new-made men are often the worst snobs.

✝

DURING THE afternoon clouds began rolling in from the west and it turned cooler. I saw Leacon looking at the sky. A fierce downpour such as had been common in June would soon turn the road from dust to mud. Leacon nodded at the drummer, who began a fast beat to get the men to pick up their pace.

We stopped briefly on another woodland road at about four to water the horses at a pond and give them some rest. Beer was passed round and I took the chance to tell Barak of my conversation with Dyrick.

'Hobbey will probably lodge Feaveryear and me in the woodshed.' He nodded to where the clerk sat on a bank a little way off, reading a psalter.

'I think we'll need three days to take depositions and see what case Hugh Curteys is in. Then we get ourselves back.'

'What if they are doing something nasty to him?'

'Then we will bring him back with us, and Dyrick can—'

'Fuck himself with a red-hot poker. I heard one of the lads telling in detail how he'd do that to Snodin.'

'Look at that!' We turned at the sound of a shout. One of the soldiers was pointing over the trees to the east. 'A forest fire.' I saw a column of smoke rising up a mile or so away. It grew denser, and I caught the first smell of smoke.

'It's not a fire,' young Llewellyn said. 'It's charcoal burners. We're on the western fringes of the iron-working area here.'

I looked over at him curiously. 'How do you know?'

'I've been there, sir. When I finish my apprenticeship I plan to move to Sussex to work. Anyone with skill at the forge can command good money in the blast furnaces. I went to Sussex last year to look for opportunities – there are ironworks everywhere, making everything from arrowheads to decorated firebacks. I went to Buxted, where they cast cannon. What a place.' He shook his head in wonder. 'Dozens of men working in huge buildings. You can hear the noise miles away, but the wages are good.' He bent and picked a blade of grass, slowly tearing it. 'Tess and my parents do not wish me to go.' He looked at me seriously. 'But it is a way for a man like me who cannot write to better himself. Is that not a good thing to do?'

'I suppose so. But for those around you, perhaps not. Though it is easy for me to say.'

'I will do it.' He frowned and picked another blade of grass.

'So we are near the Sussex border?' I asked.

'Yes. The ironworks here in the west are fewer and more old-fashioned, but there is still plenty of work for them.' He turned and looked at me, the light blue eyes in his tanned face anxious. 'Do you not think my idea a good one, sir?'

'I hear the foundries are dangerous places to work.'

'Less dangerous than soldiering,' Llewellyn answered with feeling.

✟

TOWARDS SIX the company halted outside the little town of Liphook, where a local man waited beside our allotted meadow. The soldiers marched in and began unloading the tents under Snodin's supervision. The clouds above were still heavy and thick, the air cool, but it was not yet raining. Leacon told us he was sleeping with the company again, but advised us to find an inn; the man whose field it was had assured him there would be heavy rain before the evening was out. Leacon's manner towards me still had that new remoteness, which saddened me.

'You don't let the men into the towns?' I asked him.

'No. Strict orders. They'd just get drunk and there is always someone who will cause trouble.'

'What of Sir Franklin?'

'He'll stay with the men. He believes it's a captain's place, though sleeping in a tent gives him gout. Now I should go and supervise things; I will come into town with the purser later, and try to get some decent food for the men. Meet us in the town square tomorrow morning at seven. Leave your horses in camp if you like,' he said. 'We'll bring them.'

'Seven. A late start, then.'

'I have promised the men a shave before we leave tomorrow morning. One of the recruits is a barber.'

'I could do with one too.'

'For archers it is a point of pride. Long hair and a beard may get in the way if you are drawing arrows at the rate of half a dozen a minute.'

'Perhaps we might meet in Liphook later, for a drink?'

'No, I had best return with the supplies. Goodnight.' He walked away.

✠

LIPHOOK WAS small, a village rather than a town, and there were only two inns. As at Cobham, there were carts everywhere. There was only one room at the better inn, which I let Dyrick and Feaveryear take. A small bribe secured Barak and I a little room at the other. Barak flopped down on the bed, sending up a cloud of dust from his clothes.

'I wonder if Dyrick will let Feaveryear crouch praying in their room. Dear God, I hope Master Hobbey doesn't make me share with him.'

'Maybe he will convert you to his saintly ways.'

'Let's hope we find Hugh Curteys happy as a pig in muck.'

'Amen to that.' I stretched my legs. 'God's death, I swear I heard the bones creak.' I hesitated, then said, 'I think I will go for a walk, stretch my legs. And see if I can find a barber.'

Barak looked up in surprise. 'Are you not going to rest?'

'I will be back later.' I went out quickly, uncomfortable that I had not told the truth. I had decided Liphook was a good place to begin my enquiries about Ellen. Having sworn not to involve Barak, I had not mentioned her name since we left London. Nor had he, though I knew he would not have forgotten my intention to investigate her past.

✝

I DECIDED to ask first at the larger inn. I paused, though, at a barber's shop in a side street and had a shave. Dyrick, had mentioned earlier that he would look for a barber in Liphook and I found myself hoping he would not find it; let him turn up at Hoyland Priory looking unkempt. I shook my head: his endless competitiveness was infecting me.

The inn parlour was busy and I had to elbow my way to the serving hatch, where a plump, weary-looking man stood handing out mugs of beer. I waited my turn, ordered a beer, then laid a groat on the bar and leaned forward. 'I am looking for information about a place over the Sussex border,' I said quietly. 'Rolfswood.'

He looked at me curiously. 'I come from near there.'

'How far is it?'

'You need to get off the Portsmouth road south of Horndean, then take the road east about five miles.'

'Is it a big place?'

'No. A little market town.' He looked at me curiously. 'What d'ye want at Rolfswood? Not much there since the ironworks went.'

'They work iron there?'

'Used to. There's a small seam to the north. There was a little bloomery furnace in Rolfswood, but since it burned down the ore gets taken east.'

'Burned down?' I remembered Ellen's face, her words: *He burned! The poor man, he was all on fire!*

'When I was a young man the owner and his assistant were killed. It must be twenty years ago.'

'An accident while they were — what is it — casting?'

The potman took the groat, then leaned over the bar. 'No. It was during the summer, the old bloomery foundries only operate in the winter. What's your interest, sir?'

'Can you remember the names of the people who were killed?'

'I've been gone a long time, but I remember the owner's name: Fettiplace.'

My mind raced. Twenty years ago, the very time Ellen had been attacked and put in the Bedlam. Something else had happened in Rolfswood, as well as the rape. Two people had died. *He burned!*

My heart pounded. I turned abruptly from the hatch, and found myself looking straight at Feaveryear, who had been standing behind me, his greasy locks dangling over his sunburned brow.

Three days of irritation with Dyrick's jibes and Feaveryear's sour face boiled over. 'God's death, clerk,' I cried. 'Have you been eaves-dropping?'

Feaveryear's mouth dropped open. 'No, sir, I was behind you in the queue. I came in for a beer.'

I looked around. 'Where's Dyrick? You are a spy, clerk!'

'I am not, Master Shardlake.' Feaveryear spoke hotly, his big Adam's apple twitching. 'Master Dyrick wanted to sleep, he sent me out and I came here. On my honour as a Christian, I heard you say something to that man about an ironworks that burned down, that is all.'

He seemed genuinely outraged. I saw how tired he looked, dark rings under his eyes. 'I am sorry,' I said quietly. 'I should not have shouted. Come and sit down.'

Feaveryear followed me reluctantly to a place on a bench. 'I apologize if I was mistaken,' I said. 'I have other business in Sussex, for another client.'

'You are apologizing to me, sir?' He looked surprised. 'Then I thank you.'

There was silence for a moment, then I said, 'The journey has been harder than I expected. The soldiers keep a fast pace.'

His face closed again, went sour and disapproving. 'My master says it is all unnecessary.'

I wondered whether Dyrick had used Feaveryear to spy out our plans before the hearing. Perhaps he had even been to the Court of Wards and bribed Mylling. I remembered the corner boys, the sack over my head. 'Well,' I answered neutrally, 'we shall see what we find.' I looked at him curiously. 'Have you worked for Master Dyrick long?'

'Three years. My father worked in the kitchens at the Temple, he sent me to school and afterwards asked for a place for me as a clerk. Master Dyrick took me on. He has taught me much. He is a good master.' Again that self-righteous look.

'So you sometimes work at the Court of Wards.'

'Yes, sir.' He hesitated then added, 'I see, like many, you think it a bad place.'

I inclined my head.

'Maybe it is, but my master seeks only justice there, as in the other courts where he pleads.'

'Come, Feaveryear. Lawyers take the cases that come to them, just or no.' I remembered my conversation with the Lady Elizabeth.

Feaveryear shook his head firmly. 'My master takes only cases that are just. Like this one. I am a Christian man, sir, I could not work for a lawyer who represented bad folk.' He coloured. 'I do not mean you do that, sir, only that you are mistaken in this cause.'

I stared at him. How could he believe that Vincent Dyrick, of all people, represented only the just? Yet he obviously did. I drew a deep breath. 'Well, Feaveryear, I must go back to my inn, get some food.'

'And my master asked me to find a barber.'

We went out into the street. Dusk was falling, candles lit in the windows. Some of the carters were bedding down in their wagons.

'Probably all going to Portsmouth,' I said. 'Like our company of archers.'

'Poor fellows,' Feaveryear said sadly. 'I have seen the soldiers look at me on the journey, I know they think me a weakling. Yet I think what they may be going to, and pray for them. It is wicked they have no preacher. Most of those men have not come to God. They do not realize that death in battle may be followed by a swift journey to Hell.'

'Maybe there will be no battle. Maybe the French will not land.'

'I pray not.'

I felt a drop of rain on my hand. 'Here it comes.'

'They will get wet in the camp.'

'Yes. And I must get back to my inn. Goodnight, Feaveryear.'

'Goodnight, Master Shardlake.'

'Oh, and Feaveryear, there is a barber's in the next street. Tell your master.'

✝

IT WAS POURING with rain by the time I reached my inn, another summer storm. Dressed as I was in only shirt and jerkin, I was soaked through. The man I had bribed to get us a place at the inn invited me to come through to the kitchen and sit by the fire, hoping no doubt for another coin. I was glad to take up the offer; I needed somewhere to think hard about what the man at the other inn had told me.

I stared into the flames as they rose. A foundry had burned down in Rolfswood two decades before, and two men had died. From her words at the Bedlam Ellen had seen a fire, seen at least one man burn.

Could this have been some accident she witnessed that had driven her out of her wits? But then where did the attack on her fit in? Despite the fire I felt chilled. What if the deaths of the foundrymaster and his assistant had not been accidental? What if Ellen had seen murder and that was why she was hidden away in the Bedlam? It began to seem that Barak had been right to warn me of danger.

The thought crossed my mind of not journeying to Rolfswood after all. I could return to London and leave things as they had always been. Ellen had been safe, after all, for nineteen years; if I meddled with murder I could bring danger down on her again.

The flames in the fireplace were growing higher. Suddenly they lit, from below, some words on the fireback that made me start back and almost fall from my stool.

Grieve not, thy heart is mine.

A middle-aged woman pouring ingredients for a pottage into a bowl at the kitchen table looked at me in surprise.

'Are you all right, sir?' She hurried across. 'You have gone very pale.'

'What is that?' I asked, pointing. 'Those words, there, do you see them?'

She looked at me oddly. 'You often get words and phrases carved on firebacks in these parts.'

'What does it mean? Whose heart?'

She looked more worried than ever. 'I don't know, maybe the maker's wife had died or something. Sir, you look ill.'

I was sweating now, I felt my face flush. 'I just had a — a strange turn. I will go upstairs.'

She nodded at me sympathetically. ''Tis the thought of all those Frenchies sailing towards us, it makes me feel strange too. Such times, sir, such times.'

Chapter Sixteen

THE NEXT DAY, our fourth on the road, was uneventful. It was hot and sunny again, the air muggy. Fortunately the rain had not lasted long enough to damage the roads. We passed through more country of wood and pasture, reaching Petersfield towards midday and halting there to rest.

We moved on through a countryside that was starting to change; the ground beneath us chalky, with more open fields, rising steadily as we climbed into the Hampshire Downs. There was ever more activity on the highway, many carts that stopped to let us pass at the sound of our drummer's trumpet. Once we saw a company of local militia training in a field; they waved at us and cheered. I began to notice tall structures on hilltops, thick posts supporting piles of wood soaked in tar, always with a man standing guard – the beacons that would be lit should the enemy fleet be sighted, which I knew ran in a chain across the coastal counties.

At one point a post rider in royal colours passed us, and for once it was the soldiers' turn to pull aside. Barak's eyes followed the rider as he disappeared in a cloud of dust; I guessed he was wondering when a letter might come from Tamasin. He gave me a quizzical look. Last night he had noticed my agitated state on my return to our room, but had seemed to believe me when I said I was only chilled from my soaking. I remembered the fireback and suppressed a shiver. It had been an extraordinary thing to see just when I had been thinking of abandoning my investigations into Ellen's past. I did not believe in omens, but it had unsettled me deeply.

Towards six we halted again outside a field. As on previous

evenings a local man had been posted to wait for us, a pile of brushwood beside him for the soldiers' bedding. The drummer had sounded a slow, steady beat for the last hour, for the men were tired. Looking ahead to the front of the column, I saw that Leacon's shoulders were held tight, his head hunched down. He spoke to the man by the field, ordered Snodin to lead the men in, then rode back to us.

'I am afraid, gentlemen, you must spend the evening in camp. We are outside Buriton: the man tells me it is full to bursting with travellers and carters. No chance of a place at the inn.'

'You mean we'll have to sleep in this field?' Dyrick asked in outraged tones.

'You can sleep in the roadway of you like, sir,' Leacon answered shortly, 'but I will offer you a place in our camp if you wish.'

'We should be grateful,' I said.

'I will see if I can find a tent for you.' Leacon nodded to me and rode off. Dyrick grunted. 'We should arrive at Hoyland tomorrow morning, with luck. I'll be glad to get away from these stinking soldiers.'

'And you were telling me how you sprang from common stock, Brother Dyrick. After this journey we all stink the same.'

✝

AN HOUR LATER I sat on the tussocky grass outside our tent, massaging my tired legs. Blankets had been provided from the carts, but it would be a hard night lying on the earth. I was glad the journey was nearly over; I had found the fast, steady pace increasingly taxing.

I looked across the tented camp. The sun was setting, the men sitting in little groups around their tents, some of them mending their jacks. I was impressed anew by the skilled organization of the company. On the edge of the field I saw Dyrick walking slowly with Sir Franklin, the older man limping. I had noticed Dyrick took whatever chance arose to talk to him, though he ignored Leacon. No more determined social climber than a new man, I thought. Perhaps this characteristic had drawn him to Nicholas Hobbey; like attracting like.

Leacon was walking from group to group, stopping for a word with the men. Unlike Sir Franklin he made a point of being with the soldiers, listening to their complaints. Snodin, I saw, was sitting in front of a tent on his own, drinking slowly and steadily from a large flagon of beer, frowning at anyone who looked at him. On the edge of the field Barak sat round a campfire with a dozen soldiers from the rearward section. I envied his ease with the young men; since the encounter in the village most had been pleasant enough to me, but with the cautious reserve due to a gentleman. Carswell, the corporal, was there with the Welsh boy Llewellyn. I had noticed the two seemed to be friends, though they were quite unalike: young Llewellyn was a fine lad but with little humour, while Carswell was brimming with it. But every jester needs his foil. Sulyard, the troublemaker, was sitting there, wearing his brightly dyed brigandyne. He cuffed his neighbour on the head and spoke, in loud slurred tones I could hear across the field.

'You call me master.'

'Piss off, you lumpish puttock!'

I decided to go and join them; I still liked to keep an eye on Barak when there was drink around, for all he would call me an old hen, and I had a couple of questions for Llewellyn.

As I crossed the field, I noticed Feaveryear sitting with Pygeon outside a tent. That poor young fellow, how his ears stuck out. Feaveryear was talking animatedly, though Pygeon was carving something on his knife handle, peering at it closely in the fading light. As I watched, Feaveryear got up and walked away. Pygeon gave me a hostile look.

'Have you come to convert me too, sir?'

'I do not know what you mean, fellow.'

'Yonder clerk would have me deny the blood of Christ is in the

Eucharist. He should be careful, men have been burned for less. We cleave to the old ways in Harefield.'

I sighed. If Feaveryear was starting to preach his radical views to the soldiers, it was as well we would part company with them on the morrow. 'No, Pygeon,' I said. 'I am no preacher of any doctrine.' He grunted and returned to his carving. The knife was one of the long ones carried by all the soldiers, serviceable equally as tool and weapon. I saw what he was carving, MARY SAVE OUR SOULS, in lettering of remarkable intricacy and skill.

'That is well done,' I said.

'I look to the Virgin to save us if we come to battle.'

'I am going to join the men by the fire,' I said. 'Will you come?'

Pygeon shook his head and bent again to his carving. I wondered if he feared more mockery from Sulyard. I went across to the fire, lowering myself gingerly to the earth next to Llewellyn and Carswell. I saw the men were slowly roasting a couple of rabbits and a chicken.

'A mug of beer, sir?' Carswell offered. I took it and glanced at Barak, but he was deep in conversation with some of the other men.

'Thank you. What are you cooking? If you've been poaching you had best make sure Captain Giffard does not see you.'

He laughed. 'The local man said we could hunt some rabbits. There's too many of them round here, they're eating the crops. Some of the men had a little practice with their bows in the woods.'

'That looks like a chicken. Not taken from some farm, I hope.'

'No, sir,' Carswell answered, his face suddenly solemn. His features, unremarkable enough, had the mobility of a comic. 'That's a type of rabbit they have down here.'

'It's got wings.'

'Strange place, Hampshire.'

I laughed, then turned to Llewellyn. 'There is something I would ask you,' I said, in a low voice so Barak would not hear.

'Yes, sir?'

'You spoke yesterday about the ironworks in the Weald. What is the difference between the new furnaces and the old ones – the bloomeries, I believe they are called.'

'The new blast furnaces are much bigger, sir, and the iron comes out molten, rather than in a soft lump. The blast furnaces cast it into prepared moulds. They have started to mould cannon.'

'Is it true the bloomeries do not operate in summer?'

'Yes. They mostly employ local people who work the fields in summer and the foundries in winter. While the new furnaces often have dozens of men who work all year round.'

'So a bloomery furnace is empty all summer?'

'Probably they would have a man there to keep an eye on things, taking supplies of charcoal and the like ready for the winter.'

I saw Barak looking across at me. 'Thank you, Llewellyn,' I said.

'Thinking of leaving the law for the iron trade, sir?' Carswell called after me as I went to sit next to Barak. The light was fading fast, and an extraordinary number of moths had appeared, grey-white shapes wheeling and circling in the dusk.

⟊

BARAK LOOKED AT me shrewdly. 'What were you muttering to Llewellyn about? Wouldn't be anything to do with Ellen, would it?'

'Let's concentrate on Hugh Curteys for now,' I answered snappishly.

'You've found where Rolfswood is, haven't you? You're going to go there and nose around if you get the chance.'

'I'll have to see.'

'I think you should leave well alone.'

'I know what you think!' I burst out with sudden anger. 'I'll do what I think best!'

There was another raucous laugh from Sulyard. 'Lovers' tiff!' he called out, staring at Barak and me. He was very drunk, gobbling and tumbling his words, his face alight with malice.

'Shut your face, or I'll shut it for you.' Barak half-rose, his look threatening.

Sulyard pointed at me. 'Hunchbacks bring bad luck, everyone knows that! Though we're probably fucked already, with a dozy old captain and a tippling whiffler to fight under.'

I looked round the circle of faces; a swirl of smoke made my eyes sting. The men looked away uncomfortably. Sulyard rose unsteadily to his feet and pointed at me.

'Don't you give me the evil eye! You – '

'Stop it!' Everyone turned at the shout. Pygeon had followed me and stood some feet off. 'Stop it, you fool! We're all in this together! You're not in the village any more. You can't steal game and ducks from poor folk as you like, spend your days telling people to call you master!'

Sulyard roared, 'I'll have your balls!' Pygeon stood uncertainly as Sulyard, shaking off the restraining hand of another soldier, reached for his knife.

Then a tall, white-coated figure appeared and hit Sulyard a mighty smack across the face. He staggered, rallied, and reached for his knife again.

Leacon faced him. 'Strike me, you foul-mouthed rogue, and it's mutiny!' he shouted, then added more softly, 'but I'll deal with you man to man if that's what you want.'

Sulyard, a trickle of blood dripping from a cut, let his arms fall to his sides. He stood swaying, like a puppet with the strings cut. 'I meant no mutiny,' he said. He swayed again, then yelled out, 'I want only to live! To live!'

'Then stay sober and work with your fellows. That's a soldier's best chance of surviving.'

'Coward!' someone shouted from the dark. Sulyard turned to the voice, hesitated, then stumbled off into the dark. Leacon turned back to his men. 'He'll probably fall over soon. Someone go and find him in a while, dump him in his tent. He can apologize to Master

Shardlake in front of you all tomorrow morning.' He turned away. I followed, catching him up.

'Thank you for that, George. But no public apology, please. He would not mean it and I would not wish to leave the company on such a note.'

Leacon nodded. 'Very well. But there should be some restitution.'

'Such things have happened to me before. They will again.' I hesitated, then added, 'He is frightened of what may come.'

Leacon looked at me. 'I know. As we near Portsmouth a lot of them are becoming apprehensive. But what I said was true: if it comes to battle, discipline and working together are everyone's best chance of survival. Though it is a matter of chance and chaos in the end.' He was silent a moment, then said, 'This afternoon, those drums made me want to scream.' He paused again. 'Master Shardlake, after what I said at Godalming, do you – do you truly think me fit to lead? I will have to, Sir Franklin will be no use. He is good for pulling the men into line – last night a bunch of them got to drinking and rowdiness, and a few words from him shut them up. But you have seen him – he is too old to lead men into battle.'

'I told you last night, you are as fine a leader as any they could have.'

'Thank you,' he answered quietly. 'I feared you thought otherwise.'

'No. On my soul.'

'Pray for us, after we part.'

'Right readily. Though it is long since I felt God listens to my prayers.'

✝

IT WAS STRANGE passing the night in a tent with Dyrick. He snored mightily, disturbing my sleep. Next morning we all rode out, saddle-sore, and I, painfully conscious of my aching back. It was our final day's journey. Sulyard's face was heavy as a bladder from his drinking the evening before. As he took his place in the ranks some of the soldiers gave him unpleasant looks – I guessed because he had shown his fear. Snodin, though, looked no worse than usual – the sign of a true drunkard.

We set off again. The tramp of marching feet, the rumble of the carts behind us, the dust rising up and covering us, had become a familiar daily routine. But this was the last day; the soldiers would go all the way to Portsmouth, but according to Dyrick we had only a few miles to travel before passing a village called Horndean and turning off to Hoyland.

It was another hot, sultry day. The soldiers sang through most of the morning, more bawdy versions of courtly love songs, so inventive in their obscenity they made me smile. We passed into forested country again, interspersed with stretches of downland and meadow and the occasional village, where people were going to church for Sunday service. The soldiers ceased their bawdy songs out of respect.

Then, two miles on, where the road narrowed and ran between high forested banks, we found an enormous cart that had lost a wheel and turned over, blocking the road from side to side. It had been carrying a huge iron cannon, fifteen feet long, which had slipped the thick ropes securing it and lay on the ground. The four great horses that had been pulling it stood grazing by the bank. The carter persuaded the soldiers to stop and help repair his vehicle; the cannon had come from Sussex and, he said, should have been taken to Portsmouth by sea.

While some of the men lifted the empty cart and others put the spare wheel on the axle and tried to tighten it, the rest of the company fell out, finding places to sit on the banks of the narrow lane. Dyrick strolled up and down with Feaveryear, looking at the wood, then came over to where Barak and I sat.

'May we join you?' They sat down. Dyrick waved a gloved hand at the trees. 'This land, like Master Hobbey's, is part of the ancient Forest of Bere. Do you know its history?'

'Only that it is an ancient royal forest from Norman times.'

'Well done, Brother. But little used: successive kings have preferred the New Forest. Bere Forest has been shrinking little by little for centuries, cottagers establishing the squatters' rights you are so keen on, hamlets growing into villages, land sold off by successive kings or granted to the Church like the Hoyland Priory estate. It comprises miles and miles of trees like this.'

I looked up into the forest. The growth here seemed very old, huge oaks and elms, the green undergrowth below heavy and tangled. Despite the days of hot weather a damp earthy smell came from it.

There was a crash from the cart: the new wheel had been fixed, but as soon as the men released their hold it fell off again, the cart lurching once more onto its side. Dyrick groaned. 'We shall be here all day.' He stood up. 'Come, Feaveryear, help me adjust my horse's harness.' He walked away, Feaveryear rising hastily to follow him.

'He doesn't want his little clerk telling us his secrets,' Barak said scoffingly. 'He need not fear. Feaveryear is loyal as a dog.'

'Have you got to know him any better?'

'All he seems willing to talk about is his salvation, the wickedness of the world, and how this journey is a waste of his honoured master's time.'

We looked up as Carswell approached us, a serious expression on his face. He bowed. 'Sir, I am sorry for the trouble last night. I wanted you to know, few think like Sulyard.'

'Thank you.'

He hesitated. 'May I ask you something?'

'If you wish.' I waved a hand to the bank beside me. I smiled encouragingly, expecting some legal query.

'I hear the London lawyers have their own band of players,' he said unexpectedly.

'Plays are often performed at the Inns of Court, but no, the actors' companies are independent bodies of men.'

'What sort of people are they?'

'A roistering lot, I believe, but they must work hard or they could not perform as they do.'

'Are they well paid?'

'No, badly. And life is hard in London these days. Have you a wish to be an actor, Carswell?'

His face reddened. 'I want to write plays, sir. I used to go and see the religious plays when they were allowed and as a boy I wrote little playlets of my own. I learned to write at the church school. They would have had me for a scholar, but my family is poor.'

'Most plays today are full of religious controversy, like John Bale's. It can be a dangerous occupation.'

'I want to write comedies, stories to make people laugh.'

'Did you write any of the naughty songs you sing?' Barak asked.

'Many are mine,' he said proudly.

'Most comedies in London are foreign,' I said. 'Italian mainly.'

'But why should there not be English ones too? Like old Chaucer?'

'By God, Carswell, you are a well-read fellow.'

'Archery and reading, sir, those were always my pastimes. To my parents' annoyance; they wanted me to work on the farm.' He pulled a face. 'I needed to get away, I was happy to join up. I thought once this war is over I might come to London. Maybe earn my bread with some players, learn more about how plays are made.'

I smiled. 'You have thought this out, I see. Ay, we need some English comic writing today if ever we did.'

We were interrupted by Snodin marching across. 'Come, Carswell,' he snapped. 'We're going to have some archery practice in a field down the road. Leave your betters alone, you mammering prick.'

'He's doing no harm,' Barak said.

Snodin narrowed his eyes. 'He's a soldier and he'll do as I say.'

'Yes, Master Snodin.' Carswell hastily got up and followed the whiffler. I called after him, 'Ask for me at Lincoln's Inn when you return.'

'There's an unusual fellow,' I said to Barak. 'And you should be careful of antagonizing another officer. One was enough.'

'Arsehole. As for Carswell, you'd do better not to encourage him. Half those actor folk drink themselves into the gutter.'

'You are in a poor humour today. Missing Tamasin?'

'I wonder how she is faring all the time.' He looked at me. 'And I wonder what you are planning to do about that Ellen.'

I did not reply.

✝

IT WAS AFTERNOON, and we had eaten by the roadside, before the cart was finally repaired. It took twenty men with ropes to reload the cannon. The cart pulled in to the side of the road to let the company past. We continued south, ever deeper into the Forest of Bere.

I made my way up to the head of the company, where Leacon rode with Sir Franklin. 'George,' I said, 'we will be parting shortly.'

'Ay. I am sorry for it.'

'And I. But before we go I wonder if I could ask another favour.'

'I will help if I can. What is it?'

'If Portsmouth is full of soldiers, I imagine a good proportion of those who served professionally in the past will be there.'

'Yes. Portsmouth is becoming the focus of all the military activity.'

'If you get the chance, I wonder if you could ask whether anyone ever heard of a man called William Coldiron. He is my steward, for the time being at least.' I told him the story of Coldiron and Josephine, how from what I had overheard in the tavern it seemed he had never married. 'If anyone knows his history, I would be interested to hear it. I do not believe his tales of killing the King at Flodden, but certainly he has been a soldier.'

'I will ask if I get the chance.'

'If you do, maybe you could write to me at home.'

'I will. And if you should come to Portsmouth while you're here, look for me. Though I will have a busy time keeping these fellows in order. I hear the town is chaos, full of foreign soldiers and sailors. The company will be pleased to see you too.'

'They do not all think me an unlucky hunchback?'

'Only a few joltheads like Sulyard.'

'Thank you. That means a lot.'

I rode back to the rear of the company. The road began slowly ascending and the pace slowed. I was half asleep in the saddle when Dyrick roughly shook my arm.

'We turn off here.'

I sat up. To our right a narrow lane led into deep, shadowed woodland. We pulled aside. I called out, 'George! We leave you here!'

Leacon and Sir Franklin turned. Leacon gestured to the drummer, who ceased drumming. The company halted, and Leacon rode back to us. He gripped my hand tightly. 'Farewell, then.'

'Thank you for letting us ride with you.'

'Yes,' Dyrick added with unaccustomed grace. 'I think we would have had another two days' riding without you to speed us on.'

I looked into the captain's tired, haunted eyes. 'I am glad we met again,' I said sincerely.

'And I. We must move on now, it will be late when we reach Portsmouth.' Dyrick called a farewell to Sir Franklin, and he half-raised a gloved hand.

Some of the soldiers called goodbyes. Carswell waved. Leacon rode back to the head of the company.

'God go with you all,' I called out.

The trumpet sounded, the supply carts trundled past us, and the company marched away, the tramp of their footsteps fading as they rounded a bend. We turned into the lane.

✝

THE FOUR OF US rode under the trees. All at once everything was silent, no sound apart from the chirking of birds. I was conscious of how tired I was, how dusty and smelly we all were. Suddenly the path ended at a high old stone wall. We passed through a gateway into a broad lawned area dotted with trees, a knot garden full of scented summer flowers to one side. Straight ahead stood what had once been a squat Norman church, with a wide porch and arched roof. But now large square windows had been put in at each side of the door and in the walls of what had once been the attached cloister buildings. Tall new brick chimneys rose from the cloister roof. I heard dogs barking in kennels somewhere behind the house, alerted by the sound of the horses. Then three men in servants' smocks appeared in the porch. They approached us and bowed. An older man with a short blond beard followed, wearing a red doublet and a cap which he swept off as he came up to Dyrick.

'Master Dyrick, welcome once more to Hoyland Priory.'

'Thank you. Your master had my letter?'

'Yes, but we did not think you would arrive so soon.'

Dyrick nodded, then turned to me. 'This is Fulstowe, Master Hobbey's steward. Fulstowe, this is Master Shardlake, of whom I wrote.' A bite in his tone at those words.

Fulstowe turned to me. He was in his forties, with a square, lined face, his short fair beard greying. His expression was respectful but his sharp eyes bored into mine.

'Welcome, sir,' he said quietly. 'These fellows will take your horses.' He turned to the porch. 'See, Master Hobbey and his family wait to greet you.'

On the steps four people now stood in a row, a middle-aged man and woman and two lads in their late teens: one stocky and dark, the other tall, slim and brown haired. All four seemed to hold themselves rigid as they waited silently to receive us.

Part Three

HOYLAND PRIORY

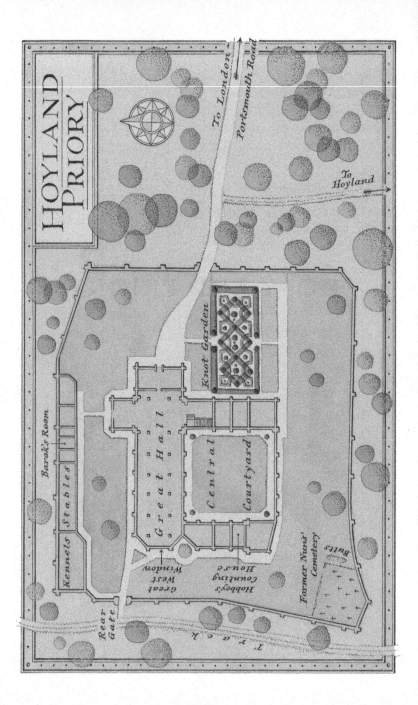

HOYLAND PRIORY

To London
Portsmouth Road

To Hoyland

Knot Garden

Barak's Room

Kennels
Stables

Great Hall

Central
Courtyard

Great
West
Window

Hobbey's
Counting
House

Former Nuns'
Cemetery

Butts

Rear Gate

Track

Chapter Seventeen

W E DISMOUNTED. Fulstowe gave Feaveryear a formal smile. 'You are well, master clerk?'

He bowed. 'Thank you, Master Fulstowe.'

Fulstowe looked at Barak. 'You must be Master Shardlake's clerk?'

'I am. Jack Barak.'

'The groom will show you both your quarters. I will have your masters' panniers taken to their rooms.'

I nodded to Barak. He and Feaveryear followed the groom, other servants leading the horses. Dyrick smiled. 'You will miss your amanuensis, Master Shardlake. Well, it is time you met our hosts and their ward.'

I followed him towards the steps, where the quartet waited. I saw that near the rear wall of the enclosed gardens a butts had been set up, a mound of raised earth with a round cloth target at the centre. Behind it was what looked like a jumble of gravestones. I followed Dyrick up the steps.

Nicholas Hobbey was a thin, spare man in his forties, with thick grey hair and a narrow, severe face. He wore a blue summer doublet of fine cotton with a short robe over it. He clasped Dyrick's hand warmly. 'Vincent,' he said in a clear, melodious voice, 'it is good to see you here again.'

'And you, Nicholas.'

Hobbey turned to me. 'Master Shardlake,' he said formally, 'I hope you will accept our hospitality. I look forward to relieving the anxieties of those who sent you.' His small brown eyes assessed me closely. 'This is my wife, Mistress Abigail.'

I bowed to the woman Michael Calfhill had called mad. She was tall, thin-faced like her husband. The whitelead powder on her cheeks could not conceal the lines beneath. She wore a wide-skirted, grey silk dress with yellow puffed sleeves and a short hood lined with pearls; the hair at her brow was a faded blonde, turning grey. I bowed and rose to find her staring at me intently. She curtsied briefly, then turned to the boys beside her, took a deep, tense breath and spoke in a high voice. 'My son, David. And my husband's ward, Hugh Curteys.'

David was a little under normal height, solid and stocky. He wore a dark brown doublet over a white shirt with a long lacework collar. His black hair was close-cropped. Black tendrils also sprouted at the collar of his shirt. Reverend Broughton had said David was an ugly child and he was on the verge of becoming an ugly man; his round face heavy-featured and thick-lipped, shaved close but still with a dark shadow on his cheeks. He had protuberant blue eyes like his mother, his only resemblance to either parent. He looked at me, his expression conveying contempt.

'Master Shardlake,' he said curtly, extending a hand; it was hot, damp and, to my surprise, callused.

I turned to the boy we had travelled over sixty miles to meet. Hugh Curteys was also dressed in dark doublet and white shirt, and he too wore his hair cropped close. I remembered Mistress Calfhill's story of the time he had nits, and chased his sister round the room laughing. I was conscious of Emma's cross round my neck, where I had worn it for safe-keeping on the journey.

Hugh was a complete contrast to David. He was tall, with an athlete's build, broad-chested and narrow-waisted. He had a long chin and a strong nose above a full mouth. Apart from a couple of tiny brown moles his would have been the handsomest of faces were it not for the scars and pits of smallpox marking its lower half. The scarring on his neck was even worse. His upper face was deeply tanned, making the white scars below even more obvious. His eyes, an unusual shade of blue-green, were clear and oddly expressionless. Despite his obvious good health I sensed a sadness in him.

He took my hand. His grip was dry and firm. His hand was callused too. 'Master Shardlake,' he said in a low, husky voice, 'so you know Goodwife Calfhill.'

'Indeed.'

'I remember her. A good, fond old lady.' Still no expression in those eyes, only watchfulness.

The steward Fulstowe had come up the steps and stood beside his master, observing us carefully. I had the odd sense he was watching the family to see how they performed, like a playmaster.

'Two letters arrived for you this morning, Master Shardlake,' he said. 'They are in your room. One for your man Barak too. They were brought by a royal post rider on his way to Portsmouth, I think he had ridden through the night.' He looked at me keenly. 'One letter had the Queen's seal on it.'

'I am fortunate to have the Queen's solicitor for a friend. He arranged to have correspondence sent on to me by the post riders. And collected too, from Cosham.'

'I can arrange for a servant to take letters there for you.'

'Thank you.' I would make sure they were well sealed.

'Master Shardlake is modest,' Dyrick said. 'He sometimes gets cases from the Queen.' He looked meaningfully at Hobbey. 'As I told you in my letter.'

Hobbey said smoothly. 'Shall we go inside? My wife dislikes the sun.'

⸸

WE PASSED THROUGH what had once been the doors leading into the church. Inside was a curious smell, dust and fresh wood overlaying a faint, lingering tang of incense. The south transept had been converted into a wide staircase leading to the old conventual buildings, while the old nave had been transformed into an impressive great hall, the ancient hammerbeam roof exposed. The walls were bright with tapestries of hunting scenes. The old windows had been replaced by modern mullioned ones, and new ones had been added, making the hall well lit. A cabinet displayed bowls of Venetian glass and vases of beautifully arranged flowers. At the far end of the hall, though, the old west window remained, a huge arch with its original stained glass showing saints and disciples. Below it a large dining table was covered with a turkey cloth. An elderly woman servant was laying out tableware. A fireplace had been installed against one wall. This conversion would have taken time and much money; the tapestries alone were worth a considerable amount.

'You have done more work since I last came, Nicholas,' Dyrick said admiringly.

'Yes,' Hobbey answered in his quiet voice. 'The west window needs plain glass put in, otherwise all is done save for that wretched nuns' cemetery.'

'I saw what looked like headstones by the far wall,' I said. 'Next to the butts.'

'The locals will not pull them down for us. No matter what we offer.' He shook his head. 'Superstitious peasants.'

'Played on by that rogue Ettis,' Abigail said bitterly. I looked at her; she seemed strung tight as a bow, her clasped hands trembling slightly.

'I will get someone from Portsmouth, my dear, as soon as things are quiet again there,' Hobbey answered soothingly. 'I see you admire my tapestries, Master Shardlake.' He stepped over to the wall, Dyrick and I following. The tapestries were exceptionally fine, a series of four making up a hunting scene. The quarry was a unicorn, startled from its woodland lair in the first tapestry, chased by horsemen in the second and third, while in the last, in accordance with ancient legend, it had halted in a clearing and laid its horned head in the lap of a young virgin, who sat smiling demurely. But her allure was a trap, for in the trees around the bower archers stood with drawn bows. I studied the intricate weave and beautifully dyed colours.

'They are German,' Hobbey said proudly. 'Much of my trade was along the Rhine. I got them at a good price, they came from a merchant bankrupted in the Peasant Wars. They are my pride and joy, as the garden is my wife's.' He ran the flat of his palm almost reverently over the unicorn's head. 'You should see how those villagers look at my tapestries when they come here for the manorial court. They stare as though the figures would leap off the wall at them.' He laughed scornfully.

The boys had come close, David looking at the archers poised to shoot the unicorn. 'Hard to miss at that range,' he said dismissively. 'A deer would never let you get that close.'

I remembered how Hugh's and David's hands had felt callused. 'Do you boys practise at the butts outside?'

'Every day,' David answered proudly. 'It is our great sport, better even than hawking. The best of manly pastimes. Is that not so, Hugh?' He slapped Hugh on the shoulder, hard I thought. I noticed a suppressed anxiety in David's manner. His mother was watching him, her eyes sharp.

'It is.' Hugh looked at me with that unreadable gaze. 'I have a copy of Master Ascham's new-printed *Toxophilus* that he presented to the King this year. Master Hobbey gave it to me for my birthday.'

'Indeed.' The book the Queen had told me Lady Elizabeth was reading. 'I should like to see that.'

'Have you an interest in archery, sir?'

I smiled. 'An interest in books, rather. I am not built for the bow.'

'I shall be pleased to show you my copy.' For the first time Hugh's face showed some animation.

'Later, perhaps,' Hobbey said. 'Our guests have been on the road five days. Hot water waits in your rooms, sirs, let it not get cold. Then come down and join us. I have told the servants to prepare a good supper.' He snapped his fingers at the old woman. 'Ursula, show Masters Dyrick and Shardlake to their rooms.'

She led us upstairs, into a corridor through whose arched windows I saw the old cloister, set to more flowerbeds and peaceful in the lengthening shadows. Ursula opened the door to a large guest room with a canopied tester bed. A bowl of water steamed on a table beside three letters.

'Thank you,' I said.

She nodded curtly. Behind her in the doorway, Dyrick inclined his head. 'You see how well Master Curteys is?' he said.

'So it would seem. On first impression.'

Dyrick sighed, shook his head and turned to follow Ursula. I closed the door, crossed quickly to the bed and picked up the letters. One was addressed to 'Jack Barak' in a clumsy hand. I opened the other two. The first, from Warner and dated three days before, was brief. He apologized again for being unable to send one of his men to accompany us, and said the King and Queen would be leaving for Portsmouth on July 4th – yesterday, so they were already on their way. He said they hoped to arrive on the 15th, and would stay at Portchester Castle. He had set enquiries in train about Hobbey's financial history, but had nothing to report yet.

I turned eagerly to Guy's letter, written on the same day, in his small neat handwriting:

Dear Matthew,

All is quiet at the house. Coldiron does all I ask, though with a surly air. The mood against foreigners grows even worse; today I went to see Tamasin, who I thank God remains well, and suffered some insults on my way. Simon says he has seen more soldiers passing through London, many marching to the south coast. I have been in England over twenty years and have seen nothing like it. Under their bravado I think people are afraid.

One strange thing; yesterday I entered the parlour and startled Josephine, who was dusting. She jumped and dropped a little vase, which broke. I was sure I heard her utter a word, 'Merde', which I know for a French oath. She was apologetic and frightened as ever, so I made little of it, but it was an odd thing.

Today I go to the Bedlam to visit Ellen; I will let you know how she fares. Having prayed much on the matter I feel all the more that the

best help you can give her is to leave her be. But you must decide.
Your true and loving friend,

Guy Malton

I folded the letter. Despite what he said, I had already decided to visit
Rolfswood on the way home; I felt I must. I sighed and went to look
out of the window. I could see the little cemetery, a jumble of stones
set amidst unkempt grass. I thought, Dyrick is right, Hugh is glowing
with health. And Nicholas Hobbey's tone had never varied from
urbane politeness. He hardly seemed the man to have set those corner
boys on me. But something was wrong here, I felt it.

✝

A SUBSTANTIAL SUPPER was served in the great hall. Dusk was
falling and candles were lit in sconces round the chamber. Hobbey
sat at the head of the table, Hugh and Dyrick on one side and David
and Abigail on the other. I took the remaining chair, next to Abigail.
The steward stood behind Hobbey, presiding as servants brought in
the food, their footsteps clicking on the worn, decorated tiles of the
old church. Apart from Ursula, most were young men. I wondered
how many servants the Hobbeys would keep; a dozen perhaps.

I was conscious of a wheezy, snuffling noise beside me. I looked
down and saw what seemed like a bundle of fur on Abigail's lap.
Then I saw two small button eyes staring up at me with friendly
curiosity. It was a little spaniel, like the Queen's dog, but very fat.
Abigail smiled down at it with an unexpectedly tender expression.

'Father,' David said in a disgusted tone, 'Mother has Lamkin on
her lap again.'

'Abigail,' Hobbey said in his quiet even voice, 'please let
Ambrose take him out. We do not want him climbing on the table
again, do we?'

Abigail allowed Fulstowe to take the dog, her eyes following as
he carried it from the room. She glanced at me, a flash of something
like hatred in her eyes. Fulstowe returned and stood behind his master

again. Ursula set down an aromatic bowl of ginger sauce. Dyrick studied the food with an anticipatory smile. Hugh stared ahead, his face expressionless.

'Let us say grace,' Hobbey said.

✝

It was a splendid meal, cold roast goose with rich sauces and fine red wine in silver jugs. Dyrick and I, both hungry, set to eagerly.

'How are things in London?' Hobbey asked. 'I hear the currency has been debased again.'

'It has. It is causing much confusion and trouble.'

'I am glad I moved to the country. How was your journey? We have had storms here, but I know they were worse in London. I worried the roads would be muddy, and full of the King's traffic coming to Portsmouth.'

'So they were,' Dyrick agreed. 'But we were lucky, thanks to Brother Shardlake. We met up with an old client of his, a petty-captain of a company of archers, who let us ride with them. A blast from his trumpeteer and everyone moved out of the way.'

I saw Hugh turn and look at me intently. 'A grateful client?' Hobbey asked with a smile. 'What did you win for him?'

'The freehold of some land.'

He nodded, as though that was what he had expected. 'And they were heading for Portsmouth?'

'Yes. Country lads from Middlesex. One wants to go to London to be a playwright.'

'A country soldier writing plays?' Hobbey gave a little scoffing laugh. 'I never heard such a thing.'

'I believe he composed the rude ditties the soldiers sang on the road,' Dyrick said. 'Saving your presence, Mistress Abigail.' Abigail smiled tightly.

'Country lads should stay at the plough,' Hobbey said firmly.

'Except when they are called to defend us all?' Hugh asked quietly.

'Yes. When they are full grown.' Hobbey's look at his ward was suddenly severe.

Dyrick said, 'More men are marching south. And the King and Queen are coming to Portsmouth to review the ships, I hear.'

Hugh turned to me. 'The soldiers were archers, sir?'

'Yes, Master Curteys. Their skill with a bow had to be seen to be believed.'

'You should see Hugh and I practising at the butts,' David said, leaning across his mother. 'I am the stronger,' he added proudly.

'But I am the one who hits the mark,' Hugh countered quietly.

'I was a fine archer in my youth,' Dyrick said complacently. 'Now I am teaching my son. Though I thank God he is only ten, too young to be called up.'

'Master Shardlake will not want to see you boys practising that dangerous sport,' Abigail said. 'One of the servants will end with an arrow through his body one of these days.'

Hugh turned cold eyes on her. 'Our only risk of being shot, good mistress, is if the French land. They say they have over two hundred ships.'

Hobbey shook his head. 'All these rumours. A hundred, two hundred. What a tumult. Three thousand men have been levied in north Hampshire and sent to Portsmouth. Hoyland village, like all the coastal villages, is exempt from recruitment, with the men kept in the militia ready to march to the coast when the beacons are lit.'

'They are recruiting heavily in London,' Dyrick said.

'I accompanied our local magistrate on a review of the village men. For all that some of them are ruffians, they are stout fellows who will make good fighting men.' Hobbey's face took on a preening expression. 'As lord of the manor I have had to supply them with harness. Fortunately the nuns had a store of old pikes and jacks, even a few rusty helmets, to meet the manor's military obligations.'

There was silence round the table for a moment. I thought of Leacon's men repairing the musty old jacks they would have to fight in. Hobbey looked at me, eyes glinting sharp in the candlelight.

'I believe you are personally acquainted with the Queen, Master Shardlake.'

'I have that privilege,' I answered carefully. 'I knew her majesty when she was still Lady Latimer.'

Hobbey spread his hands, smiling coldly. 'I, alas, have the patronage of no high personages. I have risen only to be a country gentleman.'

'All credit to you for that, sir,' Dyrick said. 'And for your fine house.'

'These smaller religious houses can be turned to fine residences. The only disadvantage is that this one was also used as Hoyland parish church, so we have to go to the next parish on Sundays.'

'With all the oafs from the village,' Abigail added tartly.

'And our status means we need to go each Sunday,' Hobbey added in a weary tone. Clearly, I thought, this is no religious family.

'How many nuns were here, Nicholas?' Dyrick asked.

'Only five. This was a subsidiary house of Wherwell Abbey, in the west of the county. I have a picture of the last abbess but one in my study, I will show you tomorrow.'

'Her face all wrapped up so tight in her wimple,' Abigail said with a shudder.

'They used to send disobedient nuns here,' David said. 'Ones that had had monks' hands at those wimples, and elsewhere—'

'David, fie, for shame,' his father said. But he spoke mildly, giving his son an indulgent look.

Hugh said quietly, 'Some nights, sitting here, I seem to hear faint echoes of their prayers and psalms. Just as we still faintly smell the incense.'

'They deserve no sympathy,' Hobbey said flatly. 'They lived as parasites on the rents from their woodland.' I thought, as you do now.

'They would be able to make fine profits today,' Dyrick said. 'The price wood is fetching.'

'Yes. This is the time to sell, while the war is on.'

'There will be good profits from your land and Master Hugh's too,' I observed.

Dyrick raised his eyebrows at me. 'Master Hobbey is laying up a fine store of money for Hugh.'

'You are welcome to see my accounts,' Hobbey said.

'Thank you,' I answered neutrally, knowing those could be doctored.

'For when I am twenty-one, a grown man,' Hugh said quietly, then laughed, a bitter little sound. Abigail sighed deeply. I thought, that woman is wound so tight she could explode.

Hobbey passed the wine around. Dyrick placed his hand over his cup. 'I will have no more, thank you,' he said. 'I prefer to keep my mind sharp.' He looked at me meaningfully.

'What happened to the nuns when they left?' I asked.

'They got good pensions.'

'Old Ursula was one of the nuns' servants,' Abigail said. 'She wishes they were back, you can see it in her.'

'We needed someone who knew the place,' Hobbey said, an impatient note entering his voice.

'She looks at me insolently. And those other servants, they're all from the village. They hate us, they'll murder us in our beds one night.'

'Oh, Abigail,' Hobbey said, 'these fears and fantasies of yours.'

The servants came in again, carrying trays of custards and comfits. As we ate I noticed something odd about the light. The candles seemed to be flickering and dimming. Then I realized that huge numbers of moths were flittering round them, as they had been at the campfire the night before. They caught their poor wings in the flames and fell and died, more moths at once taking their place. 'Some fool servant has left a window open,' Abigail said.

Hobbey looked at the candles curiously. 'I have never seen so many moths as this summer. It must be to do with the strange weather we had in June.'

Dyrick looked at Hobbey, then me. 'Well, Master Hobbey, a

delightful meal. But perhaps now we should discuss the business that brought us here.'

'Yes,' Hobbey agreed. 'Abigail, boys, perhaps you could leave us.'

'Should not Hugh stay?' I asked.

'No,' Dyrick answered firmly. 'He is a boy and this is men's business. You will have ample chance to talk to him tomorrow.'

I looked at Hugh. His face was impassive as he rose and accompanied Abigail and David from the hall. As the door closed I heard Abigail calling out for Lamkin. Fulstowe remained where he was behind his master, still as a soldier on guard. 'I would like Ambrose to stay,' Hobbey said. 'He manages my business down here.'

'Certainly,' I agreed.

Hobbey leaned back in his chair. 'Well, Master Shardlake. This is a strange business. Upsetting for my family. My wife has had delicate health ever since poor Emma died.'

'I am sorry.'

'She always wanted a daughter.' But Hugh, I thought, has no affection for her with his coldly formal manner, addressing her as 'Mistress'. And David had treated his mother like dirt.

'And just now she is anxious about the hunt,' Hobbey added in a lighter tone. 'We are having a hunt on my land, Master Shardlake. It will be an occasion, the first in my new deer park.' Pride had entered his quiet voice, as when he showed me the tapestries. 'It was to be this week but we have postponed it to next Monday to allow this business to be dealt with.' He shook his head. 'And all because Michael Calfhill chose to burst in on us out of the blue last spring.'

'May I ask what happened then? Informally, for now?'

Hobbey looked at Dyrick, who nodded. 'It is simply told,' Hobbey said. 'One afternoon in April the boys were at the butts — they think of nothing but their bows since this war began. I was in my study when a servant ran in and said a strange man was outside, shouting at Hugh. I called for Ambrose and we went out. I did not recognize Calfhill at first, it was five years since he worked for me. He was raving, shouting at Hugh that he must come away with him. He said he loved him better than anyone else in the world.' He inclined his head, looking at me meaningfully, then turned to Fulstowe. 'It was an extraordinary scene, was it not, Ambrose?'

Fulstowe nodded gravely. 'Master David was there as well, he looked terrified.'

'What was Hugh's reaction, Master Hobbey?'

'He was afraid. Both boys said later that Calfhill just appeared from the old nuns' cemetery.'

'He must have been hiding there,' Fulstowe added. 'It is very overgrown.'

So you see,' Dyrick said, 'Michael Calfhill was a pervert. Probably thoughts of what he would like to do with Hugh had been roiling in his mind for years and driven him mad.' He reached across the table and slapped his hand down on a moth which had fallen to the table and fluttered there, desperately beating its burned wings. He wiped the mess on a napkin. 'Forgive me, Nicholas, but it was annoying me. Now, Brother Shardlake. How do you wish to proceed with the depositions?'

I addressed Hobbey. 'I would like to talk to Hugh, of course, and yourself and your wife.'

Hobbey nodded. 'So long as Master Dyrick is present at all the interviews.'

'And Master David.'

'No,' Dyrick said firmly. 'He is a minor. Hugh is too, but the court will wish to see his evidence despite his youth. David is a dif-ferent matter.'

I went on, 'And Fulstowe, and such servants as have dealings with the boys.'

'God's death,' Dyrick said. 'We will be here till the leaves fall.'

'Fulstowe certainly.' Hobbey leaned forward, speaking in the same quiet, even tone but with a steely note now. 'But my servants know the boys only as masters.'

'The Court of Wards would not permit random interrogation of servants,' Dyrick said firmly, 'unless they had particular knowledge. It undermines the relationship between master and servant.'

Dyrick was right; I had been testing the water. I could not force the servants, or David, to give depositions unless I believed they had particular evidence. I would, though, have liked to talk to David; there was an uneasiness under his spoiled foolishness. And Abigail had spoken of the servants murdering them in their beds, while Dyrick had told me Hobbey wished to enclose the village lands. If the servants were village folk, that might explain Abigail's fear. It might also mean some would be willing to talk to me.

'We will leave David and the servants,' I said, 'for now.'

'For good and all,' Dyrick said emphatically.

'Then there is the feodary,' I added. 'Sir Quintin Priddis.'

Hobbey nodded. 'I have written to him and had a letter back today. At the moment he is in Christchurch, but he is coming to Portsmouth on Friday. I would suggest we go to see him there.'

'I would prefer to meet him here,' I answered. 'Over the next couple of days I would like to see Hugh's woodlands, then I hoped Sir Quintin and I could ride Hugh's lands together. So that I might ask him about the stretches of woodland which have been cut, how much each part fetched.'

'I doubt he would be able to do that,' Hobbey replied. 'Sir Quintin Priddis is an old man, infirm of body though not of mind. And those woods are hard going. If lands have to be ridden his son, Edward, usually does that. And I do not know whether Edward Priddis is with him.'

Dyrick nodded agreement. 'I think the court would expect you to accommodate Master Hobbey where possible, Brother Shardlake. Can you not see Sir Quintin in Portsmouth? If his son is with him, perhaps he could ride back with us if you insist on riding Hugh's lands.'

I considered. The King's party would not be arriving for ten days. Portsmouth was still safe for me. 'Very well. Provided, Master

Hobbey, that you write to him making clear I may request him or his son to come here afterwards.'

Hobbey looked at me seriously. 'I wish only to cooperate, Master Shardlake, to meet all reasonable demands.' He emphasized the 'reasonable'. 'I will have my books of account sent up to your room,' he added.

'Thank you.' I rose. 'Then until tomorrow, sir. Fulstowe, I would like to take this letter to Barak. His wife has a baby due soon. Perhaps you would tell me where his quarters are.'

The steward stepped forward. 'Certainly. He is in one of the old outhouses. I will take you there.'

'I will not trouble you. I can walk round.'

'It is dark out there now,' Hobbey said.

'No matter. I was brought up in the country.'

✝

WE LEFT THE great hall. Master Hobbey bade us goodnight and climbed the stairs; Dyrick gave me a curt nod and said, 'Till tomorrow.' I followed Fulstowe outside. He stood on the steps, looking up at the stars.

'A fine night, sir,' he observed, smiling deferentially. I thought, this is a proper steward, loyal to his master, not an oaf like Coldiron. But I did not trust him an inch.

'Indeed. Let us hope this better weather continues.'

Fulstowe indicated a row of substantial buildings against the side wall of the enclosure. 'Your servant is in the fourth building down. You are sure you would not like me to accompany you?'

'No, thank you. I will see you tomorrow.'

He bowed. 'Then goodnight, sir. I will leave the door open a little for you.'

I walked down the steps. I took a deep breath, relieved to be away from them all. I breathed in the country scents, grass and the rich fragrance of flowers from Abigail's garden. I had still not got used to the silence after those days on the road.

There was a footstep behind me, I was sure. I looked round. The only light came from the moon, and a few candles shimmering at the priory windows. I could see nobody, but the lawn was dotted with trees behind which someone could hide. Fear came on me again, the fear that had been with me since the corner boys' attack, and I realized how much I missed the security of riding with Leacon's company. I hurried on, turning back every few seconds to signal to anyone looking that they had been heard. I counted along the squat, functional outhouses, knocking heavily on the door of the fourth. It opened and Barak looked out, dressed in his shirt.

'It's you. God's teeth, I thought someone was trying to batter the door down. Come in.'

I followed him inside. A mean little room with a truckle bed in the corner, lit by a cheap, smoky, tallow candle. I took out the letter.

'News from Tamasin?' he said, his face suddenly bright.

'I have had a letter from Guy, he says she continues well.'

Barak tore open the letter and read it. He smiled broadly. 'Yes, all is well. Tammy says she is doing everything Jane Marris tells her. I'm not sure I believe her, though.'

'Is not the letter written in Guy's hand?' I asked curioulsy.

Barak flushed, then looked at me. 'Tamasin can barely write, did you not know?'

'No.' I was embarrassed. 'I am sorry, I thought—'

'Tamasin is a woman of low birth, she was taught little more than to sign her own name.' His tone was sharp, I had annoyed him. 'Did Guy tell you how Ellen was?'

'Guy had not visited her when he wrote.' He grunted. 'No Feaveryear for company?' I asked in an effort to lighten the atmosphere.

'No, thank heaven. He's next door. I heard him at his prayers through the wall a while ago.'

'Well, we cannot grudge him his belief.'

'I grudge his deference to that Dyrick. He thinks the sun shines out of his arse.'

'Yes. 'Tis well said that a faithful servant shall become a perpetual ass.'

Barak looked at me closely. 'Are you all right? You seemed scared when you came in.'

'I thought I heard someone following me. I was probably mistaken.' I laughed uneasily. 'No corner boys here.'

'We still don't know who set them on you. Do you think it could have been Hobbey?'

'I don't know. He is a hard man for all his civility.' I shook my head. 'But there was no time for him to instruct anyone.'

'What of Hugh Curteys? How does he seem?'

'Well. I have just dined with the family. I think he would like to go and join the army.'

Barak raised his eyebrows. 'Rather him than me. When do you think we will get home?'

'We have to go to Portsmouth on Friday to see Priddis, the feodary. Then we shall see.'

'Friday? Shit, I thought we would be on the road home by then.'

'I know. Listen, I want you to help me take the depositions tomorrow, give me your view of these people. And try to make friends with the servants, see what they may have to tell. Quietly – you know how.'

'That might not be easy. Fulstowe told me not to go to the house unless I was asked for. Haughty fellow. I took a walk by myself in the grounds, greeted a couple of gardeners but only got a surly nod. Hampshire hogs.'

I was silent a moment. Then I said, 'That family . . .'

'What?'

'They try to hide it, but it breaks through. They are angry and frightened, I think. All of them.'

'What of?'

I took a long breath. 'Of me. But I think also of each other.'

Chapter Eighteen

O N RETURNING TO the house I spent two hours going over Hobbey's accounts. He had given me the books dating back to 1539, the year they had all moved to Hoyland. Everything was clearly recorded in a neat hand that I guessed was Fulstowe's. Much woodland had been cut down in the last six years, and the payments had accumulated into a considerable sum. Hugh's land was accounted for separately, and the amount of different types of wood – oak, beech and elm and the prices each had fetched – neatly entered. But I knew well enough that even accounts as clearly set out as these could be full of false entries. I recalled the old saying that there was good fishing in puddled waters. I sat awhile, thinking back to the meal, the terrible tension round the table. There was something very wrong here, I sensed, more than profiteering from a ward's lands.

At last I went to bed and slept deeply. Just before I woke I dreamed of Joan, welcoming me home on a cold dark night, saying I had been away too long. I heaved myself out of bed, then sat thinking. It struck me that if we were not travelling to Portsmouth until Friday, then instead of visiting Rolfswood on the way home, finding some excuse to send Barak on, I should have the opportunity to ride to Sussex while we were here. I estimated the journey at perhaps fifteen miles; I would have to stay overnight to rest the horse.

I heard youthful shouts outside. I opened the window and looked out. Some distance away – I guessed the regulation two hundred and twenty yards – Hugh and David stood shooting arrows at the butts. I watched Hugh loose an arrow. It sped through the air and landed smack in the centre of the target. He seemed as fast and accurate as Leacon's men.

I would have benefited from a session of the morning exercises Guy had given me for my back, but there was much to be done. So I dressed in my serjeant's robe and went downstairs. It felt uncomfortable; it was another hot, sticky morning.

The great hall was empty, but I heard Barak's voice somewhere and followed it to a large kitchen, where he and Feaveryear sat at a table eating bread and cheese, their tones more amicable than I had heard before. The old woman Ursula stood at the big range, sweat on her thin face. Abigail Hobbey's lapdog, Lamkin, stood by Feaveryear's feet, gobbling at a lump of cheese. It looked up as I entered, wagging its feathery tail as though to say, see what a lucky fellow I am.

'Tamasin has a good woman to care for her,' Barak was saying to Feaveryear, 'but I cannot help worrying. I imagine her out in her garden, weeding when she should be sitting indoors.'

'I did not know you were married. I took you for a roistering fellow.'

'That's all done now – ah, good morning,' he said as I came in. Feaveryear stood, bowing briefly.

'You've let me sleep in,' I said, joining them at table.

'They only woke me half an hour ago,' Barak answered cheerfully. 'And the old need their sleep.'

'Less of the old, churl.' Feaveryear looked shocked at our familiarity.

From the kitchen we had a better view through an open window of the boys practising. David was shooting now, leaning back then bending his strong square body forward and loosing his arrow. He too hit the target, though offcentre.

'This is a beautiful place,' Feaveryear said. 'I have never seen the country before.'

'Never left London?' I asked.

'This is my first journey. I wanted to see it. The smells are so different, so clean.'

'Ay,' Barak agreed. 'No rotten meat or sewage stink.'

'And so quiet. Hard to think that only a few miles away the army is gathering at Portsmouth.'

'Yes,' I agreed, 'it is.'

'Master Hobbey has made a marvellous house. And a good thing this estate is no longer used to support those nuns mumbling prayers to idolatrous statues,' Feaveryear added sententiously. The old woman turned and gave him a vicious look.

'Those lads know what they're doing,' Barak said, looking through the window at Hugh and David. David shot again, and I followed the arcing trajectory of the arrow to the target. 'There,' I heard him shout, 'I win! Sixpence you owe me!'

'No!' Hugh called back. 'I shot nearer the centre!'

Feaveryear was looking at the boys too, his face sad. 'Do you pull the bow at all?' I asked him.

'No, sir. God gave me but little strength. I envy those strong lads.'

'A cosy scene,' a sneering voice said. We turned to find Dyrick in the doorway, Hobbey beside him. Dyrick too had donned his lawyer's robe.

'Who has been feeding that dog?' Hobbey asked sharply.

'Me, sir,' Feaveryear answered nervously. 'He is such a merry little fellow.'

'You will be no merry fellow if my wife finds out. Only she feeds him – she thinks he has a delicate stomach. Lamkin, go find Mistress.' The dog turned and waddled obediently out of the kitchen. Hobbey turned to Ursula. 'You should not have allowed him to feed Lamkin,' he snapped.

'I am sorry sir. I could not see through the steam.'

'I think you saw well enough. Be careful, goodwife.' Hobbey turned to me, his voice smooth again. 'Well, Brother Shardlake, perhaps you could say how you wish to proceed. As you see, Hugh is available now.'

I had decided to interview the others before Hugh, to try and get some sense of this strange family. 'I thought we might take your deposition first, sir. Then Fulstowe's and your wife's.'

Hobbey looked at Dyrick. 'Is that agreeable to you?'

Dyrick inclined his head. 'Very well.'

'Then I will tell the boys they may go hawking this morning; they asked if they might.' Hobbey took a deep breath. 'Let us begin. We can use my study.'

'I wish Barak to be with me, to take notes,' I said.

'I have brought some paper and a quill, Master Hobbey,' Barak said cheerfully. 'If you could let me have some ink.'

'We do not need clerks,' Dyrick snapped.

'Clerks usually attend when taking depositions, do they not?' I looked at him levelly. 'It makes for greater accuracy.'

'If we must,' Dyrick said with a sigh. 'Come, Feaveryear,' he continued, 'if Barak is attending you must too. More unnecessary costs for Master Shardlake's client to pay.'

☦

HOBBEY'S STUDY was a large ground-floor room, lavishly decorated. There was a wide desk with many drawers, pigeonholes on the wall above, and several beautifully decorated wooden chests. Chairs had been set in a semicircle facing the window. On one wall I saw a portrait of a Benedictine nun, her neck and head swathed in starched white folds and a black veil.

'The second to last abbess of Wherwell,' Hobbey said.

'An interesting face,' I replied. 'Watchful yet contemplative.'

'You appreciate painting, Master Shardlake.' His face relaxed and he gave me an oddly shy smile.

'We should begin, sir,' Dyrick said a little sharply. He took two inkpots from the desk, passing them to Barak and Feaveryear.

Hobbey invited us to sit and took a chair by his desk. There was a large hourglass on it, a beautiful greenstone one with clear glass, full of white sand. He turned it so the sand began to fall.

'To begin, sir,' I said. 'Would you tell me a little of your background? You said last night you had lived in Germany?'

Hobbey glanced at his hourglass, then folded his slim, well-manicured hands in his lap. 'As a boy I got a job as a messenger, running between the wool merchants and the German traders at the Steelyard. Then I went to Germany to learn the trade myself, came back and in time became a member of the Mercers' Company.'

'When did you meet the Curteys family?'

'It was seven years past,' Hobbey continued in the same quiet, even tone. 'The monasteries were going down like bowling pins, everyone was looking for bargains at the Court of Augmentations. And I wanted to retire from my business.'

'An early retirement, was it not?' I would not ask whether he had been in debt; not yet.

'I had been in the trade since I was ten, I was bored with it. I learned the lands of this priory were for sale and came down here. I met John Curteys at a local inn, God rest him. He was interested in buying some of the priory woodland. I could not afford to buy it all as well as the nunnery, so we agreed he would take the larger portion. We were both wool merchants and we became friends. But then John and his wife died suddenly, as you will know.'

'And you applied for Hugh and Emma's wardship.'

Hobbey spread his hands. 'That is no mystery. I knew the children. And as the lands they inherited marched with mine it made commercial sense for everyone for Hoyland to be managed as a unit. I paid a good price, and every penny went into Hugh and Emma's account at Wards.'

I looked at Dyrick, who was nodding slowly. I guessed they had rehearsed all this last night. I had been in practice long enough to tell.

'So taking the children's wardship was a commercial venture?'

'Certainly not.' Hobbey looked angry for a moment. 'I felt sorry for them, left orphaned with no one to care for them. Who better to look after them than Abigail and I? We had always wanted more children, but after David was born we had two babies who died.' A shadow crossed his face. 'And Hugh and Emma had no other relatives, save an ancient aunt in the north whom John and Ruth's vicar wished to involve. But that proved rather difficult,' he added scornfully, 'as she turned out to be dead.' I thought, that is the tone Reverend Broughton heard when he protested. And Abigail shrieking, which I could imagine.

I paused a moment to let Barak catch up. His and Feaveryear's pens scratched away.

'To turn to Michael Calfhill,' I continued, 'you kept him as tutor. He had been with the children some years then. Yet when you moved to Hampshire you dismissed him. Why was that?'

Hobbey leaned forward and made a steeple of his hands. 'First of all, sir, the children had no real attachment to Calfhill. After their parents died they withdrew into each other's company. And within the year Emma, too, was dead.' He gave a sigh which seemed full of genuine emotion. 'And when we moved, yes, I dismissed Michael Calfhill because Hugh was now alone, and I feared Michael's influence was becoming unhealthy. Frankly I feared what paths he might lead the boy down. Impropriety,' he added slowly.

'What evidence did you have for that?'

'Remember, Brother Shardlake,' Dyrick said, 'Master Hobbey's answer could be read out in court, in front of Michael Calfhill's mother.'

'I know.' I looked fixedly at Hobbey; Dyrick would not blackmail me thus.

'It was a matter of looks and gestures. Once I saw him touch Hugh's bottom.'

'I see. Speaking of impropriety, Michael told his mother David said something improper to Emma, and Hugh fought him over it.'

'I believe Hugh once objected to something David said. My son – well, he has no good control of his tongue. They had a boyish tussle. But David and Hugh are fast friends now.'

'Did you hope David might marry Emma? If that happened Emma would have brought her portion of her lands to her husband.'

'Of course we considered that, but it would have been up to the children.'

'Did you find another tutor for Hugh and David?'

'We had a succession of tutors till last year.' He smiled wryly. 'They all had to be good archers. Hugh had begun his craze for the bow by then, and David followed.'

'A succession? How many?'

'Four, I think.'

'In five years? That seems a great many.'

'They were not always satisfactory. And many tutors see teaching as a stopgap, rather than a career.'

'Michael Calfhill did not.'

'He might have had his reasons for that,' Dyrick said, real venom in his tone.

'And David is not an easy boy to teach.' Again that sadness in Hobbey's face. 'The last man was good, but he left us to travel, visit the continent. That was before this war began.'

'Might I have their names?' I asked.

'If you wish. Though I do not know where they would be now.'

'Coming to the present, it is surely past time for the boys to consider university or a profession.'

'I want David here, to learn about the estate. As for Hugh, he has the wit for a scholar and loves book learning. But he has a boyish fancy to go to the war. So I am keeping him here till it ends. Does that not sound a reasonable course, Master Shardlake?'

'I think you will agree it is in Hugh's interest,' Dyrick interjected.

'Perhaps.' I paused. 'Master Hobbey, you gave an account at dinner last night of Michael Calfhill's reappearance last Easter. Could you tell me again what happened, for the record this time?'

Hobbey repeated the story of Michael's appearance in the old churchyard, his telling Hugh that he loved him more than anyone. I had hoped Hobbey might slip, say something inconsistent with what he had said last night. But either he spoke true, or he had been well rehearsed by Dyrick.

'How far must we press this unsavoury episode?' Dyrick asked when Hobbey had finished.

'One more thing, Master Hobbey. You have been selling off wood from the land which is part of Hugh's patrimony.'

Hobbey spread his hands. 'I would be a poor custodian of his interests if I did otherwise. Between the need for timber for ships and the demand for charcoal for the Sussex ironworks the price has never been so high.' Mention of the Sussex ironworks again, I thought. 'I am having part of my own woods felled. There is little other profit to be made here. The rents from Hoyland village and a few cottagers in the woods bring in less than seventy pounds a year, which becomes worth less and less with this great rise in prices. You have seen my accounts.'

'Indeed. And I would like to take a ride through the woodland Hugh owns, before we meet Sir Quintin Priddis on Friday.'

'Please do. But it is a large area, several miles deep in parts. Men are at work on the outer fringes now, felling trees, but further in it is old, wild growth, not easily penetrated.'

Dyrick laughed. 'Do not get lost in there, Brother, or Mistress Calfhill will have to find another lawyer.'

'I won't.' I made my voice as smooth as Hobbey's. 'And thank you, sir. I think that will be all, for now.'

Dyrick looked up sharply. 'For now? You are not allowed innumerable depositions.'

'I will only ask if something new arises.' I smiled. 'And now, if I may, I will see the steward, Fulstowe.'

'Certainly. He is with my hounds, supervising their feeding.' Hobbey glanced at the hourglass, where the sand was still falling.

'I will go and find him,' I said. 'I would like a little breath of air. Barak, come with me. And I think I will ride out and see Hugh's woodlands tomorrow.'

✝

WE WALKED OUT into the fresh morning. A peacock strutted on the lawn, bright feathers glistening in the sun. As we approached, it uttered its mournful cry and stalked away. We followed the sound of barking to the outhouses, and I noted again the many hiding places behind the trees dotting the lawn.

'What did you think of Hobbey?' I asked.

'No fool. But I don't trust him: his story was too smoothly told.'

'I agree. But Hugh Curteys is clearly not mistreated.'

'They intended to marry David to Emma.'

'That is the way of wardship. But there is something hidden here, I am sure of it.' I frowned. 'I was thinking just now of the corner boys. If there is some roguery going on over selling the woodland, and either Sir Quintin Priddis or his son were in London, they would probably be in and out of the Court of Wards all the time. They might have learned of my involvement in this case.'

'And feared corrupt dealing being exposed, and so tried to frighten you off?'

'They would not then know I had the Queen behind me. Though Hobbey will have told them since, in his letter.' I smiled. 'I look forward to this meeting on Friday.' I took a deep breath, and added, 'Before that, given time, I think I may ride out to Rolfswood, see what I might find. Alone.'

'You should not go at all. And certainly not alone.'

'It will do me good to have a night away from here.' I was not going to tell Barak what I had heard of two deaths at the foundry. 'And I want you here, finding out all you can. That servant Ursula, she at least has no love for the Hobbeys. You could try and talk to her.'

He put his head to one side. 'Are you hiding something about Ellen?' he asked shrewdly.

'God's death, Jack,' I snapped, reddening. 'Leave it alone. It is for me to judge what to do. Now, later this morning I am going to reply to Warner. Do you want to write a letter to Tamasin for the post rider to collect?'

'Of course.'

'Then let us get our work done.' I strode on towards the con∕

tinuing sound of barking, which came from a building near the stables. I looked through an open door into a kennels where a dozen black-and-white hunting dogs stood on thick straw, tethered to the walls by long iron chains. Also chained up were two of the largest greyhounds I had ever seen, their lean bodies a mass of muscle. A man was feeding the hunting dogs chunks of meat from a pail, watched keenly by Fulstowe. The steward looked round, surprised to see me, then bowed.

I nodded at the greyhounds. 'Those are big dogs.'

'They are Hugh and David's greyhounds, Ajax and Apollo. The boys will be here to collect them shortly. Master Avery, they are going hunting. Do not feed them.' He turned back to me. 'On the hunt the other dogs will be sent after the does.

'This hunt of your master's, I gather it is the first here?'

Fulstowe nodded. 'It is. We have been keeping the hounds hungry, to get them keen for the scent of meat. That is Master Avery, whom we have hired as our Master of Hunt.'

The young man stood up and bowed. He was as thin and sinewy as the dogs, with a sharp intelligent face, his leather apron spattered with blood from the meat.

'Master Shardlake is here on legal business,' Fulstowe said.

'I heard.' Avery looked at me keenly.

'Avery is working with our forester,' Fulstowe said. He seemed to have decided to play the bluff steward. 'They have found a large stag in our park.'

'We have, sir,' Avery agreed. 'A fine beast. I look forward to next Monday.'

'The boys must be anticipating the hunt too,' I said.

'They are,' Avery agreed. 'They have come tracking deer with me. But as I said, Master Fulstowe, I would rather Master David did not come again. He makes too much noise. Though Master Hugh is a born tracker, silent as a fox. He has the makings of a fine huntsman.' He smiled. 'You should ask him to show you his heartstone.'

I stared. 'His what?'

'The piece of bone a deer has next to its heart,' Fulstowe explained. 'Master Hugh went on a neighbour's hunt last year and brought a hart down with his arrow.'

Avery smiled. 'Do you not know the old custom, sir, for the heartstone to be given to the lord who brings down the deer?'

'I fear I am a townsman.'

'It is said to have great healing properties.'

'Hugh wears it in a little bag round his neck,' Fulstowe said. His nose crinkled a little. I thought of Emma's cross round my own neck. I took a deep breath.

'Master Fulstowe,' I said. 'We would like to take your deposition now.'

'Very well.' He set his lips tight.

☘

THE STEWARD said not a word more as we walked back to the house. As we neared the stables, David and Hugh passed us on horseback. Each wore a leather glove on which a hooded goshawk stood balanced. The sun emphasized the scars on Hugh's face, and I looked away. The boys looked curiously at my serjeant's robes, and David gave a little scoffing laugh. Hugh doffed his cap as they passed, riding away to the gate.

We entered Hobbey's study. Fulstowe's face showed relief as he saw Dyrick. Hobbey had left. 'Good morning, master steward,' Dyrick said cheerfully. 'Do not worry, I will make sure Brother Shardlake keeps to the point.' I saw the hourglass had been turned over again; the sand was just beginning to fall. Fulstowe sat, looking at me as steadily as his master had.

'Well, Fulstowe,' I began in a light tone, 'tell me how you became Master Hobbey's steward.'

'I was steward at his house in London. Before Master Hobbey came here.'

'To be a country gentleman.'

'There is no more honourable calling in England.' A touch of truculence entered Fulstowe's voice.

'You will remember when Hugh and his sister came to your master's London house six years ago. And Master Calfhill.'

'I do. My master and mistress treated those poor children as their own.'

Clearly there was no question of shaking Fulstowe's loyalty. I could not catch him out either. I questioned him for twenty minutes, and his recollections echoed those of his master. He repeated that Hugh and Emma were devoted to each other, excluding all others. He recollected little of Michael Calfhill, saying Michael held himself aloof from the rest of the household. Only once did his coolness slip, and that was when I asked about the smallpox. 'It took all three children at once,' he said. 'They must have been out together and caught it from the same person, there was much of it in London that year.' His voice wavered momentarily. 'I remember Mistress Abigail saying all the children had headaches, and felt so tired they could scarcely move. I knew what that meant.'

'Did you help care for them?'

'I carried water and clean bedclothes upstairs. The other servants were too frightened to help. The physician said they should be wrapped in red cloth to bring out the bad humours. I remember I had a job finding red cloth in London then, everyone was after it.'

'I understand Mistress Hobbey insisted on caring for David herself.'

'Yes, though she visited Hugh and Emma constantly. My mistress has never been the same since Emma died.'

'And afterwards Michael was dismissed from the household.'

'My master did not want him near Hugh any more,' Fulstowe answered. 'You must ask him why.' He inclined his head meaning-fully.

'How much do you have to do with Hugh now?'

'Most of my dealings are with Master David. I am trying to teach him the running of the estate accounts.' His tone indicated he had a thankless task. 'But I look after both their wardrobes.'

'I see. What about Hugh's lands?'

'He shows little interest in them, says he will sell all when he reaches his majority. Just now he wants to join the army.'

'So you have relatively little to do with Hugh.'

'We all live in the same house. One thing I always do for both boys, since they were fourteen, is shave them. Every few days, and cut their hair too, for that is the fashion with archers. My father was a barber. Master Hugh will go to no barber for fear of being cut, given what his face and neck are like.'

'It must be a very different life for you here, Fulstowe. You are a Londoner, I think, by your voice.'

'It has taken time for us to be accepted down here. Most of the local people did not approve of the Dissolution. And the villagers suffer no master lightly.'

'Different work too. You are responsible for managing the whole estate?'

'I am. Under my master. But all trades are the same, blessed is the penny that gains two. That is my master's principle, and mine.'

'That I can believe.' I smiled. 'Well, that is all, I think. For now,' I added once again.

✝

ABIGAIL, Dyrick told me, was still ill with a sick headache; they came on her often and sometimes lasted all day. In my room I changed into lighter clothes, then wrote a reply to Warner, asking him to let me know as soon as he had news of Hobbey's affairs. I also mentioned that I had seen Richard Rich on the journey south. Then I ate lunch with Dyrick, who spent the meal telling me how honest Hobbey and Fulstowe had shown themselves. The boys, he said, would not be back till late afternoon. I left the house, taking my copy of the estate plan which I had brought, and made my way round to Barak's quarters. He gave me a letter he had just written to Tamasin.

'What say you we take a look at Hoyland village?' I asked.

'Dyrick won't like that. He'll think you're suborning the villagers against their master.' His tone was curt; he was still annoyed with me for not taking him to Rolfswood.

'To the devil with Dyrick. Come on.'

'All right. Feaveryear has just left me. He was going over our notes of the depositions, trying to change things here and there. I wouldn't be surprised if his master told him to make difficulties for the sake of it.'

'Then you need some air.'

As we walked round to the gates I glanced over at Abigail's garden, where a servant knelt weeding, noting how much effort she had made in choosing the pretty combinations of flowers. I also noticed the flower beds were designed to form a large H, for Hobbey.

We passed through the gates and followed a dusty path. To one side was a meadow where sheep and a few cattle grazed; I saw the familiar raised shape of a butts there, and wondered how Leacon and the soldiers were faring in Portsmouth. On the other side of the road dense woodland began.

'Whose woods are those?' Barak asked.

I consulted the plan. 'Hobbey's. And that meadow belongs to the village. What did you think of Fulstowe's testimony, by the way?'

'Rehearsed, like his master's.'

'I agree. I wonder if that was why they let us sleep in this morning, to give Dyrick more time to brief them. Well, I have left the door open, to come back with more questions. Ones they can't rehearse.'

We had now passed into a cultivated area, fields divided into wide ploughed strips where men and women and children were busy working. I thought of my own ancestors, generation upon generation of men and women who had spent their lives in hard labour in the fields. Some of the villagers looked up at us. 'Hard work this hot day,' Barak called out cheerfully. They lowered their heads without replying.

We arrived at Hoyland village. Perhaps twenty-five thatched houses straggled along the street. Many were small, little more than one-storey wattle and daub cottages where both people and animals would sleep. A few, though, were larger, with a second storey, and there were a couple of good timber-framed dwellings. Old people and children were working in some of the vegetable patches out front. Again they gave us cold stares, and at one house three children ran inside at our approach.

We had reached the centre of the village. The door of a large building was open, revealing a smith working at his forge, hammering something on his anvil. Coals in the furnace glowed richly red, shimmering in a heat haze. I thought of young Tom Llewellyn.

'The welcoming party's coming,' Barak said quietly.

Three men were walking up the street towards us, all powerfully built, their expressions hostile. Two wore coarse smocks, but the third had a leather jerkin and good woollen hose. He was in his thirties, with a hard, square face, brown hair and keen blue eyes. He stopped a few feet away.

'What's your business, strangers?' he asked in a broad Hampshire burr.

'We are guests at Hoyland Priory,' I answered mildly. 'Out for a walk.'

'Listen to him, Master Ettis,' another said. 'I told you.'

Ettis stepped forward. 'Not too close, fellow,' Barak warned, placing a hand on his dagger.

'Are you the lawyers?' Ettis asked bluntly.

'I am a lawyer,' I answered. 'Master Shardlake.'

'See,' the other said. 'He's come to do us out of the commons. A fucking hunchback too, to make sure we have ill luck.'

Ettis stared at me. 'Well? Is that why you're here? You should know the men of Hoyland fear no lawyers. If you try to cheat us out of our land we'll go to the Court of Requests. We have friends in other villages that have protected their rights. And if Master Hobbey's tree-fellers come on our commons again we'll stop them.'

'That is not my business. I am sent by the Court of Wards to enquire into the welfare of Master Curteys.'

'He means the pocky lad,' Ettis's confederate said.

Ettis continued studying us. 'I heard there were two lawyers at the priory.'

'Master Hobbey's own lawyer is here too. On the same business as I.' I paused and looked at him meaningfully. 'That is not to say he does not have other business too, but I am no part of that.'

Ettis nodded slowly. 'Your interest is only with Master Curteys?'

'Yes. Do you know him?'

He shook his head. 'He doesn't come here. Master David comes sometimes, with his childish airs and graces that would make my old cow laugh.'

'I understand some people from the village work as servants at the house.'

'Some. Most care not to.'

'The servants seem reluctant to speak to us,' I said. 'A pity. Exchanges of information can be useful. Master Hobbey's lawyer's name, by the way, is Vincent Dyrick.'

'Leonard Ettis. Yeoman of this village.'

'Be assured we mean you no harm. We will go back now. But perhaps we might walk this way again, and talk some more?'

'Maybe,' Ettis answered non-committally.

We turned back the way we had come. Barak glanced over his shoulder. 'They're still watching us.'

'They're frightened and angry. They need their commons for grazing and wood.' I smiled. 'But they have a leader, and they know about the Court of Requests. Hobbey and Dyrick will have a fight on their hands.'

'You could have told them that you work there. That would get them on our side.'

'I don't want to anger Hobbey and Dyrick unnecessarily. Not yet. Now come, Hugh should be back soon.'

Chapter Nineteen

W E WENT BACK to the house to find the boys had just returned. Two servants were leading their horses away. Hugh and David stood in front of the entrance, showing their hawks to Feaveryear. Each held one of the big greyhounds on a leash; as Barak and I approached, the dogs sniffed the air. David's dog growled and he jerked its leash. 'Quiet, Ajax.'

Feaveryear was looking with fascination at the speckled plumage of the bird Hugh held at the end of his extended arm. The hawk turned fierce eyes on us, the bells on the jesses securing it to Hugh's gloved hand jingling. Hugh laid his other hand lightly on its back. 'Tush, Jenny, tush.' David had a bag slung over his shoulder, from which a little blood dripped.

'Good catch?' I asked him.

'A brace of plump wood pigeons, and three pheasants. We caught the pigeons on the wing,' he added impressively, his heavy features lighting up. 'A goodly feast for dinner, eh, Hugh?' It struck me David Hobbey seemed very young for eighteen. I remembered the villagers talking of his childish airs and graces.

'It would have been four had your Ajax not half-eaten the one he fetched,' Hugh said.

Feaveryear held out his hand to Hugh's bird. He smiled, his thin face full of wonder. 'Not too close, Master Feaveryear,' Hugh warned. 'She will tolerate none but me.' The hawk flapped its wings and screeched, and Feaveryear jumped back hastily. He tripped and nearly fell, windmilling his thin arms to keep his balance.

David laughed uproariously. 'You look like a scarecrow caught in the wind, clerk.'

Hugh gently pushed the hawk's spread wings back into a folded position. With his free arm he drew a leather hood from his doublet and put it over the bird's head.

Feaveryear's interest was undiminished. 'Did you raise that bird, Master Hugh?'

'No.' Hugh fixed Feaveryear with those cool, unreadable eyes. 'The bird is raised by a falconer. As a chick it is blinded by having its eyelids sewn together, so it comes to depend on people for food. When it is a year old its eyelids are unsewn and it is trained to hunt.'

'But that is cruel.'

David slapped Feaveryear on the shoulder, nearly knocking him over again. 'You are new to the ways of the country.'

Hugh turned to me, the watchful look in his eyes again. 'You wished to take my deposition, I think, Master Shardlake?'

'Yes, please. Feaveryear, will you fetch your master? Then we can begin.'

'We will take the birds to their perches,' Hugh said, 'and get the greyhounds away. Mistress Abigail does not like them near the house.' Again, that coldly formal reference to Abigail. The boys headed for the outhouses, and Feaveryear went indoors.

'That David is a taunting little knave,' Barak said. 'Needs a good slap.'

'He is childish, with no great brains. Yet all his father's hopes must rest on him. As for Hugh – I think he left childhood behind long ago. Let us see if we can find out why.'

✟

WHEN WE ARRIVED in Hobbey's study Dyrick and Feaveryear were already present. A few minutes later Hugh walked in, confidently, almost defiantly. The afternoon sunlight emphasized the marks on his face and neck. I looked away, remembering Bess's comment about his ruined handsomeness. It was not quite so bad as that, but bad enough.

'Pray sit down, Master Hugh,' Dyrick said. He reached across to the hourglass and turned it over. 'To record time spent, for my bill of costs,' he explained with a cold smile. Hugh sat and stared at me, slim, long-fingered hands at rest in his lap. I saw that Feaveryear looked embarrassed.

'I think it best to come straight to the point,' I began. 'No beating the bushes with lawyer's words, as they say.'

'Thank you.'

'We are here because of accusations made by Michael Calfhill, God rest him. He said that when he visited here earlier this year, he found monstrous wrongs had been done to you. Have you any idea what he might have meant?'

He looked me straight in the eye. 'None, sir.'

A triumphant smile crossed Dyrick's face. 'Well,' I said, 'let us see. Tell me, what do you remember of the time when you and your sister became wards?'

'Very little. We were so grief shot we scarcely cared what went on around us.' Despite his words Hugh's tone remained unemotional.

'Michael Calfhill had been your tutor then for over a year. Were you close to him?'

'I liked and respected him. I would not say we were close.'

'Did you know that Michael tried to prevent Master Hobbey from obtaining your wardship?'

'We knew there were some arguments. But we did not care where we went.'

'You barely knew the Hobbeys.'

He shrugged. 'We knew they were friends of Father's. As I said, we did not care.'

'Did you care whether Michael Calfhill came with you?'

He considered the question for a moment. 'He was good to us. But Emma and I thought only of each other then.' His voice wavered and he clutched his hands together. I was sorry for the pain my questions must bring, though the boy tried not to show it. He said, very quietly, 'Emma and I could communicate by looking across a room, without words, as though we had been taken to our own private sphere of the universe.'

'We are upsetting Master Curteys,' Dyrick said. 'Perhaps we should adjourn—'

'No,' Hugh said with sudden fierceness. 'I would have this over and done.'

I nodded. 'Then can I ask, Hugh, were you and your sister well treated by Master and Mistress Hobbey?'

'They gave us good food and clothing, shelter and learning. But no one could replace our parents. No one could feel that loss save Emma and I. I wish people could understand that.'

'It is indeed understandable,' Dyrick said. This deposition was going his way.

'A last word concerning your poor sister,' I said quietly. 'Michael Calfhill said you had a fight with David over some improper words he used to her.'

Hugh smiled tightly and humourlessly. 'David is always saying improper words. You have met him. Once he made a coarse sug, gestion to Emma. I struck him for it and he learned not to do it again.'

'Was there ever talk of Emma marrying David?'

A fierce look sparked in Hugh's eyes for a moment. 'That would never have happened. Emma never liked him.'

'Yet you and David are friends now?'

He shrugged. 'We go hawking and practise archery together.'

'Michael Calfhill's mother said Michael first taught you and your sister to pull the bow.'

'He did. I am grateful to him for that.'

'Yet Master Hobbey dismissed him. He says he feared impropriety between him and you.'

Hugh met my look, then shook his head slowly. 'There was nothing improper between us.'

'But Master Hobbey must have thought he had reason to dismiss him,' Dyrick put in sharply.

C. J. Sansom

'Perhaps Master Hobbey believed he saw something. But I have no accusations to make against Michael Calfhill.' Hugh looked at Dyrick, and now there was a challenge in his eyes.

'Perhaps you do not care to remember,' Dyrick suggested.

'I have nothing to remember.'

'I think that is quite clear, Brother,' I said. 'Now, Hugh, after Michael left you had other tutors. They seem to have come and gone.'

He shrugged. 'One got married. One went to travel. And David did not make life easy for them.'

'And then this Easter Michael suddenly reappeared, running up to you in the garden?'

Hugh was silent for a long moment. He looked down. 'That I do not understand,' he said at length. 'He appeared like a thunderbolt. He must have been hiding among the headstones in the old cemetery, watching David and I shoot our arrows. He pulled at my arm and demanded I come away with him, said I did not belong here.'

'Master Hobbey says he told you he loved you as no other,' I said quietly.

The boy looked up, challenge in his eyes again. 'I do not remember him saying that.' He seeks to protect Michael, I thought. Is he speaking the truth or not?

'You were upset,' Dyrick said. 'Maybe you did not hear.' He smiled encouragingly. Hugh stared back at Dyrick with a cold dislike that discomfited even him for a moment. Then Dyrick said lightly, 'Master Hobbey tells us you would go for a soldier?'

'Truly I would.' Hugh stared at him, emotion entering his voice. 'Less than ten miles from here our ships and men make ready to fight. What Englishman would not wish to serve in this hour? I am young, but I am as good an archer as any. But for my wardship I would serve.'

'You forget, Master Hugh, you are responsible for a large estate. A gentleman with responsibilities.'

'Responsibilities?' Hugh laughed bitterly. 'To woods and badgers

244

and foxes? I have no interest in those, sir. David has his family to consider. But I have none.'

'Come,' Dyrick said reprovingly, 'you are part of the Hobbey family.'

Hugh looked at me. 'The family I loved are all dead. The Hobbeys – ' he hesitated – 'can never replace those I lost.'

'But you are young,' Dyrick said, 'and quite rich. In time you will marry and have your own family.'

Hugh continued to look at me. 'I would rather defend my country.'

Dyrick inclined his head. 'Then I say, young man, thank heaven for the Court of Wards, and Master Hobbey's authority over you. Do you not agree, Brother Shardlake?'

'I applaud your honourable nature, Master Hugh,' I said quietly. 'But war is a matter of blood and death.'

'Do you think I do not know that?' he answered scornfully.

There was silence for a moment. Then Dyrick asked, 'Are there any more questions?'

I repeated my formula. 'Not for now.' Hugh rose, bowed, and walked from the room. Dyrick looked at me triumphantly. Hugh had not accused Michael, but neither had he accused the Hobbeys of anything, anything at all.

✝

AFTERWARDS I invited Barak to my room to talk. 'Well,' he began, 'so much for our main witness.'

I paced up and down, frowning. 'I don't understand it. Hobbey and Fulstowe were practised, but Hugh—'

'It was almost as though he did not care.'

'Yet he did not endorse what Hobbey said about Michael. Neither that Michael behaved improperly when he was a boy, nor that he said he loved him this spring.'

'He said nothing against the Hobbeys. You can see he thinks David a fool, but who could think otherwise?'

'Why does he care nothing for his estates?'

Barak looked at me seriously. 'Maybe he just never got over his parents and sister dying.'

'After all this time? And if he despises David, why spend so much time with him?'

'There is no one else his age here. We don't choose our families, nor our adopted ones.'

'There is more to it than that,' I insisted. 'He bit down hard on his feelings when I mentioned Michael.'

'Maybe he is trying to protect his memory. For Mistress Calfhill's sake.'

'He barely knew her.' I looked at him. 'I swear he is hiding something. They all are. It is just a feeling, but a powerful one.'

Barak nodded slowly. 'I feel it too. But if Hugh will make no complaint, there is nothing to be done.'

'I must think. Let us go for a walk after dinner. I'll come to your room.'

'Meantime I suppose I'll have Feaveryear arguing every dot and comma of the deposition again.'

Barak left for his quarters, and I lay down to rest. Yet my mind was too agitated for me to settle. After a while I decided to go and see if dinner was ready. A little way up the corridor a door stood open. It was dark within, the shutters must be drawn. I heard quiet voices, Nicholas and Abigail.

'He will be gone soon,' Nicholas was saying in impatient tones.

'I can't stand the sight of his bent back.' Abigail sounded utterly weary. 'And that snarling cur Dyrick is loathsome. And I still don't want to have the hunt.'

'Wife, I cannot stand this isolation any longer,' Hobbey replied angrily. 'I tell you, it is safe.'

'We are never safe.'

I started as a little face appeared at the bottom of the doorway. Lamkin came out and waddled towards me, tail wagging. I stepped quickly back into my room, quietly closing the door on the dog. I stood there, thinking hard.

✝

ALTHOUGH the birds taken by the boys were served in more rich sauces from the Hobbey kitchen, dinner was a miserable meal. Abigail was last to arrive, pale and obviously still in pain from her headache. As she entered, Fulstowe, positioned behind Hobbey's chair again, bowed. Dyrick and I stood and Hobbey half-rose, but neither Hugh nor David troubled to rise for her. It was an insult to the mistress of the house, but Abigail seemed hardly to notice. She had taken no trouble over her appearance today, her long grey-blonde hair drooping from the back of her hood. She said nothing during the meal, picking at her food and wincing at the clatter of plates. Hobbey engaged Dyrick in talk about the conversion of the nunnery. He tried to draw David into the discussion, but the boy seemed to have no interest in the house. I saw Hobbey look at him both lovingly and sorrowfully. Hugh sat opposite me. I took the opportunity to lean forward and speak quietly. 'I am sorry if my enquiries stirred sad memories, Master Hugh. Unfortunately asking difficult questions is a lawyer's lot.'

'I understand, Master Shardlake,' he said sadly. He hesitated, then added, 'I promised to let you see my copy of *Toxophilus*. I will have a servant fetch it to your room. I would welcome another view on it.'

'Thank you. That is kind.'

I saw David had been listening to us, caught a strange look on his heavy features. He met my eye and said loudly, 'Where were you and your servant coming back from earlier, Master Shardlake? Was it the village?'

'Yes.'

Hobbey gave me a sharp look.

'Did you see any of those jumped-up serfs?' David asked with a laugh.

'We just went for a walk.'

Ursula, the old servant, was reaching forward just then to pick up an empty dish. David leaned back and his shoulder caught her arm, making her drop the dish on the table with a clatter. Abigail wailed at the noise and put her hands to her ears. 'Will you be careful?' she screeched. 'You foolish booby!'

'Abigail,' Nicholas said warningly. A smile of cruel amusement crossed Fulstowe's face, instantly suppressed. Abigail glared at her husband, then rose from the table and left the room.

'I am sorry,' Nicholas said quietly. 'My wife is unwell.'

I looked at the boys. Hugh's face was expressionless again. David looked crushed.

✝

AFTERWARDS I went round to Barak's quarters. The summer evening had begun, casting long shadows over the lawns. The old stones of the priory looked warm and mellow. Barak was in his room, reading Tamasin's letter again. We walked round to the front of the house, where Lamkin lay dozing on his back under a tree. We went past the butts and into the little graveyard. It was very overgrown. I saw a flash of colour among the greenery. Flowers had been laid by a headstone. *Sister Jane Samuel, 1462–1536.*

'Probably one of the last nuns to die here,' I said. 'I wonder who put these flowers here.'

'Ursula perhaps,' Barak suggested. 'Hobbey would not approve.'

'No. Listen, I overheard something earlier.' I told him about the Hobbeys' conversation. 'Abigail is frightened, she said she and Hobbey would never be safe. And why is she afraid of having the hunt?'

'You sure you heard right?'

'Yes. I have a duty to find out what is happening,' I said firmly. 'It is what the Queen would wish.'

He shook his head. 'You and the Queen. I just want to go home.'

✝

I RETURNED to my room. A book had been laid on my bed. *Toxophilus*, by Roger Ascham. I lay down on the bed and opened it. It began with a flowery dedication to the King, and his 'most honourable and victorious journey into France'. Victorious, I thought. Then why are we poised against a French invasion? And honourable – I recalled what Leacon had said about the waging of war on women and children in Scotland. I leafed through the text. The first part was a dialogue in which Toxophilus – clearly Ascham – described the virtues of archery to an appreciative student. Archery, as an exercise that trained all parts of the body, was contrasted to the risks and dangers of gambling. Ascham praised war: 'Strong weapons be the instruments with which God doth overcome that part which he will have overthrown.'

I thought back to my childhood. I had tried pulling a bow at our village butts just once, my father had taken me when I was ten with a little bow he had bought for me. My deformity had meant I could not take a proper stance with the bow; my arrow, released, had dropped to the ground. The village boys laughed, and I ran home in tears. Later my father had said, in the disappointed tones I had already come to know, that I was not formed for the art and need not go again.

I took up the book once more, persisting. I passed to the second part, where the dialogue changed to a discussion of the skills and techniques of archery: what to wear, how to stand, the types of bows and arrows – thorough and detailed knowledge.

I laid down the book and went to stand by the open window, looking out on the lawn. What was happening here? Hobbey might be creaming off the profits from felling trees on Hugh's lands, but there was more to it than that. Yet Hugh seemed to have complete freedom. I knew from long experience that families will sometimes make one member a scapegoat for their troubles, but from what I had seen it was not Hugh but Abigail who had that role here. What was she so frightened of?

✝

TO MY SURPRISE I slept well. A servant woke me at seven as I had asked. Outside the spell of fine weather seemed over; it was cloudy, close and sticky. I dressed once more in my serjeant's robes. I still had Emma's cross round my neck, I should give it to Hugh. I remembered Avery saying he wore this gruesome heartstone.

There was a knock at my door. Dyrick stood there. He too had put on his robe, and slicked down his coppery hair with water.

'Fulstowe says we may have a storm before the day is out. Perhaps you should postpone your ride through the woods.'

'No,' I answered briefly. 'I shall go today.'

He shrugged. 'As you wish. I came to tell you Mistress Hobbey is better, she is willing to be deposed. Unless, having seen Hugh, you will end this nonsense now.'

'No,' I answered. 'Can you ask Fulstowe to have Barak fetched?' Dyrick made an impatient sound and turned away.

✞

WE GATHERED again in Nicholas's study. Abigail was already there, sitting under the portrait of the abbess of Wherwell. She had taken care of her appearance today, her hair was tied up, her face powdered. Lamkin sat on a little rug on her lap.

'I hope you are feeling better, Mistress Hobbey,' I began.

'Better than I was.' She glanced nervously at Barak and Feaver-year, their quills poised. 'Then I will begin,' I said. 'I wonder, madam, what you thought when your husband suggested buying Hugh and Emma's wardship.'

She looked me in the eye. 'I was glad of it, for I could have no more children. I welcomed Hugh and Emma. I had always wanted a daughter especially.' She sighed deeply. 'But the children would not let me close to them. They had lost their parents. Yet do not many children lose their parents young?' Her look had a sort of appeal in it.

'Sadly they do. I understand Reverend Broughton, the Curteyses' vicar, opposed the wardship. You and he had words.'

Abigail raised her chin defiantly. 'Yes. He defamed my husband and me. Everything about the wardship was done properly.'

'Master Shardlake cannot dispute that,' Dyrick said. He was watching Abigail carefully, anxious I guessed lest she lose control.

'It must have been terrible when all the children took smallpox. I understand you took care of David yourself, despite the danger.'

A flash of anger in her face. 'And neglected Hugh and Emma, is that what you imply? Well, sir, whatever Michael Calfhill may have said, that is not true. I constantly visited Hugh and Emma. But they only wanted to see each other, only each other.' She lowered her head and I realized she was weeping. Lamkin whined, looking up at his mistress, and she stroked his head as she reached for a handkerchief. 'I lost Emma,' Abigail said quietly. 'I lost the girl I wanted for my daughter. It was my fault, all my fault. God forgive me.'

'How was it your fault, Mistress Abigail?'

Her tear-stained face suddenly closed and her eyes flickered away from mine. 'I – I sent for some red cloth, it draws the bad humours out, but I had left it too late, there was none—'

I said, 'But yesterday Fulstowe told me he managed to get some.'

Dyrick looked quickly at Abigail. 'Perhaps you meant to say he got it too late to save Emma.'

'Yes, that was it,' she said hurriedly. 'I was mistaken, it was too late.'

'You are leading the witness, Master Dyrick,' I said angrily. 'Barak, make sure his intervention is entered in the record.'

'I apologize,' Dyrick said smoothly. Abigail took deep breaths, visibly bringing herself under control. I thought, why does she really hold herself responsible for Emma's death?

I asked how she and Hugh got on now. She answered curtly, 'Well enough.' Finally I asked her about Michael Calfhill. 'I never liked him,' she said defiantly. 'He tried to drive a wedge between me and the children.'

'Why would he do that?'

'Because he wanted them to cleave to him, not to my husband and me.'

'Both Hugh and Emma?'

'Yes,' she answered quietly. Then she said in a rush, her voice shaking, 'But Michael Calfhill had such a terrible, agonized death. God pardon him, God pardon him.'

'Do you know why he was dismissed?'

She took a deep breath, bringing herself under control again. 'Only that it was for impropriety. My husband told me the reasons were such as a woman should not know. That is all.'

'Is there anything else, Master Shardlake?' Dyrick asked.

'No.' I had plenty to digest already. 'I may have further questions later.'

'Master Shardlake always says that,' Dyrick told Abigail wearily. 'Thank you, Mistress.'

Abigail wrapped the rug round Lamkin, rose from the chair, and carried the dog out of the room, hugging it to her bosom. I thought of her fear of the servants, her endless snappish battling with her son, her husband's impatience with her and Hugh's cold indifference. Poor woman, I thought. That dog is all she has left to love.

Chapter Twenty

AFTER LUNCH Barak and I fetched two of the horses we had hired in Kingston, and set out to look at the woodland. I took Oddleg, the strong, placid horse that had brought me from London. The pall of grey cloud had thickened, and the air was uncomfortably heavy. We took the Portsmouth road south; Hobbey had told us that in that direction trees were being cut on both Hugh's estate and his.

To the right one of the communal village fields sloped gently away, its strips of different crops a riot of colour. Villagers working there glanced up, some staring at us. As we rode on the woodland to our left gave way to the cleared area, stretching back a good half-mile to where the forest remained untouched, a line of unbroken green. Thin young trees were thrusting up from the undergrowth, mostly pollarded so that the trunks would divide into two trees.

We stopped. 'This area was felled some time ago,' Barak observed.

'They felled everything, not just the mature trees. It will be decades before the forest returns here. That is Hugh's land. How much the timber fetches depends on the type of tree. Prime oak, or elm or ash?' I shook my head. 'Fraud is so easy.'

Behind us a trumpet sounded suddenly. We pulled in to the side as a company of soldiers tramped by, raising clouds of dust. The men looked tired and weary, many footsore. A whiffler walked up and down the line, calling on laggards to raise their feet. The baggage train rumbled past and the company disappeared round a bend. I wondered how Leacon was faring in Portsmouth.

We rode on a further mile or two. To the left the cleared area gave way again to dense forest. There was woodland to the right, too, which from the plan was the village woodland Hobbey wanted. The road sloped gently upwards, and now we could see the line of a high hill in the distance; Portsdown Hill, with the sea on the other side. Then we came on an area where men were felling trees. Almost all had been cut, back to a distance of a hundred yards. One group of men was sawing up a felled oak, another stripping leaves from branches piled on the ground. Long sections of trunk were being loaded onto an ox cart.

'Let's talk to them,' I said. We rode carefully past the stumps, most still gleaming raw and yellow, and halted a little distance from the work. A man came across to us, a tall stringy fellow. He removed his cap and bowed.

'Good afternoon, gentlemen.'

'I am Master Shardlake, lawyer to Hugh Curteys that owns this land. I am staying with Master Hobbey at Hoyland Priory.'

'Master Fulstowe said you might be coming,' the man answered. 'As you see, we are working hard. I am Peter Drury, the foreman.' He had watchful little button eyes.

'You seem to be cutting a great swathe here. What trees are you felling?'

'Everything, sir. Some oak, but the cleared part was mostly ash and elm. The oak goes to Portsmouth, the branches to the charcoal burners.'

'It will be years before there are trees worth cutting here again.'

'It may be long before prices rise so high again, sir. So Master Hobbey says.'

'You are contracted to him, then?'

'Ay. He has the lad's wardship, has he not?' A touch of truculence entered his voice.

'So he does. Are your men local, from Hoyland perhaps?'

Drury laughed. 'Those hogs wouldn't work here. When some of my men went on to their village woods they made great complaint. No, my lads are from up beyond Horndean.' Beyond the reach of local loyalties, I thought. I thanked him, and we rode back to the road.

We continued south, to an area the felling had not yet reached. I saw a narrow path leading into the forest. 'Come,' I said, 'let's see what types of trees these are. There seems to be more oak than that fellow suggested.'

Barak looked up dubiously at the darkening sky. 'It looks like rain.'

'Then we'll get wet.'

We began riding into the forest, picking our way in single file along the narrow path. The air seemed even heavier among the trees.

'Do you still wear that old Jewish symbol round your neck?' I asked over my shoulder.

'The old mezuzah my father left me? Yes, why do you ask?'

'I have Emma Curteys' little cross around mine. I will give it to Hugh, but not in front of the Hobbeys. Did you know he wears some piece of bone from the heart of a deer round his neck?'

'The heartstone? Yes, I talked to Master Avery last night, the huntmaster. He seemed a decent fellow.'

I glanced round. 'Did he say anything about the family?'

'He closed up when I asked. Under orders from Fulstowe, I would guess.' He halted suddenly, raising a hand.

'What is it?'

'I thought I heard hoofbeats, back on the road. Then they stopped.'

'I can't hear anything.' There was nothing but the buzz of insects, little rustlings in the undergrowth as small animals fled from us. 'Maybe you imagined it.'

'I don't imagine things.' Barak frowned. 'Let's get this over with before we get soaked.'

The path narrowed to little more than a track winding through the trees. This was true ancient forest, some of the trees gigantic, hundreds of years old. They grew in profusion and great variety, but oaks with wide spreading branches dominated. The undergrowth was heavy, nettles and brambles and small bushes. The earth, where it could be seen, was dark, soft-looking, a pretty contrast to the bright summer green.

'How far does the Curteys land extend?' Barak asked.

'Three miles here according to the plan. We'll follow the path another half mile or so, then come back. This is mainly oak, and that fetches twice what the other trees will. That foreman was lying, and I think Hobbey's accounts have been doctored.'

'Different types of trees can grow in different places.'

'That is what makes anything difficult to prove.'

We rode on. I was bewitched by the silence among the great trees. According to the Romans, all England looked like this once. I remembered a boyhood visit to the Forest of Arden, riding with my father along a similar path, the one time he took me hunting.

Then I saw a brown shape move ahead, and raised a hand. I saw we were by a little clearing where a deer, a fallow doe, stood cropping the grass, two little fauns at her side. She looked up as we appeared, then turned and in a moment all three had fled into the trees in a rapid, fluid movement. A crashing of undergrowth, then silence.

'So that's a wild deer,' Barak said.

'You've never seen one?'

'I'm a London boy. But even I can see this track is fading out.' He was right, the pathway was becoming mossy and hard to follow.

'A little further.'

Barak sighed. We rode past the trunk of an enormous old oak. Then a sudden ruffle of wind set the leaves waving, and a large raindrop landed on my hand. A moment later the heavens opened and a sheet of rain fell down, soaking us in an instant.

'Shit!' Barak exclaimed. 'I said this would happen!'

We turned back to the enormous old oak, making the horses push through the undergrowth so we could gain shelter by the trunk. We sat there as the rain pelted down, the wind that had come with it making the whole forest seem to shiver.

'That path'll be just mud when we ride back,' Barak said.

'Hard rain soon passes. And these are good horses.'

'If I get congestion of the lungs, can I charge that up to Master costs—'

He broke off at a sudden, reverberating thud. We both turned. An arrow projected from the trunk above our heads, the white-feathered tip still trembling.

'Ride!' Barak yelled.

He gave his horse a prick of the spurs. We crashed out onto the path, which was slippery now. Every second I expected to feel an arrow in my back or see Barak fall, for on the path we were hardly less easy targets than under the tree. But nothing happened. After ten minutes' desperate and difficult riding we stopped in a clearing.

'We've outrun him now,' Barak said. Even so we both stared wide-eyed through the pelting rain at the trees, aware of just how helpless we were against a concealed archer.

'Come on,' Barak said.

It was with relief that we reached the highway again. The rain was easing now. We stopped, staring back the way we had come.

'Who was it?' Barak asked, almost shouting.

'Someone scaring us off? That was a warning; under that tree a bowman with any skill could have killed us both easily.'

'Another warning? Like the corner boys? Remember I heard those hoofbeats on the road? Someone rode after us, someone who knows these woods.'

'We'll have to tell Hobbey, report it to the magistrate.'

'What's he going to do? I tell you, the sooner we're out of here the better. God damn it!'

We rode back to Hoyland Priory. Once Barak would have dashed recklessly in pursuit of that archer, I thought. But now he has Tamasin and the coming child to consider.

✠

WE ARRIVED back at the house. The rain had stopped, though there was still a breeze freshening the air. Old Ursula was in the great hall, polishing the table, and I asked her to fetch Hobbey.

'He's out, sir. Gone to the village with Master Dyrick. Mistress Hobbey is unwell again. She's in bed with that dog,' she added with a disgusted grimace.

'Then please fetch the steward.'

Moments later Fulstowe strode into the hall. He looked at us curiously as I told him what had happened in the wood. 'A poacher, without doubt,' he said when I had finished. 'Perhaps a deserter from the army, they say some are living wild in the forests. We have a forester to patrol Master Hugh's woods but he is a lazy fellow. He will be sorry for this.'

'Why should a poacher draw attention to himself?' Barak asked sharply.

'You said you disturbed some deer. Maybe he was stalking them. They would be a great prize for a deserter, or one of those hogs from the village. Maybe he shot to send you out of the woods.' He frowned. 'But it is a serious matter, the magistrate should be told. A pity you did not see him. If we could get one of those Hoyland churls hanged, it would be a lesson to all of them.'

'Barak thought he heard hoofbeats on the road.'

'They stopped just where we had entered the wood.' Barak looked hard at Fulstowe. I could see he was wondering, as I had, whether the archer had come from the house.

Fulstowe shook his head. 'A poacher would not be on a horse.'

'No,' I agreed. 'He would not.'

'I will have you informed as soon as Master Hobbey returns. I regret this should happen while you are his guest.' He bowed and left us.

'I am sorry I brought you to peril after all,' I said quietly to Barak. 'After what I promised Tamasin.'

He sighed heavily. 'If I weren't here, I'd be in the army. And you're right, we weren't in danger. He shot that arrow to miss.' He looked at me. 'Are you still going to ride to Rolfswood tomorrow?'

'This may be my only opportunity.'

'I'll come if you like.'

'No,' I replied firmly. 'I want you to stay here, work on the servants. See if you can learn anything from Ursula. Maybe visit the village again.'

'All right,' he agreed reluctantly. I turned and went upstairs, feeling his concerned eyes on my back.

✟

I LOOKED OVER my copies of the depositions in my room. Then I went over to the window, drawn by the sound of voices. Hugh and David were by the butts. Fulstowe was with them, Barak and Feaveryear too. I went downstairs to join them. The sun had come out again, making the wet grass sparkle prettily as I walked up to the group. There was still a little wind, high white clouds scudding across the sky. Hugh was instructing Feaveryear in pulling a bow, while David stood watching with Barak. Fulstowe looked on with an indulgent smile. Arrows had been stuck in the grass, their white-feathered tips reminding me of what had happened in the forest.

Feaveryear had put on a long, thick shooting glove and held a beautiful bow, a little shorter and thinner than those I had seen the soldiers use, the outer side golden and the inner creamy white, polished to bright smoothness. Decorated horn nocks were carved into teardrop shapes at each end. Feaveryear had fitted a steel-tipped arrow to the bow, and was pulling with all his strength. His thin arms trembled, but he could only pull the hempen string back a few inches. His face was red and sweating.

Beside him Hugh held up an arrow, watching as the wind ruffled the goose-feather fletches slightly. 'Swing your body a little to the left, Master Samuel,' he said quietly. 'You have to take account of the wind. Now bend your left leg back, and push forward, as though you were making a throw.' Feaveryear hesitated. 'See, I will show you.' Hugh took the bow. He stood, thrusting his weight backward as he pulled on the string. Through his shirt I saw the outline of tight, corded muscles.

'Concentrate on the target,' he told Feaveryear, 'not the arrow. Think only of that and loose. Now, try it.'

Feaveryear took the bow again, glanced round at us, then pulled the bow back a little further and loosed the arrow with a grunt. It rose a little in the air, then buried its point in the grass a short way off. David laughed and slapped his thigh. Fulstowe smiled sardonically. 'Well done, Feaveryear,' David said sarcastically. 'Last time it only dropped from the bow!'

'I am useless,' Feaveryear said with a sad laugh. 'I succeed only in pulling my arms from their sockets.'

'Ignore David,' Hugh said. 'It takes years of practice to strengthen your arms to pull a bow properly. But anyone may learn, and see, already you improve a little.'

'It is hard work.'

'"The fostering of shooting is labour, that companion of virtue,"' I quoted from *Toxophilus*.

Hugh looked at me with interest. 'You have read the book, Master Shardlake.'

'He makes some pretty phrases.'

'It is a great book,' Hugh replied earnestly.

'I would not go quite so high as that.' I noticed Hugh and David had both been shaved, David's dark stubble reduced to the merest shadow on his cheeks while Hugh had a little cut by one of the scars on his neck. 'Perhaps we may discuss the book sometime.'

'I should like that, Master Shardlake. I have little opportunity to discuss books. David can barely read,' he added jestingly, but with an edge. David scowled.

'I shoot better than you,' he said. 'Here, Feaveryear, I will show you how a truly strong archer shoots.' He picked up his own bow from the grass. Like Hugh's it was beautifully made, though not quite so highly polished.

'Such achievement for a youngling,' Barak said, straight faced. David frowned, unsure if he were jesting. Then he strung the bow, bent to it, came up and loosed the arrow. It sped through the air and hit the target, missing the centre by a few inches.

'Not quite so good as Hugh,' Fulstowe said quietly, with a little smile.

David rounded on him. 'I have the greater strength. Set the butts further off and I would beat him easily.'

'I think perhaps your argument is groundless,' I ventured to the boys. '*Toxophilus* says range and accuracy are both needed. You both excel, and if one has a little more of each quality than the other, what matter?'

'David and I have been jesting and bickering these last five years, sir,' Hugh said wearily. 'It is what we do, the subject matters not. Tell me,' he added earnestly, 'what is it you find to criticize in *Toxophilus*?'

'His liking for war. And his praise for the King has a crawling quality.'

'Should we not foster the arts of war to protect ourselves?' Hugh asked with quiet intensity. 'Are we to allow the French to invade and have their will with us?'

'No. But we should ask how we came to this. If the King had not invaded France last year—'

'For hundreds of years Gascony and Normandy were ours.' For the first time I heard Hugh speak with real passion. 'It was our birthright from the Normans before upstart French nobles started calling themselves kings—'

'So King Henry would say.'

'He is right.'

'Do not let Father hear you talking like that,' David said. 'You know he will not let you go for a soldier.' Then, to my surprise, his voice took on a note of entreaty. 'And without you who should I have to hunt with?' David turned to me. 'We went out this morning, and our greyhounds caught half a dozen hares. Though my fast hound caught more—'

'Be quiet,' Hugh said with sudden impatience. 'Your endless who-is-better-than-who will drive me brainsick!'

David looked hurt. 'But competition is the spice of life. In Father's business—'

'Are we not supposed to be gentlemen now? Do you know what a hobby is, Master Shardlake?'

'A hunting hawk,' I answered.

'Ay, the smallest and meanest of birds.'

David's eyes widened with hurt. I thought he might burst into tears.

'That's enough, both of you,' Fulstowe snapped. To my surprise he spoke as though he had the authority of a parent. Both boys were silent at once.

'Please do not argue,' Feaveryear said with sudden emotion, his prominent Adam's apple jerking up and down. 'You are brothers, Christians—'

He was interrupted by a loud voice calling his name. Dyrick was striding across the lawn. He looked angry, his face almost as red as his hair. 'What are you doing shooting with the boys? And you, Barak! You were told to keep to the servants' quarters. Master steward, do you not know your master's instructions?'

Fulstowe did not reply, but gave Dyrick a cold look. 'The boys invited us,' Barak said, a dangerous edge to his voice.

'So we did, sir,' Hugh said. 'For some new company.'

Dyrick ignored them. 'Come with me, Sam! Quick! Ettis and a bunch of clods from the village are shouting Master Hobbey down in his own study. I want what they say recorded!'

'Yes, sir,' Feaveryear answered humbly. Dyrick turned and strode away, Feaveryear following.

'Come boys,' Fulstowe said. 'I think we should go in. And it is not sensible to argue in front of our guests.' He looked at Hugh and David, and some understanding seemed to pass between the three. They went off after Dyrick and Feaveryear. Barak glanced over the building, eyes narrowed. 'We could go for a little walk and pass under the study window. It's at the back of the house. We might find something out. See, they have opened all the windows to let in the breeze.'

I hesitated, then nodded. 'This case leads me into bad habits,' I muttered as I followed him round to the back of the house, where a stretch of lawn faced the old convent wall. Raised voices could be heard from Hobbey's study. I recognized the Hampshire burr of Ettis, whom we had met in the village. He was shouting. 'You want to steal our commons. Then where will the poor villagers get wood and food for their pigs?'

'Take care, Goodman Ettis!' Dyrick's loud rasp cut like a knife. 'Your boorish ways will serve you ill here. Do not forget that some of the cottagers have already sold their land to Master Hobbey. So less common land will be needed.'

'Only four. And only when you threatened them with repossession when they got behind with their rent. And the grant is clear! The priory granted Hoyland village our woods near four hundred years ago.'

'You have only your poor English translation of it—'

'We cannot read that Norman scribble!' another voice with a Hampshire accent shouted.

We were right under the window now. Fortunately the sill was above our heads. I looked round uneasily, fearing some servant might appear round the side of the house.

Dyrick replied forcefully, 'This grant only says the village should have use of all the woodland it needs.'

'The area was mapped out, clear as day.'

'That was done before the Black Death, since when Hoyland, like every village in England, has far fewer people. The woodland area should be correspondingly reduced.'

'I know what you have planned,' Ettis shouted back at Dyrick. 'Fell all our woodland, make great profit, then take the village lands and turn everything over to more woodland. No knife-tongued lawyer will talk us out of our rights! We will go to the Court of Requests!'

'You'd better hurry, then,' I heard Hobbey answer smoothly. 'I've ordered my woodsmen to start again on the area you wrongly call yours next week. And you people had better not impede them.'

'Note they've been warned, Feaveryear,' Dyrick added. 'In case we need to show the magistrate.'

'Who is in your pocket,' Ettis said bitterly.

Then we heard a bang, which must have been the door opening and slamming against the wall. Abigail's voice cried out shrilly, 'Rogues and vagabonds! Nicholas, Fulstowe tells me they shot an arrow at the hunchback lawyer in the forest! You villains!' she screamed.

'Shot?' Hobbey sounded shocked. 'Abigail, what do you mean?'

'I have just seen Master Shardlake,' Dyrick said. 'He looks no worse than he ever does.'

'He wasn't hit! But they did it!'

Then I heard Fulstowe's voice: he must have heard the commotion and come in. 'Shardlake and his clerk were shot at while riding Master Hugh's woodland. They surprised a deer: it must have been a poacher warning them off. No one was hurt, nor meant to be,' he added impatiently.

'You stupid woman!' It was the first time I had heard Hobbey lose control. Abigail began to cry. The room had fallen silent. I inclined my head, and we began moving quietly away, round the side of the house.

'That was getting interesting,' Barak said.

'I was concerned someone would come out and see us. And I think we heard enough.' I frowned. 'That woman is so frightened.'

'She's mad.'

'It's hard to know. By the way, did you notice the way the boys took orders from Fulstowe earlier? And from what we heard there Fulstowe doesn't bother showing much respect to Abigail.'

'Who is right about the woods?' Barak asked.

'I'd need to see the land grant. But if there's a defined area, that stands well for the villagers.'

'If I go into the village while you're away, maybe it's time to tell them you are counsel at Requests. Then we might get some information.'

I considered. 'Yes. Do it. See Ettis. Tell him if they write to chambers I'll apply for an injunction as soon as I get back. On condition they say nothing to Hobbey.' I smiled. 'I can tell Hobbey about it on the day we leave.'

'You are turning into a Machiavelli since becoming a Court of Wards lawyer.'

I looked at him seriously. 'Ask Ettis to tell us in return all he can about Hugh. Something is going on in this house that we cannot see. I swear it.'

Chapter Twenty-one

SEVEN O'CLOCK the next morning found me riding north along the Portsmouth road, already a mile from Hoyland Priory. Once again I had taken Oddleg. He walked along rapidly, seeming happy to be on a long journey again. The weather was fine, a scent of dewy grass on the air which was still cool at that hour. It would be hot later, and I wore a doublet of light wool, grateful to have left my robes behind. As I rode I pondered the conversation I had had, just before I left, with Hugh.

I had asked to be called at six, and been woken by a knock on the door. Fulstowe put his head round. 'There is some breakfast downstairs, sir,' he said, adding, 'I understand you are travelling to Sussex and will not be back until tomorrow afternoon.'

'Yes. A piece of business for another client. Thank you.' I had already told Hobbey that, and no more – I was not going to tell them anything about Ellen. I rose and dressed. Then I picked up Emma's decorated cross from my bedside table and Hugh's copy of *Toxophilus*. I stepped quietly into the corridor and walked along to Hugh's room. I hesitated briefly, then knocked. I had gone there the previous evening, but either he was not there or was not answering. Here was a rare chance to speak with him undisturbed.

This time he answered the door, already dressed in shirt and doublet.

'I am sorry to disturb you so early,' I said, 'but I am setting out for Sussex now, and I wanted to return your book.'

He hesitated a moment before inviting me in, as courtesy demanded. The room was furnished with a bed, a chest and a table, and a wall hanging in green and white stripes, the Tudor colours. On a shelf above the table I saw, to my surprise, a collection of perhaps two dozen books. The room smelled strongly of wax and Hugh's bow, unstrung, leaned against a corner of the bed. A box of wax and a rag lay beside it.

'I am polishing my bow.' He gave a little smile. 'Mistress Abigail prefers me to do it outside, but at this hour who will know?'

'It is early indeed.'

'I like to rise before everyone else, have some time to myself before *they* are all up.' I caught a note of contempt in Hugh's voice and looked at him keenly. He coloured and put a hand to his neck. He is very conscious of those marks, I thought.

'You have many books,' I said. 'May I look?'

'Please do.'

There were Latin and Greek classics, a book on manners for young gentlemen, and copies of *Sir Gawain and the Green Knight*, *The Book of the Hunt* and Boorde's *Dietary of Health*, as well as Sir Thomas More's *Utopia*. There were, unusually, no religious works save a New Testament.

'A fine collection,' I observed. 'Few people your age have so many.'

'Some were my father's, and Master Hobbey fetched some for me from London. But I have no one to discuss them with since our last tutor left.'

I took down *The Book of the Hunt*. 'This is the classic work on hunting, I believe.'

'It is. Originally by a Frenchman, but translated by the Duke of York, who died at Agincourt. When nine thousand English archers routed a huge French army,' he added proudly. He sat down on the bed.

'Are you looking forward to the hunt next week?' I asked.

'Very much. It will only be my third. We do not socialize much here.'

'I understand it has taken time for the local gentlefolk to accept the family.'

'It is only the prospect of the hunt that is bringing them. So Mistress Abigail says at least.' I realized how isolated Hugh was down here, David too.

'At my last hunt it was I who brought down the hart,' Hugh added proudly.

'I was told you were awarded the heartstone, that you wear it round your neck still.'

His hand rose to his neck again. His eyes narrowed. 'By whom?'

'Master Avery.'

'You have been questioning him about me?'

'Hugh, the only reason I am here is to look into your welfare.'

Those unreadable blue-green eyes met mine. 'I told you yesterday, sir, I have no complaints.'

'Before I left London, Bess Calfhill gave me something for you. Something Mistress Hobbey gave to Michael. It was your sister's.' I opened my hand and showed him the decorated cross. At once tears started to his eyes. He turned his head away.

'Michael kept it till he died?' Hugh asked, his voice hoarse.

'Yes, he did.' I laid the cross on the bed beside him. Hugh reached out and grasped it. He took out a handkerchief, wiped his eyes, then looked at me.

'Mistress Calfhill remembers my sister?'

'Very fondly.'

He was silent a moment, grasping the cross tightly. Then he asked, 'What is London like now? I have been here so long. I remember little more than the noise, people always shouting in the streets, and then the quiet of our garden.' Again I sensed a weariness in him that a boy of his age should not feel.

'If you went to university you could meet new people your age, Hugh, discuss books from morn to night. Master Hobbey must make provision if you want to go.'

He looked up, gave a tight smile, then quoted: '"In study every part of the body is idle, which encourages gross and cold humours."'

'*Toxophilus*?'

'Yes. You know I wish not to study but to go to war. Use my skills at the bow.'

'I confess I think Master Hobbey right to stop you.'

'When you go to Portsmouth on Friday, will you see your friend the captain of archers?'

'I hope so.'

'David and I are coming. To see the ships and soldiers. Tell me, were there lads my age among those archers? I have seen companies on the road to Portsmouth where some soldiers looked no older than me.'

I thought of Tom Llewellyn. 'In truth, Master Hugh, the youngest recruit I met was a year or so older than you. A right well-built lad.'

'I am strong enough, and skilled enough, too, I think, to bury a well-steeled arrow in a Frenchman's heart. God give them pestilence.' He spoke with passion. I must have looked surprised, for he flushed and lowered his head, rubbing one of the little moles on his face. Suddenly the lad seemed terribly vulnerable. He looked up again. 'Tell me, sir, is Master Dyrick your friend? They say lawyers argue over cases but are friends outside the court.'

'Sometimes they are. But Master Dyrick and I – no, we are not friends.'

He nodded. 'Good. I dislike him. But often in this life we must spend our time associating with those who are not friends, must we not?' He gave a bitter little laugh, then said, 'Time goes on, sir. I should not detain you.'

'Perhaps when I return we may discuss *Toxophilus*, and your other books.'

He looked up, his composure restored. 'Yes, perhaps.'

'I look forward to it.'

I left him clutching Emma's cross.

✠

AS I RODE along I thought again of Abigail saying she did not feel safe to have the hunt, her husband replying that he could not bear the isolation here any more. What were they frightened of? Was there some connection to our being shot at the day before? Whatever was being kept hidden at Hoyland, I felt Hugh knew at least something of it. Then there was the trouble with the villagers. I reflected that the chain of events at Hoyland was typical of a landlord seeking to destroy a village and take the land for his own purposes. I had seen the pattern many times at the Court of Requests. Village politics here was typical too: independent small landowners such as Ettis taking the lead, and some of the poor villagers being intimidated into selling their leases back to the landlord.

By the time I reached the turning for Rolfswood the sun was well up and it was becoming hot. I had expected a poor country track, but the road into Sussex was well maintained. I had ridden about a mile when I noticed a smell of burning, and remembered the charcoal burners from our ride down. To my right a wide path cut through a high bank into the forest. Curious, I urged the horse onto the path.

A few hundred yards in I came to a glade where a large, beehive-shaped clay structure stood, taller than a man, smoke rising from an opening at the top. Piles of small branches were set around the clearing. Two young men sitting on a mound of earth rose as I appeared.

'Burning charcoal?' I asked.

'Ay, sir,' one answered. Both had black faces from their work. 'We don't usually work in summer, but they want as much charcoal as they can get for the foundries these days.'

'I understand they are casting cannon now.'

'That's over in the east, sir. But there is plenty of work for the small West Sussex foundries too.'

'The war brings good profits,' his friend added, 'though we see little of them.'

'I am heading for Rolfswood. I believe there used to be an ironworks there that burned down.'

'Must have been a while ago. There's no iron worked round here now.' The man paused. 'Would you take a drink of beer with us?'

'Thank you, but I must get on my way.' They seemed disappointed and I thought it must be lonely work out here, with only the charcoal pile for company.

✞

IT WAS PAST THREE when I arrived at Rolfswood. It was a smaller place than I had expected, a main street with several good houses built of brick but not much behind except poor hovels. A straggling path led to a bridge across a little river, then across a field to an ancient-looking church. There was, I was pleased to see, a sizeable inn on the main street. Two carts passed me, full of small branches, new-cut and giving off a raw smell of sap.

I dismounted outside the inn. There I found a room for the night, which was comfortable enough. I went to the parlour to see what information I could raise; I had considered the story I would tell to explain my interest.

The parlour was empty save for an old man sitting alone at a bench. A big scent hound, a lymer, lay beside him. It raised its heavy, lugubrious face to look at me. I crossed to the serving hatch, and asked the elderly woman behind it for a beer. Her plump wrinkled face under its white coif looked friendly. I gulped down the beer, for I was sore thirsty.

'Have you travelled far, sir?' she asked.

'From near Portsmouth.'

'That's a good day's ride.' She leaned her elbows comfortably on the counter. 'What's the news from there? They say the King's coming.'

'So I hear. But I have not been to Portsmouth. I am a London lawyer; I have some business at a house north of Portsdown Hill.'

'What brings you to Rolfswood?'

'A friend in London believes he may have relatives here. I said I would come and enquire.'

She looked at me curiously. 'A good friend, to make such a long journey.'

'Their name is Fettiplace. He heard from an old aunt they once had an iron foundry here.'

'That's gone, sir,' she said gently. 'The foundry burned down near twenty years ago. Master Fettiplace and one of his workers were killed.'

I paused, as though taking in the news for the first time, then said, 'Had he any family?'

'He was a widower. He had a daughter, whose story is even sadder. She saw the fire and lost her reason because of it. They took her away, I heard to London.'

'If only my friend had known. He only recently learned he might have a Sussex connection.'

'Their house and the land the foundry stood on were sold to Master Buttress, our miller. You'll have passed the house in the main street, it's the one with the fine carvings of animals on the doorposts.'

Sold, I thought. By whom? Legally, surely, it would have gone to Ellen. 'No other Fettiplaces locally?'

'No, sir. Master Fettiplace was from somewhere in the north of the county. He came here to build the foundry.' She leaned out of the hatch, and called to the old man. 'Here, Wilf, this gentleman is enquiring after the Fettiplace foundry.' He looked up. The serving woman spoke to me quietly. 'Wilf Harrydance used to work there. He's a poor old fellow, buy him a drink and he'll tell you all he knows.'

I nodded and smiled. 'Thank you. Fetch us two more beers, will you?'

I took them over to the old man. He nodded thanks as I set a mug before him, and studied me with interest. He was well drawn in years, wearing an old smock and bald save for a few straggling grey hairs. His tanned face was wrinkled but his blue eyes were intelligent, eager with curiosity. The dog wagged its tail, no doubt looking for scraps.

'You want to hear the Fettiplace story, sir?' He waved a hand. 'I heard all you told Goodwife Bell. I may be old but my ears are good.'

'If you would. My name is Master Shardlake. You worked at the foundry?'

'I'd been with Master Fettiplace ten years when the fire happened. He wasn't a bad master.' He was silent a moment, remembering. 'It was hard work. Loading the ore and the charcoal into the furnace, checking the progress of the melt through the flue – by Mary, when you looked in there the heat near melted your eyeballs. Then scraping the bloom of melted iron out into the hearth – '

I heard Ellen's voice again. *The poor man! He was all on fire!* Wilf had paused and frowned, noting my inattention. 'I am sorry,' I said. 'Please go on. What sort of foundry was it? Was it what they call a bloomery?'

He nodded. 'A small one, though the bellows were water powered. Master Fettiplace came to Rolfswood as a young man, he had already made some money in the iron trade over in East Sussex. There's an outcrop of iron ore here, a small one, we're on the western fringes of the Weald. Master Fettiplace bought some woodland that he could use for making charcoal. The river goes through there too, so he put his money into damming the river to make the mill pond, and built the furnace. The flow of water turns the wheel that powers the bellows, you see?'

'Yes.'

'The iron ore gets brought in, in our case from a little further upriver where the ironstone outcrop lay, and you put it in the furnace with the charcoal. The iron melts out of the ore and falls to the bottom. You see?' he repeated, in a schoolmasterly manner.

'I think so. Another beer?'

He nodded gravely. 'Thank you.'

I fetched two more beers and set them on the table. 'What was Master Fettiplace like?'

Wilf shook his head sadly. 'William Fettiplace wasn't a lucky man. Rolfswood furnace never did very well, the quality of the ironstone was low, and with the competition from the new blast furnaces the price of charcoal kept going up. Then his wife that he was devoted to died young, leaving him with a young daughter. And he died in the fire, with my friend Peter Gratwyck. That mysterious fire.' Wilf was looking at me keenly now.

'Mysterious? I would have thought there was always a risk of fire in such places.'

He shook his head. 'It was summer, the furnace wasn't even working.' He leaned forward. 'This is how it was. The furnace was an enclosed area, a courtyard inside a wooden wall. The enclosure was mostly roofed over, except for the centre – it got very hot when the furnace was working. Inside the enclosure was the main building with the furnace at one end, and the big bellows connected to the water wheel. The rest of the enclosure was storage space – ore and coke and building materials. It was a small, old-fashioned foundry. Master Fettiplace hadn't the money to build a blast furnace. There were only a few workers. We worked our lands during the summer, and in the winter did the casting. See?'

'Yes.'

'Someone always had to be there during the summer, to take deliveries of coke and ore ready for the winter, and keep an eye on the mill pond and the wheel. Peter usually did that, he lived very close by. But that summer – it was 1526, the year before the great dearth when the crops failed through the rains. That August I remember was cold and windy, like October—'

'And the fire – ' I prompted.

He leaned in very close, so I felt his warm beery breath. 'That summer Peter was living at the furnace. His wife, who was a vicious old shrew, had thrown him out, saying he drank too much. I suppose he did, but never mind that. Peter asked Master Fettiplace if he could stay at the furnace for a while, and he agreed. There was a little straw bed there, people often stayed overnight during the winter campaigns, but he was the only one there that night.' Wilf took another draught of beer and sat back. 'Ah, sir. It hurts me still to remember.' He sighed. The dog looked up at him and gave a little whine.

'Towards nine that night I was at home here in the town. A

neighbour came banging at my door, saying the furnace was on fire. I ran out. Lots of people were heading for the woods. As you came close to the furnace you could see the flames through the trees, the mill pond all red, reflecting the fire. It was dreadful, the whole enclosure was ablaze from end to end when I got there. It was built of wood, you see. Ellen Fettiplace blamed Peter afterwards, said he had lit a fire in the foundry building to warm himself and started the blaze.'

'Ellen? The daughter?' I had to pretend not to know.

'That's right. She was the only witness. She and Master Fettiplace had gone for an evening walk to the furnace – Master Fettiplace wanted to check that an ore delivery had come – and found Peter drunk by the fire. Master Fettiplace shouted at him, he jumped up and somehow his clothes caught light. He fell over on the straw bed and that caught light too. There was a lot of coke dust about and the whole place went up. Peter and Master Fettiplace were burnt to death; only young Ellen got out, and it drove her mad. Too mad to appear at the inquest, a statement from her was read out.' I remembered Ellen screaming. *I saw his skin melt, turn black and crack! He tried to get up but he fell!*

'That was the end of my work there,' Wilf said. 'Me and half a dozen others. The foundry was never rebuilt, it didn't make enough profit. The ruins are still out there in the woods. The following year the harvest failed, we had a hard time making it through.' He looked round the empty parlour. 'Peter Gratwyck was my best friend. The nights we've sat here drinking when we were young men.'

'Do you know where the daughter went?' I asked.

'The night of the fire she ran to the local priest, old John Seckford that's still curate here. Her reason had gone. She wouldn't leave the vicarage. After the inquest she was taken away, to relatives in London they said. But your friend's never come across her?' he asked curiously.

'No.'

I thought, this is not what I expected, there is no rape in this story. 'This Ellen, what was she like?'

'A pretty enough girl. About nineteen then. But spoiled by her father, full of her own opinions. The sad thing was, at the time of the fire there was talk of her getting married.'

'To whom?'

'Master Philip West, his family have lands here. He went to serve on the King's ships after.'

'I take it the verdict at the inquest was accidental death.'

'It was.' Wilf was suddenly alert. He said, 'There were questions I wanted to ask about that fire. I didn't see why Master Fettiplace couldn't have got out. But I wasn't called. Master Quintin Priddis hurried the inquest through.'

I sat up. 'Priddis?'

Wilf's eyes narrowed. 'You know him?'

'Only by name. He is responsible for the Court of Wards in Hampshire.'

'He was one of the Sussex coroners then.'

'Did Mistress Fettiplace say how it happened that neither her father nor your friend escaped?'

'Peter's clothes were on fire and somehow Master Fettiplace's clothes caught too. So she said, and hers was the only evidence. The foundry was gone, nothing left of poor Peter or Master Fettiplace save a few bones. You are sure you don't know Quintin Priddis?' His look was anxious now.

'I have never met him.'

'I must go,' the old man said suddenly. 'My wife is expecting me back. How long are you staying in Rolfswood?'

'I leave tomorrow morning.'

He looked relieved. 'Then I wish you a safe journey. Thank you for the beers. Come, Caesar.'

He got up, the dog following. Then he paused, turned back and said, 'Talk to Reverend Seckford. Many round here think something was covered up back then. But that's all I'll say.'

He hurried out.

Chapter Twenty-two

I WALKED SLOWLY up the hill to the church. I was dusty, my legs and back stiff and aching, and I wanted nothing more than to rest. But I had little time here. I considered what old Wilf had said. He had seemed suspicious of the official version of what had happened at the foundry – but clearly knew nothing of a rape. I remembered Ellen's words, that terrible day she lost control. *They were so strong! I could not move!*

The church was small, a squat Norman building. Within little had changed since popish days; statues of saints were still in their places, candles burned before the main altar. Reverend Broughton would not approve, I thought. An elderly woman was replacing candles that had burned down. I went up to her.

'I am looking for Reverend Seckford.'

'He'll be in the vicarage, sir, next door.'

I went to the adjacent house. It was a poor place, wattle and daub, old paint flaking away. But Seckford was a perpetual curate, subordinate to a priest who perhaps held several parishes. I felt guilty at the thought that I was about to lie to Seckford, as I had to Wilf. But I did not want anyone here to know where Ellen was.

I knocked on the door. There were shambling footsteps, and it was opened by a small man in his fifties, wearing a cassock that could have done with a wash. He was very fat, as broad as he was long, his round cheeks covered in grey stubble. He looked at me with watery eyes.

'Reverend Seckford?' I asked.

'Yes,' he answered mildly.

'I wondered if I could speak with you. About a kindness you did many years ago to a woman called Ellen Fettiplace. Wilf Harrydance suggested I call on you.'

He studied me carefully, then nodded. 'Come in, sir.'

I followed him into a shabby parlour. He invited me to sit on a wooden settle covered by a dusty cloth. He took a chair opposite, which creaked under his weight, and looked at me curiously. 'I think you have been travelling, sir.'

'Yes. I apologize for my dusty state.' I took a deep breath, then repeated the story I had told Wilf about a friend looking for Fetti- place relatives. Seckford listened carefully, though his eye occasionally strayed to the open window behind me, and to a large jug on the buffet, where some tarnished silver plate was displayed. When I had finished he stared at me, his face full of sadness.

'Forgive me,' he said quietly, 'but I hope your client's interest is no mere matter of idle curiosity. Ellen's is a sad, terrible story.'

'My — my friend, I am sure he would help her if he could.'

'If she is still alive.' Seckford paused, gathering his thoughts. 'William Fettiplace, Ellen's father, was a good man. He got little profit from that foundry but he was charitable, gave money to the poor and to the church. His wife, Elizabeth, died young. He doted on Ellen. Perhaps he indulged her too much, for she grew into a strong-willed girl. But kind, charitable. She loved the church: she used to bring flowers for the altar, sometimes for me too, to brighten this poor place.' His eyes went blank for a moment, then he continued. 'The fire was nineteen years ago.'

'Wilf said the August of 1526.'

'Yes. Next year came the harvest failure and the great dearth. I buried many parishioners then.' His eyes wandered again to the window. I turned, but there was only a little garden with a cherry tree.

'That day was cold and cloudy, as it had often been that summer. I was here. It was getting dark, I remember I had lit a candle, when there came a frantic hammering at the door. I thought it was someone needing the last rites, but it was poor Ellen that staggered in. Her hood was gone, her hair wild, her dress torn and stained with grass. She must have fallen on her way from the foundry in the dark.'

But, I thought, something else could have happened to explain that.

'I could get no sense from her. Her eyes were staring, she kept taking great whooping breaths but could not speak. Then she said fire, fire at the foundry. I ran and shouted for help and soon half Rolfswood was running there. I stayed with Ellen. They told me after that by the time people got there the whole enclosure was ablaze. All they found of Master Fettiplace and his man Peter Gratwyck was some charred bones. God rest their poor souls.'

'Goodman Harrydance said Ellen moved in here afterwards?'

'Yes.' He raised his chin. 'But there was nothing improper, I got Goodwife Wright, one of the Fettiplace servants, to come and stay.'

'How long did she remain?'

'Near two months. She never recovered from that night. At first she would barely talk at all, and would say nothing about what happened. If we asked her she would start crying or even screaming. It alarmed us. If someone knocked on my door she would jump or even scream and run to her room. After a while she could be got to talk a little of commonplace things, the weather and suchlike, but only to me or Goodwife Wright. And she wouldn't go outside, she would just shake her head wildly if I suggested it. She refused to see anyone else. Not even the young man people had said she would marry, Master Philip West, though he came several times. You could see in his face how troubled he was. I think he loved her.'

'He went to the King's ships, Goodman Harrydance said.'

'Yes, soon after. I think he had a broken heart. You see, the word was Philip West was going to propose to Ellen. His family had obtained a junior position for him at the King's court. He was often in London, but that summer the King had come on Progress to Sussex and Master West had ridden over to visit for the day.' Seckford shook his head sadly. 'Master Fettiplace would have been pleased for them to marry, for the Wests are a wealthy landowning family. And Master West was a handsome young fellow.'

'Are the West family still here?'

'Philip West's father died some years ago. His mother, Mistress Beatrice West, still manages his lands. He owns much round here, but leaves all the management in his mother's hands, only visiting when he is home from sea. She is a – formidable woman. She lives in a big house outside the town. Philip was here last month, when his ship arrived at Portsmouth.' He looked at me. 'I hear all the King's ships are coming there, and the King himself is on his way to review them.' The curate shook his head sorrowfully. 'We live in terrible times.'

'We do, sir.'

'I saw Philip West last month, passing down the main street on his horse. Still a handsome man but middle-aged now, and stern faced.' Seckford stood abruptly. 'Forgive me, sir. I made a resolution to drink no strong beer till the shadow on that cherry tree strikes the gate. But remembering all this – ' He stepped to the buffet and took two pewter mugs. 'Will you drink with me, sir?'

'Thank you.'

He filled the mugs from the jug. He drank his straight off in a few gulps, sighed deeply and refilled it, before passing the other to me and lowering himself back into the chair.

'It was after they took Ellen away that I started drinking too much. It seemed so cruel, the foundry burning down, that poor girl with her wits gone. And I have to preach that God is merciful.' His plump face sagged into an expression of great sadness.

'And was Ellen the only witness to what happened?' I asked quietly.

Seckford frowned. 'Yes, and the coroner was very persistent in trying to get the story out of her.' His voice took on a harsh note. 'Mistress West wanted the matter out of the way so her son would not be reminded of it, and it would cease to be the talk of the locality.

And the Wests could help Coroner Priddis's advancement. An ambitious man, our former coroner,' he concluded bitterly.

'I know of Priddis,' I said. 'He is now Sir Quintin, feodary of Hampshire. A post of some power.'

'So I have heard. The Priddis family were mere yeomen, but they were ambitious for their son and sent young Quintin to law.' The curate drained his mug. 'Ambition, sir, I believe it a curse. It makes men cold and hard. They should stay in the station God set them.' He sighed. 'Perhaps you will not agree.'

'I agree ambition may lead men into harshness.'

'Priddis was keen to be in with all the gentry. A busy, bustling little fellow. From the day after the fire he kept calling here, demanding to see Ellen and take a statement. But as I told you, she wouldn't see anyone. Master Priddis had to adjourn the inquests on Master Fettiplace and Peter several times. I think it rankled with him, his power thwarted by a mere girl. He had no sympathy for her state of mind.'

'Well, it was his duty to discover what happened.'

'The knave got his statement in the end. I'll tell you how.' Seckford took another mighty quaff of beer. Unlike Wilf he had shown no suspicion of me and it struck me there was something unworldly about him.

'After a few weeks Ellen improved, as I said, but still she would not say what had happened and she would not go out, not even to the church next door. She kept inventing excuses, became – crafty. Ellen Fettiplace, that had been so honest and open before. It saddened me. I think in the end she agreed to see Priddis so he would leave her alone. That was all she wanted now, to stay in this house with me and Jane Wright and never leave.'

'Were you there when he saw her?'

He shook his head. 'Priddis insisted it just be him and Goodwife Wright. They went into my kitchen over there and came out an hour later, Priddis looking pleased with himself. Next day he sent a draft statement to Ellen and she signed it. It said she and her father went to the foundry for a walk that evening, he wanted to check the delivery of some coke, they found Peter drunk and he fell into a fire he had made to warm himself. Peter's clothes caught fire and somehow William Fettiplace's did too. Priddis allowed the statement at the inquest without Ellen attending because of her state of mind. Got a verdict of accidental death.' Seckford slapped his fist angrily on the side of his chair. 'Case closed, tied up in red ribbon and put away.'

'You think Ellen's statement was untrue?'

He looked at me keenly. 'My guess is Master Priddis pieced together the little Ellen had said, worked it up into a likely chain of events and Ellen signed it to be rid of him. As I said, she had become calculating. They say that can happen to folks that are sick in their minds. She wanted only to be left alone.'

'What do you think really happened?'

He looked at me. 'I have no idea. But if the fire had only just started I do not see how Master Fettiplace at least could not have escaped.'

'Did he have any enemies?'

'None. No one wished him ill.'

'How did Ellen come to leave you?'

The curate leaned back in his chair. 'Oh sir, you ask me to remember the worst part of all.'

'I am sorry. I did not mean to press.'

'No, you should hear it to the end now.' Seckford got up, took my mug, waddled to the buffet and poured more beer.

'Goodwife Wright and I did not know what to do about Ellen. She had no relatives, she was heiress to her father's house here in Rolfswood, a little land, and the burnt-out foundry. I thought to keep her with us in the hope that eventually she might recover and be able to deal with her affairs. But Quintin Priddis took a hand again. Not long after the verdict he was back. Sat where you sit now and said it was improper for Ellen to remain here. He threatened to tell my vicar, and I knew he would order her put out.' Seckford drained his mug again.

I leaned forward. 'Goodman Harrydance said she was taken to London, to relatives.'

I saw the hand holding the empty mug was trembling. 'I asked Master Priddis what was to become of her. He said he had made enquiries and found relatives in London, and that he was willing to arrange for her to be taken to them.' He frowned and now he did look at me sharply. 'You say this friend of yours lives there, but does not know her.'

'He knows nothing of this.' I hated lying to the old man, and realized how once started on a course of lies it becomes ever harder to stop. But Seckford seemed to accept my reply.

He said, 'My guess is Mistress West asked Priddis to search for relatives, gave him some fee. There would have to have been some profit in it for him to act.'

I thought, but for whoever placed her in the Bedlam there has been no profit, only continual expense. Keeping her out of the way could only be for their safety. Was it Mistress West, protecting her son?

'Priddis played a dirty trick.' Seckford spoke quietly. 'Jane Wright, you see, had had no wages since the fire. Nor had the other servants in Master Fettiplace's house. Who was to pay them? Priddis told her that placing Ellen with these relatives meant that things could be put on a proper footing, Master Fettiplace's house sold and her arrears of wages paid. He said he would put in a word with whoever bought the house, see if they would keep her on. That brought her over to his side. I cannot blame her, she had no income, we were all living out of my poor stipend.'

'Did you ask who these relatives were?' I asked gently.

'Priddis would not say. Only that they lived in London and would take care of her. He said that was all I needed to know.' Seckford leaned forward. 'Sir, I am only a poor curate. How was I to stand up to Priddis, a man of authority and power with a stone for a heart?'

'You were in an impossible position.'

'Yet I could have done more. I have always been weak.' He bowed his head. 'A week later a coach arrived, one of those boxes on wheels that rich people use. Priddis had told me people were coming to take Ellen to London. He said the best thing was not to tell her anything, otherwise she might become wild. Jane Wright persuaded me that was the kindest thing to do. Ah, I am too easily led.

'Priddis came early one morning with two men, big ugly ruffians. They marched into Ellen's room and hauled her out. She was screaming, like a poor animal caught in a trap. I told her it was for the best, she was going to kind relatives, but she was beyond listening. Such a look she gave me, she thought I had betrayed her. As I had. She was still screaming as the coach drove away. I hear her still.'

As I do, I thought, but did not dare to say. Seckford rose unsteadily to his feet. 'Another drink, sir? I know I need one.'

'No, thank you.' I stood as well. Seckford looked at me, something desperate in his eyes. 'Drink with me, sir,' he said. 'It eases the mind. Come.'

'I have travelled far, sir,' I answered gently. 'I am very tired, I must rest. But thank you for telling me the story. I see it was hard for you. I would not have liked to be in your place.'

'Will your client try to find Ellen?'

'I promise something will be done.'

He nodded, his face twisting with emotion as he went and poured another mug for himself.

'One last question, if I may. What happened to the Fettiplace house?'

'It was sold, as Priddis said it would be. To Master Humphrey Buttress, that owns the corn mill. He is still there.' The curate smiled mirthlessly. 'An old associate of Master Priddis – I'll warrant it was sold cheap. Master Buttress brought his own servants, and Jane Wright and the other Fettiplace servants were all out on the street. She died the next year, during the great dearth, she starved, and she was not the only one. She was old, you see, and had no work.' Seckford steadied himself on the buffet with one hand. 'I pray your friend will find Ellen in London and help her, if she still lives. But I beg you, do not repeat what I have said about Priddis, or the Wests, or Master Buttress, to anyone in authority. It could still bring me trouble. My vicar wants me out, you see, he is a radical reformer while I – I find the new ways difficult.'

'I promise.' I shook his trembling hand and left him.

✠

MY CONSCIENCE troubled me as I walked back down the lane towards the town. I wished I could have told him Ellen was alive, that she had had at least some semblance of a life before I brought fresh trouble to it. I believed there had been a rape on that long-ago night, as well as the fire. I remembered Ellen's words – *They were so strong! I could not move! The sky above – it was so wide – so wide it could swallow me!* And Ellen's dress had been torn and had grass on it. But who were the men who had done it?

Thinking hard, I was paying little attention to my surroundings. The lane ran between hawthorn hedges, and suddenly two men stepped from a gap and stood in front of me. They were in their thirties, labourers by the look of them. They looked vaguely familiar. One gave a little bow. 'Evening, master,' he said.

'Good evening, fellows.'

'I hear you've been cozening old tales out of our father.' Now I recognized the resemblance to Wilf in their thin sharp faces.

'I was asking about the fire at the Fettiplace foundry, yes.' I looked round. We were quite alone in the shady lane. I heartily wished Barak were with me.

'Been talking to old John Seckford too, have you?'

'Yes. Your father suggested it.'

'Father is an old gabblemouth. He's been full of theories about that fire for years, saying the verdict didn't make sense, something was kept quiet. We tell him it's all long past and he shouldn't be making trouble. The Wests are powerful people, they own the land we farm. Father doesn't know anything, he wasn't there. We thought we'd tell you, sir.' His tone was quiet, even respectful, but threatening nonetheless.

'Father said you were leaving Rolfswood tomorrow,' his brother added. 'Our advice is not to come back, and certainly not to talk to our father again.' He leaned forward. 'Or you might be found with your head broken. Not that we ever told you that, or even spoke to you at all.' He nodded at me significantly, then the two turned and disappeared again through the gap in the hedge. I took a long, deep breath, then resumed my way.

✟

I SPENT a troubled night at the inn. What had happened here nineteen years ago? Theories chased each other round my tired mind as I lay in bed. Could Peter Gratwyck have been one of the rapists? Had he and Philip West attacked Ellen and her father, then set fire to the foundry to dispose of the body? Had Gratwyck then run away? I shook my head. There was no evidence to support that theory, nor any other. But I wondered all the more whether murder had been done that night.

Priddis's involvement had been a shock. In two days I was to meet him in Portsmouth. And Philip West was probably there too. That was no surprise, for all the prominent officials of the region, and the army and the King's ships, were gathering in Portsmouth now. The King himself would be there in a week.

Tomorrow I would return to Hoyland Priory and its strange family. I realized I had scarcely thought about them since I arrived here. I tossed and turned, remembering how Seckford had described Ellen: like a poor animal caught in a trap.

✟

NEXT MORNING I rose early. There was one more thing I could do before I left.

I left the inn and walked up the main street. I soon found the house Goodwife Bell had mentioned. It was the largest, new-painted in blue, with diamond-paned windows and a doorway framed by posts beautifully carved with animal figures. I knocked at the door. A servant answered, and I asked if I could speak to Master Buttress regarding the Fettiplace family. That should bring him, I thought.

I was asked to wait in the parlour. It was a well-appointed room, dominated by a wall painting of Roman officials in togas, arguing outside the Senate. A large vase of summer flowers stood on a table. I looked at them, remembering what Seckford had said about Ellen bringing flowers to him. This was the house where she had been brought up, lived all her life until the tragedy. I looked around it, my senses heightened, but felt nothing, no connection.

The door opened and a tall, burly man with curly iron-grey hair entered, wearing a wool doublet with silver buttons over a shirt embroidered with fine lacework. He bowed.

'Master Buttress?' I asked.

'I am. I am told you have an enquiry about the Fettiplace family, who once lived here.' His manner was civil, but there was something both watchful and aggressive about him.

'I am sorry to trouble you so early, but I wonder if you could help me.' I told him my story about making enquiries for a friend.

'Who told you I owned the house?'

'I heard it at the inn.'

Buttress grunted. 'This town is full of gossip. I only knew the family slightly.'

'I understand. But I have been thinking. Mistress Fettiplace would have had to put her London address on the deed of conveyance when she sold the house. That might help me trace her. Unless,' I added, 'her sanity was an issue, in which case the conveyance would have gone through the Office of Wards, as it was then.'

Buttress looked at me narrowly. 'As I recall, she sold it herself. It was all done properly, she was past sixteen, of an age to sell.'

'I have no doubt it was, sir. But if you could be so kind as to find the conveyance, it would be a great help if I could find an address.' I spoke deferentially, reckoning that was the best approach with this man. He frowned again, then drew himself up to his full height. 'Wait,' he said, 'I will see if I can find it.'

Buttress left, returning a few minutes later with a document with a red seal at the bottom. He brushed the dust off with a sweeping motion and laid it on the table. 'There, sir,' he said stiffly. 'You will see everything is in order.' I studied the conveyance. It sold the house, and the freehold of some woodland, to Humphrey Buttress on the fifteenth of December 1526. Two months after Ellen had been taken away. I did not know the price of land round here then, but it was less than I would have expected. The address was care of a solicitor, Henry Fowberry of Warwick Lane, off Newgate. The signature above it, Ellen Fettiplace in a round childish hand, was nothing at all like her signature I had seen at the Bedlam. It was a forgery.

I looked up at Buttress. He smiled urbanely. 'Perhaps this solicitor is still in practice,' he said. 'You may be able to find him.'

I doubted that. 'Thank you,' I said.

'If not, your friend may be best advised to drop his search.'

'Perhaps.'

'Have you heard?' Buttress said. 'The King has just ordered the second instalment of the Benevolence to be paid now instead of at Michaelmas. Every man of means has to pay fourpence in the pound on the value of his assets.'

'I had not heard.'

'To pay the men and supplies for this great levy en masse. You will have seen much activity on the roads if you have come from London.'

'Yes, indeed.'

'If you are going to be away any length of time you should arrange to pay your assessment in London, or they will be after you.'

'My business near Portsmouth should only keep me a few days.'

'And then you will be returning home?' His hard eyes were fixed on mine.

'That is my plan.'

Buttress seemed to relax. 'I am a magistrate,' he said proudly. 'I have to help collect the payments locally. Well, we have to stop the French from landing, Pope's shavelings that they are. The price of grain is high, so I should not complain.'

'You are lucky if you have more coming in than going out this year.'

He smiled tightly. 'Wars need supplies. Well, I would offer you some breakfast. Better than you will get at that inn – '

'Thank you,' I answered. I wanted to learn more about this man.

' – but unfortunately I must leave. There is much to do at the mill. I am a man short, one of my workers was gored to death by a bull last week.'

'How sad.'

'The fool forgot to shut a gate and it went after him.' He smiled thinly. 'Bulls, fires, these rural parts can be dangerous places.'

✝

I BREAKFASTED at the inn. I received sour glances from the old woman who had introduced me to Wilf, and wondered if she had become suspicious of my close questioning of him and told his sons. I fetched Oddleg from the stables and rode out of Rolfswood, which was stirring into life on another fine summer's morning. I patted the horse. 'Back to Hampshire, good beast,' I said, settling myself in the saddle. And soon, I thought, to Portsmouth.

Chapter Twenty-three

BY THE TIME I rode once more through the gate of Hoyland Priory it was around four o'clock, the shadows lengthening. All was peaceful. A gardener was working on Abigail's flower beds. Insects buzzed and a woodpecker tapped somewhere in the woods. Two peacocks strutted across the lawn, watched by Lamkin as he sprawled under a tree. I rode round the side of the house, Oddleg quickening his pace at the prospect of returning to the stables.

I gave the ostler instructions to ensure the horse was properly washed down and combed. He was surly and uncommunicative like all the Hobbey servants. As I left the stables, a door in the rear wall of the enclosure opened and the huntsman Avery entered. He wore a green jerkin, green scoggers on his legs and even a green cap above his thin, deeply tanned features. He bowed. I walked across to him.

'Only – what – four days till your hunt?' I asked.

'It is.' Barking sounded from the kennels; the dogs had heard his footsteps. He smiled tiredly. 'Feeding time. They always hear me.'

'You must be busy now.'

'Ay. The dogs cause much labour – feeding them, keeping them clean, walking them twice a day. And more work in the park, making ready for the hunt. Master Hobbey wants everything just right.'

'So some in the village will work for him.' Avery smiled wryly and shrugged.

'How big is the park?' I asked.

'Around a mile each way. It was a deer park under the nuns, I believe. They used to lease it out to local gentry. But it has been allowed to deteriorate these last few years.'

'I wonder why Master Hobbey did not use it before now.'

'Well, sir, that is really his business.' A cautious note entered Avery's voice. Yes, I thought, he has been warned against me by the family.

'You are right, I apologize. But tell me, what will happen on the day of the hunt?'

'The guests and members of the family will take places along a prearranged route and the stag will be driven towards them. I saw the stag again yesterday. A magnificent beast.'

'And whoever brings it down will be entitled to the heartstone?'

'That's right.'

'Might it be Master Hugh again, I wonder?'

'It might be him, or one of the guests. I do not know how good shots they are. Or Master David, he is a fine shot, though he cannot seem to learn that you must keep quiet and hidden when you are tracking.'

'Is that why you are wearing green? To blend in with the wood?'

'It is. All the hunters will wear green or brown.'

'Do you travel the country organizing hunts, Master Avery?'

'I do now. I was in charge of a monastery hunting park until eight years ago. Then it was put down, the land sold off in parcels.'

'Which house?'

'Lewes Priory, over in Sussex.'

'Really? Lewes? The engineers who demolished Lewes for Lord Cromwell also took down a monastic house I had – connections with – just afterwards.'

Avery shook his head sadly. 'I watched Lewes come down in a great roar and cloud of dust. A terrible sight. Did you see this other place come down?'

'No. I did not wait for that.' I sighed, remembering.

Avery hesitated, then said, 'I will be glad to leave this place after the hunt. All the bad feeling with the village, the family hissing round each other like snakes. You are here to look out for Master Hugh's welfare?'

'Yes. Yes, I am.'

'He is the best of them. A fine lad.' Perhaps thinking he had said too much, Avery bowed quickly and walked away to his dogs.

☩

I WALKED thoughtfully past the outhouses to Barak's room.

'Master Shardlake.' I turned at a sudden voice behind me. Fulstowe had just emerged from the laundry building.

'You startled me, master steward.'

He gave his deferential smile. 'I am sorry. I saw you through the open doorway. You have just returned?'

'Yes.'

'Is there anything you need?'

'Only a wash and a rest.'

'I will arrange for hot water to be sent to your room. Some more letters have arrived for you, Barak has them.'

'Thank you. Is everyone in the house well?'

'Yes. We have had a quiet time.' Fulstowe's eyes quested over my face. 'Was your business in Sussex successful, sir?'

'It was – complicated.'

'We shall be leaving for Portsmouth early tomorrow, if that is convenient.'

'You are coming with us?'

'Yes. Master Hugh and Master David too. They are determined to see the fleet.' He smiled. 'Boys will be boys.'

'Near grown men now.'

He stroked his neat blond beard. 'Yes, indeed.'

'And now I will have a word with my clerk before I go in, see my letters.'

Fulstowe looked along the row of outhouses. 'I believe Barak is in his room.'

I smiled. 'You seem to know everyone's movements, master steward.'

'That is my job, sir.' He bowed and left me.

✝

I KNOCKED on Barak's door. He answered at once. 'Good, you're back.'

I looked at him curiously. 'Why are you skulking indoors on a fine afternoon?'

'I'm tired of that arsehole steward and his minions watching my every move. Jesu, you're dusty.'

'Let me sit down.' I sat on the straw bed. Two letters addressed to me lay there, one from Warner and one from Guy. 'Any news of Tamasin?'

'She wrote again the day we arrived.' He leaned against the door and pulled a letter from his shirt. 'Guy says she still comes along well. She is still determined the child is a girl. I miss her.'

'I know. Next week we shall be home.'

'I pray we are.'

'How have the Hobbeys been?'

'I haven't seen Hobbey or Abigail. They let me take my meals in the kitchen, apart from that they don't let me in the house. The boys were practising archery again this morning. Feaveryear and I joined them. Then Dyrick came out and shooed us off, said he needed Feaveryear and we should not be mixing with the young gentlemen.' He frowned. 'I wanted to put my boot up his arse and kick him all the way back to the house.'

'I would like to myself. But he would like me to lose control.'

'I felt sorry for little Feaveryear. He could no more make an archer than that dog Lamkin could. David mocks him, but Hugh was patient. I think he welcomes someone to talk to apart from David.'

'Feaveryear doesn't look as if he's had much patience from anyone before.'

'I have some news from Hoyland village.'

'Tell me.'

'I went there yesterday evening, sneaked out the back gate. They have a tavern there, and I asked for Master Ettis. Someone fetched him, we had a drink, then I went to his house. It's the best in the village. He leads the faction that wants to fight for their commons. I told him you work for Requests.'

'Will he keep it quiet?'

'Yes. I helped him draft a letter to the court. I said when we return to London you may take the case. If he would help us with information.'

'How did he react?'

'Said he'd cut my throat if I played him false. It was bluff: he told me after they have a spy in the house, who confirmed we were here about Hugh.'

I was about to open Warner's letter, but now I sat up. 'Who?'

He smiled. 'Old Ursula that worked for the nuns. They're furious angry, Ettis's people. Apparently Hobbey has not only been threatening to take half their woodlands under his interpretation of that old charter, but he's also trying to buy people out. Fulstowe has been offering a good price for the poorer cottagers' smallholdings if they'll go. And some of them have been given work helping set up this hunt.'

'Divide and rule. What is the mood among the rest of the Hoyland people? Would they take it to court?'

'I think so. Most are behind Ettis. They know that if the commons go down the village will die. Hobbey made a mistake by threatening to put his woodcutters on the villagers' woods, Ettis said. He's brought things to a head. Ettis thinks that was Hobbey's decision, by the way. Fulstowe has a more crafty approach. Ettis says he is the brains behind what's going on.'

'Interesting. What did Ettis say about the Hobbey family?'

'Nothing new there. David's a spoilt fool. Hobbey brings him riding through the village sometimes, and David raises a stink if some stiff-jointed old villager doesn't pull his cap off in time. Hugh they never see, nor Abigail. Ettis said Hugh goes walking in the lanes on his own sometimes, but he turns his head away and hurries past with a mumble if he meets a villager.'

'He is too conscious of his face, I think.'

'Some of the village women say Abigail is a witch, and Lamkin her familiar. Even the servants at the house are frightened of Abigail, they never know when she's going to start screaming and shouting at them. And apparently it's not true the local gentry shunned Hobbey because he bought the priory. It's rather that the family have isolated themselves. They never go anywhere, except for Hobbey making the occasional trip to Portsmouth or London.'

I frowned. 'What is it Abigail is frightened of?'

'I asked Ettis that. He had no idea. I told him too about that arrow shot at us in the forest. He was pretty sure we disturbed a poacher who wanted to warn us off.'

'That's a relief.'

'And I spoke to Ursula. I told her I was in with Ettis, and persuaded her to talk to me. She hates the Hobbeys. Said Master Hobbey told her off about leaving those flowers in the graveyard. Consecrated ground that's been left to rot, she called it. She said Abigail has always been high strung, with a sharp temper, but recently she seems to have withdrawn into herself.' He raised his eyebrows. 'Ever since she heard you were coming.'

'What did she say about the boys?'

'Just that David is a little beast. I got the impression she might know something more, but she wouldn't be drawn. She said Hugh is well mannered, but too quiet for a boy his age. She doesn't like any of them. I asked her if she saw anything the day Michael Calfhill came.'

'Did she?'

'Afraid not. That day she was working on the other side of the house.'

'Damn it.'

'This place is as full of watchers and factions as the King's court.'

'Yes,' I agreed. 'I spoke to Avery on my way in, he said much the same. He used to work at Lewes Priory. Cromwell had it demolished by the same people who demolished Scarnsea, where he sent me after his commissioner was murdered. And do you remember, during the Dark Fire business, that Wentworth household? Another family full of factions and secrets.' I sighed. 'Strange. I had one of my dreams of drowning last night; they always remind me of what happened in York, and the nightmare of the Revelation murders. Strange how the past revisits you.'

'I've always tried not to let it.' Barak looked at me keenly. 'What happened in Rolfswood? Something did, I can tell.'

I met his gaze. He looked tired, from the strain of living in this place combined with anxiety over Tamasin. I was tired too; tired of lies. I needed, self-indulgently perhaps, to tell someone about Rolfswood. So I told him about the fire, and all I had learned from Wilf, Seckford, and Buttress, as well as the threat from Wilf's sons.

'People are still scared of loose tongues nineteen years later,' he mused. 'What do you think happened?'

'Rape.' I looked at him. 'Perhaps murder. And tomorrow we go to Portsmouth and meet Priddis, who conducted the inquest. I don't think I should mention Rolfswood.'

'You think he may be linked to people who might endanger Ellen?'

'Yes. And Philip West is in Portsmouth too. I asked Guy to visit Ellen, and paid Hob Gebons to look after her, but still I fear for her. It is a nightmare tangle. If murder was involved, Ellen's safety has been only provisional for nineteen years. What if she has another outburst and lets out more of what happened? Whoever is paying her fees may decide she is safer out of the way. And if they can afford Bedlam fees and coaches, perhaps they can afford to find a hired killer too.'

'You shouldn't have started this, in my opinion.'

'Well, I did,' I snapped. 'I only learned about the fire and the deaths on the way here.' I grimaced. 'I swore to myself not to involve you. I am sorry.'

'For what? You're not going back there, are you?'

'I don't know.'

'I think the damage is done now, anyway,' he said bluntly. 'If this Buttress was involved in what happened I imagine he'd soon tell these West people someone was making enquiries.'

'Yes. I thought about it all through the ride home. I charged ahead without thinking, I was so keen to get information. I hadn't expected to find that conveyance was forged.' I hesitated. 'I have been wondering whether to try and seek out this Philip West in Portsmouth.'

'Having come this far perhaps you should. Leacon may know where we can find him. But be careful what you say to him.'

'Yes.' I realized that our roles had become reversed, Barak was the one advising me what to do, not to be impulsive. But he did not have my driving need to discover all I could about Ellen, to rescue her somehow. Through guilt for the damage I had done to her, through being unable to return her love.

I sighed, and opened my letters. The first was from Guy. It was dated 6 July, three days before, and would have crossed with the one I sent.

Dear Matthew,

I write on another hot and dusty day. The constables have been rounding up more sturdy beggars to send to Portsmouth to row on the King's ships. They are made slaves, and I think of that when Coldiron talks of English freedom being set against French slavery.

I have been to see Ellen. I think she has returned somewhat to her old self; she is working again with the patients but there is a deep melancholy about her. She did not look pleased when I came into the

Bedlam parlour. I had spoken first with the man Gebons, who was pleasant enough after the money you gave him. He says Keeper Shawms has told his staff to restrain Ellen and lock her away immediately should she have another outburst.

When I told Ellen you had asked me to come and see how she was, I am afraid she became angry. She said bitterly that she had been locked up because of you, and did not wish to speak to me. Her manner was odd, something almost childish in it. I think I will wait a few days then go again.

At home I have had words with Coldiron. I rise early these days and I heard him giving Josephine foul oaths in the kitchen, calling her a stupid mare and goggle-eyed bitch in front of the boys, all because she had slept late and not woken him as usual. He threatened to box her ears. I went in and told him to leave her alone. He was surly but obeyed. What pleased me is that as I told him to keep a decent tongue before his daughter I saw Josephine smile. I still ponder over that time I heard her swear in French.

Tamasin, by God's grace, continues very well and I am giving the post rider a letter from her, for Jack.

I put the letter down with a sigh. I was greatly relieved Ellen was improved, but her bitterness towards me cut deeply. She was right, it was my clumsiness that had done it. I cut the seal on Warner's letter. To my surprise he had already received mine.

Esher, 7th July 1545

Dear Matthew,

The rider brought your letter so I am replying early in the morning, before we move on. The King has brought a small retinue compared to a normal Progress, and we are to move as fast as we can. We travel via Godalming and Fareham, and will be at Portsmouth on the 14th or 15th. The fleet under Lord Lisle is now at the Channel Islands, watching to see when those French dogs sail, and to harry their ships. Then all our great ships will gather at Portsmouth for his majesty's arrival. It now seems certain the French will attack there. They have their spies, but we have ours.

I have had word from the man I sent to enquire about Nicholas Hobbey. I ensured he was discreet. Apparently Hobbey indeed suffered greatly through poor investments in the continental trade seven years ago, just at the time he was buying the house and woodland in Hampshire. He ended in debt to moneylenders in London. My guess would be he bought the wardship of those children in the hope he could bind their lands to his through marriage, and make illicit profit from their woodland in the meantime to pay his creditors. Sir Quintin Priddis I believe, even more than most feodaries, is known for corrupt dealing and would help them cook the accounts.

There is a strange piece of news from the Court of Wards. The senior clerk, Gervase Mylling, has been found dead in their records office, which I am told is a damp underground chamber full of vile humours. He shut himself in there accidentally some time on Tuesday evening, and was found dead on Wednesday morning, the day you left. Apparently he had a weak chest and was overcome by the foul air. I had to go to court on her majesty's business that day and all the lawyers were talking of it. Yet they say he was a careful fellow. But only God knows when a man's hour may strike.

Her majesty asks me to send you her good wishes. She hopes your enquiries progress. She thinks it would be a good thing if you were to be on your way back to London as soon as you can.

Your friend,

Robert Warner

I laid the letter in my lap and looked at Barak. 'Mylling is dead. Found locked in the Stinkroom. He suffocated.' I passed the letter to him.

'So Hobbey was in debt,' he said when he had read it.

'Yes. But Mylling – he would never have gone into the Stinkroom without leaving that stone to prevent the door closing. He feared the place, it set him wheezing.'

'Are you saying someone shut him in? They'd have had to know he had a weak chest.'

'I can't see him taking any risks with that door.'

'You're not suggesting some agent of Priddis or Hobbey had him killed, are you? And why would they? You'd seen all the papers already.'

'Unless there was something else Mylling knew. And remember Michael Calfhill? He is the second person connected with this case to die suddenly.'

'You were sure Michael's death was suicide.' Barak's voice rose impatiently. 'God's nails, if Hobbey has been defrauding Hugh over the sale of wood, it can't be worth more than a hundred or so a year at most. Not enough to be killing people for, surely, and risking the rope—'

We were interrupted by a knock at the door. Barak threw it open. A young man, one of the Hobbey servants, stood outside. 'Sir,' he said, 'Master Hobbey and Mistress Abigail are taking a glass of wine outside before dinner with Master Dyrick. They ask if you would join them.'

✟

I WENT TO my room, where I washed my face and neck in the bowl of water Fulstowe had sent up, then changed into fresh clothes and went outside. Chairs had been set out beside the porch, and Hobbey, Abigail and Dyrick sat there, a large flagon of wine on a table between them. Fulstowe had just brought out a plate of sweetmeats. Hobbey rose and smiled.

'Well, Master Shardlake.' His manner was at its smoothest. 'You have had a long ride. Come, enjoy a glass of wine and the peace of this beautiful afternoon. You too, Fulstowe, take a rest from your labours and join us.'

Fulstowe bowed. 'Thank you, sir. Some wine, Master Shardlake?'

He passed me a cup and we both sat. Abigail gave me one of her sharp, hostile glances and looked away. Dyrick nodded coldly.

Hobbey looked out over his property, his face thoughtful. The shadows were lengthening over the garden. Lamkin was dozing under his tree. In an oak tree nearby a wood pigeon began cooing. Hobbey smiled. 'There,' he said, pointing. 'Two of them, high up, see?'

I looked to where two of the fat grey birds sat on a branch. 'A far different scene from the stinks of London,' Dyrick observed.

'Yes,' Hobbey answered. 'How many days in my office there, looking out at the rubbish on the Thames bank at low tide, did I dream of living somewhere like this. Peaceful, quiet.' He shook his head. 'Strange to think they are preparing for war so near.' He sighed. 'And we will see those preparations tomorrow at Portsmouth. All I have ever aimed for is a peaceful life for me and mine.' He looked at me, real sadness in his face. 'I wish Hugh and my son were not so keen on war.'

'There I agree with you, sir,' I said. I was seeing another side of Hobbey. He was greedy, snobbish, probably corrupt, but he was also devoted to his family and what he had hoped would be a quiet country life. And surely he was not a man to arrange two murders.

'Vincent too had a letter today.' Hobbey turned to Dyrick. 'What news of your wife and children?'

'My wife says my daughters are fractious and miss me.' Dyrick gave me a hard look. 'Fine as your house is, sir, for myself I would fain be back home.'

'Well, hopefully you soon will be.'

'When Master Shardlake allows,' Abigail said with quiet bitterness.

'Come, my dear,' Hobbey said soothingly. She did not reply, only looked down and took a small sip of wine.

'How went your work in Sussex, Brother Shardlake?' Dyrick asked. 'Fulstowe said there were complications.' He smiled, demonstrating he was within the household's network of information.

'It is more complex than I expected. But so many matters turn out that way.' I returned his gaze. 'To have unexpected layers.'

'Some tenant dragging an unfortunate landlord to Requests?'

'Now, Brother,' I answered chidingly. 'I may say nothing. Professional confidentiality.'

'Of course. Why, this poor landlord may come to me for advice.'

'Master Shardlake,' Hobbey asked. 'Do you think you will have completed your business before our hunt?'

'I am not sure. I must see what Priddis has to say.'

Dyrick's face darkened. 'Man, we are surely done. You are dragging this out—'

Hobbey raised a hand. 'No arguments, gentlemen, please. Look, the boys have returned.'

Hugh and David had appeared in the gateway, their big greyhounds on their leashes. David carried a bag of game over his shoulder.

Abigail spoke sharply. 'Those hounds. I've told them to take them in by the back gate—'

Then it happened so quickly that none of us had time to do more than stare in horror. Both hounds turned their long heads towards Lamkin. The little dog got to his feet. Then his greyhound's leash was out of David's hand, flying out behind the big dog as it ran straight at Lamkin with huge, loping strides. Hugh's hound pulled forward, jerking the leash from his hand too. Lamkin fled from the dogs, running towards the flower garden with unexpected speed, but few animals on earth could have outrun those greyhounds. David's hound caught the little spaniel just inside the flower garden, lowering its head then lifting it with Lamkin in its mouth. I saw little white legs struggling, then the greyhound closed its jaws and the spaniel's body jerked, blood spurting. The greyhound loped back to David and dropped Lamkin, a limp pile of blood and fur, at its master's feet. Abigail stood, hands clawing at her cheeks. A terrible sound came from her, less a scream than a wild keening howl.

David and Hugh stared down at the bloody mess on the ground, which the dogs had started to pull apart. David looked shocked. But I had seen the tiny flicker of a smile as he let go the leash. Hugh's face was composed, expressionless. I thought, was this something they both planned, or only David?

Abigail's grief-stricken wail stopped abruptly. She clenched her fists and marched across the lawn, the hem of her dress making a hissing sound on the grass. David stepped back as Abigail raised her fists and began pummelling at his head. She screamed, 'Evil, wicked brute! Monster! Why do you torment me? You are no normal creature!'

David lifted his arms to protect his face. Hugh stepped forward and tried to pull Abigail away, but she slapped his arm down. 'Get away!' she screamed. 'You are as unnatural a creature as he!'

'Abigail!' Hobbey shouted. 'Stop, in heaven's name! It was an accident!' He was trembling. I exchanged a glance with Dyrick. For once we were in the same position, not knowing whether to intervene.

Abigail turned to us. I have seldom seen such anger and despair in a human face. 'You fool, Nicholas!' she yelled. 'He let go the leash, the evil thing! I have had enough, enough of all of you! You will blame me no more!'

Fulstowe walked quickly towards Abigail and took her by the arm. She turned and smacked him hard on the cheek. 'Get off me, you! Servant! Knave!'

Hobbey had followed the steward. He seized Abigail's other arm. 'Quiet, wife, in God's name quiet yourself!'

'Let go!' Abigail struggled fiercely. Her hood fell off, long grey-blonde hair cascading round her shoulders. David had backed against a tree. He put his head in his hands and began to cry like a child.

Suddenly Abigail sagged between Nicholas and Fulstowe. They let her go. She raised a flushed, tear-stained face and looked straight at me. 'You fool!' she shouted. 'You do not see what is right in front of you!' Her voice was cracking now. She looked at Fulstowe and her husband, then at Hugh and the weeping David. 'God give you all sorrow and shame!' she cried, then turned her back on them and ran past Dyrick and me into the house. There were servants' faces at every window. Hobbey went to David. The boy collapsed in his arms. 'Father,' I heard David say in an agonized voice.

Hugh looked expressionlessly at the greyhounds, their long muzzles red as they growled over a scrap of bloody fur.

Part Four

PORTSMOUTH

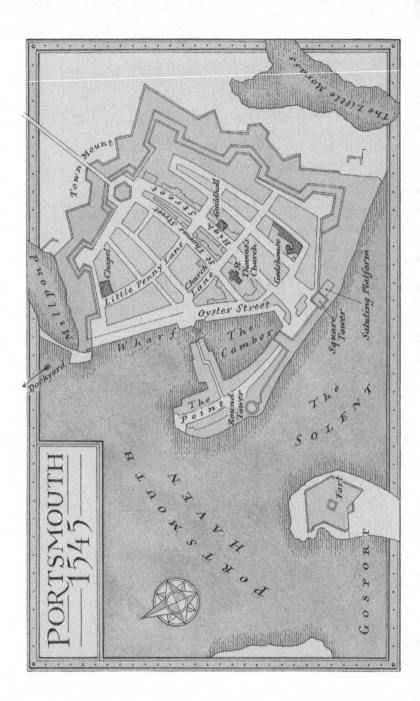

PORTSMOUTH
1545

The Little Moras

Town Mount

Millpond

Dockyard

Chapel

Little Penny Lane

St Thomas Street

High Street

Guildhall

Godshouse

Church Lane

St. Thomas's
Church

Oyster Street

Wharf

The Camber

Square Tower

Saluting Platform

The Point

Round Tower

The SOLENT

PORTSMOUTH HAVEN

Fort

GOSPORT

Chapter Twenty-four

AN HOUR LATER I was sitting in Barak's room.

'It was only a lapdog,' he said. 'Are you sure it wasn't an accident?'

'You didn't see David's smile when he let go the leash. Abigail is his mother, yet he seems to hate her, while Hugh treats her with indifference.'

'Hugh's greyhound attacked the spaniel too?'

'I think he lost hold of its leash. Abigail loved that dog. David couldn't have done anything worse to her. But what did Abigail mean, calling me a fool, saying, "You do not see what is in front of you"? *What* don't I see?'

Barak considered. 'Something to do with Fulstowe? He is such a haughty fellow, you'd think he owned the place.'

'Whatever it is, I don't think Dyrick knows. When Abigail shouted that out he looked completely astonished. Oh, in God's name, what is going on here?' I pulled my fingers through my hair, as though I could drag an answer from my tired brain, then groaned and stood up. 'It is time for dinner. Jesu knows what that will be like.'

'I'll be glad to get out of here tomorrow. Even to go to Portsmouth.'

I left him and returned to the house. The sun was starting to sink behind the tall new chimneys of the priory. A servant, supervised by Fulstowe, was wiping a patch of grass with a cloth; removing Lamkin's blood, that his mistress might not see. The steward came across.

'Master Shardlake, I was about to look for you. Master Hobbey asks if you would see him in his study.'

✝

HOBBEY SAT in a chair by his desk, looking sombre and pale. He had upturned his hourglass and was watching the sand trickle through. Dyrick sat opposite, frowning. I guessed the two had been conferring. Whatever the outcome it had not pleased Dyrick. For the first time I saw anxiety in his face.

'Please sit, Master Shardlake,' Hobbey said. 'There is something I would tell you.'

I sat. He said quietly, 'My wife has not been truly well for years, ever since poor Emma died. She has unaccountable fears, fantasies. Please discount her outburst earlier. I confess I have concealed how – how agitated she can become.' His pale skin reddened. 'Master Dyrick, too, was not aware of her – state of health.'

I looked at Dyrick. He frowned at the floor. Hobbey continued, 'Abigail loves the boys. But how strange she can be sometimes – that explains Hugh's distance from her. David's, too. This afternoon – I think she really believed David set Ajax on Lamkin deliberately.'

I stared at him. Had Hobbey not seen David's smile? I turned to Dyrick. He looked away and I thought, you saw it. I asked Hobbey, 'What do you think your wife meant, saying I was a fool for not seeing something before my eyes?'

'I do not know. She has – such fantasies.' He sat up and spread his thin white hands wide. 'I ask you only to believe she has never touched Hugh in anger, nor my son until this afternoon.'

I thought, that is probably true, judging by David's shock when his mother set about him; though, given what he had done, her reaction was hardly surprising. 'She said both Hugh and David were unnatural creatures. What could she have meant?'

'I do not know.' Hobbey looked away, and I thought, you are

lying. He turned back to me, the sad look settling on his face again. 'It is because of Abigail we mix so little with our neighbours. She does not want to see them.' He set his lips. 'But we *will* go ahead with the hunt.'

'I am sorry, sir, that she is so unhappy. The loss of her dog will distress her greatly.'

'Oh yes,' Hobbey said with a touch of bitterness. 'Lamkin had become the centre of her life.' He stood up, something heavy and reluctant in his movements. 'Well, dinner is ready. We must eat. And preserve appearances before the servants. Abigail will not be joining us, she has gone to her room.'

✝

IT WAS A sombre meal. Fulstowe joined us at table. For the steward of a substantial house to join the family at dinner sometimes was not unusual, but the way his eyes kept darting between Hobbey, Hugh and David, as though monitoring their behaviour, was strange. I remembered Barak saying Fulstowe acted as though he owned Hoyland Priory.

There was little conversation. I looked between them all, searching for something that was before my eyes but which I had not noticed before; there was nothing. David's eyes were red-rimmed and he looked crushed, somehow smaller. Next to him Hugh concentrated on his meal, eyes downcast and face expressionless, though I sensed the tension in him.

Towards the end of the meal David suddenly laid down his spoon and put his face in his hands. His heavy shoulders shook as he began, silently, to cry. His father reached across and took his arm. 'It was an accident,' Hobbey said gently, as though to a small child. 'Your mother will realize that in time. All will be well. You will see.' On David's other side, Hugh looked away. I wondered, was he jealous that Hobbey favoured David? But no, I thought, he does not care about any of them.

After dinner I went to Dyrick's room. I knocked, and his sharp voice bade me enter. He was sitting at a little desk, reading a letter by candlelight. He looked up, his thin face unwelcoming.

'Is that the letter from your wife, Brother?' I began civilly.

'Yes. She wants me home.'

'That was a horrible scene earlier. The killing of the dog, and Mistress Hobbey's reaction.'

'She didn't touch Hugh,' Dyrick answered sharply.

'She said some strange things. Calling Hugh and David unnatural creatures, saying I could not see something before my eyes.'

He waved a hand dismissively. 'She is deranged.'

'Did Hobbey tell you something, Brother, before he called me in? You seem worried.'

'I worry about my children!' he snapped. 'But what do you know of a parent's affection?' He smacked angrily at the letter. 'I should be at home with them and my wife, not here.' He glared at me, then said, 'I have watched you on this journey. You are a soft man, always looking for some poor creature to rescue. You dig and dig away at this matter, though you find nothing. You would do better to cease this obstinacy and go home. Look for another widow to chase.'

I stiffened with anger. 'What do you mean?'

'It is common gossip around the courts that you doted on Roger Elliard's widow after he died, and would bark and bite at everyone for months after she left London.'

'You churl, you know nothing—'

Dyrick laughed, an angry bitter laugh. 'Ah, at last I have drawn a manly response from you! Take my advice, Brother, marry, get a family of your own to worry over like an anxious hen.'

I stepped forward then. I would have struck Dyrick but I realized that was what he wanted. He had distracted me from my questioning, and if I assaulted him he would report it to the Court of Wards and I would be in trouble. I stepped back. I said quietly, 'I will not strike you, Brother, you are not worth it. I will leave you. But I believe you know what Abigail meant. Your client told you.'

'Leave this matter,' Dyrick said, his voice unexpectedly quiet. To my surprise his face looked almost haggard. 'Let us go home.'

'No,' I answered. I went out and closed the door.

✟

NEXT MORNING I rose early again. It was another fine summer's morning. The tenth of July, ten days already since we left London. As I dressed in my robes for my visit to Priddis, I thought of Dyrick's words the night before. Characteristically vicious, they had nonetheless unsettled me. But I was still sure Hobbey had told him some secret — he had looked worried ever since.

I breakfasted with Barak in the kitchen. Ursula was there, but apart from a brief nod she ignored us. We crossed the great hall to the porch, past the tapestries of the unicorn hunt, their colours shining brightly in the sunlight. I glanced at the representation of the hunters with their bows stealing through the trees. I wondered, would we be gone by the time of Hobbey's hunt on Monday?

'You're quiet this morning,' Barak said.

'It's nothing. Come on.'

The horses had been brought out, and I was pleased to see Oddleg had been fetched for me. Two young manservants were already on horseback; evidently they were to accompany us. Hobbey stood with Dyrick, bent over some papers, Dyrick's black robe shining in the sun like a raven's wings. Nearby, Hugh and David were talking with Feaveryear. Hugh, like Dyrick, wore a broad-brimmed hat. I went up to them. David flushed and looked away. I wondered whether he felt shame for what he had done.

'Ready for the journey?' I asked Hugh.

'Yes. Master Hobbey suggested David and I should stay behind, but I will not be done out of seeing the fleet. Master Hobbey has agreed that we may ride along the side of Portsdown Hill so we can get a view of Portsmouth Haven.'

I looked at the two young servants. 'They are coming too?'

'Gentlemen travellers should be accompanied, and Fulstowe is staying behind, to look after David's mother.' There was a touch of contempt in his voice. I thought, with unexpected anger, you do not care about poor Abigail at all. I turned to Feaveryear. 'Are you looking forward to seeing Portsmouth?'

'I do wonder what it will be like,' he answered soberly.

'We are ready, Master Shardlake,' Hobbey called.

'Ay,' Dyrick said in a biting voice. 'We must not keep Sir Quintin Priddis waiting.'

One of the servants brought the mounting block and helped Hobbey to the saddle. Then he fetched it over and Barak and I mounted. I settled myself in the saddle, patting Oddleg's side.

Then something odd happened. Hugh was about to mount. As he did so Feaveryear said, 'What will we see in Portsmouth, eh, Master Hugh?' and touched him lightly on the arm. There was nothing unusual in the gesture, though it was presumptuous given their difference in status. But Hugh thrust Feaveryear's arm violently aside, nearly toppling the skinny clerk. 'Do not touch me!' he said with sudden anger. 'I will not have it.'

He climbed into the saddle. Dyrick snapped savagely at Feaveryear, 'Don't ever do that again. Who do you think you are, you little booby? Now get on your horse!' Feaveryear obeyed, his face full of hurt.

As we rode through the gate I remembered Hobbey's deposition, the allegation that Michael had touched Hugh in a way a man should not touch a boy. And I thought, what if that were true after all? Could that be why he had reacted so fiercely just now?

⚜

THE ROAD was dusty, the sun already hot. We rode past the area where the foresters were still at work, then south, up a long, increasingly steep slope, towards the crest of Portsdown Hill. We passed one of the beacons that would be lit if the French landed; a long sturdy pole with a wooden cage suspended by a chain from the top, filled with dry kindling soaked in tar. A man stood on guard. I rode up to Hugh, who was at the head of our group beside Hobbey and David. I passed Dyrick, who still seemed preoccupied, his coppery eyebrows knitted in a frown.

I said, 'Thank you again, Hugh, for lending me *Toxophilus*.'

Hugh turned to me, his face shadowed by his wide hat. 'Do you think any better of it on reflection?'

'I agree he is a most learned scholar. I know little of archery, but I know that many worthy people praise it.' I had a sudden memory of the Lady Elizabeth sitting with Catherine Parr, her questions about the virtue and conscience of lawyers. 'But I still think that in the first part of the dialogue Master Ascham rather preened himself, as well as over-flattering the King. And I have read better dialogues. Christopher St Germain, now there is a writer, though he talks of law and politics.'

'I do not know him.'

'Thomas More, then. You have *Utopia*. With all his faults More never took himself too seriously.'

Hugh laughed. '*Utopia* is but a fantasy. A world where all live in peace and harmony, where there is no war.' He looked me in the eye. 'That is not the real world, Master Shardlake, nor one that could ever exist.'

'Strong words for a lad your age. You are too young to remember, but England had twenty years of peace till the King invaded France.'

'Listen to Master Shardlake,' Hobbey said tersely from Hugh's other side. 'He speaks true.'

David had been silent, but now he turned to his father. 'I have an idea,' he said. 'Perhaps in Portsmouth we can find a puppy, bring it back for Mother.'

'No.' Hugh turned and spoke sharply across Hobbey. 'She will need time. You cannot just replace a pet, any more than you can a person.'

David glared at him. 'What do you know about it?'

'You forget, fool, how much I know about mourning.' The cold anger in Hugh's husky voice was chilling.

'Perhaps later you can bring your mother a new dog,' Hobbey

said soothingly. Again, he spoke to David as though he were a child. I wondered if this was why David was so immature.

Just then one of the servants called a warning, and we pulled into the side of the road as two big carts rumbled past. They were full of boxes of iron gunballs. From Sussex, I thought, for the Portsmouth guns.

'We should try and pass them, in single file,' Dyrick suggested. 'Otherwise we shall be behind them all day.' We formed a line and rode carefully past the carts. I was behind Hugh. I looked at the back of his scarred neck and thought, I would give a chest of gold to know what goes on inside that head. When we passed the carts I rode up beside him again.

'Your friend the captain of archers,' he asked, 'will he be in Portsmouth?'

'I believe so.' I looked across him to Hobbey. 'Master Hobbey, after we have seen Sir Quintin Priddis, Barak and I will stay behind to seek out my friend.'

Hobbey inclined his head. 'As you wish. Though I warn you, Portsmouth is a rough place just now, full of soldiers and sailors.'

'I would like to meet your friend,' Hugh said.

'No,' Hobbey countered firmly.

'Perhaps you think I would take the chance to run away for a soldier?' Hugh said mockingly.

Hobbey turned on him, his manner suddenly sharp and forceful. 'If you ever tried that, I would have the authorities bring you back at once. You would look a fine fellow then to the brave soldiers.'

Hugh gave me a sardonic half-smile. 'Master Shardlake would help you.'

'Assuredly I would,' I agreed firmly.

We rode on in silence. The ground grew ever steeper as we approached the crest of the hill. We had almost reached it when we turned left. We rode along for a mile or so, through a little town, halting near a large windmill. We rode up to the crest of the hill and I drew in a long breath at the view.

Before us lay a complicated vista of sea and land. The hill descended steeply to an area of flat land cradling an enormous bay, the narrowest of mouths giving onto the Solent, the green and brown of the Isle of Wight beyond. The bay had a sheen like a silver mirror in the noonday heat. The tide was out, revealing large brown mudbanks. Directly below us, at the head of the bay, was a huge square enclosure of white stone that I realized must be Portchester Castle. Over to the west I could see another wide bay, more sand-banks.

Hobbey followed my gaze. 'That is Langstone Harbour. It is too shallow for big ships. The land between Langstone Harbour and Portsmouth Haven is Portsea Island.'

I looked at the wedge of land between the two bays. At the south-western end of the island, hard by the harbour mouth, I made out a dark smudge that must be Portsmouth. There were numerous ships in Portsmouth Haven. From here some were mere tiny dots but several which had their white sails up looked to be very large. The warships. At anchor out in the Solent there were many more, forty or fifty, ranging from tiny to gigantic in size.

'The fleet,' David said wonderingly. 'Gathering to await the King.'

'And the French,' Barak added soberly.

Hugh looked at me with a smile. 'Have you ever seen such a sight?'

'No,' I answered quietly. 'No, I have not.'

'Those out in the Solent are in deep water. There are many sandbanks there: with luck the French will not know where they are and will ground themselves.'

'They will have their pilots, as we have,' Hobbey observed im-patiently.

I said quietly to Hobbey, 'I had not expected Portsmouth Haven to be so large, or to see so many mudbanks.'

'Near the harbour mouth, there is deep water.'

'The whole fleet can get in if they need to, I am sure,' David said proudly. 'Then the guns on either side of the harbour will keep the French out.'

I looked along the long crest of Portsdown Hill, which I realized was part of the long chain of the South Downs. As far as I could see, all along the hilltops, a chain of beacons marched, each with a guard beside it. To my right, the beacons continued, past a large encampment of soldiers' tents.

'Let us go on,' Hobbey said. 'It is near four miles to Portsmouth. Be careful, the road down is steep.'

We began to descend, towards the island.

Chapter Twenty-five

WE RODE SLOWLY down the steep southern escarpment of Portsdown Hill. Ahead, two ox carts stacked with long tree trunks were descending the steep road with difficulty. We could not safely pass, so slowed our pace to ride behind them. I heard a clatter and turned. Feaveryear's horse had stumbled and almost pitched him from the saddle. 'Clumsy oaf,' Dyrick snapped. 'If I'd known you couldn't ride properly I'd never have brought you.'

'I'm sorry,' Feaveryear mumbled. I looked back at him, wishing that just for once he might answer Dyrick back.

Hobbey was looking at the fields of Portsea Island below us. 'There is some good growing land there, David,' he told his son. David did not seem interested. Like Hugh, he was absorbed in watching the ships, the distant specks in the harbour slowly becoming larger.

I said to Hobbey, 'Porchester Castle seems very large, but there are few buildings in the enclosure.'

'It is Roman, that is how they built their castles. It was the key to the defence of Portsmouth Haven till the silting up of the upper harbour isolated it.'

I looked down at Portsea island, a chequerboard of fields, the parts not under cultivation full of cattle and sheep. I made out movement on the roads, people and carts in the lanes heading for the town. I looked out at the Haven; sometimes trees and buildings hid the view but gradually I began to distinguish the ships more clearly. Several long, low craft were moving rapidly through the water, while four enormous warships stood at anchor; all were still like tiny models at this distance. I wondered whether Leacon and his men might be on one of the warships already. I could just make out a blur of movement along the sides of the smaller ships, like the scuttling legs of an insect.

'What are those?' I said to Hugh.

'Galleasses – ships that have both sail and oars. The oarsmen must be practising.'

We rode on, the road thankfully beginning to level out. It was another still, muggy day and I was sweating in my robes again. A bank of trees obstructed our view of the sea, but now I had a clearer view of the island. Several patches of white dots, soldiers' tents I imagined, were scattered along the coast. Next to the narrow mouth of the harbour the town was surrounded by walls, more white tents outside. There were large marshy-looking lakes on two sides of the town walls. Portsmouth, I realized, was a natural fortress.

Hugh pointed to a square white construction halfway along the shore. 'South Sea Castle,' he said proudly. 'The King's new fortress. The cannon there can fire far out to sea.'

I looked out on the Solent, remembering my voyage home from Yorkshire in 1541, all that had happened afterwards. I shivered.

'Are you all right, Master Shardlake?'

'A goose walking over my grave.'

✝

AT THE FOOT OF the hill the road was raised on earthen banks, passing over an area of marsh and mud with a narrow stretch of water in the middle spanned by a stone bridge. On the far side, where the land rose again, was a soldiers' camp. Men sat outside the tents, sewing or carving, a few playing cards or dice. On the bridge soldiers stood inspecting the contents of the cart in front of us.

'This is the only link between Portsea Island and the mainland,' Hobbey said. 'If the French were to take it the island would be cut off.'

'Our guns will sink their fleet before they land,' David said confidently. Absorbed in the view, he seemed to have forgotten about Lamkin, and his mother's attack on him. Yet there was something haunted in his face.

A soldier came up and asked our business. 'Legal matters, in Portsmouth,' Hobbey answered briefly. The soldier glanced at Dyrick's and my robes and waved us on. We clattered over the bridge.

We rode across the island, along a dusty lane between an avenue of trees. Hugh turned to Hobbey, unaccustomed deference in his voice. 'Sir, may we ride across and get a closer look at the ships in the Haven?'

'Yes, please, Father,' David added eagerly.

Hobbey looked at him indulgently. 'Very well.'

We turned along a side lane and rode towards the water. We passed close to a large dockyard where dozens of men were labouring. There were several wooden derricks and a number of low structures including a long, narrow one which I recognized as a rope-walk, where lengths of rope would be coiled together to form thicker ones, dozens of feet long if necessary. Piles of large tree trunks lay around, and carpenters were busy sawing wood into different shapes and sizes. A small ship stood on a bed of mud carved into the shore, supported by thick poles. Men were working hard repairing it. There was a constant sound of hammering.

A little to the south of the dock we turned aside from the lane and halted the horses by a mudflat next to the sea, from which a welcome breeze came. There was a smell of salt and rot, the mud spattered with green seaweed. Here we had a clear view of the ships across the water. Eight of the galleasses, sixty feet long and each with an iron-tipped battering ram in front and several cannon protruding from gun ports at the side, moved across the calm, blue-green water, smooth and fast despite their boxy shape. They were using both sails and long lines of oars. I heard the regular beat of drums marking time for the oarsmen. They made impressive speed. We jumped as one fired its guns, puffs of black smoke rising from their mouths followed by loud reverberating cracks. Then it turned round, astonishingly fast.

Dyrick gave it an anxious look. Hugh gave a little mocking laugh. 'Do not worry, sir, they are only practising. There are no gunballs in the cannon. No need to be afraid.' Dyrick glared at him.

'It is their manoeuvrability that makes them so dangerous to an enemy,' Hugh said with pride.

My attention was focused on the four great warships, anchored at some distance from each other in the harbour. Their sails were reefed now and they rode gently on the calm water. They were enormous, like castles on the sea, dwarfing the galleasses. A big rowing boat was tied to the stern of each, no doubt for transporting men and supplies from shore. It was an extraordinary sight, one I realized few would ever witness. The warships were beautiful, with their clean lines and perfect balance on the water. The sides of the soaring fore and after castles, and the waists in the middle, were brightly painted, the Tudor colours of green and white predominating. Each had four enormous masts, the largest rising a hundred and fifty feet into the air, flags of England and the Tudor dynasty flying at the top. The largest warship made my head spin to look at it; I guessed it was the *Great Harry*, the King's flagship. A massive flag bearing the royal arms flew from the aftercastle. I saw tiny figures moving to and fro along the decks, and other ant-like figures clambering in the mesh of rigging. High in the masts I made out more men standing in little circular nests.

David said, 'Those are the fighting tops. Your archers may go there.'

Even at this distance and on horseback I had to look up to see the topmasts. Hundreds of seagulls wheeled and swooped among the ships, uttering their loud sad cries.

'That men can make such things,' Hugh said wonderingly.

Two of the galleasses approached the *Great Harry*. With remarkable speed they turned side on, the oars almost ceasing to swing. The drums stopped. They held position as though about to fire a broadside at the great warship, then the drum sounded again; the galleasses wheeled round and shot down towards the mouth of the harbour. Other galleasses were making the same quick manoeuvres with the other ships. Practice, I thought, for when the French warships come.

David pointed eagerly at the second largest ship. It was the nearest, perhaps a quarter of a mile away. It had a long, high aftercastle and an even higher forecastle from which a long bowsprit, supporting meshed lines of rigging, stretched out fifty feet. At the bottom of the bowsprit a large circular object was fixed, brightly coloured in concentric circles of red and white. 'A rose,' David said. 'That is the *Mary Rose*.'

'The King's most favoured ship,' Hugh said. 'If only we could see them move. That must be astounding.'

On top of the aftercastle of the *Mary Rose* I saw a cage of what looked like netting, held in place by wooden struts. I wondered what it was.

Dyrick pointed to what looked like the ribs of some giant beast protruding from the mudflats near us. 'What's that?' he asked Hobbey.

'The ribs of some ship that foundered there. Those sandbanks are treacherous, the big warships have to be careful in the Haven. That is why most are outside, at Spitbank.' He shook his head. 'If the French come it will be difficult, perhaps impossible, to get all our ships in the Haven. At anchor they need two hundred yards to turn, I am told.'

'Just within bowshot of each other,' Hugh observed.

'There may be more dead ribs rising from the sea in a few weeks,' Feaveryear said sombrely.

'You're cheerful,' Barak told him.

'You joke,' Feaveryear said angrily, 'but war is ungodly and God will punish ungodly things.'

'No,' Hugh said. 'Our ships will deal with the French as Harry the Fifth did. Look at them — they are wonders, marvels. If the French come close we will board and destroy them. I wish I could be there.'

'Can you swim?' I asked.

'I can,' David answered proudly.

But Hugh shook his head. 'I never learned. But I am told few sailors can. Most would be carried down by the weight of their clothing.'

I looked at him. 'Do you feel no fear at the thought?'

He stared back with his usual blank expression. 'None.'

'The heartstone he wears protects him.' David said, a touch of mockery in his voice.

'How so?'

'It's supposed to prevent a stag from dying of fear,' Hobbey said wearily.

'Perhaps it does,' Hugh said.

I looked across the boys' close-shaven heads to Hobbey, who raised his eyebrows. On this matter we were on the same side.

✝

WE RODE UP to the town walls, joining the end of a queue of carts waiting to get in. I noticed a gallows a little way outside the walls, a body dangling from it. On a patch of slightly higher ground between the road and one of the large ponds flanking the city was another soldiers' camp, near a hundred conical tents. Men sat outside. I saw one man repairing a brigandyne; he knelt, sewing the heavy armoured jacket, which lay on the ground. Away from the shore the air was muggy again: most of the men had cast off their jerkins and were in their shirts. One small group, though, wore short white coats, each with two red crosses stitched on the back; some village had evidently put together a home-made version of the official costume.

Hugh and David's attention had been caught by a sight familiar enough to me now; a couple of hundred yards away mounds of earth had been thrown up to make butts and some soldiers were practising with their longbows, shooting at oyster shells.

'Come along,' Hobbey said warningly and reluctantly the boys looked away.

We approached the city walls. They were thirty feet high, surrounded by a moat-like ditch and to my surprise built not of stone but of packed mud. Only the small crenellated battlements on top and the large bastions set at intervals were of stone. Men were still working on the walls, some hanging by ropes from the top, piling up new layers of mud and stabilizing them with hurdles and wooden planks. The stone bastion enclosing the main gate was massive, its circular top bristling with cannon. Soldiers patrolled the fighting platform running along the top. Close to, Portsmouth seemed more like a hurriedly erected castle than a town.

We joined the end of a long queue of carts waiting to enter the gate, which stood on a little rise, approached by a bridge across the moat. This town was, indeed, a fortress.

'This earth wall is a far cry from the walls of York,' I said to Barak.

'It's part of the fortifications Lord Cromwell built everywhere along the coasts in '39, when it seemed the French and Spanish might attack together to bring us back under the Pope. They were cobbled together in a hurry. I know that it kept him awake at nights,' he added sadly.

'By heaven, this place stinks,' Hobbey said. He was right, a cesspit smell hung heavy in the air. He looked across to the tents. 'It's the soldiers, using the mill pond as a sewer. Pigs.'

'Where the fuck else are they supposed to go?' Barak muttered under his breath. I thought, he is right; the ordure had nowhere to go in the flat marshy land around the city. The foul odours would only get worse as time passed, threatening disease.

We all turned at the sound of a loud, angry animal bellow. Behind us a heavy wagon drawn by four great horses had pulled up. The sound came from an enormous, muscular bull in a heavy iron cage.

'There's going to be a bull-baiting,' I said to Barak.

'With dogs probably, for the soldiers.'

Looking ahead, we saw that inside the gate was a complicated enclosed barbican, and that a cart loaded with barrels had got itself stuck. More carts pulled up behind us.

'We'll be here for ever,' Dyrick said impatiently.

'Master Shardlake!' I turned as I heard my name called. A young man was running across from the tents. I smiled as I recognized Carswell, the recruit in Leacon's company who hoped to be a playwright. His mobile, humorous face was as tanned as leather now. He bowed to our company. 'You have come to Portsmouth then, sir?'

'Ay, on business. We have just seen the ships in the harbour. We wondered if you might be on one of them.'

Carswell shook his head. 'We haven't been out on a ship yet. We've been stuck in camp. Captain Leacon's around. I can take you to him, I am sure he would be glad to see you. You'll be a while here,' he added, casting an experienced eye at the men struggling with the cart inside the gate.

The bull gave another angry bellow, rocking its cage. One of our servant's horses reared and plunged, the man desperately trying to control it. People in the crowd laughed. 'Your horses will be happier if they wait beside the road till that bull is past,' Carswell observed.

Hobbey nodded, dismounted, and led his horse out of the queue. The rest of us followed, leaving a servant to keep our place. 'I think Carswell here is right,' I told Hobbey. 'I will go and see my friend, just for a few minutes. We are still in good time for our meeting with Sir Quintin.'

'A few minutes only, sir, please.'

Barak and I walked over to the tents with Carswell. This was a chance to see Leacon, ask him about Philip West. I had decided I was going to talk to him if I could.

'This place stinks, doesn't it?' Carswell observed.

'Worse than the Thames banks,' Barak agreed.

Carswell looked at me. 'You'll remember what you said about helping me, sir? When you get back to London?'

I smiled. 'I had not forgotten.'

'I yearn to be home – I hate this waiting, sitting amid this stench like pigs in a sty. We're not allowed into town without passes, and I hear the sailors must stay on the ships. They fear we might fight, or disturb all those merchants negotiating with each other to get the best price for our poor rations. But I am told much of a soldier's life is spent in waiting.'

'So you haven't been on a ship yet?' Barak asked.

'No.' For once Carswell's tone was serious. 'One of our men near fainted when he saw the ships close to – many of us had never seen the sea.' He laughed uneasily. 'Imagine trying to stage that sight in a play. The warships and those galleasses. They're manned by criminals and beggars, not strong enough for such work. Some collapse and die, bodies are brought ashore in the evenings.' His voice took on its jesting note again. 'Do you think, sir, if I brought you before our commander the Earl of Suffolk in your lawyer's robes, you might argue a case for me to leave the army? Say the prospect of danger does not agree with me?'

I laughed. 'Alas, Carswell, the powers of lawyers do not extend so far.'

We were in among the tents now, stepping over guy ropes. Some of the soldiers from the company waved or shouted greetings. Sulyard, sitting outside his tent carving something on his knife handle, gave me a nasty stare. Carswell halted before a large tent, the cross of St George on a little pole at the top. Leacon had just stepped out. 'Captain, sir,' Carswell called. 'A visitor.'

Leacon wore a round helmet, half-armour over his surcoat, his sword at his waist. The tent flap opened and I saw the Welsh boy Tom Llewellyn carrying a document case. Leacon's expression had been anxious, but his face relaxed into a smile as he saw us.

'Master Shardlake! Jack Barak!'

'We have come to Portsmouth on business. There is a hold-up at the gates, young Carswell saw us and brought us over.'

'Good! How is your wife, Jack?'

'Very well, according to her last letter.'

'George,' I said, 'there is something I would speak with you about.'

'About your steward who said he was at Flodden? I have some news there.'

'Have you? I would like to hear it. And George, there is someone else I seek, who may be in Portsmouth. It is important. A man called Philip West, who I believe is an officer on the King's ships.'

'Then he'll be here. Did you hear Lord Lisle's ships had just arrived? There was a skirmish near the Channel Islands. But listen, I must leave now, there is a meeting of the captains in the town: I have to join Sir Franklin Giffard there.' He turned to Llewellyn. 'I am taking young Tom here with me: many of the captains are from Wales and he knows some Welsh from his father.' He raised his eyebrows. 'Diplomacy.' The boy smiled nervously. 'Could you meet me in town later?' Leacon asked. 'Perhaps this afternoon.'

'Certainly. We have a meeting at ten, but after that will be free.'

'The Red Lion tavern for lunch then, say at twelve?'

'I should be pleased.'

'I will arrange for one of the officers I am meeting to stay behind to talk to you. He has an interesting tale to tell about good Master Coldiron.'

'What news of your company? How fare you, Llewellyn?'

'Well, sir. Though those ships fair affrighted us when we saw them.'

'Ay,' Leacon agreed. 'If the men are to go on them, they need to accustom themselves to being at sea. But those in charge keep arguing how best to use us, and nothing is done, for all they tell me how they value us as principal archers.' He sighed heavily. 'Come, will you walk with me back to the road?'

We made our way through the rows of tents. 'What news of the French?' I asked quietly.

He drew a little ahead of Llewellyn. 'Bad. Over two hundred ships gathering at the French ports, packed with thirty thousand soldiers. Lord Lisle encountered a host of their galleys off the Channel Islands last week. The weather turned bad, though, and there was no real action. We are going to need every man if they land here.' He looked at me seriously. 'Those galleys of theirs are large and fast, much superior to our galleasses, and rowed by slaves experienced in Mediterranean warfare. They have two dozen.' He gave me a sombre look. 'You know how many such galleys we have?' I shook my head. 'One.'

'When might they come?'

'A week, perhaps two. Much will depend on the weather, as always at sea.'

I was eager to talk about Coldiron, but saw Leacon was keen to move on. We were beyond the tents now. Then Barak pointed to where the men were practising at the butts and laughed. 'Look at that!'

Hugh and David, in defiance of Hobbey's orders, had dismounted and joined the archers. Hugh was bending to a longbow which he must have borrowed, and as I watched he sent an arrow flying. It hit the oyster shell, shattering it into a dozen pieces. The soldiers clapped. I saw Sulyard in the group, his enemy Pygeon standing at a little distance. A man at the other end of the range hurried up to the butts and fixed another oyster shell to the centre.

'Look at that fellow, sir,' Llewellyn said admiringly to Leacon.

Hugh handed the bow to David. David's arrow just missed the oyster shell and he scowled.

'Who are those lads?' Leacon asked curiously.

'My host's son and his ward.' I saw Hobbey and Dyrick talking agitatedly to Snodin the whiffler, who stood with hands on hips, an aggressive expression on his red face. Hugh bent to the bow again as we walked across to Hobbey and Dyrick.

'Get them away from there!' Hobbey was shouting to Snodin, more angry and agitated than I had ever seen him. 'Tell your men to stop their practice *now*.'

'But they have been ordered to practise,' Snodin replied in his deep voice, 'by Sir Franklin Giffard himself.' He waved a meaty hand at Leacon as we came up. 'Here, talk to Master Petty-Captain if you like.'

Leacon gave Hobbey and Dyrick a curt nod, then watched as

Hugh sent another arrow flying to the oyster shell. Again he broke it. Hobbey grabbed Leacon's arm. 'Are you the captain of this rabble? Get my boys away from those butts. They are defying my explicit orders—'

Leacon pushed Hobbey's arm away. 'I do not care for your manners, sir,' he said sharply. 'Boys they may be, but few enough adults could pull a longbow like that, let alone shoot so well. They must be very well practised.'

'They'd make good recruits,' Snodin said maliciously. 'Especially the taller lad.'

'You insolent dog,' Hobbey snapped.

Dyrick spoke up. 'Captain Leacon, we have an appointment in the city with the feodary of Hampshire. We shall be late.' He looked over to the gates. The obstruction had been cleared and the carts were going slowly in. The bull's cage was just entering.

'I think you had better call Hugh and David over,' I said quietly to Leacon.

'For you, Master Shardlake, certainly. You keep a civil tongue in your head.' He called to the archers. 'Cease firing! You two young fellows, over here!'

Reluctantly, Hugh handed the bow back to its owner, and he and David walked over to us. Leacon smiled at them. 'Well done, lads. Fine shooting.' He looked at Hugh. 'You hit the mark twice in succession, young fellow.'

'We practise every day.' Hugh was staring at Leacon with something like awe. 'Sir, will we repel the French?'

'*You* won't!' Hobbey, still angry, grabbed him by the shoulder. David flinched and backed away, a frightened expression on his face. So he had not forgotten about yesterday after all.

Hugh turned on Hobbey, his face suddenly red with fury. 'Let me go!' For a second I thought he might lash out.

'Hugh,' I said quietly.

To my relief, Hugh brushed off Hobbey's arm and walked back to the horses. 'Till later,' I said to Leacon. 'I am sorry about that.'

He nodded. 'Back to practice, Goddams,' he called to the soldiers. We remounted and rode up to the gates; Leacon and Llewellyn had already passed through. Once again we were asked our business by the soldiers on guard before we were allowed through. As we rode through the barbican into the sunlight, I heard the steady beat of drums from within.

Chapter Twenty-six

W ITHIN THE WALLS, Portsmouth reminded me even more of the interior of a castle. The town was surrounded on all sides by the earth walls, sloping gently down on the inner side, where turf had been laid to stabilize the earth. Much of the enclosed area was given over to market gardens, the town itself being surprisingly small. The street facing us was the only one wholly built up with shops and cottages, the better ones with jutting upper storeys. I saw only one church, down towards the seafront, with another signal lantern on top of its square tower.

'This is the High Street,' Hobbey said. 'We are meeting Master Priddis at the new Guildhall halfway down.'

The street was unpaved, dusty from all the traffic, the air full of the heavy, cloying smell of brewing. We rode past tired-looking labourers, sunburnt sailors in woollen smocks with bare feet, soldiers in their round helmets who must have obtained passes into the town. A well-dressed merchant, a fine lace collar on his shirt, rode along with a pomander held to his nose, a clerk riding alongside calling out figures from a list. Like many others the merchant kept a hand on the purse at his belt.

People were haggling loudly at the open shopfronts. I heard a remarkable babel of tongues among the passers-by: Welsh, Spanish, Flemish. At every corner a little group of soldiers, in half-armour and carrying halberds, stood watching all who passed. I remembered the corner boys. The town crier, resplendent in his red uniform, passed up and down ringing a bell, shouting, 'All women who cannot prove residence by tomorrow will be removed as prostitutes!' A drunk staggered into the road, swigging from a pigskin gourd. 'Join King Harry's navy!' he shouted. 'Six and sixpence a month and all the beer you can drink!' He tottered towards Feaveryear, who pulled his horse aside. 'Godless creature,' he muttered angrily.

'Don't you like a drink now and then, Feaveryear?' Barak asked teasingly.

'My vicar says to keep out of taverns.'

'Sounds like my wife.'

'Hugh and David put up a remarkable show back there,' I said to Feaveryear.

'I envy Master Hugh his prowess.' The little clerk sighed.

'I would not envy him too much. I think his life is no bed of roses.'

Feaveryear stared at me. 'No, sir. You are wrong. Hugh has been brought up well. He is strong, skilled and learned. A true gentleman. It is as my master says; you have no cause against this family.' He spurred his horse and pulled ahead.

✟

THE GUILDHALL was a large, brightly painted wooden building of three storeys. An ostler took our horses to some stables behind. Hobbey told David to wait outside with the servants until we returned, warning them sternly to stay out of the taverns.

'I suppose you want Barak with you,' Dyrick said.

'Yes, Brother, I do.'

Dyrick shrugged. 'Come then, Sam.'

We stepped into a large central hall. A wooden staircase rose to an upper floor. People passed busily to and fro, royal officials and townsmen in their guild uniforms. Hobbey accosted a harassed looking clerk and asked for Sir Quintin Priddis.

'He's upstairs, sir. In the room facing the staircase. Are you the gentlemen come to see him? I fear you are a little late.'

Hobbey rounded on Hugh. 'That business at the butts! Gentlemen do not keep each other waiting.' Hugh shrugged.

We walked upstairs. Barak looked round disparagingly. 'A wooden Guildhall?'

'There can't be more than a few hundred living here normally. The townsfolk must feel swamped.'

We knocked on the door the clerk had indicated. A cultivated voice bade us enter. Inside was a meeting room, sparsely decorated and dominated by a large oaken table at which two men sat, a neat stack of papers before them. The younger wore a lawyer's robe; he was a little over forty, his dark hair worn long, his square face coldly handsome. The elder was in his sixties; grey-haired, wearing a brown robe. He sat crouched, one shoulder much higher than the other, and for a moment I thought Sir Quintin Priddis was another hunchback. Then I saw that one side of his face was frozen and that his left hand, which lay on the table, was a desiccated claw, bone white. He must have had a paralytic seizure. As coroner of Sussex, this was the man who had ordered Ellen to be forced screaming into a coach. Reverend Seckford had described him as a busy, bustling little fellow. Not any more.

We bowed and raised our heads to find two identical pairs of sharp, bright blue eyes examining us across the table.

'Well, this is quite a deputation,' the older man said. His voice was slurred, lisping. 'I had not thought to see so many. And a serjeant, no less. You must be Master Shardlake?'

'Yes, sir.'

'Sir Quintin Priddis, feodary of Hampshire. This is my son Edward, my assistant.' He glanced at the younger man, without affection I thought. 'Now, Master Hobbey I know, and this well-set-up young fellow must be Hugh.' He studied the boy closely. Hugh put up a hand to cover his scars. 'You have grown much, lad, since last I saw you. But why do you keep your hair polled so close? A good head of hair suits a young gentleman.'

'I am an archer, sir,' Hugh answered unemotionally. 'It is the way among us.'

A sardonic smile briefly distorted the right half of Sir Quintin's face. Hobbey said, 'This is Master Vincent Dyrick, my legal representative. The other two are the lawyers' clerks.'

'I am afraid there is a shortage of chairs in this poor place,' Priddis said. 'I cannot ask you to sit. But we shall not be here long; I have a meeting at eleven that cannot wait. Well, Master Shardlake, what questions have you for me?' He gave me a cold smile.

'You will know this case well, sir—'

'Not as a legal dispute.' Edward Priddis spoke quietly and precisely. 'My father knows this as an ordinary wardship, in his capacity as feodary. He assessed the initial value of the lands and has dealt with routine queries from Master Hobbey since then.'

Sir Quintin gave his crooked, mirthless half-smile. 'You see, my son too is a lawyer. As I was at the start of my career. He is right, but you, Master Shardlake, you believe there is some reason for concern.' I looked into those bright blue eyes, but could read nothing of the man except that he still had force and power.

'Sir Quintin,' I asked, 'when you refer to routine queries do you mean the cutting of Master Hugh's woodlands?'

'Indeed. Master Hobbey has always thought these were good times to exploit the demand for wood. I advised him that would be legal if Hugh was credited with the profits. Exploiting a resource on those terms is not waste, rather a wise benefiting from market conditions.'

Edward laid his hands on the papers. 'There are notes here of my father's discussions with Master Hobbey. You are welcome to see them.'

'I am concerned that the amounts recorded in Master Hobbey's accounts may not reflect the amount of prime oak I have seen in the remaining woodlands.'

Hobbey looked at me sharply. Dyrick addressed Priddis. 'The woodland that has been cut had much less oak than that which remains.'

'You will have seen the lands before the woods were cut down, sir,' I said to Priddis.

'I remember seeing mixed woodland. But that was five years ago, at the first cutting. And travel through woodland presents difficulties for me now.' He nodded at his dead white hand.

'Master Hobbey said your son rides the lands for you.'

'That is true,' Edward said. 'And I am sure my father's assess, ment is right. However,' he added smoothly, 'we will be staying in Portsmouth a few days more, and can journey out to Hoyland. I have no objection to riding out with you to look at the lands. You can show me what you mean.'

And you can interpret it as you like, I thought, for there is no real proof; it is too late to do anything. But, if nothing else, I wanted to get to know this pair better, for Ellen's sake. Edward Priddis would have been around twenty at the time of the fire, I thought, his father in his forties.

Sir Quintin smiled. 'Good. I will come out to Hoyland with you. I could do with a day away from this stinking town. I can still just about ride, but I will have to rest at Master Hobbey's fine house. Well, Master Shardlake, you see how we make every effort to co, operate with the court. We could come next Monday, the thirteenth. In the afternoon.'

Hobbey looked worried. 'Sir, we are having a hunt on Monday. It has been planned for many weeks. It would be awkward—'

'Ah, the hunt,' Priddis said wistfully. 'I used to love hunting. Well, Monday is the only day I can come. I am due to set off for Winchester on Tuesday. We need not get in your way. The hunt should be over by three o'clock, I hazard.'

Dyrick spoke then. 'I see little point in riding through the remains of long-felled woodland to try and work out what sort of trees once grew there. And the Bill of Information that started this matter spoke of monstrous wrongs. But Master Curteys has no complaints, I believe.'

Sir Quintin turned to Hugh. 'What say you, lad? Has any wrong been done to you by Master Hobbey or his family?' I looked at the feodary. He was relaxed, he knew what answer the boy would make.

'No, sir,' Hugh answered quietly. 'Only that I am not allowed to join the army, which is what I wish.'

Priddis laughed creakily. 'So many avoiding their obligations, and here is a fine lad offering to serve. But, young man, your place is at home. And in three years' time, you will be able to sue out your livery and take your place as a gentleman with your own lands.' He waved his good arm. 'Take your hand from your face; I of all people have reason not to be put off by blemishes. Stand forth boldly! If one attracts stares, that is how one must react. Eh, Master Shardlake?'

I did not reply. Hugh lowered his hand, and Priddis studied him a moment more. Then he looked at Hobbey. 'The boy has a pleasant aspect, despite those scars. Is there a marriage in prospect?'

Hobbey shook his head. 'I am leaving Master Hugh free to choose whom he would marry. There is no one at present.'

Priddis looked at me severely. 'It seems, Master Shardlake, that you may have been sent on a fool's errand. Your client risks heavy costs when the case returns to Wards.'

'It is my duty to investigate everything.'

Priddis inclined his head. 'I suppose that is your prerogative.'

Dyrick spoke scathingly. 'I fear Brother Shardlake will be pulling up the floorboards at the priory to see if there are any mice that might bite Hugh.'

Sir Quintin raised a reproving finger. 'Now, Master Dyrick, I am sure he would not go quite that far.'

Edward Priddis murmured to his father, 'We must consider the papers on Sir Martin Osborne's case this morning—'

'Quite right,' Sir Quintin agreed. 'Thank you, gentlemen, I will see you on Monday.' He smiled at Hobbey. 'If your hunting guests see me, tell them I am an old friend who has called by.' He gave his little cackle.

We bowed and left. Outside, Dyrick rounded on me angrily. 'God's blood, Shardlake, why will you not let this go? You saw what Sir Quintin thought of it all. Are you out to embarrass Master Hobbey on the day of his hunt?'

'Calm yourself, Brother. You heard Sir Quintin, he will not advertise his business.'

We walked downstairs in silence. The clerk who had shown us up was talking in deferential tones to two men standing in the doorway of the Guildhall. Both were dressed in fur-lined robes and caps despite the July heat, and each had a fat gold chain round his neck. They turned, and I recognized Sir William Paulet and Sir Richard Rich. I was so shocked I stopped dead at the bottom of the staircase, so that Hobbey bumped into me from behind. Paulet threw me a severe look, but Rich gave a little snort of laughter.

'Master Shardlake,' he said. 'We will not eat you. On my oath, you are turned into a nervous fellow since your time in the Tower.'

Mention of the Tower brought the buzz of conversation among the people in the hallway to a halt. Everyone looked round.

'Your enquiries are still proceeding, Brother Shardlake?' Paulet asked coldly. 'You must have been here, what, a week?'

'Five days, Sir William.'

Rich gave his thin smile. 'Oh, Master Shardlake was ever a persistent fellow. No matter what trouble his persistence may land him in.'

'I act only within the confines of the law,' I answered steadily.

'So must all men,' Rich answered.

'I take it you have been seeing Sir Quintin Priddis?' Paulet asked.

'We have, sir.'

'Quintin Priddis, eh?' Rich's grey eyes widened with curiosity.

'He is the feodary of Hampshire,' Paulet said.

'I knew Sir Quintin when I was studying for the Bar thirty years ago. He gave me some interesting insights about the use of the law. Well, it is a small world at the top. And everyone of importance is heading for Portsmouth now. You should not be so astonished to see me, Master Shardlake.'

'I knew you were coming, Sir Richard. You passed us on the road last week.'

'I did not see you.'

'I was travelling with a company of soldiers.'

'Soldiers, eh? Well, I am in charge of finance for supplying the army, as I was in France last year. Making sure the merchants do not cheat the King.' He snuggled his pointed little chin into his fur collar, a courtier enjoying the display of power. 'Governor Paulet has been seeking my advice on security matters,' he went on. 'There is fighting between the soldiers and sailors who find their way to the city every night. If we could hang a few more—'

'We're short enough of men,' Paulet answered curtly. 'We can't go hanging the ones we've got. I'll speak to the officers again. Now, Sir Richard, the mayor is waiting within – '

'A moment, Sir William,' Rich said softly. 'I would have a brief word with my friend Shardlake.' He waved a hand at our party. 'The rest of you, go.' Barak hesitated, and Rich snapped, 'You too, Jack Barak. Always nosing around, ever since you served Lord Cromwell that lost his head.' Barak turned reluctantly and joined the others at the entrance.

'Now, Matthew Shardlake.' Rich stood close, I saw the heavy gold links of his chain, the smoothness of his narrow cheeks, smelt garlic on his breath. 'Listen to me, well and carefully. It is time for you to complete your business and hasten back to London. The King and Queen are at Godalming, they will be here in the middle of next week. My intelligence is that the King does not know you are Queen Catherine's friend. And if he did, and saw you here, he might be displeased with you again.' He leaned forward, poked my chest with a narrow finger. 'Time to be gone.'

'Sir Richard,' I asked quietly, 'why does it matter to you where I am or what I do?'

Rich inclined his head and smiled. 'Because I do not like you. I do not like the sight of your bent back or your long nose or your busy little eyes with their censorious look. And I am a member of his majesty's Privy Council, so when I say it is time for you to go, you go.' He turned away, his long robe billowing as he walked back to where Paulet stood watching inside the doorway. I went back to the others, my stomach churning. Dyrick looked at me curiously.

'Was that Sir Richard Rich?'

'It was.'

Dyrick laughed. 'I think he does not love you, Brother.'

'No,' I answered quietly. 'No, he does not.'

✞

THE OSTLER brought the horses round. There was little space to mount in the crowded street; one of the horses almost backed into a water carrier bent double under his huge conical basket.

'What did that evil little arsehole want?' Barak whispered.

'Not now. I'll tell you when we're on our own.'

Hobbey looked at David and Hugh. 'We shall ride down to the bottom of Oyster Street. We should be able to see the big ships anchored at Spithead from there. But then we will leave Master Shardlake to meet his friend and go home.'

'Could we not ride out to South Sea?' David asked. 'Look at the new castle?' There was still a sadness in his face; I thought, he seeks distraction.

'I have preparations to make for the hunt. And I want you boys back home. Apart from anything else, these scabby crowds will be alive with fleas.'

I wondered if the boys would argue further, but Hugh merely shrugged. David looked surly.

We rode on down the High Street, past the church, a solid Norman building with heavy buttresses. At a little distance I saw the walls of what looked like a former monastic house; tall, narrow buildings were visible over the wall, and the round tower of a large church.

'That is the old Godshouse,' Hobbey said. 'It was a monastic hospital, and lodging for travellers. It is being used as a meeting place now, and a storehouse for military equipment. We must turn here.'

We had halted in a broad space where several streets met. Opposite us the walls ended at a large square tower. Bronze and iron cannon pointed out to sea, the sun glinting on the bronze barrels. Some soldiers were drilling on a wide platform. Hugh and David looked at them with keen admiration. We turned right into a paved street fronting a little tidal bay almost enclosed by a low, semi-circular spit of land. 'That little harbour is the Camber,' Hobbey said. 'God's death, it smells foul today.'

'The marshy spit is the Point,' Hugh added.

'If we ride down to the other end we can see the ships across the Point,' Hobbey said. 'Come, let us get on.'

It took only a few minutes to ride down Oyster Street. The town wall continued along the eastern half of the spit opposite us, ending in a high round tower topped with more heavy cannon. Oyster Street was full of shops and taverns. Labourers stood outside, drinking beer. We rode carefully past soldiers and sailors, carters and labourers, and numerous merchants engaged in busy argument. At the far end of the street the circular spit of land ended at a narrow opening to the sea. Opposite the opening, at the end of Oyster Street, a broad stone jetty stood surrounded by warehouses. Goods were being carried in constantly from carts that pulled up outside, while other men brought out supplies and loaded them onto little supply boats.

We rode to the jetty, passing a group of well-dressed merchants disputing the price of biscuit with an official. Hugh's gaze was drawn by two labourers carrying a long, slightly curved box carefully to the jetty.

'A longbow box,' he said wistfully.

✝

WE HALTED a little beyond the jetty, where a walkway ran under the town walls. From here we could see across the narrow harbour entrance to the Gosport shore. There several more forts stood, mightily armed with cannon.

Hugh waved an arm across the wide vista. 'See, Master Shardlake, the harbour is protected on all sides by guns, from the Round Tower over to the Gosport forts.'

But my attention had been drawn by a sight even more extraordinary than we had seen in Portsmouth Haven – the forest of high masts in the Solent. Perhaps forty ships stood at anchor, varying in size from enormous to a third the size of the ones we had seen in the Haven. The upper parts of the bigger ships were brightly painted with shields and other emblems, and their decks all bristled with cannon. One large ship was furling its giant sails; a drumbeat sounded across the water as men laboured at the rigging.

Then, as we watched, an extraordinary vessel sped up the Solent towards them. Near two hundred feet long, it had only one mast. The sail was furled, and it was propelled by two dozen giant oars on each side. A large cannon was mounted at the front, and there was an awning at the back, decorated in cloth of gold that sparkled in the sun. There an overseer stood, beating time on a drum. I saw the heads of the rowers moving rapidly to and fro.

'Jesu, what is that?' Dyrick asked, his voice hushed for once.

'I heard the King had built a great galley,' Hobbey answered. 'It is called the *Galley Subtle*.'

I thought, according to Leacon the French have two dozen.

'Beautiful,' Hugh said quietly. The huge galley changed course, moving past the moored warships towards the mouth of the harbour, leaving a long ribbon of churning white wake.

'There, Shardlake,' Dyrick said. 'Something to tell your friends in London when you get home. Maybe the sight will be some compensation when you see my bill of costs!'

'*If* we get home,' Barak murmured in a low voice.

Hobbey turned his horse. 'Now, boys, we must go back to Hoyland.'

'Do we have to?' David asked.

'Yes. We can ride up one of the side streets, it will be quieter. Until later, Master Shardlake.' He looked at me steadily. 'And as Vincent said earlier, you saw what Sir Quintin Priddis thought of this matter. I hope and expect it will all be over on Monday. Come, boys.'

✝

HOBBEY AND his party rode away, leaving Barak and me on the walkway. 'It must be almost twelve,' I said.

'Let's get on, then.' The sight of all the ships seemed to have disturbed him. We rode back towards the jetty.

'Hobbey wants this hunt so much,' I mused. 'Yet Abigail said it is not safe. And we still have no clue why—'

He cut across me, his tone sharp, anxious. 'What happened with Rich?'

I told him, adding, 'It is odd he should be waiting there, just like at Whitehall. And with Paulet of all people.' I hesitated. 'And Richard Rich is one who could easily engage some corner boys to set on somebody.'

To my surprise Barak turned his horse round, blocking my way. It whickered nervously, and Oddleg jerked his head back.

'What are you doing?' I asked.

'Trying to make you listen!' Barak's eyes glistened with anger. 'I can't believe you just said that. You see Richard Rich and now you try to tangle *him* in this. The army is here, all the King's ships are here, nearly everyone important is coming here. Rich is on the Privy Council and Paulet is governor of Portsmouth. Where the hell else would they be? There is nothing to this. Hugh is safe and well and if Mistress Hobbey sees bogles under the bed, who gives a rat's arse?'

I was surprised by the force of his outburst. I said stiffly, 'I think Hobbey and Priddis have been creaming the profits off Hugh's woodland for years.'

Barak grabbed his cap and threw it on the dusty road in frustration. 'But you can't *prove* it, and Hugh doesn't give a shit anyway! And why in Jesus's holy name would Richard Rich care twopence about the affairs of a small estate in Hampshire? God's death, Mistress Hobbey is not the only one seeing bogles everywhere.'

Barak had been angry with me before, but never like this. 'I only want to ensure Hugh is safe,' I said quietly. 'And you have no need to speak to me like that.'

'You can surely see that he is safe. The little shit.'

'Why do you call him that?'

'Didn't you see him back there, calling that galley thing beautiful. Who were the oarsmen, eh? People picked up off the London streets, like those Corporal Carswell said are brought ashore as corpses. I was on the streets as a child and if I learned anything it was how damned hard it is for any human creature to cling onto this earth. Plenty don't, they get struck down by disease like Joan, or like my first baby that never even saw the light of day. But people like Hugh just want to bring more blood and death. But he's safe enough, living in that damned priory, waited on hand and foot.'

'He would serve in the army if he could!'

'Damn the army! And damn him! We need to get out of here, get home before the fucking French come and blow all those ships to fragments!'

I looked at him. My mind had been so concentrated on Hugh and Ellen that I had forgotten what was going on around us. 'Very well,' I said quietly. 'Unless I find some evidence of serious wrong-doing against Hugh, we will leave on Tuesday, after Priddis and his son have visited. Perhaps you are right. But I want to see what Leacon has to say about Coldiron and this man West.'

'You'd leave Ellen's matter alone too if you'd any sense. Who knows what you may stir up? But so long as we leave on Tuesday.'

I raised a hand. 'I said so. Unless I find this monstrous wrong Michael said had been done to Hugh.'

'You won't. There isn't one.'

Barak turned his horse round and we went past the jetty, back into Oyster Street. Two soldiers, unsteady with drink, shoved a labourer aside. He turned and let out a stream of angry curses. Barak pointed at an inn sign, the royal lion of England painted bright red.

'That's it,' he said. 'Let's get this done.'

Chapter Twenty-seven

BARAK FOUND an ostler to take the horses, and we entered the inn. The interior was hot, noisy, the floor covered with filthy straw. A group of carters were arguing loudly over whether hops or corn were harder to carry; a circle of Italians in striped woollen jerkins sat dicing at a table. Leacon waved to us from a small alcove by the window, where he sat with Tom Llewellyn and an older man. I asked Barak to fetch half a dozen beers from the hatch, and went over to them. Leacon had removed his half-armour and helmet, which lay on the straw beside him.

'A useful meeting?' I asked.

'Not very. They still haven't decided whether we are to be posted on the ships or on shore to repel the French.'

'Pikemen are more use on the shore,' the older man said.

Leacon clapped Llewellyn on the shoulder. 'Tom here tried his Welsh with two captains from Swansea.'

'I'm glad my father was not there to see me stumble,' the boy said ruefully.

'Now, Master Shardlake,' Leacon said, 'I have found your Philip West. He is assistant purser on the *Mary Rose*. And the ships' officers too are meeting this morning. At the Godshouse.'

'We saw the Godshouse as we rode in.'

'I will take you there afterwards. But first let me introduce Master John Saddler. He is whiffler to a company of pikemen here.'

I nodded to Saddler. He was short and stocky, with small, hard blue eyes and a lantern jaw framed by a short grey beard. I sat, removing my cap and coif with relief. Barak joined us with the drinks and passed them round.

'Now, sir,' Leacon addressed Saddler. 'Tell my friend what you know of that good man William Coldiron.'

Saddler studied me, his eyes coldly speculative. 'That's not his real name, if it's the man I knew. Though he had good reason to change his name. He was christened William Pile. Captain Leacon here has been asking all the old veterans if they'd heard of him. It was the description I recognized. Tall and thin, around sixty now, an eye out and a scar across his face.'

'That's Coldiron.'

'How do you know him, sir?' Saddler asked curiously.

'I have the misfortune to have him for my steward.'

Saddler smiled, showing stumps of discoloured teeth. 'Then watch your silver, sir. And when you return home, ask him what he did with our company's money when he deserted.'

'Deserted? He told me he was at Flodden and killed the Scottish King.'

Saddler laughed. 'Did you believe him?' he asked, mockery in his voice.

'Not for a second. Nor would I continue to employ him, for he is a lazy, lying drunkard, but I feel sorry for his daughter that came with him.'

Saddler's eyes narrowed. 'A daughter? How old would she be?'

'Mid-twenties, I would say. Quite tall, blonde. Her name is Josephine.'

Saddler laughed. 'That's her! That's our old mascot.'

'Your *what*?'

Saddler leaned back, folding his arms over a flat stomach. 'Let me tell you about William Pile. He was a Norfolk man, like me. We were both levied into the army for the war against the Scots, back in 1513. We were in our twenties then. William was at Flodden, that's true, but unlike me he wasn't standing on that moor as the Scotch pikemen ran down the ridge at us. William Pile's father was an estate reeve and got him a job working in the stores. He was well in the rear that day, as always. Killed the Scottish King, my arse.' He smiled coldly. 'And that's just the beginning. After the 1513 war, which got us fuck all like every war this King's made, we both stayed in the army. Sometimes we'd be with the garrison at Berwick, sometimes in Calais. Boring times mostly, hardly any action. That suited William, though. He liked to spend his days drinking and dicing.'

'So, you knew Coldiron – Pile – well?'

'Surely. Never liked the old shit, but I used to marvel at how he got away with things. We served together for years, I was promoted to whiffler, but William stayed an army clerk, no ambition beyond creaming what he could from the men's rations and cheating at cards. He'd no prospect of marrying, not with that face. Let me guess, he told you he got his injuries at Flodden.'

'That's right.'

Saddler laughed sardonically. 'This is what really happened. One evening in Caernarfon Castle William was playing cards. There was a big Devon fellow with us, six feet tall and with a vile temper when he was drunk, which they all were that night or William would have been more careful in his cheating. When the Devon man realized he'd been done out of a sovereign, he stood up, grabbed his sword and slashed William across the face.' He laughed again. 'God's nails, you should have seen the blood! They thought he would die, but stringy fellows like William are hard to kill. He recovered and came with us to France two years later on campaign.'

'I remember that war. I was a student then.'

'The campaign in '23 was a pathetic affair, the soldiers did little more than raid the countryside round Calais. Put a few French villages to the fire.' He chuckled again. 'Sent the village women running out over the muddy fields screaming, skirts held up round their big French bums.' Saddler looked up, enjoying my look of distaste.

'There was this one village, all the people ran like rabbits as we came down the road. We went in to see what we could take from the houses before we burned them. Don't look like that, master, spoil from stripping the countryside is the only money soldiers make from war. The French will take plenty if they land here. Anyway, there wasn't much in this dump to take back, just a few pigs and chickens. We were setting the houses afire when this little girl ran out of one, screaming at the top of her voice. About three she was. She'd been left behind. Well, some soldiers get soft-hearted.' Saddler shrugged. 'So we took her back to Calais with us. The company cared for her, shared rations with her. She was quite happy, we sewed her a little dress in the company colours, and a little hat with the Cross of St George on.' Saddler took a drink of beer and sniggered. 'You should have seen her, toddling about the barracks waving the little wooden sword we'd made for her. Like I said, our mascot.'

Leacon was staring at Saddler, his face bleak. I fought down my disgust at the man. He went on, 'Her name was Josephine. Jojo we called her. She learned some English from the men. Well, after a while the army was ordered to sail home, tails between our legs again. We were going to leave her behind, find someone in Calais to take her. But William Pile, your Coldiron, he said he'd take Jojo with him. He was thinking of retiring from the army and he would raise her to keep house for him. Maybe other things if she turned out pretty.' Saddler glanced at us, leering. Tom Llewellyn looked shocked. Leacon stared at Saddler as though he were the devil.

'Well, William did retire, but not in the usual way. As soon as we got back to England he stole the company's supply money and disappeared. Took Josephine with him. We were sent to Berwick afterwards and kept on short rations, the officers weren't going to put their hands in their pockets. Never heard of William again till now. He would have been hanged if he'd been caught.' Saddler crossed his arms, still smiling. 'That's the story. Did Josephine turn out pretty, by the way?'

'Pretty enough,' I answered coldly.

Saddler frowned. 'I remember that three months on short rations on the Scottish border. If you can get William Pile hanged that would be a favour to me.'

Leacon stood up and put on his helmet and gorget. Llewellyn followed. 'Thank you, Master Saddler,' Leacon said stiffly. 'Master Shardlake and I have someone to meet and then I must go back to camp. We are grateful for your help.'

Saddler raised his glass and smiled at me. 'Goodbye, sir. Remember me to Madame Josephine.'

✟

OUTSIDE the street seemed more crowded and noisy than ever.

'I'll walk to the Godshouse with you,' Leacon said. 'You may need my authority to get in. I don't have to go back to camp just yet, I just had to get away from Saddler.'

'I understand.'

'What did you make of his story?'

'It fits with what I know of Coldiron.' I smiled grimly. 'I have a hold over him now. I plan to kick him out, but keep Josephine on if she wishes to stay.'

'How does he treat her?'

'Badly. But she obeys every word he says. She believes herself his daughter.'

Leacon looked doubtful. 'Then she may not want to part from him.'

I smiled wryly. 'A meddler may make a worse muddle, eh?'

'That he may,' Barak agreed pointedly. Then he scratched his head fiercely. 'I think I've got lice.'

I shuddered. 'And I can feel fleas. That tavern must be full of them.'

Leacon smiled. 'You should get your hair cut, Jack.'

'Everyone in camp has lice,' Llewellyn added gloomily. 'And I've lost my comb.'

'You're not the only one,' Leacon said. 'I wish you men would remember to keep track of your things.'

Barak looked out over the stinking Camber. Beyond, the masts of the ships moored in the Solent were just visible. 'The foul humours of this place will bring disease before long.'

'Well,' Leacon said firmly, 'here we must stay till the French come.' He turned to Llewellyn. 'Would you go back to camp? Tell Sir Franklin I will return soon.'

'Yes, sir.'

I said to Barak, 'Go back with him, Jack, take the horses and wait for me in camp. I think it would be best if I spoke with Master West alone.'

'All right,' he agreed reluctantly. He and Llewellyn walked back to the tavern. Leacon and I continued down Oyster Street. Leacon said quietly, 'Saddler was on the Scottish campaign last year, he told me about all the plate and cloth he took from Edinburgh. But he is right, soldiers have always seen spoil as the legitimate fruit of war, waited for the cry of "Havoc!" Men like Saddler though – nothing they see affects them, they have hearts like stones. Thank God I only have one or two like that under my command, like Sulyard, who insulted you. When Saddler talked about those villagers running across the fields – ' He broke off.

'It reminded you of the woman by the roadside in France with the dead baby?'

His blue eyes had that staring look again. 'The strange thing is I didn't think much of it at the time. I saw so many things. But afterwards she and that dead baby would suddenly jump into my mind's eye. Let us change the subject,' he said wearily. 'It does me no good to dwell on it.'

'What do you know of Master West? Thank you for finding him so quickly, by the way.'

'We in the army are making it our business to find out about the ships' officers; we may be serving under them.' He looked at me seriously. 'What is this about, Matthew?'

I hesitated. 'A private matter. Legal.'

'Well, I am told West is an experienced officer, stern but fair with

those under him. When the French come he will have the hardest
test of his life before him.' Leacon looked at me. 'Is this a question
affecting his abilities as an officer? If it is, I should know.'

'No, George, it is not.'

Leacon nodded, relieved.

✟

WE HAD RETURNED to the open area in front of the Square Tower.
We walked on to a gatehouse giving entrance to the walled Godshouse.
A cart full of crates of cackling geese was going in, watched by soldiers
with halberds who stood guard. Leacon walked across to them.

'Is the meeting of ships' officers still going on?' he asked one.

'Yes, sir. They've been in a while.'

'This gentleman has a message for one of the officers.'

The guard looked at my lawyer's robe. 'Is it urgent, sir?'

'We can wait till they are finished.'

The man nodded. 'They're meeting in the great chamber.'

We passed into the enclosure. Inside was a wide yard, dominated
by a large Norman church surrounded by a jumble of tall buildings.
At the rear of the complex what had once been a garden was now
full of animals in pens – pigs, cows and sheep.

'I'll go across to the great chamber,' Leacon said. 'Leave a
message that someone wants to speak to Master West after the meeting.
See, there are some benches by the garden, I'll tell the clerk you'll
wait there.'

He walked away to the largest building, and I went over to some
stone benches set in the shade of the wall. I guessed they had been
built for patients and visitors to rest on and look at the garden. It was
not a restful place now. The cartload of geese was being unloaded,
the geese hissing and cackling as they were carried into a penned-off
area. Nearby some large wicker baskets had been piled up. The
brightly coloured heads of fighting cocks, brought no doubt for the
soldiers' entertainment, stared out angrily.

A few minutes later Leacon marched back across the yard. He

sat down beside me, took off his helmet with relief, and ran a hand through his blond curls. 'I've got those damned lice,' he said. 'This hair comes off today. Well, I've left the message. 'Look for Master West when they come out. I am told he is a tall grey-bearded man.'

'Grey-bearded already? He can't be much past forty.'

'He may be greyer yet before this is done.'

'What do you think will happen?' I asked quietly.

'It could be bad, Matthew. You've seen the fleet?'

'Ay. I never saw such a sight, even at York. Those great ships. We saw a huge galley rowing in earlier. The *Galley Subtle*, Hugh Curteys called it.'

'The boy who shot so well? He was remarkable. Yes, I heard the *Galley Subtle* was coming in. Much good it will do against the twenty-two Lord Lisle has reported the French have. Equipped with powerful cannon and rowed by slaves experienced in Mediterranean fighting. If they get in close, they could sink our big ships before they can fire on them. Our galleasses are clumsy in comparison. And the French have over two hundred warships; even if our ships get close enough to grapple with theirs we are greatly outnumbered. There was word today of our company going on the *Great Harry*, but nothing is certain. In some ways that would be good, for it is one of the few of our ships which is taller than the French ones. If our archers are up in the castles we would be able to fire down on their decks. Though if they have netting we would have to shoot through that.'

'I saw what looked like netting on top of the *Mary Rose* aftercastle as we arrived.'

'All the big warships have netting secured across the tops of their decks to stop boarders. If the ships grappled together, and French soldiers tried to clamber onto our decks, they would be caught on top of the netting. There will be pikemen positioned below the netting to stab up at them before they can cut through it with their knives.' He looked at me. 'It will be hard and brutal fighting if the warships do grapple.'

'Hugh said the guns in the forts will stop the French getting into Portsmouth Haven.'

'If the French manage to disable our fleet, the French galleys could land men on the Portsea coast. That's why there are so many soldiers posted along there. And if the French have thirty thousand men — well, we have maybe six thousand soldiers, many of them foreign mercenaries. Nobody knows how the militia will do. They are stout-hearted but little trained. The fear is that the French may land somewhere on Portsea Island and cut it off from the mainland. The King himself could end besieged in Portsmouth. You've seen they're preparing for a siege.'

'Is it really so bad?'

'Chance will play a big part. In a sea battle all depends on the winds, which the sailors say are unpredictable here. That could make or mar us.' He paused. 'My advice to you is to get away as soon as you can.'

I thought of Rich. 'Someone else gave me that advice earlier today.'

'There could be hard fighting on the beaches.'

'Do you think you will go there or on the ships in the end?'

'I don't know. But either way my men and I will fight to protect the people. Do not doubt it.'

'I don't. Not for a moment.' Leacon had placed his hands on his knees and I saw one was trembling again. He made a fist of it.

'Pray God it does not come to that,' I said quietly.

'Amen.' He looked at me. 'You have changed much since York, Matthew. You seem to have a weight of anxiety and sadness in you.'

'Do I?' I sighed heavily. 'Well, perhaps I have reason. Four years ago I drowned a man. Then two years after that I was nearly drowned myself, shut in a sewer with a madman. Since then – ' I hesitated. 'I am used to the Thames, George, but the sea – I haven't seen it since I sailed back from Yorkshire. It seems so vast, I confess it frightens me.'

'You are no longer young, Matthew,' he said gently. 'You are well past forty now.'

'Yes, my hair has grey well mingled with the black.'

'You should marry, settle down, have a quiet life.'

'There was one I would have married, a while ago, the widow of a friend. She lives in Bristol now. She writes from time to time. She is my age and in her last letter said she will soon be a grandmother. So yes, I begin to grow old.'

The sound of voices from the infirmary made us look up. In the doorway men in bright doublets were buckling on swords. Servants were leading horses round from the outhouses. Leacon stood. 'I will leave you now. I will see you back at camp. Take care.' He laid a hand on my shoulder, then turned and walked away to the gates. I watched him go, with his soldier's straight back and long stride.

✝

OUTSIDE THE infirmary two men were arguing, surrounded by a group of interested onlookers. One was tall and grey bearded, well dressed and with a sword at his waist; the other wore a clerk's robe. I heard the tall man shout, his voice carrying. 'I tell you, with three hundred soldiers as well as two hundred sailors and all those cannon she'll be overloaded! And what about the weight of all the supplies, if we're victualled for five hundred?' The clerk said something in reply. 'Nonsense,' the grey-bearded man shouted. The clerk shrugged and walked away. The other man detached himself from the group and marched across to where I sat. As he came close I saw Philip West was not only grey but half-bald. He wore a short jacket and a high-collared doublet with satin buttons, his shirt collar raised to make a little ruff in the new fashion. He halted before me. His tanned, weathered face was deeply lined, his expression strained. He gave me a puzzled frown. 'Is it you left a message for me?' he asked in a deep voice.

I rose stiffly. 'Yes, sir, if you are Master West.'

'I am Philip West, assistant purser on the *Mary Rose*. What does a lawyer want with me?'

I bowed. 'I am Serjeant Matthew Shardlake. I regret to trouble you now, sir, but I am trying to trace someone. For a client.' I studied West's face. If he was around forty now he had aged far beyond his years. His small, deep-set brown eyes were searching, his whole bearing that of a man burdened with responsibility.

'Who do you seek? Quick, man, I have little time.'

I took a deep breath. 'A woman from Rolfswood. Ellen Fetti-place.'

West's shoulders sank, as though I had placed a final, unbearable burden upon them. 'Ellen?' he said quietly. 'What is this? I have not heard of her in nineteen years. Then two days ago I saw Priddis riding in the town, or what is left of him. And now you come.'

'I have a client who is seeking relatives; he heard there was a family called Fettiplace in Rolfswood. I have come to Hampshire on business and I called in there.'

West was looking at me intently now. 'So you do not know whether she is still alive?'

I hesitated. 'No.' I felt as though each lie was drawing me further into a bog. 'Only that after the accident her reason was affected, and she was taken away to London.'

'Then you have come to me with this, now, for no other reason than someone's fool curiosity?' West's voice rose in anger.

'My client, I am sure, would help Ellen if he knew where she was.'

'And he is called Fettiplace? Does he not know others of that name in London? Does he know nothing of her?' He frowned, his eyes searching me hard.

'No, sir. That is why he seeks relatives.'

West sat down on the bench I had vacated, looked away and shook his head a couple of times as though trying to clear it. When he spoke again his tone had changed completely. 'Ellen Fettiplace was the love of my life,' he said with quiet intensity. 'I was going to ask her to marry me, despite –' He did not finish the sentence. 'On the day of the fire I rode over from Petworth to tell her father my intentions. I was with the King's court, which was on summer Progress at Petworth. Master Fettiplace said he would support the match if Ellen agreed. I had asked him to meet me in private, Ellen was not present. He agreed to the match. Duties meant I had to ride back to Petworth that night, but I planned to travel back and see her two days later, make my proposal. It is not a thing one wants to rush.'

'No.'

'But next day a message arrived at Petworth from the curate, telling me about the fire and that Master Fettiplace was dead.'

'Reverend Seckford? I spoke with him when I went to Rolfs-wood.'

'Then he will have told you Ellen refused to see me after the fire?'

'Yes. Or anyone else. I am sorry.'

West seemed to want to talk. 'Ellen liked me, I knew that. But I was not sure she would have me. She would not want to lose her precious independence. Her father allowed her too much.' He hesitated a long moment, then said, looking at me with haunted eyes that reminded me of Leacon, 'She was – wilful. She needed someone to master her properly.' He spoke with a sort of desperate sincerity.

'You think women should be mastered?'

Anger flared in West's face again. 'You presume, sir.'

'I apologize.'

He continued quietly, 'What happened to her, it broke me. I never saw her again. So I went to sea. Is that not what men do when their hearts are broken?' He gave a humourless smile, a rictus showing strong white teeth that seemed to split his brown face in two. He collected himself. 'Your friend should leave this be. Ellen was taken away to London, she may be dead by now.'

'I know Sir Quintin Priddis conducted the inquest, and after-wards arranged for her to be taken away. In fact I have business with him, in his capacity as feodary of Hampshire.'

'Have you spoken with him about this?' West asked sharply.

'No.'

'Then I advise you not to, and to tell your friend to leave this alone. There were things about that fire it is better not to go into, especially after all this time. Priddis did right: it was better Ellen was taken away.'

'What do you mean?'

He did not answer directly. 'How much did Seckford tell you about Ellen?'

'He told me her father indulged her, yes, but also that she was good and loving before the fire.'

'People outside families often do not see what goes on behind closed doors.'

I thought of the Hobbeys. 'That is true.'

West clasped his hands together, began wringing them slowly. 'Ellen was a woman of fierce moods and passions. She used to throw pots and vases at her father when she was angry.' He hesitated again. 'There were other things she did, too, that I learned of later.'

I felt a chill run down my back. 'What things?'

'When she was younger, if she was angry, she used to set fires sometimes out in the woods. One of my family's servants told me about it after the foundry fire – he knew one of the foresters.' West closed his eyes. 'So you see, sir, though I loved her I knew it was important she be not indulged too much. I can prove nothing, but I think that night when Master Fettiplace told Ellen of my proposal she became angry, and something happened. I do not know what.'

'You mean Ellen set that fire, killed two people?' I asked incredulously. 'How could a woman alone have done that?'

'God's death, sir, how should I know? I have never been able to puzzle it out. But two men died. So tell your friend to leave this matter alone. There are no more Fettiplaces in Rolfswood. Now leave me to try and save this country from invasion.'

West stood abruptly, gave me a final hard look, then turned and marched back to the infirmary building. Everyone else was gone now save for a groom who stood silently waiting, holding the reins of a horse. I stayed on the bench, my mind in turmoil.

Chapter Twenty-eight

I RODE BACK through Portsmouth with a head full of dark thoughts. It had never occurred to me that Ellen herself might have started the fire. Could West's hints be true? I had not liked him, he had a harshness and bitterness in him, but clearly whatever happened at Rolfswood had weighed hard on him ever since. My heart sank further as I remembered Ellen's words: *He burned! The poor man, he was all on fire — I saw his skin melt, turn black and crack!* That could be consistent with her causing the fire. But it did not prove it. And there were her other words: *They were so strong! I could not move! The sky above — it was so wide — so wide it could swallow me!* I remembered Reverend Seckford saying she had had a torn dress, grass stuck to it.

I was drawn back to the present by angry shouts in front of me. A dozen men, barefoot in the dusty street, sailors perhaps, had stepped into the road and were shouting insults at four foreigners passing on the other side of the street. They were barefoot too, dressed in patched, worn shirts and jerkins. A carter behind me pulled up sharply to avoid hitting the Englishmen.

'Fucking Spanish dogs!' one shouted. 'Can't that ape Emperor Charles even give you decent clothes?'

'Why should we serve with dirty papists? You're from that bunch shipwrecked in Devon last winter, ain't you, that the King took into service? You couldn't even sail a fucking ship properly!'

The four Spaniards had halted. They glared back at their tormentors, and one of their number stepped into the road facing the Englishmen. '*Cabrón!*' he shouted angrily. 'You think we wan' serve on your ships! Our *capitánes* make us!'

'Cappytanis! What's a fucking cappytanis?'

'I fight with Cortés in the New World!' the Spaniard shouted, 'Against the Mexica! Heathen dogs like you!'

Both groups were reaching for their knives now. Then half a dozen soldiers in half-armour, the corner guards, appeared and stepped between the two groups, swords drawn.

'Enough! You're blocking the King's highway!'

Casting fierce looks at each other, the two groups moved on. The soldiers waved the traffic back into motion.

I was now almost parallel with the Guildhall. Two men stood talking animatedly outside, both in lawyers' gowns, the elder resting his weight on a stick. Sir Quintin and Edward Priddis. I was not close enough to hear them, but Edward's expression was worried, a far cry from his air of cold superiority at our meeting. His father seemed to be trying to reassure him. Edward saw me and fell silent at once. I made a bow from the saddle. They bowed back, coldly and formally.

✝

I RODE THROUGH the city gate to the camp. The smell of urine and ordure seemed stronger than ever. A queue waited outside a barber's tent; the men who came out were close shaved, their hair cropped. Nearby a group had formed a ring around two soldiers, stripped to the waist, who were wrestling. I saw Barak among those watching, standing beside Carswell. Both had been shaved and Carswell's hair was cut to a short fuzz like Hugh and David's. I dismounted and led the horse over to them.

'What did this West have to say?' Barak asked curtly. I could tell he was still angry with me.

'Something that shook me. I'll tell you later.' I turned to Carswell. 'We should return to Hoyland now. I would like to say farewell to Captain Leacon. Do you know where he is?'

'Talking with Sir Franklin in his tent. I don't think they'll be long.'

I looked at the wrestlers. One was a big stocky fellow in his twenties, the other, I saw, was Tom Llewellyn. He had a powerful chest and shoulders for one so young. As I watched Llewellyn managed to throw his opponent on the ground, where he lay panting. Some cheered, others looked morose. Many had the big leather pouches in which they carried their belongings at their waists, and various small items were taken out and handed over. Carswell's neighbour gave him a double-sided nit comb, the thin side black with dead lice, and a tiny bone spoon.

'What's that?' I asked, pointing to the spoon.

'Ear-wax scoop,' Carswell answered cheerfully. 'Useful stuff for waxing your bows.' He threw a cloth to Llewellyn, who wiped his sweating chest. 'Well done, lad.'

'See who's next,' Barak murmured. 'This should be interesting.' I saw that Sulyard and Pygeon had stepped into the ring. They glared at each other as they removed jerkins and shirts. Sulyard was bigger, and his body looked to have a raw-boned strength; but Pygeon, though stringy, had not an ounce of fat on him. Sulyard put his hands on his hips and turned to the crowd. 'We won't be long – those who've put bets on lop-ears get ready to lose your stakes!'

Pygeon did not reply, only stared at Sulyard. He shook his arms to loosen them, then shifted his weight from foot to foot to get his balance. He was taking this seriously. Sulyard grinned at him. 'We should have our own bet, lop-ears,' he said loudly. 'Tell you what, if I win I'll have that rosary you use to say Hail Mary on the quiet. His family are our village recusants, lads!'

'And if I win,' Pygeon shouted, 'I'll have your brigandyne.'

Sulyard looked taken aback. Several in the crowd laughed. Some-one shouted, 'Take the bet, Sulyard, as you're so sure of winning.'

Barak said to Carswell, 'Bet you a half groat Sulyard wins.'

'Done.'

The fight went on for ten minutes, Sulyard's thrusting power against Pygeon's unexpected strength. I realized Pygeon meant to tire Sulyard out. Slowly the camp bully weakened. In the end Pygeon put him down, not with a throw but with a steady, powerful movement that made his stringy muscles stand out. The taller man's legs buckled, and then Sulyard was on the ground, panting heavily. Pygeon smiled, savouring his triumph.

'Shake hands and share a loving cup!' Carswell called out.

Pygeon looked down at Sulyard. 'Fetch the brigandyne to me when you are recovered, *Master.*' He picked up his clothes and walked away. The gamblers who had lost — most of them — reached ruefully for their bags. Barak paid over the half groat. I saw that Leacon had come out of his tent, accompanied by Sir Franklin and Snodin. They stood talking.

'Come, Jack,' I said, 'the afternoon wears on. We must say farewell to Leacon and return to Hoyland.'

Barak raised a hand to the soldiers. 'Farewell, lads, I must return my master to our gracious hosts!'

'You're picking up Carswell's style of humour,' I told him as we walked away.

'No, 'tis my own.'

As we approached Leacon I saw he too had had a barbering. The whiffler Snodin was talking loudly and angrily, 'Milk bellies that can't do without beds. Simpering, mumping weaklings—'

'All right, Snodin,' Sir Franklin said testily. He stared at me as I approached. 'Sir Franklin, I am sorry to interrupt, but I would say goodbye to Master Leacon—'

Sir Franklin waved a hand impatiently. 'A moment. Snodin, send a message about the deserters to Sir William Paulet. He must alert the shires to look for them.'

'Yes, Sir Franklin. The fools,' Snodin burst out with sudden emotion. 'Why did they do it? I trained those men, I know them.' He looked at Sir Franklin. 'Will they hang if they're caught?'

'The King has ordered every deserter to be hanged.'

The whiffler shook his head, bowed and walked off. 'Deserters,' Leacon told me. 'Two went last night.'

'They'll be caught if they return home.'

Barak and I exchanged glances. If we had followed Alderman Carver's advice, Barak would have been a deserter. Leacon shook his head sadly. 'Poor fools. It will be a public hanging if they're caught. All the companies are below strength now. As are the ships – they say the West Country is stripped of fishermen, the women are having to take the boats out.'

'I saw some Spanish sailors in town.'

'They'll take any foreigner that can sail, save French and Scots.'

Even more with his head shaven Leacon looked, like West, far older than his years. Yet West's eyes had been clear and sharp, while Leacon's had that vacant, staring look again. 'George,' I said quietly, 'I fear we must leave you now.'

He nodded. 'Will you be coming back to Portsmouth?'

'I think not. We return to London on Tuesday.' I put out my hand. 'But my prayers, for what they are worth, go with you and your men. And I hope we may meet once more in London, in happier days. Bring Carswell, I will find him a company of actors.'

'Happier days. Yes, I long for those.'

✝

BARAK SEEMED to have got over our argument, perhaps because of the reminder about deserters. As we rode back across Portsea Island, I told him what had passed with West.

'So Ellen could have done it herself.'

'If West is to be believed.'

'Is he?'

'I don't know. If he was responsible for the attack on Ellen, he has a strong motive for saying something likely to make me – or at least, my imaginary client – drop the matter.' I looked at him. 'But do not worry, we will go back on Tuesday as I said. I have no power here, I cannot compel anyone to answer my questions. Least of all Priddis, the one man who could give me information. But back in London,' I added grimly, 'there could be ways of bringing pressure.'

'The Queen?'

'Maybe. When she returns from Portsmouth.'

'And what of Hugh?'

I sighed heavily. 'Unless Priddis's visit produces something, I have no evidence even that there has been fraud. I cannot in good faith incur more costs.'

'I'm glad you are seeing sense,' he said.

We were forced to pull aside from the road by a long line of carts rumbling past, well guarded by soldiers. They were covered with tarpaulins, but protruding from the carts' tails I saw piles of thick fabric, decorated with elaborate, colourful designs in cloth of gold. Barak looked at me. 'Are they – ?'

'They look like the royal tents we saw at York.'

Cart after cart rumbled by, heading not for the town but towards the sea.

'Is the King going to set up camp on the coast?' Barak asked incredulously.

'It looks like it. So he's going to come right to the front line. Well, he never lacked courage.'

'Even if they land, the French could never hold England.'

'The Normans did. You're right, though, the people would resist hard. But if there's a chance of bringing us back to Rome the Pope will jump behind the French if they gain a foothold. Emperor Charles too perhaps. God's death,' I burst out angrily, 'has there ever been such a tangle?'

'Lord Cromwell would have been seeking a way out. But the King won't do that.'

'Never. He'll see England drowned in blood first.'

'Well,' Barak said more cheerfully, 'at least back in London you can do something about Coldiron. Thank you,' he said, 'for agreeing to go back.'

I nodded in acknowledgement. 'You worry about Tamasin, don't you?'

'All the time,' he said with feeling.

We rode on, towards Portsdown Hill.

Chapter Twenty-nine

WE ARRIVED AT Hoyland towards seven, exhausted. I washed and combed myself thoroughly to rid myself of the fleas and lice I had picked up, then lay on my bed thinking about Ellen and Hugh. I could see no way out of either impasse.

I was so tired I slept deeply that night. The next day passed peacefully enough. At meals Abigail barely spoke; she seemed listless, defeated. Dyrick was his usual sharp, aggressive self. Hobbey was guarded, Hugh civil enough, seeming indifferent now to my presence. David, though, was in a strange mood, quiet and restive. A couple of times I caught Fulstowe casting sharp looks at the boy. During the day everyone except Abigail was out, making final preparations for the hunt.

In the afternoon I took a walk in the grounds to try and clear my head, for I thought endlessly of Ellen and who could have started that fire, my mind fairly spinning with it all. In Abigail's garden the flowers drooped in the endless sultry heat.

✟

THAT EVENING came the first of the events that was to change the life of the Hobbey family for ever.

I was sitting at the table in my chamber, trying to work out the costs that might be awarded against us at the next hearing. They were considerable. The light was beginning to fail. I was vaguely aware that outside the boys were at the butts again, I could hear them through the open shutters. Then I heard a sudden anguished cry. 'No!'

I rose and looked out of the window. To my amazement Feaver-year was running across the lawn. Hugh and David stood looking at

362

him, too far away for me to make out their expressions. Feaveryear ran as though the devil were after him. He disappeared from view, then I heard running footsteps on the stairs, and a frantic knocking on Dyrick's door.

✝

THE FOLLOWING MORNING, yet another hot, close July day, we all walked to church. Hobbey led the little procession. Abigail was on his arm, in her best clothes but with her head cast down. Then came Dyrick, Barak and I, followed by Fulstowe at the head of the servants. Barak had not wished to go but I had roused him out, saying we should give no cause for criticism. To my surprise, though, Feaveryear was absent.

'Is young Feaveryear unwell?' I asked Dyrick. He had been frowning to himself, preoccupied.

He gave me a sharp, sidelong look. 'I've sent him back to London. There was a letter waiting when we returned from Portsmouth, about a case. I sent him back to deal with it early this morning. There's no point us both wasting our time here,' he said, as ever making a point against me.

'We have had no letters. Barak hoped there might be one from his wife.'

'It came by special messenger from London. It concerns an important case.'

'I thought I saw Feaveryear running across the lawn last night.'

He gave me another sharp look. 'I had called him.'

It was a long walk to the church in the neighbouring village of Okedean. Long too, on their one day of rest, for the Hoyland villagers we passed, who had used the priory church when the nuns were there. Ettis, a pretty wife and three children at his side, crossed our path at the end of a country lane. He bowed and stood aside to let us pass. Abigail gave him a look of hatred.

✝

OKEDEAN CHURCH was small, crowded with the people of both villages. Here, as in Reverend Seckford's church, they evidently cleaved as much as possible to the old ways, the church smelling heavily of incense, saints still in their niches. I wondered what Hugh's parents, the reformers, would have made of it. Hobbey, Dyrick and I took places at the front of the congregation in accordance with our rank, next to a stocky, middle-aged man and his haughty-looking wife, whom Hobbey introduced to us as the owner of the neighbour-ing manor, Sir Luke and Lady Corembeck. Sir Luke, Hobbey said proudly, was a justice of the peace who would be attending his hunt tomorrow. For the first time I heard deference in his voice.

The vicar gave a sermon calling on all to pray and work for the defence of the country, for the men to attend practice with the local militia. I looked at the Doom painting behind him, Christ on a throne in judgement, his face serene, angels guiding the virtuous to heaven while below the pale and naked sinners tumbled into a lake of fire. I remembered Feaveryear saying soldiers and sailors who died in battle without finding salvation must end in Hell. What had he been running from last night? Where was he?

After the service Hobbey paused for some more words with Sir Luke in the doorway, the servants and villagers walking past us. Lady Corembeck addressed Abigail a couple of times, but she answered in monosyllables, sunk in apathy. At length Hobbey parted from the Corembecks with much bowing, and we walked down the path to the lych gate. Then we saw that a group of about thirty Hoyland villagers were waiting just outside the church, whole families blocking our way. Ettis was at their head. I heard a sharp intake of breath from Hobbey.

Ettis walked over to stand boldly in front of him, his square face set hard. Fulstowe stepped to Hobbey's side and put his hand to his dagger.

'No need for that, Master Fulstowe,' Ettis said quietly. 'I want only to say something to your master.' He indicated the villagers behind him. 'See those people, Master Hobbey. Look hard, you will see some that your steward here has been pressing to abandon their land. My support is growing. We intend to bring a case in the Court of Requests.' Dyrick looked at me suspiciously. Ettis continued, 'So be warned, sir, keep your men off our woodlands, for they will shortly be subject to legal proceedings. I tell you this before all these people here assembled, including Sir Luke Corembeck, our justice of the peace.'

Abigail marched up to him. 'Churl and knave to torment us so!' she shouted, right into his face.

Ettis stared back at her with contempt. Then David ran past his mother and stood before the villagers, his face red. 'Hedge-pigs! Lumps! Cattle! When I am lord here I will drive you all out, you will all beg, beg!'

Some of the villagers laughed. 'Get back to the nursery!' one shouted.

David looked round in helpless frustration. Then he gave a strange, puzzled frown. His limbs started to jerk, little flickering spasms, his eyes rolled up in his head and he collapsed on the ground. The villagers took a step back; there were frightened murmurs from some of the women. Abigail put her hands to her cheeks and uttered a gasping groan. On the ground David was twitching wildly now, like a puppet.

'What's he doing?' someone called out.

'He's possessed, get the priest!'

Then someone said, 'It's the falling sickness,' and Abigail groaned once more.

It was; I had seen it in London. That dread disease where those afflicted seem normal most of the time but can be struck down, out of the blue, to lie jerking on the ground. Some believed it a type of madness, others a form of possession.

Abigail sank on her knees and tried to still her writhing son. 'Help me, Ambrose, for pity's sake!' she cried. 'He'll bite his tongue!' I thought, so this has happened before.

Fulstowe unbuckled his dagger from his belt and thrust the leather scabbard between David's teeth. His lips were flecked with white foam now. I saw Dyrick looking on, astonished. Hobbey stared at his son, then at the watching crowd. He called out, in a voice full of rage and pain, 'Well, you have seen! Now in God's name go, leave us!' Next to him, Hugh stood looking blankly at David. No pity, nothing.

The villagers did not move. A woman said, 'Remember that carpenter who came to live in the village – he had the falling sickness!'

'Ay, we stoned him out!'

Sir Luke Corembeck came to life. 'Disperse, I order you!' he called.

People began to move away, though they looked back at David, with fear and loathing. He lay still a moment, then sat up, groaning. He looked up at his mother. 'My head hurts,' he said and began to cry.

Hobbey came over to him. 'You had an attack,' he said gently. 'It is all right, it is over.'

'They all saw?' David asked in horror. His face wet with tears, he looked wildly round. Hobbey and Fulstowe helped him to his feet. Hobbey clasped his son's arm.

'I am sorry, David,' he said gently. 'I feared this would happen one day. It was the fault of Ettis and his people.' He turned to Sir Luke. 'Thank you, sir, for dispersing them.' At that moment I had to admire Hobbey's dignity. He swallowed hard, then continued, 'I fear, as you have seen, my son has the falling sickness. It comes on seldom, a little rest and he will be as normal again.'

'Ettis and his churls caused this,' Sir Luke said. 'Jesu, it is a fine day when yeomen defy gentlemen.'

We followed the family back down the lanes, Fulstowe and Hugh each with an arm under David's shoulders. I knew this was very serious for the family; among both gentry and villagers David would now be seen as tainted. I gestured to Barak to hang back.

'What about that?' he asked.

'My guess is they've been hiding this for years. Dyrick didn't know – he was amazed. Dear God, that couldn't have happened in a more public way. David Hobbey may be a churl, but he didn't deserve that. By the way, I think there is more to Feaveryear's going than Dyrick said.' I told him what I had seen from the window the previous evening. 'I saw him running as though he'd seen the devil. And Dyrick looks very worried about something.'

'Maybe David had an attack yesterday, too.'

'No. He was standing at the butts with Hugh. Whatever happened, Feaveryear ran to tell Dyrick about it. And now he's gone.'

'When Abigail said after Lamkin was killed that you couldn't see what was before your eyes, she must have meant David.'

I shook my head. 'No. She meant something else. She of all people wouldn't draw my attention to David's condition.' I looked at the group ahead of me: Abigail hovered behind her son. 'Feaveryear's lodging is hard by yours. Did you hear him go?'

'I heard a door slam just after dawn, then his quick little steps. I thought he was going for an early prayer.'

'What made him run like that, I wonder?' I knew his disappearance was important, but not why.

Chapter Thirty

THE WOOD WAS delightfully peaceful in the early morning. The birds sang lustily in the trees; a squirrel watched me from the branch of a beech, its bushy red tail bright against the green leaves. I was sitting on a fallen log beside an oak tree in a little glade, comfortable in the loose jerkin and shirt I had donned for the hunt. Behind me, though, I could hear the murmuring voices of the breakfast party on the the other side of the trees, while stealthy rustlings deeper in the park indicated Master Avery and his men were checking the deer tracks. But I had had to get away from them all, just for a minute. Soon enough we would be riding pell-mell through the hunting park. I reflected on all that had happened on the previous day.

✝

WHEN WE HAD returned from church David had been taken upstairs to lie down, protesting all the while that he was quite recovered. Hobbey asked Dyrick to follow him to his study. I was on my way upstairs when Dyrick appeared once more and asked if I would attend Master Hobbey.

The master of Hoyland Priory sat at his desk, his face grave. He asked me quietly to sit. He picked up the hourglass from his desk and turned it over, sadly watching the grains run through. 'Well, Master Shardlake,' he said quietly, 'you have seen that my son has – an illness. It is something we have tried to keep to ourselves. It has been a great strain on my wife; seeing him in a fit strikes her to the heart. Apart from the family only Fulstowe knew. Mercifully David has never had an attack in front of the servants. We kept it even from Master Dyrick.' He smiled sadly at his lawyer. 'I am sorry for that, Vincent. But now everyone knows. Ettis and his crew will be mocking David in the village tavern tonight.' He put down the hourglass and clenched his hand into a fist.

I spoke quietly. 'Hugh, I take it, has known about David for some time.'

'David had his first attack shortly after Hugh and Emma came to us, when we were still in London.'

'And yet still you wanted Emma to marry David. To marry a ward to someone with such a disability as the falling sickness is not allowed.'

Dyrick said curtly, 'The girl died.' He looked anxiously at Hobbey, as though he might give away more than he should. But what more could there be?

I asked Hobbey, 'Hugh has kept it secret all this time?'

He nodded. His eyes were watchful now. 'He agreed he would tell nobody. And he never has.'

'It seems a hard thing to impose on the boy.'

'The fact he has kept silent surely indicates his loyalty to this family,' Dyrick put in.

'But for you coming, but for this business – ' Hobbey's voice trembled angrily for a moment, but he quickly brought himself under control – 'it has all put my wife and son under great strain. I think that is why David's attack came now.' He gathered himself. 'I would ask you, as a matter of charity, not to report this to the Court of Wards, not to spread our secret throughout London.'

I studied him. There was a quiet desperation in Hobbey's face, his mouth trembled for a second. 'I will have to consider,' I said.

Hobbey exchanged a look with Dyrick. He sighed. 'I should go, there are arrangements regarding the hunt.'

'You are sure it is still wise to go ahead with that?' Dyrick asked.

'Yes. I will hold my head high,' Hobbey added with a touch of his old firmness. 'Face them. And you must come, Vincent, as my lawyer it would be expected. Master Shardlake,' he said, 'will you attend too?'

I hesitated, realizing this was a change of tactics, an attempt to ingratiate himself with me. Then I nodded. 'Thank you. It may ease me of the stiffness I feel after all my days of riding.'

Hobbey stood. 'Bring your clerk, if he wishes to come.' He looked utterly exhausted. 'And afterwards, Sir Quintin and his son will be arriving. I must arrange hospitality for them.'

✝

I WENT TO my room and sat down heavily on the bed. Should I report David's condition to the Court of Wards? I had no wish to. But just how far had living with this tense family and its secret affected Hugh? After a few moments' more thought, I walked up the corridor and knocked at Hugh's door. After a moment he opened it. 'Master Shardlake,' he said quietly. 'Come in.'

I followed him into the tidy room. It was dim, the shutters half-drawn against the bright afternoon light. A book lay open on his desk, More's *Utopia*.

'You have been giving More another try?' I asked.

'Yes, last night. I fear, Master Shardlake, I still find him a dreamer. And Sam Feaveryear said he burned many good men as heretics while he was Lord Chancellor.'

'Yes, he did.'

'Then who was he to condemn the violence of war?'

I thought, this boy could make a scholar. I said, 'Feaveryear has gone.'

He crossed to the window and looked through the shutters. 'Yes, I got used to seeing his strange little face about. I am told Master Dyrick has sent him back to London.'

'An urgent case, apparently. He left this morning.' I hesitated. 'I saw him running across the lawn yesterday evening.'

Hugh turned, his face expressionless. 'Master Dyrick had shouted for him.'

'I did not hear him call. I thought I heard someone shout, "No!"'

'You must have misheard, sir. Master Dyrick came out and called. His master's call would always bring poor Sam running.' He looked at me, his blue-green eyes keen. 'Was that why you came to see me?'

'No.'

'I thought not.'

'David's secret is out.'

'I wish it were not.'

'Master Hobbey told me you and your sister learned of his condition shortly after you came to the Hobbeys.'

Hugh sat down on his bed, looking up at me. 'One day not long after we joined the Hobbeys, David and Emma and I were at class with Master Calfhill. He was angry with David, he had not done his set work and Master Calfhill threatened to tell his father. David told him to go and do something abominable with a sheep. Then suddenly David fell off his chair and began shaking and foaming, just like you saw today. Emma and I were frightened, we thought his bad words had called God's justice down on him. We still believed such things in those days,' he added with a bitter little smile. 'But Master Calfhill recognized the symptoms. He settled David and held his tongue down with a ruler, as Fulstowe did today with his scabbard.'

'And David's parents made you and your sister keep the secret?'

'They asked us to.' His voice was toneless.

I said, 'You do not love them as a family, do you? Any of them?'

Hugh's long, scarred face twitched and for a moment he looked like a child again. Then his composure returned and he stared back at me. 'Despite everything,' he said quietly, 'they spent the next months pressing my sister to marry David. Despite his falling sickness, despite his braggart, bullying ways.'

'Emma disliked David?'

'She *loathed* him. Already when she was thirteen he was pawing at her skirts.' Hugh's face darkened. 'I hit him for it. Master Calfhill took our part. He told us Emma could refuse to marry David. She could go to Wards and tell them David had a taint of body.'

'That is quite right. It would be what is called a Ravishment of Wards,' I said quietly. 'But Master Hobbey still wanted to tie her share of your father's lands to his family.'

'Emma and I made plans.' Anger entered Hugh's voice. 'If Master and Mistress Hobbey persisted with their pressure we would threaten to take them to their precious Court of Wards. Master Calfhill had researched the law, he told us that although boys cannot come out of wardship till they are twenty-one, girls can inherit their lands at fourteen.'

'Yes, unless they refuse a suitable marriage.'

'A *suitable* marriage. We planned to wait a few more months till Emma was fourteen, then we would take her lands, sell them, and run away together.'

'Did you tell Master Calfhill your plans?'

'No. Perhaps we should have trusted him,' Hugh added sadly.

'It would have been complicated, you would have needed a lawyer.'

Hugh gave a high-pitched, bitter laugh. It startled me. 'It was never put to the test, was it? My sister died, and then it did not matter any more.' His face twitched again; for a second I thought he would cry but his expression settled into blankness again. I thought, if only Michael Calfhill and Reverend Broughton had known of David's condition before the wardship was granted. Hugh sighed, then scratched his chest in sudden irritation.

'I hope you do not have fleas,' I said. 'I brought some back from Portsmouth, but thought I had got rid of them.'

'No, I have more scars there, they itch.' He scratched again, but carefully.

'Do you wear Emma's cross there?' I asked gently.

He looked up. 'No, Master Shardlake, I keep it in my drawer. I find it hard to look at.'

'That is sad.'

'Perhaps you should not have brought it. No, I still wear my heartstone. You are right, I do not love the Hobbeys. You are good at getting people to talk, sir. But if I cannot go to war, then I will stay here. That is my wish, and you may say so to the Court of Wards.'

'Why, Hugh?'

He spread his long-fingered hands, gave another bitter laugh. 'Where else would I go? I am used to the life here, and I do not want a court battle with Master Hobbey. In three years I can sue out my livery and leave.'

'And then what will you do? Go for a soldier?'

'Perhaps.'

'If I can help you then, Hugh, you will find me at Lincoln's Inn.'

He smiled sadly again. 'Thank you, Master Shardlake.' He looked at me intently. 'In three years — yes, then I may need a friend in the world beyond this place.'

✝

SOME BIRDS flapping their wings in one of the trees surrounding the glade brought me back to myself. I stood and walked back through the wood to a big clearing; there were about thirty people there. Hobbey and the huntsman Avery, together with Fulstowe and Sir Luke Corembeck and two other well-dressed middle-aged men, were bent over a plan of the park set on a sawn-off tree trunk. Large white cloths had been set on the grass, strewn with cushions. There Lady Corembeck sat with two middle-aged ladies. All were dressed for company, the women's dresses silk and satin, fashionable hoods covering their hair, faces and necks powdered with whitelead. Servants brought glasses of wine and plates of bread and cheese. A little way off some twenty men, those from Hoyland village recruited to help with the hunt, stood with half a dozen horses and the hunting dogs, held on leashes. Barak was talking to them. I was pleased to see Oddleg among the horses.

Hugh and David, with two other boys who looked to be sons of the guests, stood talking with Dyrick. The boys were dressed in different shades of green, as were the villagers. The men with Hobbey wore pinked or slashed doublets, but in pale shades, the usual bright colours of fine clothes absent. The four boys held their unstrung bows and had arrowbags at their belts. I saw swan and peacock feathers on the arrows' fletches, marks of status, and all wore gloves and wrist guards of horn or embossed leather. David showed no sign of his attack the previous day, but cast worried glances at the two young guests, no doubt wondering if they knew.

The hunt breakfast was the prelude; the ladies would stay here while the menfolk hunted the stag, hopefully returning with it in the large wheeled cart that stood nearby, next to the cloth set with knives and clamps where the animal would be dissected before the company. Sometimes ladies hunted, but not today. I remembered Princess Elizabeth and the Queen telling me she already accompanied the hunt.

The women were conversing with Abigail, lightly but, I saw, uneasily too. They would probably know what had happened outside the church yesterday. Abigail was trying to make conversation, but her voice was high with tension and she fiddled constantly with her napkin. 'This will be my son's first hunt,' she said. 'It is time such a fine strong boy enjoyed a hunt.' She looked at the other women defiantly, gave a frightened whinny of a laugh. One of the hunting dogs barked sharply and she flinched. I remembered the whispered conversation I had overheard, Abigail saying it was not safe to have the hunt.

Barak left the servants and came over to me. 'Sure you want to do this?' he asked.

'I have been on a hunt before,' I replied sharply.

'It's more than I have. But they say you should experience everything once, save incest and the plague.'

'Master Shardlake!' Hugh was walking over to us. He seemed relaxed now. 'Are you ready?'

'Yes,' I replied. 'What is to happen?'

'Myself and the other three archers – ' he nodded at David and the other boys — 'will lie in wait at different points along the route. Fulstowe, too.'

'A great honour for a steward.'

'Master Hobbey believes he deserves it,' he answered blandly.

'I thought usually the young men rode with the chase rather than waiting in ambush in the woods.'

'Ah, but we want to test our archery skills. Master Stannard there is second in command of his local militia, ten miles off. Here, lads!' He waved an arm, and David came across with the two others and Dyrick. Dyrick looked ill at ease. I was introduced to Master Stannard and Master Belton, the sons of the two men looking over the plan with Hobbey. Both were only in their late teens; but it was social rank that counted in the military. I thought of Sir Franklin Giffard, past command yet still in charge of Leacon's company.

'We saw some militiamen training on the way here last week,' I said.

'I'm getting them well trained up in my district,' Master Stannard said proudly. He was a tall well-built lad, with a round face and swaggering manner. Master Belton was smaller, still with spots peppering his face. 'Equipment is the problem,' Stannard went on. 'By law they should all have their own weapons but many do not even have bows. But they will be ready to march when the beacons are lit.'

'No greater army ever seen in England,' David said. I looked at him. There seemed a hectic quality to his excited tones. He met my eye and looked away.

Master Stannard nodded. 'If we have to, we will crush them by sheer numbers. And I shall lead my militia. Today will be good practice, perhaps I shall take down the stag and gain the heartstone.'

Young Stannard turned to Hugh. 'You gained the heartstone at my father's hunt two years ago, did you not? At only sixteen.'

'I did,' Hugh answered with pride.

'It can heal many ills, I am told.'

'Normally I wear it round my neck. But today I brought it to show you.' Hugh took off his gloves and reached into the pouch at his belt. He took out a tiny leather bag with a cord attached, opened it and tipped a small, round whitish object into his palm. Barak wrinkled his nose with distaste, but the boys studied it with interest.

'Even should I gain another, I will always keep this one,' Hugh said with quiet pride. The boys looked impressed.

Dyrick stepped up to me. 'I see the horse you have been riding has been brought out for you. He looks a steady beast.'

'He is.' I looked at Dyrick in surprise. For once he was making amiable conversation.

Hobbey called out, 'All of you that are going on the hunt, over here please!' He waved an arm, and the male guests and the Hoyland men walked across to him. Dyrick put a detaining hand on my arm.

'Brother Shardlake,' he said quietly, 'Feodary Priddis and his son will be here this afternoon. You will have a chance to take young Priddis to view the woods. But afterwards I would ask you to agree that we leave tomorrow. The case I sent Feaveryear away to deal with is difficult. I should be there.'

'A Court of Wards matter?'

'An injunction.' He took a deep breath. 'And if we leave tomorrow, Master Hobbey has agreed each side in this matter will pay their own costs, out of court. It is a very pretty bargain for your client, you must agree. But otherwise,' he resumed his usual aggressive manner, 'I promise we shall press for full costs in court.'

'Hobbey has agreed this?' I asked, astonished. It was a very good offer, not one a lawyer would normally make when his opponent's case had effectively fallen apart.

'He has. He wants you gone. Christ's blood, man, has he not enough trouble?' Dyrick spoke with unusual passion.

I considered. There was only one reason for Hobbey to make this offer; he wanted to make sure David's condition was not made public in London.

'My client is not here,' I said.

'Come, man, you can agree informally. She will do what you advise. She and the Queen,' he added bitterly.

'I will consider, once I have viewed Hugh's lands with Priddis.' I looked up, to see Hobbey staring at me intently. 'Come. We should join the rest.'

✝

WE GATHERED round the tree trunk, and Hobbey introduced Dyrick and me briefly to his new guests as his lawyers. I glanced at Avery. The young man was dressed in leaf-coloured green, a silver hunting horn slung from a baldric round his neck. He had a new air of authority about him as he pointed at the map.

'This is how we plan to conduct the hunt.' The map showed the rectangular hunting park, pathways through the trees sketched in. Avery took a piece of charcoal and drew a cross near the outer edge. 'We are here,' he said. 'We will all ride along this path until we reach this track, which turns off. When we are riding, gentlemen, it is important to be as quiet as possible so as not to startle the deer, which are here.' He drew a circle at a point some way up the track. 'My men have been tracking them constantly; this is where they lay down to rest last night.'

'And then we will have them,' Hobbey said with quiet satisfaction.

Avery looked at him seriously. 'Not quite, sir. That is when the real hunt begins. Then, and only then, may you forget about silence. The dogs will be loosed, and all the riders must concentrate on separating the stag from the does and fauns, which are only a secondary quarry.'

'The rascal, as they are called.' Corembeck smiled knowledgeably. 'It is all right, sir, I have been hunting many a time.'

'But if you will excuse me, sir,' Avery said, 'not everyone present has.' He looked around the company, his expression serious. 'This stag is large, perhaps seven years old, with ten tines on his antlers. It is important to guide him onto the path we wish him to take, but not to get too close lest he turn at bay. As for the rascal, set the dogs on them, with six of the Hoyland villagers to ride after them. The rest of you villagers should wait by the hurdles set across gaps in the trees on the main path, and shout to scare the stag should he try to break through. There are only eight does and some fauns among the rascal, the dogs should bring some down and you men can finish them off with swords or bows.' Avery studied the villagers. 'Master Clements, you are in charge of the dogs.'

The young cottager he had addressed smiled broadly. 'I am ready, sir.'

'The rest of you, is there anything you do not understand?'

'If we kill a doe or faun, do we get a choice of the best meat?' a villager asked.

'You have been told so,' Hobbey answered sharply.

'We'll take a haunch back for Master Ettis,' another said, and they laughed. Even among the men Hobbey had recruited, it seemed, there was a rebellious mood. Abigail, sitting on her cushions, turned and glared at the villager who had spoken. 'Nicholas,' she called, 'see that man gets no meat for his rudeness.'

'Gentlemen!' Avery slapped a gloved hand on the map. 'Please, your attention! We will be dealing with a strong and fierce beast!'

'My apologies,' Hobbey said. He glared at Abigail. 'My wife will ruin all with her tongue.'

There was a gasp of indrawn breath among the women at Hobbey's public insult to his wife. Abigail flushed and turned away. A muscle twitched in Hobbey's cheek. Then he looked back to Avery. 'Continue,' he snapped.

The huntsman took a deep breath. 'Once the stag is roused out, the hunt proper will begin. We chase him back to the main path, then on to where the archers lie in wait. You men at the hurdles must do your job well, not be frightened if the stag rushes towards you. Away from the path, in the wood, a stag is far fleeter than a horse.'

'That is right,' Corembeck agreed portentously.

Next Avery drew five crosses at points well up the path. 'The archers will be waiting here – Master Hugh, Master David, Fulstowe and our two young guests. You set off ahead of the rest. To one of you will go the honour of loosing the fatal shot, bringing down the stag.' He looked at the archers. 'Remember, find good cover and a clear line of shot. And keep still.' He surveyed the company. 'As the stag is driven to the archers I will sound my horn – like this – to warn them to be ready. If I need to summon the archers for any reason I will blow my horn thus.' He sounded a different note. 'Now, is all clear?'

There was a chorus of assent. Avery nodded. 'Very well, sirs, to your mounts. Handlers, keep careful hold of the dogs!'

✝

WE WATCHED AS David and Hugh, Fulstowe and the two other boys rode into the wood in single file. A few minutes later Avery gave a signal and the rest of us followed. The only sound was the occasional jingle of harness, quickly silenced. The dogs, though straining at their leashes, knew to be silent. I was between Barak and Dyrick, just behind Hobbey, who rode with Corembeck. At the head Avery set a slow, steady pace. I sensed Oddleg was uneasy at this strange, silent progress and patted him gently.

After half an hour Avery raised a hand and pointed down a narrow side track. It was hard to make no noise as the horses rode along it, brushing against the branches which grew to the edges. And then, as suddenly as when Barak and I had stumbled upon the doe, we were facing a clearing full of deer. It was as Avery had said, several does and fauns, and a large stag too, all feeding peacefully. The animals turned, tensing instantly. The stag raised its head.

And then it began, the rush of quickening blood and the pell-mell chase we had been waiting for. In an instant the does and fauns had turned and fled. The hunting dogs, loosed, sped past us. Six riders rode after them, crashing through the wood.

The rest of us faced the big stag. On my one previous hunt, long ago, I had not seen the stag until it was dead. This one was bigger, the great antlers with their sharp points waving menacingly. It lowered its head at Corembeck, who was nearest. 'To the side, sir,' Avery said quietly but clearly. Corembeck guided his horse slowly to the left, smiling with tense excitement. In a second the stag had shot through the resulting gap, back down the path, the massive muscles of its hind legs flexing as it ran. Avery blew his horn and we all followed him, urging our horses on. Barak grinned, his face alight. 'Jesu, this is something!' he called out breathlessly.

We chased the stag down the track. A group of men stood on the road, calling 'Hey! Hey!' and waving their arms to make it turn right, towards the archers. It shot on down the path and we careered after it. At one point where the trees thinned the stag turned aside, but a big wooden hurdle had been erected across the gap. It turned back to the path and fled on, precious moments lost. As it turned I glimpsed the whites of its eyes, full of terror.

The stag picked up speed, outrunning the horses. I had to focus every sense on riding, watching for overhanging branches. Barak might have been enjoying this but I was not; I feared the dangers of riding so fast in a forest; dreaded the crack of a protruding branch against head or knee.

Then the great beast turned its head towards another gap in the trees, and plunged sideways. There was another hurdle there but it was low. The stag crouched; it was going to try and jump, but villagers had appeared beside the hurdle, waving and shouting. But the stag did not run on; it turned and stood facing us. The riders skidded to a halt. I was still at the front, next to Hobbey now. The stag made a sound, more like a bellow than a grunt, lowered its head and waved its great antlers from side to side. Avery blew his horn, the note that would summon the archers. Then the stag lowered its head and charged.

It ran straight at Hobbey's mount, catching his horse on the neck. The horse screamed and reared; Hobbey gave a loud cry and toppled backwards, onto me. Oddleg plunged and I felt myself falling, Hobbey on top of me. We landed in a thick bank of stinging nettles, their softness saving us from serious injury, Hobbey's weight driving the breath from my body. I pushed him off, before he suffocated me, sharp nettle stings biting at my hands and neck. Then I heard a loud 'thwack', a soft grunt from the stag and a crash.

I drew deep whooping breaths as Barak ran across and helped me into a sitting position. Avery was helping Hobbey to his feet. Gasping, I looked round. A villager was holding Oddleg, who did not seem injured, though Hobbey's horse lay kicking in the undergrowth. The men from the village were running up to us. In the centre of the path lay the stag, surrounded by the hunters, an arrow protruding from its chest. As I watched, it took a long, shuddering breath, twitched and lay still. Hugh came up and stood over it, bow in hand, his face a sheen of sweat. Young Master Stannard ran up and clapped him on the shoulder. 'Well done, Master Curteys. What a shot!'

A slow smile of satisfaction spread across Hugh's features. 'Yes,' he said. 'Yes, I did it again.'

Hobbey was breathing fast, clearly shaken. Hugh glanced at him, then looked at me. 'You are hurt, sir,' he said. 'There is blood on your wrist.'

I touched my arm, there was what felt like a deep cut below the elbow. I winced. 'I must have landed on a piece of wood.'

'Let me look,' Barak said.

I removed my doublet and rolled up my sleeve. There was a nasty cut on my forearm, blood leaking fast. 'You need that bound up,' Barak said. 'Here, let me cut off that sleeve, the shirt's ripped anyway.'

As Barak tended my wound, Hobbey stepped over to his ward. 'Hugh,' he said, his voice shaking, 'thank you, you saved the hunt. Maybe even my life.'

Hugh gave him a wintry smile. 'I told you, sir, I would make a good shot on the field of battle.'

A horn sounded from somewhere deep in the wood. 'They've killed the does,' Sir Luke said. 'Here, you men, move the stag to the side of the path so the cart can come up. And help Master Hobbey's horse.' The fallen animal was brought to its feet, fortunately uninjured though trembling violently. Four villagers grabbed the stag by the antlers, and dragged it, trailing blood, to the verge.

☦

THE HUNT DISPERSED, Hobbey ordering everyone to walk or ride back to the clearing. A servant led his limping horse away. Hugh left with the two young gentlemen, enjoying their congratulations. Avery went up the path to fetch Fulstowe and David, who must have been too far up the path to have heard the horn. Hobbey stood, dusty, his clothes torn, rubbing his pale hands. 'I am sorry I fell on you, sir,' he said. 'Will your arm be all right?'

'I think so. Come, Barak, let us go back to the house.' I stood, but at once the wood spun round me. Barak helped me sit down again.

'You've had a shock. Rest here awhile.'

Dyrick laughed. 'Be careful, Nicholas, or he'll find some way of suing you for trespass against the person.'

'Be quiet,' Hobbey snapped. Dyrick's face darkened and he looked as though he were about to say something, but then he turned and stalked away down the path, just as Avery reappeared with Fulstowe and David. David looked at the stag, the arrow stuck deep in its chest. Fulstowe stepped close. 'A fine shot,' he said admiringly. 'We should raise cups to Master Hugh tonight. He deserves the heartstone as a new trophy.'

'Had the stag run on to us,' David said sulkily, 'I would have got him. It should have been my kill.'

'God's death, boy,' Hobbey snapped. 'It knocked Master Shardlake and I over. It could have hurt us badly! Fulstowe is right, you should be congratulating Hugh.'

David's eyes widened. I had never heard Hobbey shout at his son before. David cried out, 'Oh yes, Hugh is always better than me! At everything. Hugh, Hugh, Hugh!' He glared at me. 'Hugh that the hunchback thinks so badly treated.'

'Go home!' Hobbey pointed at his son with a trembling finger.

David muttered an obscenity and crashed away into the wood, clutching his bow. I glimpsed angry tears on his face. Hobbey turned to Fulstowe in time to catch him smiling at the exhibition. His eyes narrowed. 'Go, steward,' he said. 'Meet the cart and tell them to get this stag loaded up.'

'Yes, sir,' Fulstowe said, an ironic touch in his voice. He too walked away.

'Agh, my hands,' Hobbey said. 'I need to find some dock leaves. Avery, come with me, you know these woods.'

Avery's eyes narrowed at being addressed like a household servant; nonetheless he accompanied Hobbey down the path. Barak and I were left alone with the dead stag. The birds, driven from the scene by all the clamour, slowly returned to their roosts, and their song began again.

'This'll be some story to tell Tammy when I get home,' Barak said.

'Dyrick offered me a deal on costs before the hunt,' I said quietly. 'If we leave tomorrow after Priddis's visit, each side will pay their own. I think it's because of David. I think I must accept.' I sighed. 'The mysteries of this house will have to be left to themselves.'

'Thank God for that.' Barak looked at me, a rueful smile on his face.

Creaking wheels sounded on the path. Half a dozen men guided the big cart we had seen at the clearing down the lane. It was dripping blood from the does and fauns, which must already have been taken to the clearing.

'Come on,' I said. 'I'm all right now. Let's go.'

We rode slowly down the path, the servants with the cart doffing their caps as we passed them. It was further than I had realized. My arm throbbed painfully.

I was thinking we must be at the glade soon when Barak touched my shoulder. 'Look,' he said quietly. 'What's that? Through there?'

'Where?' I looked through the trees. 'I can't see anything.'

'Something bright, like clothing.' He dismounted and walked into the wood. I dismounted too and followed, then almost walked into him from behind as he came to a dead stop.

'What is it? – '

I broke off at the extraordinary scene before us. Ahead of us was the little dell I had found that morning, with the fallen log leaning against a tree. For a second my mind whirled, for it seemed I was seeing the unicorn hunt on the tapestry in Hobbey's hall brought to life. A woman with long fair hair sat on the log, her back against the tree, arms folded on her lap. She stayed quite silent, not moving at our appearance. The images were mixed up and for a second I thought I saw a unicorn's horn projecting from her brow. Then I realized what was really there. Abigail Hobbey, pinned to the tree behind her by an arrow through her head.

Part Five

THE UNQUIET DEAD

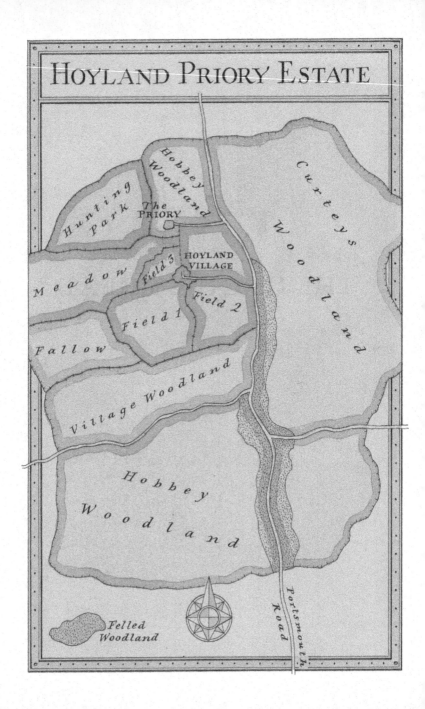

HOYLAND PRIORY ESTATE

Hobbey Woodland

Hunting Park

The PRIORY

Curteys Woodland

Meadow

Field 3

HOYLAND VILLAGE

Field 2

Field 1

Fallow

Village Woodland

Hobbey Woodland

Felled Woodland

Portsmouth Road

Chapter Thirty-one

BARAK AND I sat at the end of the big dining table in the great hall of Hoyland Priory. Fulstowe, Dyrick and Sir Luke Corembeck stood talking in low, intent voices under the old stained-glass window. Sir Quintin Priddis sat on a chair by the empty fireplace, his good hand on his stick and the dead white one in his lap, watching them with a cynical smile. Behind him Edward Priddis stood in his dark robe, his expression serious. They had been sitting in the hall when we returned from the discovery of Abigail's body.

'Ettis had every reason to hate her,' Fulstowe was saying. 'He had suffered from her tongue; he knew my poor mistress was strong against his defiance.'

'She faced him when he was shouting at my client in his own study a few days ago,' Dyrick agreed. 'I was there.'

Fulstowe nodded grimly. 'I know him well as a troublemaker. He is the only one with the fire and recklessness to risk his neck. Sir Luke, I beg you, use your authority as magistrate to have him brought back here. Question him; find out where he was today.'

Sir Luke scratched a plump cheek, then nodded. 'That would perhaps be a reasonable step, until the coroner arrives. I can get my servants to bring him in. There is a cellar at my house where we can keep him.'

Priddis cackled suddenly. 'You have found your murderer, then?' he called out. 'A village leader, opposed to your enclosure plans. Convenient.'

Sir Luke bridled. 'Ettis is a hot-headed rogue, Master Feodary, and an enemy of this family. He should be questioned.'

Priddis shrugged. 'It matters naught to me. But when the coroner arrives from Winchester he might think efforts would have been better spent checking the movements of everyone on the hunt.'

'That is being done, sir,' Dyrick replied.

'Ettis would not run,' I said. 'He has a wife and three children.'

'Full enquiries will be carried out by the coroner,' Corembeck replied haughtily, 'but in the meantime it will do no harm to secure Ettis.'

'When will the coroner be here?' Dyrick asked Fulstowe.

'Not until the day after tomorrow at the earliest, even if our messenger finds clear roads between here and Winchester, which I doubt.'

Barak looked downcast. As first finders of the body we would have to stay until the inquest. But I could not help feeling pleased. The carapace of mystery around this family would surely crack open now. Then I thought, guiltily, poor Abigail.

Sir Quintin looked at his son. 'Well, Edward, you might as well go and look at Hugh Curteys' property, that is why we are here after all. Unless you and Master Shardlake fear another arrow flying from those woods. Fulstowe tells me someone shot at you too, a few days ago.'

'Yes,' I replied. 'Though it was a warning shot, intended to miss.'

'I am not afraid, Father,' Edward said sharply.

I said, 'We will be riding through a cleared area. The big trees have all been felled; there is nowhere for an archer to hide.' I looked across at Dyrick. 'Will you come?'

'I should stay with Master Hobbey. And, Fulstowe, I want you to give the messenger going to fetch the coroner a letter to my clerk Feaveryear. It must be forwarded to London as fast as possible, I do not care what it costs.'

Edward Priddis looked at me. 'Then I will change my clothes, sir, and we can go.'

✝

BARAK HAD BEEN the first to recover from the awful sight in the glade. He had walked silently over the grass and gently touched Abigail's hand. 'She is still warm,' he said.

I approached the body. Abigail's eyes were wide open, her last emotion must have been sudden shock. I saw that a yellow woodland flower lay beside the body, some of the petals torn off. I thought, she must have picked it as she walked here. I looked at the arrow protruding obscenely from her white brow. The fletches were of goose feather. I remembered the boys had carried peacock and swan, but could not remember if they had had ordinary goose-feather arrows in their arrowbags too. There was hardly any blood, just a small red circle round the arrow shaft.

'We'll have to go and tell them,' Barak said quietly. I could hear, faintly, the murmur of voices just on the other side of the trees. I put a hand on his arm.

'Let us take a minute to look round before this dell is full of people.' I pointed to the trees. 'He shot from that direction. Come, help me see if we can find the place.'

We tried to follow the killer's line of sight. A little way into the trees, an oak blocked my path. I turned; I was looking straight at poor Abigail's body. I glanced down and saw the faint imprint of the sole of a shoe in the soft earth.

'He stood right here,' I said. 'He could have been walking along the road, as we were, and like us caught a glimpse of that bright yellow dress through the trees. Then he walked here silently, put an arrow to his bow and shot her.'

'So it wasn't planned?'

'Not if it happened that way.'

'What if she arranged to meet someone here, and they killed her?'

'That's possible. But she may have come here to get away from all the company, as I did. It can't have been easy sitting with those women, knowing they had probably been told about David.'

Barak looked at the body. 'Poor creature. What harm did she ever really do anyone? She was bad-tempered and rude, but so are many. Why kill her?'

'I don't know. Unless she had other secrets besides David, and someone took the chance to silence her.' I remembered the conversation I had overheard between Abigail and Hobbey. 'She was afraid that something would happen on the hunt. And now it has.'

✝

WHEN WE WALKED into the clearing I saw everyone had returned. Hugh and David, with Hobbey, Fulstowe and Dyrick, stood watching with the rest of the party as servants in bloody smocks cut open the stomach of a large doe under Avery's supervision. Five more had been dumped in a heap nearby. The unmaking of the quarry, I remembered they called this.

The dogs had been leashed and were held by the villagers. They pulled forward, panting and wagging their tails. Avery reached deep into the doe's innards and with a hefty tug pulled out a long trail of intestines. He cut them to pieces with a large knife and threw chunks to the dogs; their reward.

I told Fulstowe first, taking him aside. He was shocked out of his normal calm, his eyes opened wide and he stepped backwards, crying, 'What?' in a voice that made everybody turn. Then he collected himself, his face setting in tight lines.

'Best not tell everyone at once,' I said quietly.

'I must tell Master Hobbey and the boys.'

I looked on as Fulstowe went to Hobbey, then Hugh, then David, speaking quietly to each in turn. Their reactions were entirely different. Hobbey had been watching the unmaking with an indulgent smile, his composure restored after his fall. When Fulstowe told him he stood still for a moment. Then he staggered backwards and would have fallen had not a servant grasped him. He stood, half-supported by the man, staring at Fulstowe as he approached Hugh and David. Hugh frowned, looked unbelieving, but David screamed, 'Mother! My mother!' He reached out his hand in a strange gesture, as though clawing at the air for support, but when Fulstowe reached out to him he batted his hands away, then began weeping piteously.

Everyone was looking at the family now, in puzzlement and fear. The women rose from their cushions. Fulstowe stood and addressed everyone.

'There has been – ' he paused – 'an accident. To Mistress Abigail. I fear she is dead. Sir Luke, would you please come with me?'

There were gasps and exclamations. 'Please,' Fulstowe said, 'Master Dyrick, Master Shardlake, come too.'

I stepped forward. 'Fulstowe, are there any servants who have been on duty waiting on the women the whole morning?'

Fulstowe considered, then pointed to a boy Hugh and David's age. 'Moorcock, you've been here all the time, haven't you?'

The boy nodded, looking frightened.

'Lad,' I asked, 'when did Mistress Abigail leave the clearing?'

'About twenty minutes ago. I heard her tell Mistress Stannard she needed to go to the pissing place.'

One of the ladies spoke up. 'She did, but she went in the wrong direction. The appointed place is over there.' She pointed to a little path some way off.

'Who from the hunting party was back in the clearing by then?' I asked the servant.

'Hardly anybody, sir. Sir Luke had returned, then Master Avery, who said the stag had turned at bay. I think everyone else came back after Mistress Hobbey left.'

Mistress Stannard looked at Fulstowe. 'What has happened to her?'

He did not reply. I said, 'Master Avery, would you come too?' He rose, brushing bloody hands on his smock, and followed us back into the trees.

✠

IN THE DELL bluebottles were buzzing round the wound on Abigail's brow. Corembeck's mouth dropped open. 'Murder,' he breathed. Dyrick for once said nothing, staring at the corpse in horror.

'I thought it best to keep that quiet for now,' Fulstowe said. 'You, Sir Luke, are the magistrate. What should we do?'

'Who found the body?'

I stepped forward. 'My clerk and I.'

'We must send to Winchester, for Coroner Trevelyan. At once.' Corembeck put a hand to his brow, where sweat stood out.

'Why is Avery here?' Fulstowe asked me, nodding to the blood-stained huntmaster. 'This is hardly appropriate—'

'Because he knows these woodlands,' I answered curtly. 'Master Avery, there is something I would show you if you would follow me.'

I led the way to the place where the half-footprint was. 'Yes,' Avery said quietly. 'He fired from here.' He bent to a branch just in front of me; a twig was broken off, hanging by its stem. 'See, this was in his way. He broke it, quietly enough not to disturb her.' He looked at me. 'I think this man was an experienced archer. Not one of the household servants or the villagers I have been training up. He – well, he hit the centre of his mark.'

'Thank you.' I led the way back to the glade. Abigail, who had been constantly fidgeting in life, sat horribly still. But as I stepped into the glade I saw someone else had arrived there. Hugh Curteys was in the act of picking up the flower Abigail had dropped. He placed it gently in her lap, then muttered something. It sounded like, 'You deserved this.'

✟

WHEN WE RETURNED to the clearing the stag had been brought in on the cart. It was left with the does, and a long procession of shocked guests and servants filed back to the house. David, still weeping, was supported by his father. Hobbey's face remained blank with shock. Behind them Hugh walked with Fulstowe, saying nothing.

'It could have been Hugh or David,' Barak said quietly.

'Or Fulstowe. Why, almost nobody from the hunt was back when Abigail left the clearing.'

Dyrick fell into step with us. 'Avery's wrong,' he said. 'It could have been someone from the village. So many young men practise archery nowadays. Older ones too. Well, we won't be leaving here tomorrow,' he added bitterly. 'We'll have to wait for the coroner. Me as Master Hobbey's lawyer, you two as first finders. We'll be here till the inquest. Damn it.'

Did he feel nothing for Abigail? I stared at him. 'I want to see my children,' he snapped.

You could have done it, I thought, you flounced off alone after Hobbey snapped at you. And you are an archer: you were talking about teaching your son.

Barak's shoulders slumped. 'I begin to wonder if I'll ever see my child born now,' he said sorrowfully. 'I must write to Tamasin.'

'And I to Warner.'

We arrived back at the house. As we approached the steps to the porch, the front door banged open and Leonard Ettis marched out, a frown on his face. He stopped and stared at the procession, the weeping David supported by the pale, shocked Hobbey.

Fulstowe strode over to Ettis. 'What are you doing here?' he barked.

'I came to see you,' he retorted. 'To find out if your men still intend to enter our woods this week. Or try to. But there was nobody here but that savage-mouthed old cripple sitting in the hall.'

'Mind your tongue,' Fulstowe snapped.

'Oh yes, watch what I say.' Ettis laughed. 'It'll be a different story when I lead the village militia to fight the French.'

Barak and I exchanged glances. 'Priddis,' I said. 'I had forgotten all about him.'

'It was the hunt today.' Fulstowe looked narrowly at Ettis. 'Surely you had not forgotten that?'

'I thought you might be back and this matter can't wait. We need an answer from you.' He looked over the little crowd, stared again at Hobbey and David. 'Has something happened?'

'Mistress Hobbey is dead,' Fulstowe replied bluntly.

Ettis stared. 'What?'

'Shot dead with an arrow by an unknown assailant. Which way did you come to the house, Ettis?'

The yeoman's eyes widened. 'You – do you accuse me?'

Corembeck stepped forward. 'Which way did you come, Ettis?'

Ettis glared at him. 'From the village.'

'Not through the woods?'

'No!'

'Alone?' Fulstowe asked.

Ettis took a step forward and for a moment I thought he would strike the steward. Then he turned and marched away down the drive. Dyrick looked meaningfully at Corembeck.

We walked into the hall, where Priddis and his son sat waiting. Fulstowe told them what had happened. I saw the old man's eyes light up with greedy curiosity. For him, I realized, this was an unexpected piece of excitement.

✢

I WENT UPSTAIRS to change for my ride with Edward Priddis. I felt guilty now for wanting to stay. Barak wanted so much to return to Tamasin. Looking out of the window, I remembered, sadly, Feaveryear and the two boys practising at the butts. David and Hugh had both disappeared to their rooms when we returned; I did not know who, if anyone, was with them.

When I went back downstairs Sir Quintin was still ensconced in his chair by the fireplace with his son, watching all that was going on with horrible amused interest. I asked Barak to stay in the great hall, and listen to all that was said. Edward rose and we went to fetch the horses. As we rode out, Edward's manner was cool and distant, but civil enough.

'This is a terrible thing for you to find here,' I said.

He nodded seriously. 'These are strange and dreadful times.'

'What news of the French in Portsmouth?' I asked.

'They say their fleet has been sighted off the Sussex coast. People are becoming fearful.'

'Yes, there is much fear underneath people's show of confidence.'

'Nonetheless,' he said firmly, 'we must face whatever comes.'

I studied him. Edward had bushy eyebrows like his father, and a firm, obstinate set to his mouth. 'I believe your father knows Sir Richard Rich,' I said.

He gave me a wintry smile. 'Yes, he is an old acquaintance. We met and had a talk with him at the Portsmouth Guildhall. The day you brought Hugh Curteys there. I hear the merchants who have overcharged the army or provided bad food come to Sir Richard Rich in fear and trembling. I imagine he will soon cut through their excuses about having to charge more because of the new coinage. Sir Richard learned the art of interrogation under a master. Cromwell. But you will know that.' Again that wintry smile, a piercing look from those blue eyes.

'Rich spoke of me?'

Edward smiled coldly. 'A little. He asked my father about the case you have on down here. He said you can become – very strongly involved with your clients.'

'No bad thing in a lawyer, surely, Brother.' I inclined my head, hiding the anxiety I felt at Rich's continued interest in me.

'True.'

'Did you qualify at Gray's Inn, like your father?'

'I did. I worked on official service in London for a while. After a few years I came back to Winchester, to help Father in his work.'

'You must do the bulk of it now, I hazard.'

'Oh, Father still holds the reins. I am but his trusty steed.' I caught a note of bitterness. Are you waiting to succeed him? I wondered.

'Look over to your right, Brother,' I said. 'Those are Hugh Curteys' lands that were cleared some years ago.'

We came to a halt, near the area of cleared woodland Barak and I had seen on our ride. New trees, little more than saplings, stood amid thick undergrowth and the mossy stumps of old trees. It was hot, still and quiet. I said, 'I think there was more oak in this land than the accounts allow.'

'And the evidence for that?' Edward asked sharply.

'The fact the uncleared area of woodland to the south has a great deal of oak.'

'The soil may be different.'

'It looked very similar when I rode through it a few days ago.'

'The day an arrow was shot at you?' He looked at me curiously.

'Yes. Everyone thought it was a poacher. But after today I wonder.'

'A madman roaming these woods,' Edward mused. He glanced apprehensively at the distant trees.

'Sir Luke seems to think he has his suspect.'

'He may be wrong. Perhaps some deserter from the army is in hiding out in the trees. He tried to kill you, then came across poor Mistress Hobbey. He may have wished to rob her.'

'I do not believe she had a purse with her. The family would have noticed if one was gone.'

'Still, you will forgive me if I say I would like to keep the inspection brief.'

'This area is quite open, and we are out of bowshot from the trees. I suggest we ride through the cleared area, look at how many oak stumps we can see.'

'If you insist.' Edward looked across at the treeline, about five hundred yards away. He was nervous; I wondered whether pride had made him accede to his father's suggestion that we still make this ride. We rode on, guiding the horses carefully.

'I gather your family comes from near Rolfswood,' I said casually. I had decided to see what I could find out. Edward Priddis was clever, and a smooth talker, but I sensed he lacked his father's strength of character.

'That is so. Though my father moved to Winchester when he became feodary of Hampshire.'

'Do you ever visit there now?'

'Not since my mother died ten years ago, God rest her. It was her family who came from those parts. Do you have connections there, Serjeant Shardlake? I do not recall hearing your name before.'

'I have a client who thought he may have family in Rolfswood. He asked me to visit, see if I could trace them. I went there a few days ago.'

'Did you find them?' Edward smiled pleasantly, though his eyes were keen as ever.

'No. But I stayed overnight, learned of a tragedy there nineteen years ago. A foundry burned to the ground, the founder killed with one of his assistants. The founder's daughter went mad afterwards. Their name was Fettiplace, that is the name my client was looking for. Your father was coroner then, I believe.'

Edward considered. 'I remember it vaguely. I was not at home then, I had started at Cambridge. I did a degree before going to Gray's Inn,' he added proudly. 'I seem to remember my father helped the girl, who went mad.'

'That was good of him,' I said neutrally. I thought, I have seen enough of your father to see there is no shred of charity in him. I remembered Reverend Seckford telling me how Priddis had supervised Ellen's forced removal from her place of safety.

'He is not as hard as people think,' Edward said stiffly. 'He does a difficult job.'

'There is another family I heard of, that you may know. The Wests.'

'Oh yes, they are important landowners. Mistress West has always ruled the roost around Rolfswood. Did you meet her too?'

'I only heard of her and her son. He is an officer on the King's ships now. Philip West. He would have been about your age.'

'I met him once or twice when I was a boy. But I returned seldom after I went to Cambridge. You seem to have made detailed enquiries, Brother Shardlake.'

'It was an interesting story.'

Edward brought his horse to a halt and surveyed the landscape. 'In truth, sir, I think it impossible to tell what trees once grew here. The old trunks are all overgrown. And we are approaching a little too near the treeline for my comfort.'

'Look at the new young trees growing up,' I answered quietly. 'Fully half must be oaks. And see all the high old oaks in the forest ahead.'

Edward made a show of looking carefully, though I was sure he had noticed everything I had. Then he turned to me, and asked quietly, 'What do you wish to achieve from this case, Master Shardlake?'

'Justice for Hugh Curteys. It is clear to me this land was mainly forested with oak, though Master Hobbey's accounts show oaks as barely a quarter of the trees felled.'

'Yet Hugh Curteys himself said, at the Guildhall, that he is quite content.'

'He is a young man with no head for business. And when these woods were felled he was a child.'

'So you would go back to the Court of Wards and ask for what – restitution? It would take great time, Brother, and expense, trouble to a whole family, including Hugh, that has just suffered a great tragedy. A surveyor would have to be paid for, and he would likely find nothing conclusive. Consider, Master Shardlake, is it worth it? Especially when Master Hobbey has offered to be more than reasonable over costs.'

'You know of his offer?'

'Brother Dyrick told me, just before we left.' He raised his heavy eyebrows. 'He seems greatly fumed with this matter.'

I met his gaze. You and your father took a cut of those profits, I thought. But I had already decided to accept Dyrick's offer. Without

Hugh's support I could do nothing. But there was no need to commit myself just yet as we had to stay here anyway. 'I will think more on it,' I said.

He shrugged. 'Very well. Even so, I think you know you must settle. And now may we go back? I am anxious Father does not get overtired.'

'Very well.'

As Edward turned his horse I caught him smiling secretively, sure the case was over.

✞

WHEN WE RETURNED the house was still and hushed, old Priddis sitting alone by the empty fireplace. He looked up. 'Well, Edward,' he asked, 'is all well with the woodlands?'

'Master Shardlake and I have had a sensible discussion.'

Sir Quintin gave me a long stare, then grunted. 'Help me, Edward, I would get up.'

Edward helped the old man to his feet. Sir Quintin stood, breathing heavily, his useless arm swinging by his side. The whiteness of his withered hand reminded me of poor Abigail's dead face, and I had to suppress a shudder.

'I have had enough of this place,' Sir Quintin said pettishly, 'everyone in such a state. I want to get away.'

'Very well,' Edward answered soothingly. 'I will prepare the horses. By the way, Father,' he added lightly, 'Master Shardlake has visited Rolfswood. He was talking of that tragedy at the foundry – you remember, when you were coroner?'

Sir Quintin's eyes narrowed and he looked at me hard for a moment. Then he waved his good hand and said, 'I barely remember it, it was an age ago. I have dealt with so many cases in my life. Come, Edward, help me outside.' He leaned forward, staring into my face. 'Goodbye, Master Shardlake. I hope you will see the sense in letting this matter drop. These people have enough trouble, it seems to me.'

I went up to my room, stood looking out of the window at the butts. I had learned nothing from the Priddises. I felt helpless frustration and anger. There was a knock on the door, and Barak came in. He seemed anxious.

'How are the family?' I asked. 'None of them was in the great hall.'

'Fulstowe told me to get out of the house shortly after you left. But as I was leaving a rider arrived with a letter for you. I hoped it might be more news from London, but I don't recognize the hand.'

He reached into his doublet and pulled out a piece of cheap paper, crudely sealed with wax. My name and 'Hoyland Priory' were scrawled on the front. I opened it.

'Is it from home?' Barak asked eagerly.

I shook my head. 'No.'

The note was in a scrawled hand, it was dated 12 July, the day before, and signed John Seckford, Curate of Rolfswood.

Master Shardlake,

I am sorry to trouble you, but old Master Harrydance has been to see me. He has found something dreadful, that concerns the matter we talked of. We ask you please to come and help us. We are in sore fear about what to do.

Chapter Thirty-two

I PASSED BARAK the note. He read it, then handed it back, looking at me hard. 'What the hell does he mean?'

'I don't know.' I paced the room. 'Something serious. I could ride there tomorrow and come back the next day — Wednesday — the coroner won't be here before then.'

He said quietly, 'You're glad we can't go home tomorrow, aren't you?'

'That's not fair,' I answered, all the more hotly because his words had struck home. 'We would have gone but for Abigail's death. How could I know this would happen? And you cannot think I am glad that poor woman was killed. Even though an inquest may reveal what has been going on here.'

'All right. But part of you is still glad, isn't it?'

'Here is a chance to solve both matters.'

'You forget there may be a battle eight miles south of here any day now. And, if we lose, French troops may be marching up that road and in here. It's a fine property for soldiers to loot.'

'That risk we are stuck with. But — ' I looked at him — 'I will go to Rolfswood alone tomorrow.'

'Oh, I'm coming,' Barak replied in definite tones. 'I'm not staying by myself in this madhouse.'

✟

I KNOCKED ON the door of Hobbey's study. He said quietly, 'Come in.' He was sitting at his desk, watching the sand run through the hourglass. I realized it was the first time I had ever been alone with him. I felt a stab of sympathy. Within two days the secret of his son's illness had been exposed and his wife murdered. He looked bereft.

'Well, Master Shardlake,' he asked with a sigh, 'did you and Master Priddis ride the woods?'

'We did.'

He waved a hand. 'Perhaps you could discuss it with Vincent. I cannot concentrate just now.'

'I understand. Sir, may I express my condolences for your poor wife's death? God rest her soul.'

He lowered his eyes, then said, in a voice suddenly full of emotion, 'Everyone disliked poor Abigail. I know they did. But you should have seen her when I married her, she was so pretty, so light-hearted. If she had not married me – ' His voice trailed away.

'How are the boys?' I asked. I thought, in a normal family Hugh and David would have been with Hobbey, they would all have been comforting each other.

'David is in great distress. Fulstowe is with him. And Hugh – ' He sighed. 'Hugh is about the house somewhere. Sir Luke is organizing a search of the woodlands, by the way. People from the village are helping, they are much disturbed at the prospect of some madman roaming the woods. Sir Luke suggests none of us leave the house and gardens for now.'

'Has Ettis been taken in for questioning?'

'Yes. He hated this family.' Hobbey frowned. 'Vincent says that if there is no trace of a stranger in the woods, he must be a suspect. Surely that must be right.' He frowned. I thought, Dyrick will be running things here now, Dyrick and Fulstowe between them.

'Well,' I answered quietly, 'it will be up to the coroner when he arrives. The reason I came, Master Hobbey, is to tell you a messenger has brought a letter from the Sussex village where I have another matter in hand. I plan to go there tomorrow, then return the following day to see the coroner. I know he will need to speak to me and Barak as first finders.'

'Very well,' he replied without interest.

I hesitated, aware that what I had to say next should really be said with Dyrick present. But it was eating away at me. 'Last week, sir, I accidentally overheard you and your wife talking in her room. She said she did not want to have the hunt, she indicated she did not think it was safe.'

Hobbey was silent a moment. Then he spoke, without raising his head, but slowly and clearly. 'My wife had become afraid of everyone and everything, Master Shardlake. I told you before, she was not well. She had come to feel that nothing and no one was safe.' He picked up the hourglass, stared at the falling sand, then up at me, a strange expression on his thin face. 'All my life,' he said slowly, 'everything I have striven to build, those I have loved, everything is running out, like the sand in this glass. Do you believe in fate, Master Shardlake, in nemesis?'

'No, sir. I do not understand how God orders the world, but I do not think it is like that.'

'It all began with you coming here.' His voice was still quiet, his tone strange, one of mild curiosity. 'This wretched case. I doubt David would have had his fit without it. You encourage my tenants to rebel; do not deny it, I have my informants in the village. And now my wife is dead. I wonder if perhaps you are my nemesis.'

'I wish to be no one's nemesis, Master Hobbey.'

'Do you not? I wonder.' Still he spoke quietly, but now he looked at me, his eyes suddenly as sharp and questing as they had ever been. 'Well, perhaps I am wrong, perhaps it started with Michael Calfhill, with –' A spasm of pain crossed his face, and he seemed to come back to himself. 'We should not really be discussing such things without Vincent here,' he said, his tone formal again. 'I will see you in two days, Master Shardlake.' And he nodded dismissively.

✣

BARAK AND I left for Rolfswood early the next morning. I could have done without another ride; my bandaged arm was sore and my back ached after the hunt. The weather was close again, the sky grey.

I said little as we rode; Hobbey's words the previous day had unsettled me. I had told myself I had only encouraged Ettis against a bullying landlord, that David could have had a seizure at any time, and above all that nobody knew who had killed Abigail, or why. But I could understand why Hobbey might see me as his nemesis.

The evening before I had written to Warner, telling him what had happened. I told him too about Dyrick's offer on costs. Then I wrote to Guy, saying we were not coming home just yet. Afterwards I walked round to the stables to fetch the letter Barak had written to Tamasin; we would leave them at Cosham for the post rider to collect. On my way out I passed David's room, and heard deep, wrenching sobs, Fulstowe's voice talking in low, reassuring tones.

On my way back to the house with the letters I saw Hugh in the distance, sitting on the half-tumbled wall of the old nuns' cemetery. I went up to him. His long face was sad, his mouth pulled down. He looked up at me, a dreadful weariness in his eyes.

'My condolences,' I said quietly.

He bowed his head slightly. In the fading light his scars could not be clearly seen, he looked boyishly handsome but somehow all the more vulnerable. 'Thank you,' he said, 'but you should know I felt nothing for Mistress Hobbey. I thought I might, now, but I do not.'

'You put a flower in her lap this morning.'

'Yes. I felt sorry for her then.'

I said quietly, 'You were saying something when we came on you with the body.' I looked him in the eye. 'It sounded like, "You deserved this."'

He was silent a moment, then said, 'God preserve me, I may have done.' He stared ahead.

'Why?'

He spoke very quietly. 'When we first knew her, I think in her way she did want to mother me, and especially my sister. But for both her and Master Hobbey, that came second to –' his voice caught for a moment – 'to money. They wanted the use of our lands, and they tried to make Emma marry David, as I told you. When I saw her I felt sorry for her but angry too. So, yes, I did say that.'

'Have you ever seen a dead person before?'

'Yes. My mother and father. They would not let me see my sister – her face was ravaged by smallpox. I wish they had.' He looked at me. 'Will you tell the coroner of my words?'

'I think you should tell him yourself, Hugh. Tell him how you felt about Abigail.'

He looked at me hard. I wondered whether, like Hobbey, he was thinking of all the trouble that had come here since I arrived.

I asked him, 'Who do you think murdered Mistress Hobbey?'

'I have no idea.' He frowned. 'Do you believe it was me?'

I shook my head. 'Like you, Hugh, I have no idea.' I looked across at the graveyard. Ursula had left some flowers at the nun's grave again.

'But you heard my words, and thought it might be me?' Hugh's face flushed with anger, highlighting his scars.

'I only wondered, Hugh, what you meant.'

'You said you would be my friend.' He stood then, clenching his fists. I was aware that he was as tall as me, and stronger.

'I accuse no one, Hugh. But from the beginning I have sensed this entire family has been hiding something. As well as David's condition.'

'You are wrong,' he said.

'I rode your lands with Edward Priddis today. I believe Master Hobbey has been falsifying his accounts. Probably in league with Sir Quintin. I think they may have robbed you of hundreds of pounds.'

An expression of contempt crossed his face. 'When will you realize, sir, I care naught, one way or the other? And now, Master Shardlake, please leave me alone.'

✝

ON THE RIDE we saw more supply carts heading south, carrying everything from carpenters' equipment to pikes and helmets. We pulled in to allow another company of archers to pass. I wondered how Leacon's company was faring, whether they had been on board the ships yet.

Around noon we turned into the road to Sussex. We stopped for some food at the inn I had visited on my previous journey. 'You've been very quiet,' Barak said to me over his beer. 'You have that inward expression you wear when something bites at you.'

'I am thinking I have done little but make enemies since I came to Hoyland.' I told him of my talk with Hugh, and of Hobbey saying I was his nemesis. 'Hobbey set me wondering whether, if I had never come, Abigail might still be alive.'

'Something was likely to happen to that family sooner or later. They are all as mad as a box of frogs.'

'Who killed Abigail, Jack? Hobbey was right – everyone disliked her – but to *murder* her?'

'They'll set Ettis up for it if they can.'

'I think Dyrick is considering just that possibility. But there's no evidence.'

'Juries get rigged in these country places. If you want to do something useful, see the inquest is handled lawfully.'

'Yes. And you are right about the family. Their relationships are so – distorted – I cannot help thinking someone in that house killed her.'

'But who?'

'Fulstowe has a lot of power there for a steward. When servants have power over an employer it is usually because they know a secret. One they would not wish to risk through an unstable woman blurting it out.'

'But what secret?'

'I don't know.' I looked at him. 'Thank you again for coming with me.'

'Truth to tell, if I was there I would only be pacing around waiting for another messenger. I'm famished for news of Tamasin.'

'Maybe even the royal messengers are finding it hard to get through.'

'If only I could get home,' he said with sudden intensity.

I smiled sadly. 'Is it not strange how even in death, poor Abigail seems to be a nuisance to everyone? She was killed by an archer of some skill. But that covers so many possibilities. The boys, Fulstowe, Ettis. Even Dyrick said he was once a skilled archer and is teaching his children.'

'But not Hobbey?'

I shook my head. 'He does not have the skill or the – the passion, that is the word. It was a passionate, angry act. Someone who knew he would be hanged if he were caught but, at the moment he saw her at least, did not care.'

'Not old Ursula then. She hated Abigail all right, but I can't see her pulling a bow.'

'Now you are being foolish.' I drained my mug of beer. 'Come, we should be back on the road.'

'Only trying to lighten your mood a little. God knows we could both do with it.'

Chapter Thirty-three

IT WAS MID-AFTERNOON when we reached Rolfswood. The clouds had thickened; it looked as though another summer rain-storm was on the way. The little town presented the same sleepy aspect it had before. I pointed out Buttress's house. 'That was once Ellen's. He got it cheap. He's a friend of Priddis, or was.'

'Could he be paying Ellen's fees at the Bedlam as part of some deal?'

I shook my head. 'The house is not worth that much.' I pointed over the fields to the church. 'Seckford lives in the vicarage there.'

Barak squinted at the building. 'Looks tumbledown.'

'It is. So is he, I'm afraid.'

He said quietly, 'There's a woman looking at us from the doorway of that inn.'

I glanced across. The old woman who had introduced me to Wilf was standing in the doorway, arms folded, looking at us coldly.

'That's the woman who introduced me to Wilf Harrydance. I don't think I'm popular here either. I doubt we'll get rooms there tonight.'

'Then where will we sleep? It's been a long ride.'

'Maybe Seckford can help us. Come, we follow that path to the church.'

We rode up to the vicarage and tied the horses up outside. They were tired and dusty, as were we. As we walked up the path, I looked at the cherry tree and wondered if Seckford still kept to his resolution not to drink before the shadows reached a certain length. I knocked on the door and heard the old man's shuffling steps. He opened it, and his plump face broke into a look of relief. 'You came, sir,' he said. 'Thank God.' He saw Barak and asked sharply, 'Who is this?'

'My assistant.'

The curate nodded. 'I am sorry, only we have been worried. Come in. Wilf has been here most of the morning, hoping you would come – ' I caught a whiff of Seckford's breath, and guessed the two old men had already been sharing a drink. He led us into the shabby parlour. Wilf Harrydance rose from a stool. His big dog, which had been lying at his side, got up and wagged its tail. The bright eyes in Wilf's thin, weathered face were anxious. 'I didn't think you'd come, sir,' he said, 'not after my sons . . . I am sorry for that, they were only trying to protect me – '

'I understand, Wilf.'

'What news of the French?' Seckford asked.

'They are said to be sailing up the Channel towards Portsmouth.'

'God help us all. Please, sit down.'

We sat gratefully on the settle, raising little clouds of dust. 'A drink, sirs?' Seckford asked, reaching for the jug on the buffet.

'Yes, please,' Barak answered. 'We're parched.'

Seckford poured two beers, his hands shaking even more than I remembered. He brought them over, then sat in his chair. Wilf glanced at the curate, who leaned forward. Mildly drunk as he was, there was a new keenness and authority in Seckford's voice.

'After your visit, Master Shardlake, Master Buttress was going all over the town, trying to find out who had been telling you about the fire. He knew you had spoken to me, and came here in a great rage, saying you seemed to be querying his ownership of his house.'

'I did no such thing. I only told him you had told me the old story. I am sorry, I should have let you know before I left.' I looked at Wilf. 'I did not say I had spoken to you.'

'He came to the inn and asked me, though. He knows I've always thought Priddis covered something up at that inquest. I said I had not spoken with you. It made me uneasy, sir.'

Seckford added, 'Master Buttress is a hard man, with much power in this town. Forgive me, sir, but I must ask. Were you really enquiring about the Fettiplace family on behalf of a client looking for relatives?'

I took a deep breath. 'No. Forgive me for misleading you, but I am trying to find out what happened to Ellen Fettiplace, for – personal reasons.'

'You told an untruth, sir.'

'I did. I am sorry.'

'You are not acting for anyone else? Priddis, for example?'

'No, I promise. No one else at all. I can say no more, but I will happily swear on the Bible that I am acting only from personal interest and concern, because of some information that came my way in London indicating that something was indeed covered up at that inquest. But I do not know what, and it may be unsafe to say more. Please, sir, fetch your bible and I will swear.'

'I told you there was more to it,' Wilf said.

'And I told you Master Shardlake was a good man. I believe you, sir, there is no need to swear.' Seckford looked at Wilf, then clasped his hands together. 'You are a lawyer, sir. Am I right, then, that you could take Wilf on as a client, advise him about a certain problem he has, and would then be bound by an oath of confiden-tiality, as I am in confession?'

'Yes, that is true.' I looked at Wilf. 'But this matter – if is it anything to do with who started the fire at the foundry, I could not keep it secret.'

'It isn't.' Wilf shook his head vigorously. 'It's about something I found.'

Seckford said, 'It concerns the circumstances in which Wilf found it.'

'Then I will do what I can to advise you.'

Seckford said, 'I heard that for a lawyer to be bound to a client money has to pass.'

'That is not strictly true. I can act *pro bono*, for the public good.'

'I'd rather money changed hands,' Wilf said firmly. 'In front of

Master Seckford.' He reached to the purse at his belt and pulled out a sixpence, an old coin of true silver. 'Is this enough?' he asked.

I hesitated, then reached out and took the coin. 'Yes. There, Wilf, you are my client. By law I may not reveal anything you tell me, to anyone.'

Wilf took a deep breath, then bent to pat the big dog. 'Me and Caesar here, this time of year we go hunting for truffles in the woods. Master Buttress owns the woods now, and everything in them. Though he talks of having them cut down to sell the timber, he's still jealous of his property.'

'You could call what Wilf does poaching,' Seckford said quietly. 'The penalties are severe, and Master Buttress is one to ensure a prosecution. He's a magistrate.'

I said, 'There would need to be evidence.' I looked at Wilf. 'Is there any?'

His eyes bored into mine. 'Yes.' He paused, then continued. 'Two days ago, I took Caesar into the woods. He has a wonderful nose for truffles. I know the foresters' movements, see. I know when they are in another part of the woods.'

'I understand.'

'It's early for truffles yet, and I don't usually go anywhere near the old foundry. It's full of sadness for me, that place. I remember how it was, busy, the mill wheel turning. I hate seeing those ruins –' Wilf broke off, took a swig of beer, then said bitterly, 'But this time I went up there. I'd heard the mill pond had broken through the dam, after the storms of rain and hail in June, but I hadn't wanted to go and see. But you asking about what happened at the foundry, it brought it all back, and I decided to take Caesar that way and take a look at the place.'

'I see.'

Wilf wiped his mouth and went on. 'No one had attended to the mill pond since the fire. Those gates were bound to give way eventually. Well, when I went up there they had: the mill pond had quite drained away, only silt left at the bottom, which with the warmer weather this month has dried and shrunk. It was a strange, sad sight, the empty pond with the ruins by the broken dam. Then Caesar ran out onto the dried mud, began sniffing and digging at something sticking out of it.' He closed his eyes briefly, then continued.

'I called him, but he wouldn't come, he was worrying at what looked like a tree root. In the end I took off my shoes and walked over to get him. The dried mud was only a crust over softer stuff: once I sank in almost to my knees, but I made it over to Caesar. Then I saw what he was worrying at.' The old man paused and took another swig of beer. 'It was an arm, a human arm, all withered but preserved by the silt. There's a whole body down there. So then I came to Master Seckford.'

'Who do you think it was?' I asked urgently.

'I don't know. You couldn't tell.' He fell silent.

Barak said, 'Someone could have fallen in the pond over the years since the foundry went.'

Wilf shook his head. 'It was in the middle of the pond. Someone took that body out there in a boat – there used to be a little rowing boat – and dropped it in.'

I asked, 'Could a swimmer not have drowned in there sometime?'

'The body's clothed, sir. There's what looks like the remains of a doublet sleeve on the arm.'

'Mary help us,' Seckford said. He rose and headed for the buffet.

'No, sir,' I said to him sharply. 'Please, we should stay sober.'

Seckford hesitated and looked longingly at the jug, but made himself come and sit down again. He looked at me. 'Wilf was afraid of reporting it, sir, you see. Because he'd been poaching. His dog had dug up some truffles on the way, and he'd be hard put to explain what he was doing in the woods. That is our problem. And there are footprints in the mud now, going out to where the body is.'

'I see.'

Seckford said carefully, 'What we thought, sir, is that you could say you came back here today to make more enquiries, and got Wilf to agree to take you to the foundry to look at it. Then the dog can find – what it found.' He smiled uneasily.

'You are asking my master to perjure himself,' Barak said.

Seckford met his gaze. 'It may be Wilf's only hope.' He looked at me. 'He would not have gone up there but for your visit. And you, sir, wanted to discover what happened there. Well, finding the body would put you at the centre of any new enquiry. You could tell them what you told us, that you were seeking members of the Fettiplace family for a friend.'

I leaned back, sighing. Again I had set out on an enquiry in good faith, with the aim of helping someone in trouble, and brought more trouble to everyone involved. Yet Seckford, it seemed, still trusted me.

'I'll take you there now, show you,' Wilf said eagerly. 'Then you could say afterwards that you asked me to go there today. You're my only hope,' he added desperately. 'My sons agree.'

I looked at Barak. He shook his head, spread his hands.

'I'll do it,' I told Wilf. 'Take me to the foundry now, show me and we'll pretend we've just found the body.'

Wilf let out a long sigh of relief and smiled at the curate. 'You were right about him, Master Seckford. He'll save me.'

✝

SECKFORD REMAINED behind. I was not sorry, for he would have slowed us down, and I had a horrible anxiety that someone else might find the body in the meantime. I saw the old fellow reach for his jug as we headed for the door. Outside, Wilf pointed to a path which led up into woodland. I was hungry, dusty, my legs tired beyond measure. But this had to be done now.

We followed Wilf into the woods, the dog at his heels. The sky was very dark; it could start raining at any moment.

'What the fuck are we getting into this time?' Barak muttered.

'Something that should have been dealt with a long time ago. But no secret lasts for ever.'

He shook his head. 'This one might have, if that dog hadn't gone digging. You realize there'll be another inquest. You'll be first finder again. Only this time you'll have set that up.'

'I couldn't leave that old man in the briars. But you don't have to come, you don't have to be involved in this.'

'That woman saw us riding together through the town. They'll be asking later who was with you.'

'You are right. I'm sorry.'

'It looks like murder again, doesn't it?'

'Yes, Jack, it does.'

We followed Wilf along an overgrown path between the trees, alongside the large stream that ran through the town. This would have been a pretty scene in other circumstances. 'This stream fed the mill,' Wilf called over his shoulder. 'Here, Caesar!' He called to the dog, which had got a little ahead and seemed impatient. He stopped, running a hand over his bald brown pate. 'I walked this way to work for many years,' he said quietly. 'It was so busy then, carts coming down here with loads of iron. We come to the foundry first, the pond's behind.'

We reached the clearing where the foundry had stood just as heavy drops of rain began to fall. All that was left was a pile of low ruins, jagged remnants of wooden walls, black and burned, festooned with ivy. At one end the smashed remains of a water-wheel leaned against a tall, round structure with rooks' nests on top. The furnace chimney no doubt. Beyond the ruined building I glimpsed a long, rectangular expanse of brown mud, through the centre of which the stream now ran. Large overgrown mounds stood on the banks. 'What are those?' I asked Wilf, pointing.

'Slag heaps.'

Seeing the empty pond, the dog tried to dart ahead. Wilf reached out and put a hand on its collar. 'We'll need to find something to dig with,' he said. He led us into the ruins through a gap in the broken walls. Inside, the wide stone floor was covered with weeds. At one end stood the old furnace shed. The walls had almost gone but the big stone furnace stood blackened but untouched, a dark hole at the bottom: no doubt the hatch through which the semi-molten iron was collected. Wilf began picking among the rubbish on the floor. Barak and I stood looking around. The rain had started to come down steadily, pattering on our heads and on the stone floor.

'The building is larger than I thought,' I said. Even now I caught the tang of iron in the air.

Wilf looked up. He had unearthed the remains of a spade, the blade half rusted away. 'If a fire started here it would take a long time to burn up the whole enclosure. And those walls weren't high, anyone active could climb over.'

Ellen's words came back to me again: *He burned! The poor man, he was all on fire* – One man, I thought. Was the other already in the pond?

'I see what a wreck this place must have been after the fire,' Barak said.

'Burned almost to the ground,' Wilf replied. 'They found bones, of course. Burned right through, charred.' He pointed to the furnace. 'Just there.'

'How many bones?' I asked.

Wilf shook his head. 'It was hard to say which bones were there, they were so burned. But there was only the remains of one pelvis. Priddis said the other bones must have been been burned beyond recognition. Now, sirs, come. Let us see what Caesar found.'

We left the ruined foundry. The rain was still coming down, and I blinked water out of my eyes. We went over to the muddy depression, which gave off a rotten stink. It was surrounded by reeds, dying now from lack of water. Wilf produced a length of cord and tied Caesar to a tree. The dog whined, looking longingly out at the mud. Wilf pointed at a spot near the centre of the pond, perhaps twenty yards in. I saw a trail of footprints leading to what looked like a large blackened stick protruding from the mud. Barak whistled softly.

Wilf pointed to a wooden pole protruding from the reeds. 'The boat used to be tied to that post, see, there. When Master Fettiplace's daughter was little she used to go rowing out on the pond. Someone could have taken that boat on the night of the fire and dumped the body in the middle.' I suddenly thought, Ellen could. But why not leave it in the foundry?

Wilf's mouth set firmly. 'We'd best do it now, sirs.'

He put the rusty spade over his shoulders, and Barak and I removed our shoes and followed him onto the dried, cracked mud, walking carefully. Once the crust gave and Barak sank to mid-calf, swearing mightily as he pulled his leg out.

Wilf was first to reach the middle. 'See, sir?' he said quietly.

I looked down at the shrivelled remains of a human arm, dried skin and wasted tendons over bone. I was reminded of the saints' relics that were forbidden now. Wilf took the spade from his shoulders and set it in a crack in the dried mud. 'Stand back, sirs,' he said.

'Let me do it,' Barak said roughly. 'I'm younger than you.'

'No, sir. It's easy enough, even with this broken thing. I just have to dig through the crust into the mud. But you'll have to help me get it out.' Wilf thrust the spade into the mud. Barak and I watched, the rain tipping down relentlessly on our heads, as he dug. Underneath was a layer of stinking, viscous ooze. Once Wilf stopped, winced, then stood with his head lowered.

'What's the matter?' Barak asked.

'I think I hit the body.' He had gone pale.

'Do you want me to take over?' Barak asked.

'Yes, please.'

After about twenty minutes Barak had exposed an area of thick silty mud perhaps seven feet by three. Then he leaned over and reached down. He felt around, then tugged gently, dragging up another arm. He turned his head from the smell of the ooze. 'Try to find the feet,' he said. 'If we try pulling it out by the arms it might come apart.'

Wilf and I knelt carefully on the wet crust and reached into the mud. The rain still beat down on us all and on those exposed, withered arms. 'I've got a leg,' Wilf said in a shaking voice.

'I have the other.' It felt horrible, just cloth and bone.

Barak said, 'One, two, *three*,' and we all pulled. Slowly the body of a man rose from the bottom of the pool, the mud sucking at it. The leg I had hold of seemed particularly hard to get out; as it rose slowly from the mud I saw why. A rope was tied round the thigh, a lump of iron on the other end. There was no doubt now: this body had been hidden here.

We hauled the dark, dripping thing to the bank. Caesar strained at his leash, barking. We sat down, taking deep breaths of fresh air, the rain running into our mouths. Then Wilf rose and, gently turned the body over. Producing a rag from his smock, he wiped the mud-encrusted head. It was little more than a skull with skin stretched over the bones, but it still had hair.

He wiped the neck and the collar of what I saw were the rags of a doublet. He bent down and rose with a large button in his hand. He showed it to me, his hand shaking.

'See, sir, the button hasn't rotted. See the design, a big square cross. I remember it, these were the buttons Master Fettiplace wore on the doublet he often wore to work. And the hair is fair, as his was. It is him.' Wilf looked stricken, then he began to weep. 'Forgive me, this is hard for me.' Barak put a hand on his shoulder.

'How did it happen?' I asked Barak quietly. 'Ellen said one man burned. That must have been Wilf's friend Peter Gratwyck. Her father was killed and put in here.' I looked at the body, but it was too mummified to show any sign of a wound now.

Barak said, 'If he was killed, why not leave the body in the foundry to burn?' He leaned close. 'And *who* was there? Ellen was, we know, but was anyone else?'

I turned to Wilf. 'Did anyone from round here, apart from Master Fettiplace and your friend Gratwyck, go missing at the time of the fire? Someone who might have done this and fled?'

Wilf's face was streaked with mud and tears and rain. 'No sir,' he said, 'nobody.'

Chapter Thirty-four

WILF INSISTED we put Fettiplace's body under cover, and we placed the desiccated corpse against an inside wall of the ruined foundry, protecting it with loose planks. It was sickening to carry; I feared it might come apart. Afterwards I looked over the cracked mud where the body had lain; already the space, and our footsteps, were filling with rainwater. Then we walked back, sodden and dripping.

'Now I suppose we have to go to Buttress,' Barak said quietly, 'as magistrate.'

'Yes. He will have to set enquiries in motion, and notify the Sussex coroner.' I shook my head. 'Murder follows me on this journey.'

'The common factor in each is Priddis's involvement.' Barak lowered his voice to a whisper, though Wilf was ahead with Caesar. 'You said Ellen's signature on the deed conveying the house was forged. Do you think Buttress knows?'

'He could do. I didn't like what I saw of him.'

The vicarage came into view. I took Wilf's arm. 'You should send for your sons,' I said gently. 'You have had a shock.'

He came to himself, looked at me. 'You'll say nothing about my poaching?'

'No. I promised. We shall tell the story as we agreed, that I asked you to show me the old foundry buildings today.'

Seckford had seen us approaching and came into his garden. 'What did you find?' he asked apprehensively.

'The body of Master Fettiplace.' I took the curate's soft plump arm, and looked him in the face. 'Sir, Wilf will need you sober now. We all will.'

He took a deep breath and turned to Wilf. 'His body will have a Christian burial. I shall see to it.'

We went into the parlour. Seckford spoke with sudden firmness. 'That jug, Master Shardlake, will you take it out to the kitchen?'

I took his beer to a filthy little room behind the parlour, where flies buzzed over dirty plates. Seckford seemed barely able to care for himself, but once he had cared for Ellen. I returned to the parlour, where Wilf was hunched on the settle. Seckford was in his chair.

'Master Seckford,' I said, 'I think we must go to Master Buttress, now. All four of us.'

'Will the truth be found?' he asked. 'This time?'

'I hope so. Now listen please, both of you. I beg you to stay quiet about my personal interest. Let Buttress continue to think I have merely been trying to trace family links for a client.'

Seckford looked at me with sudden sharpness. 'But if you found something out in London, surely that must come out now.'

'There are reasons I should say nothing yet. Please trust me.' More than ever now I did not want Buttress, or his allies, to discover where Ellen was – assuming they did not know already. I hoped desperately that I had done enough to protect her, and suddenly wished Wilf had never stumbled on that body. The old man was looking at me doubtfully again.

Seckford came to my rescue. 'We must trust Master Shardlake, Wilf. Do not say more than you have to in dealing with people like Buttress, eh, Master Shardlake?'

'Exactly.' I felt a rush of gratitude for Seckford's trust. He stood, went over to Wilf and patted his arm. 'We can call at the church on the way, I will write a note for the verger to take to your sons.'

✝

AN HOUR LATER I sat again in Master Buttress's well-appointed parlour. There was a fresh vase of flowers on the table, their scent cloying. Seckford sat beside me, his plump cheeks sweating a little, while Barak and Wilf stood behind us. Buttress had offered chairs only to Seckford and me, though Wilf looked shocked and ill.

Buttress himself walked up and down the room, hands clasped behind his broad back, as I told him of the discovery in the pond. When I had finished he ran a big hand through his grey curly hair, thinking. Then he came and stood looking down at me.

'What I do not understand, Master Shardlake,' he said with blustering aggression, 'is why you went ferreting about at the foundry. When you came before your concern seemed to be in querying my right to this house.'

'I did not imply anything of the sort, sir. I merely wished to see if there was an address for Mistress Fettiplace on the deeds. You agreed to show the document to me.' I had not questioned his ownership of the property, but the guilty, I thought, easily take alarm. Buttress, I realized, was quite a stupid man.

He grunted, little brown eyes narrowing. 'In my experience, when a lawyer asks to see a conveyance it is usually because he wishes to query the title.'

'Then I apologize if I caused you unnecessary concern. I see I must have done, since Master Seckford and Goodman Harrydance tell me you made enquiries about my visit afterwards.'

'But why ride back all this way to look at the ruins of that foundry?'

'I had a day without business in Hampshire, and felt like a ride. Master Seckford had told me Goodman Harrydance knew the site.'

'And all this because you have a client interested in tracing family links. Who is this client, anyway?'

'You know I cannot answer that, sir. It would be a breach of professional confidentiality.'

'You'll have to tell the Sussex coroner when he gets here.' Buttress's eyes continued to probe mine a moment longer, then he turned away and made an irritated gesture. 'I suppose now I must arrange for the remains to be fetched back to Rolfswood. It's market day tomorrow –

this will be a rich piece of gossip for the goodwives. And I must write to the Sussex coroner at Chichester. Though heaven knows when he will be able to get here. Well,' he continued, looking round the four of us, 'at least there is no urgency. Master Fettiplace was in that pond nineteen years; it won't hurt him to wait a little longer.'

'With respect, sir,' I said, 'this *is* still a newly discovered murder. Sir Quintin Priddis's old verdict of accidental death was clearly wrong.'

'Ay.' Wilf spoke up boldly. 'I always said that first inquest was not done properly.'

Buttress leaned his heavy body forward, glaring into the old man's face. 'Are you accusing one of the region's leading men of incompetence? Watch your step, old nid-nod.'

'Goodman Harrydance is upset,' Seckford said placatingly.

Buttress turned his baleful look on him. 'I know you and this other old fool like a drink together, Master Curate. More than one. And I hear your services have a papist flavour. Don't provoke me into making life difficult for either of you.'

'Sir,' I said. 'I protest. You are the magistrate, it is not fitting you should bully witnesses.'

Buttress's face darkened, but he kept his control. 'I brought Goodman Harrydance to order for insulting the former coroner. And Master Seckford is no witness to anything. He did not accompany you to the foundry.'

Seckford said quietly, 'I am, though, a witness to the state of mind of Mistress Fettiplace after the foundry burned down, and to the fact she was hurried away by Master Priddis himself.'

I winced, wishing he had not drawn attention to Ellen's disappearance. I said, mildly, 'If she witnessed a murder, that could explain her state of mind.'

'And what,' Buttress asked, rounding on me, 'if the death was suicide? What if Master Fettiplace, for some reason we do not know, set the fire, killed his man, then rowed out to the middle of the pond, tied a lump of iron round his leg, and drowned himself? Such things happen; there was a silly village girl a couple of years ago got herself with child and drowned herself in a local pond.'

I suddenly thought of Michael Calfhill, swinging from that rope in his lodgings. I said, 'Then surely the empty boat would have been found floating in the pond next morning.'

'Maybe it went unnoticed; everyone was concerned with the fire.'

'Why should Master Fettiplace have killed himself?' I asked.

Buttress shrugged. 'Who knows? Well, we shall have to bring the witnesses together. Some of the men from the foundry are still alive.'

'I understand Ellen Fettiplace had spent the day with a young man who was interested in her, Philip West.'

Buttress flicked me an angry look. 'The Wests are an important local family. Self-important anyway. Master West is now an officer on the King's ships.'

'Nonetheless, he, too, will need to be questioned.' I realized that when all these people were brought together it would come out how thoroughly I had been investigating Ellen's history. But the important thing was to get them together and questioned properly. And I would be there.

'It will take time to put these wheels in motion,' Buttress said. I realized he would do everything he could to delay. But why? To keep a forged conveyance secret?

He said, 'I expect by the time the Sussex coroner has been able to get all these people together for an inquest, you will be back in London. He will write to you. Unless the French land and we are all so mired in war down here that nothing can be done about anything.'

'I shall keep in touch with matters through Master Seckford.' I gave the old man a meaningful glance, and he nodded.

'Yes, Master Shardlake,' Buttress said heavily, 'I imagine you will.'

✝

EVENING FOUND US lodging at Rolfswood inn; Buttress, unsurprisingly, had offered us no hospitality. When we left the house Wilf's sons were waiting for us a little way up the street. This time their manner towards me was friendly. After all, I had just lied to save their father from a possible charge of poaching.

'You should have left that body be, Father,' one brother said chidingly. 'Let someone else find it. Look at you, you're half dead.'

'I couldn't leave Master Fettiplace there,' Wilf said. 'Master Shardlake will keep me safe.'

'I promise I will see justice done,' I said. I hoped I would be able to. Buttress might not be clever, but he was cunning and ruthless.

Seckford and Wilf came with us to the inn. The woman who had first introduced me to Wilf, a widow named Mistress Bell, turned out to own it. She agreed to give us a place for the night. When we parted I grasped Seckford's flabby hand. 'Sir,' I said, 'please protect Wilf so far as you can. A letter will bring me here.' I had given him the address of Hoyland Priory, and of my chambers in London.

He looked at me with bleary eyes, then smiled sadly. 'You fear I will be too far gone in my cups to be of use. No, sir, I will control myself. God has given me a task to perform, as once he did with Ellen. I will not fail this time.'

'Thank you,' I said, hoping he could keep his resolution.

Barak and I were shown up to a room where we both collapsed, exhausted, on the bed, until an hour later hunger sent us down to eat. The inn was full; I remembered Buttress saying tomorrow was market day. As we ate, someone brought the news that the body of old Master Fettiplace had been found in the mill pond and an excited hubbub of conversation began. Barak and I retired upstairs before we could be connected with the gossip.

'Where does this leave us?' he asked.

'With the chance to bring everyone involved together to be questioned. Buttress will drag his heels, I must keep on at him.'

'From London? And Ellen? If this all comes out, will she be safe?'

'I took steps to ensure she was protected. I will take more on my return.'

'And now you'll have to keep coming back here.'

I sat up on the bed. 'I must bring some order out of this chaos, Jack. I must.' I heard the rising passion in my voice. Barak gave me a long, serious look, but said nothing.

'Buttress is hiding something,' I said at length.

'Probably. But where does finding Fettiplace's body actually leave things? An inquest might agree with Buttress, decide Fettiplace could have killed Gratwyck, then gone out on the pond and killed himself.'

'What if some third party came to the foundry, raped Ellen, then killed both her father and Gratwyck? She said at least two men attacked her, she said *they* were too strong for her, she could not move.'

Barak was silent again for a minute, then said, 'You place much weight on the shrieks of a madwoman.'

'She spoke the truth that day.'

'How can you be so sure?' He folded his arms and looked at me, holding my eye in a way that reminded me oddly of some judges I had known.

'You did not see her, you did not see the horror those memories brought.'

'What if West's insinuations are true, that Ellen herself killed her father and Gratwyck, then set the fire? Priddis could still have had her removed from the area to please the Wests, and done some deal with Buttress so he bought that house cheaply and they shared the profits. You know what these county officials are like, they're at it all the time.'

'I got the impression Buttress did not like the Wests. Rivals for local power, perhaps.'

'You don't want to believe she could possibly have done it, do you?'

I sat on the edge of the bed, frowning. 'I think that, whatever happened, Philip West was involved somehow. That day marks him still.'

'Just because you think so doesn't make it true.'

I said impatiently, 'I want to get West, and Priddis too, questioned at an inquest. That will bring out the truth.'

He still looked dubious, and concerned. 'What is the Sussex coroner like?'

'I know nothing about him. I will make enquiries when we return to London.'

'If we ever do.'

'We'll go back as soon as the Hampshire coroner lets us go. I made a promise and I'll keep to it.'

Barak walked to the shutters at the sound of loud voices from the street, shouting and calling. I had been conscious of growing noise but thought it was traders preparing their stalls for market day. He opened the shutters, then whistled. 'Come and see this.'

I joined him at the window. Outside a large group of people, some carrying torches, had gathered round a pile of brushwood in the middle of the street. As we watched the little crowd parted, shouting and cheering, to allow four men through. They carried the straw effigy of a man, dressed in a ragged smock with the fleur-de-lys of France painted prominently on the front.

The crowd began to shout: 'Burn the Frenchy! Kill the dog!'

The mannikin was laid on the brushwood, which was set on fire. The figure was outlined in flames for a moment, then quickly consumed. 'That's what invaders get!' someone shouted, to loud cheers.

'We'll neuter the French King's gentlemen cocks for him!'

I turned away with a grunt. 'They might pause to ask who started all this. The King, taking on a far larger power.'

'That's the problem,' Barak said, 'you set something in motion and before you know where you are it's all out of control.' He looked at me meaningfully. I did not reply, but lay down again on the bed, watching the reflected flames dancing redly on the ceiling.

✝

NEXT MORNING we rose early for the long ride back to Hoyland. The weather was clear and bright again. Outside the ashes of the fire had been cleared away, and market stalls with bright awnings were being set up along the street. We had breakfasted and were gathering our things together when old Mistress Bell knocked and entered, looking flustered. 'Someone has called to see you, sir,' she said.

'Who is it?'

She took a deep breath. 'Mistress Beatrice West, widow of Sir John West and owner of Carlen Hall.'

Barak and I exchanged glances. 'Where is she?' I asked.

'I have shown her to my poor parlour,' Mistress Bell continued in a rush of words. 'She has heard about the body in the mill pond. Please sir, do not say anything to upset her. Many of my customers are her tenants. She is a proud woman, easily offended.'

'I have no wish to make an enemy of her.'

'Trouble,' Mistress Bell said with sudden bitterness. 'Each time you come, trouble.' She went out, closing the door with a snap. Barak raised his eyebrows.

'Wait here,' I said.

✝

MISTRESS BELL'S parlour was a small room containing a scratched table, a couple of stools and an ancient wall painting of a hunting scene, the paint cracked and faded. A tall, strongly built woman in her sixties stood by the table. She wore a wide, high-collared blue dress, and an old-fashioned box hood framing a clever, haughty face with small, keen, deep-set eyes that reminded me of her son.

'Mistress Beatrice West?' I asked.

She nodded her head in curt acknowledgement, then said abruptly, 'Are you the lawyer who found that body in the pond? At the Fettiplace foundry?'

'I am, madam. Matthew Shardlake, Serjeant-at-Law, of London.' I bowed deeply.

Mistress West nodded, her pose becoming slightly less stiff. 'At least I am dealing with someone of rank.' She waved a manicured hand at the stools. 'Please, sit if you wish. Perhaps you find standing for long uncomfortable. I will not sit on a stool, I am used to chairs, but I see this is a poor place.'

The indirect reference to my condition made me bridle slightly. But I realized that temperate words and a modest manner were the best way of dealing with this woman. 'I am quite happy to stand, thank you.'

She continued staring at me with those sharp little brown eyes. Despite her haughty demeanour I read anxiety there. She spoke abruptly: 'I came to Rolfswood last night, to visit the market. I am staying with friends. I had scarce arrived when I received a letter from that boor Humphrey Buttress. He told me the body of Master Fettiplace, that we all thought burned in his foundry nineteen years ago, had been found in the pond. By you.'

'That is correct, madam.'

'He said he required as magistrate – required, oh, he loves that word – to know the whereabouts of my son, given his former – connection – to Mistress Ellen Fettiplace. Well, that is easily enough answered. Philip is at Portsmouth, preparing to defend England. Buttress said you wanted him questioned.' She paused for breath. 'Well, sir, what have you to say? What is this old matter to do with you?'

I answered quietly, 'I can tell you only what I told Master Buttress. I have been making enquiries on behalf of a client about the Fettiplace family. I visited the foundry with old Goodman Harrydance yesterday, and we found the body. I am sorry to cause inconvenience, but clearly the discovery in the pond must be investigated. Your son is one of those who must be part of that. I only wish to see justice done, to see the relevant people are called.'

'Why are you in Sussex?'

'A legal case in Hampshire. I am staying at a house some miles north of Portsmouth. Hoyland Priory. I am engaged on a Court of Wards matter there.' I judged it best not to tell this woman my normal work was at the Court of Requests. Her face relaxed a little. I said, 'Master Seckford told me your son came out on the day of the fire to ask Master Fettiplace's approval of a marriage to his daughter.'

'That girl,' Mistress West said bitterly. 'She was below our station, Philip should never have involved himself with her. She went mad after the fire – she was taken away. Will you have an official part in the investigation?' she asked suddenly.

'I am involved now, as a finder of the body.' I looked closely at Mistress West. Was it her who had arranged Ellen's abduction?

Suddenly she seemed to wilt. 'We thought it was all done, but now – a murder, and my son to be questioned.'

'I want to see the truth found, madam. That is all.'

She stared at me, long and hard, then seemed to reach a decision. 'Then there is something I should tell you. It must come out, and I would rather tell you first than Buttress. You may understand, Master Shardlake, that in small towns there is often rivalry between those of good old birth like my family and men like him.'

'Having met him, I can imagine he is – difficult.'

'If I were to tell you something that showed my son did not meet Mistress Fettiplace on that day, perhaps Philip would not have to be called to the inquest.'

'Possibly.'

'He would not want to reveal it, even now. But I must do what I can to protect him. He should have told them at the first inquest. Though we all thought it was an accident then.' She began wringing her hands and I realized she was a frightened woman, on the edge of panic. She looked at me again, then composed herself and began speaking rapidly.

'Nineteen years ago, my son was twenty-two. For his age he had risen high. Two years before, my late husband and I had found him a place in the King's household, working for his majesty's Master of Hunt. We were well pleased.' Her face relaxed into a fond smile for a moment. 'You should have seen Philip then. A fine, strong boy, carefree, devoted to manly pursuits. Those were the last of the

old days, sir, when everything in England seemed settled and secure. The King had been married to Queen Catherine of Aragon near twenty years, happily we thought, though they had no son. We did not know he had already set his eyes on Anne Boleyn.'

'I remember it well.'

'My son, as I said, helped organize the King's hunts. I am told he can scarce walk now, but in those days he was always hunting. Philip caught the King's eye, he favoured young men who shared his taste for sport. By 1526 he was in the outer circle of the King's boon companions and sometimes he would be asked to join the King at games of dice and cards.' She spoke with pride, then added in a heavier tone, 'And sometimes, the King would use Philip as a messenger, to deliver private letters. He had come to trust my son greatly. Letters to – ' Mistress West set her lips in a tight line – 'to Anne Boleyn.'

I remembered Anne Boleyn's execution that Lord Cromwell had insisted I attend; her head flying out when severed from the body, the jets of blood. I closed my eyes for a moment. Strange I had not recalled that when I saw Lady Elizabeth, her daughter.

Mistress West sighed. 'It does not matter now, Catherine of Aragon and Anne Boleyn are both long dead, but by heaven it mattered then. In 1526 no one outside the court had even heard of Anne Boleyn. The King had had mistresses before, but Anne Boleyn insisted he divorce Catherine and marry her. You know the story. She promised him a son.' Mistress West laughed bitterly. I thought, but she only gave him Elizabeth. I remembered the little girl looking keenly up at me as she questioned me about lawyers.

'Well, in 1526 the King went on one of his hunting Progresses to the royal parks in Sussex. Queen Catherine was with him, as was Philip. Anne Boleyn was at her family home in Kent. But the King wrote to her regularly, and Philip was one of the trusted messengers he used. What those letters said, how far matters had gone by then, I do not know and nor did Philip. But Queen Catherine was worried—'

'As early as that? I had not known—'

'Oh, Queen Catherine always had her spies.'

Mistress West began walking restlessly around the room, her skirt swishing on the rush-strewn boards.

'The court was at Petworth Castle in Sussex that August, over twenty miles from here. You should understand, Master Shardlake, my son's position meant he spent much of his time in London; he could only visit Rolfswood occasionally. There were often gaps of many weeks between his visits to Ellen Fettiplace. I think now, if he had seen more of her, he would have realized how unsuitable she was for a bride.'

'You did not like her.'

'I did not,' she answered vigorously. 'Her father had allowed her too much independence, she would blow hot and cold with my son. But her impertinence just made him more lovelorn.' She gave a bitter laugh. 'Just as the King was with that false, faithless Boleyn creature, and look how that ended.' She continued sadly, 'And there was something wild, unstable in Ellen's nature already. She was not one to be crossed.'

'What do you mean?'

'There are things I know.'

I frowned, remembering what Philip West had told me about setting fires.

'Philip had written to tell us he planned to propose to Ellen Fettiplace, and had obtained leave from the Master of Hunt to visit us. Then, just before he left, the King himself called for him. He asked that after Philip came here he take a letter over to Hever. A letter with the King's own seal.'

'Did the King know of your son's planned proposal?'

'Yes. That was why he allowed Philip to come here first.' Mistress West came over and looked at me. I wished she would sit. 'But when Philip rode from Petworth to Hampshire, Master Shardlake, he was not alone.' Her voice shook slightly. 'He had a friend at the court, a young lawyer, who asked if he could come with my son for the ride and his company. He was going on to Hampshire.'

I felt a catch in my throat. So there had been two of them. *They were so strong. I could not move!* It was an effort to keep my voice even. 'Who was the friend?' I asked.

Mistress West looked at me, and now there was a sort of desperate appeal in her eyes. 'That is the difficulty, sir. I do not know.'

'But if Philip came to stay with you—'

'Let me tell you how it happened. Philip's letter came by fast messenger from Petworth, saying he would be with us the following day. Because he had to go on afterwards to deliver the King's message – we did not know to whom, then – he could only stay here one night. He planned to ride straight to the Fettiplace house that afternoon and speak to William Fettiplace. If he agreed to the marriage, Philip would propose to Ellen that day.' I thought, that is not quite what Philip said, he spoke of asking for Master Fettiplace's approval and seeing Ellen later.

His mother continued, 'If Ellen accepted he would bring her and Master Fettiplace to the Hall afterwards. He said a friend would be riding with him. So we made everything ready for his arrival. The ninth of August, a date I remember each year.'

'The date of the fire.'

She gave me a long, considering look, then she went and sat heavily on a stool. She was starting to look very tired. She went on, 'My late husband and I waited at home, the best wine brought out in anticipation of a celebration, though in truth we hoped Philip would arrive alone, that Ellen Fettiplace would have refused him. But the hours passed, it grew dark and still nobody came. We waited and waited. Then, towards midnight, Philip arrived. My poor boy, he had been so happy to be part of the King's court, so full of life and energy. But it had all gone out of him, he looked crushed, bereft – ' Mistress West paused – 'afraid.'

So, I thought, she turned him down. 'Had she rejected him?' I asked.

Mistress West shook her head. 'No. Philip had not seen Ellen: he knew nothing of the fire. Because something else had happened that had frozen his blood and froze ours when he told us. His friend, Master Shardlake, had betrayed him. During the journey, some miles from Rolfswood, they stopped for a drink at a country inn. There they had an argument. Philip can be fierce when he is provoked. It was nothing, some foolish quarrel about some horses, but the two of them ended on the ground, fighting.'

'Such things happen between young men.'

'After the fight Philip's friend gave him hard words and said he would ride back to Petworth. Later Philip realized he had probably manufactured the quarrel. For shortly after, as he rode on here, Philip found the King's letter was gone. He had had it on his person. And you see, his friend was employed in Queen Catherine's household. She must have learned about the letter somehow, and used this lawyer as one of her spies.'

'So his friend stole a letter from the King to Anne Boleyn?' I asked incredulously. 'To give to Catherine of Aragon? He took his life in his hands.'

'Oh, the Queen would have protected him. She was known for her loyalty to her servants.' I thought, someone else had said that to me: Warner, the current Queen's solicitor. Who would have been a young lawyer in Catherine's service in 1526. My heart began to thud.

'Philip thought at first he had dropped the letter during the fight. He raced back to the inn but there was no sign of it. So he was left with the prospect of returning to court and telling the King it was lost.'

'But it was stolen—'

Mistress West shook her head impatiently. 'My husband told him to say it was lost. Do you not see? Better for the King to think the letter was lost than probably in Queen Catherine's hands already. My husband told Philip not even to tell us the man's name, it would be safer for us if we did not know. But this inquest will enquire about Philip's movements that night and then he must give the name or be a suspect. This man is his alibi.' Then she spoke with some venom: 'Let him pay for his crime at last.'

I said, 'Jesu, that letter could have spoken of the King's intention to marry Anne Boleyn. If Catherine of Aragon had early notice of that, it could explain her refusal to consider a divorce from the start. Madam, if the King learned of your son's lie, even now it could go hard for him.'

Mistress West clasped her hands together. 'Better my son's carelessness be known than risk a charge of murder. I have thought about it all night, Master Shardlake. And I have decided.' She looked at me, waiting for a response. I could see why she did not want Buttress to be the first to hear this story.

'So your son did not see Ellen?'

'No. He stayed the night with us, then rose early the next morning and rode straight back to Petworth. News of the fire had not yet reached us. He told the King the letter had been lost on the journey. He was dismissed, of course. Then a messenger brought him news of the fire. He came home at once, and went to see Ellen, but she would not receive him. My husband and I implored him to leave her alone, but he persisted almost until she was taken away.'

I looked at her. For the first time she dropped her eyes. And I thought, yes, it was you that conspired with Priddis to have Ellen taken to the Bedlam.

She said, 'Philip went to sea, took service on the King's ships. For him it was a matter of honour, he felt he had betrayed the King. He has been at sea ever since. I am sure the King would consider his honourable service if the truth about that letter came out now.'

I looked at her. From my knowledge of the King, I doubted it.

'Since my husband died Philip has left the running of the estate in my hands. It is as though he is punishing himself still for losing that letter, after near twenty years.' She looked at me again with a sad smile. 'And that is the story, Master Shardlake. So you see, my son knew nothing of the fire, of those deaths.'

I made a steeple of my hands. It was a coincidence, to say the least, that the letter had vanished on the night of the fire. Mistress West clearly believed her son's story implicitly, and was perhaps arrogant and self-absorbed enough to think others would too. But there was only Philip's word that the letter and his friend even existed. I remembered him at Portsmouth – he was a haunted man, but haunted only by a lost letter, or something darker? And if there was a friend was he alibi or accomplice?

'Did your son ever say what became of his friend, the lawyer?' I asked. 'If he was allied to Catherine of Aragon, he was backing the losing side.'

She shrugged. 'I do not know. I imagine he changed his loyalties, turned his coat during Queen Catherine's fall. Many did.'

'That is true.'

She took a deep breath. 'Do you think if that story is told now it would help my son?'

I looked at her. 'In truth, madam, I do not know.'

'I would ask one more thing of you,' she said. 'Please do not tell Master Buttress what I have told you. Not just yet. Give my son – give him a chance to acquit himself in the battle that may be coming.'

I thought it would do no harm to keep the matter quiet for the moment. And it would give me time to make my own further investigations.

'Very well. I promise to say nothing yet.'

Her manner had changed completely now, it was almost imploring. 'Thank you. You are a thoughtful man, a neutral party. And perhaps – '

'Perhaps what, Mistress West?'

'Perhaps there is some way, some private way, of dealing with this matter without Philip being shamed at the inquest.'

'What might that be?'

'I do not know. If you could use your influence . . .'

'I will consider,' I answered flatly.

'If you wish to speak further, a message to my house, Carlen Hall, will reach me.'

'And I am at Hoyland Priory, eight miles north of Portsmouth on the Portsmouth road.'

I looked at her, and thought, anxious and afraid for your son as you are, I have no pity for you. When the time comes I will have the story of Ellen's forced removal out of you.

She gave a desolate smile. 'Of course, long before the inquest, my son may have given his life for his country. I think he would prefer to die with honour than live to see the story told.' Her mouth trembled and tears came to her eyes. 'Die for the King, and leave me alone in the world.'

Chapter Thirty-five

AN HOUR LATER we were on the road south to Hoyland. Mistress West had given me much food for thought. Barak's reaction when I told him her story had been instantaneous: 'I don't believe a word. West told his mother that story to keep her quiet. More likely he and his friend attacked Ellen, then his friend disappeared.'

'And the fire, and the murders at the foundry?'

'Maybe Ellen's father, and Gratwyck, came on them when they were attacking Ellen. Maybe she had refused to marry West and it maddened him. There was a fight and Gratwyck and Master Fettiplace got killed. And there never was a letter.' He looked at me. 'That would put Ellen in the clear for you.'

'Well, whether you are right, or West's story has truth in it, clearly now he holds the key to what happened. Either way I think Mistress West bribed Priddis to get a verdict of accidental death at the inquest. She may have been paying Ellen's fees at the Bedlam ever since.'

'If so, Philip West will already know where she is.'

I nodded slowly. 'And if he was responsible for all that happened, guilt may have driven him to the King's ships. To look for danger and death.'

'He may find those very soon.'

'But who was his friend who rode with him that day and then vanished?' I frowned. 'If that story was a lie, it was a dangerous one. The King would have been angered if he heard a junior courtier had put such a story about. And the timing sounds right – 1526, when the King was lusting after Anne Boleyn, but no one had any inkling yet he planned to marry her. There is only one way to find out,' I said decisively. 'I am going back to Portsmouth, to ask West.'

Barak stared at me. 'You can't! It's the fifteenth of July, the King's supposed to arrive today. To say nothing of the French fleet sailing towards us. For Jesu's sake, you can set these enquiries in motion when we return to London.'

I met his gaze. 'West may no longer be alive by then.'

'I thought you were starting to see things in proportion,' Barak said. 'You can't go back to Portsmouth now.'

'It may be the only way to get the truth. And I have had a thought, one I do not like. About who West's friend might have been.'

'Who?'

'Master Warner has been in the service of the Queen's household since Catherine of Aragon's time, and he is a lawyer. He has survived five changes of Queen. He is about the right age.'

'I thought he was your friend.'

'Friends have betrayed me before.'

'Queen Catherine Parr trusts him.'

'Yes. And she has good judgement. But there would not be many lawyers of his age in the Queen's household. And he said once that our present Queen was the kindest to her servants since Catherine of Aragon.'

Barak considered. 'Edward Priddis would have been a young lawyer in London around that time. So would Dyrick, come to that.'

'And Dyrick worked in the royal service. And Priddis said he was in London for a while, but not what he did there.'

'If he was involved, his father would have a real incentive to cover things up.'

We turned at the sound of wheels creaking loudly. Two large carts passed us, each drawn by four straining horses and loaded with boxes of iron gunballs; new cast, no doubt, in the Wealden furnaces.

'I hope we have some letters when we get back to Hoyland,' Barak said. 'It's about time.'

†

THERE WERE no servants working in the gardens of Hoyland Priory when we rode through the gates. Already Abigail's flower beds were starting to look neglected. To my surprise, I saw Hugh practising at the butts on his own. He looked at us but made no acknowledgement, bending to string a new arrow to his bow.

As we dismounted, Fulstowe came round the front of the house, neat as ever, with his beard freshly trimmed. His manner was even more proprietorial. He bowed briefly. I asked if there had been any letters.

'None, sir. But the coroner has got here. He wishes to see you.'

'Thank you. Could a servant take the horses to the stables for us?'

'I fear everyone is too busy just now,' Fulstowe said with a little smile. 'And now, if you will excuse me.' He walked away.

'That fellow's getting too big for his boots,' Barak said, then added angrily, 'Damn it, I need to know how Tamasin fares.'

'If the King has arrived at Portchester, maybe the roads will be clearer tomorrow.'

He shook his head angrily. 'I'll take the horses round to the stables, since nobody else will.'

I went into the great hall. I stopped and stared as I saw the tapestries of the hunting scenes had been removed, leaving the walls blank. Then to my astonishment I saw that old Sir Quintin Priddis was again sitting in the chair by the empty fireplace. He raised the half of his face that was not paralysed in that sinister, sardonic half-smile.

'We meet again, Master Shardlake. I hear you have been over to Sussex.'

'I have, sir.'

His blue eyes narrowed. 'A successful journey?'

I took a deep breath. But he would find out soon enough. 'I was at Rolfswood, where the Fettiplace family came from. A body has been found in the mill pond there, weighted down, and it seems to be the late William Fettiplace. It appears he was murdered. There will be a new inquest,' I added.

Sir Quintin's self-control was remarkable. His sharp gaze did not flinch. I wished Edward had been there too, so I could have seen his reaction. 'Well, well,' the old man said. 'Death seems to follow you about, sir.' He changed the subject. 'I trust my son was helpful when you went to visit Master Curteys' woodlands.'

'Indeed.'

'And have you decided to abandon the silly nonsense? I am sure this poor family would be relieved to have one less thing to worry about.'

'I am still considering. I did not expect to see you here again, Sir Quintin.'

He laughed, that strange rusty sound. 'A matter I was due to deal with in Winchester has been cancelled. An assessment of a young ward's lands, but the boy has died. The fellow who took the wardship made a bad investment, and thus we are not required in Winchester till next week. So I decided to stop here on the way, to see the outcome of Mistress Hobbey's inquest. And the local Hampshire coroner is a useless fellow, I may be able to render him some assistance.' He winced and adjusted his body to a more comfortable position. It crossed my mind that he might have come back to discover more about my connection to Rolfswood.

A door opened and Edward entered, dressed like his father in sober black, and accompanied by a small, cross-looking fellow of around sixty in a lawyer's robe. Edward's cold blue eyes narrowed when he saw me. As I bowed I wondered whether this self-contained man could be capable of rape, and reflected that those who keep themselves most under control can be the most dangerous when they lose it.

Sir Quintin raised his good arm and gestured to me. 'This man and his clerk are the first finders of the body, Sir Harold. Serjeant

Matthew Shardlake. Serjeant Shardlake, this is Sir Harold Trevelyan, coroner of Hampshire.'

Sir Harold looked at us peevishly. 'So you have returned. As first finders you should have stayed till my arrival. A lawyer should know that. I want to start the inquest tomorrow afternoon. I have enough to do in Portsmouth with these deaths in the galleasses. I don't know what the King was thinking of, filling them with the drunken refuse of London. Still, hopefully this inquest should be quick enough, with a suspect in custody.'

'You may find there are one or two problems with evidence,' I answered sharply.

Sir Harold looked offended. 'Master Dyrick says this Ettis is a rebellious fellow with a grudge against the family. His only alibi is his servant. Well, I'll see for myself later.'

'Has a jury been selected?'

'It has. I authorized Master Hobbey's steward to select some villagers.'

'But loyalties in this village are divided,' I replied forcefully. 'Fulstowe will choose only villagers loyal to Master Hobbey.'

'It is established procedure to use the steward to select jurors. And might I ask, sir, what business it is of yours? I am told you are here to conduct an enquiry into the ward Hugh Curteys' lands. But I am also told you are one of the serjeants at the Court of Requests, so perhaps you have some bias against landowners.'

Sir Quintin cackled from his chair. 'Sir Harold is a major landowner up near Winchester.' I cursed silently. There could be few worse men to conduct this inquest.

Sir Quintin looked at me. 'There is a surfeit of inquests these days. Master Shardlake says there is to be another one, at the town he has just visited in Sussex. Though that one, I fancy, will be slower, with an uncertain outcome. A body found after near twenty years.'

Sir Harold nodded in agreement. 'That will not be a priority for the Sussex coroner.' Priddis exchanged a glance with Edward, who had been watching silently.

'If you will excuse me,' I said, 'I should pay my respects to Master Hobbey.'

✝

HOBBEY WAS IN his study again, with Dyrick, but now it was Dyrick who sat at the big desk, while Hobbey sat in a chair with the picture of the former abbess on his knee, staring at it. He barely looked up as I entered. His face was grey and sunken.

'Well, Master Shardlake,' Dyrick said, 'so you are back. The coroner was quite agitated to find you absent.'

'I have spoken to him. I hear Master Fulstowe has selected a jury from the villagers. Ettis's enemies, I imagine.'

'That is up to the steward. Now, tell me, Brother, have you decided to accept our proposals on costs?'

'I am still considering it,' I answered shortly. 'If the inquest finds that Ettis committed the murder, he will be committed for trial at Winchester. They will have to find a jury of townsmen there. I will be called to give evidence as first finder, and I promise you I will ensure that any trial is fair.'

Dyrick turned to Hobbey. 'You hear him, sir? Now he thinks he can interfere with the trial of your wife's murderer. Was there ever such a fellow?'

Hobbey looked up. He seemed barely interested, sunk in melancholy. 'What will happen will happen, Vincent.' He turned the picture round on his lap, showing us the old abbess, the dark veil and white wimple, the enigmatic face in the centre. 'Look how she smiles,' he said, 'as though she knew something. Perhaps those who say we who have turned monastic buildings into houses are cursed are right. And if the French invade, who knows, they may even burn this house to the ground.'

'Nicholas – ' Dyrick said impatiently.

'Perhaps that is why she is smiling.' He turned to me with a strange look. 'What do you think, Master Shardlake?'

'I think that is superstition, sir.'

Hobbey did not answer. I realized he had retreated completely into himself. Dyrick and Fulstowe were in charge here now. And if it took hanging Ettis to end opposition to the enclosure of the village, they would do it, whether he was guilty or not.

✝

Supper that evening was one of the most melancholy meals I have ever attended. Hobbey sat slumped at the end of the table, picking listlessly at his food. Fulstowe stood watchfully behind him, and several times exchanged glances with Dyrick. Hugh sat staring at his plate, oblivious of everyone, including David, who sat next to him. David was unkempt, his doublet stained with food, his pale face furred with black stubble and his protuberant eyes red from crying. Occasionally, he would stare wildly into space, like someone trying to awaken from a horrible dream. Hugh, though, was as neatly dressed as ever, and had even had a shave.

I tried to engage Hugh in conversation, but he made only monosyllabic replies. He was, I guessed, still angry after our conversation about his words over Abigail's corpse. I looked round the table: those sitting there were all men. I wondered if a woman would ever sit here again, in this place which a decade before had housed only women. I stared up at the great west window and remembered my first evening – the hundreds of moths that had come in. There were few this evening; I wondered what had become of them all.

I glanced again at the bare walls. Dyrick said, 'Master Hobbey had the tapestries taken down yesterday. He cannot bear to look at them now.'

'That is understandable.' Hobbey, next to Dyrick, had taken no notice.

Edward Priddis was next to me. He spoke quietly. 'My father says there has been a discovery at Rolfswood. That William Fettiplace did not die in that fire, but ended in the mill pond.' His tone, as always, was quiet and even.

'That is true. I was there when the body was found.' I told him how the body had been exposed when the mill pond dam burst. I saw that on Edward's other side his father was listening intently, ignoring Sir Harold's tale of how some villagers along the coast had accidentally lit one of the beacons while practising what to do if the French landed.

'I suppose the Sussex coroner will have to be brought in to conduct a fresh inquest?' Edward asked.

'Yes. Do you know him?'

'No. But Father does.' Edward leaned across and said loudly, 'Master Shardlake is asking about the Sussex coroner.'

Priddis inclined his head. 'Samuel Pakenham will let such an old matter lie. As I would. He'll get round to it in time.'

'They will want to call you, sir,' I told him, 'as you conducted the first inquest.'

'I dare say. But they won't find anything new, not after twenty years. Maybe Fettiplace killed his workman and then himself. There's insanity in the family, you know: his daughter went mad.' He fixed me with his keen eyes. 'I remember now that I helped arrange for her to be sent to relatives in London. I've forgotten who they were. You forget things, Master Shardlake, after twenty years, when you are old and crippled.' He gave his wicked-looking half-smile.

More determined than ever to be at the Sussex inquest, I turned back to Edward, forcing a disarming smile. I said, 'They will also want to call the young man who was connected to Mistress Fettiplace at the time. Philip West, who comes from the local family I mentioned to you.'

'I remember the name. Father, did he not go to the King's court?'

'Yes.' Sir Quintin nodded. 'His mother was a proud woman, full of herself.' He cackled again. 'Everyone knew from her that Philip West went hunting with the King.'

'You did not go to court yourself when you were young?' I asked Edward.

'No, sir. My time in London was spent at Gray's Inn. Working like a dog to become qualified. My father kept my nose to the grind-stone.'

The old man answered sharply, 'Law students should work like dogs, that is what they are there for, to learn how to snap and bite.' He leaned across, supporting his weight on his good arm, and said to Dyrick, 'Something you seem to have learned well, sir.' He laughed again, like old hinges creaking.

'I will take that as a compliment,' Dyrick answered stiffly.

'Of course.'

There was silence round the table. Edward and his father flicked looks at me from two pairs of hard blue eyes. Then Sir Quintin said, 'You seem very interested in matters at Rolfswood, sir, going there twice and digging up all this information.'

'As I explained to your son, a client was trying to find the Fettiplace family.'

'And now at some point you will have to trail back to Sussex from London. It does no good to meddle, I always think. Master Dyrick told me meddling landed you in trouble with the King once, at York.'

He leaned back in his seat, his barb delivered, while Dyrick gave me a nasty smile.

✝

THE INQUEST ON Abigail Hobbey was held the following afternoon in the great hall. Outside it was another bright, sunny day, but the hall was shadowed and gloomy. The big table had been set under the old west window. Sir Harold Trevelyan sat behind it, with Edward Priddis on his right, evidently pressed into service to take notes. On his left – in defiance of all procedure – sat Sir Quintin. He surveyed the room, his good hand grasping his stick. The jury, twelve men from the village, sat on hard chairs against one wall. I recognized several who had worked for the hunt. Men who would likely be in Fulstowe's pocket.

Barak and I, Fulstowe and Sir Luke Corembeck sat together.

Behind us were some of the servants, including old Ursula, and perhaps twenty people from the village. One was Ettis's attractive wife, her body tense and her face rigid with fear and anger. From the way her neighbours gave her words and gestures of comfort, I guessed they represented Ettis's faction in the village. The jury, I saw, gave them some uneasy glances.

In the front row the Hobbey family sat with Dyrick. David was slumped forward, head in hands, staring at the floor. I saw he was shaking slightly. Next to him Hugh sat bolt upright. When he came in I had looked at him hard, to remind him I remembered what he had said over Abigail's body. On Hugh's other side Nicholas Hobbey still looked dreadful; he watched people coming in with a sort of bewildered wonderment.

Last to arrive was Ettis. I heard a clanking of chains outside, and exchanged a look with Barak; we both knew that sound from the London jails. Two men led Ettis in; the proud, confident yeoman had turned into an unshaven, hollow-eyed figure. He was set roughly on a chair against the wall. Behind me there was muttering among the villagers, and one or two of the jurors looked shamefaced.

'Silence!' Sir Harold shouted, banging the table with a little gavel. 'I won't have jangle and talk in my court! Any more noise and I will clear the benches.'

Sir Harold called me first, to give evidence about finding the body. Barak was called next and confirmed what I had said. The coroner then proceeded immediately to call Fulstowe. The steward spoke with cold clear fluency of Ettis's leadership of the faction in the village that wanted to oppose the enclosures, the antipathy between him and the Hobbeys, particularly Abigail, and his known skill as an archer.

'Yes,' Sir Harold said. 'And Master Ettis's only alibi is the servant he says was with him marking his sheep. Call him.'

An old countryman was called. He confirmed he had been with his master that day. Sir Harold, in a bullying tone, got him to confirm he had worked for Ettis for twenty years.

'So you would have every incentive to say anything to protect your master,' he said coldly.

Sir Quintin intervened. 'If he is hanged his property is forfeit to the State, and you will be out on the street.'

'I – I only speak the truth, Master.'

'So we would hope, fellow. There are penalties for those who perjure themselves.'

'Isn't there anything we can do?' Barak whispered. 'That crippled old goat hasn't any right to question anyone.' I shook my head.

Sir Harold dismissed the old servant. As he did so, Sir Quintin looked straight at me, raising his eyebrows. He was showing me his power. Sir Harold banged his gavel to quell a fresh outbreak of muttering. I waited till it had died down, then rose to my feet.

'Sir,' I said, 'in fairness, it must be asked whether there were others who might have a motive to kill Abigail Hobbey.'

Sir Harold spread his hands. 'Who else could have wanted to kill the poor woman?'

I paused. I realized that what I was about to say would be terrible for the Hobbey family, but Ettis had to have justice. I said, 'I have been here over a week, sir. I fear almost everyone I met disliked Mistress Hobbey. Master Hobbey himself admitted it to be so. There was – an incident, the killing of her dog.'

A fresh murmur spread along the benches, and David turned and looked at me in utter horror. Dyrick and Nicholas Hobbey turned and stared, wide-eyed. Hugh, though, sat looking straight ahead. Hobbey stood up, suddenly connected to the real world again. 'Coroner, that was an accident.'

Dyrick stood too. He said, 'And there was certainly an incident with Ettis. He had the insolence to call and argue with Master Hobbey and me in Master Hobbey's study; Mistress Hobbey came in and gave him hard words. I was there, I heard all.'

Sir Harold said to me, 'Are you implying a member of her family could have killed her?'

'I'm saying it is possible.' I hesitated. 'I could say more.'

Then Hugh did turn and look at me, fury in his face. I stared back. Hesitantly, he stood up. 'May I say something?' he said.

The coroner looked at Sir Quintin. 'The ward,' Sir Quintin said. 'Well, boy?'

Hugh said, 'Master Shardlake is right, everyone disliked poor Mistress Hobbey. If you were to enquire of all who suffered from her tongue you would be calling many witnesses.'

'Did *you* dislike her?' Sir Harold asked.

Hugh hesitated, then said, 'I did. Perhaps I was wrong –' his voice almost broke – 'she had been strange, unwell, for many years. When I saw her dead I said, "You deserved this." But at the same time I placed a flower in her lap, for she made a most piteous sight.'

Sir Harold and Sir Quintin stared at each other, taken aback. 'Deserved it?' Sir Harold asked. 'Why did you say such a thing?'

'It was how I felt, sir.'

Sir Quintin said sharply, 'When I spoke with you in Portsmouth last week, you said you had no complaints to make about your life here.'

'I did, sir, but I did not say I was happy.'

There was the loudest murmur yet from the benches. Then there was an unexpected sound. Nicholas Hobbey had burst into tears. Burying his face in his handkerchief, he rose and walked out of the hall. Dyrick turned to me, his face furious. 'See what you have done!'

I noticed Fulstowe watching his master. For the first time I saw anxiety in the steward's calculating face. Did he, like Hobbey, begin to see his world crumbling around him? Or did he have some other reason for anxiety? Ettis, sitting in his chains, looked at Hugh with something like hope.

There was another interruption. David stood, sending his chair crashing over. He pointed at Hugh. 'You lie,' he shouted. 'You are a viper this family has taken to its bosom! You have always envied us because you are not like us, you can never be like us! My father, he loved my mother, and so did I. I did love her!' He stared round the room, his face anguished.

Sir Harold was looking anxious. He whispered to Sir Quintin. I caught the word 'adjournment'. Sir Quintin shook his head vigorously, then banged his stick on the floor. 'Be quiet! All of you!' He turned to me, his eyes savage. 'Your behaviour is disgraceful, sir. You are turning this inquest into a circus. You have brought no evidence forward. This whole family, it is clear, is racked by grief. Sir Harold, let us proceed.'

The coroner stared round the room, then asked me, 'Serjeant Shardlake, have you any evidence associating anyone with the commission of this crime?'

'No, sir. I say only that given that many had – difficulties – with Mistress Hobbey, and the lack of any proper evidence against Master Ettis, the verdict should be murder by person or persons unknown.'

'That is for the jury to decide. Sit down, or I will hold you in contempt.'

There was nothing more I could do. Sir Harold called no other witnesses. The jury was sent out. They soon returned with their verdict. Murder – it could be nothing other than that, of course – by Leonard Ettis, yeoman of Hoyland, who would now be held in custody in Winchester jail till the next assizes in September.

As he was led out Ettis looked at me again in appeal. I nodded once, vigorously. In front of me Hugh sat straight as a stock again, his back rigid. Beside him David still wept quietly. Fulstowe came across, took David's arm, and led him from the hall. I had failed to widen the inquest's investigation, at terrible cost to the family. Now nothing further would happen for months. I put my head in my hands. The room was clearing. I heard the tap of Sir Quintin's stick as he came down the hall. The tapping stopped beside me. I looked up. Sir Quintin seemed exhausted, but triumphant too. Edward was supporting him. Sir Quintin leaned slowly down, and spoke quietly. 'There, Master Shardlake. See what happens when people are awkward at inquests.'

Chapter Thirty-six

WE FILED OUT OF the hall into the sunshine. The jurors walked down the drive in a group, while most of the villagers gathered round Ettis's wife. She had broken down and stood sobbing. I walked across to her.

'Mistress Ettis,' I said quietly.

She looked up and wiped her face. 'You spoke up for my husband,' she said quietly. 'I thank you.'

'I can do little now, but I promise, when he comes to trial at Winchester, I will ensure all is fairly done. There is no actual evidence against him,' I added encouragingly.

'What should we do about going to Requests about our woodlands, sir? My husband would want us to continue.'

Behind me I saw Dyrick and Fulstowe standing on the steps, watching. I looked round the villagers; some seemed cowed, but many had a defiant aspect. I said, loudly, 'I think it vital you lodge your case. You must not let what happened today intimidate you from taking action. I think that was partly the intention; I do not consider a jury can convict Master Ettis. Appoint someone else from the village to lead you until he is freed.' I took a deep breath, then added, 'Send the papers to me, I will fight the case for you.'

'Listen to my master,' Barak added approvingly. 'Fight back.'

Mistress Ettis nodded. Then everyone turned at the sound of approaching hoofbeats. A messenger in royal livery was riding fast up the drive. He came to a halt at the steps, dismounted, and approached Fulstowe. They spoke briefly, then the messenger went inside. The steward hesitated, then walked down the steps to us. Dyrick stayed where he was. I had, reluctantly, to admire Fulstowe's courage; there were near twenty villagers there, in hostile and angry mood, but he marched straight up to me. 'Master Shardlake, that messenger has a packet of letters for you. He is waiting in the kitchen.' He turned to the villagers. 'Go, all of you, unless you wish to be arrested for trespass.'

One or two men glared back at him. One called out, 'You sure that mad boy didn't kill his mother?'

'Ay,' another added. 'He's possessed by a demon, that one.'

'No!' Mistress Ettis spoke up. 'He is but a child, leave him alone!' Then she said loudly to Fulstowe, 'It is not the boy that has sent my husband to jail, it is you.' She pointed to Dyrick. 'And that black crow!'

There was fresh murmuring. A man bent down, picked up a pebble from the driveway, and shied it at Dyrick. He jumped aside, then turned and ran into the house. The group laughed.

I raised my hands. 'Go! Do not make a disturbance! And make no trouble for the jurors in the village. Lodge your complaint with me at Lincoln's Inn!' I looked at Fulstowe. 'Now, master steward, I will see this messenger. Come, Barak.'

✟

THE MESSENGER was sitting at the kitchen table, where Ursula had given him some beer with bread and cheese. He stood and bowed at our entrance, then handed me a packet of letters. I opened it: inside was a letter addressed to me in Warner's writing, one from Guy, and a third for Barak, which I handed to him. 'Thank you, fellow,' I said to the messenger. 'How far have you come?'

'From Portchester Castle. The royal party arrived there yesterday. Master Warner said to come at once, there have been delays with private letters. The ones from London are a few days old.'

I thanked him again. 'Let us go to your room,' I said to Barak. 'Get some privacy.'

As we walked round the side of the house he said, 'There could have been trouble with the villagers there.'

'I know.'

He laughed scornfully. 'Did you see Dyrick twist and run when that pebble was thrown? He's like many who are free with bold words, he ran at a hint of violence. I wish young Feaveryear had been here to see it.'

'I was never able to fathom why Feaveryear was sent away so suddenly. It had something to do with Hugh and David, I am sure.'

He looked at me seriously. 'You finally shot your bolt with the family in there. You were hard on them.'

'I had to do something for Ettis. I thought if they knew how Abigail was regarded we might get a verdict of murder by persons unknown. Priddis helped stop that. Did you hear what he said to me afterwards?'

'Yes. He's dangerous.'

'I know. I wonder whether Mistress Ettis has the stomach to take the issue of the woods forward? I suspect the villagers will rely on her.'

'She seemed a woman of spirit to me. Reminded me a little of Tamasin, only older. Now come, let's get these letters open.'

In his room, Barak tore open Tamasin's letter and read it eagerly, while I perused Guy's. It was dated four days previously, the twelfth of July:

Dear Matthew,

I have received your letter. You will be pleased to hear that Tamasin continues very well, though increasingly tired as her time approaches. At home Coldiron has been surly since I called him to order, yet not impertinent. Josephine seems to have gained a little confidence — I heard her tell young Simon, who was saying again how he wished he could go to fight, that war is a wicked thing and she wished heartily God would stir up a universal peace among his people. I was pleased to see it, though it turned my mind back to that time she swore in French.

I have visited Ellen again. On the surface she seems returned to normal, cheerful and working with patients as though nothing had happened. She told me she was in good sort and I need not call again. But she did not mention you at all, and I sensed much hidden feeling under the smooth surface.

As I was leaving the Bedlam, Hob Gebons came to me and said that two days before Keeper Shawms had a visit from Warden Metwys. Gebons, knowing your concern to be informed of all that might concern Ellen, tried to overhear, but they spoke low and he could hear little. He told me though that at one point voices were raised: Metwys shouted that 'she' must be moved if her mouth is no longer safe, and Shawms replied you had the Queen's protection and he would not do it.

Matthew, I think you should return, as soon as you can.

Your loving friend,

Guy

I looked up at Barak. 'What does Tamasin say?'

He smiled. 'That she is bored, and tired, and heavy. She wants me home.' He took a long breath of relief. 'What about Guy?'

I passed the letter over to Barak and opened the one from Warner. It was dated yesterday, he had got it to me fast. When I opened the letter I understood why; inside was a little folded note in the Queen's own handwriting. I broke the seal. It was dated the day before, 15 July, from Portchester.

Dear Matthew,

I have received your letter, and was shocked to hear of the death of poor Mistress Hobbey. It seems there is little or nothing against Master Hobbey, and if that poor boy does not wish to proceed we should not entangle him in the coils of Wards at this time. I know that Mistress Calfhill will agree.

We have just arrived at Portchester Castle. The King will be travelling to Portsmouth in two days. Latest reports of French numbers and the progress along the Channel of their ships are very troubling. You should leave now, return to London.

I turned to Warner's letter; it was brief, the script without his usual care and written in a hurry.

Dear Matthew,

The court is arrived at Portchester Castle. I enclose a letter from the Queen; we agree you should return to London as soon as possible. Please accept Brother Dyrick's offer on costs. I hope and trust the inquest has found the killer. On that subject, I heard the inquest's verdict into Master Mylling was one of accidental death.

Here the King is much concerned by the approach of the French fleet. I may be unable to write further till this desperate crisis is resolved, one way or another.

With greetings and salutations,

Robert Warner

I passed both letters over to Barak. 'I never had a letter from the Queen before.'

'Lucky you. Well, that's the end of the Curteys case.'

'I know. This room is sticky. Let's get out.'

We stepped out into the windless summer evening. I looked over at the tiled roof, solid old walls and new high chimneys of Hoyland Priory.

'This will be our last night at this place, thank God,' Barak said. He looked at me. 'D'you still think Warner could be connected with Ellen somehow?'

'I don't know.' I took a deep breath. 'Tomorrow morning we can leave first thing. I will go to Portsmouth, and you take the road for London. With luck I will only be there a few hours, and can catch you up on the road the next day.'

'Don't go.'

'I must.'

'The French could arrive.'

'I must speak to West. It was I stirred up the hornets' nest at Rolfswood.'

'And you're going to try and get the hornets back in?'

'I am going to try and find out what happened at that foundry.'

He shook his head. 'Fuck it. Listen, I'll come with you to Portsmouth tomorrow.'

'No. Go back to London. I'll find Leacon, maybe he can help me reach West again.'

'You shouldn't go alone.'

I looked at him. 'Are you sure?'

'Provided we leave as soon as you've seen West. If I let you go alone, I fear you'll stay and land in more danger.'

I smiled. 'Then – thank you.'

He spoke with a sudden forcefulness; 'When we get back to London, you have to change. You can't go on living like this. And nor can I.' He looked at me hard again, but there was concern as well as censure in his eyes.

I smiled sadly. 'Leacon said something similar to me. About getting old.'

'And obsessive. Never more so.'

I took a deep breath. 'Then it seems that now I need you to guide me. Thank you, Jack.'

✝

WE RETURNED TO the house. I thought, he is right, when we get back it is time I made a life for myself, instead of living through other people's tragedies. I realized that was what I had been doing for years: there had been so many, brought by the wild changes and conflicts the King had forced on England, perhaps it was my response to the wider madness.

Fulstowe stood in the great hall, looking at the space where the tapestries had been. He turned to me with a hostile look, his fair beard and hair contrasting with his jet-black mourning doublet.

'Do you know where Sir Quintin and his son are?' I asked shortly.

'Departed.'

'And the family?'

The steward glared at me, any last shred of deference gone. 'I will not have you trouble them. Not after the state you reduced them to at the inquest.'

'You should mind your manners, steward,' I said quietly.

'I am in charge of this household under Master Hobbey. I say again, I will not have you disturb them.'

'Where is Master Dyrick?'

'With Master Hobbey.'

'We leave tomorrow. Tell Master Dyrick I will need to speak with him before we go.'

He looked relieved at that news. 'I will. There will be no dinner in the hall tonight. Food will be served to people in their rooms.' He turned on his heel and walked away.

I went up to my room. Soon after there was a knock at my door and Dyrick entered, his face dark and angry. 'You will be pleased to know, sir,' he said, 'that Master Hobbey is prostrate. And David is much upset.'

'Not as upset as Master Ettis, I'll wager.'

I looked at him. I felt guilty for what I believed I had had to do at the inquest, but for Dyrick I felt only anger and contempt. I had believed earlier that, ridiculously unpleasant as he was, he genuinely thought I was treating Hobbey unjustly over Hugh; but after his role in the pursuit of Ettis I knew he was corrupt and cruel.

He sneered. 'Ettis. Whose wife no doubt will take his place as your client.'

I said, 'You will be pleased to hear I have authority to accept your offer to end Hugh Curteys' case on the basis of no costs.'

'Ah yes, that royal messenger.' He smiled nastily. 'And I noticed you and Master Hugh seem no longer to be friends. And after what you made him do this afternoon I imagine he will be as glad to be rid of you as everyone else here.'

'Oh, it is not over yet, Brother Dyrick,' I answered quietly. 'There is the villagers' case to come. And still a murderer to be found, incidentally.'

'He has been found.'

'I do not think even you believe Ettis guilty.'

'Body of our Lord!' he burst out. 'You are the most troublesome fellow I ever encountered!'

'Calm yourself, Brother.'

'I will be calm when you and your impertinent clerk leave this house.'

'And I hope you remain calm when next we meet, at Ettis's trial or in the Court of Requests. I have your mark now, Dyrick, I see you clearly.'

'You see nothing. You never have. Master Hobbey and the family, by the way, can I think do without your farewells.' Dyrick flounced out, closing the door with an ear-splitting bang.

☦

WE ROSE EARLY the following morning. We breakfasted in the kitchen, and said farewell to old Ursula, toiling there as usual, who thanked us for our interest in Hugh. 'Though you never found why they told that wicked lie about Master Calfhill saying he loved Hugh, did you, sir?'

'No, Ursula. And without Hugh's cooperation, I do not think anyone can.'

She looked at me imploringly. 'You will help Master Ettis, though? He's a good man. He never killed Mistress Hobbey.'

'Of course.' I looked at her seriously. 'Have you any idea who could have, Ursula?'

'None, sir. It was a wicked act, for all her strange ways. God pardon her.'

'Amen. I will not be returning here, but if you hear anything I should know, will you tell Mistress Ettis? She knows how to contact me.'

'I will, sir. Unless the French get us all first.' She curtsied deeply, but I could see my lack of success had disappointed her.

Outside it was another hot, still day. We loaded our saddlebags onto Oddleg and the horse Barak had been using. I thought, in three or four days we shall be returning them to the supplier at Kingston.

'What will you do about the Rolfswood inquest?' Barak asked after we had mounted.

'When we get back to London I will make contact with the Sussex coroner. I will ensure Priddis is questioned. I'll ask the Queen to use her influence if need be.'

'That will all take time.'

'I know.'

'Look there,' he said quietly. I followed his gaze to where David and Hugh were walking together from the house to the butts with their bows and arrowbags. Hugh turned and saw us. He laid down his bow and came over to me, his expression cold. David simply stood and stared.

'You are leaving then?' Hugh said abruptly.

'Yes. And you will shortly hear the claim in the Court of Wards is to be abandoned.'

'I wish it had never been started.'

I held out my hand. 'Farewell, Hugh.'

The boy looked at it, then stared at me coldly again.

'Will you give farewell to my master?' Barak asked hotly. 'Impertinent puppy, all he has done has been to try and help you.'

Hugh met his gaze. 'Like making me tell the inquest what I felt about Mistress Hobbey? A strange kind of help. And now, I am going to try to distract David with some practice of honest archery.

We may be needed, mere boys as we are, if the French approach up that road.' He turned on his heel and walked away.

'Come, Jack,' I said quietly. 'Time we were gone.'

✞

AGAIN WE TRAVELLED south through the summer woodland. Trees were still being felled in Hugh's woods. Two carts loaded with oak trunks, the ends still damp with sap, pulled out of a side track and rumbled south towards Portsmouth.

We pressed on, through the rich summer landscape, the air becoming hotter as the morning advanced. We rode up the long steep incline of Portsdown Hill, hard going for the horses, and crested the escarpment. There we halted and looked down again on that extraordinary view. Nearly all the fleet seemed to be anchored out in the Solent now, only a few small ships lay in Portsmouth Haven. The ships were gathered together in three long lines, except for three – a giant, which had to be the *Great Harry*, and two other big ships that were sailing east along the coast of Portsea Island.

'They're lined up for battle,' Barak said quietly.

I looked out to the eastern end of the Isle of Wight. Somewhere, out of sight still, the enemy was approaching across that calm blue sea.

✞

AT THE BRIDGE between the mainland and Portsea Island there were large soldiers' encampments now on both sides of the tidal stream, and heavy cannon. I had put on my lawyer's robes and we were allowed through when I said we had business in the town. Supplies were still coming, many of the loaded carts heading towards the long line of tents along the coast.

As we rode downhill, Barak said, 'Those are the royal tents behind that little lake.'

'Yes.' I counted twenty of the huge tents, in a myriad of different colours and designs, strung out parallel to the coast. More were being erected.

'Do you think the King is going to camp there and watch the sea battle if it comes?'

'Perhaps. Maybe the Queen too.'

'You have to admire old Henry's courage.'

'Or foolhardiness. Come, let's find Leacon.'

✝

OUTSIDE THE city walls, where men still laboured hard to thicken the mud walls, companies of soldiers were practising manoeuvres: running with long pikes held before them, staging mock battles with bills, improving their archery at makeshift butts. All the men were brown from their time in the sun. Officers, mostly on horseback, rode to and fro supervising them, but I did not see Leacon. There were so many more tents that it was hard to get our bearings. The stink of ordure was unbearable.

We found the place where Leacon's company had been billeted and dismounted. All the tents in this part of the camp, though, were closed and empty except for one some way off, where a young soldier sat alone, eating bread and cheese from a wooden trencher. I recognized him as one of Leacon's men. His face was spotted with mosquito bites, and I noticed the long collar above his tunic was frayed, the tunic itself filthy. I asked if he knew where the rest of the company was.

'Gone to the ships, sir,' he answered. 'To get their sea legs and practise shooting from a ship. I've been left to guard the tents. They'll be back tonight.'

'We saw some warships out at sea.'

'Yes. The *Great Harry* and the *Mary Rose* and the *Murrain* are out, they said. There's five companies gone on them.'

'Thank you.'

Barak asked him, 'How do you find this life, mate?'

'Never seen anything like it. The King is coming to view the fleet tomorrow. And they say the French will be here in a few days. Two weeks ago I was a churchwarden's assistant. That'll teach me to practise archery.'

'Ay, it can be a dangerous thing.'

The soldier gestured at his trencher. 'Look at this shit they're giving us to eat. Half-mouldy cheese and bread like a stone. Reminds me of the famine back in '27, when I was a child. I've walked with bent legs ever since.' He took a drink from a wooden tankard at his side. I saw a Latin phrase embossed in large letters: *If God be for us, who can be against us?*

'I hope you find a safe billet, fellow,' I said.

'Thank you.'

We rode away. 'What now?' Barak asked.

'To the Godshouse, see if they can tell us where Master West might be.'

'Probably out in harbour, on the *Mary Rose*.'

'He may be ashore, or come ashore tonight.' I said hesitantly, 'We should try to find an inn in town. We may have to stay the night.'

He sighed and said, 'All right, one night if need be. Jesu, that soldier, I thought, he could have been me. So I owe you one night here.'

I looked up at the walls as we rode on to the town, the soldiers patrolling to and fro along the fighting platform at the top. The great guns bristled at the towers, long black barrels pointing outwards at us.

Chapter Thirty-seven

W E HAD TO WAIT a long time at the gate. The soldiers were questioning everyone about their business in Portsmouth, wary no doubt of French spies. I said I had legal business at the Guildhall, and that got us through.

Portsmouth was even more crowded now, tents pitched everywhere within the walls, soldiers practising drill. We rode down the High Street, steering through the crowd of merchants and labourers, soldiers and sailors, English and foreign. Many of the servicemen, like the soldiers at the camp, were starting to look ragged and dirty. Heavy carts still lumbered towards the wharf, drivers shouting at people to get out of the way. The sour stench of sweat was everywhere, mingling with the harsh smell from the brewhouses.

Barak wriggled. 'Shit, I've got fleas again already.'

'Must have been from the camp. Let's try to find a clean inn, then go to the Godshouse.'

We turned into Oyster Street and rode towards the wharf. The tide was full, the Camber filled with rowboats waiting their turn to deliver goods from the wharf to the ships. We rode almost to the wharf; from here we could see out across the low-lying Point to where the triple line of ships stood at anchor in the Solent. They looked even more breathtaking than on our first visit, for now there were well over fifty, of all sizes from the giant warships to small forty-foot vessels. Few had any of their sails up; even the *Galley Subtle* stood with its oars at rest. The very stillness of the fleet added to its solid might, the only moving things the flags on the masts of the large warships flapping in the light breeze. An enormous flag of St George flew from the foremast of the *Mary Rose* above the brightly painted triple decks of the forecastle. I saw the giant bulk of the *Great Harry* sailing slowly away into the Solent, some of its great white sails raised.

Barak followed my gaze. 'Maybe Leacon and the company are there.'

'Then they won't be back for hours.'

✟

WE FOUND an inn in Oyster Street. It catered for the wealthier clientele, *No Brawlers or Chiders* scrawled on a large sign by the door. The innkeeper charged a shilling to take us. He would not be beaten down, saying we were lucky to get accommodation at all.

'I hear the King comes tomorrow,' I said.

'Ay. In the morning, to view the ships. The populace have been told to line the streets.'

'There must be many royal officials seeking accommodation in town.'

He shook his head. '*They're* all comfortable in the royal tents along the coast. If Portsmouth is besieged, they'll ride off. It's us poor citizenry who'll be trapped here.'

We stabled the horses, took our panniers to our little room, then went out again. We walked back up Oyster Street, hands on belts for fear of cutpurses among the milling crowds, towards the open space in front of the Square Tower. On the platform soldiers with spiked bills marched and turned to drumbeats. A group of small boys stood watching and cheering.

There was a sudden tremendous crash that sent me jumping backwards. Barak flinched too, though the soldiers did not break step. One of the boys pointed at me and laughed. 'See the hunchback jump! Yah! Crookback!'

'Fuck off, you little arseholes!' Barak shouted. The boys fled, laughing. We stared up at the Square Tower, where wreaths of grey-black smoke were dispersing into the sky. A group of soldiers bent to reload one of the huge cannon pointing out to sea. Practice, I guessed.

We walked down to the Godshouse gate. This time we did not have Leacon to help us gain entry; I told the guard we had business with a senior officer on the *Mary Rose*, Master Philip West, and asked where he might be. 'It is a legal matter,' I said, 'important family news. We would not have come to Portsmouth today unless it were necessary.'

'No one's coming now if they can avoid it. You should talk to one of the clerks at the old infirmary.'

'Thank you.' We passed into the Godshouse courtyard. Barak looked at me dubiously. 'Should we be lying to these people?' he asked.

'It's the only way I'll get to see West.'

'You realize he may not be happy to answer your questions.'

'I'll tell him the information I have came from his mother. As it did.'

I looked around. Everywhere men in uniform or the bright robes of senior officials were walking and talking. We went up to the door of the old infirmary, where I told the guard my story about needing to see West. He let us pass inside.

The infirmary, still with its stained-glass windows showing saints in postures of prayer and supplication, had been partitioned off into a series of rooms. Through an open doorway I saw two officials arguing, a paper on the table between them. 'I tell you she can't take the extra hundred soldiers,' one said in urgent tones. 'The refit's made her even heavier—'

'She made it safe from Deptford, didn't she?' the other answered dismissively. He slapped the paper. 'These are the complements decided for each ship, approved by the King. Do you want to go to Portchester and argue with him?' The man looked up and caught my eye. Frowning irritably, he reached over and slammed the door shut.

A black-robed clerk passed, accompanied by a man in a lawyer's robe. I stepped in front of him. 'Excuse me, Brother, might you help me? I need to speak urgently with of one of the ship's officers, Philip West. I believe he is on the *Mary Rose*.'

The clerk paused, impressed by my serjeant's robe. 'All the officers are staying on the ships now. I doubt they'd let a civilian on board. Perhaps you could send a message.'

That was bad news. I considered. 'I know one of the army officers; I understand his company are out at sea today.'

'They'll be rowed back to harbour at dusk. There's not room for the soldiers to sleep on the ships.'

'I see. Thank you.'

The two men hurried on. 'I want to find Leacon when he comes back,' I told Barak. 'See if he can get me aboard the *Mary Rose*.'

'What, you're going to try and speak to West on his ship? If it was him that attacked Ellen, you'll be at his mercy.'

'On a ship full of soldiers and sailors? No. And I'll go alone,' I added. 'A private talk would be best. No arguments, it is decided. Now come, let's pass the afternoon at that inn, keep away from these foul humours.'

Barak gave me a searching, worried look. I turned and walked back out to the busy courtyard. Near the infirmary steps two men in their thirties were talking. One had a stern face, short black beard, and a long dark robe. The other was familiar, a green doublet setting off his coppery beard, a cap with a string of pearls on his head. Sir Thomas Seymour, whom I had last seen with Rich in that doorway at Hampton Court. He stood listening attentively to the other man.

'D'Annebault's a soldier, not a sailor,' the black-bearded man said confidently. 'He can't command a fleet that size—'

'The militia between here and Sussex are ready to stop any landing,' Seymour answered proudly.

Barak and I veered away so that Seymour's back was to us. 'So he's ended up here along with everyone else,' I said quietly. 'And that was Thomas Dudley, Lord Lisle, with him. The Lord Admiral, in charge of all the ships. He was pointed out to me at Westminster once.'

'Looks a fierce fellow.'

I glanced over my shoulder at the commander. He was known as a doughty warrior, a skilled administrator, and a hard man. Dudley caught my look and stared back for a second, his eyes dark in his pale face. I turned quickly away.

'I don't think you should go on that ship,' Barak said insistently.

'I must speak to West, I have to see how he reacts to learning Ellen's father's body has been found. We'll get out of Portsmouth first thing tomorrow, before the King comes,' I added impatiently. 'I'll go on the ship tonight if I have to.'

✝

WE RETURNED TO the tavern and ordered a meal brought to our room. Afterwards we tried to rest, but the endless talking and shouting from Oyster Street and the wharf made that impossible: and I was impatient, conscious of how little time I had to see West. Then we heard cannon firing again, very close, rattling the shutters which we had closed against the stink. The shot was answered by another, further away.

Barak jumped up from the bed and opened the shutters. 'Christ, is that the French?'

I joined him, looking across Oyster Street at the Camber. The tide was going out, revealing the filthy mud underneath. Men were labouring at the cannon on the Round Tower. There was another tremendous crash and a burst of smoke.

'Let's see what's happening,' Barak said.

We went outside, meeting the innkeeper who was coming from the parlour with a tray of mugs. 'What was that gunfire?' I asked.

He laughed at my anxious look. 'They're testing the cannon at the Round Tower and over at Gosport. Making sure we can cover the harbour entrance if the French appear.' A sneer crossed his face. 'Did you notice a big capstan by the tower?'

'Yes.'

'There's supposed to be a chain with links a foot long stretching across the harbour mouth, that would keep any ship out. But it was taken for repair last year, and it's never come back. So we'll need guns if the French come.'

'I thought for a moment they had.'

'You'll see and hear much more if they do,' the innkeeper said. He walked away.

'That shook me,' Barak admitted. 'Let's get out.'

⚜

WE LEFT THE INN and walked up to the High Street. Outside the Guildhall a crowd had gathered to watch a strange-looking company of soldiers pass by. Instead of armour they wore knee-length tunics under short decorated waistcoats; their legs were bare and they had sandals instead of boots. Most were tall and strongly built, with hard faces under their helmets.

'More mercenaries, by the look of them,' I said. 'I wonder where these are from.'

A boy next to us piped up. 'Ireland, Master,' he said excitedly. 'They're the kerns, they're being paid to fight the French instead of the King's soldiers.'

The Irish marched by, looking neither to left nor right. The crowd dispersed, and a man who had been watching from the Guildhall doorway became visible. It was Edward Priddis. He stared at us for a second, then turned and went back inside. Barak put his hand on my arm, pointing to an open window.

'Look,' he said quietly.

Sir Quintin was seated at a table, glaring out at us. There was another man beside him. He turned, and I saw that it was Richard Rich.

'Oh shit,' Barak whispered.

Rich rose and marched smartly out of the room. A moment later he appeared in the doorway, looking angrier than I had ever seen him, spots of red in his pale cheeks. He marched across the road to me.

'What in hell's name are you doing here?' His voice was quiet as ever, but a vicious hiss rather than his usual mocking tones. 'Why are you pursuing Sir Quintin Priddis like this?' I saw a little tic jump at the corner of his eye. 'I have been hearing about your disgraceful performance at the inquest into that woman's death.'

I made myself look him in the face. 'I did not know you were acquainted with the Hobbeys, Sir Richard.'

'I am not. But I knew Sir Quintin once, and he has told me of your obsession with some supposed injustice to the Hugh Curteys boy, and your persecution – ' he almost snarled the word – 'of that family. You go too far, master lawyer. Remember where that led you once before. If you have come to trouble Sir Quintin again—'

'My presence in Portsmouth is nothing to do with that case, Sir Richard.'

'Then what are you doing here? Eh?'

'I have legal business—'

'What business? With whom?'

'Sir Richard, you know such information is privileged.'

The flat grey eyes glared into mine, the black pupils like needles. 'How long are you here?'

'I leave tomorrow.'

'When the King comes to Portsmouth. You had better be gone.' He leaned forward. 'Remember I am a privy councillor, Master Shardlake, and this is a city preparing for war. If I wanted, I could have Governor Paulet lock you up as a suspected French spy.'

Chapter Thirty-eight

WE WALKED BACK down the High Street. My mind was in a whirl. 'Jack,' I said. 'This goes deeper than I thought. Rich is personally involved.'

'Did you see his eye twitching? I thought he was going to strike you.'

'I think he went back inside before he lost control of himself. So that's it. That meeting with Rich and Seymour at Hampton Court was truly no accident. He arranged it, he set those corner boys on me. Rich is connected somehow to whatever happened to Hugh. There *was* something, there *is* something.' I paused. 'And Michael Calfhill died. And the clerk Mylling ... If that's so, the scale of this ...'

'All the more reason to get out of here. You know how dangerous Rich is.'

I considered. 'He could have had me arrested if he wanted to, right there, on some trumped-up charge. But he didn't. Whatever connects him to the Hobbeys and Hugh, he doesn't want me talking of it, to Paulet or anyone.'

'How did he learn you were being brought into that case so early?'

I spoke heavily. 'The only other person who knew what my business was with the Queen that day was Robert Warner.'

'Who you think might be connected to the Rolfswood matter too.'

'And vulnerable to blackmail if he was involved. Blackmail is one of Rich's specialities.'

Barak was looking round carefully as we walked. He said, 'With all the people in the town it would be easy for Rich to get someone to knife you in the guts.'

'No. This is where the Queen's patronage protects me. If anything happened to me now she would leave no stone unturned to find out why. For all his bombast Rich cannot touch me.'

'You think she's that fond of you? Rich still stands high with the King; he's been kept on despite that corruption scandal last year.'

'The Queen would not desert me. If she began an investigation, who knows what might come tumbling out? No, Rich may watch me now, but that is all.'

'Do you think Seymour is involved with Rich in the Curteys matter?'

I shook my head. 'I think it more likely Rich and Seymour were both at Hampton Court that day, and Rich invited Seymour to wait with him for me to come out. It would have been an entertainment for Seymour and would help Rich intimidate me.'

Barak stopped suddenly in the road, ignoring a curse from a passing water carrier. 'Look, can't we just leave now?'

'You can, but I'm staying. Until tomorrow morning, as we agreed.'

He sighed. 'Well, for God's sake keep a careful eye out. Come on, we'll be safer at the wharf. Tonight we sleep with knives at the ready and tomorrow we get out of here first thing.'

'What can it be?' I asked. 'What can connect Rich to second-rank gentry like the Hobbeys?'

He answered curtly, 'Wait till we're back in London, then you can try to find out.'

✝

RETURNING TO Oyster Street, we walked towards the wharf. Across the Point we saw the *Great Harry* moving back towards the lines of warships with a heavy, stately slowness, the masts and raised topsail rearing high into the sky. The leviathan confidently manoeuvred its way over to a place in the outer line of ships, in front of the *Mary*

Rose. A number of other ships had untied the big rowboats they pulled behind them, and these now moved carefully round to the side of the giant warship. I made out tiny figures descending some sort of ladder to the rowboats. Two more warships, smaller than the *Great Harry* but still huge, appeared and made slowly for the line.

'Looks like the soldiers are returning,' Barak said.

We sat on a bench outside one of the warehouses, leaning our backs against the wall. I looked across the harbour to the Gosport shore, where another fort stood opposite the Round Tower. The sun was low now, in a fiery red sky that presaged another hot day.

✝

THE FIRST GROUP of soldiers to disembark were strangers. They came ashore quietly, with none of the usual talking and jesting, some stumbling a little on the steps. A whiffler drew the men into line and marched them away.

Several more groups landed before Leacon at last appeared at the top of the steps. About half the company followed. Among them familiar faces appeared: Carswell and Tom Llewellyn, Pygeon and Sulyard. Like the earlier groups some wore jacks, others leather or woollen jerkins, and Pygeon wore the brigandyne he had won from Sulyard. Snodin brought up the rear, puffing and blowing as he mounted the steps. Like the earlier groups the men were unusually silent; even Carswell seemed to have no jests this evening. Only the oafish Sulyard seemed in high spirits, his swagger returned. The men formed a ragged line on the wharf, not noticing us in the shadow of the warehouse. One man cast off his helmet and scratched his head. 'These fucking lice!'

'Stop making your moan!' Snodin yelled at him. The whiffler was evidently in a bad temper. 'Whining miserable cur.' Several of the men gave Snodin nasty looks.

I stepped forward and called out to Leacon. He turned, as did the soldiers. Carswell's face brightened a little. ''Tis our mascot! Come with us on board the *Great Harry* again tomorrow, sir, bring us luck!' The other soldiers looked on, surprised that I had turned up again. I heard Sulyard mutter, 'Hunchbacks bring bad luck, not good.'

'Fall out, men,' Leacon ordered. 'Wait over there till the rest of the company arrives.' The men walked wearily to an open space between two warehouses, and Leacon came over and took my hand. 'I thought you had left, Matthew,' he said.

'Tomorrow.'

'The King comes then. As principal archers we have to parade before him outside the town in the morning.'

'We shall be gone before then.'

'That we shall,' Barak agreed firmly. 'We leave first thing.'

Leacon glanced over to where his men stood, many looking weary and anxious. Pygeon cast his brigandyne to the ground, where it made a tinkling noise. Sulyard glared at him. Carswell asked the whiffler, 'Master Snodin, may we get back to camp, get some food?'

'Proper food,' another man said, 'not biscuit you have to knock the weevils out of!' There were murmurs of agreement.

Snodin shouted, 'We'll leave when the rest arrive, with Sir Franklin!'

'Was today their first day on the ships?' I asked Leacon.

'Yes. Not a good day either.'

Everyone jumped and looked round at a tremendous boom. Another cannon shot from the Round Tower. There was an answering flash and boom from the Gosport side.

'What are they doing?' I asked Leacon.

'Practising covering the harbour, should the French try to gain entrance. We should be able to stop them, those cannon have a range of over a mile. But if they defeat our fleet at sea, there will be nothing to prevent them making a landing elsewhere.'

'George,' I said, 'I wonder if I might ask yet another favour.'

He looked at me curiously. 'Yes?'

I nodded at the men. 'It is confidential.'

He sighed. 'Come round the side of the warehouse.'

We went round the corner, out of earshot of the company.

'Did it not go well today?' I asked.

'The whole company has been on the *Great Harry*. God's death, the size of that ship. It has enough cannon to conquer Hell itself. None of the lads had encountered anything like it. Even when we were climbing up the rope ladder, a gust of wind came and it started swinging to and fro, us clinging on like snails to a drainpipe. I could see the men were terrified of tumbling into the sea. Then on board they all slid and fell with every little movement of the sea. And they didn't like being under that netting.'

'I have heard of it. Fixed above the decks, so boarders would fall on top of it. With soldiers carrying small pikes standing underneath.'

'The mesh on the netting is thick, you feel hemmed in standing under it. And if anything happened to the ship, if it went over, you'd be trapped under it.' He laughed; something wild in the sound made me frown. 'Not that most of the men can swim. We should have been given more time to practise; we've been here a week. The men are getting bored and irritable doing nothing, hence the desertions. You can't easily replace skilled archers. The sailors laughed at them sliding about, which didn't help. The sailors go barefoot, clinging to the deck like cats.'

'Soldiers and sailors must fight the same battle. If it comes.'

'In two or three days, from what they say.' The haunted look was back in his eyes. 'We've been told we're going to the *Great Harry*. As the flagship she will be at the head of the line. The men are all cast down, and Snodin doesn't help, snarling at them over every grumble they make. Being on the ship, he hasn't had a drink all day and that doesn't aid his temper.' He sighed. 'Well, Matthew, what is this favour?'

'George, I would not trouble you were it not important. But a woman's fate may be at stake. I need to speak again to Philip West, that I saw at the Godshouse.' I took a deep breath. 'He is on the *Mary Rose*. I want to know if you can help me get on board there, this evening, to talk to him.'

Leacon looked doubtful. 'Matthew, they are only allowing people with official business on the ships.' He looked out to sea. The big rowboats had lit their lanterns now, little points of light dancing on the water. The setting sun outlined the ships from behind in a fiery glow.

'Please,' I said. 'It's important.'

He considered. 'Easy enough to pay a boatman to take us over to the *Mary Rose*, but getting on board may be another matter even with me there. You certainly won't get on without me. Very well. But I cannot take long, I need to get back to camp; the men are downhearted and they must make ready to parade before the King tomorrow morning.' He brushed away a mosquito; now dark was coming they were starting to whine around our ears.

'George, I am more grateful than I can say.'

'First I must wait until the rest of the men arrive with Sir Franklin. He can lead them back to camp, then – '

He broke off. Snodin, out of sight, was yelling furiously. 'Stand up! Stand, you lazy slugs!'

'God's death,' Leacon muttered. 'He'll go too far – ' He walked rapidly round the warehouse, Barak and I following. Many of the men now lay sprawled on the ground. Snodin was haranguing them furiously. 'Lazy bastards! Stand up! You're not in your dirty houses now!'

Nobody moved. Carswell said, 'We're tired! Why shouldn't we rest?'

'The captain told you to wait, not lie on the ground like fucking toads!' The whiffler was almost beside himself, purple jowls trembling with fury.

Everyone turned as Leacon appeared. 'Don't talk to Master Snodin like that, Carswell!' he snapped.

Pygeon stood, pointing a shaking finger at the whiffler. 'Sir, he's been throwing abuse at us all day, all we wanted was to rest our legs after being on that ship!'

'Afraid, jug ears?' Sulyard called out contemptuously.

C. J. SANSOM

Then a new voice spoke up. 'If going on the flagship's such an honour, let the King come and serve on it!' Snodin turned and stared at Tom Llewellyn. The boy, normally so quiet, had stood up to face him. 'Let King Henry come and do this for sixpence a day, that's worth less than fivepence now!'

'And let us go back and get ready for the harvest!' another man called. Snodin whirled from speaker to speaker, so quickly it made some of the men laugh. Leacon stepped forward and grasped the whiffler by the shoulder. 'Calmly, Master Snodin,' he said in a low voice. 'Calmly.'

Snodin stood, breathing heavily. 'They have to be ready for battle, sir.'

'And they will be!' Leacon raised his voice. 'Come, lads, it's been a hard day, but I have been on ships before and you soon find your balance. And I have seen to it that a cow has been slaughtered for your meal tonight. Stand now, ready for Sir Franklin. See, the rest of the company are pulling up at the wharf!'

For a second nothing happened. Then, slowly, all rose to their feet. Leacon walked Snodin away a short distance and spoke quietly in his ear. Barak and I went over to where Carswell and young Llewellyn stood together nearby. 'Bold words, lad,' Barak said to Llewellyn.

The boy still looked angry. 'I'd had enough,' he answered. 'After today – we've all had enough.'

Carswell looked at me. There was no humour in his face any more. 'It's real now,' he said. 'I see what it'll be like if there's a battle. If the *Great Harry* grapples with a French warship it'll be cannon tearing into us, pikes thrust up at our bowels from their decks if we board. I always thought I had a knack for imagining things, Master Shardlake, but I could never conjure anything like that ship.'

'The size of it,' Llewellyn said wonderingly. 'It's as big as our church back home; those masts are like steeples. I thought, how can such a thing float? Each time the deck shifted I thought it was sinking.'

'The pitching of a ship is strange at first,' I said, 'but Captain Leacon is right, you get used to it.'

'We practised shooting our bows from the upper decks,' Carswell said, 'but the ship kept moving and throwing us off balance. The sailors were all laughing and guffawing, the malt worms. And it's hard to draw fully under that netting.'

Pygeon had come over to us. 'You spoke well, Tom,' he said. 'All this to save King Harry, that doesn't give a toss if we live or die.'

Carswell said, 'But if the French win they'll do to our people what we did to them last year. There's no help for it, we must fight.'

Sulyard shouted across, 'What're you plotting, Pygeon, you treasonous papist?'

'He's been trying to keep his courage together all day,' Carswell said contemptuously. 'The more he shouts the more you know he's frightened.' He looked at me. 'Why have you come back to this damned place, sir?'

Suddenly a well modulated voice called out, 'How now, what's this?' Sir Franklin had appeared at the top of the stairs, dressed as usual in fine doublet, lace collar and sleeves, the rest of the company behind him. 'Where's Leacon?' Leacon went over to him, followed by Snodin, who looked surly. Sir Franklin peered at them. 'Ah, there you are. All well?'

'Yes. Sir Franklin, I wonder if you would lead the men back to camp? Master Shardlake has asked me to do something for him.'

'Legal business?' Sir Franklin looked at me dubiously. 'You here again, sir? You don't want to get yourself too tangled up with lawyers, Leacon.'

'It should not take much beyond an hour.'

I said, 'I would be grateful indeed if you would allow it, Sir Franklin.'

He grunted. 'Well, don't be long. Come, Snodin, you look as though someone had dropped a bag of flour on your head.'

'Wait for me at the inn, Jack,' I told Barak.

He leaned close. 'You can't ask Leacon to go with you, not with his men in the mood they are. They'd have put Snodin in the water if he hadn't stopped them.'

'He's agreed,' I said brusquely.

'I think you would like to stay and tackle Rich too.'

'Maybe so, to see this done.'

'Then I begin to fear for your reason.'

Barak walked away. I returned to where Leacon stood, watching as Sir Franklin led the men away.

'Will the men be all right?' I asked.

'I've told Snodin to go easy, and they won't challenge Sir Franklin.' He took a deep breath. 'Right. The *Mary Rose*.'

✟

THE CAMBER was full of rowboats tying up for the night. We found a boatman, a stocky middle-aged man, who agreed to take us across to the *Mary Rose*, then wait and bring us back. We followed him down the slippery steps. Above us music and voices sounded from the Oyster Street taverns. The man set the oars in the rowlocks and pushed out into the open sea towards the lines of ships. Behind them the sunset was shading into dark blue, starkly outlining the forest of masts.

All at once we were in a world of near silence, the sounds from the town fading. The air, too, was suddenly clean and salty. The water was calm, but out at sea for the first time in four years I felt uneasy. I gripped the side of the boat hard and looked back to shore. I could see the city walls, the Square Tower and, beyond the town walls, the soldier's tents lining the coast, all turned pink by the setting sun.

'Thank you for doing this,' I said to Leacon. 'After that trouble with the men.'

'Thank God I thought to ensure fresh meat tonight. The biscuit's going bad. There's a couple of men down with the flux. And one man accidentally slashed himself with his knife yesterday. At least I think it was an accident. The company's down to eighty-eight.'

I looked back again to the retreating shore. Now I could see all the way down to South Sea Castle, a little pink block in the sunset, becoming tiny as we rowed out further into the Solent. Reluctantly, I turned my head away.

Slowly, we approached the warships. As we drew closer we saw haloes of dim light flickering above the decks from candles and lamps. The sound of a pipe and drum drifted across the water. Leacon stared ahead, preoccupied, then said with a sort of quiet desperation, 'I have to encourage my men, I must. I must try and lighten their mood, though I know the nightmare they may face.'

'God knows you are doing what you can.'

'Does He?'

We had almost reached the warships now, their masts and high castles seeming impossibly tall, gigantic plaited ropes stretching down to the water securing the anchors. The light was almost gone, the bright paintwork on the upper decks turned to shades of grey. The boatman swung away to avoid a stream of ordure running from a beakhead latrine. Voices and more music drifted down as the vast hull of the *Great Harry* reared before us. Something was happening on the main deck. A little platform had been built projecting out over the water, a pulley dangling from it. It was being used to heave something up from a large rowboat. I realized to my astonishment that it was a large, high-backed chair, covered with an oilcloth, in which an enormous dead pig had been tied.

'Careful,' I heard someone shout. 'It's bumping the side!'

'What on earth is going on?' I asked the boatman.

'Some freak of sailors' humour,' he answered disapprovingly.

We rowed past the flagship to the *Mary Rose*, the rose emblem above the bowsprit dimly outlined. I craned my neck to stare up.

The lowest, central section of the ship was perhaps twenty feet high; the long aftercastle, of at least two storeys, double that. The forecastle was taller still, three levels of decks projecting out over the bow like enormous steps. A sudden breeze came, and I heard a strange singing noise in the web of rigging that soared from decks to topmast. As we drew in close I heard a cry from the fighting top, high on the mainmast. 'Boat ahoy!'

The boatman steered in to the centre of the ship, between the high castles. I looked apprehensively at the great dark hull, wondering how we would get on board. My eye travelled upwards to squares outlined in tar that must be the gun ports, stout ropes running up from rings in the centre to holes in the painted squares above, the green and white Tudor colours alternating with red crosses on a white background, the colours of St George.

'How do we get up?' I asked apprehensively.

Leacon nodded up at the painted squares. 'Those panels can be slid out. They'll drop a rope ladder down from one.'

We came athwart, and the rowboat knocked against the hull with a bump. A panel was removed and a head looked out. A voice called down the watchword I had heard in camp: 'God save King Henry!'

'And long to reign over us!' Leacon shouted back. 'Petty-Captain Leacon, Middlesex archers! Official business for Assistant-Purser West!'

The head was withdrawn, and a moment later a rope ladder was thrown down. It uncoiled, the end splashing into the water beside us.

Chapter Thirty-nine

Our boatman hauled the ladder aboard, then turned to us. 'Climb up, sirs. One at a time, please.'

Leacon grasped the ladder and climbed onto it. He began to ascend. I watched apprehensively as he moved upwards steadily, hand over hand. I started with surprise as, a little above my head, a gun port suddenly swung outwards. There was the sound of squeaking wheels from within, and the mouth of a huge cannon appeared in the gap with a strange, juddering movement. 'That axle needs greasing,' a sharp voice called. The cannon was withdrawn, and the gun-port lid banged shut. I looked up to where Leacon had reached the top of the ladder. Hands reached through the opened blind and he squeezed through the narrow gap.

'Now you, sir,' the boatman said. I took a deep breath, grasped the rungs, and climbed up. I did not look down. The gentle bobbing of the boat was disorientating. I reached the blind and hands stretched out to help me through. It was a drop of several feet to the deck, and I stumbled and nearly fell. 'It's a fucking lawyer,' someone said in wonderment.

Leacon took my arm. 'I've asked a sailor to go and look for Master West.'

I looked around. Thick rope netting with a small mesh enclosed the deck, secured to the rail above the blinds and, in the middle, to a wooden central spar seven feet above our heads supported by thick posts running the length of the open weatherdeck. The wide spar formed a walkway above us, running between the two castles; a sailor was padding across in bare feet. I looked up at the twenty-foot-high aftercastle. Two long, ornate bronze cannon projected from it, angled to fire outwards. Two more projected from the forecastle, pointing in the opposite direction.

'What a creation,' I said quietly. I looked along the weatherdeck. It was around forty feet wide and almost as long, dominated by three iron cannon on each side, a dozen feet long and lashed to wheeled carriages. The deck was illuminated by haloes of dim light from tallow candles inside tall horn lanterns. Perhaps sixty sailors sat in little groups between the guns, playing dice or cards; they were barefoot, most with jerkins over their shirts and some with round woolly hats, for there was a cool breeze now. Many were young, though already with weatherbeaten faces. A small mongrel greyhound sat beside one group, avidly watching a game of cards. Some of the sailors looked over at me with cool curiosity, doubtless wondering who I was, their eyes little points of light. One group was talking in what I recognized as Spanish, another sat listening intently to a cleric reading aloud from the Bible: 'Then he arose, and rebuked the winds and the sea; and there was a great calm.' A rancid meaty smell and little wafts of steam rose from some of the hatches with heavy wooden grilles set along the deck.

'First time aboard a warship, sir?' One of the sailors who had helped me aboard had stayed with us, from curiosity perhaps.

'Yes.' I looked up, through the netting, to the fighting top high on the foremast. There the man who had called out our presence stood looking out to sea once more. A small boy was clambering up the rigging, as rapidly as the Queen's monkey in its cage at Hampton Court.

A sailor sitting nearby turned and spoke to me in a heavy, jocular tone. 'Have you come to make them fetch up our dinner, master lawyer?' I noticed that nearly everyone had wooden spoons and empty bowls beside them. 'Our bellies are barking.'

'Let's hope it's edible,' another man grumbled. He was poking something from under his fingernails with a tool from a tiny steel manicure set. He winced as he extracted a large splinter.

'That's enough, Trevithick,' our sailor answered. 'This gentleman's on official business.' He lowered his voice. 'The food's corrupted through lying too long in the barrels, sir. We don't like the smells coming from below. We were supposed to get fresh supplies today but they ain't come.'

'Food is ever the main concern among the soldiers too,' Leacon said. He looked at the barefoot sailors. 'Food and shoes, though you sailors don't seem to worry about those.'

'The soldiers should go barefoot like us, then they wouldn't slip and slide whenever they come on board.'

The *Mary Rose* moved slightly with the breeze, and I almost stumbled again. On the walkway above me two sailors, carrying a long heavy box between them, barely checked their stride as they walked across. They disappeared through a doorway into the aftercastle. Our sailor, bored with us, moved away.

'I can see why your men were intimidated,' I said quietly to Leacon. 'I've been on ships before, but this – '

He nodded. 'Ay, though I don't doubt their courage in the rush of battle.' I looked up again at the aftercastle. I saw more netting there on the top deck, secured to a central spar, dimly illumined by light from lamps below. Someone up there was strumming a lute, the sound drifting down. Leacon followed my gaze. 'We practised on the aftercastle of the *Great Harry* today, firing through the blinds on the top deck. It was hard to get a good shot.'

'The sailors seem in a poor humour.'

'They're hard to discipline, they've been dragged together from all over the realm and beyond. Some are privateers.'

I smiled. 'Are you showing your prejudices, George?'

'They didn't mind showing theirs earlier, laughing at my men.'

A thin wiry man in a striped jerkin picked his way towards us; he carried a horn lantern whose light was brighter than the sailors', a good beeswax candle inside. He bowed briefly, then addressed Leacon in a Welsh accent. 'You have business with Master West, Captain?'

'This man does. He needs to speak with him urgently.'

'He's down in the galley with the cook. You'll have to go to him, sir.'

'Very well. Can you take me?'

He looked at me dubiously. 'The galley is down in the hold. Can you manage it?'

I answered sharply, 'I got up on the ship, didn't I?'

'Your robe will suffer, sir. Best take it off.'

Leacon took it. 'I'll wait for you here,' he said. 'But please do not be long.'

I stood in my shirt, shivering slightly. 'Don't worry, sir,' the sailor said. 'It's warm enough where we're going.'

He led the way along the deck to the forecastle. As I followed I tripped beside a group of card players, accidentally sending a tiny dice flying; a man retrieved it with a quick scooping motion. 'I am sorry,' I said. He looked at me with hard hostility.

Just before the aftercastle we reached an open hatch where a wide ladder descended into darkness. The sailor turned to me. 'We go down here.'

'What's your name?'

'Morgan, sir. Now, please follow me down carefully.'

He put his feet on the ladder. I waited till the top of his head disappeared, then began to descend.

I had to feel carefully for the rungs in the semi-darkness, and thanked God the ship was barely stirring. It grew hotter. Water dripped somewhere. At the foot of the ladder there was some light, more lanterns hanging from beams. I saw it was the gundeck. Well over a hundred feet long, it ran below the castles, almost the whole length of the ship. Further down the gundeck some areas were partitioned off into little rooms, the backs of cannon projecting between them. To my surprise there was enough headroom to stand. I looked down at the cannon on their wheeled carriages. The nearest was iron; the one next to it bronze, stamped with a large Tudor rose, a crown above, gleaming with an odd sheen in the lantern light. A harsh smell of powder mixed with the cooking smell; pods of broom and laurel leaves tied against the walls to sweeten the air had little effect.

Men were checking stone and iron gunballs for size against wooden boards with large circular holes, then stacking them carefully inside triangular containers beside each cannon. Two officers looked on: one bearded and middle-aged, a silver whistle round his neck on a silk sash, the other younger. 'This job should have been finished before dark,' the older officer growled. He saw us and stared at me, raising his chin interrogatively. Morgan bowed deeply.

'This gentleman has a message from shore, sir, for Master West. He is down in the galley.'

'Don't get in the men's way,' the officer told me curtly. Morgan led me some way down the gundeck. We came to another hatch, with a ladder leading down. 'This goes right down to the galley, sir,' Morgan said.

'Who was that?'

'The master. He's in charge of the ship.'

'I thought that was the captain.'

Morgan laughed. 'Captain Grenville doesn't know the *Mary Rose*, though at least he's a seaman, unlike some of the captains. Most are knighted gentlemen, you see, to put us in awe.' Like Sir Franklin with the soldiers, I thought.

Morgan stepped to the ladder and began nimbly descending again. I followed.

We passed another deck, full of stores in partitioned areas. I made out barrels and chests, coils of immensely thick rope. Billows of hot steam rose up from below now. The ship shifted slightly, groaning and creaking, and one of my feet almost slipped. A red glow was visible underneath us, accompanied by a wave of heat, the smell of bad meat increasingly powerful. I glanced down at Morgan; his face was redly illuminated from below. 'Where are you from?' I asked.

'St David's, sir. I have a fishing boat, or did till I was enlisted like half west Wales. Though they still haven't enough sailors, a third of the crew are Spaniards or Flemings.'

'How many sailors on board?'

'Two hundred. And three hundred soldiers if we go to battle, so we're told. Too many, some say enough to overset the ship if they all go on those high castle decks.'

We passed through another hatch, my arms aching now. Then we were in the hold. Thick, stinking steam made me gasp and almost retch, and my face was instantly covered in sweat. There was, too, a rotten salty smell that I guessed came from the beach pebbles used as ballast. I saw, to my left, two large brick kilns, set on a brick flooring, yellow flames dancing underneath bubbling vats of pottage in which thick pieces of grey flesh floated. The flames, the bubbling cauldrons and the sweating walls made it look like some radical preacher's vision of Hell. Two young men, stripped to the waist, stirred the vats. One broke off to feed a piece of wood from a little pile into one of the fires. On the other side of the vats two men in their shirts were examining something in a ladle. One was Philip West, the other, I guessed, the cook.

The cook said, 'We can't serve this up, sir. We should put it overboard and try to find a barrel of stockfish that isn't tainted.'

'Are there any left?' West answered with angry impatience. 'We should have had a week's supply of new barrels delivered today! But you're right, we can't give the men this. It's rotten.' Then he saw me; his face took on an expression of astonishment and something like horror. He stepped forward. 'What's this?' he barked at Morgan.

'This gentleman's here to speak to you, sir,' the sailor answered humbly. 'He says it's urgent.'

'Sir,' the cook said, 'there are three barrels of stockfish left, we can try cracking one open.'

'Do it,' West snapped. He was still looking at me, his face red and mottled from the heat and steam. The cook beckoned to one of the men stirring the pottage, and they went out through a sliding door. West turned to me, anger in his deep-set eyes.

'Sir,' I said. 'I have come from your mother—'

'My mother! You –' He broke off, conscious of curious glances from Morgan and the remaining man. 'Wait a minute,' he said. I stood silently, listening to grunts and bangs from the other side of the door. Then the cook and his assistant rolled a heavy barrel into the galley. They set it quickly upright and the cook opened the lid with a chisel. I saw a white mass of fish within, the gleam of salt. The cook reached in with a skinny arm, pulled out a handful of fish and sniffed it. 'This is still fresh,' he said with relief.

'Get rid of the pork and start cooking the fish,' West said. 'Have you any fresh water barrels left in there?'

'Yes, sir.'

West turned to Morgan. 'Go up, tell Master Purser what we're doing. Say we must get those fresh supplies on board tonight: there's hardly anything left.' He watched Morgan as he climbed back up the ladder, then bent and took a candle holder from the floor, lighting it with a taper. He gestured to the ladder. 'Now, Master Shardlake,' he said grimly, 'let us go up and talk.'

✝

I FOLLOWED West up to the storage deck. As we stepped off the ladder, I heard rats pattering away from us. West stepped a few feet away from the hatch, set the candle atop a barrel and stood facing me. In the dim light I could not see his expression. Around me I saw chests and boxes piled one on another in the partitioned sections. Away from the stifling heat the sweat dried instantly on my face, leaving me cold. The ship shifted slightly and I grabbed at the ladder to steady myself.

'Well?' West asked.

'Something has happened at Rolfswood.' I told him of the discovery of Master Fettiplace's remains, his mother's visit to me and what she had said about the lost letter to Anne Boleyn.

'So the letter is to be made public at last,' West said when I had finished. His voice was steady, angry. I wished I could see his face properly.

'There will have to be a new inquest,' I said quietly. 'Your mother told me the story of the letter must be revealed to protect you.'

He laughed, bitterly. 'They cannot call me away to an inquest now. In case you have not noticed, Master Shardlake, I have business. I may die here soon. Protecting people like you. For my sins,' he added bitterly.

'I know as well as you what may be coming,' I answered earnestly. 'That is why I came tonight, to ask what happened at Rolfswood nineteen years ago. Master West, who was your friend that stole the letter?'

He darted forward then, grabbing me and slamming me against the side of the ship. He was very strong; a sinewy forearm pressed my neck against the hull. 'What is your interest in this?' he said with savage intensity. 'This has to be personal for you to follow me here. Answer!' He lightened the grip on my throat just enough to allow me to speak. Close to, I saw his deep-set eyes were burning.

'I want to find out exactly what happened to Ellen Fettiplace that night.'

'Do you know where she is?' West asked.

'Do you?'

He did not answer, and I realized then he knew Ellen was in the Bedlam. The fight seemed to go out of him suddenly and he stepped away. He said, bitterly, 'My friend betrayed me that day. Then I discovered what had happened to Ellen. It was because of both those things that I went to sea.'

'Tell me who your friend was. Now, while there is still time.'

'Are you working for someone at court?' The aggression had returned to his voice. 'Who is interested in reviving that old story?'

'I am not. I swear, my concern is only with what happened at Rolfswood. Was the man's name Robert Warner?'

West stared at me. 'I never heard that name.' He hesitated a long moment. 'My friend was called Gregory Jackson.'

'A lawyer in the Queen's household?'

'The King's. But he was in the Queen's pay.'

'What happened to him, Master West?'

'He is dead,' West answered flatly. 'Years ago, from the sweating sickness.'

I stared at him. Was he lying? I did not trust that long pause before he gave the name; he should have remembered it instantly. West had stepped back from the candlelight, his face dim again. I asked once more, 'Do you know what happened to Ellen Fettiplace?'

'I have never seen her since that day.' His voice had taken on a dangerous edge again.

'What's going on here?' We both turned at a sharp, angry voice from the ladder. A man had climbed down, a middle-aged officer in a yellow doublet. He glared at me, then at West, who had straightened up and stepped away from me. 'Master Purser,' West said with a bow.

'I had your message from Morgan. I've got the crew banging spoons against their plates and mewling for food.'

'There's a barrel of good stockfish cooking now. It's all that's left. The pork was bad. We must get those fresh supplies tonight.'

The purser looked at me. 'Are you the lawyer with the message?'

'Yes, sir.'

'Delivered it?' He looked at West, who had composed his face.

'I have – '

'Then get out. They shouldn't have let you on board.'

'I—'

'God's death, get out! Now!'

✝

ON DECK the men sat with bowls and spoons in their laps, faces sullen. Officers now patrolled the deck. As I watched, the master appeared from a doorway in the forecastle. He stood on the walkway above us, blew his whistle shrilly, and shouted down in a loud clear voice: 'Men! Your food is coming! The pork was bad, but there's stockfish cooking! More stores will be brought across tonight! And I have had word that when the King comes to Portsmouth tomorrow he is coming to inspect the *Mary Rose*! He is to dine on the *Great*

Harry, then come here afterwards. All know the *Mary Rose* is his favourite ship! So come, lads, cry "God save King Harry!"'

The sailors looked at each other, then ragged cries of 'God save King Harry!' sounded along the deck. Some of the foreign sailors, not understanding, looked at each other in puzzlement. 'Hail the King, dogs!' someone shouted at them. The master stepped across the walkway to the aftercastle. I made my way to Leacon, who stood watching by the blinds. He gave me my robe; I was glad to put it on, feeling chilled in the night air after the heat of the galley.

'What's the matter, Matthew?' he asked. 'You look as though you'd seen a ghost.'

'For a moment I thought I was in Hell, down in that galley.'

'I hope they really do have some food.'

'They do.' I heard the master's voice from high up in the aftercastle, more cheers for the King.

'And you?' Leacon asked. 'Did you find Master West? Did you get the answers you sought?'

I sighed. 'Only some. The purser arrived and ordered me off. I got enough answers to worry me, though.'

He looked at me seriously. 'I have to get back to camp.'

'Of course. There is no more I can do here.'

Leacon leaned through the blind, signalling to the boatman below. He helped me clamber through. I found my footing on the rope ladder and we descended to the boat. The boatman pulled out again, over the moonlit sea. I looked back at the *Mary Rose*, then across to the *Great Harry*. 'Now we know what they were doing with that pig,' I said. 'Practising lifting the King aboard. He'd never get up a ladder.'

'No. The master did well to marshal the sailors then, that was a nasty mood developing on deck. By Mary, the people organizing the supplies – cheating merchants, corrupt officials.'

Like Richard Rich, I thought.

'Best the French come soon and make an end of this waiting,' Leacon said passionately. 'Get it over, one way or the other.'

I looked at his troubled face, but did not reply. When we reached the wharf again it was a relief to climb back on land. A group of ragged-looking men were being led up Oyster Street by constables armed with staves. One was protesting angrily. 'I've a job at the warehouse!'

'I've seen you begging by the churchyard. All beggars out of Portsmouth tonight!'

I looked at Leacon. 'Remember the beggars thrown out of York before the King arrived there?'

'I do.' He called over to the man in charge. 'Do you know what time the King arrives tomorrow?'

'At nine. He is riding down from Portchester, across Portsea Island and through the town gate. With Admiral Lord Lisle and all the Privy Council. He will be taken out to the ships, then spend the night at the royal tents.'

'Will the Queen be with them?' I asked.

'No women in the party, I'm told. Now sir, if you please I have to see to these rogues from the city.' Leacon took a long, deep breath, then reached out his hand. 'This is where we must part, Matthew.'

'Thank you, George. Thank you for everything.' There was a moment's silence, then I said, 'When this is over, come to London, stay with me a while.'

'I will. My good wishes to Jack.'

'Good luck, George.'

'And you.' I looked into his drawn face. He bowed, then turned and marched quickly away, leaving me with sadness in my heart. As I walked back to the inn, I forced my mind back to the information West had given me, what it meant and where it led.

✞

BARAK LAY ON his bed, re-reading his letters from Tamasin. I pulled off my boots and sat on the side of my own bed, wondering how to tell him what I had decided.

'George Leacon sends his good wishes,' I told him. 'I have said farewell. The King will be in Portsmouth at nine tomorrow. He is going on the ships.'

'We must be gone before then,' Barak answered firmly.

'Yes, we must.'

'Did you get on the *Mary Rose*?'

'Yes.'

'What's it like?'

'Extraordinary. Beautiful and terrifying.'

'You saw West?'

'Yes.' I rubbed my neck. 'He was angry with me, he grabbed at me.'

'I told you it was dangerous,' he said impatiently.

'There were people near. In fact the purser interrupted us and ordered me away before I found out all I needed.'

'Did you get the name of that friend of his?'

'I asked him straight out if the other man was Warner, but he denied it. He gave me a name I have never heard of. I fear he was making it up. Jack, I am sure West knows Ellen is in the Bedlam.'

'If the story of the letter was true, why keep the man's name secret now?'

'Perhaps because they raped Ellen together.'

He lay back on the bed. 'More imagining.'

'If only that purser hadn't interrupted us –'

'Well, you did what you could. Now let's get back to London.'

'Tomorrow I am going first to Portchester Castle. I have to see the Queen. And Warner. She is not accompanying the King, it is an ideal opportunity. I am going to find out if Warner was at Rolfswood that day.'

He sat up. 'No,' he said quietly. 'You are going to let this go and come back to London.'

'What if it was Warner that betrayed me to Rich? An agent of Rich's in the Queen's household!'

'Even if that's true, you know everyone at court spies on each other. And if it's not true, you could lose Warner's friendship and patronage.'

'I owe the Queen. If one of her trusted advisers is in Richard Rich's pay – '

'You *don't* owe the Queen,' he answered with slow intensity. '*She* owes *you*. She always has: you saved her life, remember? I wish you had never let her drag you back anywhere near the court.' His voice rose. 'Go to Portchester? It's mad. What if Rich is there?'

'All the privy councillors are going to the tents. But the Queen is staying behind, so her household will be too.'

'What would you say to Warner anyway?'

'Ask some hard questions.'

'This isn't courage, you know. It's wilful, blinkered stubbornness.'

'You don't have to come.'

He looked at me and I saw he was utterly weary, tired beyond belief. He said quietly, 'That's what you said about coming back here today. But I came, just like I've come almost everywhere on this damned journey. You know why? Because I was ashamed, ashamed from the moment we met those soldiers on the road, of how I'd dodged their fate. But I'm not so ashamed I'll follow you into that lion's den. So there, that's it. If you go to Portchester Castle, this time you go alone.'

'I didn't know you felt—'

'No. I've just been useful to have around. Like poor Leacon.'

'That's not fair,' I said, stung.

'Isn't it? You used him twice to get you to West, though he has a company of soldiers to lead. But there are only so many favours a man can call in from anyone.' He turned away and lay back down.

I sat in silence. Outside two drunks were walking down the streets, shouting, 'King Harry's coming! The King's coming, to see off the Frenchies!'

Chapter Forty

B ARAK AND I SPOKE LITTLE during the remainder of the evening, only discussing the practicalities of the morrow's journey with uncomfortable, restrained politeness. Now I fully understood how reluctant he had been to support me in each successive stage of what he increasingly saw as my folly: he seemed to have given up arguing with me, which disturbed me more than any harsh words. We went early to bed, but it was long before I slept.

We had asked the innkeeper to be sure and wake us at seven, but the wretched man forgot and did not call till past eight. Thus one of the most crowded and terrible days of my life began with Barak and I struggling hastily into our clothes, pulling on our boots, and hurrying breakfastless to the stables. When we rode out into Oyster Street it was already lined with soldiers, helmets and halberds brightly polished, waiting for the King. A sumptuous canopied barge was drawn up at the wharf, a dozen men resting at the oars. Out at sea the ships stood waiting, great streamers in Tudor green and white, perhaps eighty feet long, fluttering gently from the top-masts.

To save time we avoided the main streets, riding up a lane between the town fields to the gate. It was another beautiful summer morning, Saturday, the 18th of July. All around soldiers waited outside their tents in helmets and jacks and, occasionally, brigandynes, captains on horseback facing the road in burnished breastplates and plumed helmets that reminded me of that first muster in London near a month ago.

'Is the King coming this way?' Barak asked.

'I would think he'll go down the High Street. But they all have to be ready.'

'Shit!' he breathed. 'Look there!' He pointed to a bearded man standing to attention beside a mounted captain, halberd held rigid, frowning with solemn importance.

I stared. 'Goodryke!' Barak averted his head from the whiffler who had tried so hard to conscript him, and we rode swiftly past.

✟

WHERE THE town streets converged at the gate there was a milling throng. Many were on horseback, merchants by their look. They were trying to get through, but soldiers were pressing them back. 'I've to fetch five cartloads of wheat in today,' a red-faced man was shouting. 'I have to get out on the road to meet them.'

'It's to be kept clear for the King. No one enters or leaves till he has passed through. He'll be here in a few minutes.'

'Damn!' I breathed. 'Come, let's get to the back of the crowd.' I tried to turn Oddleg round, but people were packed too closely together. 'He's coming!' A captain shouted from the gate. 'Everyone stay where they are!'

So we sat waiting. Looking down the High Street, I saw behind the soldiers facing the road hundreds of townsfolk, some holding up English flags. Brightly coloured wall hangings and carpets hung from the first-floor windows of the houses, and there were even people standing on the roofs. I looked behind me at the crowd and saw, at the back, Edward Priddis and his father on horseback. They stared at me, Edward stonily and Sir Quintin balefully. I turned away and looked up at the walkway atop the town walls, crowded with soldiers. I patted Oddleg, who, like many of the horses in the tense crowd, was nervous.

A soldier on the walls cupped his hands and shouted down, 'He comes!' I pulled my cap forward to hide my face as the soldiers cheered. There was a sound of tramping feet and a company of pikemen marched in through the gate. A group of courtiers followed, in furs and satins, Rich among them. Then the unmistakable figure of the King rode slowly in, his gigantic horse draped in a canopy of cloth of gold. He wore a fur-trimmed scarlet robe set with jewels that glinted in the sun, a black cap with white feathers on his head. When I had seen him four years before he had been big, but now his body was vast, legs like tree trunks in golden hose sticking out from the horse's side. Beside him rode Lord Lisle, stern as when I had seen him at the Godshouse, and a large man whom I recognized from York as the Duke of Suffolk; his beard now was long, forked and white; he had become an old man.

Cheers rose from the streets, and a crash of cannon from the Camber sounded a welcome. I risked a glance at the King's face as he passed, fifteen feet from me. Then I stared, so different was it from four years before. The deep-set little eyes, beaky nose and small mouth were now surrounded by a great square of fat that seemed to press his features into the centre of his head. His beard was thin, and almost entirely grey. He was smiling, though, and began waving to the welcoming crowds, tiny eyes swivelling keenly over them. In that grotesque face I thought I read pain and weariness, and something more. Fear? I wondered whether even that man of titanic self-belief might think, as the French invasion force approached, what will happen now? Even, perhaps: *What have I done?*

Still waving, he rode away down the High Street, towards the barge that would take him to the *Great Harry*.

✝

HALF AN HOUR passed before the King's entire retinue had entered the town and we were able to ride out. From the seafront more cannon resounded as the King arrived at the wharf. Beyond the gate the soldiers lining the road were now falling out of line, wiping sweat from their brows.

'Christ's blood, he's aged,' Barak said. 'How old is he now?'

I calculated. 'Fifty-four.'

'Is that all? Jesu. Imagine the Queen having to sleep with that.'

'I prefer not.'

'That I believe.' He ventured a smile and I smiled sadly back, glad the ice was broken.

We crossed the bridge to the mainland and rode quickly to the little town of Cosham. There one road continued north, past Hoyland and on to London, while another forked left to Portchester Castle. We halted. Barak said quietly, 'Let's ride on, get home.'

'No. I am still going to Portchester. An hour to ride there and back, an hour or two at the castle. I'll try and catch you up tomorrow.'

'I'm still not coming.'

'I understand. You think me mad, I know.' I tried to smile.

'I'll wait for you at the inn over there till three,' he said. 'But if you're not back by then I'll ride on.'

'Agreed.'

So I turned and rode west. I passed along the coastline for a couple of miles; slowly the high white Roman walls of Portchester Castle, set on a peninsula protruding into the head of Portsmouth Haven, became clearer. Twice I passed a company of soldiers heading in the opposite direction.

The castle, an almost perfect square of high stone walls surrounded by a moat, enclosed a site of several acres. In the centre of the walls was a large gatehouse, and at the western end an enormous square keep, immensely solid. A group of soldiers in half-armour, with swords and halberds, stood guard before the drawbridge in front of the gatehouse. I handed the letter I had written to Warner the previous night asking for an interview, to a young officer, a petty-captain I guessed. He looked at me interrogatively. 'I understand the Queen and her household have remained at Portchester,' I said.

'They're here.'

'I have been engaged on a piece of legal business for the Queen at Portsmouth. There has been a development and I need to speak with Master Warner.'

The captain stared. 'I'd have thought they'd be too busy there to bother with lawyer's quibbles.'

'This matter started before the present crisis. I think Master Warner will want to see me.'

He grunted disapproval, but beckoned a young soldier across, gave him the letter, and told him to find Warner. The soldier ran off to the drawbridge.

'Did you see his majesty enter Portsmouth?' the petty-captain asked.

'He arrived just before I left. He had a fine welcome.'

He jerked his head back at the castle behind him. 'We may have to defend this place from the French. They say there's thirty thousand of them.' He laughed bitterly, muttered 'Lawyer's quibbles,' again. We waited in silence, the hot sun beating down on us, till the young soldier ran back. 'He'll see the lawyer, sir,' he told the officer.

✝

ONE OF THE soldiers took the horse, and the officer, with ill grace, led me across the drawbridge. We passed through the big gatehouse, guarded by more soldiers, which gave entrance to the castle and came out into a huge open space where there were yet more soldiers' tents. Men were drilling and practising with their bows on the cropped grass. Ahead of me was an enormous storehouse. The door was open and I saw it was near empty; most of the stores would have been taken to Portsmouth. A path ran straight across the enclosure to another gate on the opposite side, giving on to the harbour. Soldiers patrolled the walls and I saw the dark shapes of cannon; if the French managed to enter the harbour they might try to land here.

We turned left towards the tall inner keep; it was surrounded by a complex of smaller buildings, closed off by internal walls and protected by a continuation of the moat. The petty-captain had to explain his mission to the guards stationed there before he was allowed to lead me across the inner moat into a central yard. With the King away few people remained there. We passed through a high ornate door, then climbed a flight of steps to a great hall with a splendid hammerbeam roof. I was handed on to an official who led me down a narrow corridor into a small antechamber, telling me to wait. There were some cushioned chairs; I sat down wearily. It was quiet; a clock on the buffet ticked steadily. The sun streamed in through an arched window.

The door opened and Warner entered, my letter in his hand. He looked agitated. 'Matthew, what is this?' he asked. 'I hope it is urgent.'

I stood and bowed. 'It is. I need to speak with you, Robert.'

'Why are you still here?' he asked sharply. 'The Queen recommended you to leave. You know the King is here?'

'I saw him enter Portsmouth two hours ago.'

'Please tell me nothing more has happened at Hoyland Priory. The Queen was most concerned to learn of that woman's death.'

'A man has been arrested for Abigail Hobbey's murder, a local yeoman. I believe he is innocent.'

He waved a hand impatiently. 'The Queen cannot deal with that now.'

'And I have been warned to drop the Curteys case. By none other than Sir Richard Rich.'

I watched carefully for Warner's reaction, but he only looked surprised. 'What on earth has Rich to do with Hoyland?'

'I do not know. But I remember the day I came to Hampton Court to see the Queen, Rich was standing in a doorway in Clock Court when I left her. With Sir Thomas Seymour. They took the opportunity to bait me a little, but I thought the meeting was ill chance. Now I am not so sure.'

He shook his head. 'I can make nothing of this.'

I continued, 'I believe I mentioned I wished to take the opportunity to look into another matter down here.'

'You did.' He frowned. 'If there is a connection to the Hugh Curteys case, you should have told the Queen.'

'I have only recently discovered there may be a link. A man called Sir Quintin Priddis.'

'Matthew, the Queen cannot be troubled with this now,' he said sharply. 'The King needs her full support. You were told to leave—'

I said quickly, 'I have been investigating how a woman called Ellen Fettiplace came to be placed in the Bedlam nineteen years ago, despite there being no certificate of lunacy. Sir Quintin Priddis was involved. My trail led me to a town near the Sussex border, Rolfswood, where the body of her late father was recently discovered. It looks like murder. I have been talking to the man who was to marry her. He is now assistant purser on the *Mary Rose*. His name is Philip West.'

I watched Warner's face as I recited those names, but he still only looked puzzled and annoyed. 'Master West told me an extraordinary tale,' I continued. 'When he was young he was at court. He was favoured by the King and chosen to take a letter from Petworth to Hever Castle, the same summer of 1526 that Ellen's father disappeared and she went to the Bedlam. The letter was stolen by the man West was travelling with, a young lawyer in Catherine of Aragon's service.'

'What is all this to do—'

I continued relentlessly. 'He believes the lawyer was a spy for Catherine of Aragon and took the letter to her. It may have given her early warning of the King's intention to divorce her. West told the King the letter was lost, not stolen. He told me the man who stole it was named Gregory Jackson, and that he is dead, but I have wondered whether West might have been lying.'

Warner stared at me; then he reddened and his face grew hard. 'What are you saying?' I did not answer. 'You know I was a young lawyer in Catherine of Aragon's household then.' He said quietly, 'You think it might have been me.' He took a deep breath. 'Very well.'

He turned round and walked to the door. 'Wait here,' he said. Before I could move he had gone, closing the door. I heard him call out to a guard to watch it.

✟

FOR HALF AN HOUR I waited and sweated. And I thought, Barak was right, I have become obsessed; if he had come here with me, I would have led us both into danger. When the door opened I jumped involuntarily, my heart in my mouth. Warner was there, two guards with halberds behind him. 'Come with me,' he said abruptly. I went out, the guards taking positions behind me.

Warner led me downstairs, our feet clattering on stone flags, and I thought with horror, this is a castle, it will have dungeons. But he stopped on the ground floor, took me along a corridor and then opened a door that led, to my surprise, into a small, secluded garden surrounded by trees. Vines hung from trellises and flowers grew in little banks by the walls. There, shaded by a trellis, the Queen sat, the spaniel Rig on her knee, two maids-in-waiting standing behind her. She wore a dress in her favourite crimson and a hood patterned with flowers, tiny diamonds sewn into the petals. She looked up at me and I saw her face was tight with strain, dark circles under the eyes. Her body was tense, rigid, her face angry. I bowed deeply.

'Matthew!' The Queen's tone was low, hurt. 'Master Warner tells me you have accused him of being in the pay of that scoundrel Richard Rich.'

I turned to Warner, who gazed back at me steadily. 'I made no accusation, your majesty. But I feared—'

'He has told me. It sounds scant reason to come here and accuse him. Now, of all times.'

'Your majesty, my concern was for the integrity of your household.'

The Queen closed her eyes. 'Oh, Matthew, Matthew,' she said. She looked at me again, steadily. 'Have you told anyone else this story?'

'Only Barak.'

'Well, it is true at least that this man West lied to you.' The Queen gestured wearily to her lawyer. 'Tell him, Robert.'

Warner said coldly, 'There was indeed a young lawyer in Catherine of Aragon's household named Gregory Jackson. He worked for me, in fact. But he died in 1525, the year before West lost this letter. From the sweating sickness. I remember, I went to his funeral. So the man West and his mother spoke of could not have been Jackson. But nor was it me. Queen Catherine of Aragon had her spies, certainly, who would try to ferret out whatever they could about the King's mistresses. But they were mostly servants in the King's household. And on my oath I was no spy, I was a lawyer then as I am now. And I have no connections with Richard Rich, no dealings with that man if I can avoid it. I thought it best to lay your – insinuation – directly before the Queen.'

'And I trust Robert.' The Queen's voice rose. 'Do you think me a fool, Matthew, not to be sure whom I can trust in my service, when I know what can happen to queens in this country?'

I looked between her and Warner, saw the anger in both their faces. I realized I had been wrong. 'I apologize most humbly, your majesty. And to you, Master Warner.'

The Queen turned to Warner. 'I wonder if there even was a letter.'

'I do not know, your majesty. I never heard anything, but I was not greatly in Catherine of Aragon's confidence. She knew or guessed by then that I was beginning to have reformist sympathies.'

I said, 'Either way, West lied about this man Jackson.'

He nodded stiffly in agreement. I looked back at the Queen. 'And there is still the question of Rich's involvement in the Curteys affair. There is a common link between the Curteys case and the Sussex matter – the feodary Sir Quintin Priddis, who was once a Sussex coroner. He is an old friend of Rich's.'

The Queen considered. 'The death of poor Mistress Hobbey – you told Robert a man had been accused?'

'A local yeoman. He had been contesting attempts by Master Hobbey to enclose Hoyland village.'

'You believe him innocent?'

'Yes. There is no real evidence.'

'Is there any evidence against anyone else?'

I hesitated. 'No.'

'Then he will stand trial. The truth will be investigated there.'

'He is in prison now. I have offered to take up the villagers' case at the Court of Requests.'

'You have been busy,' Warner said sarcastically.

The Queen said, 'And the man found dead at Rolfswood, the father of your – friend – in Bedlam. What will happen there?'

'There will be an inquest. I do not know when.'

The Queen looked at me. 'Then that will be the time to ferret out the truth. As for Hugh Curteys, whatever corruption there may have been in the administration of his lands, if he does not wish to pursue the case, there is nothing to be done. Matthew, I know you never like to let a matter rest once you have taken it up, but some, times in this life you must. These matters will have to await due process. And you should not be here. The French are coming, there could be mortal danger.' She raised a hand and pinched the bridge of her nose.

'Are you all right, your majesty?' I asked.

'Tired, that is all. The King slept badly last night and called me to talk with him. Often now he cannot sleep from the pain from his leg.'

'You do not know how difficult life is for the Queen just now,' Warner said angrily. 'Why do you think the King has left her here today? I will tell you,' he went on. 'Because if, which God forbid, he should be killed or captured in these next few days, the Queen will be Regent for Prince Edward as she was when the King went to France last year, and she will have to deal with all of them. Gardiner, Norfolk, the Seymours, Cranmer. And Rich.' He moved a step closer to his mistress, protectively. 'These last two years she has kept her patronage of you as unobtrusive as she can, lest the King remember your past encounter and be annoyed. And now you stay in Hampshire against her wishes, you come swaggering in here, making ridiculous accusations against me – '

The Queen looked up and now she was smiling faintly. She put

C. J. SANSOM

her hand on Warner's sleeve. 'Come, Robert. Swaggering is something Matthew does not do. Leave us to talk, just for a few moments, then take Matthew out and he can make haste straight back to London.'

Warner bowed deeply to the Queen, then walked stiffly away without another look at me. The Queen nodded to the maids-in-waiting and they stepped to the shade of the doorway. She looked at me, the half-smile still on her face.

'I know you meant well, Matthew. But never forget that, as the Gospels tell us, the road to Hell is paved with good intentions.'

'I am sorry. Sorry that I accused Master Warner, and sorrier that you have cause to be angry with me.'

She looked at me intently. 'Do you see that I have cause? After you disobeyed me?'

'Yes. Yes, I do.'

She nodded in acknowledgement, then looked down at her dog. 'Do you remember that day at Hampton Court?' she said in a lighter tone. 'The Lady Elizabeth was with us. She liked your answers to her questions, she told me later. I think you made a friend there. She does not like everyone, I can tell you.'

'I have remembered it too, these last weeks. You told me she was reading Roger Ascham's *Toxophilus*. It is a great favourite of Hugh Curteys' too. He lent it to me. I confess I found it a little – self-satisfied.'

'I have met Master Ascham. He – he is one who does swagger.' She laughed. 'But he is a learned man. The Lady Elizabeth has expressed a wish to correspond with him. She is such a remarkable child. Master Grindal is teaching her well, he is one of those who believes a woman may learn anything as well as a man. That is good. I often wish I had had a better education.' She smiled again, and a little merriment came to her eyes. 'Though I wish Elizabeth would not swear like a boy. I tell her it is not ladylike.' The Queen looked round the little garden; sunlight came through the trees, making patterns on the ground as the breeze shifted the branches. Birds sang softly. 'This is a peaceful little place,' she said wistfully. 'Tell me, what is Hugh Curteys like?'

'He is somehow – unreadable. But he still mourns his sister.'

Her face clouded again. 'Many in England may be in mourning before long. I wish the King had never – ' she cut herself short, biting her lip, then reached out and touched my hand. 'I am sorry I was vexed, Matthew. I am tired.'

'Should I leave you, your majesty?'

'Yes. I may go to my chamber and rest. But I pray God we may meet again, safe, in London.'

I bowed and stepped to the door. I was full of gratitude for her forgiveness, and deeply sorry now for my accusations against Warner. I might have gained a friend in little Lady Elizabeth, but I had lost one, too. Then I frowned. Something was nagging at my mind. Something the Queen had said about Elizabeth. The maids-in-waiting moved aside to let me pass, dresses rustling. Inside, Warner waited, his manner still cold and hostile.

'Robert,' I said, 'I apologize again—'

'Come, you should leave, now.'

We went back up the stairs I had descended in such fear. 'Master Warner,' I said when we reached the top. 'There is one last question I would ask, if you will?'

'Well?' he asked roughly.

'Something you said to me at Hampton Court. You said the Queen was like Catherine of Aragon, utterly loyal to her servants.'

'Do not worry,' he said contemptuously, 'the Queen will stay loyal to you.'

'I did not mean that. It was something else you said, that Catherine of Aragon had her faults. What did you mean by that?'

'It is simple enough. She was another like you, sir, who would not let go when sense and even decency indicated she ought. When the King first said he wished to divorce her, the Pope sent her a message. That I did know of, as her lawyer. The Pope, to whom

Catherine of Aragon's ultimate loyalty lay as a Catholic, suggested that in order to resolve the problems that were beginning to tear England apart, she should retire to a nunnery, which in canon law would allow the King to marry again without a divorce.'

'That would have been a neat answer.'

'It would have been the best answer. She was past childbearing age; the King would not bed with her anyway. She could have kept her status and honours, lived an easy life. And her daughter Mary that she loved would have kept her place in the succession rather than being threatened, as she was later, with execution. So much blood and trouble would have been spared. And the irony is Catherine of Aragon's obstinacy meant that England split from Rome; the last thing she wanted.'

'Of course. I see.'

Warner smiled tightly. 'But she believed God desired her to stay married to the King. And as often happens, God's will and her own chimed nicely. So there you are, that is where obstinacy may lead. Fortunately, our present Queen has a strong sense of realism. Stronger than some men, for all that she is a weak woman.'

He turned on his heel, and led me away. And with his last words it came to me, like a click in the brain. I understood now what had happened at Hoyland, what the secret was that everyone had known and concealed. Warner turned and looked at me in surprise as I released a sound that started as a sigh but ended as a groan.

✟

AN HOUR LATER Barak and I were riding north along the London road. When I arrived at the inn I had been moved by the relief on his face. I told him Warner was innocent and that I had received a deserved rebuke from the Queen.

'Well,' he said, 'I did warn you.'

'Yes. You did.'

As we rode on I was silent; Barak probably thought I was in a chastened mood, but I was thinking hard, turning everything over since that flash of revelation as I left the Queen, afraid I might be building another castle in the air. But this time everything fitted tightly. And it would be easy to find out, very easy.

I said quietly, 'I want to call in at Hoyland on the way. Just briefly.'

For a second I thought he would fall from his saddle. '*Hoyland*? Have you gone stark mad? What sort of welcome do you think you'll get?'

'I know now what it was that the Hobbeys were keeping quiet. What caused poor Michael Calfhill such distress when he came, and why Feaveryear left.'

'Jesus Christ, another theory.'

'It is easy to test. It should only take half an hour. And if I am wrong no harm will be done, and we can be on our way.'

'Do you think you know who killed Abigail?' he asked sharply.

'I am not sure yet. But if I am right, the killer came from within the household not the village.' I gave him a pleading look. 'Maybe I am wrong, but if I am right Ettis may be proved innocent. Half an hour. But if you want, ride on and find a bed in Petersfield.'

He looked down the dusty, tree-shaded road, then at me, and to my relief he shook his head and laughed. 'I give up,' he said. 'I'll come. After all, it's only the Hobbeys we have to face this time.'

Chapter Forty-one

I KNEW THAT if we rode up to the front door of Hoyland Priory, Fulstowe might see us and order us off. Accordingly we turned onto the path along the edge of the hunting park that led to the rear gate. Overhanging branches brushed us as we rode quietly along. I remembered the day of the hunt, the great stag turning at bay. And the day we had ridden into Hugh's woodland and that arrow had plunged into the tree beside us.

We dismounted beside the gate. 'Let's tie the horses to a tree,' I said.

'I hope it's unlocked.'

'It's flimsy. If need be we can smash it open.'

'Breaking and entering?' Barak looked at me seriously. 'That's not like you.'

But it was unlocked, and we stepped quietly through into the familiar grounds. Ahead was the lawn dotted with its trees; to our left the kennels and other outhouses. Barak looked down to the little sheds where he and Dyrick's clerk had lodged. He suddenly asked, 'Feaveryear hasn't been harmed, has he?'

'No, he was sent packing back to London because he discovered something.'

'In God's name, what?'

'I want you to see for yourself.'

I looked at the great hall, the sun glinting on the windows. No one was about; it was very quiet. We started a little as a pair of wood pigeons flapped noisily from one tree to another. It was hot, the sun almost directly above. My coif chafed against my brow and I wiped away sweat. I realized I was hungry; it was well past lunchtime. I looked at the old nuns' cemetery, the practice butts, remembered Hobbey saying he wondered if he might be under a curse for taking over the old convent.

One of the servants, a young man from the village, came out of the buttery. He stared at us in astonishment, as though we were ghosts. All the servants would know how I had upset the family at the inquest. I walked across, smiling. 'Good afternoon, fellow. Do you know if Master Hobbey is at home?'

'I – I don't know, sir. He is going to the village today, with Master Fulstowe and Master Dyrick.'

'Dyrick is still here?'

'Yes, sir. I don't know if they've gone out yet. You have come back?'

'Just briefly. Something I need to speak with Master Hobbey about. I will go round to the house.' We walked away, leaving him gazing after us.

'I wonder what they're up to in the village,' Barak said.

'Trying to bully them over the woodlands, probably.'

We went down the side of the great hall and round to the front of the house. In Abigail's garden the flowers were dying unwatered in the heat. I said, 'Remember when that greyhound killed Abigail's dog? Remember her saying I was a fool who did not see what was in front of me? If I had, then, she might not have died. But they were so clever, all of them. Come,' I said savagely, 'let's get this over.'

We walked round to the front porch. Hugh was sitting on the steps, oiling his bow. He wore a grey smock and a broad-brimmed hat to shade his face. When he saw us he jumped to his feet. He looked shocked.

'Good afternoon, Hugh,' I said quietly.

'What do you want?' His voice trembled. 'You are not welcome here.'

'I need to talk to Master Hobbey. Do you know where he is?'

'I think he's gone to the village.'

'I will go in and see.'

'Fulstowe will throw you out.'

I met Hugh's gaze, this time letting my eyes rove openly over his long, tanned face, staring straight at the smallpox scars. He looked away. 'Come, Jack,' I said. We walked past Hugh, up the steps.

The great hall, too, was silent and empty. The saints in the old west window at the far end still raised their hands to heaven. The walls remained blank; I wondered where the tapestries were. Then a door at the upper end of the hall opened, and David came in, dressed in mourning black. Like Hugh and the servant before him, he stared at us wonderingly. Then he walked forward, his solid body settling into an aggressive posture.

'You!' he shouted angrily. 'What are you doing here?'

'There is something I need to see your father about,' I told him.

'He's not here!' David's voice rose to a shout. 'He's gone to the village with Fulstowe, to sort out those serfs.'

'Then we will wait till he returns.'

'What's this about?'

'Something important.' I looked into the boy's wide, angry blue eyes. 'Something I have discovered about the family.' David's full lips worked, and his expression turned from truculence to fear.

'Go away! I am in charge in my father's absence. I order you to leave!' he shouted. 'I order you out of this house!' He was breathing heavily, almost panting.

'Very well, David,' I said quietly. 'We will go. For now.' I turned and walked away to the door. Barak followed, casting glances over his shoulder to where David stood staring. Then the boy turned and walked rapidly away. A door slammed.

We stepped back into the sunlight. In the distance I saw Hugh standing, shooting arrows at the butts. Barak said, 'David looked like he'd been found out in something.'

'He has, and realized it. He is not quite as stupid as he seems.'

'He looked like he might have another fit.'

'Poor creature,' I said sorrowfully. 'There is every reason to pity David Hobbey. More than any of them.'

'All right,' Barak said in a sharp voice. 'Enough riddles. Tell me what's going on.'

'I said I wanted you to see. Come, walk with me.'

I led the way round the side of the house. Here we had a clear view of Hugh. He stood with feet planted firmly on the lawn. He had a bagful of arrows at his belt and was shooting them, one after another, at the target. Several were stuck there already. Hugh reached down, fitted another arrow to his bow, bent back, rose up and shot. The arrow hit the centre of the target.

'By God,' Barak said. 'He gets better and better.'

I laughed then, loudly and bitterly. Barak looked at me in surprise.

'There is what none of us saw,' I said, 'except Feaveryear, who realized and ran to Dyrick. I think Dyrick did not know until Hobbey told him after Lamkin died. I remember he looked perturbed after that. He had probably demanded Hobbey tell him what it was Abigail had said I could not see.'

'Know what?' Barak's voice was angry now. 'All I see is Hugh Curteys shooting on the lawn. We saw that every day for a week.'

I said quietly, 'That is not Hugh Curteys.'

Now Barak looked alarmed for my sanity. His voice rose. 'Then who the hell is it?'

'Hugh Curteys died six years ago. That is Emma, his sister.'

'What—'

'They both had smallpox. But I believe it was Hugh that died, not Emma. We know Hobbey was in financial difficulties. He could hold off his creditors by making a bond to pay them, over a period of years, and creaming off the money from the Curteys children's woodlands. I think that is why he took the wardship.'

'But that's a boy—'

'Let me continue.' I went on, in tones of quiet intensity, 'But then

Hugh died. Remember how wardship works: a boy has to be twenty-one to sue out his livery and gain possession of his lands, but a girl can inherit at fourteen. Emma would have inherited Hugh's share of the lands automatically. Hobbey no doubt had thought he would have control at least for nine years, but now he faced losing them in one. Not long enough to pay off his debts. So I think they substituted Emma for Hugh.'

'They couldn't – '

'They could. It helped that the children were so close in age and looked alike, though no one who knew them both would have been deceived. So they dismissed Michael Calfhill at once and left London quickly.'

'But Michael said he saw Emma buried.'

'It was Hugh in that coffin.'

'Jesus.'

'Michael never did anything wrong with Hugh. And when he came to visit last spring he recognized Emma.'

Barak leaned forward, watching the figure on the lawn intently as another arrow was loosed at the target. Like the last, it hit dead centre. 'You're wrong, that's not a girl. And what on earth would be in it for her?'

'Not marrying David, I would guess. Of course, she might have learned from Michael that David's falling sickness meant she could go to the Court of Wards and say a marriage to him would be disparagement. But, with Michael gone and her fate in the hands of the Hobbeys, it would be a hard thing for a thirteen-year-old girl to do on her own. And the impersonation would have given her some power over the Hobbeys. She held their fate in her hands. I would guess Emma agreed to the substitution because it meant there could never be a marriage. That was probably all she thought of then,' I added sadly. 'But once it was done they were all trapped.'

Barak shaded his eyes with his hand, looked again at Hugh. 'That is no girl. It can't be.'

'Keep your voice down. No, you wouldn't think so. But a girl may learn skill at the bow, may be educated as well as a man. I think that is why the time I met Lady Elizabeth kept coming back into my mind. She too is a good archer. And if a girl has learned to walk as a boy, dress as a boy, behave as a boy and shoot arrows like a boy, then among strangers the deception may be kept up for years. If she is tall, that helps too.'

'But her breasts? And the stubble – Hugh gets shaved regularly.'

'Breasts can be flattened with padding. And though they have taken trouble to tell us Hugh is shaved regularly I have never seen any stubble on his face. Have you?'

'But he had shaving cuts – '

'He had cuts on his face. Or rather, hers. Those are easy enough to make.'

'No Adam's apple – '

'Some boys have a prominent one, like Feaveryear. Others have one that is barely noticeable. And her scars prevented anyone from looking too closely at her neck.'

Barak stared harder. 'But to keep it up for years – '

'Yes. It must have been a terrible strain on them all, one that unbalanced Abigail and David. They told Fulstowe, of course – his help was essential. And that gave him a hold over the family. The Hobbeys must soon have realized they were caught, trapped for ever. Because once it started there was no going back. If they were found out they could have ended in prison.'

'But why would Emma keep up the pretence now? Jesu, he – or she – wants to go and be a soldier!'

I said angrily, 'Perhaps by now she scarcely knows who or what she is.'

'Listen. I know it fits, but you'd better be sure – '

I said sadly, 'I looked at Hugh properly for the first time, on the steps when we arrived. Full in his scarred face. Then I saw he could easily be a girl.'

Barak turned to me. 'Did Hugh – Emma – kill Abigail?'

He spoke too loudly. The slim, lithe figure at the butts had just risen to fire another arrow. He – or rather she – lowered the bow and turned to face us. We stood quite still for a moment, all three of us, like some strange tableau. Then, in seconds, the person we had known as Hugh had strung an arrow to the bow, raised it and taken aim at my chest. I knew there was nothing Barak or I could do; before we could run a few paces Emma Curteys could loose the arrow, string another, and shoot us both dead.

I raised my arms, as though I could ward off that steel-tipped shaft. 'Don't!' I shouted. 'You will gain nothing!'

I could not see her face properly at that distance; it was shaded by the hat, which I realized now was one of the many ruses, like putting her hand to her scars, that Emma had developed over the years to prevent people looking her fully in the face. I saw the bow move slightly and stepped back with a cry, but then I realized it was trembling, shaking slightly from side to side in her hand though she still aimed at me.

'Run!' Barak cried.

I seized his arm. 'No! Don't do anything sudden!' I called out to Emma. 'I'm your friend!' I called steadily. 'Haven't you realized that? I will help you!'

Still she stood, the bow trembling gently. The whole thing can only have lasted ten seconds but it seemed like an age. Then I saw a figure on the edge of my vision, a dark solid shape running towards the archer.

'Hugh!' David shouted out – he still called her Hugh – 'stop! It can't help you! They know, it's over! Put the bow down!'

Emma turned, pointing the bow at David as he ran towards her. The arrow hit him in the side, its force sending him staggering. He toppled over onto the lawn, moaned once, then was silent. Then, no doubt drawn by the shouting, Fulstowe appeared in the doorway. David had lied, he was in there after all. He stepped out. A gaggle of servants followed as Fulstowe began walking towards David. Emma reached back, flicked another arrow on to her bow, and aimed at the steward. Fulstowe stopped dead in his tracks. One of the women servants screamed. I thought Emma would shoot Fulstowe down but instead she retreated backwards, step by step, to the gate, still keeping him covered. Only once did she glance across to where David lay on the lawn, quite still now. All this time she had not uttered a single word.

She backed out of the gateway, then turned and ran. Fulstowe and some of the other servants raced over to where David lay. Someone screamed, 'Murder!'

Chapter Forty-two

D AVID, THOUGH, was not dead. From where he lay on the grass I heard a faint, desperate moan. Fulstowe turned from the gate and ran across to him, Barak and I following. Blood was pouring from the wound in David's side, from which the arrow shaft protruded obscenely.

'Help me,' he whimpered.

'Still, lad,' Barak said gently.

The steward shouted to the servants who had gathered at the side of the lawn. 'Quick! Someone ride to fetch the Cosham barber-surgeon! And tear up some sheets!'

I shouted, 'My horse is ready saddled, tied up outside the back gate. Take it!'

Fulstowe looked wildly at me. 'What the hell happened? Why are you here?'

'Hugh shot David. I think he might have killed us had David not intervened.'

'What?'

'Leave me go!' I heard a shrill, desperate voice from the doorway. Hobbey stood there, Dyrick holding his arm. He threw Dyrick off, ran across to David and knelt beside him. He began tenderly stroking his dark head, tears streaming down his cheeks. The boy lifted a hand with difficulty and his father clutched it.

I felt a hand seize my own arm, nails digging into it, and looked up into Dyrick's furious face. 'God's nails,' he snarled. 'What have you done?'

'Found out the truth,' I answered quietly. 'That Emma Curteys has been impersonating her dead brother. It's all over now, Dyrick.'

'I didn't know!' he blustered. 'All these years, they made a fool of me too. I knew nothing until—'

'Until Lamkin died, and you demanded Hobbey tell you what it was Abigail said I could not see that was in front of me. Then Feaveryear guessed.'

An angry spasm twisted Dyrick's sharp features. 'The stupid lad formed a passion for Hugh, that sent him wailing and praying to God for forgiveness. Then he realized the truth, he said he kept looking at Hugh closely and one day he understood.'

'You should have withdrawn from acting for Hobbey then.' I looked at him with scorn. 'But you couldn't bear to be made to look a fool, could you? Couldn't bear the revelation of how you had been gulled?'

'You sanctimonious bent churl!' Dyrick launched himself at me, pummelling at me with hard bony fists, even as Hobbey wept over his son. Then he was sent sprawling down on the lawn. Barak stood over him.

'You preening shit,' he said. 'You're finished. Now shut your weasel mouth or I'll give you the beating I've dreamed of for weeks!'

Dyrick lay on his back, red and gasping, his robe spread out beneath him. I looked to where Hobbey still knelt over David; he had not even turned round. 'My poor son,' he said gently. 'My poor son.'

✝

THE BARBER-SURGEON arrived shortly after. Helped by Fulstowe he took David inside, Hobbey and the servants following. Dyrick went with them. Barak and I stayed in the great hall. I asked a servant to tell Dyrick I wanted to talk to him as soon as possible. We sat down at the table, silent, shocked, waiting.

'Where do you think Emma will go?' Barak asked.

'My guess is Portsmouth, to try and enlist. I think, God help me, she may seek to end all this in a blaze of glory.'

'Did she kill Abigail?'

I shook my head. 'I think today was the first time she lost control. No, that was someone else.'

He said, 'If I hadn't raised my voice – '

We looked up at the sound of footsteps. Fulstowe approached us, pure hatred in his eyes. 'Master Hobbey would speak with you.'

I nodded assent. 'Come, Barak.' I wanted a witness to this.

We followed the steward to Hobbey's study. Hobbey sat slumped at his desk, his thin face grey, staring unseeingly at the hourglass. Dyrick sat in a chair next to him. Fulstowe stood by the window, watching, as Dyrick said to me, 'Master Hobbey wishes to talk to you. Know it is against my advice—'

'Your advice,' Hobbey said quietly. 'Where has that brought me? Since that first day you told me the children's wardship was worth paying for.' He looked at me; his eyes were sunk deep in his skull. 'David will live. The barber-surgeon has taken the arrow out. But he thinks David's spine is injured. He cannot move his legs properly. We must get a physician.' His voice broke for a moment. 'My poor boy, what a hard path I gave him to tread in this world. Harder than he could bear.' He looked at me. 'You are not my nemesis, Master Shardlake. I have been my own. I caused the destruction of my family.' He closed his eyes. 'Vincent says you know what we did.'

'Yes,' I answered gently. 'I realized only this morning.'

'We have told everyone there was an accident at the butts, that Hugh was frightened by what happened and has run away. I think they believed us.' He paused. 'Unless you tell them something different.'

I said, 'It was David who shot at Barak and me that day, wasn't it? I think he was even following me the night I arrived.'

He answered quietly, 'I think so.'

'And who killed his mother?'

Hobbey bowed his head. Dyrick raised a hand. 'Nicholas – '

Hobbey looked up again. 'I feared so from the start. David – he had come to see everyone as his enemy; except me, and Emma, whom he – whom he loved. He said to me more than once that if anyone tried to expose us he would shoot them dead.' He added sombrely, 'I think perhaps he did mean to shoot you in the woods that day, but missed. He was never as good a shot as Emma.'

'Jesu,' Barak said.

'That was why I let Fulstowe and Vincent persuade me to try and get Ettis convicted. David's mind –' He shook his head. 'But now it is all over.' He looked at the hourglass with a sad, broken smile. 'The sand has run out, as I have feared it would for so long.'

'Did you make Emma assume her brother's identity because the law allows a girl to come into her lands much sooner than a boy?'

'Six years ago, when I bought this house, I was a prosperous merchant, a *risen man*.' He spoke the words bitterly. 'But then the French and Spanish put their embargo on English trade. I invested too much at the wrong time, and faced ruin. When Hugh and Emma's parents died, I saw the opportunity to make profit from Hugh's woods. Eighty pounds a year's profits for eight years, that was what I needed to repay the bond with my creditors. Getting Hugh and Emma's wardship was the only way out I could see. I was advised by friends to see Vincent.'

I turned to Dyrick. 'So you were part of the plan to steal the children's assets from the start.'

'Many people do it,' Dyrick said impatiently. 'And it kept Master Hobbey and his family from penury. And gave the children, who had nobody else, a home.'

'And David a potential wife. Whether Emma wanted him or not.'

Hobbey said, 'We hoped Emma would come to love David in time. Abigail said she would have made a steady, sober wife for him, which he needed. She was right.'

'What of *her* needs?' I asked in sudden anger. 'That orphaned child?'

'Listen,' Dyrick said. 'Never mind the moralizing, much as you love it. The point is, what is going to happen now?'

Hobbey said, 'Yes. To Emma? And David?'

'First I need to know it all,' I answered. 'Everything. What happened, who was involved. So, Dyrick got you the children's wardship and you tried to cajole Emma into marrying David. I imagine Hugh and Michael Calfhill both counselled her to resist.'

'Yes, they did.'

'But then something went badly wrong, didn't it? Hugh died. His lands passed to Emma. Who, unless she married David, would inherit at fourteen, not twenty-one.'

Hobbey said, 'We were in a panic, we thought we would go bankrupt. After Hugh died we begged and pleaded with Emma to marry David, but she refused utterly. She said she would go to the Court of Wards and say David was not a suitable husband because of his falling sickness. Though we knew she could hardly do that alone.' Hobbey bowed his head. 'And then – then my wife had the idea of substituting Emma for Hugh.'

'And Emma agreed?'

'She agreed readily, perhaps too readily. I still do not understand why she disliked my son so much, but – she did. In fact it was David that Abigail and I needed to persuade to accept our plans.'

'And then you got rid of Michael Calfhill and moved down here. Where no one had ever seen the children.'

'Yes. It was only then that we realized that we were all trapped. Me, David, Abigail and Emma. If the truth came out we could have been in deep trouble. The only other who knew was Fulstowe.' Hobbey looked at his steward. 'He was always so good at organizing things, anticipating difficulties. And Emma – she retreated into herself, into books and archery.'

'Which she had already practised with Michael.'

'Yes. And the other tutors. We never let one stay too long. It was easy enough to deceive them at first, but it grew harder as Emma grew older. We – we became frightened of her. She never let us know what was happening in her mind. She impersonated her brother so well – sometimes I found myself thinking of her as Hugh for days at a time, somehow it eased my mind. Abigail never did – if I accidentally referred to Emma as Hugh in her presence she would shout and rail at me. But she was utterly terrified of exposure. And at the time you came there were only three years left till Emma could go to court as Hugh and claim her lands. I do not know what would have happened then.' Nor did I, I thought. Emma had truly made herself unreachable.

Hobbey continued: 'As the years passed the deception was a toll on us all. But especially on Abigail. She was the one who had to counsel Emma how to deal with the monthly woman's curse, cut and sew padding for her breasts. That only seemed to make Emma hate her, and – and somehow we all came to blame Abigail because it had been her idea. Especially David. It was not fair, it had all been done to pay my debts. But even I came to blame her. My poor wife.'

'And then Michael Calfhill returned.'

Hobbey flinched. 'He realized at once that Hugh was really Emma. The moles on her face were enough. He threatened to expose us. But Emma did not want him to.' He looked at Dyrick. 'And you had found out something about Michael, hadn't you, when he was encouraging Emma to refuse to marry David.'

'You suspected it yourself,' Dyrick answered sharply. 'You asked me to see what I could find.'

Hobbey dropped his gaze. He said, 'Someone in London told me Michael was said to have had an – improper – relationship with another student at Cambridge. And Vincent discovered there had been others.'

'So after he came this year you threatened him with exposure?'

'Yes. I got Vincent to visit him. God forgive me.'

'Sodomy is a hanging offence,' Dyrick snapped. 'I told Calfhill I would tell the world what he was if he lodged a complaint at Wards. How was I to know he would kill himself?'

'So it was suicide, after all,' I said.

'What the hell else did you think it was?' Dyrick burst out.

'You went and threatened him.' I looked at Dyrick with disgust. 'You drove that young man, who had only ever sought to help both children, to his grave.'

'I did not know he was that weak,' Dyrick said defiantly.

'You dirty shit,' Barak said.

I stared at Dyrick. 'Someone attacked me in London and warned me off the case. Was that you as well?'

Dyrick and Hobbey stared at each other, then at me. Dyrick said, 'That was nothing to do with us.'

I frowned, thinking. 'So Michael screwed up the courage to make the complaint at the Court of Wards. But then he became terrified of what you would say and killed himself. How he must have struggled with his conscience. Perhaps he hoped his mother would take up the case, maybe bring it to the Queen, who had been kind to him.'

'Conscience,' Hobbey said with infinite sadness. 'I had one once. Ambition killed it. And afterwards – you know in your heart the wrong you have done, but – you stifle it. You have to. You continue to act your part. But Michael's death has haunted me.' Tears began coursing down his thin grey cheeks. 'And poor Abigail. Oh, if only we could have seen where this imposture would lead. And it destroyed my poor son's mind.' He put his head in his hands and began weeping uncontrollably. Dyrick stirred restlessly. Fulstowe gave his employer a look of contempt.

After a minute, Hobbey wiped his face then looked at me wearily. 'What will you do now, sir, about David? Will you reveal he killed his mother?'

'Shouldn't he?' Barak asked brutally.

'My son's mind was disturbed,' Hobbey said desperately. 'It was my fault.' He looked at me, his face suddenly animated. 'If I could, I would sell Hoyland, leave the villagers alone, and go somewhere where I could spend the rest of my life looking after my son, trying – trying to heal him. Though I think he would not be sorry to die now.'

'Nicholas,' Dyrick said, 'Hoyland has been your life—'

'That is over, Vincent.' Hobbey looked at his servant. 'And you, Fulstowe, that we took into our confidence, you used that to build up power over this family. You used us, you felt nothing for any of us. I have known that for a long time. You can go, now. At once.'

Fulstowe looked at him in disbelief. 'You can't dismiss me. Listen, were it not for me—'

'I can,' Hobbey cut in, a touch of the old authority in his voice. 'Get out, now.'

Fulstowe turned to Dyrick. But his confederate in the plan to destroy the village only jerked his head sharply at the door, saying, 'Tell no one about Emma, ever. You are as implicated as your master.'

'After everything I have done for you –' Fulstowe looked at Hobbey and Dyrick again, then walked from the room, slamming the door behind him.

I looked at Dyrick. 'Ettis has to be freed,' I said. 'You and Fulstowe would have let him die to further your schemes.'

'Don't be stupid,' Dyrick snapped back. 'He would never have been found guilty. But with him in prison the villagers would have been more reasonable.'

'Master Shardlake,' Hobbey said, 'I want no charges brought against Emma. If only she could be brought back –'

'I fear she may have gone to Portsmouth to enlist. She may look for my friend George Leacon's company. They saw what a good archer she is.'

'Could you – might you find her?'

I sat back, considering. David and Emma. Both their fates were in my hands now.

Barak said, 'She nearly killed us. Let them both be exposed for what they did.'

I looked at Hobbey. 'I have two more questions. First, am I right that Sir Quintin Priddis knew Hugh was really Emma?'

'Nicholas,' Dyrick expostulated, 'don't answer. We may need Priddis –'

Hobbey ignored him. 'Yes. He knew.'

'From the beginning?'

'No, but he visited this house once, to bargain for his share when I began cutting Emma's woodlands. Sir Quintin is very observant, looking at her he realized the deception. The only one that ever has, save you and Feaveryear. He agreed to keep quiet in return for a larger cut.'

'And his son?'

'I think not. Sir Quintin is a man who even now likes his power, and secrets are power. Other people's, that is; your own are a curse.'

I took a deep breath, then asked, 'And Sir Richard Rich? What is his involvement in all this?'

A look of genuine puzzlement crossed Hobbey's face. 'Rich? The royal counsellor? I have never met him. I saw him for the first time when he came up to you at the Guildhall.'

'Are you sure, Master Hobbey?'

He spread his hands. 'Why would I keep anything back now?'

Dyrick too was staring at me in surprise. I realized neither of them had any idea what I was talking about. But then why had Rich been so agitated in Portsmouth? Why had he, as I increasingly believed, set those corner boys on me in London and killed the clerk Mylling? I thought hard, and then I understood. Again I had jumped to a wrong conclusion.

✝

AND NOW I had to decide what to do. I looked at Hobbey's desperate face, Barak's angry one, then at Dyrick, who had begun to look uneasy and frightened. If it became known he had helped to conceal Emma's true identity there would be serious professional consequences for him. I could never trust Dyrick, but for now he was in my power. I said, 'This is what I am prepared to do. If Ettis is freed I will say nothing about David killing his mother.'

Barak sat up. 'You can't! He murdered her! What else might he do? And you can believe they're not involved with Rich—'

'They're not. They never were. I think I see what happened now. But tell me, Jack, do you think David was of sound mind when he killed Abigail? Do you think his being put on trial and either certified as mad or hanged will do anyone any good? Who will it benefit?'

'He may shoot someone else.'

'That he never will,' Hobbey said. 'He may never even walk properly again. And I told you, from now on I will watch after him day and night – '

I raised a hand. 'I have three conditions, Master Hobbey.'

'Anything – '

'First, you will ensure – I care not how – that Ettis is released. If he has to stand trial for murder in due course, very well, so long as I am there to ensure that justice takes its course and he is found innocent. And I want to let him know now, in confidence, that that will be the outcome.'

Hobbey looked at Dyrick. 'We can arrange that, Vincent, I am sure. Sir Luke—'

Dyrick said, 'What are your other conditions?'

'The second, Master Hobbey, is that you do as you said, sell Hoyland – having confirmed the villagers' title to the woodland – and take David to a place where you can keep him safe and watched.'

'Yes,' he answered at once. 'Yes.'

Barak looked at me and shook his head. And though I doubted David would be a danger to anyone again, I knew I was taking a risk. But I believed Hobbey would do as he promised.

'My last condition concerns Emma. I will ride back to Portsmouth, and if I find her there and trying to join the army I will get her out.'

'No—' Barak started.

'He'd need to expose her as a girl,' Dyrick said. 'Nicholas, if he does that we could be done for after all. If she gets a lift on a supply cart she could be there already.'

'If she has joined my friend's company, or another, I do not need to tell them the whole story. Merely that a patriotic girl is impersonating a boy.'

'I agree,' Hobbey said. 'I agree to everything.'

'But I will not bring Emma back here. I will take her to London. And you, Master Hobbey, will sell Hugh's wardship to me, as wardships are constantly bought and sold. Though, of course, the transaction will only be a paper one, I will give you no money. Master Dyrick here will organize it.'

Even now, after all the death and ruin, Dyrick took the chance to score a point. 'You will make a profit for yourself – '

'I will see the Curteys lands sold for a fair price, and the money kept safe till Emma, as Hugh, comes of age. That will mean continuing the deception, so far as the Court of Wards at least is concerned. But there are a hundred deceptions there, though maybe none so dramatic as this. Again you will have to cooperate, Dyrick.'

'But Emma just tried to kill David, and nearly killed us!' Barak was proving hard to persuade.

'She didn't kill us, though she easily could have. And I don't think she meant to kill David. She could have shot him through the heart as easily as she could us, but she didn't. My guess is she will be desperately regretting what she did. I learned enough of his – her – nature when we were here before to understand that.'

'Him – her – God's nails!' Barak shouted. 'Are you going to take her home? Will you dress her in tunics or frocks?'

'I will help her to find somewhere to live in London. What she makes of her future then will be up to her. This is the one chance I have of fulfilling my promise to the Queen and Mistress Calfhill, whose son died because he felt he had to help her. We owe something to Michael, too.'

Dyrick looked at Hobbey. 'I can negotiate a better deal than that for you.'

'Don't be a fool, Vincent,' Hobbey said dismissively. He reached out a hand to me. 'Again, I agree to it all. Everything. Thank you, Master Shardlake, thank you.'

I could not take his hand. I looked him in the eye. 'I am not doing this for you, Master Hobbey. It is for Emma, and David, to try and bring some future for them out of all this ruination.'

✝

BARAK AND I left the house an hour later. It was early afternoon now, the sun high and hot. We pulled the horses to a halt outside the priory gate.

'You're stark mad,' Barak told me.

'Perhaps I am. But mad or no, it is time for you to go home. No more words now. With hard riding you might make Petersfield tonight. I will try to find Emma, then follow you. If I do not catch up with you tonight, ride on tomorrow and I will meet you on the road.'

'How can you trust Hobbey and Dyrick?'

'Hobbey is a broken man now, you saw that. All he has left is David. And Dyrick knows what is good for him.'

'So much for Dyrick believing his clients were always in the right. He was as corrupt as Hobbey.'

'I still think he believed Hobbey was in the right, at least until he discovered Emma's identity. Some lawyers need to believe that. But yes, after the discovery his only concern was to save his own position. And as for what he would have done to the villagers –'

Barak looked back through the gates at the untended flower beds. 'Poor old Abigail. She'll get no justice out of this, you realize that.'

'I think in her heart she would have wanted to see David and Emma safe. I think she too was haunted by guilt.'

'What about Rich? Mylling? The corner boys? Did you believe what they said?'

'I think I know what happened there, and it did not involve Hobbey or Dyrick. I will pick up that matter in London. I will say no more now – if I am right it could be dangerous to know. But I will tell the Queen. This time Richard Rich may find he has gone too far.'

'Sure you won't tell me?'

'Quite sure. Tamasin would not want me to.'

'If Emma has chosen to go for a soldier, it is what she always wanted. Why not leave her to follow her choice?'

I answered firmly, 'She has been so hemmed all these years she is in no right mind to make a decision like that.'

He shook his head. 'You are determined to rescue her whether she wants it or no. Whatever the consequences. As with Ellen.'

'Yes.'

'What if she's not in Portsmouth?'

'Then there will be nothing else I can do, and I will return alone. Now, goodbye, Jack.' I put out my hand. 'Until tonight or tomorrow.'

'Mad,' he said. 'Completely mad. Try to stay safe, for God's sake.'

He turned his horse, spurred it, and rode fast up towards the London road. He disappeared round a bend. I patted Oddleg. 'Come, back to Portsmouth.' I said.

☩

THE ROAD SOUTH was strangely quiet. I thought, it is Sunday. No, that was tomorrow. From the deep-set lanes I smelt smoke several times and thought, are the charcoal-burners working as far south as this? I heard shouts, too.

I began the slow climb up Portsdown Hill. And then, near the top, the air became thick with smoke and I saw a burning beacon, men milling round it. My heart thumping, I crested the escarpment. Smoke from beacon after beacon was visible, in a line all along the hills. I looked down, across Portsea Island to the sea. Then my jaw dropped and I gripped Oddleg's reins, hard.

Most of the warships were still at anchor in the Solent, though some of the smaller ships were in the harbour, small dots from here. In front of the warships half a dozen larger dots were manoeuvring rapidly to and fro. I heard a sound like the rumble of thunder that could only be cannon firing. I thought, those ships are moving and turning so fast they must be galleys, as big as the *Galley Subtle*. Then I saw, at the eastern end of the Isle of Wight in the distance, an enormous dark smudge. The French fleet had arrived. The invasion had begun.

Part Six

THE BATTLE

PORTSEA ISLAND AREA · 1545

0 Mile 1

Hoyland

PORTSDOWN HILLS

Cosham

Portchester Castle

Port Creek

PORTSMOUTH HAVEN

PORTSEA ISLAND

LANGSTONE HARBOUR

Dock

Mill Pond

Gosport

PORTSMOUTH

Royal Tents

Little Morass

Great Morass

English Fleet

South Sea Castle

The SOLENT

Chapter Forty-three

I SAT FOR several minutes watching the extraordinary scene in the distance. The English ships, at anchor and with sails reefed, looked terrifyingly vulnerable. I wondered why the huge French fleet did not advance and assumed the wind was against them. A little way along from me, near the burning beacon, a group of country women stood watching the fighting. They were silent, anxious-looking, and I wondered if they had menfolk down there.

My instinct was that I was too late, I should turn and ride back. But Emma had been only three hours ahead of me at most; if she had come to Portsmouth she could surely not have found her way into battle yet. I thought of her watchfulness, her carefully considered speech. With the companies short of men it was perfectly possible she could get herself taken on, all the more now the French were here. I remembered Hobbey saying how Abigail had helped her bind up her breasts as they grew, and Hugh rubbing uncomfortably at 'his' chest. How much discomfort must she have undergone these last six years?

At the bridge linking the mainland to Portsea Island everything had changed since the morning. Now people were trying to get off the island, not on to it. A stream of people was crossing from the seaward side; women with babies, children, old people hobbling on sticks, all fleeing a possible siege. Most were poor; they carried bundles or hauled their possessions stacked on rickety carts. I remembered Leacon talking of the populace of the French countryside, begging and starving beside the road. I thought, is this about to happen here?

I waited till the refugees had passed. They began wearily climbing Portsdown Hill. An old couple started to argue about whether to abandon their cart, which contained a dismantled truckle bed, some poor clothes, pewter plates and a couple of stools. People trying to get past shouted at them to get out of the way. Then I heard drums, and a company of militia with an assortment of weapons marched rapidly down the hill. The refugees jumped quickly aside. The soldiers marched rapidly past me, the half-armour some wore clinking and rattling. The guards at the bridge saluted as they tramped across in a cloud of yellow dust.

When they had gone, I rode up to the nearest guard and asked what the latest news was. He looked at me with irritation. 'The Frenchies have come, that's what.' He was an enlisted man, who normally would not have dared talk to someone of my class like that; but as I had seen many times now, the war was dissolving social boundaries.

'Can I get into the city?'

'Everyone's trying to leave.'

'There is someone I need to try and get out. A friend.'

'Well, master lawyer, if you can persuade them to let you in, I wish you the best of luck.' He gave me a glance of grudging respect, and waved me on.

✝

ON PORTSEA ISLAND the soldiers' tents still stood, but they were all empty now, the flaps open, only a handful of men on guard. Small objects were scattered here and there on the grass – a bowl, a spoon, a cap – the soldiers had been called away in a hurry.

As I approached the town walls, where men still laboured hard to strengthen the fortifications, I passed another group of refugees trudging towards the bridge, among them a group of prostitutes, their painted faces streaked and dusty. Then I had to pull into the side again to allow another company of soldiers to march past; foreign mercenaries this time in bright slashed doublets, talking in German. I had a view of the fleet: the ships still rode at anchor, among them the *Great Harry* and the *Mary Rose*; I saw the *Galley Subtle* with the galleasses, between the warships and the huge French galleys half a mile off. I wondered if Leacon and his company were already aboard the *Great Harry*. A cloud of dark smoke came from the front of a French galley, followed by a distant boom; an English galleass had fired back.

I reached the tents outside the city. As I feared, they, too, were empty. Looking up at the walls, I saw the soldiers lining the top had their backs to me, watching what was happening out at sea; the city wall now blocked my view. I turned Oddleg towards the tents, hoping someone had been left on guard who could give me information, but could see nobody. It was strange riding among the tents and hearing no noise, no shouting or clattering. The tents of Leacon's company, like the others, were empty. I was about to turn back when I heard a voice calling weakly.

'Lawyer Shardlake! Over here!'

I followed the voice to a tent from which a cesspit smell emanated. Hesitantly, I looked through the open flap. In the half-light within I saw bowls and clothing scattered about. In a corner a man lay, half-covered by a blanket. It was Sulyard, the bully who had been so full of bravado the night before. His ugly bony face was white as a sheet. 'It is you,' he said. 'I thought I was having bad visions.'

'Sulyard? What ails you?'

'There was a barrel of bad beer last night. When we went into Portsmouth this morning four of us were sent back with the flux.' He gave a little smile, and I saw that he was glad.

'Where is the rest of the company?'

'On the *Great Harry*. Listen, can you get me something to drink? There's beer in the tent with the green flag.'

I went and found the tent he described. There were some barrels of beer and drinking vessels stored there and I filled a tankard. I took it back to him. He drank greedily, then he gave me an amused, calculating look. 'Have you come for the boy?'

'What boy?' I asked eagerly. 'Do you mean Hugh Curteys?'

'The one that was with you the first time you came here, the good archer.'

'Have you seen him? Please, tell me.'

'We were supposed to go on the ships this morning, but the King was on the *Great Harry* and they weren't going to put us on till he'd gone across to the *Mary Rose*. We were waiting on the wharf, when your lad ran up. Hot and dusty, carrying a bow. He recognized Captain Leacon and asked to join the company. By then four of us were crouched against a wall shitting like dogs, and the company's already short. So the captain took him on, and sent us sick ones back.'

'I need to find that boy.'

'You'll have a job. Just after, there was a great commotion and the King's barge came speeding back to shore. Then the French fleet comes into view round the Isle of Wight.' With difficulty, Sulyard leaned up on his elbows. 'Do you know what's happened since? Have the French landed?' I understood the reason for his unaccustomed civility; it was not just drink he wanted; he was afraid the French would come and butcher him in his tent.

'No. They're skirmishing out at sea. Listen, did they take the boy on board the *Great Harry*?'

'They must have done.'

'I must try and find him. I must go into town.'

'They won't let you in, they've been clearing civilians out all morning. You'd need to go to the army quartermaster's office at the royal tents.'

'Is the King there?'

'I heard he went to South Sea Castle to watch the battle. I saw him when he landed – Christ, it took eight men to get him up the steps. Listen, can you get me out of here? Off the island?'

'No, Sulyard, I can't. I told you, I am going into Portsmouth.'

He scowled, then gave me a leering wink. 'You like the boy, eh?'

I sighed. 'Is there anything else I can do for you?'
'No. You've brought us enough bad luck.'

✝

MY ONLY CHANCE now was to try and find the quartermaster. As I had told Hobbey, I planned to say Emma was a young woman driven by patriotism to impersonate a man and join up – I had heard tavern tales of such things. But I feared she could already have been rushed on board the *Great Harry*.

I rode past the town walls where the royal tents stood behind the long shallow pond, the Great Morass. There were over thirty of them, each as large as a small house, the heavy fabric woven in the vibrant colours I remembered from York. The largest and most spectacular, heavily guarded, with elaborate designs and threaded with cloth of gold and silver, would be the King's tent. Soldiers and officials bustled to and fro. From all the tents the flags of England and the Tudor dynasty hung listlessly. I thought, it will be starting to get dark soon, ships do not fight in the dark. That will be the time to get Emma off the *Great Harry*.

On the seaward side of the pond the sandy, scrubby ground was alive with hundreds of soldiers. Companies had been joined together to form groups of several hundred, the captains patrolling in front on horseback. Nearby a troop of perhaps three hundred pikemen stood at attention, their weapons rising fifteen feet into the air; if the French attempted a coastal landing they would charge them on the beach. Somewhere a drum beat softly, regularly. All along the coastline more groups of pikemen and halberdiers stood ready. There were only a few archers at the front of each group, most would be out on the ships.

At the shore the ground shelved upwards to a little bank, blocking my view of the sea. Cannon were being set up along the top, and men were digging holes and fixing in pointed wooden stakes, angled to point seaward. I saw yet more cannon being dragged across. Ahead of me was the bulk of the new South Sea Castle, a solid, heavy square with wide-angled bastions. It bristled with cannon, as did a smaller fort a little way along the coast. On the tower at the top I saw a group of brightly coloured figures, the one at the centre far larger than the others. The King, watching what was happening out at sea.

There was a tremendous crashing roar, and smoke rose from South Sea Castle as a battery of cannon fired, presumably at the French galleys. Cheers sounded from the soldiers standing on top of the bank, so perhaps one was hit. I remembered Leacon saying the biggest cannon could hit a target over a mile away.

I turned aside, realizing my legs were shaking. Again I fought an overwhelming urge to turn back. I thought of Barak, no doubt still riding northward, and thanked God I had insisted he go. Then I set my jaw and rode on slowly towards the royal encampment. The sun was beginning to sink towards the horizon.

I was a hundred yards from the nearest tent when a soldier stepped in front of me, halberd raised. I halted. 'What do you want, sir?' the man asked roughly.

'I need to speak to someone in the army quartermaster's office. The matter is urgent. My name is Serjeant Matthew Shardlake, of Lincoln's Inn.'

'Wait here.' As at Portchester – had my meeting with the Queen really been only a few hours ago? – I was left waiting as the soldier disappeared among the tents. I looked over at South Sea Castle; the cluster of bright figures still stood looking out to sea. I heard distant cannonfire from out on the water; no doubt the French galleys firing on our ships; I shuddered at the thought of the huge target the *Great Harry* would make. The *Mary Rose*, too, where Philip West would be.

Two captains in half-armour emerged from the nearest tents. They passed me, talking fast and excitedly. 'Why has d'Annebault brought so few galleys forward? Most are still by the Wight shore – '

The soldier reappeared, a second beside him, walking fast towards me. He came up to me and spoke, this time in a respectful tone.

'You're to come with me, sir. This fellow will take care of your horse.' The second soldier placed a mounting block beside Oddleg for me to descend. I felt a wave of relief; I had doubted a busy official would find the time to see me.

I dismounted. 'Thank you,' I said. 'I will take but a little of his time.'

The soldier nodded and led me away to the tents. Some tent flaps were closed, but where they were open I saw soldiers and officials sitting at trestle tables, talking animatedly. I was led to a large conical tent in the centre of the encampment, cream-coloured with blue patterning at the top, the flap half-closed. The soldier ushered me in with a wave of his arm.

In the dimness inside a man sat at a trestle table, his head bent over papers. A bell and a sconce of candles stood on the table. The man was well dressed, his doublet green silk.

I took off my cap. 'Thank you for seeing me, Master Quarter-master,' I said. 'I crave—' Then, as the man raised his head, I broke off abruptly.

Richard Rich smiled. 'Good,' he said quietly, satisfaction in his voice. 'Welcome to my working quarters. So you came for the boy. Or, I should say, the girl. I thought you might.'

I stared at him. 'Where is Emma?'

He smiled, again showing his sharp little teeth. 'Quite safe, for now. She is with Captain Leacon's company, who are now under the trusted care of Master Philip West. On the *Mary Rose*. And now, Master Shardlake, I think we must have a proper talk.'

Chapter Forty-four

S TOOLS WERE SET in front of the trestle table; Rich motioned me to sit. Then he leaned forward, linked his small, manicured hands together, and rested his chin on them. His sleeves rustled. His expression was childishly mocking, though his grey eyes were cold and hard.

'I hear the French galleys have retreated,' he said conversationally. 'My servant just brought me word. I think today has just been a skirmish before the main battle.' His tone was still smoothly pleasant. 'Though tomorrow it may be a different matter.'

'I hear our guns can keep them out of Portsmouth Haven.'

'Yes. But if they were to bottle our fleet up there – which perhaps is what they sought to do today – or sink it, they could use their galleys to make a landing on Portsea Island. You will have seen the cannon being dragged up, and the stakes set in the ground to protect the archers.' He paused and held my gaze a moment. 'Well, then there may be a great fight. Perhaps right out there on the seafront.' He nodded towards the tent flap. I did not reply. I thought, let him talk, see what he reveals. Does he know how much I have guessed? He must do, or he would not have had me brought here. The skin under Rich's eye twitched and I realized just how much he was on edge.

'To business,' he said abruptly. 'That girl, eh? Coming here and enlisting as a boy. What a strange thing to do.'

'You know Hugh Curteys is really Emma?'

'Yes. Though only since yesterday, when my old associate Sir Quintin Priddis told me, just before I came out to you at the

536

Guildhall. He told me because he was afraid you had discovered it. He is implicated in the fraud.'

'I know.'

'When did you find out?'

'Today. It was my unmasking her that sent Emma Curteys fleeing to Portsmouth. She had always wanted to enlist. Now she has nothing to lose.'

Rich inclined his head, like a predatory bird. 'Only today, Master Shardlake? I would have thought you would have ferreted that amusing fact out before. I have overestimated you.' He thought a few seconds. 'I imagine young Curteys is another of those people you try to do good works for, hey? Like Elizabeth Wentworth when we first met, or old Master Wrenne in York?'

'If you know Hugh Curteys is really Emma, why have you let her on board the *Mary Rose*?'

He smiled. 'It was an opportunity, Brother Shardlake. I spend my life watching for opportunities. That is why I am a privy councillor. With my responsibilities for supply I see the daily reports on manpower; how many men have deserted, or fallen ill, how many new ones have come forward. Two hours ago I was brought this.' He flicked a finger through the documents on his desk, then pulled out a list and passed it to me. A name leaped out at me. *Hugh Curteys, 18 yrs, Hoyland. Company of Sir Franklin Giffard.*

'You may imagine,' Rich said, 'how my eyes widened too at that name. And knowing from Priddis that he – or rather she – was one of your protégées, I wondered whether you might follow her. Had you not, I was not sure what to do with you. Since you ignored my first warning from the apprentices.' His tone had turned vicious. 'If you had some fatal accident your friend Barak would be on the case, and no doubt involve your patron the Queen. You have to watch Catherine Parr, she is no fool.' His eye twitched again. 'But now, I think, we may come to an agreement. That is why, though I knew Emma Curteys' true identity, I allowed her to enlist.'

'You will use her to make a bargain with me.'

Rich leaned forward. 'After seeing the list I rode straight into Portsmouth. The French fleet had appeared, the King had left the *Great Harry*, soldiers were milling around, waiting to go on the ships. Some of the senior officers had come ashore to ensure every ship got its correct complement, including Philip West.' He looked at me.

'Yes,' I said quietly. 'West.'

'Your friend Captain Leacon's archers were due to go on the *Great Harry*, but I spoke to West and arranged for them to go with him on the *Mary Rose* instead. So he can keep an eye on Emma Curteys for me. Then I came back here to see if you would follow her. She matters nothing to me, of course, she never did. Those corner boys I set to attack you failed to make themselves clear. For which they were punished.' His icy eyes stared into mine. 'The case you were meant to drop was not Hugh Curteys'. It was the other one my agent, Master Mylling of the Court of Wards, told me you had been enquiring about.'

'Ellen Fettiplace,' I said heavily. 'That is your connection to West. It was you with him at Rolfswood nineteen years ago.'

Rich leaned back in his chair again. His face was impassive now. 'So you know.'

'When I realized you had no connection to the Curteys case, I knew it had to be that.'

'Who else knows?' he asked abruptly.

'Barak,' I lied. 'And I have sent him back to London.'

Rich sat, considering. Then a voice called from outside, 'Sir?'

A spasm of annoyance crossed Rich's face. 'Come in, Colin,' he said heavily.

The door opened and a large, heavy-faced young man, the letters RR emblazoned on his tunic, entered with a taper. Rich gestured to the sconce, and the servant lit the candles, illuminating the tent with yellow light. 'What news?' Rich asked.

'The French have gone.'

'The soldiers will stay on board tonight?'

'Yes, sir. They must be ready to engage the French at first light if need be. Sir, a messenger came. The Privy Council is meeting in the King's tent in an hour.'

'God's death,' Rich snapped, 'why didn't you tell me immediately you came in?'

The man reddened. 'I—'

'Messages from the Privy Council must be conveyed at once – how many times have I told you? Get out,' Rich snapped. 'But stay near enough to hear if I ring my bell for you.'

'Yes sir.' He bowed and left. Rich shook his head. 'Peel is a dolt,' he said, 'but it can be useful sometimes to have people around who understand little, and who fear you.' He composed his features into that superior, contemptuous smile again. I saw it cost him an effort.

'Now, Brother Shardlake, let me tell you what I propose. A letter from me to Philip West will get you on the *Mary Rose*. Then you can tell your friend Leacon that the boy he recruited today is a girl, and bring her back. My servant will get a boat to row you there and back. In return, you will say nothing to anybody about what happened at Rolfswood nineteen years ago. It is Philip West, by the way, who has been paying Ellen Fettiplace's fees at the Bedlam all these years.'

'I guessed that.'

'You can take over responsibility for payment yourself if you like, I don't care.'

'You have left her safe all this time? If she had ever talked about the rape—'

'She never knew my name. And West has always threatened to tell the whole story if anything happened to her.' Rich's eye twitched again and he blinked angrily. 'Well, Brother Shardlake, what do you say? There will likely be a battle tomorrow, next day at the latest.'

'I need to know the whole story,' I answered steadily. I needed time to think, too.

'Do we really have to go into that?' he snapped impatiently.

'I do,' I answered. 'West's mother told me of the letter he carried from the King to Anne Boleyn that day.'

'He told me she had. Stupid old mare.'

'And I want to know what happened at that foundry.' I needed to know if Ellen had played any part in the deaths of her father and Gratwyck.

Rich's eyes narrowed.

'You must have been near thirty then,' I said. 'Much older than West. From what he said it was only a junior official that accompanied him.'

'I *was* junior then. Despite my striving, despite my attempts to get the patronage of Thomas More, I had advanced only to a lowly position working for the King's chamberlain.' He smiled, an odd smile. 'Do you believe in fortune, Master Shardlake? Fate?'

'No.'

'I like to gamble. The world is like the cards. You wait for a run of luck, then when you have it you use your skill to increase it. What happened with that letter began the run of luck that has led me on to the Privy Council.'

'How did you know what it contained?'

'I didn't.' He laughed. 'I wouldn't have dared touch it if I had. I thought it was just a matter of old Queen Catherine nosing out how long the King's affair with Anne Boleyn might last. Ridiculous old creature, you should have seen her then. Waddling around with her rosary, fat and shapeless from carrying all those children that died. I had put much effort into getting to know anyone I could at court, and had made friends with an elderly maid-in-waiting in the Queen's household, one of those wonderful old gossips who knows what everyone is doing. I told her I was a loyal servant of the Queen, someone who did not like to see her disgraced by the Boleyn, and so on.' He smiled at his cleverness. 'She told Queen Catherine, and through her it was suggested that I cultivate West; the Queen knew he sometimes carried letters to Anne Boleyn. Then she suggested that I intercept this one. Queen Catherine's spies in the King's household must have told her it contained something important. So I arranged to accompany Philip West to Rolfswood.'

'How did you get hold of the letter?'

'It is enough for you to know that I did.'

'No, Sir Richard, if we are to make a bargain I must know everything. Remember, Barak is on the road to London even now.'

Rich set his narrow lips. 'You have met Philip West. He is a man dominated by his passions, even more when he was younger. And like many who think themselves honourable fellows, what really matters to him is his dignity. His reputation, his vanity. What his mother thinks of him.' He wrinkled his sharp nose in contempt. 'I rode to Rolfswood with him that day, and waited at an inn nearby while he went to propose marriage to Ellen Fettiplace.'

'I thought there was a fight, and that he had not intended to propose to her that day, just talk to her father.'

'No, no. That was a lie he made up for his parents.' He raised his eyebrows. 'He had quite a passion for the woman. She was no great beauty but there it is.' He paused. 'Ah, you mind my saying that. Perhaps you have a liking for this Ellen, too.'

'No. I do not.'

Rich shrugged. 'Well, Philip West was convinced she would accept him, he thought someone of his station would be a good catch for her. But when he returned he told me that she had said no; she did not love him. He was furious, outraged, humiliated. Ranting like a demon in a play. I listened to him maundering on, encouraged him to get more and more drunk in case it gave me a chance to take the letter, but his hand kept going to his shirt where he kept it. He was not going to forget it. Not unless something dramatic happened to distract him. In the end he decided to ride back to Petworth. We had just started out on the road when my second good card turned up. Ellen Fettiplace herself.'

It was warm in the tent, but I felt cold. A moth flew in from a gap somewhere and began fluttering round the candles. I remembered Dyrick slamming his arm down on the moth at Hoyland. Rich ignored it. 'What does Ellen Fettiplace mean to you?' he asked. 'Are you sure she is just another of your waifs and strays, not something more?'

'No,' I answered sadly. 'Nothing more.'

He looked at me hard. 'She has been a worry to me for years.' His eye gave a little twitch again. 'Do you really need me to go on?'

'Yes, Sir Richard. If we are to bargain, I must know everything that happened to Ellen. And to her father, and his worker.'

'I can deny this conversation ever happened, you realize that. There are no witnesses.'

'Of course.'

He frowned, then continued in clipped tones. 'The girl saw us riding towards her and stopped. West's face frightened her, I think. Then I said to him, have her anyway, there's no one else around. He said that by damnation he would. He was too drunk to think of consequences. I had to help him unbuckle his sword – as gentlemen, we both wore swords – then help him off his horse. I thought the girl would run but she stood there with her mouth open as we ran over and seized her. West had his way. I helped hold her down, and while he was on her I took the letter. He did not notice, he was inside her by then, and the girl was beating and clawing at him. I'm surprised he was able to do it, he was very drunk. I took the letter and ran. Unfortunately I had to leave my horse.'

'What if the girl talked?'

'I planned to say she was confused, that I had tried to stop West and fled for help when I realized I couldn't.' He considered. 'And I was willing to take the risk, to gain the Queen as a patron.'

I frowned. 'But your promotion came through Thomas Cromwell, Catherine of Aragon's enemy.'

'Oh, Cromwell saw I could be a useful man.'

'Please continue, Sir Richard.' He gave me a long cold stare, and I suppressed a shudder at the thought of what he would have liked to do to me had I not had the Queen's protection.

'After I left West I planned to go to the nearest town and hire a horse. But I got lost in those woods and it soon became too dark even to see my way. Then I heard West blundering about in the trees, cursing and shouting my name. He had missed the letter. And he knew those woods, he had been brought up there. I managed to lose him, then I saw a light ahead, and made for it. I thought it was some house or inn where I could seek shelter.' A cloud crossed Rich's face, and I realized he had been afraid that night, alone in the woods.

'The foundry,' I said.

'Yes, it was the Fettiplace foundry. There was some old man sitting on a straw bed there, drinking. I said I was lost and he told me the way to Rolfswood. He invited me to stay, I think he was awe-struck having a gentleman appear out of the blue. I decided to wait, hoping West would give up or fall down drunk, which I learned later is what he did. While I sat I read the letter. The damned seal had broken when I took it off West. I was astounded, for in it the King said he intended to marry Anne; he thought he could get the Pope on his side if Catherine refused. I hadn't realized that, I thought it was just some silly endearments to his mistress.'

'So you took the letter to Catherine of Aragon and gave her warning of the King's intentions.'

'Yes. God's death, the King must have been angry when West said he had lost it. I wonder West kept his head. Next year when the King went to Catherine saying he believed their marriage contravened biblical law and that was why they had had no sons, she already knew what his plans were. She'd had months to stew in her anger.'

'If the King found out what you had done —'

'Catherine of Aragon never told him she had intercepted that letter. She always protected her servants, that was her strategy to keep people loyal. I began my way up the ladder that night — and changed my loyalties when in the struggle that followed I saw Anne Boleyn would be the victor.'

'So what you helped West to do to Ellen, that set you on your upward path.'

'If you like. But it wasn't quite as simple as that. That night, as I was sitting in that old foundry, the door banged open. I feared West had found me but it was the girl who appeared, dishevelled and wild-looking. When she saw me she screamed and pointed and shouted,

"Rape!" That man Gratwyck forgot his drink, got up and came towards me with a stick in his hand. Fortunately I had kept my sword. I slashed at him with it. I didn't kill him, but he fell into the fire he had lit and a moment later he was on fire himself, stumbling and shrieking around the place.' Rich paused and looked at me. 'It was self-defence, you see, not murder. I confess it shocked me, and when I turned back to the girl she was gone.

'I ran out into the night after her, but she had disappeared. I had to think what to do. I went back to the foundry, but it was already well on fire, Gratwyck still shrieking somewhere inside. So I walked up the path by that pond, looking for the girl.'

'What would you have done, had you found her?'

He shrugged. 'I did not find her. Instead I stepped straight into an older man in a robe.'

'Master Fettiplace.'

'He yelled, "Who are you?" I think he had been out looking for his daughter and come to the foundry to see whether she might be there, though I do not know. He grabbed at me, so I put my sword through him.' Rich spoke quite unemotionally, as though reading a document in court. 'I knew I had to get rid of him before people were attracted by the fire. I couldn't put him in the building, it was ablaze from end to end by now. But it was a moonlit night, I saw a boat by the pond, I rowed him out and sunk him with a discarded lump of iron I found nearby. I walked until dawn broke, then I hired a horse from an inn and rode back to Petworth.'

You were afraid, I thought: walking through the night in a terrified panic after what you'd done.

Rich said, 'Next day West sought me out. I denied I had anything to do with the fire, I said I rode straight back to Petworth, and though he suspected me there was no proof. As for the letter and the rape, I told him we must both keep quiet. But the fool rode back to Rolfswood again, to try and speak to Ellen. That was dangerous, it gave me some sleepless nights. But fortunately the girl had lost her wits, and after a while West and his family arranged with Priddis for her to be taken to the Bedlam. Priddis, as you can imagine, was well paid to ask no questions.'

'So now you have made a new bargain with Philip West.'

'Yes. I am good at bargains.'

'He had insisted Ellen be left alive.'

Rich frowned. 'He said if she ever came to harm he would tell the whole story. He was full of remorse then, he had decided to go to the King's ships. He is half mad — I think part of him wants to die. Though with his honour preserved.' Rich sneered. 'That is why, when I met him today, he agreed to take the Curteys girl on board his ship, so I could bargain for your silence.'

'My silence over what happened at Rolfswood, in return for getting Emma Curteys off that ship. I see. And what of Ellen?'

He spread his little hands. 'I will leave her safe in the Bedlam, under your eye. I understand she would never leave, even if she could.'

I thought hard. But Rich was right. I could perhaps destroy him, but then I would never get Emma Curteys off the *Mary Rose*. I thought, you will get away with murder. But he had already; I remembered his betrayal of Thomas More, his persecution of heretics in Essex. I asked, 'How can you be sure I will not take Emma off the ship, see her safe, and expose you anyway?'

'Oh, I have thought of that.'

'I guessed you would.' I added, 'You killed Mylling, too, didn't you?'

'He was in my pay, with standing instructions to inform me if anyone asked after Ellen Fettiplace. He told me you had been nosing around. And then, do you know, he tried to blackmail me, asked for more money. He did not know his young clerk was in my pay too. I could not afford any risks, so I arranged for the clerk to deal with him. Shutting him up in that Stinkroom place was a good idea; if he had survived it could be said the door shutting on him was an accident. Young Master Alabaster has his job now.' He bent his head to search among his papers. 'And now,' he concluded briskly, 'here it is.' He pulled out a paper and passed it across to me. 'Your will.'

I jerked backwards, nearly falling off my stool, for wills are made in contemplation of death. Rich gave a mocking laugh. 'Do not worry. Everyone is making wills in this camp with the battle coming. Look through it, there are spaces for your legacies.'

I looked down. *I make this will at Portsmouth, the French fleet before me, in contemplation of death.* Then the executor's clause: *I appoint Sir Richard Rich, of Essex, Privy Councillor to his majesty the King, as my sole executor.* Afterwards, the first legacy was already inserted: *To the aforesaid Sir Richard Rich, with a request for forgiveness for dishonourable accusations I have laid against him over many years, but who has now shown me his true friendship, 50 marks.* There was space for more gifts, then the date, *18th of July 1545,* and space for me and two witnesses to sign.

Rich passed over two blank sheets of paper. 'Copy it out twice,' he instructed briskly, in charge again. 'One copy for me to keep, for I have little doubt you will make a new will when you return to London. That matters not, the fifty marks is a nominal amount, as anyone can see. I want this will, which will be witnessed by a couple of reputable men from this camp who do not know me or you, and who can testify later that your will was made quite freely, for I shall show it in court should you ever make accusations against me.' He tilted his neat little head. 'No legacies to Ellen Fettiplace, by the way.'

I read the draft will again. Neat, tidy, like everything Rich did, except for that first venture at Rolfswood when he had taken huge risks and murdered a man in a panic. He held out a quill and spoke quietly. 'If you betray me, if you leave me with nothing to lose, then believe me something will happen to Ellen Fettiplace. So there you are, we have each other tied up neatly.'

I took the quill and began to write. As I did so I heard voices outside, clatter, noise: the King's party, returning from South Sea Castle. I heard people talking in low, serious tones as they passed Rich's tent.

When I had finished, Rich took the will and read both copies carefully. He nodded. 'Yes, large gifts to Jack and Tamasin Barak and to Guy Malton, as I expected. Small gifts to the boys who work in your household.' Then he looked up with an amused expression. 'Who is this Josephine Coldiron you leave a hundred marks to? Are you keeping some whore with you at Chancery Lane?'

'She, too, works in my household.'

Rich shrugged, studied the documents once more for some slip or trick, then nodded, satisfied, and rang the little bell on his desk. A moment later Peel came in. 'Fetch a couple of gentlemen here,' Rich said. 'The higher their status the better. Officials, not anyone who may be involved in any fighting tomorrow. I want them to survive to remember witnessing my friend Shardlake here signing his will.' He looked at the hourglass. 'Be quick, time runs on.'

When Peel had gone, Rich said, 'When the witnesses come we must pretend to be friends, you understand. Just for a moment.'

'I understand,' I said heavily.

Rich looked at me, curious now. 'You were once a friend of Lord Cromwell's; you could have risen to the top had you not fallen out with him.'

'His price was too high.'

'Ah, yes, we councillors are wicked men. But you, I think, like above all to feel you are in the right. Helping the poor and weak. Justified, as the radical Protestants say. As consolation for how you look, perhaps.' He smiled ironically. 'You know, there are men of conscience on the Privy Council. People like me and Paulet and Wriothesley sit round the council table and listen to them; Hertford snarling at Gardiner and Norfolk about correct forms of religion. We listen afterwards as they plot to put each other in the fire. But some of us, as Sir William Paulet says, bend to the wind rather than be broken by it. Those with conscience are too obsessed with the rightness of their cause to survive, in the end. But the King knows the value of straight, hard counsel, and that is why men like us survive while others go to the axe.'

'Men without even hearts to turn to stone,' I said.

'Oh, we have hearts. For our families, our children whom we educate and make prosperous with the help of our grants of land from the King, and incomes and presents from our clients. But of course,' he said, his face twisting into a sneer, 'you would know nothing about families.'

Footsteps sounded outside. Peel returned with two gentlemen I had never seen, who bowed deeply to Rich. He came round the table, putting a slim arm round my shoulder. I suppressed a shudder. 'Thank you for coming, gentlemen,' he said. 'My friend Master Shardlake here wishes to put his affairs in order, given what may be about to unfold here. Would you witness his will, as a kindness to me?'

The two assented. They told me their names and watched as I signed the will and the copy, then each signed in turn as witness. Rich picked up his cap and papers from the table, together with two folded letters and his copy of the will. 'Thank you, gentlemen,' he said. 'And now, I must go, I have to attend the Privy Council.' Then he said loudly, for the witnesses to hear, 'I am glad, friend Shardlake, to have been of service regarding the girl.'

'You have done what I would expect of you, sir,' I answered evenly.

The gentlemen bowed and left. Rich still had his hand on my shoulder. He moved it and gave my hump a sharp little smack, whispering in my ear, 'I have often wanted to do that.' Then he turned to Peel, brusque and businesslike. 'Now, Colin, I want you to go with Master Shardlake into Portsmouth, find a boat, and take him out to the *Mary Rose*.' He placed the two letters in a leather satchel, and handed it to Peel. 'The unsealed one is my letter of authority: it will let you into Portsmouth and get you a boat. The other you are to give into the hands of the addressee, Philip West. No one else. If some ship's officer asks for it, tell them that and invoke my name. Then you are to wait with the boat till Master Shardlake returns, and get him back to shore. There will be someone else with him. Now go. Is my horse at the stables?'

'Yes, Sir Richard.'

'Sure you understand all that?' he asked mockingly.

'Yes, sir.'

'Brother Shardlake, put him right if he gets it wrong. And now, goodbye.' He bowed, turned, and walked out of the tent. Peel stared at me.

'You have the letters safe?' I asked.

'Yes, sir.'

'Then please, come. Our business is urgent.'

Chapter Forty-five

'Y OU HAVE A HORSE, sir?' Peel asked.
    'Yes. A soldier took it.'
'I'll fetch it. It will be quickest to ride to the Camber wharf.' He bowed and hurried away. I stood waiting by the tents, looking out to sea. The sun was sinking towards the horizon; it was yet another peaceful summer evening. At South Sea Castle soldiers milled round the cannon. Men were dragging another big gun across the sandy scrub of the foreshore. Some soldiers had lit small cooking fires; others were dispersing to the tents. The air was cooling rapidly as the sun lowered.

Peel returned with Oddleg and another horse. 'Can I help you mount, sir?' he asked politely.

I looked at him curiously, remembering how he had taken Rich's insults in his stride. 'Thank you. You must have seen much of the preparations for this invasion, fellow, working for Sir Richard.'

His face became guarded. 'I don't listen, sir. I'm just a servant, I do my little jobs and keep my ears closed.'

I nodded. 'That's a safe way to live.'

We rode away to the town, skirting the Great Morass. 'Well,' I asked, 'what do you think of all this?'

'I pray my master gets away if the French do land. But he is a clever man.'

'That he certainly is.'

There were no fowl on the still waters of the Morass; the guns must have scared them away. We approached the town walls, where the labourers working on the fortifications were packing up their equipment.

'Were you with your master in Portsmouth today?' I asked Peel.

'No, sir. I stayed in camp. We all ran out of the tents when they shouted the French ships were coming. Then the King rode in from Portsmouth.'

We came round the town walls to the main gate. Peel showed the guard Rich's letter of authority and we were allowed in at once.

The High Street was deserted now apart from patrolling guards, the windows of the houses and shops all closed and shuttered; I wondered whether the owners had all left. Inside one a dog howled. A solitary cart laden with freshly slaughtered sides of beef lumbered past, dripping blood onto the dust.

Oyster Street, by contrast, was as crowded as ever, soldiers and sailors jostling with labourers. Now the French had gone more supplies were being loaded onto boats at the wharf. We halted by the warehouses. Across the Camber there were now soldiers on guard even on the empty spit beyond the Round Tower. The English warships stood at anchor out in the Solent.

'Will we be able to get a boat?' I asked Peel worriedly.

'We should with my letter, sir. Wait here a minute, if you please. I'll get the horses stabled.'

'You have the other letter? For Master West?'

He patted his satchel. 'Safe in here. I am not a fool, sir,' he added in a hurt tone.

'Of course not.' I looked across at the ships. 'But please, be quick.'

We dismounted and Peel led the horses away. I saw the huge bulk of the *Great Harry*. There must have been a great panic on board when they saw the French coming. My eye found the *Mary Rose*, where Emma was with Leacon's company. A company of soldiers marched down Oyster Street. They must have come straight in from the country, for they kept staring out to sea, eyes wide.

I heard a shout from below me. Looking down, I saw Peel standing with a boatman in a tiny rowboat at the bottom of some steps. 'Hurry, sir,' he called urgently. 'Before someone requisitions it.'

✝

THE BOATMAN, a young fellow, rowed quickly out, past heavily laden supply boats. I had a view of the French ships in the distance, the setting sun casting a red glow on a close-packed forest of masts. A sudden volley of gunfire sounded from them, booming across the still water. Peel sat up, eyes wide.

'They're trying to make us jumpy,' the boatman said. 'Bastard French serfs. They're too far off to hit anything.' He turned the boat and headed for the line of warships. Some of the smaller ones had retreated to the harbour, but forty or so rode in a double row, two hundred yards apart, turning slowly on their anchors as the tide ebbed. We rowed out to the *Mary Rose*. It had been night when I boarded her before, but now, in the fading daylight, I could see how beautiful she was, as well as how massive: the powerful body of the hull, the soaring masts almost delicate by contrast; the complex web of rigging where sailors were clambering; the castles painted with stripes and bars and shields in a dozen bright colours. The gun ports were closed, the ropes by which they were opened from the deck above hanging slack. A boat was already drawn up at the side, and what looked like boxes of arrows were being hauled up through gaps in the blinds to the weatherdeck.

'I'll row round to the other side,' the boatman said. He pulled past the bow and the immense ropes of the twin anchors, then under the tall foremast with the red and white Tudor Rose emblem at its base. There were no supply boats on the other side. We pulled in. Again someone on the tops shouted, 'Boat ahoy!' and a face appeared on deck, looking down through an open blind.

Peel shouted up, 'Letter from Sir Richard Rich for Assistant-Purser West!' A few moments later a rope ladder came down, splashing as the end hit the water. Peel and I stood up carefully as the boatman grabbed the end. Peel looked at it anxiously.

'Climb up behind me,' I told him. 'It's not that bad, just keep a firm hold and don't mind the swaying.' I turned to the boatman. 'You may have to wait a little.'

'Yes, sir.' He stood too, flexing stiff arms.

I began climbing the ladder, Peel behind me.

✞

AGAIN I WAS helped through a gap in the blinds by a sailor. This time I was able to descend to the planks of the weatherdeck with a little more dignity. Peel followed, looking shaken. There was an immense bustle on the deck, which was full of soldiers as well as sailors. A young officer with a whistle on a purple sash was waiting for us. 'You have a message from Sir Richard Rich for Master West?' he asked abruptly. Peel took the letter from his satchel and held it up for the officer to see the seal.

'Is it about those supplies we were waiting for?' the officer asked me.

I hesitated. 'The letter may only be given to Master West, then I must speak with him. I am sorry.'

The officer turned away. 'Wait here with them,' he ordered one of the sailors, and marched away to the forecastle.

I looked over the deck. Many of the soldiers sat with their backs against the blinds, between the cannon, some cleaning long arque, buses. Everyone is preparing for battle, I thought. The setting sun cast a red glow, broken by the shadow of the netting, making a strange latticework effect on the deck. Sailors carried pairs of gunballs to the guns in slings, cursing at stray soldiers to get out of the way, setting them up next to the guns in triangular battens. Boxes of equipment were being carried from forecastle to aftercastle across the walkway above the netting. I looked up at the aftercastle, saw heads moving under the netting there. It was too high to distinguish whether any of them were from Leacon's company.

I turned to the sailor. He was a little bearded man, perhaps forty – old among all the young men. 'How many soldiers on board now?' I asked.

'Near three hundred,' he answered quietly in a Welsh accent. He looked at me with sudden eagerness. 'Sir, forgive me, but I heard you have a message from Sir Richard Rich. Are they taking some of the soldiers off? We think there are too many; most of the officers agree, but the King's put Vice-Admiral Carew in command of the ship and he won't listen. He's never been aboard till today—'

'I am sorry, that is not the subject of my message,' I answered gently. 'Where are the new archers that came aboard today?'

'Up on the ship's castles. They'll sleep up there tonight, the French may come at dawn if the wind favours them. Sir, many of the soldiers can't even walk properly on deck. There was a gust of wind earlier and they were puking up all over the place, the aftercastle deck stinks already. God knows what they'll be like on the open sea. Sir, if you could get a message to Sir Richard Rich—'

'I fear I have no influence there.' I looked at Peel, who shook his head vigorously. The sailor turned away. A little way off I saw a small group standing between two cannon, talking in a foreign tongue; Flemish I thought. One was nervously reading a rosary, clicking the beads through his fingers. It was something I had not seen for some time, as it had been forbidden by law since Lord Cromwell's time. I guessed the rules would be relaxed for foreign sailors in wartime.

I caught snatches of conversation: 'I saw a swan today, riding in and out of our ships without a care. Maybe it's an omen, sent by the Lord. A royal bird – '

'I wish He'd send us one big enough to climb on and fly away – '

'If the French board, thrust your pike up between their legs – '

'They'll send the galleys back come dawn, we're sitting targets – '

I looked up at the high forecastle with its triple decks, where the senior officers' cabins were. I thought again what an astonishing thing the warship was, every part of it intricately interconnected.

A sharp gust of wind made the *Mary Rose* roll. It only lasted a moment, but though the sailors ignored it two soldiers nearby staggered, and I heard shouts from the castles above. Some of the sailors laughed, others frowned worriedly. Then I saw West approaching from the forecastle alone, men stepping aside to let him pass.

✝

WEST STOOD before us, fists clenched at his sides. His deep-set eyes were bloodshot. 'You,' he said thickly.

Peel bowed and held out the letter. 'From Sir Richard Rich, sir.' West tore the seal and read it, then stared at me, perplexed. He said quietly, 'Rich says you are to fetch back one of the archers that came on board today.'

So he did not know Hugh was really a girl. Rich had not told him that, perhaps fearing he would put him off the ship anyway.

I looked at the man who had ruined Ellen's life. 'That is right, Master West. In accordance with your bargain.'

'I must talk to the master. He is in control of this ship, not Sir Richard. He will need persuading to let an enlisted man go.'

'If we tell him something I know about Hugh Curteys, he will let him go.'

He glanced again at the letter, then at me. 'Sir Richard says that you and he have made a bargain. About the – the other matter.'

'We have. A bargain of necessity.'

West looked at Peel. 'You are one of Sir Richard's bodyservants?'

'Yes, sir.' Peel lowered his gaze.

'Then you will know how to keep your mouth shut.' West had spoken quietly. Now he looked at the men around us. 'Come with me, Master Shardlake, let us find somewhere quiet to talk, see how we can best get this Curteys back on shore.' He looked up at the forecastle, then said, 'Not my cabin, we'll get no peace. I'm waiting for food supplies, they should have been here by now. I know a place.'

He began walking across the crowded deck to the hatch below the aftercastle, near the huge mainmast, which I had descended before. A group of sailors stood on deck, hauling at the rigging to the sound of a beating drum. I looked up at the aftercastle again, wondering if

Leacon could hear the sound which brought back the siege of Boulogne. A sailor knelt, carefully lighting the candles inside a row of lanterns on the deck. West took one and then, with a flinty look at me, turned and began descending the ladder. I took a deep breath and followed him.

We went down to the gundeck. West stood at the foot of the ladder as Peel and I followed. There was nobody there. I looked again at the double row of cannons facing the closed gun ports. Cannonballs and other equipment were stacked neatly by the guns in battens. A barrel was tied securely to the wall. It was marked with a white cross: gunpowder. The light from the grilles in the deck hatches above us was dim, bare feet padded to and fro across them. The floor planks were swept clean.

'Ready for action tomorrow,' West said grimly. 'Come with me. There's a storeroom up here. Thanks to the disorganization on shore there's nothing but a barrel of rotten pork in it.'

It was well he had the lamp, for he led me to the part of the gundeck that lay right under the aftercastle. Between an iron gun and a large cabin projecting out onto the gundeck was a small room. It had a sliding door secured with a padlock; West produced a key and slid it open. It was a tiny storeroom, barely five feet square, empty save for a large barrel secured to hooks on the wall with ropes to prevent it sliding with the movement of the ship. There was a lid on it, but the smell of rotten meat still escaped.

Once inside, West looked at me in silence for a moment. Sounds rose up through the planks from the orlop deck below, muttered voices and scrapings and curses. 'I have taken care of that woman for nineteen years,' he said. 'Rich would have had her killed.'

'I know.'

'I protected her.' He spoke with sudden fierceness, his voice shaking.

'You raped her.'

'She provoked me.'

I felt my face twitch with disgust. I said, 'I have made the bargain. Your secret is safe.'

'Yes.' He nodded. 'It is.' He stared at me a moment longer, then reached back and slid the door open. Peel was standing outside. Somehow it was a different Peel, the blank, deferential servant's expression replaced by a wide, smiling leer. He stepped inside as West pushed me back against the wall. There was barely room for the three of us, but they managed to twist me round and force my arms behind my back. West slid the door shut again with his foot as Peel brought a handkerchief from his doublet and thrust it in my open mouth, nearly choking me. Then West pulled out a dagger and held it to my throat. 'Move and we'll kill you now,' he said quietly. 'You, tie him up.'

Peel reached into his satchel and pulled out a long length of cord. My arms were pinned. Now I realized why Rich had insisted he place the letter in West's hands himself. I had made a mistake in thinking I could bargain with him. He had planned the whole thing, right down to pretending that Peel was a half-witted servant.

My legs were kicked from under me and I crashed heavily to the deck. I gasped, then looked up wildly. Peel was staring down at me, grinning wolfishly. I remembered young Carswell talking of the skills of actors; he could have taken lessons from Peel. No doubt it was a skill that Rich found useful. Peel bent and tied my legs together with more cord, which he also used to bind the gag firmly round my head. He sat me upright against the barrel and ran the cord twice round my middle and the barrel. I was pinioned, voiceless, helpless.

West stood over me, hands on hips. He looked angry, as though it were he who had been wronged. 'I told you,' he said in a low, trembling voice, 'I have protected that woman for nineteen years. If it consoles you I have felt ashamed all this time. But I have redeemed my honour in the King's service, and I will not let a worthless pen-scraping lawyer take that from me on the eve of battle, not even the merest chance of it. I may die, and then what would the truth do to my poor mother? Not that you care. Well, Rich worked out this way of dealing with you, and I shall be glad to see you dead.'

'Shall we kill him now?' Peel asked. 'I've got a dagger –'

West shook his head impatiently. 'No. He has the Queen's patronage, we must be careful. It has to look like an accident if his body is washed ashore. I'll knock him out when it's dark, then weight him and get him over the side somehow. I have the only key to that padlock.'

Peel smiled at me. 'Accidents happen on ships, you see, Master Shardlake. Civilians who come on board at nightfall can fall overboard.'

West bit his lip. 'I've got to go and get that food onto the ship, we haven't enough for tonight –' His eyes widened at the sound of footsteps. He stepped quickly outside, shutting the door and leaving me with Peel. I recognized the purser's voice. 'What are you doing in there?' he asked West. His voice was puzzled, but not suspicious.

'Checking that last barrel of pork, sir. It's rancid.'

'The supplies still aren't here. The cook says there's barely enough stockfish left with all the soldiers staying on board overnight. The master says you've to go over to the warehouses now yourself, bring those supplies across at once. Or we'll have nothing and there'll be trouble. Get one of the rowboats going back.'

'Does it have to be me?'

'You're the one that's supposed to be negotiating with them. Go now.'

I heard the purser's footsteps retreating again, then the door slid open. 'You heard that?' West asked.

'Yes.' Peel gave my shin a vicious kick. 'You're going to be trouble to the end, aren't you?'

'Listen,' West said urgently. 'You must get off the ship, people will be asking who that boatman is. I'll deal with Shardlake later. I have to go now. After I come back I'll find a time when it's quiet, it usually is for a while about three, then kill him and sling him through one of the gun ports.' West looked down at me. His face was anguished, I realized that unlike Peel he did not relish cold-blooded murder. But I knew, too, that he would do it. He was, as Rich had said, a man concerned ultimately with his own honour. He would die for his vanity, and kill for it too.

☩

I WAS LEFT IN total darkness. I heard, faintly, footsteps and murmuring voices from the aftercastle above, an officer's whistle. I thought, Leacon and his men are up there, and Emma. There would be no taking her off now. I lay helpless on the floor. The smell from the barrel behind me was horrible. I felt a savage anger against West and Rich but also against myself. My obsessive quarrying for the truth about Ellen and Hugh had ended here. And Ellen: would West still protect her from Rich after this? Better I had never left London in the first place.

I heard someone moving about in the cabin next door, but there was no way I could call for attention. I tried banging my feet on the floor, every movement sending sharp twinges of pain into my back, but I was so tightly bound I was able only to make a light scraping noise, too faint to be noticed next door.

After a while I noticed tiny points of flickering light above and below me. Lamplight, I realized, coming through minute gaps in the planking. Darkness must have fallen.

The smell from the barrel of rotten meat grew worse than ever in the hot, thick, stinking air. Twice footsteps sounded outside but they passed on. Then I heard bangs and grunts and muttering from outside, I thought from the companionway to the upper deck which I had descended. I wondered if West had fetched the supplies and they were being brought down to the kitchen. I heard a voice. 'Do you want some in the little storeroom, sir?'

West's voice answered sharply. 'No! Down to the kitchen.'

The noise went on for a long time, then ceased. Then I heard West's voice again, on an angry note. 'What are you three men doing here?'

A Devon accent answered, 'We've to stay down here with the cannon tonight, sir, to make sure all is safe lest the ship roll. Orders from the master. There's a full barrel of gunpowder here, sir.'

There was silence. I could almost feel West, outside, wondering how he might be able to get rid of these men, kill me, and dispose of me. Then, to my relief, I heard his footsteps retreating.

For hours and hours I lay there, constantly moving my bound body to try and ease the pains that racked it, fearing that West might find some way to get rid of those sailors keeping watch on the gun-deck. All the time the dim pinhole points of light came and went, and muffled voices and occasional whistles sounded from the deck above. I doubt anyone on the *Mary Rose* slept much that night.

Chapter Forty-six

DESPITE THE PAIN, I found myself drifting in and out of an exhausted doze, starting awake from spasms in my back or shoulders. Several times footsteps outside made me start, fearing West was returning, but always they passed on. The noises of the ship quieted for a while, leaving an hour or two of uneasy near silence save for a bell tolling a change of watch. I was desperately thirsty, my mouth as dry as the gag Peel had stuffed into it.

I dozed again, and found myself dreaming. I was riding into Hampshire with the soldiers, marching along the green, tunnel-like lanes. I was at the head of the company, beside Leacon. Suddenly he turned and said, 'Who's that?' I followed his gaze and realized that some of the soldiers I knew, Carswell and Llewellyn and Pygeon and Sulyard, were carrying a bier on which a body in white grave clothes lay. It was Ellen.

I started awake. A voice, somewhere, shouting, 'Hurry!' Other noises were audible from above, footsteps and whistles, scurrying feet, and though I had no way of knowing I guessed dawn had come. Someone shouted for crews to move into position; I realized with relief that the guncrews had come down. They would probably be here the rest of the day, preventing West from dealing with me. His mission on shore and the posting of guards by the guns had made him miss the opportunity of dealing with me at dead of night.

I heard whistles, then a steady rumbling that set the plank floor of my prison vibrating. Then another whistle and a series of clatters. It sounded as though the gun ports had been opened, cannon moved forward and then back. A practice? It must have been, for it happened two or three more times. From the noises, there seemed to be activity all over the ship. I tried to work out what people were saying, but could only catch stray words.

It was impossible to calculate the passage of time. The room, which had cooled a little in the middle of the night, became very hot again, the stink of rotten meat even stronger. Sometime later I heard distant gunfire, whether from our ships or the French galleys I could not tell. At one point I heard a loud cheer from the decks above, a distinct cry of 'Got the galley!' There was more gunfire, sometimes close, sometimes far away. After one shot I felt a dull reverberation through the deck beneath me, and outside someone shouted, 'Are we hit?' Then I heard a number of men running down the companionway and continuing down to the decks below. I thought I caught the word 'Pump!' My heart raced with panic at the thought of being trapped in the tiny cabin if the ship was hit, but nothing more happened. I felt sick, and despite the pain the effort brought to my bound arms I leaned my head forward as far as I could, for were I to vomit with the gag in my mouth I would choke. Then I heard a knock on the door, a gentle hesitant knock, and a voice calling, 'Matthew?' It was Leacon.

A wave of relief ran through me. I tried to move, despite the pain that flashed through my body, terrified he would leave. I managed to scrape my bound heels across the floor. 'Matthew?' he called again. He had heard. I scraped my heels again. There was a moment's silence, then a crash as Leacon put his shoulder to the door. Someone outside called 'Hey!'

'There's someone shut up in here!' A moment later, with a tremendous crash, the flimsy door splintered open and light spilled through, searing my eyes.

The voice outside called again, 'What in God's name's going on, man?'

Leacon was staring through the open doorway, unbelievingly. 'There's a civilian in here!' he called back. He smashed his shoulder against the door again, making a gap wide enough to enter. The officer who had called out to him came across and stared in at me, wide-eyed.

'What the hell – do you know him?'

'Yes, he is a friend.'

'God's holy wounds! Who the fuck tied him up in there? Sort it out,' the officer snapped. 'Get him off the gundeck!'

Leacon stepped into the cabin. He took out his knife, cut my bonds and removed the gag. I lay on my back and groaned, sucking in air, unable for the moment to move.

'God's death, who did this to you?' Leacon's face was tired, dirty, streaked with perspiration. He wore his helmet, a padded jack and his officer's sword.

'Philip West.' My voice came out as a croak. 'I found out – something – that he once did.'

'You came on board to confront him?' Leacon asked unbelievingly.

'Yes. What time is it?'

'Past three o'clock.'

'Jesu. I've been here since last night. What's happening? I heard gunfire – '

'The French have brought five of their galleys forward again, but our guns are keeping them at a distance. We hit one. It trailed back to the main fleet, listing. There's no wind, neither our warships nor theirs can move. The French have used some galleys to land on the Isle of Wight. We can see fires. Just as well, if they'd sent them all against us we'd be in worse trouble. If there's a wind when the tide is right we're going to sail out against them.'

'What's happening outside? I heard the cannon being moved, but no firing.'

'They're making the guncrews pass the time with practice. This waiting is hard.'

'Someone shouted something about a pump. I thought we'd been hit – '

'Some men went below to see, but they don't think it's anything serious.'

I sighed with relief. 'How did you find me?'

'I overheard two sailors saying a lawyer boarded last night and went below with West, and the boat left without him. They said you were still on the ship, you never came back up. They said –' he hesitated.

'I can guess. Hunchbacks bring bad luck. Well, this time their superstition saved me.'

'I questioned them and they were definite. So I came down to look. I started by going along the gundeck, found that closed door and found you.'

'Where is West?'

'Somewhere on board. He went ashore last night to fetch supplies, but half the beer he brought back is bad. My men are parched with thirst. He's probably up in the forecastle with the purser. I told Sir Franklin I was going to try and find out what was happening with the beer.'

'Thank you. Thank you. You have saved my life. How are the men?'

'Tired and hungry. More than half are up on the aftercastle, including the section you know. I'm with them. Others have gone to the forecastle decks. But they're resolute, they'll fight and die if it comes.' Pride and pain mingled in his voice. 'I have to get back to them. Can you stand if I help you?'

I forced myself to my feet, biting my lip against the pain. 'God's death,' Leacon burst out. 'West must be mad, leaving you in here.'

'He meant to deal with me last night, but by the time he'd finished getting the stores some men had been stationed on guard. He and Richard Rich planned this yesterday. I thought I had made a bargain with Rich. Dear God, I was a fool.'

He shook his head sadly. 'West is known as a fair, hard-working officer.' He looked at me accusingly. 'You should have told me he was dangerous.'

'I did not understand how dangerous until yesterday. But Barak said I was using you and he was right. I am sorry.'

'Where is Jack?'

'Well on his way to London.' I took a deep breath. 'George, there is something else you will find hard to believe. Something Rich used to get me on the ship – and it's why your company was put on the *Mary Rose*. Yesterday you took on a new recruit. Hugh Curteys.'

'Yes,' he answered, sounding defensive. 'He came in the afternoon, he wanted to enlist and I let him. I remembered seeing him that time before, and recalled what a good archer he was. He said his guardian had agreed.'

I smiled wryly. 'Did you believe that?'

'All the companies are under-strength. If I had refused he would only have got himself into another.'

'George, Hugh Curteys is not who he says. He is not even a boy. "He" is a girl, Hugh's sister. She has been impersonating him for years.'

He looked at me blankly. 'What?'

'That wretched man Hobbey forced the impersonation on her, for gain. He has admitted it. George, please, take me up to the aftercastle with you. Let me show you.'

He looked at me dubiously. 'Can you make it up there?'

'Yes. If you help me. Please.'

He looked me in the eye. 'You realize you should try and get off this ship, now. There are a few rowboats going between the ships and shore with messages.'

'I must take Emma Curteys with me. I've got this far, against all my enemies could throw at me.'

Leacon looked round the little cabin, shook his head again, then said, 'Come.'

'Thank you again, George.'

As I moved away, my robe caught on a splinter in the planking of the wall. I threw off the filthy, dusty thing, then tore off my coif too. In my shirt, I followed Leacon from the little cabin. As I went out I heard cannonfire. It sounded close.

✣

OUTSIDE, guncrews of half a dozen men stood round the cannon in positions of readiness, in their shirts or bare-chested. The gun ports were open. The air was stifling, thick with the stench of unwashed bodies. Each member of the guncrews stood in a fixed place: one holding a long ladle; another with a wooden linstock and smouldering taper, ready to light the powder; a third with an iron gunball at his feet, ready to load. The master gunners stood behind the guns, watching an officer in doublet and hose, sword at his waist and a whistle round his neck, pacing up and down between the double row of guns. The men lifted tired, strained faces to stare at us. The officer stepped forward, glaring at me. 'Who the hell are you? Who put you in there?'

'Assistant-Purser West. He—'

A whistle sounded loudly from the top of the ladder. The officer thrust out his arm to stop us moving. 'Stay back! Wait here!'

The whistle had been a signal. The officer blew his own whistle and I watched as another practice followed, the crews swinging smoothly into motion, moving with speed and grace. The iron cannon were loaded with shot from the back, the bronze ones, which had been hauled back for the purpose, from chambers at the front. Vents on top of the guns were filled with powder and the bronze guns were rolled forward, the ropes binding them to the walls slackening. The movement made the deck tremble again. Each master gunner placed the taper next to a hole at the back of each gun, into which another man had already mimed pouring in a dob of powder from a flask. Then everyone stopped and waited, still as a tableau for half a minute, until another whistle sounded. The guns were hauled inboard again, and the gunballs removed. Everyone took up their former positions. The officer said, 'Good enough. We'll give them a hot cannonade!' He inclined his head at us. 'Get out, quick!'

We passed between the guncrews. I remember one man holding a linstock staring at me as I went by. He was shirtless, with a short, scarred, muscular body, a square bearded face. He looked at me as though I were something from another world, an apparition.

We walked to the ladder. At the bottom Leacon said quietly, 'Can you make it up?'

'After all I've been through to get here? Yes.'

I climbed after him, though the effort sent pain slicing through my shoulders. Fresh, salt air wafted down from above, making my head swim for a moment. Leacon reached the deck and helped me up. Again, through the stout netting, I saw the great masts rearing up into the blue sky of another hot July day. The sails were still furled, but on deck and up in the rigging sailors stood in position, ready to release them on command. The deck was more crowded than ever, everyone at battle positions. As below, guncrews had taken up positions of readiness beside the cannon. Half the blinds were open, giving me a view of the *Great Harry* and the other warships beyond on one side, and on the other the Isle of Wight, where, away in the distance, I saw smoke rising from several large fires.

I looked along the deck. Archers stood at some of the open blinds, and perhaps fifty pikemen stood together, nine-foot-long half-pikes raised with tips poking through the netting, ready to thrust up at boarders. An officer with a whistle round his neck stood watching; he glanced up at the fighting top in the topmast where lookouts stood, the only ones with a clear view of what was happening.

Near us, on the opposite side of the deck, three officers were arguing. One I recognized as the purser. The second was Philip West. He looked haggard as he spoke to the third man, a tall officer in his forties, richly dressed. He had a dark brown beard framing a long, frowning face, a pomander as well as a sword at his waist. Round his neck he wore a massive whistle on a long gold chain. He was examining what looked like a tiny sundial. He looked up as West finished speaking.

'If the beer's bad,' he said impatiently, 'they'll just have to do without.'

The purser answered, 'The men are parched. And starting to murmur – '

'Then give them what there is!'

'They won't drink it, Sir George,' West said impatiently. 'It's bad—'

Sir George Carew shouted back, 'Don't talk to me like that, knave! God's death, they'd best behave, all of them. The King is watching at South Sea Castle, and he'll have a special eye on this ship!'

West turned his head away. He saw me then; his mouth fell open in astonishment and horror. I met his gaze grimly. There was nothing he could do to me here. Leacon stared at him too, angrily, then turned to me. 'Let's go up.'

We mounted via the space under the aftercastle, next to the mainmast, and arrived on the lower aftercastle deck, where helmeted handgunners stood with arquebuses and hailshot pieces propped against the side of the ship. There were no blinds here, only portholes at eye-level for them to stick their weapons through. I had a view through a wide doorway giving on to the walkway between the castles, above the netting. Two sailors in check shirts stood in the doorway leading to the aftercastle, watching as a pair of soldiers carried a long box across the walkway from the forecastle end. On either side of the doorway the two long cannon I had seen from the weatherdeck on my first visit were positioned, angled to fire outwards past the ship through a gap in the rigging, guncrews beside them. The cannon were bronze, beautifully ornate. Looking back, I saw two lines of handgunners, their feet braced, their long, heavy weapons thrust through little portholes. If the *Mary Rose* grappled with a French ship, they would fire hailshot of metal and stone at the opposing crew.

'More arrows,' the soldiers said as they reached the doorway.

'Give them here.' The sailors took the box and carried it to the ladder, which continued upwards. They climbed up nimbly, then descended again to resume their positions in the doorway. Leacon and I ascended to the top deck of the aftercastle, into the sunshine, underneath another span of netting fixed to wooden supports that enclosed the deck. The aftercastle was far longer than the weatherdeck, and just as crowded. Around half Leacon's company were there, perhaps twenty men standing at open blinds on each side, with a few placed behind ready to replace any who fell. Snodin was pacing slowly up and down the deck, his plump face set hard. He saw me and stared with an astonished frown. Like the men on the deck below most wore helmets and cotton jacks – Pygeon, some way off, had on the bright red brigandyne he had won from Sulyard. The men held strung bows upright at their sides, angled carefully so the tops did not touch the enclosing netting above, arrowbags at their waists, bracers on their wrists. The box of arrows lay open in the middle of the deck. Here and there the archers were interspersed with swivel gunners, their thin, six-foot long weapons fixed to the rail above the blinds. The guns were at rest, muzzles up and long tails resting on the deck. At the far end of the aftercastle, under an enormous flag of St George, Sir Franklin Giffard stared down the deck, his face set and resolute. Through the open blind next to me I saw the sea, forty feet below. I swallowed and looked away. Then I looked backwards, and stared.

From here, looking through open blinds at the back of the after-castle, I could see not only our ships and the distant French fleet, which appeared to be in the same position as the night before, but, perhaps half a mile ahead, the French galleys. Four of the enormous, sleek things faced us. They were drawn up stern to stern, like a four-spoked wheel, turning slowly on the sparkling water, so they could, each in turn, bring the cannon in the bows round to face us. I could see the oars flashing, the dark shapes of the double cannon in the prows. Some of our galleasses, pathetically small by comparison, faced them. As I watched, a puff of smoke billowed up and out as a galley fired at one of our ships further down the line. A boom echoed across the water.

I turned and looked down the rows of archers. I saw Carswell and Llewellyn at adjacent blinds, other familiar faces, all shining with sweat.

It was hard to pick Emma out among the archers but I saw her, in helmet and jack, up near the stern. She still carried the beautiful slim bow with horn tips that I recognized from Hoyland. When she saw me her face reddened with fury and her hand went instinctively to her throat. Leacon looked along the deck at her. Their eyes met. Emma's scarred face wavered a moment, then set hard.

Sir Franklin had seen us. He marched between the rows of men, hand on sword hilt, frowning. No doubt he was astonished by my appearing yet again, this time on the *Mary Rose* herself. I followed Leacon towards him. A strong breeze rose suddenly, ruffling my hair. The ship tipped a little, and several of the archers and swivel gunners staggered. Leacon reached Sir Franklin, then bent to whisper in his ear. As he did so, I heard whistles and shouts from the main deck below.

Sir Franklin jerked upright, stared at Leacon, then at me. He laughed. 'What?'

'Easy enough to determine, sir,' Leacon said. Sir Franklin stared at Emma, then nodded. He and Leacon walked up the deck to her. I followed them.

'Is it true?' Leacon asked her sharply. 'What Master Shardlake just told me about you?'

Emma hesitated, then answered quietly, 'I do not understand, sir.'

Doubt flickered across Leacon's face. In her uniform Emma was utterly convincing. He said quietly, 'If I have to, I'll find out the truth here and now. In front of everyone.'

'There is nothing to find, Captain.' I had to admire her courage as she made her bluff.

Leacon took a deep breath, then reached out and lifted off her close-fitting helmet. He stared at the short brown fuzz, studied her face again, then said, 'Remove your jack, soldier.'

There was muttering up and down the ranks. The men still stood in position, but most had turned their heads to stare. Slowly, Emma removed her arrowbag, then took off her jack and dropped it to the deck. She stood there, the wind that had risen ruffling her white shirt.

Leacon put his hands to her collar and ripped the shirt open. The heartstone was tied round her neck in its tiny leather pouch, over a white linen band. The band was drawn tightly across her chest, but above it the tops of her breasts made a slight swell. I feared Leacon might force her to untie the band but he had seen enough. There was an excited muttering among the men.

'What's that? Is it a bandage? Is he hurt?'

'Shit, I think it's a woman.'

'Be quiet!' Sir Franklin called out. Leacon spoke quietly to Emma. 'Why have you done this? Why have you made a mockery of my company?'

Emma crossed her arms. 'I wanted to fight, sir. You've seen that I'm a good archer.'

Sir Franklin stepped up to her. He raised his hand and I thought he would strike her, but he turned to Leacon, and said, voice trembling with fury, 'Can she be got off the ship?'

'Maybe. If a boat comes over.'

'Go and find one. Get her out of sight for now. Under the aftercastle. Anywhere.' He looked round at the gawping soldiers. Emma stared at me, arms held tight across her breasts, her eyes full of pain and anger.

The *Mary Rose* lurched violently. Some of the men staggered again, grabbing at the rails or reaching up to the enclosing netting. I had been aware of more whistles and shouted commands from below, and now I heard a loud rattling from the stern; the anchors were being raised. Turning round, I saw huge white sails billow out from the bowsprit and foremast, snapping and cracking in the rising breeze. Over to the left sails unfurled on the *Great Harry* too, then on the other ships. The *Mary Rose* rocked once more, then began moving slowly forward towards the galleys. It had begun. We were going into battle.

Chapter Forty-seven

SEVERAL SHORT, PIERCING whistle blasts sounded from the foot of the ladder. Sir Franklin shouted, 'To positions!'

Leacon looked at Emma and me grimly. 'Go down to the space under the aftercastle and stay there!' he said, then walked away to his men. Most still had their heads turned in our direction but now they were looking past us to where, beyond the forecastle and the raised foresail, the galleys faced us. There was another crack and billow of canvas as the lateen sail at the back of the ship was set. Though I could feel little movement – just the ship rising and falling gently – the *Mary Rose* was approaching the galleys at considerable speed. I looked at the soldiers again; Carswell gave me a frightened smile and shrugged, as though to say, now we have all come to it, and you too. Pygeon, sweating in his brigandyne, crossed himself. Leacon went to stand in the centre of the aftercastle beside Snodin, near where Emma's jack lay. 'Stay steady, lads,' Snodin said in a quiet, sympathetic tone such as I had never heard him use before.

The deck shifted and I almost fell. A nearby sailor, in position by the topmast rigging, shouted at us, 'Get your shoes off! Then get off this deck, out of our way!'

I kicked off my shoes and ran to the ladder. Emma hesitated, then did the same. As we reached the hatch, I glanced backwards. The *Mary Rose* had pulled ahead of the rest of the fleet now, the *Great Harry* was behind us; all the other ships seemed to be following. Through the open blind of the archer next to me I glimpsed South Sea Castle in the distance. I looked down; far below I saw frothing waves as the *Mary Rose* cut through the water. My stomach lurched.

I began descending the ladder. I looked back at Emma. She hesitated again, then, with a savage look, followed me.

I clambered slowly down, trying to ignore the pain in my arms and shoulders. On the deck below the handgunners still stood with feet braced looking through their little ports, while on each side of the ladder the gun teams stood ready at the two long cannons. Through the wide door giving on to the walkway above the netting I saw we were still heading fast for the galleys. The two sailors still stood one on each side of the door, likewise staring ahead. Then the *Mary Rose* began to turn. The port side dipped, pitching me off the ladder onto the deck. I hit my shoulder and cried out with pain. The sailors next to us looked round for a moment. The ship dipped even further, then righted itself.

I tried to rise. Pain shot down my arm. I managed to get to my feet. Emma hesitated, looking at me. I said, 'I can't use the ladder.'

'We were told to go to the space under the aftercastle.'

'You go. I can't.'

For the first time her expression was indecisive, uncertain. She stepped off the ladder and stood beside me. The ship was still turning, some of the handgunners were clutching at the ports now with one hand. Staring ahead, I realized the *Mary Rose* intended to face the galleys side on, bringing her cannon to bear. I felt giddy and sank to the floor. Emma looked down at her torn shirt, the heartstone swinging on its cord. It was still hard to believe she was not a boy. She pulled the ends of the shirt together, then sat down beside me. 'Afraid, Master Shardlake?' she asked coldly.

'Leacon is right,' I answered. 'Everyone should be afraid to die.'

She laughed harshly. 'Rather die fighting than hang.' Her voice seemed perceptibly higher. Something else she had had to keep under control all these years.

I said, 'David is not dead, though he is badly hurt.'

She lowered her head, then spoke quietly. 'I did not mean to kill him. I thought I would kill you and Barak, but I couldn't.'

'I know.'

She did not answer, but sat with head bowed. I looked ahead again. The four galleys were close now, I saw their sides were richly gilded with the arms of France. They circled round, still in their square formation, bringing their guns into position to fire on the *Mary Rose*. I said, as steadily as I could given my thudding heart, 'It's coming.'

'Let it,' Emma answered without looking up.

I said, 'If we get out of this, Hobbey will pass your wardship to me. Then you can decide what you want to be.'

She looked up, her face set hard again. 'If we live I'll find another company. Fight the Scots, perhaps.'

'I risked all to try and save you.'

'Why?' she asked. 'Why did you? I never wanted – '

'To give you a chance. A choice – '

I broke off at the sound of a cracking boom. Dark grey smoke billowed out from the front of the galley facing us. There was an odd silence lasting perhaps twenty seconds, then one of the sailors said, 'That was close.'

Then from below came a shout of 'Give fire!' followed by the loudest noise I have ever heard, as all the cannon on the starboard side of the *Mary Rose* fired on the galleys, one after another after another, a series of tremendous crashing roars. I felt the impact travel up through my legs, making my very bones shake, and a dreadful pressure on the inside of my ears. The decks trembled and creaked. I turned to Emma; she had looked up, her eyes alight with excitement.

As the smoke cleared I saw the galleys were undamaged. The *Mary Rose* began turning to port, fast and steeply. I heard a cracking of sails. Then, through the doorway, I felt a sudden strong gust of wind.

'That's too fast,' one of the sailors said.

The ship heeled to starboard. I thought it would be like the earlier manoeuvre and she would right herself, but she tilted more and more. The soldiers on the port side, which rose high as the starboard side dipped lower, clung to the side of the portholes; their guns began slipping back through them and crashing down the decks. Looking through the doorway I saw a man fall off the topmast into the web of rigging, swivel guns fall from the topdeck railing, into the sea. I heard crashing and shouting below the netting enclosing the weatherdeck as men and equipment slid and fell. All this took only seconds, but the time seems to stretch out in my memory, detail after terrible detail. All the soldiers on our deck, and their guns, were now tumbling and crashing against the starboard side. The long cannon on the port side, too, began slipping from its mount.

'Get out of here!' the sailor beside us shouted to his fellow. They went down on hands and knees and began crawling rapidly out onto the walkway above the netting, grasping the sides for the ship was tilted at such an angle now it was impossible to walk. Under the netting men were screaming. I saw hands reaching up through the mesh.

'Come on!' I shouted to Emma. I began crawling after the sailors, gritting my teeth against the pain in my shoulders. For a second I thought she might stay behind, but I heard her shuffling after me. We got out onto the walkway. Men were hacking frantically up at the stout netting with their knives. A hand reached up and grasped my arm, a frantic voice shouted, 'Help us!' but then water crashed over us, the cold a sudden shock, and I felt myself carried outwards. In the seconds I rode the top of the onrushing water I saw dozens of soldiers falling from the aftercastle through open or broken blinds. I saw the red of Pygeon's heavy brigandyne as he fell past me like a stone, eyes wide with horror, and Snodin's plump form, arms windmilling frantically, mouth open and screaming. The men threw up great splashes as they hit the sea, then disappeared, the weight of their clothing and helmets taking them at once to the bottom. All those men, all of them. And from the hundreds trapped below the netting, and on the lower decks, I heard a terrible screaming. Then the cold waters came over my head and I thought, this is it, the end I feared, drowning. And suddenly all the pains in my body were gone.

✠

SEVERAL MOMENTS of utter, absolute terror, and then I felt myself carried up and outward, and my head was in the air again. I took a frantic breath, kicking wildly at the water. I had been swept some yards out from the *Mary Rose*. The giant ship was on its side now, rapidly sinking. Part of the foresail floated on the surface, and the topmast and foremast, almost horizontal, hung out over the frothing water. Tiny brown shapes were climbing up them; I realized they were rats. Amazingly a couple of the men in the fighting top high on the foremast had survived; they clung on, calling piteously for help, the great mast I had craned my neck to look up at now only a few feet above the waves. The terrible screaming from the soldiers and sailors trapped below the netting had ceased. I looked round wildly; perhaps a couple of dozen men were, like me, kicking and shouting in the water; a few bodies floated face down. More rats scrabbled in the water. A great bubble of air burst a few feet from me. The ship sank lower, below the water's surface.

I felt a force dragging me down again. Perhaps it was the ship settling on the seabed fifty feet below — as my head went under, I saw, amid hundreds more bubbles, the dim shape of the forecastle. It seemed to be moving, breaking away from the hull. I closed my eyes against the terror of it all, and seemed to see the face of the man I had once drowned staring at me sorrowfully.

Then the dragging ceased. I kicked frantically upwards, bringing my head above water again, desperately sucking in air. At a little distance the *Great Harry* was bearing straight down on the French galleys. After what had happened to the *Mary Rose* she was not going to turn broadside. One of the galleys fired and there was an answering roar from the guns near the bow of the *Great Harry*. Smoke drifted out over the water. I grasped frantically at something floating past. It was a longbow, too light to take my weight. I was fearfully cold, and suddenly light-headed. I felt myself sink again; and remembered hearing somewhere that if you are drowning, the third time you go down is the last.

Then a hand grasped my arm and pulled me up. I stared, wide-eyed, at Emma. She was clinging to something, a broad wooden circle with a short spar attached, the circle painted with alternating red and white rose petals. The emblem from the bow of the *Mary Rose*. I scrabbled at it. It was not heavy enough to support both of us, but by kicking our feet we were able to keep our heads above water. The pain in my shoulder returned from the effort of holding on, and my teeth began chattering with cold; even with the emblem to hold on to we could not survive long. Faint cries still sounded across the water from the few still left alive.

I saw the galleys break formation and retreat, rowing back to the French fleet. We were much closer to the French ships now; I could make out individual warships. Dozens and dozens of them, painted in black and yellow and green, drawn up in a long line three abreast. One at the front carried a massive papal flag, the keys of St Peter. I looked across the spar to Emma. Her face was wild, frantic. 'Where are they all?' she asked. 'The soldiers, the men?'

'Gone,' I managed to gulp out. 'Drowned.' I looked to where the *Mary Rose* had been; there was nothing to be seen now in the still-bubbling sea save the tips of the two masts a few feet above the water, men still clinging to the fighting tops, and the floating sail.

I heard a shout and turned to see a rowboat from one of the English ships approaching. Others were following, fishing the living from the water. The boat drew level and hands reached down to pull us out. Emma was landed in the boat first; I was dropped on top of her like a hooked fish. I looked round, into the horrified face of a sailor. 'The *Mary Rose* is gone,' he said.

Chapter Forty-eight

I WOKE TO semi-darkness. I realized I was on land; the ground beneath me was still. I was thirstier than ever in my life, the dryness reaching from deep in my chest to the back of my nose. I swallowed, tasted salt, and raised myself painfully up on my elbows. My shoulders were painfully stiff and sore. I saw that I was in a long, low room with small high windows; it was dark outside. I was lying on rough sacks on a dusty floor, a smelly blanket on top of me. Other men lay in rows along the walls. Someone was groaning. A couple of men with candles were moving to and fro. I tried to call out but could only manage a croak. One of the men carrying the candles came over with a heavy, limping walk. He stood over me: he was middle-aged with a seamed, lined face. I croaked out the words, 'Drink. Please.'

He knelt beside me, placing a leather pouch to my lips. 'Slowly, matey,' he said, as a blessed trickle of weak beer ran down my throat. 'Don't gulp.'

I lay back, gasping. 'Where are we?'

'In one of the Oyster Street warehouses. They brought all of you here that survived. I'm Edwin, I work on the loading usually.'

I croaked, 'How many? How many saved?'

'Thirty-five pulled alive from the water. Those of you in a bad state were brought here. There are fifteen of you. One died earlier, God rest him.'

'Thirty-five,' I breathed. 'Out of – '

'Five hundred. The rest are at the bottom of the Solent.' His face, tanned and weatherbeaten, was sombre. 'I knew some of them; I was a sailor till I smashed my leg five years ago.'

'Did any soldiers survive?'

'Two or three in the fighting tops managed to cling on. No others. The soldiers were heavy clad, they—'

'Drowned. I saw. And heard the men under the netting, screaming – ' My eyes were suddenly hot and stinging, though there was no moisture left in me for tears.

'Here,' the old sailor said, 'easy now. Drink some more beer. You brought up a lot of water in the boat before you lost consciousness.'

I asked, 'Did you see it? Did you see the ship go down?'

'Everyone on shore did. We all heard the screaming too, as the King did at South Sea Castle.'

'He saw the *Mary Rose* sink?'

'They say he cried out, "Oh, my gallant gentlemen! Oh, my gallant men!" He thought of the gentlemen first, of course,' he added bitterly.

'Why? Why did she sink?'

Edwin shook his head. 'Some are saying the gun ports weren't closed quickly enough as the ship turned. Others have it she was top-heavy with all the cannon, and too many soldiers on board. I heard she might have been hit, too, by the galleys. Whatever the cause, all those men are dead.'

'The French – what happened? The *Great Harry* fired on the galleys – '

'The galleys went back to the main fleet. They were trying to draw us into deep water to do battle with the French fleet, but Lord Lisle wasn't to be had like that. We'd have been overwhelmed.'

'I saw fires on the Isle of Wight.'

'The French have landed near two thousand men there, but they're being beaten back. The two fleets are still at a stand-off. They're badly led, luckily for us. Though if the wind favours their ships they could still attack ours. You should leave, soon as you can.'

He gave me a little more beer, then looked at me curiously. 'We've been wondering, sir, what you were doing on board. You're not a sailor or soldier. You sound like a gentleman.'

'I shouldn't have been there. I intended to get off, but then the ship sailed out.'

'Where were you on the *Mary Rose*?'

'On the aftercastle. By the walkway over the netting. I managed to crawl out onto it.'

Edwin nodded. 'And you were in your shirt, so you didn't just fall to the bottom like so many.'

I lay back again. Memories of what had happened were returning in fractured jerks: the ship heeling over at that impossible angle, the man grasping at me as I crawled across the walkway, Emma behind. I said, 'There was someone in the water with me – '

Edwin got to his feet, wincing. He had had a fracture below one knee; it had set badly, at a strange angle. 'Yes,' he said, 'there was a boy rescued with you. You were both clinging to the *Mary Rose* emblem. You were lucky. The boatmen tried to pull the emblem in, but it sank – '

'A boy?'

'Yes. Well-set-up lad, with a scarred face.' He looked at me again. 'Your son, perhaps?'

'No. But sh – he – saved me. Where is he?'

'Gone. I was one of those helping survivors off the boats. He was lying face down underneath you. He seemed unconscious, but when the boat hit the wharf he shoved you off, went up the steps like a monkey and ran away down Oyster Street. We called after him – he seemed injured, holding one arm tight across his chest. But he just kept running. You didn't know him?'

'No. I only wondered what happened to him. He pulled me onto the spar. Tell me, did any officers survive?'

'No. They were all under the netting.'

I remembered West arguing with Carew and the master. So he was dead too, they all were. Vividly, in bright, terrible flashes, I saw

Leacon's company falling into the sea, sinking to the bottom in an instant.

✞

I SLEPT INTERMITTENTLY. The man who had been groaning became quiet; he must have died, for I saw Edwin and his fellows carry a body out, draped in a blanket. It was worse being awake; I kept seeing, again and again, the deaths of Leacon and his men. Then I would remember them tramping down the country lanes, the arguments and jokes and little kindnesses; Leacon riding at the front with Sir Franklin, hating the sound of drums. Edwin and his colleague gave me more to drink, and later tried to make me take a little soup, but I could not bear to eat.

Next time I woke it was daylight. I felt rested now, in body at least. I looked at the man on the sacks next to me, a young sailor. He said something in Spanish. I was too tired to remember the few words I knew and shook my head apologetically. I struggled to get to my feet, but only managed three faltering steps before my head swam and I had to grasp at a pillar. Edwin limped towards me. 'You're still weak, sir,' he said. 'You were insensible some time, you should lie down again. Try to eat something.'

'I can't.' A horrible thought struck me. 'Have any of the king's officials been here?'

He laughed bitterly. 'No. The royal party haven't left South Sea Castle and the tents.'

'The Queen – is she there?'

'No. At Portchester. The only visitor we've had is from the town council; they're arguing with Governor Paulet over whether they or the army should pay for the care of those here.' He gave me that inquisitive look again. 'Were you expecting someone?'

I shook my head. I let go of the pillar, and staggered back to my sacks.

✞

WHEN NEXT I woke night had fallen again. I was conscious of someone sitting next to me and sat up with a start. It was Barak, on a stool, with a lamp next to him.

'Jack?' I asked hesitantly, for my dreams had been peopled with phantoms.

He took a deep breath. 'Ay.'

'How did you get here?'

'When you didn't arrive at Petersfield I rode back to Hoyland to see if they had news of you or Emma. They said neither of you had returned so I rode down here. I arrived this morning and learned Leacon's company had gone down with the *Mary Rose*. I could see the top of the masts sticking out of the water. I thought you were fucking dead,' he burst out in sudden anger. 'Then I learned some survivors had been brought here and came to see.'

'I was on the aftercastle, I managed to get off into the water. Emma rescued me.'

'She lives too?'

'Yes, but when the boat brought us ashore she ran away. On the ship – I told Leacon who she was; he made her take off her jack and helmet, open her shirt. I exposed her as a woman. But it saved her. Jack, they're all gone. Leacon, Carswell, Llewellyn, everyone we knew.' Tears sprang to my eyes. 'It was my fault, it was because of me that Rich put them on that ship – ' I started to weep.

Then Barak did something I would never have expected – he leaned forward and took me in his arms.

✝

LATER I WAS able to sit up. I told Barak the story – my imprisonment by West, the scenes on the aftercastle, escaping via the walkway and being helped by Emma in the water. He told me he had picked up some letters that had been delivered to Hoyland – Tamasin was well, but worried that he had not returned to London. Guy said Coldiron was becoming troublesome and surly over his protectiveness towards Josephine.

'That doesn't surprise me,' I said.

He did not reply for a moment, then burst out angrily, 'Why didn't you send me a message?'

'I'm sorry. All I could think of was that our friends died because of me.'

'If it hadn't been George Leacon's company, it would have been another, a different set of women and children mourning.'

'But knowing them – ' I shook my head desperately – 'knowing them makes all the difference.'

'It was Richard Rich put them on the *Mary Rose*,' he said.

'Because he knew West was there. I saw them fall into the water. They never had a chance. I should have died with them: that would have been justice.'

'What good would that do? Another man dead? Me left to tell Tamasin and Guy? I thought I was going to have to do that, you know.'

I looked at him. 'I am sorry.' I sighed. 'How is David? I should have asked – I cannot seem to order my thoughts.'

'Dyrick was still at the priory, he wouldn't let me see Hobbey or David.' Barak looked at me hard. 'You should ride out and tell them Emma's alive. They'll have heard the *Mary Rose* went down with five hundred men by now, they'll be worried if they don't hear. You could get up if you'd eat something. That Edwin says you won't.'

'I can't eat.' I sat silent for a moment. 'Philip West – he had the death in action he wanted.'

'Action? He died because the arseholes in charge of this mess overloaded the *Mary Rose* and put a man who knew nothing of ships in charge. So they're saying in the taverns, anyway.'

'Just before Leacon and I went up to the aftercastle, we saw West. I looked at him – he knew I would bring him to account. I was so full of – righteousness. As I have been all along.'

'Does Rich think you're dead?' Barak asked.

'I don't know. I thought he might come here. But no one from the court has been.'

'Then with West dead, Ellen may be in danger from him. Have you thought of that?'

I put my head in my hands. 'I can't think of anything but those men—'

He reached out and grasped my hand roughly. 'It's time you pulled yourself together. Come, rouse yourself, there are still things to be done.'

Chapter Forty-nine

IT WAS ANOTHER DAY before I felt able to set out. Barak had forced me to eat, and had even gone out into Portsmouth to find new clothes for me. Gunfire still sounded frequently during the day. He told me the French had been repelled from the Isle of Wight, but the two fleets still stood facing each other, the French were sending galleys forward to try and hit our ships and tempt us out, though after the loss of the *Mary Rose* only our galleasses had been sent against them. In Portsmouth he managed to find a tailor, who supplied me with an outfit which made me look, if not a lawyer, at least like a gentleman.

'They fear the French will try to land elsewhere,' Barak said when he had given me the clothes. 'There are still soldiers coming in – I heard the King has ordered a new levy from London, and more shot from the Sussex ironworks. We have to go,' he concluded.

We were still in the old warehouse, sitting on stools and eating pottage by the pile of sacks that had become my bed. Most of the men who had been brought to the warehouse had left now; besides me there were only three with broken limbs and one poor sailor, very young, who seemed to have lost his mind and spent most of the time weeping in a corner. I had not been able to face going outside; I dreaded the prospect of looking again at the open sea. I had thought, was this how it began for Ellen?

'They want to try and refloat the *Mary Rose* when it's safe,' Barak said. 'Bring in Italian engineers, to recover the guns, at least.' He hesitated. 'The topmasts can be seen above the water at low tide.'

I kept silent. Barak put down his bowl. 'Right,' he said in businesslike tones. 'You know what we're going to do tomorrow.'

'Yes. We go to Portchester Castle and I ask to see the Queen.'

'I've confirmed she's still there, and the King at the tents. You talk to the Queen and then we go home. The horses are still stabled at the inn. We can stop at Hoyland on the way home, if you wish.'

I smiled sadly. 'We have indeed changed places, have we not? It is you who thinks everything out, makes plans for me to implement.'

'Always was that way really, if you ask me.'

I laughed, but it was a hollow sound. My mind kept returning to those images of the *Mary Rose* sinking; sometimes they crowded at me so I could not think. It was Barak who had worked out that to ensure Ellen's safety now I must go to the Queen, tell her Rich's secret.

I said, 'West would have died on the *Mary Rose* whatever happened, wouldn't he?'

'Of course he would,' Barak answered with the sort of irritated patience that was starting to creep into his voice. 'He was a senior officer, wasn't he?'

'Yes. For his death at least I have no responsibility.'

'Nor the others. It was the ship being overloaded with soldiers, the gun ports cut too close to the water, or any one of the other reasons being bruited around. Whatever it was, it wasn't you.'

'I think I will never be the same,' I said quietly. 'This has broken me.'

'You'll see things clearly with time; you always do.'

'I hope so, Jack. I hope so.'

✝

WE SET OUT early the next morning. Yet another hot July day. My heart began thumping as soon as I stepped out of the warehouse.

'Ships all in the same places,' Barak said. 'The French haven't sent the galleys forward yet today.'

I looked out across the Point. The fleet still rode at anchor out on the Solent, in fact more small ships had joined it, but one great ship was missing. Though it set my stomach fluttering with fear, my eyes searched out over the water. 'You can't see the masts from here,' Barak said gently.

'Will they send word to the families of the men who were lost? Leacon's company came from Hertfordshire.'

Barak looked out at the ships. 'They won't be able to send anyone. Returning soldiers will tell the families when this is over.'

'I will tell Leacon's parents at least, go to Kent. Dear God, I owe them that.'

He answered gently, 'Let's get our business done and return to London first.'

We walked towards the inn where Oddleg was stabled. A company of tired-looking soldiers marched past us towards the wharf. I studied their faces, then asked quietly, 'When you were out in the city yesterday, I don't suppose there was any sign of Emma?'

'I asked around, spoke to the soldiers at the gate. No one remembers a brown-haired boy in a torn shirt. I think she's got herself away.'

✝

WE FOUND THE horses and rode out through the town gate: I left Portsmouth for the last time with head bowed, unable to look back. There were new soldiers in the tents where Leacon's company had been encamped. We spurred the horses to a canter, riding north across Portsea Island, and crossed the bridge over the muddy creek to the Hampshire mainland; then left, to Portchester Castle. I kept my gaze away from the seaward side of the road; I could not bear to look out there.

I had no letter now, no authority to get into the castle. I dared not ask for Warner. But faced with the guards by the moat I found my fear and shrinking left me, my lawyer's tricks of speech and manner came back and I told them – truthfully enough – that I was a lawyer who worked for the Queen and had been on the *Mary Rose*. I managed to get the name out, although it brought a fresh churning to my stomach.

I had expected the officer in charge to be impressed, but he only looked at me dubiously. 'What was a lawyer doing on the *Mary Rose*? There's dozens round Portsmouth now saying they're survivors of the sinking. Most are hoping for pensions. If you're a lawyer, where's your robe?'

I lost my temper. 'At the bottom of the Solent! I tell you, I was on that ship; it will haunt me all my days! Now get a message to the Queen, it's urgent. She'll see me. If she won't, you can throw me in the moat for all I care.'

He looked at me doubtfully again, but sent a soldier to take my message in. Barak clapped me on the arm. 'That's better,' he said in relieved tones. 'See, you're getting back to your old self.'

I did not reply. Seeing the soldiers had made me think again of Leacon and the company, the water splashing up around them as they fell and drowned. I gripped Oddleg's reins, saw my knuckles turn white.

✞

HALF AN HOUR later I was shown into a richly furnished chamber. Barak had been ordered to wait in the courtyard. The Queen sat at a desk, writing. As ever, two maids-in-waiting were with her, sewing in a bay window. They rose and bowed. Robert Warner stood beside the desk. He gave me an angry stare as I bowed deeply to the Queen. She got up. I saw she still looked strained and tired.

'The guard told me you were on the *Mary Rose*, Matthew?' she said gently.

'I was, your majesty.' I found I was blinking back tears. At a nod from the Queen, Warner guided me to a chair. Queen Catherine stood, hands folded over her lap, looking down at me.

'What happened?' she asked softly.

I took a deep breath, but for a moment no words came. 'I am sorry, your majesty. I hastened to get here, but – forgive me, I find it hard to speak.' My voice trembled.

'Take your time.' The Queen waved at her ladies. 'Rosamond, bring some wine.'

After a few moments I collected myself. I said, 'I have the answer to what was done to Hugh Curteys. And to poor Michael Calfhill, who was driven to kill himself. And then – I have something to tell you about Sir Richard Rich and the woman I know in the Bedlam. Something dark and secret.'

Warner spoke for the first time. 'If it involves Rich, your majesty, you should be careful. Master Shardlake, is this something safe for the Queen to know?'

I hesitated, then said, 'Perhaps you are right. My judgement of late has been wanting, God knows.'

The Queen smiled, that sudden touch of irrepressible humour. 'No, Matthew, you cannot lead me this far up the path and then abandon me. Tell me everything, and I shall judge what is to be done.'

So I told her the story of my discovery at Hoyland, and Emma's attack on David, though I minimized the extent of David's injuries and did not say that he had killed Abigail. I told of Emma's flight to Portsmouth, my bargain with Rich and the journey to the *Mary Rose*, my imprisonment by West. And the ship rolling over beneath me and sinking. At that my voice faltered again.

After I finished the Queen was silent a full minute. Her shoulders slumped, then rose again with resolution. She asked quietly, 'Have you no idea what has become of Emma Curteys?'

'No. Though she has no money, and left Portsmouth in nothing but a shirt.'

'Rogues!' she burst out, in a fury such as I had never seen before, her colour rising. 'Rogues and villains, to do that to a young girl for money. And as for what Richard Rich did, that is even worse. Well, the girl Emma may be gone but Rich shall not imperil the safety of that poor woman in the Bedlam!'

'What will you do, your majesty?' Warner asked anxiously. 'The King –'

The Queen shook her head. 'I will deal with this.' She stood. 'Sir Richard Rich, I think, is here at Portchester. Have him fetched.'

'But your majesty—'

'Have him fetched,' she repeated, steel in her voice. She turned to the ladies. 'Leave us, this is a privy matter.'

Warner hesitated, then bowed and left, the maids-in-waiting following. The Queen and I were alone. The anger in her brown eyes had changed to concern. I felt tears come to my eyes again.

'The *Mary Rose* – it must have been terrible. The King saw her go down – he was stricken by it. Lady Carew was with him, he comforted her.'

'The soldiers on the aftercastle, it was because of me they were brought there. Barak says if it had not been them it would have been another company, and he is right, but – I keep seeing them, thinking I caused their deaths.'

'That is natural, if wrong.' She smiled again, sadly. 'But words do not help, do they? Only time and prayer can do that.'

'Prayer, your majesty?' I repeated hollowly.

'Yes, prayer.'

'I have lost the art.'

She reached out her hand and laid it on mine. A soft, shapely hand, scented. Then she lifted it abruptly as a knock sounded on the door. She called, 'Enter,' and Warner ushered in Richard Rich, his sharp little head buried in the thick fur collar of his grey robe, gold chain of office round his neck. His hard little eyes swept the room. Then he saw me, his eyes widened and he stepped back. I thought, so Barak was right, you thought me dead. Rich staggered and might have fallen had Warner not grasped his thin little shoulders. Rich looked at the Queen, remembered where he was, and bowed deeply. The Queen stared at him with eyes as hard as his own.

'Sir Richard,' she said grimly, 'I see you believed Master Shardlake dead.'

Rich brought himself under control. 'I heard he was on the *Mary Rose*, your majesty. They said only a few sailors and soldiers survived.'

The Queen spoke quietly, her eyes never leaving Rich's face. 'I know you sent him on board the *Mary Rose*, to be killed by the man

West, who is dead now, and who for all his grievous faults at least tried to protect the life of the woman whose life you helped him ravage.'

Rich gave me a wolfish look. 'I do not know what this man has told you, your majesty, but he is my enemy. He will say aught—'

'I believe what he has said, Sir Richard. It makes sense, given the things I know you are capable of. The killing of the clerk Mylling—'

'He shut himself in that chamber—'

She continued as though he had not spoken. 'Your conspiracy with West to murder Master Shardlake, your allowing Emma Curteys to go on the *Mary Rose*, knowing who she was, I know everything, all the way back to the time you stole the King's letter to Anne Boleyn and took it to Catherine of Aragon –'

Rich licked his thin lips. He pointed at me. 'Nothing of this can be proved. West is dead—'

'His mother lives. She could testify that letter was stolen; there are not many left who were at court nineteen years ago, but there may be some who will remember you going with West. I could soon start an enquiry. And the King will certainly remember that letter—'

Rich's eye began twitching. 'Bring me a bible, your majesty. I will swear on it before you—'

'When did you sell your soul to the devil?' the Queen asked quietly.

Rich reddened, opened his mouth, then closed it hard, his pointed little chin jutting but the tic under his eye twitching again. The Queen said, 'Listen to me, Richard Rich. The woman Ellen Fettiplace, and Master West's mother, are now under my personal protection. As West is dead, I shall pay Ellen's fees at the Bedlam myself so long as she chooses to stay there. If anything happens to her, or to Matthew, I promise you on my oath – and *my* oath is not made lightly – I shall tell the King all you have done, starting with your theft of that letter, which gave Catherine of Aragon notice he intended to divorce her.'

Rich said nothing. The Queen's face flushed with anger.

'Do you understand? Answer your Queen, churl!'

He said, very quietly, 'I understand, your majesty.'

'One thing more,' I added. My voice sounded thick from the hatred I felt for Rich. 'There is a will, that he tricked me into making. He has a copy. It must be destroyed.'

The Queen turned to Warner. 'Robert, Master Rich will bring the copy to you within the hour. You will personally destroy it.'

Rich looked at the Queen with hunted, twitching eyes. She stared him down. 'I will bring it,' he said.

'Good. Then get out of my sight. And stay out of it.'

Rich bowed, then began walking backwards out of the room. From the doorway he gave me a look. It told me plainly that if ever I found myself at his mercy again, I would die, slowly and painfully, while he watched.

As the door closed behind him I drew a deep breath. Warner, too, visibly relaxed. The Queen alone still stared angrily at the closed door.

✝

WARNER TOOK Barak and me to the gate of Portchester Castle. He had not spoken, but as we parted he said quietly, 'Regarding Sir Quintin Priddis and his son, the Queen may want to act against them, but I shall argue against it. It would make these matters public and do no good to the Court of Wards. The King much values the profits it brings, and I do not want the Queen arguing with him.'

'I understand,' I said.

He took a deep breath. 'And after this I feel it might be safer if the Queen did not instruct you in any more cases.'

I nodded. 'Given where this one led?'

He spoke quietly. 'If you love her, as I do, you will leave her in peace now.'

'I agree, Master Warner. And I am sorry again that I accused you.'

He nodded, then reached out a hand. 'Goodbye, Matthew,' he said.

'Goodbye, Robert, and thank you.' I hesitated, 'Beware of Richard Rich. I fear I have made him into the Queen's enemy.'

'I will.'

Barak and I rode across the bridge over the moat. My eyes turned to the sea, then flickered away. I drew a deep breath.

'To Hoyland,' I said. 'Then home.'

We turned and rode away from Portchester Castle, away from the sea.

Chapter Fifty

TWO HOURS LATER we rode again down the narrow lane to Hoyland Priory. We passed through the gate and faced the house. Poor Abigail's flowers had mostly died and the grass on the once neat lawns was starting to grow high. The windows were shuttered. I saw the butts by the nuns' graveyard had gone.

I had been relieved to turn inland, but now, as we rode towards the porch, the gentle motion of the horse seemed all at once like a heaving deck. I grasped the reins, pulled Oddleg to a halt, and closed my eyes, breathing heavily.

'All right?' Barak asked anxiously.

'Yes. Just give me a moment.'

'There's Dyrick.'

I opened my eyes. Dyrick had come out onto the steps. He stood there in his black robe, frowning at us. The sight restored me; I would not let that man see my weakness. Dyrick called over his shoulder into the hall, and a boy ran out to take the horses.

'You're back at last,' Dyrick said in his grating voice as we approached. 'It's been four days. Master Hobbey has been out of his mind with worry. Where is Emma? Did you find her?'

I had to smile at how, even now, he had to be argumentative. Yet I could see he had been mightily worried; fearing no doubt that what the Hobbeys had done to Emma might have been discovered.

'I found her, Dyrick. But she would not return with me. She ran away again, I do not know where she is.'

'We heard of the *Mary Rose* sinking, the attack on the Isle of Wight.'

'The French failed to take it. Though they are still in the Solent.' I had already agreed with Barak to say nothing about being on the *Mary Rose*. There was no point. 'The lawn is starting to look unkempt,' I said.

Dyrick grunted. 'Half the servants have left. Even that old crone Ursula has gone, saying the household's cursed. They've all run back to the village, to try and ingratiate themselves with Ettis. He has been released, by the way. Master Hobbey kept his word.'

'Where is he?'

'In his study. He never leaves it now, save to go to his son.'

'How is David?'

'Recovering, but they think he will never walk properly again. And Jesu knows what is happening in his mind. I fear he may spill out the whole story,' Dyrick added in a pettish tone. 'He needs to be kept somewhere where he can be watched.'

I stared at him. His words reminded me of how West and Rich had protected themselves after Ellen's rape. Nothing like that, I would make sure, would happen to David.

✝

NICHOLAS HOBBEY sat at his desk. When we came in I saw the sad blankness that had been on his face since Abigail's death, then a kind of desperate eagerness. He had, I saw, lost weight.

'Emma! Have you news of her? We have been waiting.' There was an old man's querulousness in his voice now.

'We were detained in Portsmouth. There has been fighting—'

'Yes. They brought the news the *Mary Rose* was lost. But, sir, Emma —'

I took a deep breath. 'I found her, but she ran away again. She has left Portsmouth. I do not know where she is now.'

His face fell. 'Is she still — pretending to be her brother?'

'I think she will continue to do so. That identity is all she has known for years.'

Dyrick said, 'She can't last for long on the road. She took no money.'

'It is possible she may try to join a company somewhere.'

Hobbey groaned. 'Sleeping in hedges, stealing food from gar- dens – '

Dyrick added angrily, 'And any day she could be caught and exposed for who she really is.'

I said, 'Emma is intelligent. She will realize she cannot support herself, that she risks discovery. I think there is a chance at least that she may seek me out.'

'In London?' Hobbey asked.

'I told her I was taking her wardship, that I would leave her to decide what to make of her life.'

'Then pray God she does come to you.' Hobbey sighed, then added, 'I plan to go back to London myself, sell this wretched place and buy a small house, somewhere quiet. It will be easier for David, and I can find better help for his afflictions there.'

'Afflicted he is,' Dyrick said emphatically.

'Do you think I, of all people, do not know that?' Hobbey snapped. He turned back to me. 'I will get a good price for this house and all these woods. Sir Luke Corembeck has expressed an interest.' He turned to Dyrick, with another touch of his old sharpness. 'Make sure of the price, Vincent. I leave the negotiation to you. Whatever we make will be all David and I have to live on in the future, once – once my old debts are paid off. Master Shardlake, will you hold Emma's share if she has not returned by the time Hoyland is sold?'

'I will.'

'We'd get more if we had the village woodlands,' Dyrick grumbled.

'Well, we don't,' Hobbey said. 'Leave tomorrow, Vincent, get the negotiations moving from London. I am sick of the sight of you,' he added. Dyrick's face darkened. Hobbey turned to me. 'Master

Shardlake, I want you, if you will, to see David. To reassure him you plan to say nothing of what happened to his mother.'

I nodded agreement. I still felt the responsibility of keeping that secret; I needed to see how David was.

✟

HOBBEY AND I ascended the stairs. He walked slowly, clinging to the banister. 'Before we see David, Master Shardlake, there is something I wanted to ask you.'

'Yes?'

'I hope you are right and that Emma may come to you in London. But if she is exposed, do you think she will tell – ' he winced, gripping the banister – 'that David killed his mother? I believe she guessed it was him.' He stared at me intently. His first concern was still his son.

'I doubt it. From what she said in Portsmouth she feels a deep guilt for what she did to David.'

Hobbey took another step, then stopped again and looked me in the face. 'What was I doing?' he asked. 'What were we thinking of, all those years?'

'I do not believe any of you were thinking clearly, not for a long time. You were all too afraid. Except for Fulstowe, who was out to get what he could from the situation.'

Hobbey looked around the great hall, the culmination of all his ambition. 'And I was blind to how my son was becoming – deranged. I blame myself for what he did.' He sighed. 'Well, it is all over now. Dyrick tries to talk me out of leaving, but my mind is made up.'

He led me into David's room. It had a good four-poster bed, chairs and cushions, and an old tapestry on the wall showing a battle from Roman times. No books, unlike Hugh's room. David lay in the bed; he had been looking up at the ceiling, but when we came in he struggled to rise. Hobbey raised a hand.

'No, no. You will pull at your bandages.'

David fixed me with a frightened gaze. Lying there he looked like a trapped, terrified little boy, the stubble on his cheeks making him seem all the more pathetic.

'How do you fare, David?' I asked gently.

'It hurts,' he said. 'The doctor stitched me up.'

Hobbey said, 'David was brave. He did not cry out once, did you, my son?' He took a deep breath. 'Master Shardlake has come to tell you he will say nothing of what happened to your mother.'

Tears welled up in David's eyes. 'I think I was mad, sir. I shot at you and then I killed my poor mother. I seemed able to think of nothing else but shooting at people, all the time. I had to keep our secret, keep Emma with us. Even if I had to kill – ' He had been talking fast, almost gabbling, but suddenly he paused, looked at me, and asked in a passionate voice, 'Sir, can God ever forgive such a sin as I have committed?'

I looked into his wild eyes. 'I am no cleric, David, but if someone truly repents, they say He will forgive even the greatest sin.'

'I pray ceaselessly, sir,' he said through his tears. 'For forgiveness and for my mother.'

'That is all you can do, David,' his father said, going forward and taking his hand. His words reminded me of what Catherine Parr had said to me a few hours ago. I looked down at the floor.

'What news of Emma?' David asked tremulously.

'Master Shardlake saw her in Portsmouth. She is truly sorry for what she did to you.'

'I deserved it,' David said. He looked at me, and I saw that even now he loved her. I shuddered to think of what had gone on in his mind these last six years, warping it utterly. 'Where is she now?' he asked.

Hobbey hesitated. 'We are not sure. But we believe her safe.'

'Will I see her again?'

'I do not think so, David. If she goes to anyone it will be Master Shardlake.'

David looked at me again. 'I loved her, you see, I loved Emma all these years.' I nodded. 'I never thought of her as Hugh. That was why, when I feared we might actually be exposed, I think – I think the devil took hold of me. But I loved her. I loved my poor mother too, I realized as soon as I had – I had killed her.' He burst out sobbing, tears streaming down his face.

Hobbey hung his head.

'I wonder – ' I said. Hobbey looked at me. I hesitated, for I had brought enough nightmare cases to Guy. Yet he thrived on the most difficult patients, perhaps he even needed something like this now. And it would be a way for me to keep an eye on the Hobbeys. I said, 'If you come to London, I know a physician, a good man. He may be able to help David.'

Hobbey said eagerly, 'Might he help him walk again?'

'I cannot promise that.'

'I do not deserve to,' David burst out passionately.

I said, though again only to comfort the poor creature, 'Leave that to God.'

✝

AN HOUR LATER Barak and I rode out of Hoyland Priory for the last time and turned on to the London road. Before I left I had done one more thing; I went into Emma's room and took the little cross from where it still lay in the drawer by the bed.

'Home,' Barak said. 'Home at last. To see my son born.' I looked at him, noticing the paunch he had begun to carry in London was gone. He followed my gaze. 'Soon have the weight back on,' he said cheerfully. 'Rest and some good beer, that'll do it.'

Yet there was a delay. We passed the turning for Rolfswood, and I had looked up the road to Sussex between the steep banks. Then a couple of miles further on we found three soldiers standing across the road, blocking it. They told us that up the road a bridge had collapsed and was being repaired. It was late in the afternoon, and the soldiers told us we would have to find somewhere to stay for the night.

Barak was angry. 'Isn't there any way we can get past? There's only two of us and my wife in London has a baby due soon.'

'Nobody goes across till the repair's completed. There are soldiers and supplies waiting to go to Portsmouth.'

Barak looked ready to argue, but I said, 'Let us make a virtue of necessity, Jack, and go to Rolfswood.'

He turned away from the soldier's stare. 'Come on, then,' he muttered, waiting till we were out of their hearing to follow the comment with a string of oaths.

✝

ROLFSWOOD was quiet again, peaceful in the summer evening. We passed Buttress's house. 'What will you do about that rogue?' Barak asked.

'As with Priddis, I doubt there is anything I can do. If I try to raise the issue of whether he and Priddis got together to forge Ellen's signature, it just opens up the story of the rape. And I do not think that would be in anyone's interest now.'

'At least Rich has had his wings clipped.'

'A little. And we can leave West's mother to believe her son died a hero.'

'I wonder what the inquest on poor Master Fettiplace will decide.'

'Murder by persons unknown, I am sure. Let us leave it there.'

We rode on to the inn, where we found a place for the night. We ate dinner, then I left Barak alone, for I had a visit to make.

✝

THE VICARAGE looked as tumbledown as ever, the gnarled cherry tree in full leaf in the unkempt garden. Reverend Seckford answered my knock. He looked sober for once, though there was a beer stain on his surplice. He invited me in. I told him the whole story, about West and Ellen, and David and Emma, and the men I had seen die on the *Mary Rose*.

It was dark by the time I concluded; Seckford had lit candles in his parlour. He had prevailed on me to share a jug of beer; I had drunk one mug to his three. When I finished the story he sat with bowed head, plump hands trembling on his lap. Then he looked up. 'This King has had three wars against France, and lost all of them. All for his own glory. You know, the Church has a doctrine called just war. St Thomas Aquinas wrote on it, though the doctrine is much older than that. A State going to war must have tried all other options, must have justice on its side and have an honourable purpose in mind. None of Henry's wars has been like that. Though he claims to be God's representative on earth.'

'Which wars do have justice on their side, Master Seckford?'

He raised his cup to his lips with a shaking hand. 'Some, perhaps. But not this King's.' He spoke with sudden anger. 'Blame him, blame him for the men dead on the *Mary Rose*, the soldiers and the women and children in France. And even for Philip West, may his sins be forgiven.'

'I keep seeing my friend's face, all the other soldiers, I see them crashing into the water. Over and again.' I smiled wryly. 'A woman I admire greatly tells me to seek refuge in prayer.'

'You should.'

I burst out, 'How can God allow such things to happen? How? I think of that ship going down, of the savagery Reformers and Catholics show to each other, of Emma and Hobbey and David and sometimes – forgive me, but sometimes I think God only laughs at us.'

Seckford put down his cup. 'I understand how people can think like that nowadays. And if God were all powerful, perhaps you would be right. But the Gospels tell a different story. The Cross, you see. For myself I think Christ suffers with us.'

'What is the good of that, Reverend Seckford? How does that help?'

'The age of miracles is long gone. See – ' He picked up his mug again. 'He cannot even stop me drinking, though I would like Him to.'

'Why?' I asked. 'Why can he not?'

He smiled sadly. 'I do not know, I am only a drunken old country priest. But I have faith. It is the only way to live with the mystery.'

I shook my head. 'Faith is beyond me now.'

Seckford smiled. 'You do not like mysteries, do you? You like to solve them. As you have solved the mystery of Ellen.'

'At such cost.'

He looked at me. 'You will take care of her?'

'I will do all I can.'

'And that poor girl Emma, and the wreckage of that Hobbey family?'

'So far as possible.'

Seckford leaned forward, placed his trembling hand on my arm. '"Faith, Hope and Charity,"' he quoted. '"But the greatest of these is charity."'

'That is an old-fashioned doctrine nowadays.'

'The best, nonetheless, Master Shardlake. Remember me to Ellen when you see her. And tonight I shall light candles in the church for your friend George Leacon and his men. I shall make it a blaze of colour for them.'

He laid a shaking hand on mine. But I found it poor comfort.

Chapter Fifty-one

Barak and I arrived back in London five days later, on the afternoon of the 27th of July. We had been away almost a month. We had returned the horses at Kingston and made the final leg of the journey, like the first, by boat. Even the tidal swell of the river made me feel uneasy, though I tried to hide it.

We walked up through Temple Gardens. Dyrick would be back in his chambers soon; if Emma appeared I would have to liaise with him to get Hugh's — as the court supposed Emma to be — wardship transferred to me. But if she were never seen again I could do nothing.

Fleet Street and the Strand presented the same aspect as when we had left; groups of corner boys in blue robes boldly scrutinizing passers-by; posters pasted to the buildings warning of French spies. The boatman had told us more soldiers were being sent south; the French were still in the Solent.

Barak invited me to come to his house to see Tamasin, but I knew he would rather greet her alone so I said I must go to my chambers. We parted at the bottom of Chancery Lane. He promised to be in chambers the following morning. I walked on, turning in at Lincoln's Inn gate. I wanted to see how things fared there, and also to consider how I would tackle Coldiron when I returned home.

✟

GATEHOUSE COURT was hot, dusty-smelling in the summer sun. Barristers and clerks walked to and fro within the square of red brick buildings. Here there was no sign of war. I felt myself relax at the old familiar scene as I walked to my chambers. I had sent Skelly a note from Esher saying I would shortly be back, and he rose to greet me with a smile.

'Are you well, sir?' From the hesitation in his voice I could tell the strain of what I had been through showed on my face.

'Well enough. And you? Your wife and children?'

'We are all in good health, thanks be to God.'

'Everything well here?'

'Yes, sir. A few new cases are in, to come on in the new term.'

'Good.' I sighed. 'I want to encourage some new work.'

'We heard about the French trying to invade the Isle of Wight, the loss of the *Mary Rose* in front of the King himself. They're sending another fifteen hundred men down from London – '

'Yes, the road to Portsmouth was busy with men and supplies on our way back.'

'Nobody seems to know what will happen next. The ship *Hedgehog* blew up in the Thames the same day the *Mary Rose* sank; some say she was blown up by French spies, though others blame the stock of gunpowder she carried not being supervised properly – '

'I would guess that is more likely. Were many killed?'

'A good many. Sir, are you all right?' He darted forward as I grasped at a corner of a table, for the floor had seemed to shift beneath my feet.

'Tired, that is all. It has been a long journey. Now, are those new papers in my office? I should look at them.'

'Sir – ' Skelly asked.

I answered impatiently, 'Yes?'

'How is Jack? Is there any news of his wife? I think his baby is due soon.'

I smiled. 'Jack is well, Tamasin too I believe. I left him going to her.'

I went into my office, shut the door, and leaned against it. Sweating, I waited for the feeling that the ground was moving to stop.

✝

I LOOKED OVER the new papers, then turned my mind to the subject of Coldiron and Josephine. I was still considering how to tackle him when there was a knock at the door. Skelly came in and closed it.

'Sir, there's a young man to see you. He called two days ago, asking for you. He says he knows you from a place called Hoyland. Though he—'

I sat bolt upright. 'Show him in,' I said, trying to keep the excitement and relief from my voice. 'Now.'

I sat behind my desk, my heart beating fast. But it was not Emma that Skelly ushered in, it was Sam Feaveryear. He stood before me, brushing a lock of greasy hair from his forehead in that familiar gesture. I fought down my disappointment.

'Well, Feaveryear,' I said heavily, 'have you brought a message from your master?'

He hesitated, then said, 'No, sir. I have decided — I will work for Master Dyrick no more.'

I raised my eyebrows. Feaveryear said, in a sudden rush of words, 'I did wrong, sir. I found something out at Hoyland. I let Master Dyrick send me away, but I should have told you. It has been on my conscience ever since. Hugh was really—'

'I know already. Emma Curteys.'

Feaveryear took a deep breath. 'When I met Hugh there was something — something that attracted me to him.' He began twisting his thin hands together. 'I thought — I thought the devil was tempting me to a great sin. I prayed for guidance, but I could not stop how I felt. He did not like me looking at him, but I could not help myself. Then one day, I realized—'

'And told Dyrick.'

'I thought he would do something for — for the girl. But he said the matter was his client's secret and must be protected, and sent me away. I thought, I prayed, and I realized — it cannot be right, sir, what has happened to her.'

I spoke sharply. 'The family made her impersonate her dead

brother for years, for gain. Now she has run away, and nobody knows where she is.'

'Oh, sir.' He gulped. 'May I sit down?'

I waved him to a stool. He collapsed onto it, the picture of misery.

'Do you know,' I asked, 'what happened to Abigail Hobbey?'

'Yes,' he replied in a small voice. 'My master wrote. He said the man Ettis had been arrested for her murder.'

'He has been released. It was not him.' I leaned forward and said angrily, 'Why did you not tell anyone about Hugh?'

'I could not be disloyal to my master. But I have been thinking and praying, and when Master Dyrick wrote saying he was return, ing tomorrow I realized – ' Feaveryear looked at me with pleading intensity. 'He is not a good man, is he?'

I shrugged.

'I – I wonder, sir, whether perhaps I could come and work for you. You are known as a good lawyer, sir, a champion of the poor.'

I looked at Feaveryear's miserable face. I wondered how far his coming to me had been motivated by conscience, how much by the desire to get an alternative post. I could not tell.

'Feaveryear,' I said quietly, 'I have no room for another clerk. My advice to you is to seek work from some crusty old cynic of a lawyer, who will take whatever work he is given and not fall prey to the illusion that whoever he acts for must always be in the right. An illusion, I regret, I have sometimes had too. Then, perhaps, without someone's shadow to hide behind, you will grow up at last.'

He lowered his head, looked disappointed. I said more gently, 'I will see if I can find such a lawyer who might need a clerk.'

He looked up, sudden resolution on his face. 'I will not work for Master Dyrick again. Whatever happens, I will not go back to him.'

I smiled. 'Then there is hope for you, Feaveryear. I will see what I can do.'

✝

SOON AFTER I left and walked the short distance to my house. I let myself in and stood in the hall. I heard the boys' voices from the kitchen. I remembered Joan and felt a deep pang of sadness. Then I became aware of someone looking at me from the top of the stairs. I stared up at Coldiron. He began descending with his light step, his eye alight with curiosity. 'Sir,' he said, 'welcome back. Did you see anything at Portsmouth? I heard there was a battle, the French seen off in front of the King himself.'

I did not reply. He came to the foot of the stairs and stopped. He looked at me uncertainly, sensing something. He said, 'They're sending more men out of London. Young Simon still wants to join up if the war goes on.'

'Over my dead body,' I answered quietly. 'Where is Dr Malton?'

'In the parlour. I—'

'Join us in fifteen minutes.' I turned away, leaving him uneasy.

✝

IN THE PARLOUR Guy sat reading. He looked up at me in delighted surprise, got to his feet and came over, grasping me by the arms. I was pleased to see he seemed more like his old self, the weary sadness less marked in his brown face.

'You are back at last,' he said. 'But you look tired.'

'I have seen terrible things, Guy, worse than you can believe. I will tell you later.'

He frowned. 'Is Jack all right?'

'Yes. He has been a rock these past weeks. He has gone on to Tamasin. How is she?'

He smiled. 'Large, and tired, and irritated. But everything goes well. About ten days now till she is due, I would say.'

'And you?'

'I feel better than for a long time. You know, my energy seems to be returning. I want to go back to my house, start practising again. And if the corner boys return – well, it is in God's hands.'

'I am heartily glad.'

'You know what has helped me? Keeping Coldiron in order. By Jesu, he was an insolent rogue that first week. But I did not let him get away with his tricks. I called him out for his insolence, as I said in my letter. Then he was quiet and obedient for a while, but last week he got angry with Josephine again—'

'You said.'

'He set about her with a ladle. I took it off him.'

'Good. I have asked him to come in here shortly. But first I have something to tell you about him, something I did not trust to a letter in case the rogue opened it.'

I related what the soldier in Portsmouth had told me about Josephine's origin, and Coldiron's desertion after stealing his company's funds. 'He is a wanted man,' I concluded.

'It does not surprise me,' Guy said quietly. 'What are you going to do?'

I answered grimly, 'You will see.'

A few minutes later there was a knock and Coldiron entered. He took up a military stance in the middle of the floor. I said, 'Well, Coldiron. Or, I should say, William Pile.'

He did not move, but his stance stiffened.

'I met an old comrade of yours in Portsmouth. Someone you used to play cards with. One John Saddler.'

Coldiron took a deep breath. 'I remember Saddler. A dishonourable fellow. Soldiers with a grievance tell lies readily, sir.'

'He was at Flodden with you, when you were a purser in the rear. He remembered how later you took Josephine from France when she was a small girl.'

He gulped, his Adam's apple moving up and down in his stringy throat. His voice rose. 'Lies,' he said. 'Lies and slander – yes, slander. I rescued Jojo from a burning French village, I saved her life.'

'No, you didn't. You took her like a chattel when you decided to desert, having stolen your company's money. A hanging offence.'

'It's all lies!' Coldiron shouted. He swallowed, brought himself under control. His voice turned wheedling. 'Why would you believe Saddler, sir? A vicious liar. Old soldiers never get any justice,' he added pathetically.

'Easy enough to make enquiries. Then you will get the justice you deserve.'

His face took on a hunted look. 'Does Josephine know who she really is?' I asked sharply.

'She remembers the burning village, her life in camp. She knows I gave her a life, a place in the world. I rescued her, I'm all she has. I treated her as my daughter.'

'Guy,' I said, 'would you do me a small favour? Go and fetch Josephine.'

Coldiron turned to him as he went to the door. 'Sir,' he said pleadingly, 'you don't believe these lies?'

Guy did not answer. When he had gone Coldiron and I stood facing each other. He licked his lips. 'Sir, please don't report this. If it came to a trial they might believe Saddler's lies.'

'They will be able to check what he says with the company records. Then we will have the truth.'

'Just let Josephine and me go,' he said pleadingly. 'We'll leave, as soon as you like. Though I'm an old man, injured in the King's service—'

'Injured when you were caught cheating at cards, I heard.'

His face twisted with anger for a moment, but he said no more. The door opened again and Guy came in. Josephine trailed after him, looking afraid.

'Sir,' she said at once. 'Have I done something wrong? Father—'

'Shut your face, Jojo,' Coldiron told her warningly. 'Keep quiet.'

I said, 'Josephine, you are not in trouble. But I know William Coldiron is not your father. Coldiron is not even his real name.'

Josephine had been shifting nervously from foot to foot but now she became very still, her face watchful, eyes narrowed. And I realized her stupidity and clumsiness were largely an act. A part she had grown used to playing for Coldiron over the years, as Emma Curteys had learned to play the part of her brother. No doubt that was how Coldiron liked her to be – silly, clumsy, dependent.

'When I was in Portsmouth,' I continued. 'I learned some things about Master Coldiron. How he really got his injury—'

'It was at Flodden, sir,' she said.

'Lies. And he deserted from his company years later, when he took you.'

She looked at Guy. He nodded. She turned to Coldiron. 'You said you had to leave, Father, the men were going to do bad things to me and you wanted to protect me—'

'I said shut up,' Coldiron hissed, 'you stupid clumsy French mare.'

She stopped speaking at once. 'I am going to let you go, Coldiron,' I said. 'I will not report your crimes – I would not have your disgrace visited on Josephine. Go now. But you, Josephine, I would like you to stay and work for me. If you want to.'

Her lip trembled. 'But sir, you know – Dr Malton knows – how useless I am.'

'You are,' Coldiron said hotly. 'You need me to look after you, stop you messing everything up.'

I turned to her. 'That is not true.'

'We will look after you, Josephine,' Guy said gently. She looked between us, then her face crumpled and she raised her hands to her face, sobbing. Guy walked over and patted her shoulder.

'Leave her alone, you brown shit!' Coldiron shouted out. 'And you, you crookback bastard! You've always been against me; you hate soldiers, any real men, that aren't weaklings and cripples and cowards—'

Suddenly I lost all reason. I ran at him. Coldiron jerked away in surprise as I grasped him by the shoulders, turned him round and marched him into the hall. Simon and Timothy had heard the raised voices and were standing in the kitchen doorway, open-mouthed.

'Tim!' I shouted. 'Open the door!'

Coldiron howled, 'No, not in front of the boys! No!' He struggled as Timothy ran and threw open the door. I propelled Coldiron through it. He went flying, landing face down on the ground at the bottom of the steps. He howled like a stuck pig, then turned and stared up at me. As I slammed the door in his face the best thing was that just behind me Coldiron saw Simon and Timothy laughing and clapping their hands.

Chapter Fifty-two

I RETURNED TO the parlour. Josephine sat at the table, calmer now, Guy beside her. She looked up at me, a direct look rather than her usual averted gaze. 'Is he gone, sir?' she asked tremulously.

I breathed hard. My shoulders were hurting now. 'Yes, he is.'

Guy asked gently, 'Do you remember your last name, Josephine, from when you were small?'

'No.' She bowed her head. 'But I remember the village, the house burning.' She looked up at me. 'I remember some of the soldiers in the camp were kind. But then he took me away.' Then she gave a deep sigh. 'How will I manage without him?'

Guy said, 'Do you wish to? You could still follow him.'

'But I am nobody, nothing.'

'We do not think so, or we would not have asked you to stay.'

Josephine jumped violently as a loud knocking sounded at the front door. She grabbed Guy's hand. 'He has come back! Sir, he will be angry, help me please – '

I strode out and opened the door. Simon and Timothy were still standing beside it, their faces gleeful. I threw it open. Coldiron stood on the step. He quailed for a moment at my expression, then said, 'My things, sir. The money in my chest, my clothes, my little mementos – you can't keep them!' His voice rose to a shout. 'It's not legal! And I'm due wages! Keep Jojo, keep her, but I want my wages!'

I turned to the boys. 'Go to Coldiron's room, put everything in his chest, bring it down and put it outside. No need to be too careful in packing it.' Coldiron had stepped forward, he was trying to get back in, but I slammed the door in his face once more.

'Yes, sir!' Timothy ran quickly away up the stairs. I thought, I am setting a bad example to these boys. As Simon turned to follow I put a hand on his shoulder. 'Wait,' I said.

'Yes, sir?'

I looked into the thin face beneath the untidy blond hair. He was as tall as me now. I asked quietly, 'Do you still want to be a soldier?'

He hesitated, then said, 'After you left, sir, I came to realize – Master Coldiron told many lies, didn't he?'

'Yes, he did. But Simon, if you still think of going for a soldier, come to me first, and I will see if I can find some men who have done real fighting for you to talk to. Then if you still want to do it I will not stand in your way.'

'Sir, I was thinking. Before you left, you spoke of helping me to an apprenticeship – '

I smiled. 'Yes. I will, if that is what you want.'

He looked round. Guy and Josephine were standing in the parlour doorway. Josephine was trembling and her face was streaked with tears. She had heard Coldiron saying we could keep her. Simon looked at her, then back at me, a blush coming to his face. 'Is Josephine staying?' he asked.

'Well, Josephine?' I asked quietly.

She answered, tremblingly, 'Yes, Simon. I am staying.'

Shortly after the boys bumped and banged Coldiron's little chest down the stairs. I opened the door. He was sitting morosely on the steps. I watched him drag the chest out through my gate and off down Chancery Lane. My last sight of him was when he turned and shook a skinny fist at me.

✝

EVENING WAS drawing on. I stood in the parlour, looking out at the garden. Guy had been with Josephine in the kitchen, easing her back into her life, getting her to prepare dinner with the boys. He came back looking thoughtful. I smiled. 'I will need a new steward now. How would you like the job?'

He raised his eyebrows. 'I think going back to medicine may be easier.' He hesitated, then said with unexpected diffidence, 'I thought of returning to my house next week.'

'I will get the boys to clean it out first. They and Josephine.' I looked at him seriously. 'Will she be able to manage without Coldiron?'

'It will not be easy. If you could get some kindly decent old fellow to take Coldiron's place, that might help, give her a sense of order. She will need that, for a time at least. And you need a man in charge of the household, otherwise there may be gossip about you and her.'

I nodded, smiling. 'I think young Simon is the one with an interest there.'

'I have noticed that. I think you should tell him she needs help, but peace and quiet too. He is a good lad, I think he will understand.'

I sat down. I was silent a minute, then said, 'Well, I have seen to Coldiron. But there is something else I have to deal with.'

'Ellen?'

'While I was away I discovered what happened to her. She was raped. One of the men involved is dead, the other now in a position where he can do her no harm. And the Queen is taking over payment of her fees.'

He gave me a long, steady look. 'What happened in Hampshire, Matthew?'

'It is a long story. I may have a new patient for you if you want him, by the way, a sad unhappy boy, badly injured by an arrow.' I looked at Guy. 'He did a terrible thing, it preys much on him. He is — well, he is very sick in his mind. But he was injured trying to save my life, and Barak's.'

'Is it Hugh Curteys?'

'No. His name is David Hobbey. Guy, I will tell you everything, but first I must go to the Bedlam, tell Ellen she is safe. And free.'

'Be careful with her, Matthew. And I am not sure she can ever be free.'

'Before I had only questions for her, now I have answers. It must be me who does this.'

'You know she has been in love with you.'

'Then I owe it to her to make clear, at last, that there is no hope for us there.'

✠

I FETCHED Genesis from the stables and rode across to the Bedlam. Hob Gebons opened the door to me. His heavy face fell. 'You're back.'

'Yes. And I would like to talk to Keeper Shawms.' I lowered my voice. 'I know everything about Ellen now, Hob.'

The keeper was in his office. I sat down without asking. Shawms stared at me, a calculating look on his fat, stubbly face. He had on the same stained jerkin he was wearing when I had left. I wondered, where does he spend all the money he gets?

He grunted. 'Metwys has been to see me.'

'Let me guess what he said. Ellen is now under the protection of the Queen, who will meet her fees from now on.'

He nodded. 'That's right. How d'you swing that?'

'By finding the truth about who raped Ellen nineteen years ago. It was the one who paid her fees, Philip West. He is dead. Another man was involved, but he can do her no harm now she has the protection of Queen Catherine. Did Metwys tell you who he is?'

'No. And I don't want to know. Will Ellen leave now?' he asked. 'I don't mind, she can go when she likes if the Queen wishes. There's no —'

'No order of lunacy, nor ever was. I know that too. Beatrice West must have paid the warden well to take her in, all those years ago. Arranged by Sir Quintin Priddis I have no doubt. You would like her out of your hair now, I dare say. Well, I would like her to leave too, but I doubt she will.' I leaned forward. 'Make sure that she is well treated, and pay her, too, for the work she does, or I will ensure the Queen hears about it.'

He looked at me, shook his head. 'You're a persistent devil, aren't you?'

'Yes.' I stood. 'And now, where is she?'

'In her room. Look, I don't want you upsetting her again. That doesn't do anyone any good.'

'She needs to know where she stands. Goodbye, Master Shawms.'

✞

I LOOKED THROUGH the bars of Ellen's door. She was sitting on her bed, quietly sewing. Her expression was sad, but composed. I remembered the terror in her face the last time I had seen her. I would not bring her to that again, I swore.

I knocked and went in. She looked up. Her face went hard and cold.

'Good day, Ellen,' I said.

'You have returned,' she answered evenly.

'Yes. This morning. Have you been well treated while I was away?'

'Yes. Gebons has been unusually friendly. I wondered if you had paid him to be.'

'I wanted to see you were not mistreated while I was away.' She did not reply. I asked, 'Has Master Shawms said anything to you?'

'No.' She looked apprehensive. 'About what?'

I drew a deep breath. 'Ellen,' I said gently, 'I do not want to rake over the past again.' A tense watchfulness came into her face. I continued, 'But I have been to Sussex. You are safe now from those men.' I had decided to say nothing of the discovery of her father's body. 'The Queen herself has taken responsibility for your fees. And if you ever want to leave here, you can. You are free, Ellen.'

She looked at me, intently, fearfully. 'What has happened to him? To – Philip?'

I hesitated again. She said, 'Tell me!'

'He is dead, Ellen. He went down on the *Mary Rose*.'

She sat very still, staring into space. Then she said, quietly, with cold, whispered anger, 'He deserved it.' It was the same phrase Emma had used standing over Abigail's body, and David about what had happened to him.

'He did a terrible thing to you.'

She looked at me, her expression utterly weary. 'And the man who was with him that day? What of him?'

I hesitated. 'Do you know who he was?'

'I only remember a skinny little fellow.' She shuddered, her whole body trembling. I realized the depth of emotion she had been holding in, all these wasted years.

'He is now a high official of state. It is better you do not know his name. But he can do you no harm now.'

'Because you told the Queen what was done to me?' I heard anger in her voice now.

'It was the only way to protect you.'

She stared into space, hands trembling above her sewing. Then she put her work down, turned and looked me full in the face. 'I was content here,' she said, 'content as ever I could be. You should not have interfered.'

'I have freed you from a great threat.'

She laughed bitterly. 'To do that you should have been at Rolfswood nineteen years ago. You talk as though I cared one whit what happens to me now. I am past that. I did care for a while, when I thought you loved me. I see now that is impossible. Do you know who made me understand that?'

'No.'

'Your friend Guy. Oh, he said nothing directly, but somehow he made me realize. He is clever,' she said bitterly. 'But you let me go on believing there might be hope for two years. You did not have the courage to tell me the truth. You are a coward, Matthew.'

'I could have been killed trying to find out the truth about you!' I burst out.

'I never asked you to!' She took a couple of long, deep breaths, then said in tones of bitter contempt, 'Have you ever loved anyone, I wonder? Can you?'

'We do not choose who we love. I love – ' I checked myself.

'I do not care now,' she answered. She looked away. 'Leave me. I do not want to see you again. I hate you now.' The anger had gone from her voice, only the weariness was left.

'Is that what you really want?' I asked. 'For me never to come back?'

'Yes.' Still she looked away. 'And that is what you want too, in your heart. I see that now. When mad folks are brought to see things they see them very clearly.'

'You are not mad.'

'I said, go.'

She did not meet my gaze as I walked through the door, closed it behind me, and looked at her for the last time through the bars before turning away.

✝

I RODE HOME. My mind was a blank, I could not think, even the sight of a foreign-looking man being chased down Cheapside by a group of whooping corner boys barely registered. I stabled Genesis and walked round to the front of the house. Simon was looking out from an upstairs window. When I opened the door he was running down the stairs towards me.

'Master Shardlake—'

'What has happened? Is Josephine—'

'She is all right, sir. But Mistress Tamasin – her woman came round to fetch Master Guy. Her baby's coming early, she thinks something's wrong – '

I turned away and started running down Chancery Lane, past lawyers who stopped and stared, to Barak's house.

✝

HE OPENED the door. He was dishevelled, wild-eyed, a mug of beer in his hand. From the closed door of the bedroom across the hall I heard screams of pain.

Barak pulled me in. He sank down on the little wooden settle in the hall. I said, 'Is Guy—'

'In there with her. I'd not been back half an hour when her waters broke. It shouldn't have come for near two weeks. The last time the baby came when it was due.'

'Where is Goodwife Marris?'

'In with Guy. They shut the door on me.'

'Here – ' I took the cup of beer from his hand, he was gesticulating so wildly I feared he might spill it. 'What did Guy say?'

'He says it's just early. Goodwife Marris was frightened, she ran for him – '

'Well, second babies can come early, you know that.'

He gave an anguished look at the closed door, from behind which screams still came.

'It only means the baby's coming—'

He said wildly, 'If anything happens to her, I couldn't bear it, I'd take to drink again – she's everything – '

'I know. I know.'

'I don't care if it's a girl – ' He broke off. The screaming had stopped. There was a long, terrifying moment of silence. Then, faintly, we heard another sound, the grizzling cry of a baby. Barak's mouth fell open. The door opened and Guy came out, wiping his hands on a towel. He smiled.

'Jack, you have a fine, healthy son.'

He jumped up, ran over and pumped Guy's hand. 'Thank you! Thank you!' He was panting with relief.

'Thank Tamasin. She did the work. It was easy enough in the end – ' But Barak had rushed past him into the room. I followed more slowly.

Goodwife Marris stood by the bed, holding a tiny form wrapped in swaddling clothes. Barak threw himself on Tamasin.

'Take care, fool,' she said softly. She smiled, stroked his head. 'Go and see your son.'

He went over to the child. Guy and I looked over Goodwife Marris's shoulder. 'He's – he's wonderful,' Barak said. Gently he took one of the baby's tiny hands in his own.

'He is,' I said, though in truth all babies look the same to me, like little old men. But he seemed healthy, screaming at the top of his lungs. I saw he had a fuzz of blond hair like Tamasin's.

Barak turned to Guy, his face momentarily anxious. 'He *is* healthy?'

'As healthy a child as I ever saw.'

Barak looked again at his son. 'Just think,' he said quietly. 'He could live to see a new century. Think of that, think of that.'

'Your John,' Tamasin said quietly from the bed.

Barak thought a moment, looked at me, then said, 'Tammy, do you mind if we give him another name?'

'What?' she asked, surprised.

'Let us call him George,' he answered softly. 'Like our first baby. I'd like to name him George Llewellyn Carswell.' He looked at me. 'To remember them.'

Epilogue

There was a cold wind in the churchyard. The last leaves had fallen and it sent them whirling and whispering around my feet. I pulled my coat tighter round me as I walked towards the church. Winter was come.

I stopped at Joan's grave and placed a last rose from my garden before the headstone. I stood a moment, wondering what she would have thought of the events in my household that summer. I still had no steward; I had interviewed several men, but none had the sensitivity I felt was needed to deal with Josephine. She was much better, but any mistakes she made, any little criticism, set her to dithering clumsiness. Occasionally when I came home from Lincoln's Inn I would see her looking out on the street, with a strange, intent expression. I guessed she was looking out for Coldiron, with what mixture of fear and desire for the security of his presence I did not know.

I had returned to work, grateful now for the routine. But sometimes when I was tired I still had that dreadful sensation of the ground slipping and sliding beneath my feet. I went on to my friend Roger's grave; the autumn rains had brought dirty streaks to the marble. I thought, I must send one of the boys to clean it. Simon would be leaving my house soon, as apprentice to a mercer; I had arranged it with Alderman Carver. I remembered how after Roger's death I had wanted to marry his widow. I had heard nothing from

Dorothy in recent months. Nor had I heard from the Queen, nor Warner; but I had not expected to.

There was a bench outside the old church, and I cleared some leaves from it and sat down. I looked towards the churchyard wall, remembering the muster in Lincoln's Inn Fields back in June. The French had given up their plan to invade England now, their fleet had returned to France, where the siege of Boulogne dragged on; English troops inside the city, the French army outside. All a useless waste of time. Rumour said that the King had, at long last, realized his enterprise against France had failed utterly, and there would be a peace treaty in the New Year.

I looked towards the churchyard gate. This time I had not come here to ponder, but for a meeting, one best held away from the nosiness of Lincoln's Inn. As I watched, the gate opened and a tall, slim figure in a heavy coat and dark cap walked towards me. Emma Curteys still carried herself like a boy, dressed as a boy, looked like a boy. I invited her to sit beside me. She sat quietly for a moment, then turned and looked at me enquiringly. Her scarred face was pale.

'It is done,' I said.

'Were there any difficulties?'

'None, as everyone was agreed. Dyrick was there to confirm Hobbey's approval of the sale of the wardship. And Edward Priddis to approve the valuation. He is Hampshire feodary since his father died in September. Sir William Paulet raised no queries, so it is done.' I smiled uneasily. 'You are my ward now or, rather, Hugh Curteys is.'

She said quietly, 'Thank you.'

Emma had appeared in my chambers back in August. It was as well I was there, for Skelly would have refused entry to the thin, dirty boy who came asking for me. Emma told me she had not wanted to come, but a month penniless on the road, stealing from farmhouses, had worn her down and overcome her pride. I had given her money and found her a room in the city until the application to transfer the wardship could be heard.

I spoke hesitantly. 'Hobbey was there too, in case he was needed. Hoyland Priory has been sold to Sir Luke Corembeck.'

Emma looked at me. 'How is David?'

'He can walk a little now. But he has had more attacks of the falling sickness. Hobbey will not let him out of his sight; my physician friend thinks he protects him too much.' I looked at her. 'He is still sick with guilt and shame.'

'Master Hobbey always had to have people to be in charge of.' Emma paused, then looked at me and said with sudden passion, 'Yet I think constantly of David, what I did. I would put it right if I could.'

'I know.'

'And I think of the soldiers – I dream of them falling into the water, the screams of those trapped men.'

'So do I.' I had never told Emma that but for Rich's machinations it would have been a different company of soldiers on the *Mary Rose*. I would not have her share my unending sense of guilt. I remembered visiting Leacon's parents in Kent, to tell them their son was dead, and offer what financial help I could. The two old people had been lost, broken.

Emma said, 'Thank you, Master Shardlake. I am sorry I did not trust you from the beginning. I did not think anyone could get me away from Hoyland and the Hobbeys, and I had stopped wanting to leave.'

I leaned forward, resting my elbows on my knees, and looked at her. 'Why did you let them do it to you, Emma?'

'At first to save myself from marriage to David. But – when I became a boy, I realized how much more power a male child has in the world. And – ' she hesitated momentarily, then continued – 'in a strange way it was as though wearing his clothes and pretending to be him kept my brother alive. Can you understand that?'

'Perhaps. But later – you could have changed your identity back and claimed your lands. There would have been nothing the Hobbeys could have done.'

She shook her head. 'I had been Hugh for too long by then. There would have been a scandal. And a disfigured young woman, alone, even one with money, has little power. Far less than a man. And I wanted to be a soldier so much.' She laughed mirthlessly. 'What am I, I wonder? Perhaps something new in the world.'

I did not know how to reply. We were silent a few moments, then Emma said, 'I heard they have given up trying to raise the *Mary Rose*. The masts have collapsed, she has settled into the silt. With the remains of all those men, God rest their souls.'

We were silent a moment. Then I asked, 'What will you do? As I have said before, you can do what you like with your life now. That is what I wanted for you. The Court of Wards has permitted me to hold all your money. I have to hold it for three years, but whatever sums you want, just ask. So far as I am concerned it is yours. God knows you deserve it after what it has cost you. I have it safe in the old gold coins, protected from this endless collapse in the value of money.'

Emma shook her head. 'I do not know, Master Shardlake. I like it at my rooms. You know, I thought it might be more difficult to pass as a boy in the city. But no one looks at you twice, it is easy to blend in. Thank you, by the way, for sending me the money to buy those books.'

'You can buy what you like now. You are rich.'

'Yet still I do not know who or what I am. But I do not want to be a woman, to be an obedient, subservient creature, wear those uncomfortable clothes.'

'You should meet Barak's wife, Tamasin, nobody could ever call her subservient. And it is possible for a woman to be independent, if she has money.'

Then Emma sighed, looked away. She said, 'There is a boy who has a room in my house, who I have gone drinking with some evenings. I – I like him. His name is Bernard.' She reddened slightly, her scars showing pale, then added, 'But I fear he might guess the truth, as Sam Feaveryear did. Love,' she said bitterly, 'it is a very dangerous thing.'

'Emma, it would be difficult for you to assume the identity of a woman now, I know. But I have been thinking. Jack's wife Tamasin could help you, show you how a woman dresses and behaves. She is to be trusted with the story, and you would like her, I am sure.'

'Does she not have a new baby?'

'Yes. But she would be glad to help you, I am sure.'

She shook her head. 'I cannot bear the thought of learning how to become a different person. Not again. No matter how good and kind your friend Tamasin is, it would bring back those days when Hobbey and Fulstowe made me learn how to impersonate Hugh. And wearing skirts again would make me feel hopeless, helpless, as I did when my brother died.'

'But now you have money – '

'Even if I wanted to, I do not think I could do it.' She took a deep breath. 'Master Shardlake, I have been thinking of going abroad, perhaps to the Low Countries, away from England. Perhaps even seeing if I can get a place in one of the universities there. I could never be a soldier now, not after what happened.'

'No.'

'You see, I think you were right, perhaps I am a scholar by nature. But there are no women scholars, are there?'

'There are learned women. The Queen herself has written a book, and the Lady Elizabeth – '

Emma shook her head vigorously. 'They have a dispensation, as royalty.'

I thought, then asked, 'Are you running away from your feelings for this boy Bernard?'

Her face worked, the scars pulling. 'I need time, Master Shardlake. I need some occupation. Would you let me go abroad?'

'It is your life. I have interfered too much with people's fates. I will help you, at any time. But you must come to me.'

She stood up. 'Then I will arrange a passage to Flanders. I will write to you from there. To let you know how I fare.'

'You will go, then?'

'Yes.' Emma rose from the bench and extended a long-fingered hand.

I said, 'Emma, there is one thing I have never asked. Do you still wear the heartstone?'

She looked at me, a warmth in her eyes I had never seen, then shook her head. 'No,' she answered quietly. 'I cast it in the Thames. It was part of my old life with the Hobbeys. I wear the cross my mother gave me now, that you took from Hoyland and gave me in August.'

I smiled. 'Good.'

'I wish I could have thanked that good old lady for what she and poor Michael did, but I could not – ' her voice tailed away.

'Practise the deception with her? No. But I have sent word to her that Hugh is safe.'

She said, 'I thank you for everything, Master Shardlake. But I am on my own path now; let it lead where it will.'

I took her hand. The rough calluses formed by the years of archery practice were fading. I watched as Emma Curteys walked back down the path, to all appearances a young gentleman with a firm tread, a fine coat, short brown hair under a black cap. The dead yellow leaves swirled around her feet.

HISTORICAL NOTE

HENRY VIII's French war of 1544–6 was probably the most disastrous policy decision that even he ever made. Henry has sometimes been portrayed as a 'modernizing' monarch, but his attitude to war harked back to medieval times. From the beginning of his reign he wanted the glory of the conquests in France that had garlanded his medieval predecessors. France, however, was now a united and prosperous state, with a far larger population than England's.

Learning nothing from the failure of two previous attempts, in 1544 Henry invaded northern France in a shaky alliance with the Holy Roman Emperor Charles V. The objective was for Henry's and Charles's forces to converge on Paris, but Henry diverted his army to attack Boulogne, which he hoped to link to England's remaining French possession of Calais to form an enlarged English territory. But when, after a long and bloody siege, Henry took Boulogne, his own forces were besieged there by the French army. Charles and the French King, Francis I, made a separate peace and the English forces were to remain bottled up in Boulogne for the next eighteen months, supplied with difficulty from England. Henry now faced the weight of France alone; and in addition France sent troops to its ally Scotland, against which Henry was already waging war.

The war was extraordinarily, ruinously expensive – to pay for it Henry sold off much of the monastic land he had taken from the Church in the 1530s, bled England white with taxation, and even debased the coinage through reducing its silver content, starting an unprecedented spiral of inflation. All sections of society were affected, but it was the poor, who had no power to raise the price of their labour, who suffered most.

In the summer of 1545 the French decided to dispose of the problem by invading England. This was a real and very serious threat; the French gathered a fleet with perhaps three times the number of warships England could command, carrying around 30,000 soldiers. The Pope contributed a ship. The enterprise was larger in scale than the Spanish Armada of forty years later. To meet the threat Henry ordered a massive levy of soldiers from the civilian population. Including militia and naval forces, over 100,000 men were put under arms – as a proportion of the population the equiv-alent of well over a million men today; a proportion of the male population comparable to that mobilized to resist Hitler's threatened invasion in 1940.

Fortunately for England the French were poorly led by their commander, Admiral d'Annebault – like the English, the French always had aristocrats rather than professionals to lead their forces. If d'Annebault had concentrated his resources, it is possible the French could have gained control of the Isle of Wight, or, had they managed to land on Portsea Island, besieged Portsmouth as the English had besieged Boulogne. Large-scale amphibious landings are notoriously difficult, but there would have been, at the very least, serious fighting in southern England.

In the end, however, after the inconclusive Battle of the Solent described in the book, the war simply petered out and most of those levied went home to the harvest – though some were sent to the continuing siege of Boulogne. At the peace treaty of 1546 England was allowed to hold Boulogne – which by then had been reduced to a heap of rubble – for ten years. Henry was also awarded an indemnity that was a drop in the ocean of the vast sums he had wasted.

The war achieved absolutely nothing save the loss of the lives of thousands of soldiers and sailors; English, Scottish, Irish, Welsh,

French, and men from other European nations. To that number must be added many French and Scottish civilians.

Six months after the peace treaty Henry VIII died. He left his children a legacy of isolation in Europe, continuing war with Scotland, religious conflict, inflation, national penury, and incipient social revolt. In the 1550s Boulogne was handed back to France and in 1558 Calais, England's last possession on the continent, was lost.

✝

THE SINKING of the *Mary Rose* as it sailed into battle on 19 July 1545 has attracted many different explanations. It seems certain that the gun ports on the starboard side were not closed when a sudden gust of wind, common in the Solent, caught the sails and caused the turning ship to heel over, allowing water to flood in through them. The ship may also have been seriously overloaded with cannon and soldiers, and top-heavy with men in the high castles. It is also possible she was hit a glancing blow by gunfire from the French galleys and may have been taking in water. Whatever the cause, or combination of causes, the *Mary Rose* sank in minutes, with the vast majority of those aboard trapped under the anti-boarding netting. Their screams were audible from the shore. Around thirty-five people survived out of, it is now estimated, 500.

Henry had dined the previous day on his flagship, the *Great Harry*, and left the ship suddenly when the French fleet was sighted off the eastern end of the Isle of Wight. I have invented his plan to visit the *Mary Rose* afterwards. It is not known where Henry stayed during his 1545 visit to Portsmouth, but the most likely candidates are Portchester Castle and the royal tents erected on Southsea Common. It is also not known where Catherine Parr was in the summer of 1545, but one piece of evidence leads me to think she travelled to Portsmouth with the King. In his dispatch reporting the battle of the Solent, Charles V's ambassador Francis Van der Delft refers to being shown the ships by the Queen's chancellor. Given the structure of the royal household, the only reason her chancellor would have been at Portsmouth is surely if Catherine were there too.

I have invented the presence at Portsmouth of Richard Rich. The records show that he was not among the members of the Privy Council who accompanied Henry there. But his role in the financial organization of the invasion of France in 1544 is accurate, as are his loss of the post and the suspicion that he had been lining his pockets a little too heavily. However he remained on the Privy Council and his career was not affected.

Robert Warner was Queen Catherine Parr's solicitor, and was used by her to defend a relative of one of the Queen's servants accused of heresy in 1544.

✟

IN 1526 Henry VIII and his first wife Catherine of Aragon did go on a summer Progress which took them to Petworth. Henry was by then in correspondence with Anne Boleyn; it was also probably in 1526 that he decided to divorce Catherine and marry Anne. However, the intercepted letter is fictional. It is true, though, that the Pope did later suggest that Catherine of Aragon resolve the problems raised by Henry's desire for a divorce by going into a nunnery, and that she refused because she believed God's wish was for her to stay married to Henry. If she had agreed, paradoxically, Henry's split from Rome would probably never have happened.

✟

THE ABUSE of the Court of Wards as a source of revenue, at great financial (to say nothing of emotional) cost to many of the children involved, was yet another scheme for extracting money from the populace devised by Henry VIII. The abuse of the court continued under Elizabeth I and James I and reached epic proportions under Charles I. Curbing its exploitation of minors was a major demand of Parliament in the years before the Civil War, and its abolition is one of the forgotten achievements of the English Republic of 1649–60.

Such was public feeling that even the corrupt regime of the restored Charles II dared not bring it back.

✝

WHILE THE STORY of Emma Curteys is entirely imaginary, there are numerous accounts stretching back through history of women who impersonated men and fought as soldiers, sometimes for years. For example there were several hundred documented cases on both sides in the American Civil War, where often the women were known as fighters of particular courage.

Acknowledgements

I am very grateful to the many people who have helped and advised me on this book. It took me into areas – particularly on the military and naval side – where my knowledge was sparse. I hope the finished product does at least some justice to the expertise of those who advised me; any errors are, of course, mine.

My agent Antony Topping first came up with the idea of a book set around the war of 1544–6. I am very grateful to him, once again, for his encouragement, and for reading and commenting on the manuscript. Thanks also to Maria Rejt for another marvellously skilled job of editing, to Liz Cowen for her painstaking copy-editing, and to Becky Smith for her typing. Michael Holmes advised me on naval aspects from the beginning, chauffeured me on visits to Portsmouth, and also read the first draft of the book, as did Roz Brody, Jan King and William Shaw. Once again, I am so grateful for all their shrewd insights. James Willoughby kindly translated the Court of Wards motto for me. Glennan Carnie of the English Warbow Society (www.englishwarbowsociey.com) was very helpful on everything connected with archery – again, any mistakes are mine. Robyn Young kindly commented on the chapter dealing with the hunt at Hoyland Priory.

There is a huge amount of archaeological evidence about the warship *Mary Rose*, though documentary evidence about the sinking is rather thin. When it sank, one side was preserved in the silt at the bottom of the Solent; this was raised from the seabed in 1982. The divers also discovered, and have been bringing up ever since, hundreds of items ranging from cannon and longbows to clothing, shoes, and the personal possessions of those on board, as well as the remains of many of the unfortunate crew.

I am very grateful to those at the Mary Rose Trust, where these items are preserved and displayed in Portsmouth, for taking time out to read the manuscript in draft, and for their comments and advice. My warm thanks to Rear-Admiral John Lippiett, Sally Tyrrell, Alex Hildred and Christopher Dobbs for all their help. I have made every effort to ensure that my portrayal of the *Mary Rose* and its crew is based on fact, and any errors are mine. My description of the ship, and particularly of the ship's castles, which were never recovered, is based on Geoff Hunt's beautiful painting of the *Mary Rose*, painted in 2009 for the 500th anniversary of the building of the ship.

The Mary Rose Museum is currently fundraising for a new museum, planned to open in 2012, which will feature both the half of the ship which was preserved and a reconstructed 'mirror image' of the other half of the ship, showing the artefacts in the places where they would have been. (Some of the soldiers' possessions appear in this book.) This will provide a unique insight into the lives of the soldiers and sailors. More about current displays and activities, and future plans, can be found at www.maryrose.org.

Henry VIII's Master of Horse, Sir Anthony Browne, who was at Portsmouth, commissioned a series of large paintings for his mansion at Cowdray House in Sussex, one of which was of the English encampment at Portsmouth in 1545. It shows the English and French fleets, together with the masts of the newly sunk *Mary Rose* just above the water. It is a very interesting painting, with the ships positioned extremely accurately, though the people on land would certainly have felt far less happy than they are shown in face of the huge invasion fleet; in that sense it is a work of propaganda. Henry VIII is also shown as far younger and slimmer than he was in 1545. Unfortunately the originals were lost when Cowdray House burned down in 1793, but a series of engravings of the paintings had been made, and survives. The engraving of the encampment at Portsmouth has been closely studied by Dr Dominic Fontana of Portsmouth University, who has also studied the Tudor town. I am very grateful to him for all his help and, again, for commenting on the manuscript. More about the Cowdray engravings, the sinking of the *Mary Rose*, and Tudor Portsmouth can be found at his website www.dominicfontana.co.uk.

The 1544 campaign in France is unusual in that a first-hand account was written by a Welsh officer, Elis Gruffudd: *The Enterprises of Paris and Boulogne*, trans. M. B. Davies (Cairo, 1944). Leacon's account of the ravaging of the French countryside is based on his account. Tudor warfare often involved the spoliation of the civilian population, but usually as a by-product of the military campaigns. In 1544, however, Henry VIII specifically ordered the terrorization of civilians both in France and, especially, Scotland.

The town of Rolfswood is fictitious, as is Hoyland Priory, although its former mother house, Wherwell Priory, was real. Many former monastic establishments were sold off in the 1530s and far more in the 1540s, as noted, to raise money for Henry's war. Jeremy Hodgkinson's *The Wealden Iron Industry* (Stroud, 2009) was very useful on the iron industry, as was the display at Lewes Museum in Sussex. The fireback which Shardlake sees in Liphook can be seen at Lewes Museum. Roger Ascham's *Toxophilus* remains in print (Lightning Source, UK). On archery, Richard Wadge's *Arrowstorm: the World of the Archer in the Hundred Years War* (Staplehurst, 2007) was especially useful, as were, for the *Mary Rose*, Ann Stirland's *The Men of the Mary Rose: Raising the Dead* (Stroud, 2005) and David Childs's *The Warship Mary Rose* (London, 2007). J. J. Goring's *The Military Obligations of the English People, 1511–1558* (Ph.D. thesis, 1955) was invaluable on the recruitment of early Tudor armies. For the Court of Wards I consulted H. E. Bell, *An Introduction to the History and Records of the Court of Wards and Liveries* (Cambridge, 1953) and J. Hurstfield, *The Queen's Wards* (London, 1958).

Despite the wealth of works on Tudor history, no one has yet written a history of the war of 1544–6. Somebody should.